KU-407-374

# GREAT FRENCH ROMANCES

## OTHER PILOT OMNIBUS TITLES

*Uniform with this Volume*

•

NOVELS OF MYSTERY FROM THE VICTORIAN AGE

NOVELS AND STORIES BY ROBERT LOUIS STEVENSON

NOVELS OF HIGH SOCIETY FROM THE VICTORIAN AGE

NOVELS AND STORIES BY ANTHONY TROLLOPE

FOUR NOVELS BY THE BRONTE SISTERS

# GREAT FRENCH ROMANCES

*Four complete novels by*
Madame de Lafayette, Choderlos de Laclos,
the Abbé Prevost, Honoré de Balzac

*Selected with an Introduction by*
RICHARD ALDINGTON

LONDON
PILOT PRESS LTD
1946

*First published in February 1946*
*Second Impression 1946*
*by The Pilot Press Ltd.,*
*45 Great Russell Street, London, W.C. 1*

PRINTED IN THE NETHERLANDS BY
N.V. VAN MUNSTER'S DRUKKERIJEN
AMSTERDAM

## CONTENTS



The Publishers wish to express their thanks to Messrs. J. M. Dent and Sons, Ltd. for allowing them to reprint Ellen Marriage's translation of *The Duchess of Langeais* and to Messrs. George Routledge and Sons, Ltd. for Richard Aldington's translation of *Les Liaisons Dangereuses* which appeared in their Broadway Translations series under the title of *Dangerous Acquaintances*.

# INTRODUCTION

By Richard Aldington

I

This book is made up of four outstanding French novels of the past, novels which have so far escaped the terrific mortality of that species of writing. They have benefited by the gradual improvement in the literary status of the novel to rise from the unhealthy but interesting position of public scandals to the pure eminence of the classics. Let us never forget Oscar Wilde's definition of the classics as " books which everybody talks about and nobody reads."

It should be useful to begin by listing the books with the date of first publication. They are :

(1) *La Princesse de Clèves*. By Madame de Lafayette. 1678.
(2) *Manon Lescaut*, which is the end of Book Fifteen and the seventh volume of Mémoires d'un Homme de Qualité. By the Abbé Prévost, 1731.
(3) *Les Liaisons Dangereuses*. By Choderlos de Laclos, 1782.
(4) *La Duchesse de Langeais*. By Honoré de Balzac, 1834.

The novels having been selected for their intrinsic value as literature, it is a matter of pure chance that they appeared at intervals of approximately fifty years. There is no absolute rule about it, of course, but that is just about the length of time needed for a fashion, an epoch, even a novel to be about at its nadir—old-fashioned without being quaint, vaguely remembered without being familiar, grandmotherly without being venerable. (After another decade the pioneer revival starts—" Waverley, or 'Tis Sixty Years Since.") I have no wish to stress the point, but I think it not unreasonable to say that each of these novels illustrates a change in the sexual fashions of France which, without having any sort of monopoly, has certainly in the past gone in rather enthusiastically for that sort of thing.

Before looking at them in more detail, let us just run briefly through these books, their authors and epochs, with this in view. *La Princesse de Clèves* was the work—or rather the play—of a *grande dame* from the Court of le Roi Soleil. She was not born *grande*, barely scraped into the *noblesse* in fact, but became so by marital and other contacts and by a very judicious royal friendship or two, and—give the devil her due—by reason of her shrewd and genial character, her eminently practical common sense. It is remarkable how prosperous some virtuous people are, and equally gratifying to see how virtuous some prosperous people are.

The word for Madame de Lafayette's epoch is *majestueux*. " Majestic" is not quite right, because the adjective immediately makes one think of

Queen Victoria not being amused. But "*majestueux*" suggests the frescoes of Lebrun and the sermons of Bossuet, the "O Ciel!" of Racine's heroines and the Legs of Louis as painted by Rigault, the fountains of Versailles, the wigs of Bernini's portrait statues, and the ceremonious modesty of duchesses who bore their children *en vertugadin*—wearing hooped skirts. The Princesse de Cléves and her amorous experience, which is a renunciation of such experience, are *majestueux*. Sexual affairs have here become a matter of complicated but perfectly understood ritual, the fine flower of which—the ultimate word—is renunciation. Such is the ideal though, perhaps, not the reality of Court life at a certain moment of its evolution. So it was in Urbino when Bembo and Castiglione reasoned of Platonic love, and in the Court of Imperial Japan when the Lady Murasaki penned her delicately dreary memoirs. It is the Age of Louis XIV, not as it was, but as it hoped to make other people see it.

However stylised the emotions of *La Princesse de Clèves*, however much they have been taught to accept conventions utterly unsympathetic (if not absurd) to us of this age, I have never doubted their sincerity. Nor have I any doubt of the (temporary) genuineness of feeling in the Abbe Prévost's *Manon Lescaut*. But during the half-century or so which had passed since the Princesse de Clèves touched so many hearts by rejecting love for duty's sake, much had happened in France.

The Great King had died to the great relief of all but a few, and his body had been carried to the Abbey of St. Denis (whose distant view he had always detested as a sinister *memento mori*), carried with immense pomp but amid the execrations of an amiable if fickle people. Released from twenty years of religion *à la Maintenon*, which had reinforced the austerity of the few who were sincere and clapped a grim mask of hypocrisy on the many who were not, the younger generation rushed to an opposite extreme which is not unlike what happened in England in the golden days of good King Charles's restoration. This excessive Christmassing (when, as one of our own dramatists put it, "every Adame had his Christmas Eve") was led by no less a person than the Regent Duc d'Orléans, who was smitten by apoplexy in the midst of his uninhibited revels. Law's Bank and the Mississippi venture (ingenious schemes which were probably unintentional swindles) provided all the pleasures and illusions of reckless inflation, followed of course by the grim realities of the crash.

All this means that the reading public (that odd animal) was prepared for a different kind of hero and heroine to weep over and perhaps to emulate. Manon and the Chevalier des Grieux are at the very antipodes from that overpoweringly noble husband, the Prince de Clèves, who dies of grief at the mere suspicion of his wife's infidelity:

("Men have died, and worms have eaten them,
But not for love . . .")

from the distant, respectful, chivalric devotion of the Duc de Nemours who barely toys from afar with faint hopes of adultery and humbly asks to marry the widow: and from the virtuous Princess who so sternly subdued her love for M. de Nemours during the lifetime of the husband she had never loved, and who refused herself and her lover a (presumed) lifetime of married happiness because this unintentional passion might have contributed towards the death of the sensitive M. de Clèves.

In *Manon Lescaut* we leap at once from the highest Court circle of the *Princesse de Clèves* to the gutter. Manon is a pretty girl who elopes at a moment's acquaintance with a strange young man picked up in the yard of a coaching inn. But it is impossible for her to be even faithful to him for more than a few days. Her lover has no money to give her the luxuries and pleasures she wants, so she earns them for herself and for him by the only method she knows. What is more, when young Grieux finds this out and goes into fits of amorous despair and jealousy, she is genuinely surprised and hurt. He has her heart, and she has his, what more does he want? a girl must live, *voyons!* Manon is the type, if not the original, of the capricious but sympathetic prostitute who has haunted romantic literature ever since. Perhaps she is now extinct, though doubtless she will reappear charmingly bestowing on her *amant de cœur*, not diamonds and a seat at the opera, but a handful of political tracts and a stick of dynamite.

And des Grieux? He of course is the victim of Venus who turns up in so many postures and disguises from the time of the Tale of Troy onward. Though des Grieux "withdraws his esteem" from Manon after the first of her infidelities and bursts into tears and reproaches on each subsequent occasion, he is fatally attracted to her and must return whenever she beckons, even though he knows it is at the expense of his own self-respect and decency. He ruins himself for her, becomes a card-sharper, a criminal, an exile. Des Grieux is the type of the man, young or old (a fruity morsel for psycho-analysts) who insanely *must* ruin himself for the sake of a manifestly faithless *cocotte*. For the time being, however, I imagine des Grieux is extinct. He belongs to those fabulous far-off days when families were not annually ruined by the budgets of heroically patriotic governments. But no doubt if the contemporary des Grieux were allowed to have any money they would squander it on the Manons, if any still exist.

Yet in spite of all this few readers can help liking this reprehensible couple and being on their side, however much one wishes that Grieux wept less frequently and that Manon might once have a little common sense. The question is often asked why this is so, why nearly everyone who is not too firmly in the clutch of some hard-and-fast social or moral system finds it impossible to refuse sympathy to this worthless young couple who do absolutely nothing towards solving the problem of security? Perhaps it is because they are genuine human beings living spontaneously, symbols of that lost minority whose memory dies with a certain grace.

Another half-century brings us to the publication of *Les Liaisons Dangereuses* in 1782. The thousand year old monarchy of France was about to commit hara-kiri, just when it had achieved the sweetest of all triumphs by the defeat and humiliation of the hereditary enemy, England, by tearing away the most valuable part of its colonial empire. But this triumph brought its nemesis, as luckily for humanity mere warlike triumph so often does. With England apparently disposed of for good and all, the French had leisure to consider their internal affairs. Now was the time for all good revolutionaries to unite for the destruction of Louis XVI. Now was plucked the fruit of half a century of propaganda by Voltaireans and Encyclopædists, Rousseauites and Jacobins, Free Masons and secret political societies. The apparently indestructible edifice collapsed, and probably nobody was more surprised than its enemies.

It seems to me not at all impossible that *Les Liaisons Dangereuses* was one more of the innumerable and now forgotten propaganda writings of the pre-Revolution epoch. At any rate it was not the work of a refined dowager or of a harum-scarum young man with more good intentions than common sense, but of an embittered middle-aged man who during the Revolution played some sort of secret political game in the entourage of Philippe Egalité, though exactly what nobody seems to know. We all recollect that " hell knows no fury, etc.," but what about the cold anger of a gifted man in his forties who feels he has been completely frustrated by jacks-in-office ? Society is fortunate when such a man has no gift for action, and takes it out in writing a book.

The novel written by this suspicious person with the odd name long passed as a work of more or less pornographic interest. It seems strange today that this superficial view should have been held, for it overlooks the astringent almost diabolical bitterness of the writer and the psychological insight which, in the slang phrase, " never misses a trick." The theme of the book is not love and scarcely sex, but the abuse of sex in an over-sophisticated society. This may not have been new in life, but it was certainly new in the literature of the novel, which had treated sex as heroical or ideal or sentimental or as a test of virtue or as sensual or comic or domestic, but never as a means to wield cold destructive power. There is fiendish totalitarian efficiency about the Merteuil woman and Valmont as they slowly destroy their victims. And one must not be misled by the intentionally clumsy *deus ex machina* " punishment" which falls on them. They really do succeed in what they set out to do, and the "divine vengeance " makes such a blot on an otherwise almost flawlessly constructed and motivated novel that it is hard to believe that Laclos had not his tongue in his cheek when he wrote it. The edifying end was tacked on to stop the quacking of censors and pious folk in general.

But how, it may be asked, can this novel be considered as a piece of pre-Revolutionary propaganda ? Well, it is an obvious line of disparagement of a ruling class the propagandist hopes to discredit, to say that it is sensually profligate and at the same time cold-hearted and cruel. This is the legend about the French aristocracy which has prevailed, and is firmly believed by millions of simple-minded people whose evidence is such nonsense as the why-don't-they-eat-cake myth. Of course, life went on very much as it always does, but as a matter of fact the fashionable fad in the 1780's was not to be one of the *roués* (that belonged to an older generation) but to live the simple life, to be benevolent, sentimental, gushing and an indiscriminate admirer of Nature and the Virtuous Poor. It was therefore rather difficult for Laclos to put over his thesis, when so many of these wicked people at any rate appeared to be exactly the opposite of what was claimed. He solved the problem neatly. He does not deny the virtues or at any rate the sentimental harmlessness of the Dancenys and Céciles, the Madame de Tourvels and Madame de Rosemondes, but shows them as the victims and dupes of the Valmonts and Merteuils. The Duc de la Rochefoucauld had said long before that the results of sex more often resembled hatred than love ; but it was left to Laclos to prove this amiable theorem.

I have no wish or indeed necessity to examine the changing political phases of France between 1782 and the publication of Balzac's *La Duchesse de Langeais* in 1833–34. Yet it is impossible to ignore the changes and counter-changes which had occurred within that period of sixty years. It is important to remember that the great French Revolution began in no spirit of idle acrimony. Never before, perhaps, had there been so much universal goodwill ; never had so many happy tears been shed by virtuous patriots. A foreigner, William Wordsworth, has strikingly described those first two years as "bliss," as "very heaven" ; and subsequent researches go to show that he himself celebrated in no uncertain terms. The millennium, like Mr. Hoover's elusive prosperity, was just around the corner. But somehow matters went wrong. Louis XVI, "*ce roi adorable*," after having been copiously cheered and wept upon, woke up one fine morning to the awful embrace of Madame Guillotine. Revolutionary governments dissolved each other with great rapidity by means of this same guillotine, and finally fell to the wicked "reaction" of the Directoire after endowing France (and much of the world) with such permanent boons of freedom as compulsory military service, inflation, taxes of a new kind, and police spies disguised as doorkeepers. The Consulate, the Empire, the Restoration, the Hundred Days, Louis XVIII, Charles X, the Revolution of 1830, followed with amazing speed, and already at the publication date of *La Duchesse de Langeais* Louis Philippe had for more than three years essayed the ungrateful and perhaps impossible task of being a constitutional king of France.

In spite of this unceasing turmoil and the really frightful losses in man-power, France continued to show extraordinary energy and fertility. Among the tokens of its energy, who is more attractive, if taken on his own terms, than the exuberant Honoré de Balzac ? Pretentious and even absurd in some respects he may be, but what energy, what gusto, what creative power ! The man is a microcosm, a world in himself, a dynamo of production. A refined and nobly aspiring intelligence, like that of Aldous Huxley, cannot avoid seeing the vulgarity and ridiculousness of Balzac. Everything Mr. Huxley says against Balzac is quite true from the point of view of one aspiring towards an austere and abstract idealism. But if you are going to make mankind your study and your love, if you are going to take your "bain de multitude" without spluttering, perhaps you must be a little or more than a little pretentious, absurd and vulgar. You can say all sorts of things more or less truly against Balzac, but by God! (as the Duke of Wellington used to remark) you can't call him prim.

There is a story, evidently based on a passage in the *Illusions Perdues* that in his early days Balzac wrote two propaganda books. He was desperately hard up when he heard a journalist say that the liberals must buck up their propaganda—in order to arouse suspicions of the government somebody must write a book advocating the restoration of the right of primogeniture. Balzac undertook the job for 600 francs, and converted himself to royalism in doing so. He then wrote a book against the Jesuits, and converted himself to Catholicism. This is the kind of story people tell, but it does rather neatly bring out the synthetic quality of Balzac's royalism and catholicism. Both, I have no doubt, were fundamentally sincere, but parliamentary or Pickwickian or Balzacien. At any rate the royalists were always suspicious of him and the Catholics put most of his books on the Index, while the opposition seem to have borne him no particular grudge. Happy days, before the birth of that universal slogan of salvation, put-him-up-against-a-wall.

At all events the reader who comes to *La Duchesse de Langeais* after the three other novels in this book has a rich opportunity for gnomic reflections of no particular value from a practical point of view. In a sense the wheel has come full circle, and we are back once more in the aristocratic-religious ritual of *La Princesse de Clèves*, but with what a difference! Here are no gentlemen and ladies, controlled, hieratic, beautiful as the characters of the Lady Murasaki, but prodigious vulgarians trying to play the part in an atmosphere of plebeian meloprama.

And what a melodrama! Strictly speaking, I should keep this description of *La Duchesse de Langeais* for a later part of this essay. But in writing about Balzac the only thing to do is to break all rules, as he did. Without undertaking the superfluous task of summarising a novel which is here presented for the reader's close study, let me at least mention the dramatic or melodramatic elements of the story.

A Duchess flirts and coquets outrageously with a General who is madly in love with her. Human nature reaches its limits—he abducts her in the midst of the Paris season and is about to brand her on the forehead, like a criminal. This determined action releases all the Duchess's hidden love (could the psycho-analysts do better?) and she longs to be branded as his mistress. The General now refuses, and returns her (mysteriously) to the party from which she had been kidnapped. Now the Duchess is all for him, desperately tries to be his mistress, to compromise herself with him. He coldly refuses. In despair she writes him that if he does not come to see her by a given time, " no human power can discover her on earth." Naturally the General trots off to the rendezvous, but (a weak spot, this) his clock is slow, and she has gone. Where ?

The General is a member of a super Boy Scout organisation " The Thirteen," each one of whom is a man of immense power and pledged to support the others in their plans to the uttermost. For five years they seek the Duchess. Then, when the French invade Spain in the forgotten campaign of 1823, the General hears her voice singing in the choir of a convent. He seeks an interview, but at the crucial moment she reveals to the Mother Superior that this is her lover. With the aid of the Thirteen the General attacks the convent to carry off his beautiful nun-duchess-mistress, and arrives in time—to find her lying dead. Summarised in this crude fashion the plot sounds silly and forced. Nevertheless the novel is one which was rightly described by our grandfathers as " ve'y pahful."

The spiral of change has made another full turn, and with *La Duchesse de Langeais* we are back again at the novel of renunciation. But how different from *La Princesse de Clèves !* In that little book the exterior, the setting, even the period are only slightly indicated, and the reader has to remind himself from time to time that he is supposed to be reading about the Court of François II, not that of Louis XIV. Balzac's work simply drips with wodges of local colour. The motive for Madame de Clèves's renunciation is an over-exacting sense of duty as austere and colourless as that of any pre-Christian stoic. Balzac hits the religious note until it screams. And the General ! Far from the quiet good-breeding of M. de Nemours, he loves, so to speak, with a *rugissement de lions*. What makes *La Duchesse de Langeais* memorable, what makes it as vividly alive as the other three, is Balzac's passionate energy, his passionate belief in himself and his characters. It is that which enabled him to impose a semblance of order on the confusion of his age, and that which makes him to be forgiven for a multitude of sins against taste.

## 2

EACH one of these writers, and one might almost add each one of these novels, has become in the course of time the centre of a little library of commentary. Mr. Ashton's excellent study of Mme de Lafayette, published in 1922, lists roughly 350 books and periodicals in its bibliography. Not all nor indeed most of them are studies of Mme. de Lafayette, but each has contributed something to that work of careful reconstruction and interpretation which was so largely developed by the 19th-century Germans. Nor has the work stopped, though it has slowed. The discovery of some unpublished letters or of some interesting document (proving or disproving a disputed episode) is in itself enough to justify a new book—or so it is thought. Nor is this all. Some careful and thoughtful student excogitates new " points of view," or somebody has to write a thesis for his Ph.D., or somebody else thinks it might be a good idea if there was a " modern " book about whoever it happens to be. The knowledge is there all right but it is not so very accessible, particularly to people who don't happen to have specialised in French. The books are mostly out of print and preserved in the vaults of enormous public libraries where they are more often dusted than read. If I haven't always got the right or final dope, the reader will remember that the flesh is weak and nobody can possibly read all the books.

Earnestly and cheerfully, however, I advise the reader not to be in the least intimidated or put off by all this printed erudition, and not to bother about it unless impelled by the demon of wanting-to-know, but to sit down to each of these novels as if it had just appeared for the first time on the shelves of the circulating libraries. Novels, of all books, are primarily to be read for the fun of the thing, and if you haven't read one, then so far as you're concerned it is a new one, however old-fashioned its garment of words and outlook may be. Of course a novel one or two or three centuries old is not a modern novel—insane to pretend it is—but it was a novel before it was a bit of culture. Oscar Wilde—who seems to be haunting my memory at the moment—pointed out that the dislike for Realism is the rage of Caliban at seeing his face in a mirror, and that the dislike for Romanticism is the rage of Caliban at *not* seeing his face in a mirror. Let us be sensible little Calibans, and enjoy seeing in the mirror the faces of other people of other times, even if the mirror be a little tarnished by time. The novels are the important thing, and if they are no good, then all the comment is waste indeed.

This studying the man in his works or studying the works in the man is perhaps overdone, but it is a harmless little racket which should be allowed to survive, if possible. There is, however, quite a valid reason for including brief outlines of the lives of these writers, quite apart from the fact that this may save some readers the trouble of mugging them up in books of reference. Apparently for generations past it has been the habit of novel-readers who are not novel-writers to consider every book they read as biographical or autobiographical or both. In other words, they think every novel is an account of some episode in the author's life with nasty remarks about his friends. (Crime stories are to some extent immune from this harsh judgment, though I cannot imagine why.) At all events soon after the publication of Jones's new novel, one is bound to run into Brown who is wearing that injured look. Almost at once the following dialogue, or something of the kind, ensues :

" I say, do you know ? Jones has put me in his book."

" No really ? "

" Yes. You remember that character who was a cretin, and they gave him thyroid, and he developed homicidal mania, and killed his uncle ? '

" Well, vaguely. . . ."

" That was meant for me ! "

" You surprise me. I don't see. . . ."

" Do you mean to say you didn't notice he is described as having blue eyes ? "

Now for the first time in a not very memorable acquaintance you realise that Brown has the kind of pale glaucous eyes which his wife might have thought of as blue before she married him.

" And looked as though he had adenoids ? " Brown continues indignantly. " I can bring witnesses to prove that I described to Jones exactly how I was operated on for adenoids."

" Oh, well," you say, trying to making soothing noises, " there isn't anything to be done about it. . . ."

" Isn't there ! Pinch, Pecksniff and Sneak—my solicitors, you know, wonderful old firm—advise me it's libellous, and I'm going for thumping damages."

This is the most recent version of a process which has apparently been going on for centuries, based on the conviction that no one can write a novel except about himself and his acquaintances. Of course, I don't say that Jones is invariably wrong. It is just possible that Jones may have chosen this method of telling the world (and Brown) what a cow he thinks Brown is. But ten to one he never thought about Brown, and the blue eyes and the adenoids may have been a bit of ill-judged local colour or the most innocent of subconscious memories. On the other hand, we must remember that only too often " real characters " are " put " into novels with a view to raising the circulation. A predecessor of Mme de Lafayette, the marathonian Mlle de Scudéry, found it very profitable to insert " portraits " of well-known people and then to circulate keys giving the real names for the benefit of those who liked it to be thought they were in the highest society. But some French critics seem to me to carry this line of interpretation a bit far, especially when they read every book as some sort of revenge on a woman for turning down the author. According to them, you might consider Genesis as a book of memoirs written to discredit Madame Eve, Madame Lot and Madame Potiphar.

Yet, as is so often the case, common prejudice is not entirely wrong, or at any rate merely over-stresses a certain amount of truth. Is it not the fact that many of the most-liked novels (if not those which exclusive literary fashion would pick out) have a kernel of autobiography, in the sense that a deeply felt personal experience has been imaginatively reconstructed ?

## 3

Marie-Madeleine Pioche de la Vergne was the child of her father's second marriage. She had two half-sisters, both of whom were nuns. Her mother was Elizabeth de Péna, whose family is supposed to have come to France from Naples, though the name sounds Portuguese or Spanish. They were unimportant people, only just inside the circle of the *noblesse*, but they were blessed by distinguished patrons who acted as godparents to the young child when she was baptised in Saint-Sulpice on the 18th March, 1634. One of them, the Marquis de Brezé, was related to Cardinal Richelieu; the other became Duchesse d'Aiguillon, and was moreover Richelieu's niece. Through their influence, it is said, M. de la Vergne found employment at Pontoise and Le Havre. Indeed, at Le Havre he commanded the citadel on behalf of the Duchess, and died somewhere in 1649-50, when his daughter was about fifteen. In December 1650 the inconsolable widow married the Chevalier Renaud de Sévigné, uncle of the famous letter-writer, the Marquise de Sévigné. Although separated by several years these two girls had the same tutor, Gilles Ménage, who is always called "a pedant" because he could write poetry in four languages.

Mlle de la Vergne was twenty-one when she married, and that was almost aged in an epoch when girls were married usually at sixteen or earlier. The date of the marriage was February 14th, 1655, the husband was nearly forty, and his name was François, Comte de Lafayette. This was the senior branch of the family which received some publicity in the 18th century from the activities of a Marquis de Lafayette. The Comte de Lafayette descended from an ancient family of warriors. Among his ancestors Gilbert II went on a crusade in 1095; Gilbert III was also a crusader; Gilbert VI was knighted in the 13th century for services against the English; Jean du Mottier was killed at Poitiers; François was killed at Saint-Quentin; René was killed at Moncontour in 1569; Charles at Estampes in 1631. The last male of this line of Lafayettes, the son of our author, died a Brigadier of forty at Landau.

François de Lafayette seems to have been a mild, unliterary sort of person who liked a country life and was involved in many and complicated lawsuits. His wife bore him two children, and then he seemed rather to fade out of her life. Indeed he was supposed to have faded out of life himself somewhere about 1660, which supposition was held to excuse an equally suppositious liaison between his wife and the Duc de la Rochefoucauld. It is easy to imagine the rage of the experts when in the 1890's Comte d'Haussonville published definite proof that Lafayette outlived Rochefoucauld by several years. This ridiculous fact went contrary to all the accepted literary histories, so by way of revenge the affronted historians turned angrily against Mme de Lafayette.

She was a woman of ability and much practical common sense, since she took charge of her husband's lawsuits and brought them to satisfactory conclusions. One glance at her shrewd wooden face (as recorded in the Château de Chambord portrait, for the engravings are of a totally different person) makes one feel that in later life her exquisite conversations with M. de la Rochefoucauld probably always ended up as follows:

*M. de la Rochefoucauld : Alors, il faut profiter ?*
*Mme de Lafayette : Mais oui, mais oui, evidémment il faut profiter.*

In addition to these practical gifts, which should not be despised by those who lack them, Mme de Lafayette had a genius for friendship with important people. One has only to look through the letters she received from the Minister, Louvois, to see that she must have been a person who had to be treated with care and respect. In the 1660's she was perhaps the closest friend of Madame, to whom she was lady-in-waiting. Madame was Henrietta, youngest daughter of Charles I of England, the wife of Louis XIV's brother, the Duc d'Orléans, who was a homosexual. Louis is said to have fallen in love with her when it was too late, and to have regretted that he had not married her himself when he had the chance. Henrietta died, still little more than a girl, of appendicitis probably, though she, poor frightened thing, believed she had been poisoned. Two people knelt at her deathbed—the King and Mme de Lafayette.

It is said that Louis never forgot this. Mme de Lafayette's friendship with Henrietta was genuine, at least to the extent that she had never asked the princess to use her influence to obtain Mme de Lafayette favours. Louis, who was the most begged from man on earth, must have thought this terrific. (With sombre accuracy he used to remark when he granted a favour : " I have now made one man ungrateful and fifty discontented.") At all events, Mme de Lafayette thereafter very seldom begged from His Majesty in vain. I don't think there had been any calculation in all this. It was perfectly genuine. Moreover, when she did beg, it was not for herself, but for her friends and her not very interesting sons.

Among her numerous other friends, two must be mentioned. One was " Madame Royale," the ruling Duchess of Savoy, who need not occupy us further ; and the other was the Duc de la Rochefoucauld, who here interests us very much. Not to beat about the bush—was she his mistress ? For it is about this possible relationship that the interpretation of *La Princesse de Clèves* as autobiography was constructed. While still a young woman Mme de Lafayette retired from active Court life (except for occasional visits " of solicitation ") and lived at 16, Rue de Vaugirard, seeing a small circle of friends and occasionally her husband. She was much afflicted by " the vapours," which fashionable complaint seems to have been nothing more or less than flatulence, due to lack of exercise. When she died, May 25th, 1693, the autopsy indicated a chronic condition of this kind as well as diseases of the heart and kidneys.

A dry summary of this kind inevitably omits all the real life of the woman. In addition to the practical sense which made her existence materially successful, she must have had a strong personality and a great deal of charm. She studied Latin and Greek under Ménage, and a little Hebrew with Huet (afterwards a bishop), but nobody claims that she could read either Greek or Hebrew, and the story that in three months she learned more Latin than Ménage is plainly absurd. She seems to have read some Virgil and Horace. Even if she had been a genuine scholar she would have concealed the fact (as she concealed whatever she did know) since at that time it was not considered seductive for women to learn much about anything. Nor was it considered decent for a woman of her social position to publish her writings; which accounts for the fact that her few works (including *La Princesse de Clèves*) were published anonymously, and even positively disavowed when an enquirer was too pertinacious.

I hope these few facts will enable the reader to judge for himself how far *La Princesse de Clèves* may be considered autobiographical. There are, however, one or two other points about the book which should be touched on before coming to that. In the first place, the claim used to be confidently put forward that with *La Princesse de Clèves* Mme de Lafayette made a bold original break with the traditional long-winded novel of heroical and sentimental adventure, and invented the modern realistic novel of psychology. Now, as usual, there is something in this, but it is much too absolute and flattering to our novelist. On the one hand researches have showed that the adventure story of d'Urfé and Scudéry often had a good deal of psychology or would-be psychology; and, on the other hand, further extensive researches have brought to light a number of short novels of a rather similar type which preceded *La Princesse de Clèves*. Furthermore, the material of the book is only that of a long short story, and to make it reach even its present modest size it is padded with a series of "portraits" at the beginning and with at least three long unnecessary digressions. Therefore, if Mme de Lafayette reduced the length of the novel so drastically, this may not have been wholly due to exquisite æsthetic tact, but in part to that short-windedness, that lack of fertility and staying power, so characteristic of the highly distinguished amateur in both prose and poetry.

Again, the idea that Mme de Lafayette initiated the novel of contemporary realism is only partly true, and, in the actual circumstances not so greatly to her credit as it would have been if she had intended to produce contemporary realism. But, as a matter of fact, she set out to write an historical novel about the Courts of Henry II and François II. Picturesque local colour and more or less accurate historical detail did not come into the novel until Sir Walter Scott wrote *Waverley*. Naturally Mme de Lafayette is not to blame for not having written in a style which was only invented a hundred and twenty years after her death. Indeed, some of her attraction for later readers probably lies in the fact that she was totally innocent of local colour with which most people are surfeited. Mme de Lafayette probably did not know much more about the sixteenth century than what she read in the amusing works of Brantôme, from whom she derived most of her characters. But as the only Court she knew was that of Louis XIV, and as she didn't know the trick of faking a "period," it is difficult to read her book as anything but a study of contemporary character, which indeed it is. Perhaps she intended it as such, and merely used a conventional historical setting in order to avoid the horrible reproach of having degraded living royalty with anything so lower class as literature.

The plot of *La Princesse de Clèves* is really very little more than a Brantôme anecdote, more stately, more chaste, more edifying and less credible, but still a Brantôme anecdote. The crux of the whole thing is the "*aveu*," the wife's confession. The Prince de Clèves is in love with his wife who is not in love with him, a lamentable state of affairs only too common under the system whereby marriage was the mating of two sums of money. The Duc de Nemours, pride of the Louvre, falls in love with her, and for her sake abandons a match with Queen Elizabeth of England—though what real chance a little Frenchman had of marrying our Professional Virgin need not be debated. Touched by this sacrifice and by the Duke's innumerable virtues and gifts (which are quite terrific) the Princesse de Clèves naturally falls in love with him. But though she does not love her husband and is not specially religious, the Princesse steadily refuses him. Driven pretty well out of the Maginot Line of her virtue, as a last resort she desperately tells her husband about her feelings, which naturally worries him a lot. (This is the "*aveu.*") In spite of her unflinching virtue, appearances are against her, and her husband is led to believe the Worst. He, poor fellow, dies of the horror of it, though not before she assures him (too late, alas !) that he was mistaken. After an intolerably long delay of decency, the Duc de Nemours proposes to the widow, but though she vows she loves him, she refuses to marry him because she feels that her culpable passion may have contributed to the death of M. de Clèves. She takes refuge in a house which abuts on a convent of nuns, just like Mme de Lafayette's house in the Rue de Vaugirard.

Now, when it was thought that the Comte de Lafayette had popped off soon after his lady met M. le Duc de la Rochefoucauld ; and when it was quite certain that (in spite of his gout) M. le Duc hobbled round every day to see Mme de Lafayette, wife or widow, for years, in spite of the fact that Mme la Duchesse de la Rochefoucauld was still alive—and when you think of what had happened with Mme la Duchesse de Longueville, to mention one only—well, was it surprising that critics of the utmost eminence thought *La Princesse de Clèves* was autobiographical ? The only thing they doubted was the continuous and final break with M. de la Rochefoucauld-Nemours after the death of M. de Lafayette-Clèves.

Then, of course, as I have already mentioned, the romance was blown sky high by the pestilential discovery that M. de Lafayette had outlived M. de la Rochefoucauld. However, the eminent critics still refused to give up the *liaison*, even though he was crippled with gout and fiftyish, and she was a martyr to wind.

It was the "*aveu*" that troubled these noble minds. So original, so unheard of, so bizarre for a wife to take her husband into her confidence in such a dilemma, that it must have happened to Mme de Lafayette—that exquisite, unpractical creature whose " delicacy " was as light as wind. It is true that a certain Madame de Villedieu wrote a novel called, *Les Désordres de l'Amour*, which contained an " *aveu* " almost exactly similar, and that this novel has priority of publication. However, this is explained away on the ground that Mme de Villedieu (a venal author, it appears) plagiarised this unique episode from a manuscript copy of *La Princesse de Clèves*. And the fact that in this plebeian, not to say proletarian age, wives and husbands tell each other practically everything printable and unprintable, is irrelevant.

More relevant is a small literary fact, which appears (miraculously) to have escaped the attention of the many erudite commentators on *La Princesse de Clèves*. It is well known, as I have already mentioned, that Mme de Lafayette took many of her characters and such pallid local colour as she could muster, from that most virile and entertaining of writers, the Sieur de Brantôme, who actually has enough local colour for a battalion of historical novelists. Well, if you will look up the *Discours Septième* of the *Vies des Dames Galantes*, and read the paragraph beginning : " *Je vous fairay deux contes de deux femmes mariées . . .* " on page 354 of the cheap Garnier reprint, you will find a story of a lady who makes an " *aveu* " to her husband. It is true that M. de Brantôme jests somewhat heartlessly at her " *sotte simplicité* " and that the story ends in a far less edifying manner ; but still there is the " *aveu*," and what more was needed ?

And if you are still determined to find out the exact truth, you had better begin on those 350 books I mentioned.

Speaking from a purely personal point of view, I should say that *La Princesse de Clèves* gets off to a rather slow start and too many characters are introduced at once. It is not a bad idea to make a list of the various kings and queens and what-nots Mme de Lafayette throws at us so lavishly. The " portraits " must be borne with patiently. They were a fad of the time, derived from the " characters " of Theophrastus which had been translated and imitated. (The difference between them is that a " character " is supposed to be a type, and a " portrait " an individual.) Mme de Lafayette and friends had quite a time writing " portraits " of each other, and it is just possible that this novel began with imitating the portraits in Brantôme, and that they were gradually worked up into the novel. There is no proof of this, any more than of the possibility, not to say probability, that Rochefoucauld advised or revised or even collaborated.

It strikes me—again as a purely personal point of view—as odd that *La Princesse de Clèves* should be praised as "realism." When I think of early realism in the novel I think of Defoe, whose *Moll Flanders* for example is as down to earth and full as facts as the *Police Gazette*. But in *La Princesse de Clèves* the characters are not so much realised as idealised. They don't behave as people do or did, but as Mme de Lafayette thought they ought to behave. Compare, for instance, Mme de Lafayette's Nemours, sighing and dying at a respectful distance, with Brantôme's Nemours, whose method with women seems to have been something between persuasive mendacity and rape. What is meant by " realism " is that Mme de Lafayette abandoned imagination and invention (if she had any) and wrote a sober little tale of a matrimonial tangle. The characters themselves are even more morally noble than those of mid-Victorian novels, which is saying a lot. And they are not too convincing to anyone who has read the memoirs of Brantôme and Saint-Simon. It is curious, though perhaps not very fruitful, to reflect that Mme de Lafayette was a contemporary of Aphra Behn.

When all is said and done, we must remember that *La Princesse de Clèves* is one of the very few novels—if not the only one—of its epoch which is still entirely readable, in spite of certain drawbacks and a few long-winded passages. The reason is, I think, that Mme de Lafayette has here a genuinely interesting situation, which she has treated dramatically but sensibly. The idealisation of the characters is not so great as to spoil the situation. It is all *majestueux*, but not incredible. So far as actual prose is concerned, it is probably the best written of all these four books, with that sober stylised elegance which characterises the best work of this period in France. If we accept its conventions and limitations, it is certainly a little masterpiece.

## 4

From the very high life of Mme de Lafayette and her story, it is a come-down to the Abbé Prévost and his Manon and her lover. We leave pleasures and palaces for Grub Street and prisons. Of course it is unfair to Prévost to label him " Grub Street "—you can't do that to a man who has written a book which has remained in print for over two centuries and has had so much influence, as *Manon Lescaut*. But we have to remember that when Prévost was not either in a monastery or wanted by the police—odd alternatives—he was writing hard for a meagre living. And the position of *Manon Lescaut* in Prévost's work as a whole might be not unfairly indicated by saying that it is rather as if one of the short stories in *The Pickwick Papers* had turned out to be a masterpiece while all the rest of Dickens's work was practically forgotten except by a few students and specialists. As for the Abbé himself, he is—at this distance—a not unattractive mixture of two favourite subjects of the character-writers, the *fripon* and the *étourdi*, the rascal and the scatterbrain, with the scatterbrain predominating.

The little town of Hesdin in the Pas-de-Calais now seems as if it had been French for centuries, but though French influence must have been strong there it was in fact stormed by one of Richelieu's armies in 1639 and eventually added to French territory. On the 1st of April—significant day! —1697, a middle-class family named Prévost, of the town of Hesdin, was increased by the birth of a boy, who was named Antoine François. This family had been divided between law and the

Church. Prévost's grandfather was a brewer, his father a magistrate, both rather violent men according to tradition. The grandfather was in legal trouble in 1673 for calling a magistrate a thief.

Absolutely nothing is known of the first fourteen years of young Prévost's life, but at that age (in 1711) he went to the Jesuits' College in Hesdin, and in 1713 is said to have become a novice with the Jesuits in Paris. There is a good deal of uncertainty about the next four years—some think he stayed the whole time with his learned instructors, some think only a year. At any rate, at some time between 17 and 21, the scatterbrain in Prévost's character suddenly asserted itself. Abandoning the career in the Church for which he was evidently being groomed, Prévost joined the army as a gentleman volunteer. Luckily for Prévost, that particular war was over, so he did not have to show the heroism which was expected of gentlemen volunteers, and it seems that his chief acquirement as a soldier was a knowledge of gambling, with a not too precise attention to the rules of the games, when disregarding them unobserved was to his advantage.

What happened to him then is again a matter of uncertainty. He is said to have left the army, and either to have returned to his novitiate or to have travelled in Holland, and then to have gone back to the army. But not to stay. The 9th November, 1721, is a definitely established date in his career, for it was then that after a year as a novice he took his vows—but as a Benedictine, not as a Jesuit ! This ceremony took place at the great abbey of Jumièges, and for some years Prévost's family must have congratulated themselves on his behaviour, in the mistaken belief that he had settled down. But his story as a Benedictine is a record of restlessness, of petitions that he be allowed to move to another monastery, of alternating between teaching and preaching. Nevertheless, he was ordained priest in 1726, and next year got himself transferred to the abbey of Saint-Germain des Près in Paris, where he divided his time between working for the austere " Gallia Christiana " and writing the first part of a long picaresque novel. The first two volumes of the *Memoires et aventures d'un Homme de qualité* were published in 1728.

The publication was a success, and thus at thirty-one Dom Prévost discovered his real vocation in life. He was neither soldier nor monk, but a novelist, and his adventure both as *étourdi* and *fripon* were only just beginning. Intoxicated by his fallacious success, he determined to abandon his life as a Benedictine and applied for permission to join the less austere monks of Cluny. Scatterbrained as usual, he did not wait to see the result of his petition, but suddenly ran away from Saint-Germain des Près, and appeared in Paris in the dress of a secular priest. All this, no doubt, was very well meant—" virtuous and philosophical," as they said in the eighteenth century ; and he was doubtless astounded to learn that the Lieutenant of Police of Paris had issued a warrant for the arrest of " A. Prévost of Hesdin," " a man of medium height, light hair, wide-open blue eyes, with a fleshy face and ruddy complexion."

Advised of this enormity by his friends, the rollicking monk took to his heels and made for England with all speed.

It is a great temptation to dwell on the theme of Prévost in England, since it ought to provide a good deal of entertainment for English readers. The temptation must be resisted in the interests of proportion and space, but I cannot refrain from saying that Prévost's highest enthusiasm was aroused by the excellence of English food—just a little more lyricism in one of his gastronomic passages and it would have been an Ode to a Southdown Mutton. Having spent the money earned by his book, Prévost became tutor to a young man named Francis Eyles, with whom he travelled and ate the meals and saw the scenes he described so pleasantly in the later volumes of his *Man of Quality*. But here again the restlessness of Prévost's temperament showed itself, reinforced no doubt by the difficulty of earning a sufficient living as a man of letters in the England of Walpole. At any rate in October, 1730, Prévost went to Holland, where he busied himself with publishing a translation of the historian, de Thou, and in 1731, the last three volumes of his *Man of Quality*, which contained as a kind of appendix or afterthought the vivid and touching story of *Manon Lescaut*.

Hitherto the life of Prévost has not displayed any particular signs of evil. Some will think his flight from a monastery shows depravity; others will think it merely a flash of common sense. But these years of childishly monotonous discipline had evidently unfitted the Abbé for coping with the ways of the world. In the Hague he fell in with a siren of the pavements named Lenki, with whom he fled to England, snatching her from an unlawful "protector," said to have been a Swiss colonel. The trouble was that he left considerable debts, including "four or five thousand florins advanced by the Dutch booksellers."

This was in January, 1733, two years after the publication of *Manon Lescaut*, and it is certainly very curious to see how Prévost seemed fated to imitate his des Grieux in some of that hero's less respectable actions. Arriving in England Prévost tried to get his hands on some of the money given by George II for the aid of destitute French Protestants. He failed, and failed also to make enough money out of *Pour et Contre*, a periodical in imitation of *The Spectator* and *Tatler* of Queen Anne's time. On the 13th December of the same year he was arrested on a charge of fraud. The sum involved was fifty guineas, and the name of the person defrauded was his former pupil, Francis Eyles.

For nearly two centuries it was not known exactly what Prévost had done to get into this legal trouble, and naturally his admirers hoped it was something trifling or a mistake. To Miss Mysie Robertson belongs the sad honour of having discovered and published the truth, in 1927, in the preface to her edition of the fifth book of the *Man of Quality*. It seems that, hard pressed for money for his Lenki, Prévost adopted a method of raising cash which had become so common in France that the Government had taken special steps to deal with it. What Prévost did was to find a letter from Francis Eyles in which he had carelessly left a wide space between "your humble servant" and his signature. Carefully cutting this out the Abbé wrote an acceptance for fifty guineas over the name Francis Eyles, and cashed it. Anatole France's Abbé Coignard never practised a dirtier little trick on a friendly benefactor.

However, we have no right to say that Prévost was guilty of this charge, since he was never tried for it. Five days later he was released. Miss Robertson thinks Eyles refused to press the charge, having just discovered that forgery had recently been made a capital offence—a curious lack of knowledge in an M.P. for the City of London. He may just as well have been released for lack of evidence or any other reason. On the other hand, a man in Eyles's position would hardly have asked for a warrant against a poor refugee unless he had possessed pretty good evidence and was in addition angry about it.

The argument has been made that if Prévost had really been guilty of this charge, he would not have stayed in England a day after his release from arrest. But where on earth was he to go? There were obvious reasons for not returning to Holland or France, Prussia and Russia were not yet in the market for slightly shop-soiled Frenchmen of talent, and even an *étourdi* could not have supposed that the French or British colonies in America would welcome him. Finally, he did a comparatively sensible thing. In 1734 he went to Calais, "incognito" to avoid immediate arrest, and through friends and relatives tried to negotiate with the ecclesiastical authorities he had offended. In this he was successful. After a short time of supposed penitence in an abbey, he was released. His reputation as a writer had grown rapidly during his absence; trying to cheat an Englishman was no crime in Paris; and he was appointed almoner to the Prince de Conti. This gave him no money but protection from arrest and molestation, and he seems to have settled down to a life of novel-writing.

Alas, that he did not stick to this comparatively harmless form of activity. In 1741 he was again on the run from the police, a *lettre de cachet* having been issued against him for publishing "scandalous libels" in a periodical. The Prince de Conti (it is said) heard of it, and gave the Abbé 25 *louis* in time to get away. He fled to Brussels and then to Frankfurt, and did not receive permission to return to France until September of 1742.

The last twenty years of his life were comparatively calm and prosperous. He had a house and garden, with two servants and "an amiable widow" to look after him. He translated Richardson, and other writers of Great Britain, including Middleton and Hume. He edited a collection of travels and voyages, contributed to periodicals, and published numbers of books; but managed to keep out of further trouble.

A macabre story used to be told that he was smitten by apoplexy, but that death was prematurely certified and that he recovered only to die under the knives and scalpels of an autopsy. The certificate of death (25th November, 1763) shows that he did indeed die of apoplexy, but gives no support to the sensational part of the story.

The temptation to equate Prévost with his hero, des Grieux, has been too strong for most writers, and indeed there is much to be said for it. But the situation has been interpreted rashly. Because des Grieux is obviously much the same sort of character as Prévost, it does not follow that the adventures and crimes attributed to des Grieux by a sensitive and imaginative novelist are literally copied from the exploits of the Abbé. Demonstrably Prévost did not forestall des Grieux by shooting a man in St. Lazare or by emigrating to America. Why then must other adventures of des Grieux be Prévost's ? What is remarkable is this—that in 1731, the Abbé Prévost, sketching much of his own character in the imaginary life of des Grieux, thought that he was capable of committing a legal crime for the sake of a loose woman. Now, the only really criminal action charged against Prévost is the London forgery, which, if committed, was committed for the sake of a loose woman, and two years after the publication of *Manon Lescaut*. There is no need to invoke any fanciful 1890 hypothesis and paradox about " life imitating art." The plainer fact is that in a moment of lucidity Prévost saw where his temperament might lead him, and was unable to prevent himself from being led that way.

As to Lenki—she cannot be Manon, because Prévost did not meet her until after the publication of his book. There is no dramatic tragedy about the end of Lenki in Prévost's life. She just fades out. Did he leave her in England ? Did he send her back to Holland ? Did he take her to France ? Nobody seems to have asked, let alone to have answered these questions. Poor Lenki—nobody is going to have a good word for her, a little whore who happened to pick up with a man of genius and so got her name into the newspapers and—which is worse from the point of fairness to her—into the books of her lover's literary admirers.

A medical friend tells me that the Chevalier des Grieux has got into the books of the Viennese sex quacks as an example of " sexual bondage." This, oddly enough, is a better description of the character and a better indication of the central theme of the book than much of the literary comment. (Michelet, for example, after falsifying the date of the book and Manon's social status, gives a pre-determined political interpretation which is almost absurd.) But it is not as a case of " sexual bondage " that des Grieux and Manon have touched the hearts of generations of readers. If the book was just a case history of a weak, sensual and vicious young man, enslaved by an artful cocotte, the world would not have been moved to pity and regret for their fate. What Prévost himself felt so deeply and recorded with such sincerity was the conflict of impulses in them, a genuine love which leads them both to disaster, Antony and Cleopatra in low life. If the book has a moral it would be the not very welcome one that idealising love is more dangerous than realistic sex. If Manon were as cynical as Michelet supposes, she would be incapable of warmth and affection and would be repulsive even to des Grieux ; and if he were as selfishly depraved as he is painted by the virtuous, why then he would never have been capable of suffering so much and so long for Manon.

There are faults of taste and perhaps of structure which can be alleged against *Manon Lescaut*. The presence of characters extraneous to the action (such as the "I" of Chapter I) is due to the fact that the book is simply an episode detached from a long novel. The virtuous friend, Tiberge, is often felt as an unreasonable affliction by the modern reader. The picaresque tone makes for sensationalism. Moreover, Manon's character involves Prévost in mechanical difficulties. To hold her des Grieux must have a little money, which he acquires by shady means ; but since she prefers him to anyone and will stay with him as long as he has any money, and neither is really extravagant, accidents have to be invented to precipitate ruin. Within a few pages we have a disastrous fire and an equally disastrous robbery by servants—neither improbable in itself, but taken together obviously devised and clumsy. And then it is certain that Prévost abuses the use of tears as a means of touching his readers. I once set out to re-read *Manon Lescaut* with the intention of making a list of the tear-sheddings, but after a certain number of pages I was once more so absorbed by the story that I forgot about these lachrymose statistics. And that, after all, is what matters in a novel—that it should hold our interest. All the rules and canons and "methods" and taste worked up by the art-and-craft-of-fiction people are so much wind compared with that essential quality. There is really only one rule for a novelist—not to be a bore.

## 5

Choderlos de Laclos—what a mouthful of odd syllables ! The only equivalent I know of is the English admiral, Sir Cloudesley Shovel. Our novelist's name suggests a Spanish origin, but he was born in fact at Amiens on the 19th of October, 1741. The family was of the minor nobility, and the son became an artillery officer in 1761, vegetating on garrison duty for many years with no hope of promotion. He was over forty when he attracted a young woman at La Rochelle, and had a child by her. Two years later, in 1786, when Laclos inherited a small income they were married, and seem to have been happy. Was this another case of "life imitating art ?" At all events, *Les Liaisons Dangereuses* had been written at Aix between July, 1780, and September, 1781, and published in Amsterdam the next year. It was a success of scandal, of esteem and of sales. The early bibliography has not been fully worked out, but there were at least ten editions within ten years.

As a young man Laclos is described as "tall, thin, narrow-shouldered, with blue eyes and fine pale features." He wept over the works of Rousseau, but had "a cold exterior" and disappointed ambitions.

This is almost a classic description of the eighteenth-century French revolutionary. Though a friend of Mirabeau and of Danton, Laclos attached himself to the party of the Duc d'Orléans (Philippe Egalité). Practically all the early Revolutionists (except the Marquis de Lafayette) were in the pay of Orléans, and Laclos was in the very centre of a complicated and obscure plot to get rid of Louis and Marie Antoinette, and to place Orléans on the throne.

Had this plot succeeded, Laclos would no doubt have achieved some important if temporary position on the way to the guillotine. It failed, and Laclos joined the Jacobins, still keeping in close touch with his Duke. After the flight to Varennes (June, 1791) Laclos did his best to serve Orléans, by trying to get him appointed Regent. This led to serious riots, to a split in the Jacobins, and to the downfall of Laclos, who was expelled from the Club (henceforth a violently republican body) and lost all influence with Orléans.

Nothing daunted, Laclos now proclaimed himself a republican, and though treated with suspicion and contempt by the Jacobins, he was made Commissioner to the army with the rank of *Maréchale de camp*, through the influence of his friend, Servan. It is said that he had a considerable share in the victory of Valmy. In 1792 he was appointed Governor General of the French possessions in India, and prepared one of the many plans formed by various people at various times for driving out the English. But as the revolutionary governments rapidly fell, Laclos's friends disappeared and his enemies took over. In March of 1793 he was arrested, along with the Duc d'Orléans, the Duke's children and mistress, Mme de Genlis.

To placate his enemies Laclos resigned from his rank of general and his more or less imaginary governor generalship of India. He was released under surveillance for a short time, but re-arrested, and remained in prison for thirteen months, during much of the time in dire peril of Fouquier-Tinville and the guillotine. The Thermidore revolution—or, should one say, reaction ?—saved his life. He was released and given 10,000 livres compensation, but no military employment until Brumaire and Bonaparte came along.

Boney knew the value of trained officers, and promptly appointed Laclos a general of artillery and sent him to the front—a professional soldier who had his baptism of fire at sixty. Perhaps this was a little late in life, but evidently he failed to please the autocrat and was packed off to command the artillery train at Taranto—an immense distance from Paris in those days, and much dreaded by French officers as an unhealthy place. There Laclos died of dysentery on the 3rd September, 1803. His last thoughts and his last written words were a plea to Marshal Marmont on behalf of his wife and children—a strange end for the man who was supposed to have drawn his own character as the Vicomte de Valmont, the heartless " seducer."

In spite of what it owes to earlier writers, such as Marivaux and Rousseau, *Les Liaisons Dangereuses* is an original work as well as a book of sinister power. The novels and memoirs of the period show that situations and characters such as Laclos depicted with almost mathematical precision were by no means impossible. I should say they had more real life basis and owed less to the imagination of a gifted satirist than Major Evelyn Waugh's bright young people. As I have indicated earlier, the fundamental idea had been stated by La Rochefoucauld in his constipated way, but it was left to Laclos to demonstrate vividly that sex might be allied, not with affection, but with malice, that it could be just as destructive as it was held to be the opposite.

The notion, so almost universal during the reign of public prudery in the nineteenth century, that *Les Liaisons Dangereuses* is a pornographic work, is one of the most mistaken that can be entertained. It is true that Laclos's theme called for a frankness of presentation most detestable to the posse of humbugs who stuck the figleaves on ; but pornography relies for its effects on rather primitive methods of titillating the libido. Laclos is not interested in these effects. His interest is psychological and—perhaps—political. Still, he was so much more of an artist or a scientist—they are much closer than they think—that any propaganda is wholly subsidiary to the psychological study.

This was the epoch of the Marquis de Sade, so that the theme of sex and malice cannot be held to be illusory. The very centre and dynamo of *Les Liaisons Dangereuses* is Madame de Merteuil, who may indeed have been devised by the author as a revenge on some unresponsive lady—but of this we have no evidence. Valmont was only considered to be the villain of the piece by generations who held the idea that men seduce women, and not vice versa, as Prévost had already shown.

The Marquise de Merteuil and the Vicomte de Valmont have had an affair, have parted amiably, but the Vicomte wants to renew it. The Marquise doesn't refuse, but as a price demands that Valmont shall " seduce " the wife of a judge, the virtuous Mme de Tourvel. Later, in order to be revenged on an ex-lover she arranges for the " seduction " of Cécile, the girl he is to marry. Cécile is helped in her love affair with the young Chevalier Danceny. But—here comes in a superb piece of irony—Cécile's sexual education is taken in hand by the Vicomte, while Mme de Merteuil renders the same service to Danceny. Meanwhile, after an interminable correspondence and more scruples than even the Princesse de Clèves thought necessary, the virtuous Rousseauesque heroine, Mme de Tourvel, yields to the Vicomte. He triumphantly informs the Marquise, but she guesses that the Vicomte is really in love with the Tourvel, and, playing on his silly vanity, forces him to write an unforgivable letter to Tourvel. The Vicomte once more claims his reward, only to find Danceny present at the rendezvous. Furious, he threatens war, which the Merteuil cynically accepts. Now melodrama rears its ugly head. Mme de Tourvel, dies of grief ; Danceny kills Valmont in a duel ; Cécile is thrust into a convent. But the Merteuil ? It is true that publication of her letters will be a social disaster, but this would not be enough for the moralists. So, with amusing cynicism, Laclos smites her with smallpox and financial losses—in no way connected with the construction of the book. In other words—malice really does triumph.

An interesting example of human fondness for seeing life in terms of *a priori* conventions is furnished by the comments on this book. The very people who thought Mme de Lafayette's innocently pompous idealities were " realism," the people who thought Prévost's romantic gutter idyll was " realism," exclaimed against *Les Liaisons Dangereuses* as mere invention and perversion. But who that has looked at human life without prejudice can doubt its essential truth to human nature? Of course, it is not the whole of human nature, but it is a neglected aspect presented with masterly skill and accuracy. Life does not arrange itself quite so symmetrically—that is what art does for life—but anyone over thirty-five who does know every one of Laclos's characters has not been around much. Even that rustic little village of London could furnish them.

The political bias of the book is slight, but decisive. Think back once more to *La Princesse de Clèves*—that is how the French aristocracy wished to be thought of, as dignified, sober, restrained, ready to sacrifice themselves quixotically to the idea of honour. Laclos is cunning. He does not deny, like a modern propagandist, all virtue to his enemy. On the contrary, he shows a virtuous Mme de Tourvel, a generous Danceny, an " innocent " Cécile, a Polonian Mme de Volanges. But they are all the easy victims of the " wicked " Marquise and her unconscious tool, the Vicomte. The argument of M. de Laclos is plain : " True, there are virtuous members of the possessing class, but they are infected by the wicked ones and become like them. Therefore, let us overturn the social system, and find me a well-paid job."

The novel in letter-form is now practically extinct, but was almost the dominant form in France at this time. The *Letters of Mme de Sévigné* had given prestige to the letter as a literary form ; then came the success of Richardson's *Pamela,* followed by the immense vogue of Rousseau's *La Nouvelle Héloïse.* Laclos handles the form with amazing skill. Each writer has a style of his own—difficult to indicate in translation—and while the complex intrigue is cunningly woven the oblique analysis of character proceeds with precision. Nothing could be better done, and Laclos might claim to be the real master of Stendhal and eventually of Flaubert and the Naturalistes. But to my mind the letter-form of *Les Liaisons Dangereuses* lays itself open to a fatal objection. I feel it improbable that any group of people would have carried on so much of their most intimate erotic life by correspondence. Even the " innocent " ones might well have hesitated to put so much on paper, while two artful buzzards like Merteuil and Valmont would certainly not have put such damning evidence into anyone's hands. But every art has its conventions, and in this case the letter-form must just be accepted. It did not prevent Laclos from writing a masterpiece.

## 6

Looking at the blank paper on which I am to put all Balzac in a nutshell, I cannot help thinking of the horrible literary meals to which in the days of ignorance one was betrayed by false pretences. In spite of assurances to the contrary, the awful moment arrived when the Chairwoman rose once more and coquettishly announced: " Though you may not know it, we have among us . . . Mr. Aldington I'm sure will be glad to tell us *all* that is going on among the younger European writers—Mr. Aldington." Well, you get up reluctantly and do your best, and a fine mess it is.

Another memory presents itself—Flaubert writing of Balzac: " *C'est un immense bonhomme, mais de seconde ordre.*" Well, Flaubert no doubt had the right to speak of Balzac as second-rate, but what I am thinking about is the immensity. It is true that all sorts of reservations may be made about this " immensity "—its pretentiousness, its presumption, its falsities, its vulgarities, and so on and so on. But the fact remains that Balzac is unique, and that no other novelist has laboured so heroically to present—not a group or circle or a class—but a whole world. There is something finicky, not to say thin-lipped, about a taste which thinks itself too good to include Balzac.

His life is as curious and as full of gusto as his writings. First of all he was not " de Balzac " or even " Balzac " but " Balssa " or " Balsa," descended from a family of Auvergne peasants on the father's side. He was born at Tours in 1799, was an average sort of pupil as a schoolboy, and worked for some time in a lawyer's office. Throwing up this work he lived in a garret, wrote tragedies and a stupendous number of bad novels under pseudonyms.

In 1822 he fell in love with a married woman Mme de Berny, a godchild of Louis XVI and Marie Antoinette, twenty-three years older than he was; and she became his mistress. (In *La Duchesse de Langeais* it is written that only a woman's last love can respond to a man's first love.) This singular affair lasted for nearly ten years. Meanwhile Balzac involved himself in a series of business enterprises, for which he thought himself divinely gifted—a piece of presumption which involved him in financial losses of 100,000 francs. No more than Sir Walter Scott (one of his most admired literary heroes) did Balzac ever succeed in paying off this debt. Certainly, he made a lot of money but he was extravagant, and in the end 90,000 francs of the debt were liquidated by his mother.

He was thirty before he wrote his first real novel, *Les Chouans*, and thereafter his life was a prodigious effort of work, during which he turned out the *Comédie Humaine* along with many attempts at plays and much forgotten journalism. Meanwhile Balzac went courting with the

Almanac de Gotha in his hand—the middle-aged Duchesse d'Abrantès (widow of that Marshal Junot who was so soundly trounced by Wellington), then the Duchesse de Castries, who flirted with him and turned him down. A fan letter from the Ukraine introduced him to a Polish Countess, Mme Hanska, whom he married only a little time before his death after a long and trying courtship. He died, still harnessed to his endless labour of the pen, in 1850.

Nobody can read Balzac without perceiving that he "fancied himself," as the saying is, as a business man and a ladies' man. I do not think there is any novelist who goes into so many details about money, who attaches so much importance to the money affairs of his characters, and who tries to give the impression of being a financial genius. And, although the mysteries of a woman's heart and the way of a man with somebody else's wife are specialities of the French school of novelists, Balzac does like to give us the impression of his own omniscience and irresistible charm in such matters. His actual record in both love and money was far from brilliant.

In 1832 Balzac received an anonymous fan letter from a woman, to which he replied. In due course the unknown revealed herself, and turned out to be another Duchess, but not a mere Napoleonic creation like poor Mme d'Abrantès. This was a Duchess "out of the top drawer," a descendant of the old aristocracy, niece of the Duc de Fitz-James, wife of the Duc de Castries. She seems to have been a brilliant, handsome and attractive woman, with the excuse of a hunting accident to keep her extended half the day on a *chaise longue* and a great need to dissipate boredom. She is described as "coquettish, witty, penetrating, not of any deep emotional power, religious within the bounds of conventional good taste, with a slightly factitious warmth of manner. . . ."

One can imagine Balzac snorting with joy at the thought of such a conquest. How well it would sound in the gossip of "all Paris," what an admirable chapter in his posthumous biographies! Balzac, the catholic, the royalist, ought to have a Duchess of the old stock for a mistress. Unluckily for all these hopes, Mme de Castries, while appreciating his genius and enjoying Balzac's talk, was only amusing herself by flirtatious encouragements. Balzac, who can never be accused of under-estimating himself, bloomed and burgeoned into white waistcoats and fine linen, a blue coat with embossed gold buttons, silk stockings, a gold watch chain, new yellow gloves, an enormous beaver hat and a large cane.

The Duchess invited him to Aix, where her uncle, the Duc de Fitz-James, was most attentive to the genius. They both urged him to come on a tour of Italy. Suddenly Balzac broke off relations and returned to Paris, in a state of cerebral excitement which made his doctor apprehensive of brain fever. Evidently Mme de Castries had missed her destiny, by refusing to be Balzac's mistress.

Out of this frustrated affair came *La Duchesse de Langeais*. It is at once Balzac's compensation for his discomfiture as a would-be lover and a threat or series of threats of Mme de Castries—which must have amused that *mondaine* very much indeed. The prodigiously Napoleonic figure of General Montriveau may not strike the reader as a very realist portrait of M. de Balzac ; but there can be little doubt that the writer intended it to be. " See what grandeurs of heart and mind you have missed ! " it seems to say, and then, with a Romantic *rugissement de lion*, " Beware the vengeance of such a hero ! I am capable of treating you as Montriveau treated Mme de Langeais ! " Setting himself (in the novel) a rôle of arduous constancy and search, Balzac pleasantly revenges himself by giving Mme de Langeais-Castries five years of austerities in a convent of Carmelites, and then, just as love breaks even convent bars to snatch her away, he kills her off. Carrying off the body of the once beloved and dropping it into the sea with a cannon ball on each leg was a piece of bad taste, like the accompanying remarks of M. de Ronquerolles. But there is worse taste in Balzac's predecessor, Chateaubriand (e.g., the burial of Atala) and in his contemporaries, Victor Hugo and Bulwer Lytton. And, come to think of it, this age is not so impeccable in taste that it can afford to censure others.

*La Duchesse de Langeais* does not rank as one of Balzac's greatest works, *Le Curé de Tours* or *Le Père Goriot* or *Eugénie Grandet ;* but it does show some of Balzac's most conspicuous qualities and defects, and rounds out this collection by taking up again Mme de Lafayette's theme of renunciation in love. The enormous differences in approach and treatment illustrate the difference of two epochs as well as of two temperaments—they are almost as startling as the differences between a pseudo-classical statue in marble and a sound film in technicolour. But in Balzac's story the renunciation is not for the sake of duty or principle —though Balzac pulls out all the religious organ stops which Mme de Lafayette with impeccable taste barely touches ; the sacrifice is to Fate or rather to that vanity which Stendhal declared so often barred his compatriots from the *amour passion* known to other nations.

Undoubtedly, however, Balzac intended *La Duchesse de Langeais* to be a masterpiece of *amour passion.* The opening is capital—the old convent on the lonely island, the French general who for five years has been looking for a lost love in every European convent, the general's recognition that " she " is there from the music she plays on the organ and from her voice in the choir. This is a splendid opening to a highly romantic and tragical love story. Evidently after five years of absence the general and the mysterious nun are as much in love as ever. By interposing the maximum of obstacles between his lovers Balzac raises the amorous tension and expectancy to their highest power—a psychological truth overlooked by the advocates of sex as biology with or without culture.

Unluckily at this point Balzac's coffee régime came into full play. As everybody knows Balzac drugged himself with caffeine while writing. Caffeine, which is even more richly present in tea leaves than in coffee berries, has a strong effect on the central nervous system ; and of course can become a habit as powerful as that of alcohol, particularly with those who have a professional horror of alcohol. Balzac drank his coffee cold and almost intolerably strong, a sort of moistened coffee dust, which of course had a powerful effect on his nerves. Balzac himself has explained how his brain was stimulated and his ideas "moved like the battalions of Napoleon's army." Memories, he continues, charge up with banners flying ; the light cavalry of comparisons opens out in a magnificent gallop ; up rushes the artillery of logic ; witty remarks come up skirmishing . . . and "the paper is covered with ink, for the vigil begins and ends in torrents of black water, as a battle with black powder."

That's the trouble. So often when Balzac is at his best and going along splendidly, the caffeine gets hold of his brain and drowns the story in "torrents of ink," one of those long-winded would-be omniscient surveys which are almost fatal to the story and too often fatal to the patience of the modern reader. You have only to listen to a pack of old girls chirping over the teacups to realise the fatal loquacity engendered by caffeine.

This is what happens at this point in the *Duchesse de Langeais*. Just as the reader is all agog to know who these two are and how they got into this jam, and what will happen after that, Balzac launches out into an interminable semi-political discourse about the French aristocracy, their qualities and shortcomings—in fact, a long homily to Mme de Castries pointing out to her that her caste is doomed. In this Balzac was quite right, and much of what he says is interesting in itself, but it holds up the action too long, and is too long a digression for a full-length novel, let alone a *nouvelle*. Moreover, the build-up of the general is too lengthy, and here and there ridiculous. We do not catch up with the story and the real Balzac until the meeting of Mme de Langeais and the general, and her sudden caprice to attach him to herself as a sighing but unrequited follower.

Thereafter the story develops into a quite thrilling duel of the sexes and moves on almost flawlessly to its melodramatic finale. There is even a fine symbolism in the melodrama, for when the general and his mysterious powerful friends carry off Sister Theresa he finds they have only the body of the Duchesse de Langeais. The worst flaw is that little bit of essential machinery—the general's clock, which is so slow that he misses the supreme rendezvous which would have given them both if not happiness at least possession. An error of time is most unlikely in a professional military man, who is far more likely to be a monomaniac about punctuality. Apart from that, the tragedy moves admirably to its climax, and if you can accept Balzac's Restoration *décors*, his ornate psychological landscape, I see every reason why you should agree with me that in its own way *La Duchesse de Langeais* is also a masterpiece.

## 7

In introducing these novels I have assumed that the reader is mentally adult, sufficiently educated to understand that mankind has a past, sufficiently curious to be interested in phases of life and culture in another country, sufficiently supple to be able to entertain more than one idea at a time.

It is possible that the series of revolutions and wars which have occurred in the past thirty years will result in such changes of taste or even in such extinguishing of taste that books such as we have been discussing will be neglected and perhaps eventually lost, and a discussion like this be quite meaningless. Such changes have occurred before, sweeping away whole areas and centuries of culture and achievement, making obsolete the work of many generations of craftsmen, artists and poets. Distant posterity always agrees that these violences and changes were the best thing that could have happened, for otherwise of course distant posterity would not be made up of the same people. They survived, therefore they were the fittest.

At the present time literature and the arts generally survive chiefly as they serve commercial or political advertising or the basest kind of popular entertainment. The obsequious practitioners are enormously rewarded. Everything else is either "academic" or "long-haired" or "wild-eyed" or something of the kind, and the object of contempt, neglect or downright suppression. When the writer is not engaged in selling somebody's product or political programme, he is supposed to be entertaining (and flattering) the common man and his lady. Otherwise he (the writer) is a dilletante and a snob.

Of course, this does not prove anything against literature as an art. The eighth century preferred the droning of priests and the bellowing of intoxicated scalds to Catullus and Thucydides, but on the whole that rather disposed of the eighth century than of Catullus and Thucydides.

The error is in supposing that literature and the fine arts were ever understood or really loved at any time by more than a few persons. The philanthropists of the eighteenth and nineteenth centuries believed that you had only to put "the best" before the people—the common man and his lady—and the people would love it. The philanthropists also believed that "the people's art" would transcend in glory everything that had gone before. It seems to be the belief of many people that just this has occurred; but from this view I feel bound to dissent. Step aside a moment from the stream of life and muse over the popular novel and popular music, popular dancing and popular singing, the popular newspaper and the popular illustrated magazine, popular advertising and the popular politician. If these are the standard all I have written here is sheer waste of time and you made a great mistake in borrowing or pilfering this book.

# THE PRINCESS OF CLEVES

# THE PRINCESS OF CLEVES

## I

GRANDEUR and gallantry never appeared with more lustre in France, than in the last years of Henry the Second's reign. This Prince was amorous and handsome, and though his passion for Diana of Poitiers Duchess of Valentinois, was of above twenty years standing, it was not the less violent, nor did he give less distinguishing proofs of it.

As he was happily turned to excel in bodily exercises, he took a particular delight in them, such as hunting, tennis, running at the ring, and the like diversions. Madam de Valentinois gave spirit to all entertainments of this sort, and appeared at them with grace and beauty equal to that of her grand-daughter, Madam de la Marke, who was then unmarried; the Queen's presence seemed to authorise hers.

The Queen was handsome, though not young; she loved grandeur, magnificence and pleasure; she was married to the King while he was Duke of Orleans, during the life of his elder brother the Dauphin, a prince whose great qualities promised in him a worthy successor of his father Francis the First.

The Queen's ambitious temper made her taste the sweets of reigning, and she seemed to bear with perfect ease the King's passion for the Duchess of Valentinois, nor did she express the least jealousy of it; but she was so skilful a dissembler, that it was hard to judge of her real sentiments, and policy obliged her to keep the duchess about her person, that she might draw the King to her at the same time. This Prince took great delight in the conversation of women, even of such as he had no passion for; for he was every day at the Queen's court, when she held her assembly, which was a concourse of all that was beautiful and excellent in either sex.

Never were finer women or more accomplished men seen in any Court, and Nature seemed to have taken pleasure in lavishing her greatest graces on the greatest persons. The Princess Elizabeth, since Queen of Spain, began now to manifest an uncommon wit, and to display those beauties, which proved afterwards so fatal to her. Mary Stuart, Queen of Scotland, who had just married the Dauphin, and was called the Queen-Dauphin, had all the perfections of mind and body; she had been educated in the Court of France, and had imbibed all the politeness of it; she was by nature so well formed to shine in everything that was polite, that notwithstanding her youth, none surpassed her in the most refined accomplishments. The Queen, her mother-in-law, and the King's sister, were also extreme lovers of music, plays and poetry; for the taste which Francis the First had for the Belles Lettres was not yet extinguished in France ; and as his son was addicted to exercises, no kind of pleasure was wanting at Court. But what rendered this Court so splendid, was the presence of so many great Princes, and persons of the highest quality and merit : those I shall name, in their different characters, were the admiration and ornament of their age.

The King of Navarre drew to himself the respect of all the world both by the greatness of his birth, and by the dignity that appeared in his person ; he was remarkable for his skill and courage in war. The Duke of Guise had also given proofs of extraordinary valour, and had, been so successful, that there was not a general who did not look upon him with envy ; to his valour he added a most exquisite genius and understanding, grandeur of mind, and a capacity equally turned for military or civil affairs. His brother, the Cardinal of Loraine, was a man of boundless ambition, and of extraordinary wit and eloquence, and had besides acquired a vast variety of learning, which enabled him to make himself very considerable by defending the Catholic religion, which began to be attacked at that time. The Chevalier de Guise, afterwards called Grand Prior, was a prince beloved by all the world, of a comely person, full of wit and address, and distinguished through all Europe for his valour. The Prince of Conde, though little indebted to Nature in his person, had a noble soul, and the liveliness of his wit made him amiable even in the eyes of the finest women. The Duke of Nevers, distinguished by the high employments he had possessed, and by the glory he had gained in war, though in an advanced age, was yet the delight of the Court : he had three sons very accomplished ; the second, called the Prince of Cleves, was worthy to support the honour of his house ; he was brave and generous, and showed a prudence above his years. The Viscount de Chartres, descended of the illustrious family of Vendome, whose name the Princes of the blood have thought it no dishonour to wear, was equally distinguished for gallantry ; he was genteel, of a fine mien, valiant, generous, and all these qualities he possessed in a very uncommon degree ; in short, if anyone could be compared to the Duke de Nemours, it was he. The Duke de Nemours was a masterpiece of Nature ; the beauty of his person, inimitable as it was, was his least perfection ; what placed him above other men, was a certain agreeablencss in his discourse, his actions, his looks, which was observable in none beside himself : he had in his behaviour a gaiety that was equally pleasing to men and women ; in his exercises he was very expert ; and in dress he had a peculiar manner, which was followed by all the world, but could never be imitated : in fine, such was the air of his whole person, that it was impossible to fix one's eye on anything else, wherever he was. There was not a lady at Court, whose vanity would not have been gratified by his address ; few of those whom he addressed, could boast of having resisted him ; and even those for whom he expressed no passion, could not forbear expressing one for him : his natural gaiety and disposition to gallantry was so great, that he could not refuse some part of his cares and attention to those who made it their endeavour to please him; and accordingly he had several mistresses, but it was hard to guess which of them was in possession of his heart: he made frequent visits to the Queen-Dauphin; the beauty of this princess, the sweetness of her temper, the care she took to oblige everybody, and the particular esteem she expressed for the Duke de Nemours, gave ground to believe, that he had raised his views even to her. Messieurs de Guise, whose niece she was, had so far increased their authority and reputation by this match, that their ambition prompted them to aspire at an equality with the Princes of the blood, and to share in power with the Constable Montmorency. The King entrusted the Constable with the chief share in the administration of the Government, and treated the Duke of Guise and the Mareschal de St André as his favourites; but whether favour or business admitted men to his presence, they could not preserve that privilege without the good-liking of the Duchess of Valentinois; for though she was no longer in possession either of youth or beauty, she yet reigned so absolutely in his heart, that his person and state seemed entirely at her disposal.

The King had such an affection for the Constable, that he was no sooner possessed of the Government, but he recalled him from the banishment he had been sent into by Francis the First: thus was the Court divided between Messieurs de Guise, and the Constable, who was supported by the Princes of the blood, and both parties made it their care to gain the Duchess of Valentinois. The Duke d'Aumale, the Duke of Guise's brother, had married one of her daughters, and the Constable aspired to the fame alliance; he was not contented with having married his eldest son with Madam Diana, the King's daughter by a Piemontese lady, who turned nun as soon as she was brought to bed. This marriage had met with a great many obstacles from the promises which Monsieur Montmorency had made to Madam de Piennes, one of the maids of honour to the Queen; and though the King had surmounted them with extreme patience and goodness, the Constable did not think himself sufficiently established, unless he secured Madam de Valentinois in his interest, and separated her from Messieurs de Guise, whose greatness began to give her uneasiness. The Duchess had obstructed as much as she could the marriage of the Dauphin with the Queen of Scotland; the beauty and forward wit of that young Queen, and the credit which her marriage gave to Messieurs de Guise, were insupportable to her; she in particular hated the Cardinal of Loraine, who had spoken to her with severity, and even with contempt; she was sensible he took the party of the Queen, so that the Constable found her very well disposed to unite her interests with his and to enter into alliance with him, by marrying her granddaughter Madam de la Marke with Monsieur d'Anville, his second son, who succeeded him in his employment under the reign of Charles the Ninth. The Constable did not expect to find the same disinclination to marriage in his second son, which he had found in his eldest, but he proved mistaken. The Duke d'Anville was desperately in love with the Dauphin-Queen, and how little hope soever he might have of succeeding in his passion, he could not prevail with himself to enter into an engagement that would divide his cares. The Mareschal de St. André was the only person in the Court, that had not listed in either party: he was a particular favourite, and the King had a personal affection for him; he had taken a liking to him ever since he was Dauphin, and created him a Mareschal of France at an age in which others rarely obtain the least dignities. His favour with the King gave him a lustre which he supported by his merit and the agreeableness of his person, by a splendour in his table and furniture, and by the most profuse magnificence that ever was known in a private person, the King's liberality enabling him to bear such an expense. This Prince was bounteous even to prodigality to those he favoured, and though he had not all the great qualities, he had very many; particularly he took delight and had great skill in military affairs; he was also successful, and excepting the Battle of St. Quintin, his reign had been a continued series of victory; he won in person the Battle of Renti, Piemont was conquered, the English were driven out of France, and the Emperor Charles V found his good fortune decline before the walls of Mets, which he besieged in vain with all the forces of the Empire, and of Spain: but the disgrace received at St. Quintin lessened the hopes we had of extending our conquests, and as fortune seemed to divide herself between two Kings, they both found themselves insensibly disposed to peace.

The Duchess Dowager of Loraine had made some overtures about the time of the Dauphin's marriage, since which a secret negotiation had been constantly carried on; in fine, Coran in Artois was the place appointed for the treaty; the Cardinal of Loraine, the Constable Montmorency, and the Mareschal de St. André were plenipotentaries for the King; the Duke of Alva, and the Prince of Orange for Philip the II, and the Duke and Duchess of Loraine were mediators. The principal articles were the marriage of the Princess Elizabeth of France with Don Carlos the Infanta of Spain, and that of his majesty's sister with the Duke of Savoy.

The King, during the Treaty, continued on the frontiers, where he received the news of the death of Queen Mary of England; his Majesty dispatched forthwith the Count de Randan to Queen Elizabeth, to congratulate her on her accession to the Crown, and they received him with great distinction; for her affairs were so precarious at that time, that nothing could be more advantageous to her, than to see her title acknowledged by the King. The Count found she had a thorough knowledge of the interests of the French Court, and of the characters of those who composed it; but in particular, she had a great idea of the Duke of Nemours: she spoke to him so often, and with so much earnestness concerning him, that the Ambassador upon his return declared to the King, that there was nothing which the Duke of Nemours might not expect from that Princess, and that he made no question she might even be brought to marry him. The King communicated it to the Duke the same evening, and caused the Count de Randan to relate to him all the conversations he had had with Queen Elizabeth, and in conclusion advised him to push his fortune: the Duke of Nemours imagined at first that the King was not in earnest, but when he found to the contrary, " If, by your advice, sir," said he, " I engage in this chimerical undertaking for your Majesty's service, I must entreat your Majesty to keep the affair secret, till the success of it shall justify me to the public; I would not be thought guilty of the intolerable vanity, to think that a Queen, who has never seen me, would marry me for love." The King promised to let nobody into the design but the Constable, secrecy being necessary, he knew, to the success of it. The Count de Randan advised the Duke to go to England under pretence of travelling; but the Duke, disapproving this proposal, sent Mr. Lignerol, a sprightly young gentleman, his favourite, to sound the Queen's inclinations, and to endeavour to make some steps towards advancing that affair: in the meantime, he paid a visit to the Duke of Savoy, who was then at Brussels with the King of Spain. The death of Queen Mary brought great obstructions to the Treaty; the Congress broke up at the end of November, and the King returned to Paris.

There appeared at this time a lady at Court, who drew the eyes of the whole world; and one may imagine she was a perfect beauty, to gain admiration in a place where there were so many fine women; she was of the same family with the Viscount of Chartres, and one of the greatest heiresses of France, her father died young, and left her to the guardianship of Madam de Chartres his wife, whose wealth, virtue, and merit were uncommon. After the loss of her husband she retired from Court, and lived many years in the country; during this retreat, her chief care was bestowed in the education of her daughter; but she did not make it her business to cultivate her wit and beauty only, she took care also to inculcate virtue into her tender mind, and to make it amiable to her. The generality of mothers imagine, that it is sufficient to forbear talking of gallantries before young people, to prevent their engaging in them; but Madam de Chartres was of a different opinion, she often entertained her daughter with descriptions of love; she showed her what there was agreeable in it, that she might the more easily persuade her wherein it was dangerous; she related to her the insincerity, the faithlessness, and want of candour in men, and the domestic misfortunes that flow from engagements with them; on the other hand she made her sensible, what tranquillity attends the life of a virtuous woman, and what lustre modesty gives to a person who possesses birth and beauty; at the same time she informed her, how difficult it was to perserve this virtue, except by an extreme distrust of one's self, and by a constant attachment to the only thing which constitutes a woman's happiness, to love and to be loved by her husband.

This heiress was, at that time, one of the greatest matches in France, and though she was very young several marriages had been proposed to her mother ; but Madam de Chartres being ambitious, hardly thought anything worthy of her daughter, and when she was sixteen years of age she brought her to Court. The Viscount of Chartres, who went to meet her, was with reason surprised at the beauty of the young lady ; her fine hair and lovely complexion gave her a lustre that was peculiar to herself ; all her features were regular, and her whole person was full of grace.

The day after her arrival, she went to choose some jewels at a famous Italian's ; this man came from Florence with the Queen, and had acquired such immense riches by his trade, that his house seemed rather fit for a Prince than a merchant ; while she was there, the Prince of Cleves came in, and was so touched with her beauty, that he could not dissemble his surprise, nor could Mademoiselle de Chartres forbear blushing upon observing the astonishment he was in ; nevertheless, she recollected herself, without taking any further notice of him than she was obliged to do in civility to a person of his seeming rank ; the Prince of Cleves viewed her with admiration, and could not comprehend who that fine lady was, whom he did not know. He found by her air, and her retinue, that she was of the first quality ; by her youth he should have taken her to be a maid, but not seeing her mother, and hearing the Italian call her madam, he did not know what to think ; and all the while he kept his eyes fixed upon her, he found that his behaviour embarrassed her, unlike to most young ladies, who always behold with pleasure the effect of their beauty ; he found too, that he had made her impatient to be going, and in truth she went away immediately : the Prince of Cleves was not uneasy at himself on having lost the view of her, in hopes of being informed who she was ; but when he found she was not known, he was under the utmost surprise ; her beauty, and the modest air he had observed in her actions, affected him so, that from that moment he entertained a passion for her. In the evening he waited on his Majesty's sister.

This Princess was in great consideration by reason of her interest with the King her brother ; and her authority was so great, that the King, on concluding the peace, consented to restore Piemont, in order to marry her with the Duke of Savoy. Though she had always had a disposition to marry, yet would she never accept of anything beneath a sovereign, and for this reason she refused the King of Navarre, when he was Duke of Vendome, and always had a liking for the Duke of Savoy ; which inclination for him she had preserved ever since she saw him at Nice, at the interview between Francis I, and Pope Paul III. As she had a great deal of wit, and a fine taste of polite learning, men of ingenuity were always about her, and at certain times the whole Court resorted to her apartments.

The Prince of Cleves went there according to his custom ; he was so touched with the wit and beauty of Mademoiselle de Chartres, that he could talk of nothing else; he related his adventure aloud, and was never tired with the praises of this lady, whom he had seen, but did not know; Madame told him, that there was nobody like her he described, and that if there were, she would be known by the whole world. Madam de Dampiere, one of the Princess's ladies of honour, and a friend of Madam de Chartres, overhearing the conversation, came up to her Highness, and whispered her in the ear, that it was certainly Mademoiselle de Chartres whom the Prince had seen. Madame, returning to her discourse with the Prince, told him, if he would give her his company again the next morning, he should see the beauty he was so much touched with. Accordingly Mademoiselle de Chartres came the next day to Court, and was received by both Queens in the most obliging manner that can be imagined, and with such admiration by everybody else, that nothing was to be heard at Court but her praises, which she received with so agreeable a modesty, that she seemed not to have heard them, or at least not to be moved with them. She afterwards went to wait upon Madame; that Princess, after having commended her beauty, informed her of the surprise she had given the Prince of Cleves; the Prince came in immediately after; "Come hither," said she to him, "see, if I have not kept my word with you, and if at the same time that I show you Mademoiselle de Chartres, I don't show you the lady you are in search of. You ought to thank me, at least, for having acquainted her how much you are her admirer."

The Prince of Cleves was overjoyed to find that the lady he admired was of quality equal to her beauty; he addressed her, and entreated her to remember that he was her first lover, and had conceived the highest honour and respect for her, before he knew her.

The Chevalier de Guise, and the Prince, who were two bosom friends, took their leave of Madame together. They were no sooner gone but they began to launch out into the praises of Mademoiselle de Chartres, without bounds; they were sensible at length that they had run into excess in her commendation, and so both gave over for that time; but they were obliged the next day to renew the subject, for this new-risen beauty long continued to supply discourse to the whole Court; the Queen herself was lavish in her praise, and showed her particular marks of favour; the Queen-Dauphin made her one of her favourites, and begged her mother to bring her often to her Court; the Princesses, the King's daughters, made her a party in all their diversions; in short, she had the love and admiration of the whole Court, except that of the Duchess of Valentinois: not that this young beauty gave her umbrage; long experience convinced her she had nothing to fear on the part of the King, and she had to great a hatred for the Viscount of Chartres, whom she had endeavoured to bring into her interest by marrying him with one of her daughters, and who had joined himself to the Queen's party, that she could not have the least favourable thought of a person who bore his name, and was a great object of his friendship.

The Prince of Cleves became passionately in love with Mademoiselle de Chartres, and ardently wished to marry her, but he was afraid the haughtiness of her mother would not stoop to match her with one who was not the head of his family: nevertheless his birth was illustrious, and his elder brother, the Count d'En, had just married a lady so nearly related to the Royal family, that this apprehension was rather the effect of his love, than grounded on any substantial reason. He had a great number of rivals; the most formidable among them, for his birth, his merit, and the lustre which Royal favour cast upon his house, was the Chevalier de Guise; this gentleman fell in love with Mademoiselle de Chartres the first day he saw her, and he discovered the Prince of Cleves's passion as the Prince of Cleves discovered his. Though they were intimate friends, their having the same pretentions gradually created a coolness between them, and their friendship grew into an indifference, without their being able to come to an explanation on the matter. The Prince of Cleves's good fortune in having seen Mademoiselle de Chartres first seemed to be a happy presage, and gave him some advantage over his rivals, but he foresaw great obstructions on the part of the Duke of Nevers his father: the Duke was strictly attached to the Duchess of Valentinois, and the Viscount de Chartres was her enemy, which was a sufficient reason to hinder the Duke from consenting to the marriage of his son, with a niece of the Viscount's.

Madam de Chartres, who had taken so much care to inspire virtue into her daughter, did not fail to continue the same care in a place where it was so necessary, and where there were so many dangerous examples. Ambition and gallantry were the soul of the Court, and employed both sexes equally; there were so many different interests and so many cabals, and the ladies had so great a share in them, that love was always mixed with business, and business with love: nobody was easy, or indifferent; their business was to raise themselves, to be agreeable, to serve or disserve; and intrigue and pleasure took up their whole time. The care of the ladies was to recommend themselves either to the Queen, the Dauphin-Queen, or the Queen of Navarre, or to Madame, or the Duchess of Valentinois. Inclination, reasons of decorum, resemblance of temper made their applications different; those who found the bloom worn off, and who professed an austerity of virtue, were attached to the Queen; the younger sort, who loved pleasure and gallantry, made their Court to the Queen-Dauphin; the Queen of Navarre too had her favourites, she was young, and had great power with the King her husband, who was in the interest of the Constable, and by that means increased his authority; Madame was still very beautiful, and drew many ladies into her party. And as for the Duchess of Valentinois, she could command as many as she would condescend to smile upon; but very few women were agreeable to her, and excepting some with whom she lived in confidence and familiarity, and whose humour was agreeable to her own, she admitted none but on days when she gratified her vanity in having a Court in the same manner the Queen had

All these different cabals were full of emulation and envy towards one another; the ladies, who composed them, had their jealousies also among themselves, either as to favour or lovers: the interests of ambition were often blended with concerns of less importance, but which did not affect less sensibly; so that in this Court there was a sort of tumult without disorder, which made it very agreeable, but at the same time very dangerous for a young lady. Madam de Chartres perceived the danger, and was careful to guard her daughter from it; she entreated her, not as a mother, but as her friend, to impart to her all the gallantry she should meet withal, promising her in return to assist her in forming her conduct right, as to things in which young people are oftentimes embarrassed.

The Chevalier de Guise was so open and unguarded with respect to his passion for Mademoiselle de Chartres, that nobody was ignorant of it: nevertheless he saw nothing but impossibilities in what he desired; he was sensible that he was not a proper match for Mademoiselle de Chartres, by reason of the narrowness of his fortune, which was not sufficient to support his dignity; and he was sensible besides, that his brothers would not approve of his marrying, the marriages of younger brothers being looked upon as what tends to the lessening great families; the Cardinal of Loraine soon convinced him, that he was not mistaken; he condemned his attachment to Mademoiselle de Chartres with warmth, but did not inform him of his true reasons for so doing; the Cardinal, it seems, had a hatred to the Viscount, which was not known at that time, but afterwards discovered itself; he would rather have consented to any other alliance for his brother than to that of the Viscount; and he declared his aversion to it in so public a manner, that Madam de Chartres was sensibly disgusted at it. She took a world of pains to show that the Cardinal of Loraine had nothing to fear, and that she herself had no thoughts of this marriage; the Viscount observed the same conduct, and resented that of the Cardinal more than Madam de Chartres did, being better apprised of the cause of it.

The Prince of Cleves had not given less public proofs of his love, than the Chevalier de Guise had done, which made the Duke of Nevers very uneasy; however he thought that he needed only to speak to his son, to make him change his conduct; but he was very much surprised to find him in a settled design of marrying Mademoiselle de Chartres, and flew out into such excesses of passion on that subject, that the occasion of it was soon known to the whole Court, and among others to Madam de Chartres: she never imagined that the Duke of Nevers would not think her daughter a very advantageous match for his son, nor was she a little astonished to find that the houses both of Cleves and Guise avoided her alliance, instead of courting it. Her resentment on this account put her upon finding out a match for her daughter, which would raise her above those that imagined themselves above her; after having looked about, she fixed upon the Prince Dauphin, son of the Duke de Montpensier, one of the most considerable persons then at Court. As Madam de Chartres abounded in wit, and was assisted by the Viscount, who was in great consideration, and as her daughter herself was a very considerable match, she managed the matter with so much dexterity and success, that Monsieur de Montpensier appeared to desire the marriage, and there was no appearance of any difficulties in it.

The Viscount, knowing the power the Dauphin-Queen had over Monsieur d'Anville, thought it not amiss to employ the interest of that Princess to engage him to serve Mademoiselle de Chartres, both with the King and the Prince de Montpensier, whose intimate friend he was: he spoke to the Dauphin-Queen about it, and she entered with joy into an affair which concerned the promotion of a lady, for whom she had a great affection; she expressed as much to the Viscount, and assured him, that though she knew she should do what was disagreeable to the Cardinal of Loraine her uncle, she would pass over that consideration with pleasure, because she had reasons of complaint against him, since he every day more and more espoused the interest of the Queen against hers.

Persons of gallantry are always glad of an opportunity of speaking to those who love them. No sooner was the Viscount gone, but the Queen-Dauphin sent Chatelart to Monsieur d'Anville, to desire him from her to be at Court that evening. Chatelart was his favourite, and acquainted with his passion for this Princess, and therefore received her commands with great pleasure and respect. He was a gentleman of a good family in Dauphiny; but his wit and merit distinguished him more than his birth: he was well received at Court. He was graceful in his person, perfect at all sorts of exercises; he sung agreeably, he wrote verses, and was of so amorous and gallant a temper, as endeared him to Monsieur d'Anville in such a degree, that he made him the confidant of his amours between the Queen-Dauphin and him; this confidence gave him access to that Princess, and it was owing to the frequent opportunities he had of seeing her, that he commenced that unhappy passion which deprived him of his reason, and at last cost him his life.

Monsieur d'Anville did not fail to be at Court in the evening; he thought himself very happy, that the Queen-Dauphin had made choice of him to manage an affair she had at heart, and he promised to obey her commands with the greatest exactness. But the Duchess of Valentinois being warned of the design in view, had traversed it with so much care, and prepossessed the King so much against it, that when Monsieur d'Anville came to speak to his Majesty about it, he plainly showed he did not approve of it, and commanded him to signify as much to the Prince de Montpensier. One may easily judge what the sentiments of Madam de Chartres were, upon the breaking off of an affair which she had set her mind so much upon, and the ill success of which gave such an advantage to her enemies, and was so great a prejudice to her daughter.

The Queen-Dauphin declared to Mademoiselle de Chartres, in a very friendly manner, the uneasiness she was in for not having been able to serve her: "You see, Madam," said she to her, "that my interest is small; I am upon so ill terms with the Queen and the Duchess of Valentinois, that it is no wonder if they or their dependents still succeed in disappointing my desires; nevertheless, I have constantly used my endeavours to please them. Indeed, they hate me not for my own sake, but for my mother's; she formerly gave them some jealousy and uneasiness; the King was in love with her before he was in love with the Duchess; and in the first years of his marriage, when he had no issue, he appeared almost resolved to be divorced from the Queen, in order to make room for my mother, though at the same time he had some affection for the Duchess. Madam de Valentinois being jealous of a lady whom he had formerly loved, and whose wit and beauty were capable of lessening her interest, joined herself to the Constable, who was no more desirous than herself that the King should marry a sister of the Duke of Guise; they possessed the deceased King with their sentiments; and though he mortally hated the Duchess of Valentinois, and loved the Queen, he joined his endeavours with theirs to prevent the divorce; but in order to take from the King all thoughts of marrying the Queen my mother, they struck up a marriage between her and the King of Scotland, who had had for his first wife the King's sister, and they did this because it was the easiest to be brought to a conclusion, though they failed in their engagements to the King of England, who was very desirous of marrying her; and that failure wanted but little of occasioning a rupture between the two Crowns: for Henry the Eighth was inconsolable, when he found himself disappointed in his expectations of marrying my mother; and whatever other Princess of France was proposed to him, he always said, nothing could make him amends for her he had been deprived of. It is certainly true, that my mother was a perfect beauty; and what is very remarkable, is, that being the widow of the Duke of Longueville, three Kings should court her in marriage. Her ill fortune gave her to the least of them, and placed her in a kingdom where she meets with nothing but trouble. They say I resemble her, but I fear I shall resemble her only in her unhappy destiny; and whatever fortune may seem to promise me at present, I can never think I shall enjoy it."

Mademoiselle de Chartres answered the Queen, that these melancholy presages were so ill-grounded, that they would not disturb her long, and that she ought not to doubt but her good fortune would accomplish whatever it promised.

No one now entertained any further thoughts of Mademoiselle de Chartres, either fearing to incur the King's displeasure, or despairing to succeed with a lady, who aspired to an alliance with a Prince of the blood. The Prince of Cleves alone was not disheartened at either of these considerations; the death of the Duke of Nevers his father, which happened at that time, set him at entire liberty to follow his inclination, and no sooner was the time of mourning expired, but he wholly applied himself to the gaining of Mademoiselle de Chartres. It was lucky for him that he addressed her at a time when what had happened had discouraged the approaches of others. What allayed his joy was his fear of not being the most agreeable to her, and he would have preferred the happiness of pleasing to the certainty of marrying her without being beloved.

The Chevalier de Guise had given him some jealousy, but as it was rather grounded on the merit of that Prince than on any action of Mademoiselle de Chartres, he made it his whole endeavour to discover, if he was so happy as to have his addresses admitted and approved: he had no opportunity of seeing her but at Court or public assemblies, so that it was very difficult for him to get a private conversation with her; at last he found means to do it, and informed her of his intention and of his love, with all the respect imaginable. He urged her to acquaint him what the sentiments were which she had for him, assuring her, that those which he had for her were of such a nature as would render him eternally miserable, if she resigned herself wholly up to the will of her mother.

As Mademoiselle de Chartres had a noble and generous heart, she was sincerely touched with gratitude for the Prince of Cleves's behaviour; this gratitude gave a certain sweetness to her words and answers, sufficient to furnish hopes to a man so desperately enamoured as the Prince was, so that he flattered himself in some measure that he should succeed in what he so much wished for.

She gave her mother an account of this conversation; and Madam de Chartres told her, that the Prince of Cleves had so many good qualities, and discovered a discretion so much above his years, that if her inclination led her to marry him, she would consent to it with pleasure. Mademoiselle de Chartres made answer, that she observed in him the same good qualities; that she should have less reluctance in marrying him than any other man, but that she had no particular affection to his person.

The next day the Prince caused his thoughts to be communicated to Madam de Chartres, who gave her consent to what was proposed to her; nor had she the least distrust but that in the Prince of Cleves she provided her daughter a husband capable of securing her affections. The articles were concluded; the King was acquainted with it, and the marriage made public.

The Prince of Cleves found himself happy, but yet not entirely contented: he saw with a great deal of regret, that the sentiments of Mademoiselle de Chartres did not exceed those of esteem and respect, and he could not flatter himself that she concealed more obliging thoughts of him, since the situation they were in permitted her to discover them without the least violence done to modesty. It was not long before he expostulated with her on this subject: "Is it possible," says he, "that I should not be happy in marrying you? and yet it is certain, I am not. You only show me a sort of civility which is far from giving me satisfaction; you express none of those pretty inquietudes, the concern, and impatience, which are the soul of love ; you are no further affected with my passion, than you would be with one which flowed only from the advantage of your fortune, and not from the beauty of your person." "It is unjust in you to complain," replied the Princess, "I don't know what you can desire of me more ; I think decency will not allow me to go further than I do." "It's true," replied he, "you show some appearances I should be satisfied with, were there anything beyond ; but instead of being restrained by decency, it is that only which makes you act as you do ; I am not in your heart and inclinations, and my presence neither gives you pain nor pleasure." "You can't doubt," replied she, "but it is a sensible pleasure to me to see you, and when I do see you, I blush so often, that you can't doubt, but the seeing you gives me pain also." "Your blushes, Madam," replied he, "cannot deceive me ; they are signs of modesty, but do not prove the heart to be affected, and I shall conclude nothing more from hence than what I ought."

Mademoiselle de Chartres did not know what to answer ; these distinctions were above her comprehension. The Prince of Cleves plainly saw she was far from having that tenderness of affection for him, which was requisite to his happiness ; it was manifest she could not feel a passion which she did not understand.

The Chevalier de Guise returned from a journey a few days before the marriage. He saw so many insuperable difficulties in his design of marrying Mademoiselle de Chartres, that he gave over all hopes of succeeding in it ; and yet he was extremely afflicted to see her become the wife of another : his grief however did not extinguish his passion ; and his love was as great as ever. Mademoiselle de Chartres was not ignorant of it ; and he made her sensible at his return, that she was the cause of that deep melancholy which appeared in his countenance. He had so much merit and so much agreeableness, that it was almost impossible to make him unhappy without pitying him, nor could she forbear pitying him ; but her pity did not lead to love. She acquainted her mother with the uneasiness which the Chevalier's passion gave her.

Madam de Chartres admired the honour of her daughter, and she admired it with reason, for never was anyone more naturally sincere ; but she was surprised, at the same time, at the insensibility of her heart, and the more so, when she found that the Prince of Cleves had not been able to affect her any more than others : for this reason, she took great pains to endear her husband to her, and to make her sensible how much she owed to the affection he had for her before he knew her, and to the tenderness he since expressed for her, by preferring her to all other matches, at a time when no one else durst entertain the least thoughts of her.

The marriage was solemnised at the Louvre ; and in the evening the King and the two Queens, with the whole Court, supped at Madam de Chartres's house, where they were entertained with the utmost magnificence. The Chevalier de Guise durst not distinguish himself by being absent from the ceremony, but he was so little master of himself that it was easy to observe his concern.

The Prince of Cleves did not find that Mademoiselle de Chartres had changed her mind by changing her name; his quality of a husband entitled him to the largest privileges, but gave him no greater share in the affections of his wife: hence it was, that though he was her husband, he did not cease to be her lover, because he had always something to wish beyond what he possessed; and though she lived perfectly easy with him, yet he was not perfectly happy. He preserved for her a passion full of violence and inquietude, but without jealousy, which had no share in his griefs. Never was husband less inclined to it, and never was wife farther from giving the least occasion for it. She was nevertheless constantly in view of the Court; she frequented the Courts of the two Queens, and of Madame: all the people of gallantry saw her both there and at her brother-in-law the Duke of Never's, whose house was open to the whole world; but she had an air which inspired so great respect, and had in it something so distant from gallantry, that the Mareschal de St. André, a bold man and supported by the King's favour, became her lover without daring to let her know it any otherwise than by his cares and assiduities. A great many others were in the same condition: and Madam de Chartres had added to her daughter's discretion so exact a conduct with regard to everything of decorum, that everybody was satisfied she was not be be come at.

The Duchess of Loraine, while she was employed in negotiating the peace, had applied herself to settle the marriage of the Duke her son: a marriage was agreed upon between him and Madam Claude of France, the King's second daughter; and the month of February was appointed for the nuptials.

In the meantime the Duke of Nemours continued at Brussels, his thoughts being wholly employed on his design in England; he was continually sending or receiving couriers from thence; his hopes increased every day, and at last Lignerolly sent him word that it was time to finish by his presence what was so well begun; he received this news with all the joy a young ambitious man is capable of, who sees himself advanced to a throne merely by the force of his personal merit; his mind insensibly accustomed itself to the grandeur of a Royal State; and whereas he had at first rejected this undertaking as an impracticable thing, the difficulties of it were now worn out of his imagination, and he no longer saw anything to obstruct his way.

He sent away in haste to Paris to give the necessary orders for providing a magnificent equipage, that he might make his appearance in England with a splendour suitable to the design he was to conduct; and soon after he followed himself, to assist at the marriage of the Duke of Loraine.

He arrived the evening before the espousals, and that very evening waited on the King to give him an account of his affair, and to receive his orders and advice how to govern himself in it. Afterwards he waited on the Queens; but the Princess of Cleves was not there, so that she did not see him, nor so much as know of his arrival. She had heard everybody speak of this celebrated Prince, as of the handsomest and most agreeable man at Court; and the Queen-Dauphin had described him in such a manner, and spoke of him to her so often, that she had raised in her a curiosity and even impatience to see him.

The Princess employed the day of the wedding in dressing herself, that she might appear with the greater advantage at the ball and royal banquet that were to be at the Louvre. When she came, everyone admired both her beauty and her dress. The ball began, and while she was dancing with the Duke of Guise, a noise was heard at the door of the hall, as if way was making for some person of uncommon distinction. She had finished her dance, and as she was casting her eyes round to single out some other person, the King desired her to take him who came in last; she turned about, and viewing him as he was passing over the seats to come to the place where they danced, she immediately concluded he was the Duke of Nemours. The Duke's person was turned in so delicate a manner, that it was impossible not to express surprise at the first sight of him, particularly that evening, when the care he had taken to adorn himself added much to the fine air of his carriage. It was as impossible to behold the Princess of Cleves without equal admiration.

The Duke de Nemours was struck with such surprise at her beauty, that when they approached and paid their respects to each other, he could not forbear showing some tokens of his admiration. When they begun to dance, a soft murmur of praises ran through the whole company. The King and the two Queens remembering, that the Duke and Princess had never seen one another before, found something very particular in seeing them dance together without knowing each other; they called them, as soon as they had ended their dance, without giving them time to speak to anybody, and asked them if they had not a desire to know each other, and if they were not at some loss about it. "As for me, Madam," said the Duke to the Queen, "I am under no uncertainty in this matter; but as the Princess of Cleves has not the same reasons to lead her to guess who I am, as I have to direct me to know her, I should be glad if your Majesty would be pleased to let her know my name." "I believe," said the Queen-Dauphin, "that she knows your name as well as you know hers." "I assure you, Madam," replied the Princess a little embarrassed, "that I am not so good a guesser as you imagine." "Yes, you guess very well," answered the Queen-Dauphin; "and your unwillingness to acknowledge that you know the Duke of Nemours, without having seen him before, carries in it something very obliging to him." The Queen interrupted them, that the ball might go on; and the Duke de Nemours took out the Queen-Dauphin. This Princess was a perfect beauty, and such she appeared in the eyes of the Duke de Nemours, before he went to Flanders; but all this evening he could admire nothing but Madam de Cleves.

The Chevalier de Guise, whose idol she still was, sat at her feet, and what had passed filled him with the utmost grief; he looked upon it as ominous for him, that fortune had destined the Duke of Nemours to be in love with the Princess of Cleves. And whether there appeared in reality any concern in the Princess's face, or whether the Chevalier's jealousy only led him to suspect it, he believed that she was touched with the sight of the Duke, and could not forbear telling her, that Monsieur de Nemours was very happy to commence an acquaintance with her by an incident which had something very gallant and extraordinary in it.

Madam de Cleves returned home with her thoughts full of what had passed at the ball; and though it was very late, she went into her mother's room to give her a relation of it; in doing which she praised the Duke of Nemours with a certain air, that gave Madam de Chartres the same suspicion the Chevalier de Guise had entertained before.

The day following the ceremony of the Duke of Loraine's marriage was performed; and there the Princess of Cleves observed so inimitable a grace, and so fine a mien in the Duke of Nemours, that she was yet more surprised.

She afterwards saw him at the Court of the Queen-Dauphin; she saw him play at tennis with the King; she saw him run the ring; she heard him discourse; still she found he far excelled everybody else, and drew the attention of the company to him wherever he was; in short, the gracefulness of his person, and the agreeableness of his wit soon made a considerable impression on her heart.

The Duke de Nemours had an inclination no less violent for her; and hence flowed all that gaiety and sweetness of behaviour, which the first desires of pleasing ordinarily inspire a man with: hence he became more amiable than ever he was before; so that by often seeing one another, and by seeing in each other whatever was most accomplished at Court, it could not be but that they must mutually receive the greatest pleasure from such a commerce.

The Duchess of Valentinois made one in all parties of pleasure; and the King was still as passionately fond of her as in the beginning of his love. The Princess of Cleves being at those years, wherein people think a woman is incapable of inciting love after the age of twenty-five, beheld with the utmost astonishment the King's passion for the Duchess, who was a grandmother, and had lately married her granddaughter: she often spoke on this subject to Madam de Chartres. "Is it possible, Madam," said she, "that the King should still continue to love? How could he take a fancy to one, who was so much older than himself, who had been his father's mistress, and who, as I have heard, is still such to many others?" "'Tis certain," answered Madam de Chartres, "it was neither the merit nor the fidelity of the Duchess of Valentinois, which gave birth to the King's passion, or preserved it; and this is what he can't be justified in; for if this lady had had beauty and youth suitable to her birth; and the merit of having had no other lover; if she had been exactly true and faithful to the King; if she had loved him with respect only to his person, without the interested views of greatness and fortune, and without using her power but for honourable purposes and for his Majesty's interest ; in this case it must be confessed, one could have hardly forbore praising his passion for her. If I was not afraid," continued Madam de Chartres, " that you would say the same thing of me which is said of most women of my years, that they love to recount the history of their own times, I would inform you how the King's passion for this Duchess began, and of several particulars of the Court of the late King, which have a great relation to things that are acted at present." " Far from blaming you," replied the Princess of Cleves, " for repeating the histories of past times, I lament, Madam, that you have not instructed me in those of the present, nor informed me as to the different interests and parties of the Court. I am so entirely ignorant of them, that I thought a few days ago, the Constable was very well with the Queen." " You was extremely mistaken," answered Madam de Chartres, " the Queen hates the Constable, and if ever she has power, he'll be but too sensible of it ; she knows, he has often told the King, that of all his children none resembled him but his natural ones." " I should never have suspected this hatred," said the Princess of Cleves, " after having seen her assiduity in writing to the Constable during his imprisonment, the joy she expressed at his return, and how she always calls him Compere, as well as the King." " If you judge from appearances in a Court," replied Madam de Chartres, " you will often be deceived ; truth and appearances seldom go together.

"But to return to the Duchess of Valentinois, you know her name is Diana de Poitiers ; her family is very illustrious, she is descended from the ancient Dukes of Aquitaine, her grandmother was a natural daughter of Lewis the XI, and in short she possesses everything that is great in respect of birth. St. Valier, her father, had the unhappiness to be involved in the affair of the Constable of Bourbon, which you have heard of ; he was condemned to lose his head, and accordingly was conducted to the scaffold : his daughter, viz., the Duchess, who was extremely beautiful, and who had already charmed the late King, managed so well, I don't know by what means, that she obtained her father's life ; the pardon was brought him at the moment he was expecting the fatal blow ; but the pardon availed little, for fear had seized him so deeply, that it bereft him of his senses, and he died a few days after. His daughter appeared at Court as the King's mistress ; but the Italian expedition, and the imprisonment of the present Prince, were interruptions to his love affair. When the late King returned from Spain, and Madam the Regent went to meet him at Bayonne, she brought all her maids of honour with her, among whom was Mademoiselle de Pisselen, who was since Duchess d'Etampes ; the King fell in love with her, though she was inferior in birth, wit and beauty to the Duchess of Valentinois, and had no advantage above her but that of being very young. I have heard her say several times, that she was born the same day Diana de Poitiers was married, but she spoke this in the malice of her heart, and not as what she knew to be true; for I am much mistaken, if the Duchess of Valentinois did not marry Monsieur de Breze, at the same time that the King fell in love with Madam d'Etampes. Never was a greater hatred than that between these two ladies; the Duchess could not pardon Madam d'Etampes for having taken from her the title of the King's mistress; and Madam d'Etampes was violently jealous of the Duchess, because the King still kept correspondence with her. That Prince was by no means constant to his mistresses; there was always one among them that had the title and honours of mistress, but the ladies of the small band, as they were styled, shared his favour by turns. The loss of the Dauphin, his son, who died at Tournon, and was thought to be poisoned, extremely afflicted him; he had not the same affection and tenderness for his second son, the present King; he imagined he did not see in him spirit and vivacity enough, and complained of it one day to the Duchess of Valentinois, who told him, she would endeavour to raise a passion in him for her, in order to make him more sprightly and agreeable. She succeeded in it, as you see, and this passion is now of above twenty years' duration, without being changed either by time or incidents.

"The late King at first opposed it; and whether he had still love enough left for the Duchess of Valentinois to be jealous, or whether he was urged on by the Duchess d'Etampes, who was in despair upon seeing the Dauphin so much attached to her enemy, it is certain he beheld this passion with an indignation and resentment, that showed itself every day by something or other. The Dauphin neither valued his anger or his hatred, nor could anything oblige him either to abate or conceal his flame, so that the King was forced to accustom himself to bear it with patience. This opposition of his to his father's will, withdrew his affections from him more and more, and transferred them to his third son, the Duke of Orleans, who was a Prince of a fine person full of fire and ambition, and of a youthful heat which wanted to be moderated; however, he would have made a very great Prince, had he arrived to a more ripened age.

"The rank of eldest, which the Dauphin held, and the King's favour which the Duke of Orleans was possessed of, created between them a sort of emulation, that grew by degrees to hatred. This emulation began from their infancy, and was still kept up in its height. When the Emperor passed through France, he gave the preference entirely to the Duke of Orleans, which the Dauphin resented so bitterly, that while the Emperor was at Chantilli, he endeavoured to prevail with the Constable to arrest him without waiting for the King's orders, but the Constable refused to do it: however, the King afterwards blamed him for not following his son's advice, and when he banished him the Court, that was one of the principal reasons for it.

"The discord between the two brothers put Madam d'Etampes upon the thought of strengthening herself with the Duke of Orleans, in order to support her power with the King against the Duchess of

Valentinois; accordingly she succeeded in it, and that young Prince, though he felt no emotions of love for her, entered no less into her interest, than the Dauphin was in that of Madam de Valentinois. Hence rose two factions at Court, of such a nature as you may imagine, but the intrigues of them were not confined to the quarrels of women.

The Emperor, who continued to have a great friendship for the Duke of Orleans, had offered several times to make over to him the Duchy of Milan. In the propositions which were since made for the peace, he gave hopes of assigning him the seventeen provinces, with his daughter in marriage. The Dauphin neither approved of the peace or the marriage, and in order to defeat both he made use of the Constable, for whom he always had an affection, to remonstrate to the King of what importance it was not to give his successor a brother so powerful as the Duke of Orleans would be with the alliance of the Emperor and those countries; the Constable came the more easily into the Dauphin's sentiments, as they were opposite to those of Madam d'Etampes, who was his declared enemy, and who vehemently wished for the promotion of the Duke of Orleans.

"The Dauphin commanded at that time the King's Army in Champaign, and had reduced that of the Emperor to such extremities, that it must have entirely perished, had not the Duchess d'Etampes, for fear too great successes should make us refuse peace, and the Emperor's alliance in favour of the Duke of Orleans, secretly advised the enemy to surprise Espernai and Cheteau-Thieni, in which places were great magazines of provisions; they succeeded in the attempt, and by that means saved their whole army.

"This Duchess did not long enjoy the success of her treason. A little after the Duke of Orleans died at Farmontiers of a kind of contagious distemper: he was in love with one of the finest women of the Court, and was beloved by her. I will not mention her name, because she has since lived with so much discretion, and has so carefully concealed the passion she had for that Prince, that one ought to be tender of her reputation. It happened she received the news of her husband's death at the same time as she heard of the Duke's, so that she had that pretext to enable her to conceal her real sorrow, without being at the trouble of putting any constraint upon herself.

"The King did not long survive the Prince his son; he died two years after; he recommended to the Dauphin to make use of the Cardinal de Tournon and the Admiral d'Annebault, but said nothing at all of the Constable, who was then in banishment at Chantilli. Nevertheless the first thing the King his son did was to recall him, and make him his Prime Minister.

"Madam d'Etampes was discarded, and received all the ill treatment she could possibly expect from an enemy so very powerful; the Duchess of Valentinois amply revenged herself both of that lady, and all those who had disobliged her; she seemed to reign more absolute in the King's heart, than she did even when he was Dauphin. During the twelve years' reign of this Prince she has been absolute in everything; she disposes of all governments and offices of trust and power; she has disgraced the Cardinal de Tournon, the Chancellor, and Villeroy; those who have endeavoured to open the King's mind with respect to her conduct, have been undone in the attempt; the Count de Taix, great Master of the Ordnance, who had no kindness for her, could not forbear speaking of her gallantries, and particularly of that with the Count de Brissac, of whom the King was already very jealous. Nevertheless she contrived things so well, that the Count de Taix was disgraced, and his employment taken from him; and what is almost incredible, she procured it to be given to the Count de Brissac, and afterwards made him a Mareschal of France. Notwithstanding, the King's jealousy increased to such a heigth, that he could no longer suffer him to continue at Court: this passion of jealousy, which is fierce and violent in other men, is gentle and moderate in him through the great respect he has for his mistress, and therefore he did not go about to remove his rival, but under the pretext of giving him the Government of Piemont. He has lived there several years; last winter he returned to Paris, under pretence of demanding troops and other necessaries for the Army he commands; the desire of seeing the Duchess of Valentinois again, and the fear of being forgotten by her, was perhaps the principal motive of this journey. The King received him very coldly; Messieurs de Guise, who have no kindness for him, but dare not show it on account of the Duchess, made use of Monsieur the Viscount, her declared enemy, to prevent his obtaining what he came to demand. It was no difficult matter to do him hurt. The King hated him, and was uneasy at his presence, so that he was obliged to return to Piemont without any benefit from his journey, except perhaps that of rekindling in the heart of the Duchess the flame which absence began to extinguish. The King has had a great many other subjects of jealousy, but either he has not been informed of them, or has not dared to complain of them.

"I don't know, daughter," added Madam de Chartres, "if I have not already told you more of these things, than you desired to know." "I am far, Madam, from complaining of that," replied the Princess of Cleves, "and if it was not for fear of being importunate, I should yet desire to be informed of several circumstances I am ignorant of."

The Duke de Nemours' passion for Madam de Cleves was at first so violent, that he had no relish left for any of the ladies he paid his addresses to before, and with whom he kept a correspondence during his absence; he even lost all remembrance of his engagements with them, and not only made it his business to find out excuses to break with them, but had not the patience to hear their complaints, or make any answer to the reproaches they laid upon him. The Queen-Dauphin herself, for whom his regards had been very tender, could no longer preserve a place in that heart which was now devoted to the Princess of Cleves. His impatience of making a tour to England began to abate, and he showed no earnestness in hastening his equipage. He frequently went to the Queen-Dauphin's Court, because the Princess of Cleves was often there, and he was very easy in leaving people in the opinion they had of his passion for that Queen ; he put so great a value on Madam de Cleves, that he resolved to be rather wanting in giving proofs of his love, than to hazard its being publicly known ; he did not so much as speak of it to the Viscount de Chartres, who was his intimate friend, and from whom he concealed nothing ; the truth is, he conducted this affair with so much discretion, that nobody suspected he was in love with Madam de Cleves, except the Chevalier de Guise ; and she would scarcely have perceived it herself, if the inclination she had for him had not led her into a particular attention to all his actions, but which she was convinced of it.

She no longer continued to have the same disposition to communicate to her mother what she thought concerning the Duke de Nemours, as she had to talk to her about her other lovers ; though she had no settled design of concealing it from her, yet she did not speak of it. Madam de Chartres, however, plainly perceived the Duke's attachment to her daughter, as well as her daughter's inclination for him ; the knowledge of this could not but sensibly afflict her, nor could she be ignorant of the danger this young lady was in, in being beloved by, and loving so accomplished a person as the Duke de Nemours : she was entirely confirmed in the suspicion she had of this business, by an incident which fell out a few days after.

The Mareschal de St. André, who took all opportunities to show his magnificence, desired the King, under pretence of showing him his house which was just finished, to do him the honour to sup there with the two Queens. The Mareschal was also very glad to display, in the sight of the Princess of Cleves, that splendid and expensive manner of life, which he carried to so great a profusion.

Some days before that appointed for the entertainment, the Dauphin, who had an ill state of health, found himself indisposed, and saw nobody ; the Queen-Dauphin had spent all that day with him ; and in the evening, upon his growing better, all the persons of quality that were in the anti-chamber were admitted ; the Queen-Dauphin returned to her own apartment, where she found Madam de Cleves and some other ladies, with whom she lived in familiarity.

It being already very late, and not being dressed, she did not wait upon the Queen, but gave out that she was not to be seen, and ordered her jewels to be brought, in order to choose out some for the Mareschal de St. André's Ball, and present the Princess of Cleves with some, as she had promised her. While they were thus employed, the Prince of Conde entered ; his great quality gave him free access everywhere. "Doubtless," said the Queen-Dauphin, " you come from the King my husband, what are they doing there ? " " Madam," said he, " they are maintaining a dispute against the Duke of Nemours, and he defends the argument he undertook with so much warmth, that he must needs be very much interested in it; I believe he has some mistress that gives him uneasiness by going to balls, so well satisfied he is that it is a vexatious thing to a lover to see the person he loves in those places."

"How," replied the Queen-Dauphin, "would not the Duke de Nemours have his mistress go to a ball? I thought that husbands might wish their wives would not go there; but as for lovers, I never imagined they were of that opinion." "The Duke de Nemours finds," answered the Prince of Conde, "that nothing is so insupportable to lovers as balls, whether they are beloved again, or whether they are not. He says, if they are beloved they have the chagrin to be loved the less on this account for several days; that there is no woman, whom her anxiety for dress does not divert from thinking on her lover; that they are entirely taken up with that one circumstance, that this care to adorn themselves is for the whole world, as well as for the man they favour; that when they are at a ball, they are desirous to please all who look at them; and that when they triumph in their beauty, they experience a joy to which their lovers very little contribute. He argues further, that if one is not beloved, it is a yet greater torment to see one's mistress at an assembly; that the more she is admired by the public, the more unhappy one is not to be beloved, and that the lover is in continual fear lest her beauty should raise a more successful passion than his own; lastly he finds, there is no torment equal to that of seeing one's mistress at a ball, unless it be to know that she is there, and not to be there one's self."

Madam de Cleves pretended not to hear what the Prince of Conde said, though she listened very attentively; she easily saw what part she had in the Duke of Nemours's opinion, and particularly as to what he said of the uneasiness of not being at a ball where his mistress was, because he was not to be at that of the Mareschal de St. André, the King having sent him to meet the Duke of Ferrara.

The Queen-Dauphin, and the Prince of Conde, not going into the Duke's opinion, were very merry upon the subject. "There is but one occasion, Madam," said the Prince to her, "in which the Duke will consent his mistress should go to a ball, and that is when he himself gives it. He says, that when he gave your Majesty one last year, his mistress was so kind as to come to it, though seemingly only to attend you; that it is always a favour done to a lover, to partake of an entertainment which he gives; that it is an agreeable circumstance for him to have his mistress see him preside in a place where the whole Court is, and see him acquit himself well in doing the honours of it." "The Duke de Nemours was in the right," said the Queen-Dauphin, smiling, "to approve of his mistress's being at his own ball; there was then so great a number of ladies, whom he honoured with the distinction of that name, that if they had not come, the assembly would have been very thin."

The Prince of Conde had no sooner begun to relate the Duke de Nemours's sentiments concerning assemblies, but Madam de Cleves felt in herself a strong aversion to go to that of the Mareschal de St. André. She easily came into the opinion, that a woman ought not to be at an entertainment given by one that professed love to her, and she was very glad to find out a reason of reservedness, for doing a thing which would oblige the Duke of Nemours. However, she carried away with her the ornaments which the Queen-Dauphin had given her; but when she showed them her mother, she told her that she did not design to make use of them; that the Mareschal de St. André took a great deal of pains to show his attachment to her, and she did not doubt he would be glad to have it believed that a compliment was designed her in the entertainment he gave the King, and that under the pretence of doing the honours of his house, he would show her civilities which would be uneasy to her.

Madam de Chartres for some time opposed her daughter's opinion, as thinking it very singular; but when she saw she was obstinate in it, she gave way, and told her, that in that case she ought to pretend an indisposition as an excuse for not going to the ball, because the real reasons which hindered her would not be approved of; and care ought to be taken that they should not be suspected. Madam de Cleves voluntarily consented to pass some days at her mother's, in order not to go to any place where the Duke of Nemours was not to be. However the Duke set out, without the pleasure of knowing she would not be at the ball.

The day after the ball he returned, and was informed that she was not there; but as he did not know the conversation he had at the Dauphin's Court had been repeated to her, he was far from thinking himself happy enough to have been the reason of her not going.

The day after, while he was at the Queen's apartments, and talking to the Queen-Dauphin, Madam de Chartres and Madam de Cleves came in. Madam de Cleves was dressed a little negligently, as a person who had been indisposed, but her countenance did not at all correspond with her dress. "You look so pretty," says the Queen-Dauphin to her, "that I can't believe you have been ill; I think the Prince of Conde, when he told us the Duke de Nemours's opinion of the ball, persuaded you, that to go there would be doing a favour to the Mareschal de St. André, and that that's the reason which hindered you from going." Madam de Cleves blushed, both because the Queen-Dauphin had conjectured right, and because she spoke her conjecture in the presence of the Duke de Nemours.

Madam de Chartres immediately perceived the true reason, why her daughter refused to go to the ball; and to prevent the Duke de Nemours discovering it, as well as herself, she took up the discourse after a manner that gave what she said an air of truth. "I assure you, Madam," said she to the Queen-Dauphin, "that your Majesty has done my daughter more honour than she deserves; she was really indisposed, but I believe, if I had not hindered her, she would not have failed to wait on you, and to show herself under any disadvantages, for the pleasure of seeing what there was extraordinary at yesterday's entertainment." The Queen-Dauphin gave credit to what Madam de Chartres said; but the Duke de Nemours was sorry to find so much probability in it: nevertheless, the blushes of the Princess of Cleves made him suspect, that what the Queen-Dauphin had said was not altogether false. The Princess of Cleves at first was concerned the Duke had any room to believe it was he who had hindered her from going to the Mareschal de St. André; but afterwards she was a little chagrined, that her mother had entirely taken off the suspicion of it.

Though the Congress of Cercamp had been broken off, the negotiations for the peace were continued, and things were so disposed, that towards the latter end of February the conferences were reassumed at Chateau-Cambresis; the same plenipotentiaries were sent as before, and the Mareschal de St. André being one, his absence freed the Duke de Nemours from a rival, who was formidable rather from his curiosity in observing those who addressed to Madam de Cleves, than from any advances he was capable of making himself in her favour.

Madam de Chartres was not willing to let her daughter see, that she knew her sentiments for the Duke, for fear of making herself suspected in some things which she was very desirous to tell her. One day she set herself to talk about him, and a great deal of good she said of him, but mixed with it abundance of sham praises, as the prudence he showed in never falling in love, and how wise he was to make the affair of women and love an amusement instead of a serious business: "It is not," added she, "that he is not suspected to have a very uncommon passion for the Queen-Dauphin; I observe he visits her very often; and I advise you to avoid, as much as possible, speaking to him, and especially in private; because, since the Queen-Dauphin treats you as she does, it would be said, that you are their confidant; and you know how disagreeable that sort of reputation is: I'm of opinion, if this report continues, that you should not visit the Queen-Dauphin so often, in order to avoid involving yourself in adventures of gallantry."

The Princess of Cleves had never heard before of the amour between the Duke de Nemours and the Queen-Dauphin; she was so much surprised at what her mother had told her, and seemed to see so plainly how she had been mistaken in her thoughts about the Duke, that she changed countenance. Madam de Chartres perceived it. Visitors came in that moment; and the Princess of Cleves retired to her own apartment, and shut herself up in her closet.

One can't express the grief she felt, to discover, by what her mother had been just saying, the interest her heart had in the Duke de Nemours; she had not dared as yet to acknowledge it to her secret thoughts; she then found, that the sentiments she had for him were such as the Prince of Cleves had required of her; she perceived how shameful it was to entertain them for another, and not for a husband that deserved them; she found herself under the utmost embarrassment, and was dreadfully afraid lest the Duke should make use of her only as a means to come at the Queen-Dauphin, and it was this thought determined her to impart to her mother something she had not yet told her.

The next morning she went into her mother's chamber to put her resolves in execution, but she found Madam de Chartres had some touches of a fever, and therefore did not think proper to speak to her: this indisposition however appeared to insignificant, that Madam de Cleves made no scruple after dinner to visit the Queen-Dauphin; she was in her closet with two or three ladies of her most familiar acquaintance. "We were speaking," said she to her, as soon as she saw her, "of the Duke de Nemours, and were admiring how much he's changed since his return from Brussels; before he went there, he had an infinite number of mistresses, and it was his own fault, for he showed an equal regard to those who had merit, and to those who had none; since his return he neither knows the one nor the other; there never was so great a change; I find his humour is changed too, and that he is less gay than he used to be."

The Princess of Cleves made no answer; and it shocked her to think she should have taken all that they said of the change in the Duke for proofs of his passion for her, had she not been undeceived; she felt in herself some little resentment against the Queen-Dauphin, for endeavouring to find out reasons, and seeming surprised at a thing, which she probably knew more of than anyone else; she could not forbear showing something of it; and when the other ladies withdrew, she came up and told her in a low voice, "And is it I, Madam, you have been pointing at, and have you a mind to conceal, that you are she who has made such an alteration in the conduct of the Duke of Nemours?" "You do me injustice," answered the Queen-Dauphin, "you know I conceal nothing from you; it is true the Duke of Nemours, before he went to Brussels, had, I believe, an intention to let me know he did not hate me; but since his return, it has not so much as appeared that he remembers anything of what he has done; and I acknowledge I have a curiosity to know what it is has changed him so: it would not be very difficult for me to unravel this affair," added she; "the Viscount de Chartres, his intimate friend, is in love with a lady with whom I have some power, and I'll know by that means the occasion of this alteration." The Queen-Dauphin spoke with an air of sincerity which convinced the Princess of Cleves, and in spite of herself she found her mind in a more calm and pleasing situation than it had been in before.

When she returned to her mother, she heard she was a great deal worse than she had left her; her fever was redoubled, and the days following it increased to so great a degree, that she was thought to be in danger. Madam de Cleves was in extreme grief on this occasion, and never stirred out of her mother's chamber. The Prince of Cleves was there too almost every day and all day long, partly out of affection to Madam de Chartres, and partly to hinder his lady from abandoning herself to sorrow, but chiefly that he might have the pleasure of seeing her, his passion not being at all diminished.

The Duke de Nemours, who had always had a great friendship for the Prince of Cleves, had not failed to show it since his return from Brussels; during the illness of Madam de Chartres he frequently found means to see the Princess of Cleves, pretending to want her husband, or to come to take him out to walk; he enquired for him at such hours as he knew very well he was not at home, and under pretence of waiting for him stayed in Madam de Cleves's anti-chamber, where there were always a great many people of quality; Madam de Cleves often came there, and her grief did not make her seem less handsome in the eyes of the Duke de Nemours; he made her sensible what interest he had in her affliction, and spoke to her with so submissive an air, that he easily convinced her, that the Queen-Dauphin was not the person he was in love with.

The seeing him at once gave her grief and pleasure; but when she no longer saw him, and reflected that the charm he carried about him when present, was an introduction to love, she was very near imagining she hated him, out of the excessive grief which that thought gave her.

Madam de Chartres still grew worse and worse, so that they began to despair of her life; she heard what the physicians told her concerning the danger she was in with a courage worthy her virtue, and her piety. After they were gone, she caused everybody to retire, and sent for Madam de Cleves.

"We must part, my dear daughter," said she, stretching out her hand to her; "the danger I leave you in, and the occasion you have for me, adds to the regret I have to leave you: you have a passion for the Duke de Nemours; I do not desire you to confess it; I am no longer in a condition to make use of that sincerity for your good; I have perceived this inclination a great while, but was not willing to speak to you of it at first, for fear of making you discover it yourself; you know it at present but too well; you are upon the brink of a precipice; great efforts must be used, and you must do great violence to your heart to save yourself: reflect what you owe to your husband; reflect what you owe to yourself, and think that you are going to lose that reputation which you have gained, and which I have so much at heart; call up, my dear daughter, all your courage and constancy; retire from Court; oblige your husband to carry you away; do not be afraid of taking such resolutions, as being too harsh and difficult; however frightful they may appear at first, they will become more pleasant in time, than the misfortunes that follow gallantry: if any other motives than those of duty and virtue could have weight with you, I should tell you that if anything were capable of disturbing the happiness I hope for in the next world, it would be to see you fall like other women; but if this calamity must necessarily happen, I shall meet death with joy, as it will hinder me from being a witness of it."

Madam de Cleves bathed with tears her mother's hand, which she held fast locked in her own; nor was Madam de Chartres less moved. "Adieu, dear daughter," said she, "let us put an end to a conversation which melts us both; and remember, if you are able, all that I have been saying to you."

When she had spoke this, she turned herself on the other side, and ordered her daughter to call her women, being unwilling either to hear her reply, or to speak any more. Madam de Cleves went out of her presence in a condition one need not describe; and Madam de Chartres thought of nothing but preparing herself for death: she lived two days longer, during which she would not see her daughter again; her daughter was the only thing she had reluctance to part with.

Madam de Cleves was in the utmost affliction; her husband did not leave her, and no sooner was her mother expired, but he carried her into the country, that she might not have in her eye a place which could serve only to sharpen her sorrow, which was scarce to be equalled. Though tenderness and gratitude had the greatest share in her griefs, yet the need which she found she had of her mother to guard her against the Duke of Nemours, added no small weight to them; she found she was unhappy in being left to herself, at a time when she was so little mistress of her own affections, and when she so much wished for somebody to pity and encourage her. The Prince of Cleves's behaviour to her on this occasion, made her wish more ardently than ever, never to fail in her duty to him; she also expressed more friendship and affection for him than she had done before; she would not suffer him to leave her, and she seemed to think that his being constantly with her could defend her against the Duke of Nemours.

The Duke came to see the Prince of Cleves in the country; he did what he could to pay a visit also to Madam de Cleves, but she refused to receive him; and being persuaded she could not help finding something dangerously lovely in him, she made a strong resolution to forbear seeing him, and to avoid all occasions of it that were in her power.

The Prince of Cleves went to Paris to make his Court, and promised his lady to return the next day, but however he did not return till the day after. "I expected you yesterday," said Madam de Cleves to him on his arrival, "and I ought to chide you for not having come as you promised; you know, if I was capable of feeling a new affliction in the condition I am in, it would be the death of Madam de Tournon, and I have heard of it this morning; I should have been concerned, though I had not known her; it is a melting consideration to think that a lady so young and handsome as she, should be dead in two days; but besides, she was the person in the world that pleased me most, and who appeared to have discretion equal to her beauty."

"I am sorry I could not return yesterday," replied the Prince of Cleves, "but my presence was so necessary to the consolation of an unhappy man, that it was impossible for me to leave him. As for Madam de Tournon, I do not advise you not to be concerned for her, if you lament her as a woman full of discretion, and worthy of your esteem." "You surprise me," answered Madam de Cleves, "I have heard you say several times, that there was not a lady at Court you had a greater respect for." "It is true," replied he, "but women are incomprehensible, and when I have seen them all, I think myself so happy in having you, that I cannot enough admire my good fortune." "You esteem me more than I deserve," answered Madam de Cleves, "you have not had experience enough yet to pronounce me worthy of you; but tell me, I beseech you, what it is has undeceived you with respect to Madam de Tournon." "I have been undeceived a great while," replied he, "and I know that she was in love with the Count de Sancerre, and that she gave him room to hope she would marry him." "I can't believe," said Madam de Cleves, "that Madam de Tournon, after so extraordinary an aversion as she has shown to marriage from the time she became a widow, and after the public declarations she has made that she would never marry again, should give hopes to Sancerre." "If she had given hopes to him only," replied the Prince of Cleves, "the wonder had not been so great; but what is surprising is, that she gave hopes likewise to Etouteville at the same time: I'll let you know the whole history of this matter."

## II

"You know the friendship there is betwixt Sancerre and me. Nevertheless about two years ago he fell in love with Madam de Tournon, and concealed it from me with as much care as from the rest of the world; I had not the least suspicion of it. Madam de Tournon as yet appeared inconsolable for the death of her husband, and lived in retirement with great austerity. Sancerre's sister was in a manner the only person she saw, and it was at her lodgings he became in love with her.

"One evening there was to be play at the Louvre, and the actors only waited for the coming of the King and Madam de Valentinois, when word was brought that she was indisposed, and that the King would not come. It was easy to see that the Duchess's indisposition was nothing but some quarrel with the King; everyone knew the jealousy he had had of the Mareschal de Brisac during his continuance at Court, but he had been set out some days on his return to Piemont, and one could not imagine what was the occasion of this falling out.

"While I was speaking of this to Sancerre, Monsieur d'Anville came into the room, and told me in a whisper, that the King was so exasperated and so afflicted at the same time, that one would pity him; that upon a late reconciliation between him and the Duchess, after the quarrel they had had about the Mareschal de Brisac, he had given her a ring, and desired her to wear it; and that as she was dressing herself to come to the play, he had missed it on her finger, and asked what was become of it; upon which she seemed in surprise that she had it not, and called to her women for it, who unfortunately, or for want of being better instructed, made answer they had not seen it four or five days.

"It was, continued Monsieur d'Anville, precisely so long, since the Mareschal de Brisac left the Court, and the King made no doubt but she gave him the ring when she took her leave of him. The thought of this awaked in so lively a manner that jealousy which was not yet extinguished, that he fell into uncommon transports, and loaded her with a thousand reproaches ; he is just gone into her apartment again in great concern, but whether the reason is a more confirmed opinion that the Duchess had made a sacrifice of the ring, or for fear of having disobliged her by his anger, I can't tell.

" As soon as Monsieur d'Anville had told me this news, I acquainted Sancerre with it ; I told it him as a secret newly entrusted with me, and charged him to say nothing of it.

" The next day I went early in the morning to my sister-in-law's, and found Madam de Tournon at her bedside, who had no great kindness for the Duchess of Valentinois, and knew very well that my sister-in-law had no reason to be satisfied with her. Sancerre had been with her, after he went from the play, and had acquainted her with the quarrel between the King and the Duchess ; and Madam de Tournon was come to tell it to my sister-in-law, without knowing or suspecting that it was I from whom her lover had it.

" As soon as I advanced toward my sister-in-law, she told Madam de Tournon, that they might trust me with what she had been telling her ; and without waiting Madam de Tournon's leave she related to me word by word all I had told Sancerre the night before. You may judge what surprise I was in ; I looked hard at Madam de Tournon, and she seemed disordered ; her disorder gave me a suspicion. I had told the thing to nobody but Sancerre ; he left me when the comedy was done, without giving any reason for it ; I remembered to have heard him speak much in praise of Madam de Tournon ; all these things opened my eyes, and I easily discerned there was an intrigue between them, and that he had seen her since he left me.

" I was so stung to find he had concealed this adventure from me, that I said several things which made Madam de Tournon sensible of the imprudence she had been guilty of ; I led her back to her coach, and assured her, I envied the happiness of him who informed her of the King's quarrel with the Duchess of Valentinois.

" I went immediately in search of Sancerre, and severely reproached him ; I told him I knew of his passion for Madam de Tournon, without saying how I came by the discovery ; he was forced to acknowledge it ; I afterwards informed him what led me into the knowledge of it, and he acquainted me with the detail of the whole affair ; he told me, that though he was a younger brother, and far from being able to pretend to so good a match, nevertheless she was determined to marry him. I can't express the surprise I was in ; I told Sancerre he would do well to hasten the conclusion of the marriage, and that there was nothing he had not to fear from a woman, who had the artifice to support, in the eye of the public, appearances so distant from truth ; he gave me in answer, that she was really concerned for the loss of her husband, but that the inclination she had for him had surmounted that affliction, and that she could not help discovering all on a sudden so great a change; he mentioned besides several other reasons in her excuse, which convinced me how desperately he was in love; he assured me he would bring her to consent that I should know his passion for her, especially since it was she herself who had made me suspect it; in a word, he did oblige her to it, though with a great deal of difficulty, and I grew afterwards very deep in their confidence.

"I never knew a lady behave herself in so genteel and agreeable a manner to her lover, but yet I was always shocked at the affectation she showed in appearing so concerned for the loss of her husband. Sancerre was so much in love, and so well pleased with the treatment he received from her, that he scarce durst press her to conclude the marriage, for fear she should think he desired it rather out of interest than love; however he spoke to her of it, and she seemed fully bent on marrying him; she began also to abandon her reserved manner of life, and to appear again in public; she visited my sister-in-law at hours when some of the Court were usually there; Sancerre came there but seldom, but those who came every night, and frequently saw her there, thought her extremely beautiful.

"She had not long quitted her solitude, when Sancerre imagined that her passion for him was cooled; he spoke of it several times to me: but I laid no great stress on the matter; but at last, when he told me, that instead of forwarding the marriage, she seemed to put it off, I began to think he was not to blame for being uneasy: I remonstrated to him, that if Madam de Tournon's passion was abated after having continued two years, he ought not to be surprised at it, and that even supposing it was not abated, possibly it might not be strong enough to induce her to marry him; that he ought not to complain of it; that such a marriage in the judgment of the public would draw censures upon her, not only because he was not a suitable match for her, but also on account of the prejudice it would do her reputation; that therefore all he could desire was, that she might not deceive him, nor lead him into false expectations; I told him further, that if she had not resolution enough to marry him, or if she confessed she liked some other person better, he ought not to resent or be angry at it, but still continue his esteem and regard for her.

"I give you," said I, "the advice which I would take myself; for sincerity has such charms to me, that I believe if my mistress, or even my wife ingenuously confessed, she had a greater affection for another than for me, I might be troubled, but not exasperated; I would lay aside the character of a lover or a husband, to bestow my advice and my pity."

This discourse made Madam de Cleves blush, and she found in it a certain similitude of her own condition, which very much surprised her, and gave her a concern, from which she could not recover in a great while.

"Sancerre spoke to Madam de Tournon," continued Monsieur de Cleves, "and told her all I had advised him; but she encouraged him with so many fresh assurances, and seemed so displeased at his suspicions, that she entirely removed them ; nevertheless she deferred the marriage until after a pretty long journey he was to make ; but she behaved herself so well until his departure, and appeared so concerned at it, that I believed as well as he, that she sincerely loved him. He set out about three months ago ; during his absence I have seldom seen Madam de Tournon ; you have entirely taken me up, and I only knew that he was speedily expected.

" The day before yesterday, on my arrival at Paris, I heard she was dead ; I sent to his lodgings to enquire if they had any news of him, and word was brought me he came to town the night before, which was precisely the day that Madam de Tournon died ; I immediately went to see him, concluding in what condition I should find him, but his affliction far surpassed what I had imagined.

" Never did I see a sorrow so deep and so tender ; the moment he saw me he embraced me with tears ; ' I shall never see her more,' said he, ' I shall never see her more, she is dead, I was not worthy of her, but I shall soon follow her.'

" After this he was silent ; and then, from time to time, continually repeating ' She is dead, I shall never see her more,' he returned to lamentations and tears, and continued as a man bereft of reason. He told me, he had not often received letters from her during his absence, but that he knew her too well to be surprised at it, and was sensible how shy and timorous she was of writing ; he made no doubt but she would have married him upon his return ; he considered her as the most amiable and constant of her sex ; he thought himself tenderly beloved by her ; he lost her the moment he expected to be united to her for ever ; all these thoughts threw him into so violent an affliction, that I own I was deeply touched with it.

" Nevertheless I was obliged to leave him to go to the King, but promised to return immediately ; accordingly I did, and I was never so surprised as I was to find him entirely changed from what I had left him ; he was standing in his chamber, his face full of fury, sometimes walking, sometimes stopping short, as if he had been distracted ; ' Come,' says he, ' and see the most forlorn wretch in the world; I am a thousand times more unhappy than I was a while ago, and what I have just heard of Madam de Tournon is worse than her death.'

" I took what he said to be wholly the effect of grief, and could not imagine that there could be anything worse than the death of a mistress one loves and is beloved by ; I told him, that so far as he kept his grief within bounds, I approved of it, and bore a part in it ; but that I should no longer pity him, if he abandoned himself to despair and flew from reason. ' I should be too happy if I had lost both my reason and my life,' cried he ; ' Madam de Tournon was false to me, and I am informed of her unfaithfulness and treachery the very day after I was informed of her death ; I am informed of it at a time when my soul is filled with the most tender love, and pierced with the sharpest grief that ever was; at a time when the idea of her in my heart, is that of the most perfect woman who ever lived, and the most perfect with respect to me; I find I am mistaken, and that she does not deserve to be lamented by me; nevertheless I have the same concern for her death, as if she had been true to me, and I have the same sensibility of her falsehood, as if she were yet living; had I heard of her falsehood before her death, jealousy, anger, and rage would have possessed me, and in some measure hardened me against the grief for her loss; but now my condition is such, that I am incapable of receiving comfort, and yet know not how to hate her.'

"You may judge of the surprise I was in at what Sancerre told me; I asked him how he came by the knowledge of it, and he told me that the minute I went away from him, Etouteville, who is his intimate friend, but who nevertheless knew nothing of his love for Madam de Tournon, came to see him; that as soon as he was sat down, he fell a-weeping, and asked his pardon for having concealed from him what he was going to tell him, that he begged him to have compassion of him, that he was come to open his heart to him, and that he was the person in the world the most afflicted for the death of Madam de Tournon.

"'That name,' said Sancerre, 'so astonished me, that though my first intention was to tell him I was more afflicted than he, I had not the power to speak: he continued to inform me, that he had been in love with her six months, that he was always desirous to let me know it, but she had expressly forbid him; and in so authoritative a manner, that he durst not disobey her; that he gained her in a manner as soon as he courted her, that they concealed their mutual passion for each other from the whole world, that he never visited her publicly, that he had the pleasure to remove her sorrow for her husband's death, and that lastly he was to have married her at the very juncture in which she died; but that this marriage, which was an effect of love, would have appeared in her an effect of duty and obedience, she having prevailed upon her father to lay his commands on her to marry him, in order to avoid the appearance of too great an alteration in her conduct, which had seemed so averse to a second marriage.'

"'While Etouteville was speaking to me,' said Sancerre, 'I believed all he said, because I found so much probability in it, and because the time when he told me his passion for Madam de Tournon commence[d] is precisely the same with that when she appeared changed towards me; but the next morning I thought him a liar, or at least an enthusiast, and was upon the point of telling him so. Afterwards I came into an inclination of clearing up the matter, and proposed several questions, and laid my doubts before him, in a word, I proceeded so far to convince myself of my misfortune, that he asked me if I knew Madam de Tournon's handwriting, and with that threw upon my bed four letters of hers and her picture; my brother came in that minute; Etouteville's face was so full of tears, that he was forced to withdraw to avoid being observed, and said he would come again in the evening to fetch what he left with me ; and as for me, I sent my brother away under pretence of being indisposed, so impatient was I to see the letters he had left, and so full of hopes to find something there that might make me disbelieve what Etouteville had been telling me ; but alas ! What did I not find there ? What tenderness ! what oaths ! what assurances of marriage ! what letters ! She never wrote the like to me. Thus,' continued he, ' am I at once pierced with anguish for her death and for her falsehood, two evils which have been often compared, but never felt before by the same person at the same time ; I confess, to my shame, that still I am more grieved for her loss than for her change ; I cannot think her guilty enough, to consent to her death : were she living. I should have the satisfaction to reproach her, and to revenge myself on her by making her sensible of her injustice ; but I shall see her no more, I shall see her no more ; this is the greatest misfortune of all others ; would I could restore her to life, though with the loss of my own ! Yet what do I wish ! If she were restored to life, she would live for Etouteville : how happy was I yesterday,' cried he, ' how happy ! I was the most afflicted man in the world ; but my affliction was reasonable, and there was something pleasing in the very thought that I was inconsolable ; today all my sentiments are unjust ; I pay to a feigned passion the tribute of my grief, which I thought I owed to a real one ; I can neither hate nor love her memory ; I am incapable of consolation, and yet don't know how to grieve for her ; take care, I conjure you, that I never see Etouteville ; his very name raises horror in me ; I know very well I have no reason of complaint against him ; I was to blame in concealing from him my love for Madam de Tournon ; if he had known it, perhaps he would not have pursued her, perhaps she would not have been false to me ; he came to me to impart his sorrows, and I cannot but pity him ; alas ! he had reason to love Madam de Tournon, he was beloved by her, and will never see her more : notwithstanding I perceive I can't help hating him ; once more I conjure you take care I may not see him.'

" Sancerre burst afterwards into tears, began again to regret Madam de Tournon, and to speak to her, as if she were present, and say the softest things in the world ; from these transports he passed to hatred, to complaints, to reproaches and imprecations against her. When I saw him in so desperate a condition, I found I should want somebody to assist me in appeasing his mind ; accordingly I sent for his brother, whom I had left with the King ; I met him in the anti-chamber, and acquainted him with Sancerre's condition : we gave the necessary orders to prevent his seeing Etouteville, and employed part of the night in endeavouring to make him capable of reason ; this morning I found him yet more afflicted ; his brother continued with him, and I returned to you."

" 'Tis impossible to be more surprised than I am," said Madam de Cleves ; " I thought Madam de Tournon equally incapable of love and falsehood." " Address and dissimulation," replied Monsieur de Cleves, "cannot go further than she carried them ; observe, that when Sancerre thought her love to him was abated, it really was, and she began to love Etouteville ; she told the last, that he removed her sorrow for her husband's death, and that he was the cause of her quitting her retirement ; Sancerre believed the cause was nothing but a resolution she had taken not to seem any longer to be in such deep affliction ; she made a merit to Etouteville of concealing her correspondence with him, and of seeming forced to marry him by her father's command, as if it was an effect of the care she had of her reputation ; whereas it was only an artifice to forsake Sancerre, without his having reason to resent it : I must return," continued Monsieur de Cleves, " to see this unhappy man, and I believe you would do well to go to Paris too ; it is time for you to appear in the world again, and receive the numerous visits which you can't well dispense with."

Madam de Cleves agreed to the proposal, and returned to Paris the next day ; she found herself much more easy with respect to the Duke de Nemours than she had been ; what her mother had told her on her death-bed, and her grief for her death, created a sort of suspension in her mind as to her passion for the Duke, which made her believe it was quite effaced.

The evening of her arrival the Queen-Dauphin made her a visit, and after having condoled with her, told her that in order to divert her from melancholy thoughts, she would let her know all that had passed at Court in her absence ; upon which she related to her a great many extraordinary things ; " but what I have the greatest desire to inform you of," added she, " is that it is certain the Duke de Nemours is passionately in love ; and that his most intimate friends are not only not entrusted in it, but can't so much as guess who the person is he is in love with ; nevertheless this passion of his is so strong as to make him neglect, or to speak more properly, abandon the hopes of a Crown."

The Queen-Dauphin afterwards related whatever had passed in England ; " What I have just told you," continued she, " I had from Monsieur d'Anville ; and this morning he informed me, that last night the King sent for the Duke de Nemours upon the subject of Lignerol's letters, who desires to return, and wrote to his Majesty that he could no longer excuse to the Queen of England the Duke of Nemours's delay ; that she begins to be displeased at it ; and though she has not positively given her promise, she has said enough to encourage him to come over ; the King showed this letter to the Duke of Nemours, who instead of speaking seriously as he had done at the beginning of this affair, only laughed and trifled, and made a jest of Lignerol's expectations : He said, 'The whole world would censure his imprudence, if he ventured to go to England, with the pretensions of marrying the Queen, without being secure of success ; I think,' added he, ' I should time my business very ill to go to England now, when the King of Spain uses such pressing instances to obtain the Queen in marriage; the Spanish King perhaps would not be a very formidable rival in matters of gallantry, but in a treaty of marriage I believe your Majesty would not advise me to be his competitor.' 'I would advise you to it upon this occasion,' replied the King; 'but however you will have no competitor in him; I know he has quite other thoughts; and though he had not, Queen Mary found herself so uneasy under the weight of the Spanish Crown, that I can't believe her sister will be very desirous of it.' 'If she should not,' replied the Duke of Nemours, 'it is probable she will seek her happiness in love; she has been in love with my Lord Courtenay for several years; Queen Mary too was in love with him, and would have married him with consent of the states of her kingdom, had not she known that the youth and beauty of her sister Elizabeth had more charms for him than her crown; your Majesty knows, that the violence of her jealousy carried her so far, as to imprison them both, and afterwards to banish my Lord Courtenay, and at last determined her to marry the King of Spain; I believe Queen Elizabeth will soon recall that Lord, and make choice of a man whom she loves, who deserves her love, and who has suffered so much for her, in preference to another whom she never saw.' 'I should be of that opinion,' replied the King, 'if my Lord Courtenay were living, but I received advice some days ago, that he died at Padua, whither he was banished: I plainly see,' added the King, as he left the Duke, 'that your marriage must be concluded the same way the Dauphin's was, and that ambassadors must be sent to marry the Queen of England for you.'

"Monsieur d'Anville and the Viscount, who were with the King when he spoke to the Duke of Nemours, are persuaded that it is the passion he is so deeply engaged in, which diverts him from so great a design; the Viscount, who sees deeper into him than anybody, told Madam de Martigny that he was so changed he did not know him again; and what astonishes him more is, that he does not find he has any private interviews, or that he is ever missing at particular times, so that he believes he has no correspondence with the person he is in love with; and that which surprises him in the Duke is, to see him in love with a woman, who does not return his love."

What poison did this discourse of the Queen-Dauphin carry in it for Madam de Cleves? How could she but know herself to be the person whose name was not known, and how could she help being filled with tenderness and gratitude, when she learned, by a way not in the least liable to suspicion, that the Duke, who had already touched her heart, concealed his passion from the whole world, and neglected for her sake the hopes of a Crown? It is impossible to express what she felt, or to describe the tumult that was raised in her soul. Had the Queen-Dauphin observed her closely, she might easily have discerned, that what she had been saying was not indifferent to her; but as she had not the least suspicion of the truth, she continued her discourse without minding her: "Monsieur d'Anville," added she, "from whom, as I just told you, I had all this, believes I know more of it than himself, and he has so great an opinion of my beauty, that he is satisfied I am the only person capable of creating so great a change in the Duke of Nemours."

These last words of the Queen-Dauphin gave Madam de Cleves a sort of uneasiness very different from that which she had a few minutes before. "I can easily come into Monsieur d'Anville's opinion," answered she; "and 'tis very probable, Madam, that nothing less than a Princess of your merit could make him despise the Queen of England." "I would own it to you, if I knew it," replied the Queen-Dauphin, "and I should know it, if it were true; such passions as these never escape the sight of those who occasion them; they are the first to discern them; the Duke of Nemours has never showed me anything but slight complaisances; and yet I find so great a difference betwixt his present and former behaviour to me, that I can assure you, I am not the cause of the indifference he expresses for the Crown of England.

"But I forget myself in your company," added the Queen-Dauphin, "and don't remember that I am to wait upon Madame: you know the peace is as good as concluded, but perhaps you don't know that the King of Spain has refused to sign it, but on condition of marrying this Princess, instead of the Prince Don Carlos, his son: the King was with great difficulty brought to allow it, but at last he has consented, and is gone to carry the news to Madame; I believe she will be inconsolable. To marry a man of the King of Spain's age and temper can never be pleasing, especially to her who has all the gaiety which the bloom of youth joined with beauty inspires, and was in expectation of marrying a young Prince, for whom she has an inclination without having seen him. I do not know whether the King will find in her all the obedience he desires; he has charged me to see her, because he knows she loves me, and believes I shall be able to influence her. From thence I shall make a visit of a very different nature, to congratulate the King's sister. All things are ready for her marriage with the Prince of Savoy, who is expected in a few days. Never was a woman of her age so entirely pleased to be married; the Court will be more numerous and splendid than ever, and notwithstanding your grief, you must come among us, in order to make strangers see that we are furnished with no mean beauties."

Having said this, the Queen-Dauphin took her leave of Madam de Cleves, and the next day Madame's marriage was publicly known; some days after the King and the Queens went to visit the Princess of Cleves; the Duke de Nemours, who had expected her return with the utmost impatience, and languished for an opportunity of speaking to her in private, contrived to wait upon her at an hour, when the company would probably be withdrawing, and nobody else come in; he succeeded in his design, and came in when the last visitors were going away.

The Princess was sitting on her bed, and the hot weather, together with the sight of the Duke de Nemours, gave her a blush that added to her beauty; he sat over against her with a certain timorous respect, that flows from a real love; he continued some minutes without speaking; nor was she the less at a loss, so that they were both silent a good while: at last the Duke condoled with her for her mother's death; Madam de Cleves was glad to give the conversation that turn, spoke a considerable time of the great loss she had had, and at last said, that though time had taken off from the violence of her grief, yet the impression would always remain so strong, that it would entirely change her humour. "Great troubles and excessive passions," replied the Duke, "make great alterations in the mind; as for me, I am quite another man since my return from Flanders; abundance of people have taken notice of this change, and the Queen-Dauphin herself spoke to me of it yesterday." "It is true," replied the Princess, "she has observed it, and I think I remember to have heard her say something about it." "I'm not sorry, Madam," replied the Duke, "that she has discerned it, but I could wish some others in particular had discerned it too; there are persons to whom we dare give no other evidences of the passion we have for them, but by things which do not concern them; and when we dare not let them know we love them, we should be glad at least to have them see we are not desirous of being loved by any other; we should be glad to convince them, that no other beauty, though of the highest rank, has any charms for us, and that a Crown would be too dear, if purchased with no less a price than absence from her we adore: women ordinarily," continued he, "judge of the passion one has for them, by the care one takes to oblige, and to be assiduous about them; but it's no hard matter to do this, though they be ever so little amiable; not to give oneself up to the pleasure of pursuing them, to shun them through fear of discovering to the public, and in a manner to themselves, the sentiments one has for them, here lies the difficulty; and what still more demonstrates the truth of one's passion is, the becoming entirely changed from what one was, and the having no longer a gust either for ambition or pleasure, after one has employed one's whole life in pursuit of both."

The Princess of Cleves readily apprehended how far she was concerned in this discourse; one while she seemed of opinion, that she ought not to suffer such an address; another, she thought she ought not to seem to understand it, or show she supposed herself meant by it; she thought she ought to speak, and she thought she ought to be silent; the Duke of Nemours's discourse equally pleased and offended her; she was convinced by it of the truth of all the Queen-Dauphin had led her to think; she found in it somewhat gallant and respectful, but also somewhat bold and too intelligible; the inclination she had for the Duke gave her an anxiety which it was not in her power to control; the most obscure expressions of a man that pleases, move more than the most open declaration of one we have no liking for; she made no answer; the Duke de Nemours took notice of her silence, which perhaps would have proved no ill-presage, if the coming in of the Prince of Cleves had not ended at once the conversation and the visit.

The Prince was coming to give his wife a further account of Sancerre, but she was not over curious to learn the sequel of that adventure; she was so much taken up with what had just passed, that she could hardly conceal the embarrassment she was in. When she was at liberty to muse upon it, she plainly saw she was mistaken, when she thought she was indifferent as to the Duke de Nemours; what he had said to her had made all the impression he could desire, and had entirely convinced her of his passion; besides the Duke's actions agreed too well with his words to leave her the least doubt about it; she no longer flattered herself that she did not love him; all her care was not to let him discover it, a task of which she had already experienced the difficulty; she knew the only way to succeed in it was to avoid seeing him; and as her mourning gave her an excuse for being more retired than usual, she made use of that pretence not to go to places where he might see her; she was full of melancholy; her mother's death was the seeming cause of it, and no suspicion was had of any other.

The Duke de Nemours, not seeing her any more, fell into desperation; and knowing he should not meet with her in any public assembly, or at any diversions the Court joined in, he could not prevail upon himself to appear there, and therefore he pretended a great love for hunting, and made matches for that sport on the days when the Queens kept their assemblies; a slight indisposition had served him a good while as an excuse for staying at home, and declining to go to places where he knew very well that Madam de Cleves would not be.

The Prince of Cleves was ill almost at the same time, and the Princess never stirred out of his room during his illness; but when he grew better, and received company, and among others the Duke de Nemours, who under pretence of being yet weak, stayed with him the greatest part of the day, she found she could not continue any longer there; and yet in the first visits he made she had not the resolution to go out; she had been too long without seeing him, to be able to resolve to see him no more; the Duke had the address, by discourses that appeared altogether general, but which she understood very well by the relation they had to what he had said privately to her, to let her know that he went a-hunting only to be more at liberty to think of her, and that the reason of his not going to the assemblies was her not being there.

At last she executed the resolution she had taken to go out of her husband's room, whenever he was there, though this was doing the utmost violence to herself: the Duke perceived she avoided him, and the thought of it touched him to the heart.

The Prince of Cleves did not immediately take notice of his wife's conduct in this particular, but at last he perceived she went out of the room when there was company there; he spoke to her of it, and she told him that she did not think it consistent with decency to be every evening among the gay young courtiers; the she hoped he would allow her to live in a more reserved manner than she had done hitherto, that the virtue and presence of her mother authorised her in many liberties which could not otherwise be justified in a woman of her age.

Monsieur de Cleves, who had a great deal of facility and complaisance for his wife, did not show it on this occasion, but told her he would by no means consent to her altering her conduct ; she was upon the point of telling him, it was reported that the Duke de Nemours was in love with her, but she had not the power to name him ; besides she thought it disingenuous to disguise the truth, and make use of pretences to a man who had so good an opinion of her.

Some days after the King was with the Queen at the assembly hour, and the discourse turned upon nativities and predictions ; the company were divided in their opinion as to what credit ought to be given to them ; the Queen professed to have great faith in them, and maintained that after so many things had come to pass as they had been foretold, one could not doubt but there was something of certainty in that science ; others affirmed, that of an infinite number of predictions so very few proved true, that the truth of those few ought to be looked upon as an effect of chance.

" I have formerly been very curious and inquisitive as to futurity," said the King, " but I have seen so many false and improbable things, that I am satisfied there is no truth in that pretended art. Not many years since there came hither a man of great reputation in astrology ; everybody went to see him ; I went among others, but without saying who I was, and I carried with me the Duke of Guise and Descars, and made them go in first ; nevertheless the astrologer addressed himself first to me, as if he had concluded me to be their master ; perhaps he knew me, and yet he told me one thing that was very unsuitable to my character, if he had known me ; his prediction was that I should be killed in a duel ; he told the Duke of Guise, that he should die of a wound received behind ; and he told Descars he should be knocked of the head by the kick of a horse ; the Duke of Guise was a little angry at the prediction, as if it imported he should run away ; nor was Descars better pleased, to find he was to make his exit by so unfortunate an accident ; in a word, we went away all three of us very much out of humour with the astrologer ; I don't know what will happen to the Duke of Guise and Descars, but there is not much probability of my being killed in a duel ; the King of Spain and I have just made peace, and if we had not, I question whether we should have fought, or if I should have challenged him, as the King my father did Charles the Fifth."

After the King had related the misfortune that was foretold him, those who had defended astrology abandoned the argument, and agreed there was no credit to be given to it : " For my part," said the Duke de Nemours aloud, " I have the least reason of any man in the world to credit it " ; and then turning himself to Madam de Cleves, near whom he stood, "it has been foretold me," says he very softly, " that I should be happy in a person for whom I should have the most violent and respectful passion; you may judge, Madam, if I ought to believe in predictions."

The Queen-Dauphin, who believed, from what the Duke had spoke aloud, that what he whispered was some false prediction that had been told him, asked him what it was he said to Madam de Cleves; had he had a less ready wit, he would have been surprised at this question; but without any hesitation, "What I said to her, Madam," answered he, "was, that it had been predicted to me, that I should be raised to a higher fortune than my most sanguine hopes could lead me to expect." "If nothing have been foretold you but this," replied the Queen-Dauphin," smiling, and thinking of the affair of England, "I would not advise you to decry astrology; you may have reasons hereafter to offer in defence of it." Madam de Cleves apprehended the Queen-Dauphin's meaning, but knew withal, that the fortune the Duke of Nemours spoke of was not that of being King of England.

The time of her mourning being expired, the Princess of Cleves was obliged to make her appearance again, and go to Court as usual; she saw the Duke de Nemours at the Queen-Dauphin's apartment; she saw him at the Prince of Cleves's, where he often came in company of other young noblemen, to avoid being remarked; yet she never once saw him, but it gave her a pain that could not escape his observation.

However industrious she was to avoid being looked at by him, and to speak less to him than to any other, some things escaped her in an unguarded moment, which convinced him he was not indifferent to her; a man of less discernment than he would not have perceived it, but he had already so often been the object of love, that it was easy for him to know when he was loved; he found the Chevalier de Guise was his rival, and the Chevalier knew that the Duke de Nemours was his; Monsieur de Guise was the only man in the Court that had unravelled this affair, his interest having made him more clear-sighted than others; the knowledge they had of each other's sentiments, created an opposition between them in everything, which, however, did not break out into an open quarrel; they were always of different parties at the running at the ring, at tournaments, and all diversions the King delighted in, and their emulation was so great it could not be concealed.

Madam de Cleves frequently revolved in her mind the affair of England; she believed the Duke de Nemours could not resist the advice of the King, and the instances of Lignerolles; she was very much concerned to find that Lignerolles was not yet returned, and she impatiently expected him; her inclinations strongly swayed her to inform herself exactly of the state of this affair; but the same reasons, which raised in her that curiosity, obliged her to conceal it, and she only enquired of the beauty, the wit, and the temper of Queen Elizabeth. A picture of that Princess had been brought the King, which Madam de Cleves found much handsomer than she could have wished for, and she could not forbear saying, the picture flattered. "I don't think so," replied the Queen-Dauphin; "that Princess has the reputation of being very handsome, and of having a very exalted genius, and I know she has always been proposed to me as a model worthy my imitation; she can't but be very handsome, if she resembles her mother, Anne Boleyn; never had woman so many charms and allurements both in her person and her humour; I have heard say she had something remarkably lively in her countenance, very different from what is usually found in other English beauties." "I think," replied Madam de Cleves, "'tis said she was born in France." "Those who imagine so are mistaken," replied the Queen-Dauphin; "I'll give you her history in a few words.

"She was of a good family in England; Henry the Eighth was in love with her sister and her mother, and it has been even suspected by some, that she was his daughter; she came to France with Henry the Seventh's sister, who married Louis XII that Princess, who was full of youth and gallantry, left the Court of France with great reluctance after her husband's death; but Anne Boleyn, who had the same inclinations as her mistress, could not prevail with herself to go away; the late King was in love with her, and she continued maid of honour to Queen Claude; that Queen died, and Margaretta, the King's sister, Duchess of Alenson, and since Queen of Navarre, whose story you know, took her into her service, where she imbibed the principles of the new religion; she returned afterwards to England, and there charmed all the world; she had the manners of France, which please in all countries; she sung well, she danced finely; she was a maid of honour to Queen Catherine, and Henry the Eighth fell desperately in love with her.

"Cardinal Wolsey, his favourite and first minister, being dissatisfied with the Emperor for not having favoured his pretensions to the Papacy, in order to revenge himself of him, contrived an alliance between France and the King his master; he put it into the head of Henry the Eighth, that his marriage with the Emperor's aunt was null, and advised him to marry the Duchess of Alenson, whose husband was just dead; Anne Boleyn, who was not without ambition, considered Queen Catherine's divorce as a means that would bring her to the Crown; she began to give the King of England impressions of the Lutheran religion, and engaged the late King to favour at Rome Henry the Eighth's divorce, in hopes of his marrying the Duchess of Alenson; Cardinal Wolsey, that he might have an opportunity of treating this affair, procured himself to be sent to France upon other pretences; but his master was so far from permitting him to propose this marriage, that he sent him express orders to Calais not to speak of it.

"Cardinal Wolsey, at his return from France, was received with as great honours as could have been paid to the King himself; never did any favourite carry his pride and vanity to so great a height; he managed an interview between the two Kings at Boulogne, when Francis the First would have given the upperhand to Henry the Eighth, but he refused to accept it; they treated one another by turns with the utmost magnificence, and presented to each habits of the same sort with those they wore themselves. I remember to have heard say, that those the late King sent to the King of England were of crimson satin beset all over with pearls and diamonds, and a robe of white velvet embroidered with gold; after having stayed some time at Boulogne, they went to Calais. Anne Boleyn was lodged in Henry the Eighth's Court with the train of a Queen; and Francis the First made her the same presents, and paid her the same honours as if she had been really so: in a word, after a passion of nine year's continuance King Henry married her, without waiting for the dissolving of his first marriage. The Pope precipitately thundered out excommunications against him, which so provoked King Henry, that he declared himself head of the Church, and drew after him all England into the unhappy change in which you see it.

"Anne Boleyn did not long enjoy her greatness; for when she thought herself most secure of it by the death of Queen Catherine, one day as she was seeing a match of running at the ring made by the Viscount Rochefort her brother, the King was struck with such a jealousy, that he abruptly left the show, went away to London, and gave orders for arresting the Queen, the Viscount Rochefort, and several others whom he believed to be the lovers or confidants of that Princess. Though this jealousy in appearance had its birth that moment, the King had been long possessed with it by the Viscountess Rochefort, who not being able to bear the strict intimacy between her husband and the Queen, represented it to the King as a criminal commerce; so that that Prince, who was besides in love with Jane Seymour, thought of nothing but ridding himself of Anne Boleyn; and in less than three weeks he caused the Queen and her brother to be tried, had them both beheaded, and married Jane Seymour. He had afterwards several wives, whom he divorced or put to death; and among others Catherine Howard, whose confidant the Viscountess Rochefort was, and who was beheaded with her: thus was she punished for having falsely accused Anne Boleyn. And Henry the Eighth died, being become excessive fat."

All the ladies, that were present when the Queen-Dauphin made this relation, thanked her for having given them so good an account of the Court of England; and among the rest Madam de Cleves, who could not forbear asking several questions concerning Queen Elizabeth.

The Queen-Dauphin caused pictures in miniature to be drawn of all the beauties of the Court, in order to send them to the Queen her mother. One day, when that of Madam de Cleves was finishing, the Queen-Dauphin came to spend the afternoon with her; the Duke de Nemours did not fail to be there; he let slip no opportunities of seeing Madam de Cleves, yet without appearing to contrive them. She looked so pretty that day, that he would have fell in love with her, though he had not been so before: however he durst not keep his yes fixed upon her, while she was sitting for her picture, for fear of showing too much the pleasure he took in looking at her.

The Queen-Dauphin asked Monsieur de Cleves for a little picture he had of his wife's, to compare it with that which was just drawn; everybody gave their judgment of the one and the other; and Madam de Cleves ordered the painter to mend something in the headdress of that which had been just brought in; the painter in obedience to her took the picture out of the case in which it was, and having mended it laid it again on the table.

The Duke de Nemours had long wished to have a picture of Madam de Cleves; when he saw that which Monsieur de Cleves had, he could not resist the temptation of stealing it from a husband, who, he believed, was tenderly loved; and he thought that among so many persons as were in the same room he should be no more liable to suspicion than another.

The Queen-Dauphin was sitting on the bed, and whispering to Madam de Cleves, who was standing before her. Madam de Cleves, through one of the curtains that was but half-drawn, spied the Duke de Nemours with his back to the table, that stood at the bed's feet, and perceived that without turning his face he took something very dextrously from off the table; she presently guessed it was her picture, and was in such concern about it, that the Queen-Dauphin observed she did not attend to what she said, and asked her aloud what it was she looked at. At those words, the Duke de Nemours turned about, and met full the eyes of Madam de Cleves that were still fixed upon him; he thought it not impossible but she might have seen what he had done.

Madam de Cleves was not a little perplexed; it was reasonable to demand her picture of him; but to demand it publicly was to discover to the whole world the sentiments which the Duke had for her, and to demand it in private would be to engage him to speak of his love; she judged after all it was better to let him keep it, and she was glad to grant him a favour which she could do without his knowing that she granted it. The Duke de Nemours, who observed her perplexity, and partly guessed the cause of it, came up, and told her softly, "If you have seen what I have ventured to do, be so good, Madam, as to let me believe you are ignorant of it; I dare ask no more"; having said this he withdrew, without waiting for her answer.

The Queen-Dauphin went to take a walk, attended with the rest of the ladies; and the Duke de Nemours went home to shut himself up in his closet, not being able to support in public the ecstasy he was in on having a picture of Madam de Cleves; he tasted everything that was sweet in love; he was in love with the finest woman of the Court; he found she loved him against her will, and saw in all her actions that sort of care and embarrassment which love produces in young and innocent hearts.

At night great search was made for the picture; and having found the case it used to be kept in, they never suspected it had been stolen but thought it might have fallen out by chance. The Prince of Cleves was very much concerned for the loss of it; and after having searched for it a great while to no purpose, he told his wife, but with an air that showed he did not think so, that without doubt she had some secret lover, to whom she had given the picture, or who had stole it, and that none but a lover would have been contented with the picture without the case.

These words, though spoke in jest, made a lively impression in the mind of Madam de Cleves; they gave her remorse, and she reflected on the violence of her inclination which hurried her on to love the Duke of Nemours; she found she was no longer mistress of her words or countenance; she imagined that Lignerolles was returned, that she had nothing to fear from the affair of England, nor any cause to suspect the Queen-Dauphin; in a word, that she had no refuge or defence against the Duke de Nemours but by retiring; but as she was not at her liberty to retire, she found herself in a very great extremity and ready to fall into the last misfortune, that of discovering to the Duke the inclination she had for him: she remembered all that her mother had said to her on her death-bed, and the advice which she gave her, to enter on any resolutions, however difficult they might be, rather than engage in gallantry; she remembered also what Monsieur de Cleves had told her, when he gave an account of Madam de Tournon; she thought she ought to acknowledge to him the inclination she had for the Duke de Nemours, and in that thought she continued a long time; afterwards she was astonished to have entertained so ridiculous a design, and fell back again into her former perplexity of not knowing what to choose.

The peace was signed; and the Lady Elizabeth, after a great deal of reluctance, resolved to obey the King her father. The Duke of Alva was appointed to marry her in the name of the Catholic King, and was very soon expected. The Duke of Savoy too, who was to marry the King's sister, and whose nuptials were to be solemnised at the same time, was expected every day. The King thought of nothing but how to grace these marriages with such diversions as might display the politeness and magnificence of his Court. Interludes and comedies of the best kind were proposed, but the King thought those entertainments too private, and desired to have somewhat of a more splendid nature: he resolved to make a solemn tournament, to which strangers might be invited, and of which the people might be spectators. The princes and young lords very much approved the King's design, especially the Duke of Ferrara, Monsieur de Guise, and the Duke de Nemours, who surpassed the rest in these sorts of exercises. The King made choice of them to be together with himself the four champions of the tournament.

Proclamation was made throughout the kingdom, that on the 15th of June in the City of Paris, his most Christian Majesty, and the Princes Alphonso d'Etè Duke of Ferrara, Francis of Loraine Duke of

Guise, and James of Savoy Duke of Nemours would hold an open tournament against all comers. The first combat to be on horse-back in the lists, with double armour, to break four lances, and one for the ladies; the second combat with swords, one to one, or two to two, as the judges of the field should direct; the third combat on foot, three pushes of pikes, and six hits with the sword. The champions to furnish lances, swords, and pikes, at the choice of the combatants. Whoever did not manage his horse in the carreer to be put out of the lists; four judges of the field to give orders. The combatants, who should break most lances and perform best, to carry the prize, the value whereof to be at the discretion of the judges; all the combatants, as well French as strangers, to be obliged to touch one or more, at their choice, of the shields that should hang on the pillar at the end of the lists, where a herald at arms should be ready to receive them, and enroll them according to their quality, and the shields they had touched; the combatants to be obliged to cause their shields and arms to be brought by a gentleman and hung up at the pillar three days before the tournament, otherwise not to be admitted without leave of the champions.

A spacious list was made near the Bastille, which begun from the Chateau des Tournelles and crossed the street of St. Anthony, and extended as far as the King's stables; on both sides were built scaffolds and amphitheatres, which formed a sort of galleries that made a very fine sight, and were capable of containing an infinite number of people. The princes and lords were wholly taken up in providing what was necessary for a splendid appearance, and in mingling in their cyphers and devices somewhat of gallantry that had relation to the ladies they were in love with.

A few days before the Duke of Alva's arrival, the King made a match at tennis with the Duke de Nemours, the Chevalier de Guise, and the Viscount de Chartres. The Queens came to see them play, attended with the ladies of the Court, and among others Madam de Cleves. After the game was ended, as they went out of the tennis court, Chatelart came up to the Queen-Dauphin, and told her fortune had put into his hands a letter of gallantry, that dropped out of the Duke de Nemours's pocket. This Queen, who was always very curious in what related to the Duke, bid Chatelart give her the letter; he did so, and she followed the Queen her mother-in-law, who was going with the King to see them work at the lists. After they had been there some time, the King caused some horses to be brought that had been lately taken in, and though they were not as yet thoroughly managed, he was for mounting one of them, and ordered his attendants to mount others; the King and the Duke de Nemours hit upon the most fiery and high mettled of them. The horses were ready to fall foul on one another, when the Duke of Nemours, for fear of hurting the King, retreated abruptly, and ran back his horse against a pillar with so much violence, that the shock of it made him stagger. The company ran up to him, and he was thought considerably hurt; but the Princess of Cleves thought the hurt much greater than anyone else. The interest she had in it gave her an apprehension and concern which she took no care to conceal ; she came up to him with the Queens, and with a countenance so changed, that one less concerned than the Chevalier de Guise might have perceived it : perceive it he immediately did, and was much more intent upon the condition Madam de Cleves was in, than upon that of the Duke de Nemours. The blow the Duke had given himself had so stunned him, that he continued some time leaning his head on those who supported him ; when he raised himself up, he immediately viewed Madam de Cleves, and saw in her face the concern she was in for him, and he looked upon her in a manner which made her sense how much he was touched with it : afterwards he thanked the Queens for the goodness they had expressed to him, and made apologies for the condition he had been in before them ; and then the King ordered him to go to rest.

Madam de Cleves, after she was recovered from the fright she had been in, presently reflected on the tokens she had given of it. The Chevalier de Guise did not suffer her to continue long in the hope that nobody had perceived it, but giving her his hand to lead her out of the lists : " I have more cause to complain, Madam," said he, " than the Duke de Nemours ; pardon me, if I forget for a moment that profound respect I have always had for you, and show you how much my heart is grieved for what my eyes have just seen ; this is the first time I have ever been so bold as to speak to you, and it will be the last. Death or at least eternal absence will remove me from a place where I can live no longer, since I have now lost the melancholy comfort I had of believing that all who behold you with love are as unhappy as myself."

Madam de Cleves made only a confused answer, as if she had not understood what the Chevalier's words meant : at another time she would have been offended, if he had mentioned the passion he had for her ; but at this moment she felt nothing but the affliction to know that he had observed the passion she had for the Duke de Nemours. The Chevalier de Guise was so well convinced of it, and so pierced with grief, that from that moment he took a resolution never to think of being loved by Madam de Cleves ; but that he might the better be able to quit a passion which he had thought so difficult and so glorious, it was necessary to make choice of some other undertaking worthy of employing him ; he had his view on Rhodes : the taking of which he had formerly had some idea of ; and when death snatched him away, in the flower of his youth, and at a time when he had acquired the reputation of one of the greatest Princes of his age, the only regret he had to part with life was, that he had not been able to execute so noble a resolution, the success whereof he thought infallible from the great care he had taken about it.

Madam de Cleves, when she came out of the lists, went to the Queen's apartment, with her thoughts wholly taken up with what had passed The Duke de Nemours came there soon after, richly dressed, and lik one wholly unsensible of the accident that had befallen him; he appeared even more gay than usual, and the joy he was in for what he had discovered, gave him an air that very much increased his natural agreeableness. The whole Court was surprised when he came in; and there was nobody but asked him how he did, except Madam de Cleves, who stayed near the chimney pretending not to see him. The King coming out of his closet, and seeing him among others called him to talk to him about his late accident. The Duke passed by Madam de Cleves, and said softly to her, "Madam, I have received this day some marks of your pity, but they were not such as I am most worthy of." Madam de Cleves suspected that he had taken notice of the concern she had been in for him, and what he now said convinced her she was not mistaken; it gave her a great deal of concern to find she was so little mistress of herself as not to have been able to conceal her inclinations from the Chevalier de Guise; nor was she the less concerned to see that the Duke de Nemours was acquainted with them; yet this last grief was not so entire, but there was a certain mixture of pleasure in it.

The Queen-Dauphin, who was extremely impatient to know what there was in the letter which Chatelart had given her, came up to Madam de Cleves. "Go read this letter," says she; "'tis addressed to the Duke de Nemours, and was probably sent him by the mistress for whom he has forsaken all others; if you can't read it now, keep it, and bring it me about bedtime and inform me if you know the hand." Having said this, the Queen-Dauphin went away from Madam de Cleves, and left her in such astonishment, that she was not able for some time to stir out of the place. The impatience and grief she was in not permitting her to stay at Court, she went home before her usual hour of retirement; she trembled with the letter in her hand, her thoughts were full of confusion, and she experienced I know not what of insupportable grief, that she had never felt before. No sooner was she in her closet, but she opened the letter and found it as follows:

I have loved you too well, to leave you in a belief that the change you observe in me is an effect of lightness; I must inform you that your falsehood is the cause of it; you will be surprised to hear me speak of your falsehood; you have dissembled it with so much skill, and I have taken so much care to conceal my knowledge of it from you, that you have reason to be surprised at the discovery; I am myself in wonder, that I have discovered nothing of it to you before; never was grief equal to mine; I thought you had the most violent passion for me, I did not conceal that which I had for you, and at the time that I acknowledged it to you without reserve, I found that you deceived me, that you loved another, and that in all probability I was made a sacrifice to this new mistress. I knew it the day you run at the ring, and this was the reason I was not there; at first I pretended an indisposition in order to conceal my sorrow, but afterwards

I really fell into one, nor could a constitution delicate like mine support so violent a shock. When I began to be better, I still counterfeited sickness, that I might have an excuse for not seeing and for not writing to you; besides I was willing to have time to come to a resolution in what manner to deal with you; I took and quitted the same resolution twenty times; but at last I concluded you deserved not to see my grief, and I resolved not to show you the least mark of it. I had a desire to bring down your pride, by letting you see, that my passion for you declined of itself: I thought I should by this lessen the value of the sacrifice you had made of me, and was loth you should have the pleasure of appearing more amiable in the eyes of another, by showing her how much I loved you; I resolved to write to you in a cold and languishing manner, that she, to whom you gave my letters, might perceive my love was at an end: I was unwilling she should have the satisfaction of knowing I was sensible that she triumphed over me, or that she should increase her triumph by my despair and complaints. I thought I should punish you too little by merely breaking with you, and that my ceasing to love you would give you but a slight concern, after you had first forsaken me; I found it was necessary you should love me, to feel the smart of not being loved, which I so severely experienced myself; I was of opinion that if anything could rekindle that flame, it would be to let you see that mine was extinguished, but to let you see it through an endeavour to conceal it from you, as if I wanted the power to acknowledge it to you: this resolution I adhered to; I found it difficult to take, and when I saw you again I thought it impossible to execute. I was ready a hundred times to break out into tears and complaints; my ill state of health, which still continued, served as a disguise to hide from you the affliction and trouble I was in; afterward I was supported by the pleasure of dissembling with you, as you had done with me; however it was doing so apparent a violence to myself to tell you or to write to you that I loved you, that you immediately perceived I had no mind to let you see my affection was altered; you was touched with this, you complained of it; I endeavoured to remove your fears, but it was done in so forced a manner, that you was still more convinced by it, I no longer loved you; in short, I did all I intended to do. The fantasticalness of your heart was such, that you advanced towards me in proportion as you saw I retreated from you. I have enjoyed all the pleasure which can arise from revenge; I plainly saw, that you loved me more than you had ever done, and I showed you I had no longer any love for you. I had even reason to believe that you had entirely abandoned her, for whom you had forsaken me; I had ground too to be satisfied you had never spoken to her concerning me; but neither your discretion in that particular, nor the return of your affection can make amends for your inconstancy; your heart has been divided between me and another, and you have deceived me; this is sufficient wholly to take from me the pleasure I found in being loved by you, as I thought I deserved to be, and to confirm me in the resolution I have taken never to see you more, which you are so much surprised at.

Madam de Cleves read this letter, and read it over again several times, without knowing at the same time what she had read; she saw only that the Duke de Nemours did not love her as she imagined and that he loved others who were no less deceived by him than she. What a discovery was this for a person in her condition, who had a violent passion, who had just given marks of it to a man whom she judged unworthy of it, and to another whom she used ill for his sake! Never was affliction so cutting as hers; she imputed the piercingness of it to what had happened that day, and believed that if the Duke de Nemours had not had ground to believe she loved him she should not have cared whether he loved another or not; but she deceived herself, and this evil which she found so insupportable was jealousy with all the horrors it can be accompanied with. This letter discovered to her a piece of gallantry the Duke de Nemours had been long engaged in; she saw the lady who wrote it was a person of wit and merit, and deserved to be loved; she found she had more courage than herself, and envied her the power she had had of concealing her sentiments from the Duke de Nemours; by the close of the letter, she saw this lady thought herself beloved, and presently suspected that the discretion the Duke had showed in his addresses to her, and which she had been so much taken with, was only an effect of his passion for this other mistress, whom he was afraid of disobliging; in short, she thought of everything that could add to her grief and despair. What reflections did she not make on herself, and on the advices her mother had given her! how did she repent, that she had not persisted in her resolution of retiring, though against the will of Monsieur de Cleves, or that she had not pursued her intentions of acknowledging to him the inclination she had for the Duke of Nemours! She was convinced, she would have done better to discover it to a husband, whose goodness she was sensible of, and whose interest it would have been to conceal it, than to let it appear to a man who was unworthy of it, who deceived her, who perhaps made a sacrifice of her, and who had no view in being loved by her but to gratify his pride and vanity; in a word, she found, that all the calamities that could befall her, and all the extremities she could be reduced to, were less than that single one of having discovered to the Duke de Nemours that she loved him, and of knowing that he loved another: all her comfort was to think, that after the knowledge of this she had nothing more to fear from herself, and that she should be entirely eased of the inclination she had for the Duke.

She never thought of the orders the Queen-Dauphin had given her, to come to her when she went to rest: she went to bed herself, and pretended to be ill; so that when Monsieur de Cleves came home from the King, they told him she was asleep. But she was far from that tranquillity which inclines to sleep ; all the night she did nothing but torment herself, and read over and over the letter in her hand.

Madam de Cleves was not the only person whom this letter disturbed. The Viscount de Chartres, who had lost it and not the Duke de Nemours, was in the utmost inquietude about it. He had been that evening with the Duke of Guise, who had given a great entertainment to the Duke of Ferrara his brother-in-law, and to all the young people of the Court : it happened that the discourse turned upon ingenious letters ; and the Viscount de Chartres said he had one about him the finest that ever was writ : they urged him to show it, and on his excusing himself, the Duke de Nemours insisted he had no such letter, and that what he said was only out of vanity ; the Viscount made him answer, that he urged his discretion to the utmost, that nevertheless he would not show the letter ; but he would read some parts of it, which would make it appear few men received the like. Having said this, he would have taken out the letter, but could not find it ; he searched for it to no purpose. The company rallied him about it ; but he seemed so disturbed, that they forbore to speak further of it; he withdrew sooner than the others, and went home with great impatience, to see if he had not left the letter there. While he was looking for it, one of the Queen's pages came to tell him, that the Viscountess d'Usez had thought it necessary to give him speedy advice, that it was said at the Queen's Court, that he had dropped a letter of gallantry out of his pocket while he was playing at tennis ; that great part of what the letter contained had been related, that the Queen had expressed a great curiosity to see it, and had sent to one of her gentlemen for it, but that he answered, he had given it to Chatelart.

The page added many other particulars which heightened the Viscount's concern ; he went out that minute to go to a gentleman who was an intimate friend of Chatelart's ; and though it was a very unseasonable hour, made him get out of bed to go and fetch the letter, without letting him know who it was had sent for it, or who had lost it. Chatelart, who was prepossessed with an opinion that it belonged to the Duke of Nemours, and that the Duke was in love with the Queen-Dauphin, did not doubt but it was he who had sent to redemand it, and so answered with a malicious sort of joy, that he had put the letter into the Queen-Dauphin's hands. The gentleman brought this answer back to the Viscount de Chartres, which increased the uneasiness he was under already, and added new vexations to it : after having continued some time in an irresolution what to do, he found that the Duke de Nemours was the only person whose assistance could draw him out of this intricate affair.

Accordingly he went to the Duke's house, and entered his room about break of day. What the Duke had discovered the day before with respect to the Princess of Cleves had given him such agreeable ideas, that he slept very sweetly ; he was very much surprised to find himself waked by the Viscount de Chartres, and asked him if he came to disturb his rest so early, to be revenged of him for what he had said last night at supper. The Viscount's looks soon convinced him, that he came upon a serious business ; "I am come," said he, "to entrust you with the most important affair of my life ; I know very well, you are not obliged to me for the confidence I place in you, because I do it at a time when I stand in need of your assistance ; but I know likewise, that I should have lost your esteem, if I had acquainted you with all I am now going to tell you, without having been forced to it by absolute necessity : I have dropped the letter I spoke of last night ; it is of the greatest consequence to me, that nobody should know it is addressed to me ; it has been seen by abundance of people, who were at the tennis court yesterday when I dropped it ; you was there too, and the favour I have to ask you, is, to say it was you who lost it." "Sure you think," replied the Duke de Nemours smiling, "that I have no mistress, by making such a proposal, and that I have no quarrels or inconveniences to appiehend by leaving it to be believed that I receive such letters." "I beg you," said the Viscount, "to hear me seriously ; if you have a mistress, as I doubt not you have, though I do not know who she is, it will be easy for you to justify yourself, and I'll put you into an infallible way of doing it. As for you, though you should fail in justifying yourself, it can cost you nothing but a short falling out ; but for my part, this accident affects me in a very different manner, I shall dishonour a person who has passionately loved me, and is one of the most deserving women in the world ; on the other side, I shall draw upon myself an implacable hatred that will ruin my fortune, and perhaps proceed somewhat further." "I do not comprehend what you say," replied the Duke de Nemours, "but I begin to see that the reports we have had of your interest in a great Princess are not wholly without ground." "They are not," replied the Viscount, "but I would to God they were : you would not see me in the perplexity I am in ; but I must relate the whole affair to you, to convince you how much I have to fear.

"Ever since I came to Court, the Queen has treated me with a great deal of favour and distinction, and I had grounds to believe that she was very kindly disposed towards me : there was nothing, however, particular in all this, and I never presumed to entertain any thoughts of her but what were full of respect ; so far from it, that I was deeply in love with Madam de Themines ; anyone that sees her may easily judge, 'tis very possible for one to be greatly in love with her, when one is beloved by her, and so I was. About two years ago, the Court being at Fontainebleau, I was two or three times in conversation with the Queen, at hours when there were very few people in her apartment : it appeared to me, that my turn of wit was agreeable to her, and I observed she always approved what I said. One day among others she fell into a discourse concerning confidence. I said there was nobody in whom I entirely confided, that I found people always repented of having done so, and that I knew a great many things of which I had never spoke :

the Queen told me, she esteemed me the more for it, that she had not found in France anyone that could keep a secret, and that this was what had embarrassed her more than anything else, because it had deprived her of the pleasure of having a confidant; that nothing was so necessary in life as to have somebody one could open one's mind to with safety, especially for people of her rank. Afterwards she frequently resumed the same discourse, and acquainted me with very particular circumstances; at last I imagined she was desirous to learn my secrets, and to entrust me with her own; this thought engaged me strictly to her. I was so pleased with this distinction that I made my court to her with greater assiduity than usual. One evening the King and the ladies of the Court rode out to take the air in the forest, but the Queen, being a little indisposed did not go; I stayed to wait upon her, and she walked down to the pond-side, and dismissed her gentlemen ushers, that she might be more at liberty. After she had taken a few turns she came up to me, and bid me follow her; 'I would speak with you,' says she, 'and by what I shall say you will see I am your friend.' She stopped here, and looking earnestly at me; 'You are in love,' continued the, 'and because perhaps you have made nobody your confidant, you think that your love is not known; but it is known, and even by persons who are interested in it: you are observed, the place where you see your mistress is discovered, and there's a design to surprise you; I don't know who she is, nor do I ask you to tell me, I would only secure you from the misfortunes into which you may fall.' See, I beseech you, what a snare the Queen laid for me, and how difficult it was for me not to fall into it; she had a mind to know if I was in love, and as she did not ask me who I was in love with, but let me see her intention was only to serve me, I had no suspicion that she spoke either out of curiosity or by design.

"Nevertheless, contrary to all probability, I saw into the bottom of the matter; I was in love with Madam de Themines, but though she loved me again, I was not happy enough to have private places to see her in without danger of being discovered there, and so I was satisfied she could not be the person the Queen meant; I knew also, that I had an intrigue with another woman less handsome and less reserved than Madam de Themines, and that it was not impossible but the place where I saw her might be discovered; but as this was a business I little cared for, it was easy for me to guard against all sorts of danger by forbearing to see her; I resolved therefore to acknowledge nothing of it to the Queen, but to assure her on the contrary that I had a long time laid aside the desire of gaining women's affections, even where I might hope for success, because I found them all in some measure unworthy of engaging the heart of an honourable man, and that it must be something very much above them which could touch me. 'You do not answer me ingenuously,' replied the Queen; 'I am satisfied of the contrary; the free manner in which I speak to you ought to oblige you to conceal nothing from me; I would have you,' continued she, 'be of the number of my friends ; but I would not, after having admitted you into that rank, be ignorant of your engagements ; consider, whether you think my friendship will be too dear at the price of making me your confidant ; I give you two days to think on it ; but then, consider well of the answer you shall make me, and remember that if ever I find hereafter you have deceived me, I shall never forgive you as long as I live.'

" Having said this, the Queen left me without waiting for my answer ; you may imagine how full my thoughts were of what she had said to me ; the two days she had given me to consider of it I did not think too long a time to come to a resolution ; I found she had a mind to know if I was in love, and that her desire was I should not be so ; I foresaw the consequences of what I was going to do, my vanity was flattered with the thought of having a particular interest with the Queen, and a Queen whose person is still extremely amiable ; on the other hand, I was in love with Madam de Themines, and though I had committed a petty treason against her by my engagement with the other woman I told you of, I could not find in my heart to break with her ; I foresaw also the danger I should expose myself to, if I deceived the Queen, and how hard it would be to do it ; nevertheless I could not resolve to refuse what fortune offered me, and was willing to run the hazard of anything my ill conduct might draw upon me ; I broke with her with whom I kept a correspondence that might be discovered, and was in hopes of concealing that I had with Madam de Themines.

" At the two days' end, as I entered the room where the Queen was with all the ladies about her, she said aloud to me, and with a grave air that was surprising enough, ' Have you thought of the business I charged you with, and do you know the truth of it ? ' ' Yes, Madam,' answered I, ' and 'tis as I told your Majesty.' ' Come in the evening, when I am writing,' replied she, ' and you shall have further orders.' I made a respectful bow without answering anything, and did not fail to attend at the hour she had appointed me. I found her in the gallery, with her secretary and one of her women. As soon as she saw me she came to me, and took me to the other end of the gallery ; ' Well,' says she, ' after having considered thoroughly of this matter, have you nothing to say to me, and as to my manner of treating you, does not it deserve that you should deal sincerely with me ? ' ' It is, Madam,' answered I, ' because I deal sincerely, that I have nothing more to say ; and I swear to your Majesty with all the respect I owe you, that I have no engagement with any woman of the Court.' ' I will believe it,' replied the Queen, ' because I wish it ; and I wish it, because I desire to have you entirely mine, and because it would be impossible for me to be satisfied with your friendship, if you were in love ; one cannot confide in those who are ; one cannot be secure of their secrecy ; they are too much divided, and their mistresses have always the first place in their thoughts, which does not suit at all with the manner in which I would have you live with me : remember then, it is upon your giving me your word that you have no engagement, that I choose you for my confidant; remember, I insist on having you entirely to myself, and that you shall have no friend of either sex but such as I shall approve, and that you abandon every care but that of pleasing me; I'll not desire you to neglect any opportunity for advancing your fortune; I'll conduct your interests with more application than you can yourself, and whatever I do for you, I shall think myself more than recompensed, if you answer my expectations; I make choice of you, to open my heart's griefs to you, and to have your assistance in softening them; you may imagine they are not small; I bear in appearance without much concern the King's engagement with the Duchess of Valentinois, but it is insupportable to me; she governs the King, she imposes upon him, she slights me, all my people are at her beck. The Queen, my daughter-in-law, proud of her beauty, and the authority of her uncles, pays me no respect. The Constable Montmorency is master of the King and kingdom; he hates me, and has given proofs of his hatred, which I shall never forget. The Mareschal de St. André is a bold young favourite, who uses me no better than the others. The detail of my misfortunes would move your pity; hitherto I have not dared to confide in anybody, I confide in you, take care that I never repent it, and be my only consolation.' The Queen blushed, when she had ended this discourse, and I was so truly touched with the goodness she had expressed to me, that I was going to throw myself at her feet: from that day she has placed an entire confidence in me, she has done nothing without advising with me, and the intimacy and union between us still subsists

## III

"In the meantime, however busy and full I was of my new engagement with the Queen, I still kept fair with Madam de Themines by a natural inclination which it was not in my power to conquer; I thought she cooled in her love to me, and whereas, had I been prudent, I should have made use of the change I observed in her for my cure, my love redoubled upon it, and I managed so ill that the Queen got some knowledge of this intrigue. Jealousy is natural to persons of her nation, and perhaps she had a greater affection for me than she even imagined herself; at least the report of my being in love gave her so much uneasiness, that I thought myself entirely ruined with her; however I came into favour again by virtue of submissions, false oaths, and assiduity; but I should not have been able to have deceived her long, had not Madam de Themines's change disengaged me from her against my will; she convinced me she no longer loved me, and I was so thoroughly satisfied of it, that I was obliged to give her no further uneasiness, but to let her be quiet. Some time after she wrote me this letter which I have lost; I learned from it, she had heard of the correspondence I had with the other woman I told you of, and that that was the reason of her change.

As I had then nothing further left to divide me, the Queen was well enough satisfied with me ; but the sentiments I have for her not being of a nature to render me incapable of other engagements, and love not being a thing that depends on our will, I fell in love with Madam de Martigues, of whom I was formerly a great admirer, while she was with Villemontais, maid of honour to the Queen-Dauphin ; I have reason to believe she does not hate me ; the discretion I observe towards her, and which she does not wholly know the reasons of, is very agreeable to her ; the Queen has not the least suspicion on her account, but she has another jealousy which is not less troublesome ; as Madam de Martigues is constantly with the Queen-Dauphin, I go there much oftener than usual ; the Queen imagines that 'tis this Princess I am in love with ; the Queen-Dauphin's rank, which is equal to her own, and the superiority of her youth and beauty, create a jealousy that rises even to fury, and fills her with a hatred against her daughter-in-law that cannot be concealed. The Cardinal of Loraine, who, I believe, has been long aspiring to the Queen's favour, and would be glad to fill the place I possess, is, under pretence of reconciling the two Queens, become master of the differences between them ; I doubt not but he has discovered the true cause of the Queen's anger, and I believe he does me all manner of ill offices, without letting her see that he designs it. This is the condition my affairs are in at present ; judge what effect may be produced by the letter which I have lost, and which I unfortunately put in my pocket with design to restore it to Madam de Themines : if the Queen sees this letter, she will know I have deceived her ; and that almost at the very same time that I deceived her for Madam de Themines, I deceived Madam de Themines for another ; judge what an idea this will give her of me, and whether she will ever trust me again. If she does not see the letter, what shall I say to her ? She knows it has been given to the Queen-Dauphin ; she will think Chatelart knew that Queen's hand, and that the letter is from her ; she will fancy the person of whom the letter expresses a jealousy, is perhaps herself ; in short, there is nothing which she may not think, and there is nothing which I ought not to fear from her thoughts ; add to this, that I am desperately in love with Madam de Martigues, and that the Queen-Dauphin will certainly show her this letter, which she will conclude to have been lately writ. Thus shall I be equally embroiled both with the person I love most, and with the person I have most cause to fear. Judge, after this, if I have not reason to conjure you to say the letter is yours, and to beg of you to get it out of the Queen-Dauphin's hands."

"I am very well satisfied," answered the Duke de Nemours, "that one cannot be in a greater embarrassment than that you are in, and it must be confessed you deserve it; I have been accused of being inconstant in my amours, and of having had several intrigues at the same time, but you out-go me so far, that I should not so much as have dared to imagine what you have undertaken ; could you pretend to keep Madam de

Themines, and be at the same engaged with the Queen ? did you hope to have an engagement with the Queen, and be able to deceive her ? she is both an Italian and a Queen, and by consequence full of jealousy, suspicion, and pride. As soon as your good fortune, rather than your good conduct, had set you at liberty from an engagement you was entangled in, you involved yourself in new ones, and you fancied that in the midst of the Court you could be in love with Madam de Martigues without the Queen's perceiving it : you could not have been too careful to take from her the shame of having made the first advances ; she has a violent passion for you ; you have more discretion than to tell it me, and I than to ask you to tell it ; it is certain she is jealous of you, and has truth on her side." "And does it belong to you," interrupted the Viscount, "to load me with reprimands, and ought not your own experience to make you indulgent to my faults ? However I grant I am to blame ; but think, I conjure you, how to draw me out of this difficulty" ; "I think you must go to the Queen-Dauphin as soon as she is awake, and ask her for the letter, as if you had lost it." "I have told you already," replied the Duke de Nemours, "that what you propose is somewhat extraordinary, and that there are difficulties in it which may affect my own particular interest ; but besides, if this letter has been seen to drop out of your pocket, I should think it would be hard to persuade people that it dropped out of mine." "I thought I had told you," replied the Viscount, "that the Queen-Dauphin had been informed that you dropped it." "How," said the Duke de Nemours hastily, apprehending the ill consequence this mistake might be of to him with Madam de Cleves, "has the Queen-Dauphin been told I dropped the letter ?" "Yes," replied the Viscount, "she has been told so ; and what occasioned the mistake was, that there were several gentlemen of the two Queens in a room belonging to the tennis court, where our clothes were put up, when your servants and mine went together to fetch them ; then it was the letter fell out of the pocket ; those gentlemen took it up, and read it aloud ; some believed it belonged to you, and others to me ; Chatelart, who took it, and to whom I have just sent for it, says, he gave it to the Queen-Dauphin as a letter of yours ; and those, who have spoken of it to the Queen, have unfortunately told her, it was mine ; so that you may easily do what I desire of you, and free me from this perplexity."

The Duke de Nemours had always had a great friendship for the Viscount de Chartres, and the relation he bore to Madam de Cleves still made him more dear to him ; nevertheless he could not prevail with himself to run the risk of her having heard of this letter, as of a thing in which he was concerned ; he fell into a deep musing, and the Viscount guessed pretty near what was the subject of his meditations ; "I plainly see," said he, "that you are afraid of embroiling yourself with your mistress, and I should almost fancy the Queen-Dauphin was she, if the little jealousy you seem to have of Monsieur d'Anville did not take me off from that thought ; but be that as it will, it is not reasonable you should sacrifice your repose to mine, and I'll put you in a way of convincing her you love, that this letter is directed to me, and not to you ; here is a billet from Madam d'Amboise, who is a friend of Madam de Themines, and was her confidant in the amour between her and me ; in this she desires me to send her Madam de Themines's letter, which I have lost ; my name is on the superscription, and the contents of the billet prove, without question, that the letter she desires is the same with that which has been found ; I'll leave this billet in your hands, and agree that you may show it to your mistress in your justification ; I conjure you not to lose a moment, but to go this morning to the Queen-Dauphin."

The Duke de Nemours promised the Viscount he would, and took Madam d'Amboise's billet ; nevertheless his design was not to see the Queen-Dauphin ; he thought more pressing business required his care ; he made no question, but she had already spoke of the letter to Madam de Cleves, and could not bear that a person he loved so desperately, should have ground to believe he had engagements with any other.

He went to the Princess of Cleves as soon as he thought she might be awake ; and ordered her to be told, that, if he had not business of the last consequence, he would not have desired the honour to see her at so extraordinary an hour. Madam de Cleves was in bed, and her mind was tossed to and fro by a thousand melancholy thoughts that she had had during the night ; she was extremely surprised to hear the Duke de Nemours asked for her ; the anxiety she was in made her presently answer, that she was ill, and could not speak with him.

The Duke was not at all shocked at this refusal ; he thought it presaged him no ill, that she expressed a little coldness at a time when she might be touched with jealousy. He went to the Prince of Cleves's apartment, and told him he came from that of his lady, and that he was very sorry he could not see her, because he had an affair to communicate to her of great consequence to the Viscount de Chartres ; he explained in few words to the Prince the importance of this business, and the Prince immediately introduced him into his lady's chamber. Had she not been in the dark, she would have found it hard to have concealed the trouble and astonishment she was in to see the Duke de Nemours introduced by her husband. Monsieur de Cleves told her the business was about a letter, wherein her assistance was wanting for the interest of the Viscount, that she was to consult with Monsieur de Nemours what was to be done ; and that as for him he was going to the King, who had just sent for him.

The Duke de Nemours had his heart's desire, in being alone with Madam de Cleves ; "I am come to ask you, Madam," said he, "if the Queen-Dauphin has not spoke to you of a letter which Chatelart gave her yesterday." "She said something to me of it," replied Madam de Cleves, "but I don't see what relation this letter has to the interests of my uncle, and I can assure you that he is not named in it." "It is true, Madam," replied the Duke de Nemours, " he is not named in it but yet it is addressed to him, and it very much imports him that you should get it out of the Queen-Dauphin's hands." " I cannot comprehend," replied the Princess, " how it should be of any consequence to him, if this letter should be seen, nor what reason there is to redemand it in his name." " If you please to be at leisure to hear me, Madam," said Monsieur de Nemours, " I'll presently make you acquainted with the true state of the thing, and inform you of matters of so great importance to the Viscount, that I would not even have trusted the Prince of Cleves with them, had I not stood in need of his assistance to have the honour to see you." " I believe," said Madam de Cleves in a very unconcerned manner, " that anything you may give yourself the trouble of telling me, will be to little purpose ; you had better go to the Queen-Dauphin, and plainly tell her, without using th : roundabout ways, the interest you have in that letter, since she has been told, as well as I, that it belongs to you."

The uneasiness of mind which Monsieur de Nemours observed in Madam de Cleves gave him the most sensible pleasure he ever knew, and lessened his impatience to justify himself : " I don't know, Madam," replied he, " what the Queen-Dauphin may have been told ; but I am not at all concerned in that letter ; it is addressed to the Viscount." " I believe so," replied Madam de Cleves, " but the Queen-Dauphin has heard to the contrary, and she won't think it very probable that the Viscount's letters should fall out of your pocket ; you must therefore have some reason, that I don't know of, for concealing the truth of this matter from the Queen-Dauphin ; I advise you to confess it to her." " I have nothing to confess to her," says he, " the letter is not directed to me, and if there be anyone that I would have satisfied of it, it is not the Queen-Dauphin ; but, Madam, since the Viscount's interest is nearly concerned in this, be pleased to let me acquaint you with some matters that are worthy of your curiosity." Madam de Cleves by her silence showed her readiness to hear him, and he as succinctly as possible related to her all he had just heard from the Viscount. Though the circumstances were naturally surprising, and proper to create attention, yet Madam de Cleves heard them with such coldness, that she seemed either not to believe them true, or to think them indifferent to her ; she continued in this temper until the Duke de Nemours spoke of Madam d'Amboise's billet, which was directed to the Viscount, and was a proof of all he had been saying ; as Madam de Cleves knew that this lady was a friend of Madam de Themines, she found some probability in what the Duke de Nemours had said, which made her think, that the letter perhaps was not addressed to him ; this thought suddenly, and in spite of herself, drew her out of the coldness and indifferency she had until then been in. The Duke having read the billet, which fully justified him, presented it to her to read, and told her she might possibly know the hand. She could not forbear taking it, and examining the superscription to see if it was addressed to the Viscount de Chartres, and reading it all over, that she might the better judge, if the letter which was redemanded, was the same with that she had in her hand. The Duke de Nemours added whatever he thought proper to persuade her of it; and as one is easily persuaded of the truth of what one wishes, he soon convinced Madam de Cleves that he had no concern in the letter.

She began now to reason with him concerning the embarrassment and danger the Viscount was in, to blame his ill conduct, and to think of means to help him: she was astonished at the Queen's proceedings, and confessed to the Duke that she had the letter; in short, she no sooner believed him innocent, but she discoursed with him with greater ease and freedom, concerning what she would scarce before vouchsafe to hear; they agreed that the letter should not be restored to the Queen-Dauphin, for fear she should show it to Madam de Martigues, who knew Madam de Themines's hand, and would easily guess, by the interest she had in the Viscount, that it was addressed to him; they agreed also, that they ought not to entrust the Queen-Dauphin with all that concerned the Queen her mother-in-law. Madam de Cleves, under pretence of serving her uncle, was pleased to be the Duke de Nemours's confidant in the secrets he had imparted to her.

The Duke would not have confined his discourse to the Viscount's concerns, but from the liberty he had of free conversation with her, would have assumed a boldness he had never yet done, had not a message been brought in to Madam de Cleves, that the Queen-Dauphin had sent for her. The Duke was forced to withdraw; he went to the Viscount to inform him, that after he had left him, he thought it more proper to apply to Madam de Cleves, his niece, than to go directly to the Queen-Dauphin; he did not want reasons to make him approve what he had done, and to give him hopes of good success.

In the meantime Madam de Cleves dressed herself in all haste to go to the Queen-Dauphin; she was no sooner entered her chamber, but she called her to her, and whispered her, "I have been waiting for you these two hours, and was never so perplexed about disguising a truth as I have been this morning: the Queen has heard of the letter I gave you yesterday, and believes it was the Viscount de Chartres that dropped it; you know, she has some interest to be satisfied in it; she has been in search for the letter, and has caused Chatelart to be asked for it; who said he had given it to me; they have been to ask me for it, under pretence it was an ingenious letter which the Queen had a curiosity to see; I durst not say that you had it, for fear she should think I had given it you on your uncle the Viscount's account, and that there was a correspondence between him and me. I was already satisfied, that his seeing me so often gave her uneasiness, so that I said the letter was in the clothes I had on yesterday, and that those who had them in keeping were gone abroad; give me the letter immediately," added she, "that I may send it her, and that I may read it before I send it, to see if I know the hand."

Madam de Cleves was harder put to it than she expected; "I don't know, Madam, what you will do," answered she, "for Monsieur de Cleves, to whom I gave it to read, returned it to the Duke of Nemours, who came early this morning to beg him to get it of you. Monsieur de Cleves had the imprudence to tell him he had it, and the weakness to yield to the entreaties the Duke de Nemours made that he would restore it him." "You throw me into the greatest embarrassment I can possibly be in," replied the Queen-Dauphin; "and you have given this letter to the Duke de Nemours. Since it was I that gave it you, you ought not to have restored it without my leave; what would you have me say to the Queen, and what can she imagine? She will think, and not without reason, that this letter concerns myself, and that there is something between the Viscount and me; she will never be persuaded the letter belonged to the Duke de Nemours." "I am very much concerned," replied Madam de Cleves, "for the misfortune I have occasioned, and I believe the difficulty I have brought you into is very great; but 'twas Monsieur de Cleves's fault, and not mine." "You are in fault," replied the Queen-Dauphin, "for having given him the letter; and I believe you are the only woman in the world that acquaints her husband with all she knows." "I acknowledge myself in fault, Madam," replied the Princess of Cleves, "but let us rather think of preventing the consequences of what I have done, than insist on the fault itself." "Do you remember, pretty near, what the letter contains?" says the Queen-Dauphin. "Yes, Madam, I do," replied she, "for I have read it over more than once." "If so," said the Queen-Dauphin, "you must immediately get it written out in an unknown hand, and I'll send it to the Queen; she'll not show it those who have seen it already; and though she should, I'll stand in it, that it is the same Chatelart gave me; and he'll not dare to say otherwise."

Madam de Cleves approved of this expedient, and the more because it gave her an opportunity of sending for the Duke de Nemours, to have the letter itself again, in order to have it copied word for word, imitating as near as may be the hand it was written in, and she thought this would effectually deceive the Queen. As soon as she was got home, she informed her husband of what had passed between her and the Queen-Dauphin, and begged him to send for the Duke de Nemours. The Duke was sent for, and came immediately; Madam de Cleves told him all she had told her husband, and asked for the letter; but the Duke answered, that he had already returned it to the Viscount de Chartres, who was so overjoyed upon having it again, and being freed from the danger he was in, that he sent it immediately to Madam de Themines's friend. Madam de Cleves was in a new embarrassment on this occasion: in short, after having consulted together, they resolved to form the letter by memory; and, in order to go about it, they locked themselves up, and left orders that nobody should be admitted, and that all the Duke de Nemours's attendants should be sent away. Such an appearance of secret confidence was no small charm to

Monsieur de Nemours, and even to Madam de Cleves ; her husband's presence, and the interests of her uncle the Viscount de Chartres, were considerations which in great measure removed her scruples, and made this opportunity of seeing and being with the Duke de Nemours so agreeable to her, that she never before experienced a joy so pure and free from allay ; this threw her into a freedom and gaiety of spirit which the Duke had never observed in her till now, and which made him still more passionately in love with her : as he had never known such agreeable moments, his vivacity was much heightened ; and whenever Madam de Cleves was beginning to recollect and write the letter, instead of assisting her seriously, did nothing but interrupt her with wit and pleasantry. Madam de Cleves was as gay as he, so that they had been locked up a considerable time, and two messages had come from the Queen-Dauphin to hasten Madam de Cleves, before they had half finished the letter.

The Duke de Nemours was glad to prolong the time that was so agreeable to him, and neglected the concerns of his friend ; Madam de Cleves was not at all tired, and neglected also the concerns of her uncle : at last, with much ado, about four o'clock the letter was finished, and was so ill done, and the copy so unlike the original, as to the handwriting, that the queen must have taken very little care to come at the truth of the matter, if she had been imposed on by so ill a counterfeit. Accordingly she was not deceived ; and however industrious they were to persuade her, that this letter was addressed to the Duke de Nemours, she remained satisfied not only that it was addressed to the Viscount de Chartres, but that the Queen-Dauphin was concerned in it, and that there was a correspondence between them ; this heightened her hatred against that Princess to such a degree, that she never forgave her, and never ceased persecuting her till she had driven her out of France.

As for the Viscount de Chartres, his credit was entirely ruined with her ; and whether the Cardinal of Loraine had already insinuated himself so far into her esteem as to govern her, or whether the accident of this letter, which made it appear that the Viscount had deceived her, enabled her to discover the other tricks he had played her, it is certain he could never after entirely reconcile himself to her ; their correspondence was broke off, and at length she ruined him by means of the conspiracy of Amboise, in which he was involved.

After the letter was sent to the Queen-Dauphin, Monsieur de Cleves and Monsieur de Nemours went away ; Madam de Cleves continued alone, and being no longer supported by the joy which the presence of what one loves gives one, she seemed like one newly waked from a dream ; she beheld, with astonishment, the difference between the condition she was in the night before, and that she was in at this time : she called to mind, how cold and sullen she was to the Duke de Nemours, while she thought Madam de Themines's letter was addressed to him, and how calm and sweet a situation of mind succeeded that uneasiness, as soon as he was satisfied he was not concerned in that letter; when she reflected, that she reproached herself as guilty for having given him the foregoing day only some marks of sensibility, which mere compassion might have produced, and that by her peevish humour this morning, she had expressed such a jealousy as was a certain proof of passion, she thought she was not herself; when she reflected further, that the Duke de Nemours saw plainly, that she knew he was in love with her, and that, notwithstanding her knowing it, she did not use him the worse for it, even in her husband's presence; but that, on the contrary, she had never behaved so favourably to him; when she considered, she was the cause of Monsieur de Cleves's sending for him, and that she had just passed an afternoon in private with him; when she considered all this, she found, there was something within her that held intelligence with the Duke de Nemours, and that she deceived a husband who least deserved it; and she was ashamed to appear so little worthy of esteem, even in the eyes of her lover; but what she was able to support less than all the rest was, the remembrance of the condition in which she spent the last night, and the pricking griefs she felt from a suspicion that the Duke de Nemours was in love with another, and that she was deceived by him.

Never till then was she acquainted with the dreadful inquietudes that flow from jealousy and distrust; she had applied all her cares to prevent herself from falling in love with the Duke de Nemours, and had not before had any fear of his being in love with another: though the suspicions which this letter had given her were effaced, yet they left her sensible of the hazard there was of being deceived, and gave her impressions of distrust and jealousy which she had never felt till that time; she was surprised, that she had never yet reflected, how improbable it was, that a man of the Duke de Nemours's turn, who had showed so much inconstancy towards women, should be capable of a lasting and sincere passion; she thought it next to impossible for her to be convinced of the truth of his love; "But though I could be convinced of it," says she, "what have I to do in it? Shall I permit it? Shall I make a return? Shall I engage in gallantry, be false to Monsieur de Cleves, and be false to myself? In a word, shall I go to expose myself to the cruel remorses and deadly griefs that rise from love? I am subdued and vanquished by a passion, which hurries me away in spite of myself; all my resolutions are vain; I had the same thoughts yesterday that I have today, and I act today contrary to what I resolved yesterday; I must convey myself out of the sight of the Duke de Nemours; I must go into the country, however fantastical my journey may appear; and if Monsieur de Cleves is obstinately bent to hinder me, or to know my reasons for it, perhaps I shall do him and myself the injury to acquaint him with them." She continued in this resolution, and spent the whole evening at home, without going to the Queen-Dauphin to enquire what had happened with respect to the counterfeited letter.

When the Prince of Cleves returned home, she told him she was resolved to go into the country; that she was not very well, and had occasion to take the air. Monsieur de Cleves, to whom she appeared so beautiful that he could not think her indisposition very considerable, at first made a jest of her design, and answered, that she had forgot that the nuptials of the Princesses and the tournament were very near, and that she had not too much time to prepare matters so as to appear there as magnificently as other ladies. What her husband said did not make her change her resolution, and she begged he would agree, that while he was at Compiegne with the King, she might go to Colomiers, a pretty house then building, within a day's journey of Paris. Monsieur de Cleves consented to it; she went thither with a design of not returning so soon, and the King set out for Compiegne, where he was to stay but few days.

The Duke de Nemours was mightily concerned he had not seen Madam de Cleves since that afternoon, which he had spent so agreeably with her, and which had increased his hopes; he was so impatient to see her again that he could not rest; so that when the King returned to Paris, the Duke resolved to go to see his sister the Duchess de Mercœur, who was at a country seat of hers, very near Colomiers; he asked the Viscount to go with him, who readily consented to it. The Duke de Nemours did this in hopes of visiting Madam de Cleves, in company of the Viscount.

Madam de Mercœur received them with a great deal of joy, and thought of nothing but giving them all the pleasures and diversions of the country; one day, as they were hunting a stag, the Duke de Nemours lost himself in the forest, and upon enquiring his way was told he was near Colomiers; at that word, Colomiers, without further reflection, or so much as knowing what design he was upon, he galloped on full speed the way that had been showed him; as he rode along he came by chance to the made-ways and walks, which he judged led to the castle: at the end of these walks he found a pavilion, at the lower end of which was a large room with two closets, the one opening into a flower-garden, and the other looking into a spacious walk in the park; he entered the Pavilion, and would have stopped to observe the beauty of it, if he had not seen in the walk the Prince and Princess of Cleves, attended with a numerous train of their domestics. As he did not expect to meet Monsieur de Cleves there, whom he had left with the King, he thought at first of hiding himself; he entered the closet which looked into the flower-garden, with design to go out that way by a door which opened to the forest; but observing Madam de Cleves and her husband were sat down under the Pavilion, and that their attendants stayed in the park, and could not come to him without passing by the place where Monsieur and Madam de Cleves were, he could not deny himself the pleasure of seeing this Princess, nor resist the curiosity he had to hear her conversation with a husband, who gave him more jealousy than any of his rivals. He heard Monsieur de Cleves say to his wife, " But why will you not return to Paris ? What can keep you here in the country ? You have of late taken a fancy for solitude, at which I am both surprised and concerned, because it deprives me of your company : I find too, you are more melancholy than usual, and I am afraid you have some cause of grief." " I have nothing to trouble my mind," answered she with an air of confusion, " but there is such a bustle at Court, and such a multitude of people always at your house, that it is impossible but both body and mind should be fatigued, and one cannot but desire repose." " Repose," answered he, " is not very proper for one of your age ; you are at home, and at Court, in such a manner as cannot occasion weariness, and I am rather afraid you desire to live apart from me." " You would do me great wrong to think so," replied she with yet more confusion, " but I beg you to leave me here ; if you could stay here, and without company, I should be very glad of it ; nothing would be more agreeable to me than your conversation in this retirement, provided you would approve not to have about you that infinite number of people, who in a manner never leave you." " Ah ! Madam," cries Monsieur de Cleves, " both your looks and words convince me, that you have reasons to desire to be alone, which I don't know ; I conjure you to tell them me." He urged her a great while to inform him, without being able to oblige her to it ; and after she had excused herself in a manner which still increased her husband's curiosity, she continued in a deep silence, with her eyes cast down ; then, taking up the discourse on a sudden, and looking upon him, " Force me not," said she, " to confess a thing to you which I have not the power to confess, though I have often designed it ; remember only, that it is not prudent a woman of my years, and mistress of her own conduct, should remain exposed in the midst of a Court." " What is it, Madam," cried Monsieur de Cleves, " that you lead me to imagine ? I dare not speak it, for fear of offending you." Madam de Cleves making no answer, her silence confirmed her husband in what he thought ; " You say nothing to me," says he, " and that tells me clearly, that I am not mistaken." " Alas, sir," answered she, falling on her knees, "I am going to make a confession to you, such as no woman ever yet made to her husband ; but the innocence of my intentions, and of my conduct, give me power to do it ; it is true, I have reasons to absent myself from Court, and I would avoid the dangers persons of my age are sometimes liable to ; I have never shown any mark of weakness, and I cannot apprehend I ever shall, if you will permit me to retire from Court, since now I have not Madam de Chartres to assist me in my conduct ; however dangerous a step I am taking, I take it with pleasure to preserve myself worthy of you ; I ask you a thousand pardons, if I have sentiments which displease you, at least I will never displease you by my actions ; consider, that to do what I do, requires more friendship and esteem for a husband than ever wife had ; direct my conduct, have pity on me, and if you can still love me."

Monsieur de Cleves, all the while she spoke, continued leaning his head on his hand, almost beside himself, and never thought of raising her up. When she had done speaking, and he cast his eyes upon her, and saw her on her knees with her face drowned in tears, inimitably beautiful, he was ready to die for grief, and taking her up in his arms, "Have you pity on me, Madam," says he, "for I deserve it, and pardon me, if in the first moments of an affliction so violent as mine, I do not answer as I ought to so generous a proceeding as yours; I think you more worthy of esteem and admiration than any woman that ever was, but I find myself also the most unfortunate of men: you inspired me with passion the first moment I saw you, and that passion has never decayed; not your coldness, nor even enjoyment itself, has been able to extinguish it; it still continues in its first force, and yet it has not been in my power to kindle in your breast any spark of love for me, and now I find you fear you have an inclination for another; and who is he, Madam, this happy man that gives you such apprehensions? How long has he charmed you? What has he done to charm you? What method has he taken to get into your heart? When I could not gain your affections myself, it was some comfort to me to think, that no other could gain them; in the meantime, another has effected what I could not, and I have at once the jealousy of a husband and lover. But it is impossible for me to retain that of a husband after such a proceeding on your part, which is too noble and ingenuous not to give me an entire security; it even comforts me as a lover; the sincerity you have expressed, and the confidence you have placed in me are of infinite value: you have esteem enough for me to believe I shall not abuse the confession you have made to me; you are in the right, Madam, I will not abuse it, or love you the less for it; you make me unhappy by the greatest mark of fidelity ever woman gave her husband; but go on, Madam, and inform me who he is whom you would avoid." "I beg you not to ask me," replied she; "I am resolved not to tell you, nor do I think it prudent to name him." "Fear not, Madam," replied Monsieur de Cleves, "I know the world too well to be ignorant that a woman's having a husband does not hinder people from being in love with her; such lovers may be the objects of one's hatred, but we are not to complain of it; once again, Madam, I conjure you to tell me what I so much desire to know." "It is in vain to press me," replied she, "I have the power to be silent in what I think I ought not to tell; the confession I made to you was not owing to any weakness, and it required more courage to declare such a truth, than it would have done to conceal it."

The Duke de Nemours did not lose a word of this conversation, and what Madam de Cleves had said gave him no less jealousy than her husband; he was so desperately in love with her, that he believed all the world was so too; it is true, he had many rivals, yet he fancied them still more, and his thoughts wandered to find out who it was Madam de Cleves meant: he had often thought he was not disagreeable to her, but the grounds of his judgment on this occasion appeared so slight, that he could not imagine he had raised in her heart a passion violent enough to oblige her to have recourse to so extraordinary a remedy; he was so transported, that he scarce knew what he saw, and he could not pardon Monsieur de Cleves for not having pressed his wife enough to tell him the name of the person she concealed from him.

Monsieur de Cleves nevertheless used his utmost endeavours to know it; and having urged her very much on the subject; "I think," answered she, "that you ought to be satisfied with my sincerity; ask me no more about it, and don't give me cause to repent of what I have done; content yourself with the assurance which I once more give you, that my sentiments have never appeared by any of my actions, and that no address hath been made to me that could give me offence." "Ah! Madam," replied Monsieur de Cleves on a sudden, "I cannot believe it; I remember the confusion you was in when your picture was lost; you have given away, Madam, you have given away that picture, which was so dear to me, and which I had so just a right to; you have not been able to conceal your inclinations, you are in love; it is known; your virtue has hitherto saved you from the rest." "Is it possible," cried Madam de Cleves, "you can imagine there was any reserve or disguise in a confession like mine, which I was no way obliged to? Take my word, I purchase dearly the confidence I desire of you; I conjure you to believe I have not given away my picture; it is true, I saw it taken, but I would not seem to see it, for fear of subjecting myself to hear such things as no one has yet dared to mention to me." "How do you know then that you are loved," said Monsieur de Cleves? "What mark, what proof of it has been given you?" "Spare me the pain," replied she, "of repeating to you circumstances which I am ashamed to have observed, and which have convinced me but too much of my own weakness." "You are in the right, Madam," answered he, "I am unjust; always refuse me when I ask you such things, and yet don't be angry with me for asking them."

Just then several of the servants, who had stayed in the walks, came to acquaint Monsieur de Cleves, that a gentleman was arrived from the King, with orders for him to be at Paris that evening. Monsieur de Cleves was obliged to go, and had only time to tell his wife, that he desired her to come to Paris the next day; and that he conjured her to believe, that, however afflicted he was, he had a tenderness and esteem for her, with which she ought to be satisfied.

When he was gone, and Madam de Cleves being alone, considered what she had done, she was so frightened at the thought of it, she could hardly believe it to be true. She found she had deprived herself of the heart and esteem of her husband, and was involved in a labyrinth she should never get out of; she asked herself why she had ventured on so dangerous a step, and perceived she was engaged in it almost without having designed it; the singularity of such a confession, for which she saw no precedent, made her fully sensible of her danger.

But on the other hand, when she came to think that this remedy, however violent it was, was the only effectual one she could make use of against Monsieur de Nemours, she found she had no cause to repent, or to believe she had ventured too far; she passed the whole night full of doubts, anxiety and fear; but at last her spirits grew calm again; she even felt a pleasure arise in her mind, from a sense of having given such a proof of fidelity to a husband, who deserved it so well, who had so great a friendship and esteem for her, and had so lately manifested it by the manner in which he received the confession she had made him.

In the meantime Monsieur de Nemours was gone away from the place, in which he had overheard a conversation which so sensibly affected him, and was got deep into the forest; what Madam de Cleves said of her picture had revived him, since it was certain from thence that he was the person she had an inclination for; at first he gave a leap of joy, but his raptures were at an end as soon as he began to reflect, that the same thing that convinced him he had touched the heart of Madam de Cleves, ought to convince him also that he should never receive any marks of it, and that it would be impossible to engage a lady who had recourse to so extraordinary a remedy; and yet he could not but be sensibly pleased to have reduced her to that extremity; he thought it glorious for him to have gained the affections of a woman so different from the rest of her sex; in a word, he thought himself very happy and very unhappy at the same time. He was benighted in the forest, and was very much put to it to find his way again to his sister's the Duchess of Mercœur; he arrived there at break of day, and was extremely at a loss what account to give of his absence, but he made out the matter as well as he could, and returned that very day to Paris with the Viscount.

The Duke was so taken up with his passion, and so surprised at the conversation he had heard, that he fell into an indiscretion very common, which is, to speak one's own particular sentiments in general terms, and to relate one's proper adventures under borrowed names. As they were travelling he began to talk of love, and exaggerated the pleasure of being in love with a person that deserved it; he spoke of the fantastical effects of this passion, and at last not being able to contain within himself the admiration he was in at the action of Madam de Cleves, he related it to the Viscount without naming the person, or owning he had any share in it; but he told it with so much warmth and surprise, that the Viscount easily suspected the story concerned himself. The Viscount urged him very much to confess it, and told him he had known a great while that he was violently in love, and that it was unjust in him to show a distrust of a man, who had committed to him a secret on which his life depended. The Duke de Nemours was too much in love to own it, and had always concealed it from the Viscount, though he valued him the most of any man at Court; he answered, that one of his friends had told him this adventure, and made him promise not to speak of it; and he also conjured the Viscount to keep the secret: the Viscount assured him he would say nothing of it; but notwithstanding Monsieur de Nemours repented that he had told him so much.

In the meantime Monsieur de Cleves was gone to the King, with a heart full of sorrow and affliction. Never had husband so violent a passion for his wife, or so great an esteem; what she had told him did not take away his esteem of her, but made it of a different nature from that he had had before; what chiefly employed his thoughts, was a desire to guess who it was that had found out the secret to win her heart; the Duke de Nemours was the first person he thought of on this occasion, as being the handsomest man at Court; and the Chevalier de Guise, and the Mareschal de St. André occurred next, as two persons who had made it their endeavour to get her love, and who were still very assiduous in courting her, so that he was fully persuaded it must be one of the three. He arrived at the Louvre, and the King carried him into his closet to inform him he had made choice of him to conduct Madame into Spain, and that he believed nobody could acquit himself better of that charge, nor that any lady would do France greater honour than Madam de Cleves. Monsieur de Cleves received the honour the King had done him by this choice with the respect he ought, and he considered it also as what would take his wife from Court, without leaving room to suspect any change in her conduct; but the embarrassment he was under required a speedier remedy than that journey, which was to be deferred a great while, could afford; he immediately wrote to Madam de Cleves to acquaint her with what the King had told him, and gave her to understand he absolutely expected she should return to Paris. She returned according to his orders, and when they met, they found one another overwhelmed with melancholy.

Monsieur de Cleves spoke to her, as a man of the greatest honour in the world, and the best deserving the confidence she had reposed in him; "I am not alarmed as to your conduct," said he, "you have more strength and vitue than you imagine; I am not alarmed with fears of what may happen hereafter; what troubles me is, that I see you have those sentiments for another which you want for me." "I don't know what to answer you," said she, "I die with shame when I speak of this subject spare me, I conjure you, such cruel conversations; regulate my conduct, and never let me see anybody; this is all I desire of you; but tak it not ill of me, if I speak no more of a thing which makes me appear so little worthy of you, and which I think so unbecoming me." "You are in the right, Madam;" replied he, "I abuse your goodness and your confidence in me; but have some compassion also on the condition you have brought me to, and think that whatever you have told me, you conceal from me a name, which creates in me a curiosity I cannot live without satisfying; and yet I ask you not to satisfy it; I cannot, however, forbear telling you, that I believe the man I am to envy is the Mareschal de St. André, the Duke de Nemours, or the Chevalier de Guise." "I shall make you no answer," says she blushing, " nor give you any ground from what I say, either to lessen or strengthen your suspicions ; but if you endeavour to inform yourself by observing me, you will throw me into a confusion all the world will take notice of, for God's sake," continued she, " allow me under pretence of an indisposition to see nobody." " No, Madam," said he, " it will quickly be discovered to be a feigned business ; and besides, I am unwilling to trust you to anything but yourself ; my heart tells me this is the best way I can take, and my reason tells me so also, considering the temper of mind you are in, I cannot put a greater restraint upon you, than by leaving you to your liberty."

Monsieur de Cleves was not mistaken ; the confidence he showed he had in his wife, fortified her the more against Monsieur de Nemours, and made her take more severe resolutions than any restraint could have brought her to. She went to wait on the Queen-Dauphin at the Louvre as she used to do, but avoided the presence and eyes of Monsieur de Nemours with so much care, that she deprived him of almost all the joy he had in thinking she loved him ; he saw nothing in her actions but what seemed to show the contrary ; he scarcely knew if what he had heard was not a dream, so very improbable it seemed to him ; the only thing which assured him that he was not mistaken, was Madam de Cleves's extreme melancholy, which appeared, whatever pains she took to hide it ; and perhaps kind words and looks would not have increased the Duke of Nemours's love so much as this severe conduct did.

One evening, as Monsieur and Madam de Cleves were at the Queen's apartment, it was said there was a report that the King would name another great lord to wait on Madame into Spain. Monsieur de Cleves had his eye fixed on his wife, when it was further said, the Chevalier de Guise, or the Mareschal de St. André, was the person ; he observed she was not at all moved at either of those names, nor the discourse of their going along with her ; this made him believe, it was not either of them whose presence she feared. In order to clear up his suspicions, he went into the Queen's closet, where the King then was, and after having stayed there some time came back to his wife, and whispered her, that he had just heard the Duke de Nemours was the person designed to go along with them to Spain.

The name of the Duke de Nemours, and the thought of being exposed to see him every day, during a very long journey, in her husband's presence, so affected Madam de Cleves, that she could not conceal her trouble : and being willing to give other reasons for it, " No choice," says she, " could have been made more disagreeable for you ; he will share all honours with you, and I think you ought to endeavour to get some other chosen." " It is not honour, Madam," replied Monsieur de Cleves, " that makes you apprehensive of the Duke de Nemours's going with me, the uneasiness you are in proceeds from another cause ; and from this uneasiness of yours I learn, that which I should have discovered in another woman, by the joy she would have expressed on such an occasion; but be not afraid; what I have told you is not true, it was an invention of mine to assure myself of a thing which I already believed but too much." Having said this, he went out, being unwilling to increase, by his presence, the concern he saw his wife in.

The Duke de Nemours came in that instant, and presently observed Madam de Cleves's condition; he came up to her, and told her softly, he had that respect for her, he durst not ask what it was made her more pensive than usual. The voice of the Duke de Nemours brought her to herself again, and looking at him, without having heard what he had said to her, full of her own thoughts, and afraid lest her husband should see him with her, "For God's sake," says she, "leave me to myself in quiet." "Alas, Madam," answered he, "I disturb you too little; what is it you can complain of? I dare not speak to you, I dare not look upon you, I tremble whenever I approach you. How have I drawn upon myself what you have said to me, and why do you show me, that I am in part the cause of the trouble I see you in?" Madam de Cleves was very sorry to have given the Duke an opportunity of explaining himself more clearly than ever he had done before; she left him without making any answer, and went home with her mind more agitated than ever. Her husband perceived her concern was increased, and that she was afraid he would speak to her of what had passed, and followed her into her closet; "Do not shun me, Madam," says he, "I will say nothing to you that shall displease you; I ask pardon for the surprise I gave you a while ago; I am sufficiently punished by what I have learnt from it; the Duke de Nemours was of all men he whom I most feared; I see the danger you are in; command yourself for your own sake, and, if it is possible, for mine; I do not ask this of you as a husband, but as a man whose happiness wholly depends on you, and who loves you more violently and more tenderly than he whom your heart prefers to me." Monsieur de Cleves was melted upon speaking these words, and could scarce make an end of them; his wife was so moved, she burst into tears, and embraced him with a tenderness and sorrow that put him into a condition not very different from her own; they continued silent a while, and parted without having the power to speak to one another.

All things were ready for the marriage of Madame, and the Duke of Alva was arrived to espouse her; he was received with all the ceremony and magnificence that could be displayed on such an occasion; the King sent to meet him the Prince of Condè, the Cardinals of Loraine and Guise, the Dukes of Loraine and Ferrara, d'Aumale, de Bouillon, de Guise, and de Nemours; they had a great number of gentlemen, and a great many pages in livery; the King himself, attended with two hundred gentlemen, and the Constable at their head, received the Duke of Alva at the first gate of the Louvre; the Duke would have kneeled down, but the King refused it, and made him walk by his side to the Queen's apartment, and to Madame's, to whom the Duke of Alva had brought a magnificent present from his master; he went thence to the apartment of Madam Margaret the King's sister, to compliment her on the part of the Duke of Savoy, and to assure her he would arrive in a few days; there were great assemblies at the Louvre, the show the Duke of Alva, and the Prince of Orange who accompanied him, the beauties of the Court.

Madam de Cleves could not dispense with going to these assemblies, however desirous she was to be absent, for fear of disobliging her husband, who absolutely commanded her to be there; and what yet more induced her to it, was the absence of the Duke de Nemours; he was gone to meet the Duke of Savoy, and after the arrival of that Prince, he was obliged to be almost always with him, to assist him in everything relating to the ceremonies of the nuptials; for this reason Madam de Cleves did not meet him so often as she used to do, which gave her some sort of ease.

The Viscount de Chartres had not forgot the conversation he had had with the Duke de Nemours: it still ran in his mind, that the adventure the Duke had related to him, was his own; and he observed him so carefully, that it is probable he would have unravelled the business, if the arrival of the Duke of Alva and of the Duke of Savoy had not made such an alteration in the Court, and filled it with so much business, as left no opportunities for a discovery of that nature; the desire he had to get some information about it, or rather the natural disposition one has to relate all one knows to those one loves, made him acquaint Madam de Martigues with the extraordinary action of that person, who had confessed to her husband the passion she had for another; he assured her, the Duke de Nemours was the man who had inspired so violent a love, and begged her assistance in observing him. Madam de Martigues was glad to hear what the Viscount told her, and the curiosity she had always observed in the Queen-Dauphin for what concerned the Duke de Nemours, made her yet more desirous to search into the bottom of the affair.

A few days before that which was fixed for the ceremony of the marriage, the Queen-Dauphin entertained at supper the King her father-in-law, and the Duchess of Valentinois. Madam de Cleves, who had been busy in dressing herself, went to the Louvre later than ordinary; as she was going, she met a gentleman, that was coming from the Queen-Dauphin to fetch her; as soon as she entered the room, that Princess, who was sitting upon her bed, told her aloud, that she had expected her with great impatience. "I believe, Madam," answered she, "that I am not obliged to you for it, and that your impatience was caused by something else, and not your desire to see me." "You are in the right," answered the Queen-Dauphin, "but, nevertheless, you are obliged to me; for I'll tell you an adventure, which I am sure you'll be glad to know."

Madam de Cleves kneeled at her bedside, and, very luckily for her, with her face from the light: "You know," said the Queen, "how desirous we have been to find out what had caused so great a change in the Duke de Nemours; I believe I know it, and it is what will surprise you; he is desperately in love with, and as much beloved by, one of the finest ladies of the Court." It is easy to imagine the grief Madam de Cleves felt upon hearing these words, which she could not apply to herself, since she thought nobody knew anything of her passion for the Duke; "I see nothing extraordinary in that," replied she, "considering how young and handsome a man the Duke de Nemours it." "No," replied the Queen-Dauphin, "there is nothing extraordinary in it; but what will surprise you is, that this lady, who is in love with the Duke de Nemours, has never given him any mark of it, and that the fear she was in lest she should not always be mistress of her passion, has made her confess it to her husband, that he may take her away from Court; and it is the Duke de Nemours himself, who has related what I tell you."

If Madam de Cleves was grieved at first through the thought that she had no concern in this adventure, the Queen-Dauphin's last words threw her into an agony, by making it certain she had too much in it; she could not answer, but continued leaning her head on the bed; meanwhile the Queen went on, and was so intent on what she was saying, that she took no notice of her embarrassment. When Madam de Cleves was a little come to herself, "This story, Madam," says she, "does not seem very probable to me, and I should be glad to know who told it you." "It was Madam de Martigues," replied the Queen-Dauphin, "and she heard it from the Viscount de Chartres; you know the Viscount is in love with her; he entrusted this matter to her as a secret, and he was told it by the Duke de Nemours himself; it is true the Duke did not tell the lady's name, nor acknowledge that he was the person she was in love with, but the Viscount makes no manner of question of it." When the Queen-Dauphin had done speaking, somebody came up to the bed; Madam de Cleves was so placed that she could not see who it was, but she was presently convinced, when the Queen-Dauphin cried out with an air of gaiety and surprise, "Here he is himself, I'll ask him what there is in it." Madam de Cleves knew very well it was the Duke de Nemours, without turning herself, as it really was; upon which she went up hastily to the Queen-Dauphin, and told her softly, that she ought to be cautious of speaking to him of this adventure, which he had entrusted to the Viscount de Chartres as a secret, and that it was a thing which might create a quarrel between them. "You are too wise," said the Queen-Dauphin smiling, and turned to the Duke de Nemours. He was dressed for the evening assembly, and taking up the discourse with that grace which was natural to him, "I believe, Madam," says he, "I may venture to think you were speaking of me as I came in, that you had a design to ask me something, and that Madam de Cleves is against it." "It is true," replied the Queen-Dauphin, "but I shall not be so complaisant to her on this occasion as I was used to be; I would know of you, whether a story I have been told is true, and whether you are not the person who is in love with, and beloved by a lady of the Court, who endeavours to conceal her passion from you, and has confessed it to her husband."

The concern and confusion Madam de Cleves was in was above all that can be imagined, and if death itself could have drawn her out of this condition, she would have gladly embraced it; but the Duke de Nemours was yet more embarrassed, if possible: the discourse of the Queen-Dauphin, by whom he had reason to believe he was not hated, in the presence of Madam de Cleves, who was confided in by her more than anybody of the Court, and who confided more in her, threw him into such confusion and extravagance of thought, that it was impossible for him to be master of his countenance: the concern he saw Madam de Cleves in through his fault, and the thought of having given her just cause to hate him, so shocked him he could not speak a word. The Queen-Dauphin, seeing how thunderstruck she was, "Look upon him, look upon him," said she to Madam de Cleves, "and judge if this adventure be not his own."

In the meantime the Duke de Nemours, finding of what importance it was to him to extricate himself out of so dangerous a difficulty, recovered himself from his first surprise, and became at once master of his wit and looks. "I acknowledge, Madam," said he, "it is impossible to be more surprised and concerned than I was at the treachery of the Viscount de Chartres, in relating an adventure of a friend of mine, which I had in confidence imparted to him. I know how to be revenged of him," continued he, smiling with a calm air, which removed the suspicions the Queen-Dauphin had entertained of him: "He has entrusted me with things of no very small importance; but I don't know, Madam, why you do me the honour to make me a party in this affair. The Viscount can't say I am concerned in it, for I told him the contrary; I may very well be taken to be a man in love, but I cannot believe, Madam, you will think me of the number of those who are loved again." The Duke was glad to say anything to the Queen-Dauphin, which alluded to the inclination he had expressed for her formerly, in order to divert her thoughts from the subject in question. She imagined she understood well enough the drift of what he said, but without making any answer to it, she continued to rally him upon the embarrassment he was in. "I was concerned, Madam," said he, "for the interest of my friend, and on account of the just reproaches he might make me for having told a secret which is dearer to him than life. He has nevertheless entrusted me but with one half of it, and has not told me the name of the person he loves; all I know is, that he's the most deeply in love of any man in the world, and has the most reason to complain." "Do you think he has reason to complain," replied the Queen-Dauphin, "when he is loved again?" "Do you believe he is, Madam," replied he, "and that a person who had a real passion could discover it to her husband? That lady, doubtless, is not acquainted with love, and has mistaken for it a slight acknowledgment of the fondness her lover had for her. My friend can't flatter himself with the least hopes; but, unfortunate as he is, he thinks himself happy at least in having made her afraid of falling in love with him, and he would not change his condition for that of the happiest lover in the world." "Your friend has a passion very easy to be satisfied," said the Queen-Dauphin, "and I begin to believe it is not yourself you are speaking of; I am almost," continued she, "of the opinion of Madam de Cleves, who maintains that this story cannot be true." "I don't really believe it can be true," answered Madam de Cleves, who had been silent hitherto; "and though it were possible to be true, how should it have been known? It is very unlikely that a woman, capable of so extraordinary a resolution, would have the weakness to publish it; and surely her husband would not have told it neither, or he must be a husband very unworthy to have been dealt with in so generous a manner." The Duke de Nemours, who perceived the suspicions Madam de Cleves had of her husband, was glad to confirm her in them, knowing he was the most formidable rival he had to overcome. "Jealousy," said he, "and a curiosity perhaps of knowing more than a wife has thought fit to discover, may make a husband do a great many imprudent things."

Madam de Cleves was put to the last proof of her power and courage, and not being able to endure the conversation any longer, she was going to say she was not well, when by good fortune for her the Duchess of Valentinois came in, and told the Queen-Dauphin that the King was just coming; the Queen-Dauphin went into the closet to dress herself, and the Duke de Nemours came up to Madam de Cleves as she was following her. "I would give my life, Madam," said he, "to have a moment's conversation with you; but though I have a world of important things to say to you, I think nothing is more so, than to entreat you to believe, that if I have said anything in which the Queen-Dauphin may seem concerned, I did it for reasons which do not relate to her." Madam de Cleves pretended not to hear him, and left him without giving him a look, and went towards the King, who was just come in. As there were abundance of people there, she trod upon her gown, and made a false step, which served her as an excuse to go out of a place she had not the power to stay in, and so pretending to have received some hurt she went home.

Monsieur de Cleves came to the Louvre, and was surprised not to find his wife there; they told him of the accident that had befallen her, and he went immediately home to enquire after her; he found her in bed, and perceived her hurt was not considerable. When he had been some time with her, he found her so excessive melancholy that he was surprised at it; "What ails you, Madam?" says he; "you seem to have some other grief than that which you complain of." "I feel the most sensible grief I can ever experience," answered she; "what use have you made of that extraordinary, or rather foolish confidence which I placed in you? Did not I deserve to have my secret kept? and though I had not deserved it, did not your own interest engage you to it? Should your curiosity to know a name it was not reasonable for me to tell you, have obliged you to make a confidant to assist you in the discovery? Nothing but that curiosity could have made you guilty of so cruel an indiscretion; the consequences of it are as bad as they possibly can be. This adventure is known, and I have been told it by those who are not aware that I am principally concerned in it." "What do you say, Madam?" answered he; "you accuse me of having told what passed between you and me, and you inform me that the thing is known; I don't go about to clear myself from this charge, you can't think me guilty of it; without doubt you have applied to yourself what was told you of some other." "Ah! sir," replied she, "the world has not an adventure like mine, there is not another woman capable of such a thing. The story I have heard could not have been invented by chance; nobody could imagine any like it; an action of this nature never entered any thoughts but mine. The Queen-Dauphin has just told me the story; she had it from the Viscount de Chartres, and the Viscount from the Duke de Nemours." "The Duke de Nemours!" cried Monsieur de Cleves, like a man transported and desperate: "How! does the Duke de Nemours know that you are in love with him, and that I am acquainted with it?" "You are always for singling out the Duke de Nemours rather than any other," replied she; "I have told you I will never answer you concerning your suspicions: I am ignorant whether the Duke de Nemours knows the part I have in this adventure, and that which you have ascribed to him; but he told it to the Viscount de Chartres, and said he had it from one of his friends, who did not name the lady: this friend of the Duke de Nemours must needs be one of yours, whom you entrusted the secret to, in order to clear up your suspicions." "Can one have a friend in the world, in whom one would repose such a confidence," replied Monsieur de Cleves, "and would a man clear his suspicions at the price of informing another with what one would wish to conceal from oneself? Think rather, Madam, to whom you have spoken; it is more probable this secret should have escaped from you than from me; you was not able alone to support the trouble you found yourself in, and you endeavoured to comfort yourself by complaining to some confidant who has betrayed you." "Do not wholly destroy me," cried she, "and be not so hard-hearted as to accuse me of a fault you have committed yourself: can you suspect me of it? and do you think, because I was capable of informing you of this matter, I was therefore capable of informing another?"

The confession which Madam de Cleves had made to her husband was so great a mark of her sincerity, and she so strongly denied that she had entrusted it to any other, that Monsieur de Cleves did not know what to think. On the other hand he was sure he had never said anything of it; it was a thing that could not have been guessed, and yet it was known; it must therefore come from one of them two; but what grieved him most was, to know that this secret was in the hands of somebody else, and that in all probability it would be soon divulged.

Madam de Cleves thought much after the same manner; she found it equally impossible that her husband should, or should not have spoken of it. What the Duke de Nemours had said to her, that curiosity might make a husband do indiscreet things, seemed so justly applicable to Monsieur de Cleves's condition, that she could not think he said it by chance, and the probability of this made her conclude that Monsieur de Cleves had abused the confidence she had placed in him. They were, so taken up, the one and the other, with their respective thoughts, that they continued silent a great while; and when they broke from this silence, they only repeated the same things they had already said very often; their hearts and affections grew more and more estranged from each other.

It is easy to imagine how they passed the night; Monsieur de Cleves could no longer sustain the misfortune of seeing a woman, whom he adored, in love with another; he grew quite heartless, and thought he had reason to be so in an affair where his honour and reputation were so deeply wounded: he knew not what to think of his wife, and was at a loss what conduct he should prescribe to her, or what he should follow himself; he saw nothing on all sides but precipices and rocks; at last, after having been long tossed to and fro in suspense, he considered he was soon to set out for Spain, and resolved to do nothing which might increase the suspicion or knowledge of his unfortunate condition. He went to his wife, and told her that what they had to do was not to debate between themselves who had discovered the secret; but to make it appear, that the story which was got abroad, was a business in which she had no concern; that it depended upon her to convince the Duke de Nemours and others of it; that she had nothing to do but to behave herself to him with that coldness and reserve which she ought to have for a man who professed love to her; that by this proceeding she would easily remove the opinion he entertained of her being in love with him; and therefore she needed not to trouble herself as to what he might hitherto have thought, since if for the future she discovered no weakness, his former thoughts would vanish of themselves; and that especially she ought to frequent the Louvre and the assemblies as usual.

Having said this, Monsieur de Cleves left his wife without waiting her answer; she thought what he said very reasonable, and the resentment she had against the Duke de Nemours made her believe she should be able to comply with it with a great deal of ease; but it seemed a hard task to her to appear at the marriage with that freedom and tranquillity of spirit as the occasion required. Nevertheless as she was to carry the Queen-Dauphin's train, and had been distinguished with that honour in preference to a great many other Princesses, it was impossible to excuse herself from it, without making a great deal of noise, and putting people upon enquiring into the reasons of it. She resolved therefore to do her utmost, and employed the rest of the day in preparing herself for it, and in endeavouring to forget the thoughts that gave her so much uneasiness; and to this purpose she locked herself up in her closet. Of all her griefs the most violent was, that she had reason to complain of the Duke de Nemours, and could find no excuse to urge in his favour; she could not doubt but he had related this adventure to the Viscount de Chartres; he had owned it himself, nor could she any more doubt from his manner of speaking of it, but that he knew the adventure related to her; how could she excuse so great an imprudence? and what was become of that extreme discretion which she had so much admired in this Prince? "He was discreet," said she, "while he was unhappy; but the thought of being happy, though on uncertain grounds, has put an end to his discretion; he could not consider that he was beloved, without desiring to have it known; he said everything he could say; I never acknowledged it was he I was in love with; he suspected it, and has declared his suspicions; if he had been sure of it, he might have acted as he has; I was to blame for thinking him a man capable of concealing what flattered his vanity; and yet it is for this man, whom I thought so different from other men, that I am become like other women, who was so unlike them before. I have lost the heart and esteem of a husband who ought to have been my happiness; I shall soon be looked upon by all the world as a person led away by an idle and violent passion; he for whom I entertain this passion is no longer ignorant of it; and it was to avoid these misfortunes that I hazarded my quiet, and even my life." These sad reflections were followed by a torrent of tears; but however great her grief was, she plainly perceived she should be able to support it, were she but satisfied in the Duke de Nemours.

The Duke was no less uneasy than she; the indiscretion he had been guilty of in telling what he did to the Viscount de Chartres, and the mischievous consequences of it, vexed him to the heart; he could not represent to himself the affliction and sorrow he had seen Madam de Cleves in, without being pierced with anguish; he was inconsolable for having said things to her about this adventure, which, though gallant enough in themselves, seemed on this occasion too gross and impolite, since they gave Madam de Cleves to understand he was not ignorant that she was the woman who had that violent passion, and that he was the object of it. It was before the utmost of his wishes to have a conversation with her, but now he found he ought rather to fear than desire it. "What should I say to her!" says he; "should I go to discover further to her what I have made her too sensible of already! Shall I tell how I know she loves me; I, who have never dared to say I loved her? Shall I begin with speaking openly of my passion, that she may see my hopes have inspired me with boldness? Can I even think of approaching her, and of giving her the trouble to endure my sight? Which way could I justify myself? I have no excuse, I am unworthy of the least regard from Madam de Cleves, and I even despair of her ever looking upon me: I have given her by my own fault better means of defending herself against me than any she was searching for, and perhaps searching for to no purpose. I lose by my imprudence the glory and happiness of being loved by the most beautiful and deserving lady in the world; but if I had lost this happiness, without involving her in the most extreme grief and sufferings at the same time, I should have had some comfort; for at this moment I am more sensible of the harm I have done her, than of that I have done myself in forfeiting her favour."

The Duke de Nemours continued turning the same thoughts over and over, and tormenting himself a great while; the desire he had to speak to Madam de Cleves came constantly into his mind; he thought of the means to do it; he thought of writing to her; but at last he found, considering the fault he had committed and the temper she was in, his best way was to show her a profound respect by his affliction and his silence, to let her see he durst not present himself before her, and to wait for what time, chance, and the inclination she had for him might produce to his advantage. He resolved also not to reproach the Viscount de Chartres for his unfaithfulness, for fear of confirming his suspicions.

The preparations for the espousals and marriage of Madame on the next day so entirely took up the thoughts of the Court, that Madam de Cleves and the Duke de Nemours easily concealed from the public their grief and uneasiness. The Queen-Dauphin spoke but slightly to Madam de Cleves of the conversation they had had with the Duke de Nemours; and Monsieur de Cleves industriously shunned speaking to his wife of what was past; so that she did not find herself under so much embarrassment as she had imagined.

The espousals were solemnised at the Louvre; and after the feast and ball all the Royal family went to lie at the Bishop's Palace, according to custom. In the morning, the Duke of Alva, who always had appeared very plainly dressed, put on a habit of cloth of gold, mixed with flame-colour, yellow and black, all covered over with jewels, and wore a close crown on his head. The Prince of Orange very richly dressed also, with his liveries, and all the Spaniards with theirs, came to attend the Duke of Alva from the Hôtel de Villeroy where he lodged, and set out, marching four by four, till they came to the Bishop's Palace. As soon as he was arrived, they went in order to the Church; the King led Madame, who wore also a close crown, her train being borne by Mademoiselles de Montpensier and Longueville; the Queen came next, but without a crown; after her followed the Queen-Dauphin, Madame the King's sister, the Duchess of Loraine, and the Queen of Navarre, their trains being borne by the Princesses; the Queens and the Princesses were all of them attended with their maids of honour, who were richly dressed in the same colour which they wore themselves; so that it was known by the colour of their habits whose maids they were: they mounted the place that was prepared in the Church, and there the marriage ceremonies were performed; they returned afterwards to dine at the Bishop's Palace, and went from thence about five o'clock to the Palace where the feast was, and where the Parliament, the Sovereign Courts, and the Corporation of the City were desired to assist. The King, the Queens, the Princes and Princesses sat at the marble table in the great hall of the Palace ; the Duke of Alva sat near the new Queen of Spain, below the steps of the marble table, and at the King's right hand was a table for the ambassadors, the archbishops, and the Knights of the Order, and on the other side one for the Parliament.

The Duke of Guise, dressed in a robe of cloth of gold frieze, served the King as Great Chamberlain ; the Prince of Condè as Steward of the Household, and the Duke de Nemours as Cup-bearer. After the tables were removed the ball began, and was interrupted by interludes and a great deal of extraordinary machinery ; then the ball was resumed, and after midnight the King and the whole Court returned to the Louvre. However full of grief Madam de Cleves was, she appeared in the eyes of all beholders, and particularly in those of the Duke de Nemours, incomparably beautiful. He durst not speak to her, though the hurry of the ceremony gave him frequent opportunities ; but he expressed so much sorrow and so respectful a fear of approaching her, that she no longer thought him to blame, though he had said nothing in his justification ; his conduct was the same the following days, and wrought the same effect on the heart of Madam de Cleves.

At last the day of the tournament came ; the Queens were placed in the galleries that were prepared for them ; the four champions appeared at the end of the lists with a number of horses and liveries, the most magnificent sight that ever was seen in France.

The King's colours were white and black, which he always wore in honour of the Duchess of Valentinois, who was a widow. The Duke of Ferrara and his retinue had yellow and red. Monsieur de Guise's carnation and white. It was not known at first for what reason he wore those colours, but it was soon remembered that they were the colours of a beautiful young lady whom he had been in love with, while she was a maid, and whom he yet loved though he durst not show it. The Duke de Nemours had yellow and black ; why he had them could not be found out : Madam de Cleves only knew the reason of it ; she remembered to have said before him she loved yellow, and that she was sorry her complexion did not suit that colour. As for the Duke, he thought he might take that colour without any indiscretion, since not being worn by Madam de Cleves it could not be suspected to be hers.

The four champions showed the greatest address that can be imagined ; though the King was the best horseman in his kingdom, it was hard to say which of them most excelled. The Duke de Nemours had a grace in all his actions which might have inclined to his favour persons less interested than Madam de Cleves. She no sooner saw him appear at the end of the lists, but her heart felt uncommon emotions, and every course he made she could scarce hide her joy, when he had successfully finished his career.

In the evening, when all was almost over, and the company ready to break up, so it was for the misfortune of the State, that the King would needs break another lance ; he sent orders to the Count de Montgomery, who was a very dextrous combatant, to appear in the lists. The Count begged the King to excuse him, and alleged all the reasons for it he could think of ; but the King, almost angry, sent him word he absolutely commanded him to do it. The Queen conjured the King not to run any more, told him he had performed so well that he ought to be satisfied, and desired him to go with her to her apartments ; he made answer, it was for her sake that he would run again ; and entered the barrier ; she sent the Duke of Savoy to him to entreat him a second time to return, but to no purpose ; he ran ; the lances were broke, and a splinter of the Count de Montgomery's lance hit the King's eye, and stuck there. The King fell ; his gentlemen and Monsieur de Montmorency, who was one of the Mareschals of the field, ran to him ; they were astonished to see him wounded, but the King was not at all disheartened ; he said, that it was but a slight hurt, and that he forgave the Count de Montgomery. One may imagine what sorrow and affliction so fatal an accident occasioned on a day set apart to mirth and joy. The King was carried to bed, and the surgeons having examined his wound found it very considerable. The Constable immediately called to mind the prediction which had been told the King, that he should be killed in single fight ; and he made no doubt but the prediction would be now accomplished.

The King of Spain, who was then at Brussels, being advertised of this accident, sent his physician, who was a man of great reputation, but that physician judged the King past hope.

A Court so divided, and filled with so many opposite interests, could not but be in great agitation on the breaking out of so grand an event ; nevertheless all things were kept quiet, and nothing was seen but a general anxiety for the King's health. The Queens, the Princes and Princesses hardly ever went out of his anti-chamber.

Madam de Cleves knowing that she was obliged to be there, that she should see there the Duke de Nemours, and that she could not conceal from her husband the disorder she should be in upon seeing him, and being sensible also that the mere presence of that Prince would justify him in her eyes and destroy all her resolutions, thought proper to feign herself ill. The Court was too busy to give attention to her conduct, or to enquire whether her illness was real or counterfeit ; her husband alone was able to come at the truth of the matter, but she was not at all averse to his knowing it. Thus she continued at home, altogether heedless of the great change that was soon expected, and full of her own thoughts, which she was at full liberty to give herself up to. Everyone went to Court to enquire after the King's health, and Monsieur de Cleves came home at certain times to give her an account of it ; he behaved himself to her in the same manner he used to do, except when they were alone, and then there appeared something of coldness and reserve: he had not spoke to her again concerning what had passed, nor had she power, nor did she think it convenient to resume the discourse of it.

The Duke de Nemours, who had waited for an opportunity of speaking to Madam de Cleves, was surprised and afflicted not to have had so much as the pleasure to see her. The King's illness increased so much, that the seventh day he was given over by the physicians; he received the news of the certainty of his death with an uncommon firmness of mind; which was the more to be admired, considering that he lost his life by so unfortunate an accident, that he died in the flower of his age, happy, adored by his people, and beloved by a mistress he was desperately in love with. The evening before his death he caused Madame his sister to be married to the Duke of Savoy without ceremony. One may judge what condition the Duchess of Valentinois was in; the Queen would not permit her to see the King, but sent to demand of her the King's signets, and the jewels of the crown which she had in her custody. The Duchess enquired if the King was dead, and being answered, "No"; "I have then as yet no other matter," said she, "and nobody can oblige me to restore what he has trusted in my hands." As soon as the King expired at Chateau de Tournelles, the Duke of Ferrara, the Duke of Guise, and the Duke de Nemours conducted the Queen-Mother, the New King and the Queen-Consort to the Louvre. The Duke de Nemours led the Queen-Mother. As they began to march, she stepped back a little, and told the Queen her daughter-in-law, it was her place to go first; but it was easy to see, that there was more of spleen than decorum in this compliment.

## IV

THE QUEEN-MOTHER was now wholly governed by the Cardinal of Loraine; the Viscount de Chartres had no interest with her, and the passion he had for Madam de Martigues and for liberty hindered him from feeling this loss as it deserved to be felt. The Cardinal, during the ten days' illness of the King, was at leisure to form his designs, and lead the Queen into resolutions agreeable to what he had projected; so that the King was no sooner dead, but the Queen ordered the Constable to stay at Tournelles, with the corpse of the deceased King, in order to perform the usual ceremonies. This commission kept him at a distance, and out of the scene of action; for this reason the Constable dispatched a courier to the King of Navarre, to hasten him to Court, that they might join their interest to oppose the great rise of the House of Guise. The command of the Army was given to the Duke of Guise, and the care of the finances to the Cardinal of Loraine. The Duchess of Valentinois was driven from Court; the Cardinal de Tournon, the Constable's declared enemy, and the Chancellor Olivier, the declared enemy of the Duchess of Valentinois, were both recalled. In a word, the complexion of the Court was entirely changed; the Duke of

Guise took the same rank as the Princes of the blood, in carrying the King's mantle at the funeral ceremonies: He and his brothers carried all before them at Court, not only by reason of the Cardinal's power with the Queen-Mother, but because she thought it in her power to remove them, should they give her umbrage; whereas she could not so easily remove the Constable, who was supported by the Princes of the blood.

When the ceremonial of the mourning was over, the Constable came to the Louvre, and was very coldly received by the King; he desired to speak with him in private, but the King called for Messieurs de Guise, and told him before them, that he advised him to live at ease; that the finances and the command of the Army were disposed of, and that when he had occasion for his advice, he would send for him to Court. The Queen received him in a yet colder manner than the King, and she even reproached him for having told the late King, that his children by her did not resemble him. The King of Navarre arrived, and was no better received; the Prince of Condè, more impatient than his brother, complained aloud, but to no purpose: he was removed from Court, under pretence of being sent to Flanders to sign the ratification of the peace. They showed the King of Navarre a forged letter from the King of Spain, which charged him with a design of seizing that King's fortresses; they put him in fear for his dominions, and made him take a resolution to go to Bearn; the Queen furnished him with an opportunity, by appointing him to conduct Madam Elizabeth, and obliged him to set out before her, so that there remained nobody at Court that could balance the power of the House of Guise.

Though it was a mortifying circumstance for Monsieur de Cleves not to conduct Madam Elizabeth, yet he could not complain of it, by reason of the greatness of the person preferred before him; he regretted the loss of this employment not so much on account of the honour he should have received from it, as because it would have given him an opportunity of removing his wife from Court without the appearance of design in it.

A few days after the King's death, it was resolved the new King should go to Rheims to be crowned. As soon as this journey was talked of, Madam de Cleves, who had stayed at home all this while under pretence of illness, entreated her husband to dispense with her following the Court, and to give her leave to go to take the air at Colomiers for her health: he answered, that whether her health was the reason or not of her desire, however he consented to it: nor was it very difficult for him to consent to a thing he had resolved upon before: as good an opinion as he had of his wife's virtue, he thought it imprudent to expose her any longer to the sight of a man she was in love with.

The Duke de Nemours was soon informed, that Madam de Cleves was not to go along with the Court; he could not find in his heart to set out without seeing her, and therefore the night before his journey he went to her house as late as decency would allow him, in order to find her alone. Fortune favoured his intention; and Madam de

Nevers and Madam de Martigues, whom he met in the Court as they were coming out, informed him they had left her alone. He went up in a concern and ferment of mind to be paralleled only by that which Madam de Cleves was under, when she was told the Duke de Nemours was come to see her ; the fear lest he should speak to her of his passion, and lest she should answer him too favourably, the uneasiness this visit might give her husband, the difficulty of giving him an account of it, or of concealing it from him, all these things presented themselves to her imagination at once, and threw her into so great an embarrassment, that she resolved to avoid the thing of the world which perhaps she wished for the most. She sent one of her women to the Duke de Nemours, who was in her anti-chamber, to tell him that she had lately been very ill, and that she was sorry she could not receive the honour which he designed her. What an affliction was it to the Duke, not to see Madam de Cleves, and therefore not to see her, because she had no mind he should ! He was to go away the next morning, and had nothing further to hope from fortune. He had said nothing to her since that conversation at the Queen-Dauphin's apartments, and he had reason to believe that his imprudence in telling the Viscount his adventure had destroyed all his expectations ; in a word, he went away with everything that could exasperate his grief.

No sooner was Madam de Cleves recovered from the confusion which the thought of receiving a visit from the Duke had given her, but all the reasons which had made her refuse it vanished ; she was even satisfied she had been to blame ; and had she dared, or had it not been too late, she would have had him called back.

Madam de Nevers and Madam de Martigues went from the Princess of Cleves to the Queen-Dauphin's, where they found Monsieur de Cleves : the Queen-Dauphin asked them from whence they came ; they said they came from Madam de Cleves, where they had spent part of the afternoon with a great deal of company, and that they had left nobody there but the Duke de Nemours. These words, which they thought so indifferent, were not such with Monsieur de Cleves : though he might well imagine the Duke de Nemours had frequent opportunities of speaking to his wife, yet the thought that he was now woth her, that he was there alone, and that he might speak to her of his live, appeared to him at this time a thing so new and insupportable, that jealousy kindled in his heart with greater violence than ever. It was impossible for him to stay at the Queen's ; he returned from thence, without knowing why he returned, or if he designed to go and interrupt the Duke de Nemours : he was no sooner come home, but he looked about him to see if there was anything by which he could judge if the Duke was still there ; it was some comfort to him to find he was gone, and it was a pleasure to reflect that he could not have been long there : he fancied, that, perhaps, it was not the Duke de Nemours of whom he had reason to be jealous ; and though he did not doubt of it, yet he endeavoured to doubt of it ; but he was convinced of it by so many circumstances, that he continued not long in that pleasing uncertainty. He immediately went into his wife's room, and after having talked to her for some time about indifferent matters, he could not forbear asking her what she had done, and who she had seen, and accordingly she gave him an account: when he found she did not name the Duke de Nemours he asked her trembling, if those were all she had seen, in order to give her an occasion to name the Duke, and that he might not have the grief to see she made use of any evasion. As she had not seen him, she did not name him; when Monsieur de Cleves with accents of sorrow, said, "And have you not seen the Duke de Nemours, or have you forgot him?" "I have not seen him indeed," answered she; "I was ill, and I sent one of my women to make my excuses." "You was ill then only for him," replied Monsieur de Cleves, "since you admitted the visits of others: why this distinction with respect to the Duke de Nemours? Why is not he to you as another man? Why should you be afraid of seeing him? Why do you let him perceive that you are so? Why do you show him that you make use of the power which his passion gives you over him? Would you dare refuse to see him, but that you knew he distinguishes your rigour from incivility? But why should you exercise that rigour towards him? From a person like you, all things are favours, except indifference." "I did not think," replied Madam de Cleves, "whatever suspicions you have of the Duke de Nemours, that you could reproach me for not admitting a visit from him." "But I do reproach you, Madam," replied he, "and I have good ground for so doing; why should you not see him, if he has said nothing to you? but Madam, he has spoke to you; if his passion had been expressed only by silence, it would not have made so great an impression upon you; you have not thought fit to tell me the whole truth; you have concealed the greatest part from me; you have repented even of the little you have acknowledged, and you have not the resolution to go on; I am more unhappy than I imagined, more unhappy than any other man in the world: you are my wife, I love you as my mistress, and I see you at the same time in love with another, with the most amiable man of the Court, and he sees you every day, and knows you are in love with him: Alas! I believed that you would conquer your passion for him, but sure I had lost my reason when I believed it was possible." "I don't know," replied Madam de Cleves very sorrowfully, "whether you was to blame in judging favourably of so extraordinary a proceeding as mine; nor do I know if I was not mistaken when I thought you would do me justice." "Doubt it not, Madam," replied Monsieur de Cleves, "you was mistaken; you expected from me things as impossible as those I expected from you: how could you hope I should continue master of my reason? Had you forgot that I was desperately in love with you, and that I was your husband? Either of these two circumstances is enough to hurry a man into extremities; what may they not do both together? Alas! What do they not do? My thoughts are violent and uncertain, and I am not able to control them ; I no longer think myself worthy of you, nor do I think you are worthy of me ; I adore you, I hate you, I offend you, I ask your pardon, I admire you, I blush for my admiration : in a word, I have nothing of tranquillity or reason left about me : I wonder how I have been able to live since you spoke to me at Colomiers, and since you learned, from what the Queen-Dauphin told you, that your adventure was known ; I can't discover how it came to be known, nor what passed between the Duke de Nemours and you upon the subject ; you will never explain it to me, nor do I desire you to do it ; I only desire you to remember that you have made me the most unfortunate, the most wretched of men."

Having spoke these words, Monsieur de Cleves left his wife, and set out the next day without seeing her ; but he wrote her a letter full of sorrow, and at the same time very kind and obliging : she gave an answer to it so moving and so full of assurances both as to her past and future conduct, that as those assurances were grounded in truth, and were the real effect of her sentiments, the letter made great impressions on Monsieur de Cleves, and gave him some tranquillity ; add to this, that the Duke de Nemours going to the King as well as himself, he had the satisfaction to know that he would not be in the same place with Madam de Cleves. Everytime that lady spoke to her husband, the passion he expressed for her, the handsomeness of his behaviour, the friendship she had for him, and the thought of what she owed him, made impressions in her heart that weakened the idea of the Duke de Nemours ; but it did not continue long, that idea soon returned more lively than before.

For a few days after the Duke was gone, she was hardly sensible of his absence ; afterwards it tortured her ; ever since she had been in love with him, there did not pass a day, but she either feared or wished to meet him, and it was a wounding thought to her to consider that it was no more in the power of fortune to contrive their meeting.

She went to Colomiers, and ordered to be carried thither the large pictures she had caused to be copied from the originals which the Duchess of Valentinois had procured to be drawn for her fine house of Annett. All the remarkable actions that had passed in the late King's reign were represented in these pieces, and among the rest was the Siege of Mets, and all those who had distinguished themselves at that Siege were painted much to the life. The Duke de Nemours was of this number, and it was that perhaps which had made Madam de Cleves desirous of having the pictures.

Madam de Martigues not being able to go along with the Court, promised her to come and pass some days at Colomiers. Though they divided the Queen's favour, they lived together without envy or coldness ; they were friends, but not confidants ; Madam de Cleves knew that Madam de Martigues was in love with the Viscount, but Madam de Martigues did not know that Madam de Cleves was in love with the Duke de Nemours, nor that she was beloved by him.

The relation Madam de Cleves had to the Viscount made her more dear to Madam de Martigues, and Madam de Cleves was also fond of her as a person who was in love as well as herself, and with an intimate friend of her own lover.

Madam de Martigues came to Colomiers according to her promise, and found Madam de Cleves living in a very solitary manner: that Princess affected a perfect solitude, and passed the evenings in her garden without being accompanied even by her domestics; she frequently came into the pavilion where the Duke de Nemours had overheard her conversation with her husband; she delighted to be in the bower that was open to the garden, while her women and attendants waited in the other bower under the pavilion, and never came to her but when she called them. Madam de Martigues having never seen Colomiers was surprised at the extraordinary beauty of it, and particularly with the pleasantness of the pavilion. Madam de Cleves and she usually passed the evenings there. The liberty of being alone in the night in so agreeable a place would not permit the conversation to end soon between two young ladies, whose hearts were enflamed with violent passions, and they took great pleasure in conversing together, though they were not confidants. Madam de Martigues would have left Colomiers with great reluctance, had she not quitted it to go to a place where the Viscount was; she set out for Chambort, the Court being there.

The King had been anointed at Rheims by the Cardinal of Loraine, and the design was to pass the rest of the summer at the castle of Chambort, which was newly built; the Queen expressed a great deal of joy upon seeing Madam de Martigues again at Court, and after having given her several proofs of it, she asked her how Madam de Cleves did, and in what manner she passed her time in the country. The Duke de Nemours and the Prince of Cleves were with the Queen at that time. Madam de Martigues, who had been charmed with Colomiers, related all the beauties of it, and enlarged extremely on the description of the pavilion in the forest, and on the pleasure Madam de Cleves took in walking there alone part of the night. The Duke de Nemours, who knew the place well enough to understand what Madam de Martigues said of it, thought it was not impossible to see Madam de Cleves there, without being seen by anybody but her. He asked Madam de Martigues some questions to get further lights; and the Prince of Cleves, who had eyed him very strictly while Madam de Martigues was speaking, thought he knew what his design was. The questions the Duke asked still more confirmed him in that thought, so that he made no doubt but his intention was to go and see his wife; he was not mistaken in his suspicions: this design entered so deeply into the Duke de Nemours's mind, that after having spent the night in considering the proper methods to execute it, he went betimes the next morning to ask the King's leave to go to Paris, on some pretended occasion.

Monsieur de Cleves was in no doubt concerning the occasion of his journey; and he resolved to inform himself as to his wife's conduct, and to continue no longer in so cruel an uncertainty; he had a desire to set out the same time as the Duke de Nemours did, and to hide himself where he might discover the success of the journey; but fearing his departure might appear extraordinary, and lest the Duke, being advertised of it, might take other measures, he resolved to trust this business to a gentleman of his, whose fidelity and wit he was assured of; he related to him the embarrassment he was under, and what the virtue of his wife had been till that time, and ordered him to follow the Duke de Nemours, to watch him narrowly, to see if he did not go to Colomiers and if he did not enter the garden in the night.

The gentleman, who was very capable of this commission, acquitted himself of it with all the exactness imaginable. He followed the Duke to a village within half a league of Colomiers, where the Duke stopped and the gentleman easily guessed his meaning was to stay there till night He did not think it convenient to wait there, but passed on, and placed himself in that part of the forest where he thought the Duke would pass: he took his measures very right; for it was no sooner night but he heard somebody coming that way, and though it was dark, he easily knew the Duke de Nemours; he saw him walk round the garden, as with a design to listen if he could hear anybody, and to choose the most convenient place to enter: the palisades were very high and double, in order to prevent people from coming in, so that it was very difficult for the Duke to get over, however he made a shift to do it. He was no sooner in the garden, but he discovered where Madam de Cleves was; he saw a great light in the bower, all the windows of it were open; upon this, slipping along by the side of the palisades, he came up close to it, and one may easily judge what were the emotions of his heart at that instant: he took his station behind one of the windows, which served him conveniently to see what Madam de Cleves was doing. He saw she was alone; he saw her so inimitably beautiful, that he could scarce govern the transports which that sight gave him: the weather was hot, her head and neck were uncovered, and her hair hung carelessly about her. She lay on a couch with a table before her, on which were several baskets full of ribbons, out of which she chose some, and he observed she chose those colours which he wore at the tournament; he saw her make them up into knots for an Indian cane, which had been his, and which he had given to his sister; Madam de Cleves took it from her, without seeming to know it had belonged to the Duke. After she had finished her work with the sweetest grace imaginable, the sentiments of her heart showing themselves in her countenance, she took a wax candle and came to a great table over against the picture of the Siege of Mets, in which was the portrait of the Duke de Nemours; she sat down and set herself to look upon that portrait, with an attention and thoughtfulness which love only can give.

It is impossible to express what Monsieur de Nemours felt at this moment; to see, at midnight, in the finest place in the world, a lady he adored, to see her without her knowing that he saw her, and to find her wholly taken up with things that related to him, and to the passion which she concealed from him; this is what was never tasted nor imagined by any other lover.

The Duke was so transported and beside himself, that he continued motionless, with his eyes fixed on Madam de Cleves, without thinking how precious his time was; when he was a little recovered, he thought it best not to speak to her till she came into the garden, and he imagined he might do it there with more safety, because she would be at a greater distance from her women; but finding she stayed in the bower, he resolved to go in: when he was upon the point of doing it, what was his confusion; how fearful was he of displeasing her, and of changing that countenance, where so much sweetness dwelt, into looks of anger and resentment!

To come to see Madam de Cleves without being seen by her had no impudence in it, but to think of showing himself appeared very unwise; a thousand things now came into his mind which he had not thought of before; it carried in it somewhat extremely bold and extravagant, to surprise in the middle of the night a person to whom he had never yet spoke of his passion. He thought he had no reason to expect she would hear him, but that she would justly resent the danger to which he exposed her, by accidents which might rise from this attempt; all his courage left him, and he was several times upon the point of resolving to go back again without showing himself; yet urged by the desire of speaking to her, and heartened by the hopes which everything he had seen gave him, he advanced some steps, but in such disorder, that a scarf he had on entangled in the window, and made a noise. Madam de Cleves turned about, and whether her fancy was full of him, or that she stood in a place so directly to the light that she might know him, she thought it was he, and without the least hesitation or turning towards the place where he was, she entered the bower where her women were. On her entering she was in such disorder, that to conceal it she was forced to say she was ill; she said it too in order to employ her people about her, and to give the Duke time to retire. When she had made some reflection, she thought she had been deceived, and that her fancying she saw Monsieur de Nemours was only the effect of imagination. She knew he was at Chambort; she saw no probability of his engaging in so hazardous an enterprise; she had a desire several times to re-enter the bower, and to see if there was anybody in the garden. She wished perhaps as much as she feared to find the Duke de Nemours there; but at last reason and prudence prevailed over her other thoughts, and she found it better to continue in the doubt she was in, than to run the hazard of satisfying herself about it; she was a long time ere she could resolve to leave a place to which she thought the Duke was so near, and it was almost daybreak when she returned to the castle.

The Duke de Nemours stayed in the garden, as long as there was any light; he was not without hopes of seeing Madam de Cleves again, though he was convinced that she knew him, and that she went away only to avoid him; but when he found the doors were shut, he knew he had nothing more to hope; he went to take horse near the place where Monsieur de Cleves's gentleman was watching him; this gentleman followed him to the same village, where he had left him in the evening. The Duke resolved to stay there all the day, in order to return at night to Colomiers, to see if Madam de Cleves would yet have the cruelty to shun him or not expose herself to view: though he was very much pleased to find himself so much in her thoughts, yet was he extremely grieved at the same time to see her so naturally bent to avoid him.

Never was passion so tender and so violent as that of Monsieur de Nemours; he walked under the willows, along a little brook which ran behind the house, where he lay concealed; he kept himself as much out of the way as possible, that he might not be seen by anybody; he abandoned himself to the transports of his love, and his heart was so full of tenderness, that he was forced to let fall some tears, but those tears were such as grief alone could not shed; they had a mixture of sweetness and pleasure in them which is to be found only in love.

He set himself to recall to mind all the actions of Madam de Cleves ever since he had been in love with her; her cruelty and rigour, and that modesty and decency of behaviour she had always observed towards him, though she loved him; "For, after all, she loves me," said he, "she loves me, I cannot doubt of it, the deepest engagements and the greatest favours are not more certain proofs than those I have had. In the meantime, I am treated with the same rigour as if I were hated; I hoped something from time, but I have no reason to expect it any longer; I see her always equally on her guard against me and against herself; if I were not loved, I should make it my business to please; but I do please; she loves me, and tries to hide it from me. What have I then to hope, and what change am I to expect in my fortune? though I am loved by the most amiable person in the world, I am under that excess of passion which proceeds from the first certainty of being loved by her, only to make me more sensible of being ill used; let me see that you love me, fair Princess," cried he, "make me acquainted with your sentiments; provided I know them once in my life from you, I am content that you resume for ever the cruelties with which you oppress me; look upon me at least with the same eyes with which I saw you look that night upon my picture; could you behold that with such sweet complacency, and yet avoid me with so much cruelty? What are you afraid of? Why does my love appear so terrible to you? You love me, and you endeavour in vain to conceal it; you have even given me involuntary proofs of it; I know my happiness, permit me to enjoy it, and cease to make me unhappy. Is it possible I should be loved by the Princess of Cleves, and yet be unhappy? how beautiful was she last night? how could I forbear throwing myself at her feet? If I had done it, I might perhaps have hindered her from shunning me, my respectful behaviour would have removed her fears; but perhaps, after all, she did not know it was I; I afflict myself more than I need; she was only frightened to see a man at so unseasonable an hour."

These thoughts employed the Duke de Nemours all the day; he wished impatiently for the night, and as soon as it came he returned to Colomiers. Monsieur de Cleves's gentleman, who was disguised that he might be less observed, followed him to the place to which he had followed him the evening before, and saw him enter the garden again. The Duke soon perceived that Madam de Cleves had not run the risk of his making another effort to see her, the doors being all shut; he looked about on all sides to see if he could discover any light, but he saw none.

Madam de Cleves, suspecting he might return, continued in her chamber; she had reason to apprehend she should not always have the power to avoid him, and she would not submit herself to the hazard of speaking to him in a manner that would have been unsuitable to the conduct she had hitherto observed.

Monsieur de Nemours, though he had no hopes of seeing her, could not find in his heart soon to leave a place where she so often was; he passed the whole night in the garden, and found some pleasure at least in seeing the same objects which she saw every day; it was near sunrise before he thought of retiring; but as last the fear of being discovered obliged him to go away.

It was impossible for him to return to Court without seeing Madam de Cleves; he made a visit to his sister the Duchess of Mercœur, at her house near Colomiers. She was extremely surprised at her brother's arrival; but he invented so probable a pretence for his journey, and conducted his plot so skilfully, that he drew her to make the first proposal herself of visiting Madam de Cleves. This proposal was executed that very day, and Monsieur de Nemours told his sister, that he would leave her at Colomiers, in order to go directly to the King; he formed this pretence of leaving her at Colomiers in hopes she would take her leave before him, and he thought he had found out by that means an infallible way of speaking to Madam de Cleves.

The Princess of Cleves, when they arrived, was walking in her garden; the sight of Monsieur de Nemours gave her no small uneasiness, and put her out of doubt that it was he she had seen the foregoing night. The certainty of his having done so bold and imprudent a thing gave her some little resentment against him, and the Duke observed an air of coldness in her face, which sensibly grieved him; the conversation turned upon indifferent matters, and yet he had the skill all the while to show so much wit, complaisance, and admiration for Madam de Cleves, that part of the coldness she expressed towards him at first left her in spite of herself.

When his fears were over and he began to take heart, he showed an extreme curiosity to see the pavilion in the forest; he spoke of it as of the most agreeable place in the world, and gave so exact a description of it, that Madam de Mercœur said he must needs have been there several times to know all the particular beauties of it so well. "And yet, I don't believe," replied Madam de Cleves, "that the Duke de Nemours was ever there; it has been finished but a little while." "It is not long since I was there," replied the Duke, looking upon her, "and I don't know if I ought not to be glad you have forgot you saw me there." Madam de Mercœur, being taken up in observing the beauties of the gardens, did not attend to what her brother said; Madam de Cleves blushed, and with her eyes cast down, without looking on Monsieur de Nemours, "I don't remember," said she, "to have seen you there; and if you have been there, it was without my knowledge." "It is true, Madam," replied he, "I was there without your orders, and I passed there the most sweet and cruel moments of my life."

Madam de Cleves understood very well what he said, but made him no answer; her care was to prevent Madam de Mercœur from going into the bower, because the Duke de Nemours's picture was there, and she had no mind she should see it; she managed the matter so well, that the time passed away insensibly, and Madam de Mercœur began to talk of going home: but when Madam de Cleves found that the Duke and his sister did not go together, she plainly saw to what she was going to be exposed; she found herself under the same embarrassment she was in at Paris, and took also the same resolution; her fear, lest this visit should be a further confirmation of her husband's suspicions, did not a little contribute to determine her; and to the end Monsieur de Nemours might not remain alone with her, she told Madam de Mercœur she would wait upon her to the borders of the forest, and ordered her chariot to be got ready. The Duke was struck with such a violent grief to find that Madam de Cleves still continued to exercise the same rigours towards him, that he turned pale that moment. Madam de Mercœur asked him if he was ill, but he looked upon Madam de Cleves without being perceived by anybody else, and made her sensible by his looks that he had no other illness besides despair: however, there was no remedy but he must let them go together without daring to follow them; after what he had told his sister, that he was to go directly to Court, he could not return with her, but went to Paris, and set out from thence the next day.

Monsieur de Cleves's gentleman had observed him all the while; he returned also to Paris, and when he found Monsieur de Nemours was set out for Chambort, he took post to get thither before him, and to give an account of his journey; his master expected his return with impatience, as if the happiness or unhappiness of his life depended upon it.

As soon as he saw him, he judged from his countenance and his silence, that the news he brought was very disagreeable; he was struck with sorrow, and continued some time with his head hung down, without being able to speak; at last he made signs with his hand to him to withdraw; "Go," says he, "I see what you have to say to me, but I have not the power to hear it." "I can acquaint you with nothing," said the gentleman, "upon which one can form any certain judgment; it is true, the Duke de Nemours went two nights successively into the garden in the forest, and the day after he was at Colomiers with the Duchess of Mercœur." "'Tis enough," replied Monsieur de Cleves, still making signs to him to withdraw, "'tis enough; I want no further information." The gentleman was forced to leave his master, abandoned to his despair; nor ever was despair more violent. Few men of so high a spirit, and so passionately in love, as the Prince of Cleves, have experienced at the same time the grief arising from the falsehood of a mistress, and the shame of being deceived by a wife.

Monsieur de Cleves could set no bounds to his affliction; he felt ill of a fever that very night, and his distemper was accompanied with such ill symptoms that it was thought very dangerous. Madam de Cleves was informed of it, and came in all haste to him; when she arrived, he was still worse; besides, she observed something in him so cold and chilling with respect to her, that she was equally surprised and grieved at it; he even seemed to receive with pain the services she did him in his sickness, but at last she imagined it was perhaps only the effect of his distemper.

When she was come to Blois where the Court then was, the Duke de Nemours was overjoyed to think she was at the same place where he was; he endeavoured to see her, and went every day to the Prince of Cleves's under pretence of enquiring how he did, but it was to no purpose; she did not stir out of her husband's room, and was grieved at heart for the condition he was in. It vexed Monsieur de Nemours to see her under such affliction, an affliction which he plainly saw revived the friendship she had for Monsieur de Cleves, and diverted the passion that lay kindling in her heart. The thought of this shocked him severely for some time; but the extremity, to which Monsieur de Cleves's sickness was grown, opened to him a scene of new hopes; he saw it was probable that Madam de Cleves would be at liberty to follow her own inclinations, and that he might expect for the future a series of happiness and lasting pleasures; he could not support the ecstasy of that thought, a thought so full of transport! he banished it out of his mind for fear of becoming doubly wretched, if he happened to be disappointed in his hopes.

In the meantime Monsieur de Cleves was almost given over by his physicians. One of the last days of his illness, after having had a very bad night, he said in the morning, he had a desire to sleep; but Madam de Cleves, who remained alone in his chamber, found that instead of taking repose he was extremely restless; she came to him, and fell on her knees by his bedside, her face all covered with tears; and though Monsieur de Cleves had taken a resolution not to show her the violent displeasure he had conceived against her, yet the care she took of him, and the sorrow she expressed, which sometimes he thought sincere, and at other times the effect of her dissimulation and perfidiousness, distracted him so violently with opposite sentiments full of woe, that he could not forbear giving them vent.

"You shed plenty of tears, Madam," said he, "for a death which you are the cause of, and which cannot give you the trouble you pretend to be in ; I am no longer in a condition to reproach you," added he with a voice weakened by sickness and grief ; "I die through the dreadful grief and discontent you have given me ; ought so extraordinary an action, as that of your speaking to me at Colomiers, to have had so little consequences ? Why did you inform me of your passion for the Duke de Nemours, if your virtue was no longer able to oppose it ? I loved you to that extremity, I would have been glad to have been deceived, I confess it to my shame ; I have regretted that pleasing false security out of which you drew me ; why did not you leave me in that blind tranquillity which so many husbands enjoy ? I should perhaps have been ignorant all my life, that you was in love with Monsieur de Nemours ; I shall die," added he, "but know that you make death pleasing to me, and that, after you have taken from me the esteem and affection I had for you, life would be odious to me. What should I live for ? to spend my days with a person whom I have loved so much, and by whom I have been so cruelly deceived ; or to live apart from her and break out openly into violences so opposite to my temper, and the love I had for you ? That love, Madam, was far greater than it appeared to you ; I concealed the greatest part of it from you, for fear of being importunate, or of losing somewhat in your esteem by a behaviour not becoming a husband : in a word, I deserved your affection more than once, and I die without regret, since I have not been able to obtain it, and since I can no longer desire it. Adieu, Madam ; you will one day regret a man who loved you with a sincere and virtuous passion ; you will feel the anxiety which reasonable persons meet with in intrigue and gallantry, and you will know the difference between such a love as I had for you, and the love of people who only profess admiration for you to gratify their vanity in seducing you ; but my death will leave you at liberty, and you may make the Duke de Nemours happy without guilt : what signifies anything that can happen when I am no more, and why should I have the weakness to trouble myself about it ?"

Madam de Cleves was so far from imagining that her husband suspected her virtue, that she heard all this discourse without comprehending the meaning of it, and without having any other notion about it, except that he reproached her for her inclination for the Duke de Nemours ; at last, starting all of a sudden out of her blindness, "I guilty !" cried she, "I am a stranger to the very thought of guilt ; the severest virtue could not have inspired any other conduct than that which I have followed, and I never acted anything but what I could have wished you to have been witness to." "Could you have wished," replied Monsieur de Cleves, looking on her with disdain, " I had been a witness of those nights you passed with Monsieur de Nemours? Ah! Madam; is it you I speak of, when I speak of a lady that has passed nights with a man, not her husband?" "No, sir," replied she, " it is not me you speak of; I never spent a night nor a moment with the Duke de Nemours; he never saw me in private, I never suffered him to do it, nor would give him a hearing. I'll take all the oaths . . ." "Speak no more of it," said he interrupting her, "false oaths or a confession would perhaps give me equal pain." Madam de Cleves could not answer him; her tears and her grief took away her speech; at last, struggling for utterance, "Look on me at least, hear me," said she; " if my interest only were concerned I would suffer these reproaches, but your life is at stake; hear me for your own sake; I am so innocent, truth pleads so strongly for me, it is impossible but I must convince you." "Would to God you could!" cried he; "but what can you say? the Duke de Nemours, has not he been at Colomiers with his sister? And did not he pass the two foregoing nights with you in the garden in the forest?" "If that be my crime," replied she, "it is easy to justify myself; I do not desire you to believe me, believe your servants and domestics; ask them if I went into the garden the evening before Monsieur de Nemours came to Colomiers, and if I did not go out of it the night before two hours sooner than I used to do." After this she told him how she imagined she had seen somebody in the garden, and acknowledged that she believed it to be the Duke de Nemours; she spoke to him with so much confidence, and truth so naturally persuades, even where it is not probable, that Monsieur de Cleves was almost convinced of her innocence. "I don't know," said he, "whether I ought to believe you; I am so near death, that I would not know anything that might make me die with reluctance; you have cleared your innocence too late; however it will be a comfort to me to go away with the thought that you are worthy of the esteem I have had for you; I beg you I may be assured of this further comfort, that my memory will be dear to you, and that if it had been in your power you would have had for me the same passion which you had for another." He would have gone on, but was so weak that his speech failed him. Madam de Cleves sent for the physicians, who found him almost lifeless; yet he languished some days, and died at last with admirable constancy.

Madam de Cleves was afflicted to so violent a degree, that she lost in a manner the use of her reason; the Queen was so kind as to come to see her, and carried her to a convent without her being sensible whither she was conducted; her sisters-in-law brought her back to Paris, before she was in a condition to feel distinctly even her griefs: when she was restored to her faculty of thinking, and reflected what a husband she had lost, and considered that she had caused his death by the passion which she had for another, the horror she had for herself and the Duke de Nemours was not to be expressed.

The Duke in the beginning of her mourning durst pay her no other respects but such as decency required; he knew Madam de Cleves enough to be sensible that great importunities and eagerness would be disagreeable to her; but what he learned afterwards plainly convinced him that he ought to observe the same conduct a great while longer.

A servant of the Duke's informed him, that Monsieur de Cleves's gentleman, who was his intimate friend, had told him, in the excess of his grief for the loss of his master, that Monsieur de Nemours's journey to Colomiers was the occasion of his death. The Duke was extremely surprised to hear this; but after having reflected upon it, he guessed the truth in part, and rightly judged what Madam de Cleves's sentiments would be at first, and what a distance it would throw him from her, if she thought her husband's illness was occasioned by his jealousy; he was of opinion that he ought not so much as to put her in mind of his name very soon, and he abided by that conduct, however severe it appeared to him.

He took a journey to Paris, nor could he forbear calling at her house to enquire how she did. He was told, that she saw nobody, and that she had even given strict orders that they should not trouble her with an account of any that might come to see her; those very strict orders, perhaps, were given with a view to the Duke, and to prevent her hearing him spoken of; but he was too much in love to be able to live so absolutely deprived of the sight of Madam de Cleves; he resolved to find the means, let the difficulty be what it would, to get out of a condition which was so insupportable to him.

The grief of that Princess exceeded the bounds of reason; a husband dying, and dying on her account, and with so much tenderness for her, never went out of her mind: she continually revolved in her thoughts what she owed him, and she condemned herself for not having had a passion for him, as if that had been a thing which depended on herself; she found no consolation but in the thought that she lamented him as he deserved to be lamented, and that she would do nothing during the remainder of her life, but what he would have been glad she should have done, had he lived.

She had often been thinking how he came to know, that the Duke de Nemours had been at Colomiers; she could not suspect that the Duke himself had told it; though it was indifferent to her whether he had or no, she thought herself so perfectly cured of the passion she had had for him; and yet she was grieved at the heart to think that he was the cause of her husband's death; and she remembered with pain the fear Monsieur de Cleves expressed, when dying, lest she should marry the Duke; but all these griefs were swallowed up in that for the loss of her husband, and she thought she had no other but that one.

After several months the violence of her grief abated, and she fell into a languishing kind of melancholy. Madam de Martigues made a journey to Paris, and constantly visited her during the time she stayed there: she entertained her with an account of the Court, and what passed there; and though Madam de Cleves appeared unconcerned, yet still she continued talking on that subject in hopes to divert her.

She talked to her of the Viscount, of Monsieur de Guise, and of all others that were distinguished either in person or merit. "As for the Duke de Nemours," says she, "I don't know if State affairs have not taken possession of his heart in the room of gallantry; he is abundantly less gay than he used to be, and seems wholly to decline the company of women; he often makes journeys to Paris, and I believe he is there now." The Duke de Nemours's name surprised Madam de Cleves, and made her blush; she changed the discourse, nor did Madam de Martigues take notice of her concern.

The next day Madam de Cleves, who employed herself in things suitable to the condition she was in, went to a man's house in her neighbourhood, that was famous for working silk after a particular manner, and she designed to bespeak some pieces for herself; having seen several kinds of his work, she spied a chamber door, where she thought there were more, and desired it might be opened: the master answered, he had not the key, and that the room was taken by a man, who came there sometimes in the daytime to draw the plans and prospects of the fine houses and gardens that were to be seen from his windows; "he is one of the handsomest men I ever saw," added he, "and does not look much like one that works for his living; whenever he comes here, I observe he always looks towards the gardens and houses, but I never see him work."

Madam de Cleves listened to this story very attentively, and what Madam de Martigues had told her of Monsieur de Nemours's coming now and then to Paris, she applied in her fancy to that handsome man, who came to a place so near her house; and this gave her an idea of Monsieur de Nemours endeavouring to see her; which raised a disorder in her, of which she did not know the cause: she went towards the windows to see where they looked into, and she found they overlooked all her gardens, and directly faced her apartment: and when she was in her own room, she could easily see that very window where she was told the man came to take his prospects. The thought that it was the Duke de Nemours, entirely changed the situation of her mind; she no longer found herself in that pensive tranquillity which she had begun to enjoy, her spirits were ruffled again as with a tempest: at last, not being able to stay at home, she went abroad to take the air in a garden without the suburbs, where she hoped to be alone; she walked about a great while, and found no likelihood of anyone's being there.

Having crossed a little wilderness she perceived at the end of the walk, in the most remote part of the garden, a kind of a bower, open on all sides, and went towards it; when she was near, she saw a man lying on the benches, who seemed sunk into a deep contemplation, and she discovered it was the Duke de Nemours. Upon this she stopped short; but her attendants made some noise, which roused the Duke out of his musing: he took no notice who the persons were that disturbed him, but got up in order to avoid the company that was coming towards him, and making a low bow, which hindered him from seeing those he saluted, he turned into another walk.

If he had known whom he avoided, with what eagerness would he have returned? But he walked down the alley, and Madam de Cleves saw him go out at a back door, where his coach waited for him. What an effect did this transient view produce in the heart of Madam de Cleves? What a flame rekindled out of the embers of her love, and with what violence did it burn? She went and sat down in the same place from which Monsieur de Nemours was newly risen, and seemed perfectly overwhelmed; his image immediately possessed her fancy, and she considered him as the most amiable person in the world, as one who had long loved her with a passion full of veneration and sincerity, slighting all for her, paying respect even to her grief, to his own torture, labouring to see her without a thought of being seen by her, quitting the Court (though the Court's delight) to come and look on the walls where she was shut up, and to pass his melancholy hours in places where he could not hope to meet her; in a word, a man whose attachment to her alone merited returns of love, and for whom she had so strong an inclination, that she should have loved him, though she had not been beloved by him; and besides, one whose quality was suitable to hers: all the obstacles that could rise from duty and virtue were now removed, and all the trace that remained on her mind of their former condition was the passion the Duke de Nemours had for her, and that which she had for him.

All these ideas were new to her; her affliction for the death of her husband had left her no room for thoughts of this kind, but the sight of Monsieur de Nemours revived them, and they crowded again into her mind; but when she had taken her fill of them, and remembered that this very man, whom she considered as a proper match for her, was the same she had loved in her husband's lifetime, and was the cause of his death, and that on his death-bed he had expressed a fear of her marrying him, her severe virtue was so shocked at the imagination, that she thought it would be as criminal in her to marry Monsieur de Nemours now, as it was to love him before: in short, she abandoned herself to these reflections so pernicious to her happiness, and fortified herself in them by the inconveniency which she foresaw would attend such a marriage. After two hours' stay in this place she returned home, convinced that it was indispensably her duty to avoid the sight of the man she loved.

But this conviction, which was the effect of reason and virtue, did not carry her heart along with it; her heart was so violently fixed on the Duke de Nemours, that she became even an object of compassion, and was wholly deprived of rest. Never did she pass a night in so uneasy a manner; in the morning, the first thing she did was to see if there was anybody at the window which looked towards her apartment;

she saw there Monsieur de Nemours, and was so surprised upon it, and withdrew so hastily, as made him judge she knew him; he had often wished to be seen by her, ever since he had found out that method of seeing her, and when he had no hopes of obtaining that satisfaction, his way was to go to muse in the garden where she found him.

Tired at last with so unfortunate and uncertain a condition, he resolved to attempt something to determine his fate: "What should I wait for?" said he. "I have long known she loves me; she is free, she has no duty now to plead against me; why should I submit myself to the hardship of seeing her, without being seen by her or speaking to her? Is it possible for love so absolutely to have deprived me of reason and courage, and to have rendered me so different from what I have been in all my other amours? It was fit I should pay a regard to Madam de Cleves's grief; but I do it too long, and I give her leisure to extinguish the inclination she had for me."

After these reflections, he considered what measures he ought to take to see her; he found he had no longer any reason to conceal his passion from the Viscount de Chartres; he resolved to speak to him of it, and to communicate to him his design with regard to his niece.

The Viscount was then at Paris, the town being extremely full, and everybody busy in preparing equipages and dresses to attend the King of Navarre, who was to conduct the Queen of Spain: Monsieur de Nemours went to the Viscount, and made an ingenuous confession to him of all he had concealed hitherto, except Madam de Cleves's sentiments, which he would not seem to know.

The Viscount received what he told him with a great deal of pleasure, and assured him, that though he was not acquainted with his sentiments on that subject, he had often thought, since Madam de Cleves had been a widow, that she was the only lady that deserved him. Monsieur de Nemours entreated him to give him an opportunity of speaking to her, and learning what disposition she was in.

The Viscount proposed to carry him to her house, but the Duke was of opinion she would be shocked at it, because as yet she saw nobody; so that they agreed, it would be better for the Viscount to ask her to come to him, under some pretence, and for the Duke to come to them by a private staircase, that he might not be observed. Accordingly this was executed; Madam de Cleves came, the Viscount went to receive her, and led her into a great closet at the end of his apartment; some time after Monsieur de Nemours came in, as by chance: Madam de Cleves was in great surprise to see him; she blushed and endeavoured to hide it; the Viscount at first spoke of indifferent matters, and then went out, as if he had some orders to give, telling Madam de Cleves he must desire her to entertain the Duke in his stead, and that he would return immediately.

It is impossible to express the sentiments of Monsieur de Nemours, and Madam de Cleves, when they saw themselves alone, and at liberty to speak to one another, as they had never been before: they continued silent a while; at length, said Monsieur de Nemours, "Can you, Madam, pardon the Viscount for giving me an opportunity of seeing you, and speaking to you, an opportunity which you have always so cruelly denied me?" "I ought not to pardon him," replied she, "for having forgot the condition I am in, and to what he exposes my reputation." Having spoke these words, she would have gone away; but Monsieur de Nemours stopping her, "Fear not, Madam," said he; "you have nothing to apprehend; nobody knows I am here; hear me, Madam, hear me, if not out of goodness, yet at least for your own sake, and to free yourself from the extravagancies which a passion I am no longer master of will infallibly hurry me into." Madam de Cleves now first yielded to the inclination she had for the Duke de Nemours, and beholding him with eyes full of softness and charms, "But what can you hope for," says she, "from the complaisance you desire of me? You will perhaps repent that you have obtained it, and I shall certainly repent that I have granted it. You deserve a happier fortune than you have hitherto had, or than you can have for the future, unless you seek it elsewhere." "I, Madam," said he, "seek happiness anywhere else? Or is there any happiness for me, but in your love? Though I never spoke of it before, I cannot believe, Madam, that you are not acquainted with my passion, or that you do not know it to be the greatest and most sincere that ever was; what trials has it suffered in things you are a stranger to? What trials have you put it to by your rigour?"

"Since you are desirous I should open myself to you," answered Madam de Cleves, "I'll comply with your desire, and I'll do it with a sincerity that is rarely to be met with in persons of my sex: I shall not tell you, that I have not observed your passion for me; perhaps you would not believe me if I should tell you so; I confess therefore to you, not only that I have observed it, but that I have observed it in such lights as you yourself could wish it might appear to me in." "And if you have seen my passion, Madam," said he, "is it possible for you not to have been moved by it? And may I venture to ask, if it has made no impression on your heart?" "You should have judged of that from my conduct," replied she; "but I should be glad to know what you thought of it." "I ought to be in a happier condition," replied he, "to venture to inform you; my fortune would contradict what I should say; all I can tell you, Madam, is that I heartily wished you had not acknowledged to Monsieur de Cleves what you concealed from me, and that you had concealed from him what you made appear to me." "How came you to discover," replied she blushing, "that I acknowledged anything to Monsieur de Cleves?" "I learned it from yourself, Madam," replied he; "but that you may the better pardon the boldness I showed in listening to what you said, remember if I have made an ill use of what I heard, if my hopes rose upon it, or if I was the more encouraged to speak to you."

Here he began to relate how he had overheard her conversation with Monsieur de Cleves; but she interrupted him before he had finished;

"Say no more of it," said she, "I see how you came to be so well informed; I suspected you knew the business but too well at the Queen-Dauphin's, who learned this adventure from those you had entrusted with it."

Upon this Monsieur de Nemours informed her in what manner the thing came to pass; "No excuses," says she; "I have long forgiven you, without being informed how it was brought about; but since you have learned from my ownself what I designed to conceal from you all my life, I will acknowledge to you that you have inspired me with sentiments I was unacquainted with before I saw you, and of which I had so slender an idea, that they gave me at first a surprise which still added to the pain that constantly attends them: I am the less ashamed to make you this confession, because I do it at a time when I may do it without a crime, and because you have seen that my conduct has not been governed by my affections."

"Can you believe, Madam," said Monsieur de Nemours, falling on his knees, "but I shall expire at your feet with joy and transport?" "I have told you nothing," said she smiling, "but what you knew too well before" "Ah! Madam," said he, "what a difference is there between learning it by chance, and knowing it from yourself, and seeing withal that you are pleased I know it." "It is true," answered she, "I would have you know it, and I find a pleasure in telling it you; I don't even know if I do not tell it you more for my own sake, than for yours; for, after all, this confession will have no consequences, and I shall follow the austere rules which my duty imposes upon me." "How! Madam; you are not of this opinion," replied Monsieur de Nemours; "you are no longer under any obligation of duty; you are at liberty; and if I durst, I should even tell you, that it is in your power to act so, that your duty shall one day oblige you to preserve the sentiments you have for me." "My duty," replied she, "forbids me to think of any man, but of you the last in the world, and for reasons which are unknown to you." "Those reasons perhaps are not unknown to me," answered he, "but they are far from being good ones. I believe that Monsieur de Cleves thought me happier than I was, and imagined that you approved of those extravagancies which my passion led me into without your approbation." "Let us talk no more of that adventure," said she; "I cannot bear the thought of it, it giving me shame, and the consequences of it have been such that it is too melancholy a subject to be spoken of; it is but too true that you were the cause of Monsieur de Cleves's death; the suspicions which your inconsiderate conduct gave him, cost him his life as much as if you had taken it away with your own hands: judge what I ought to have done, had you two fought a duel, and he been killed; I know very well, it is not the same thing in the eye of the world, but with me there's no difference, since I know that his death was owing to you, and that it was on my account." "Ah! Madam," said Monsieur de Nemours, "what phantom of duty do you oppose to my happiness? What! Madam, shall a vain and groundless fancy hinder you from making a man happy, for whom you have an inclination ? What, have I had some ground to hope I might pass my life with you ? has my fate led me to love the most deserving lady in the world ? have I observed in her all that can make a mistress adorable ? Has she had no disliking to me ? Have I found in her conduct everything which perhaps I could wish for in a wife ? For in short, Madam, you are perhaps the only person in whom those two characters have ever concurred to the degree they are in you ; those who marry mistresses, by whom they are loved, tremble when they marry them, and cannot but fear lest they should observe the same conduct towards others, which they observed towards them ; but in you, Madam, I can fear nothing, I see nothing in you but matter of admiration : have I had a prospect of so much felicity for no other end but to see it obstructed by you ? Ah ! Madam, you forget, that you have distinguished me above other men ; or rather, you have not distinguished me ; you have deceived yourself, and I have flattered myself."

"You have not flattered yourself," replied she ; "the reasons of my duty would not perhaps appear so strong to me without that distinction of which you doubt, and it is that which makes me apprehend unfortunate consequences from your alliance." "I have nothing to answer, Madam," replied he, "when you tell me you apprehend unfortunate consequences ; but I own, that after all you have been pleased to say to me, I did not expect from you so cruel a reason." "The reason you speak of," replied Madam de Cleves, "is so little disobliging as to you, that I don't know how to tell it you." "Alas ! Madam," said he, "how can you fear I should flatter myself too much after what you have been saying to me ?" "I shall continue to speak to you," says she, "with the same sincerity with which I begun, and I'll lay aside that delicacy and reserve that modesty obliges one to in a first conversation, but I conjure you to hear me without interruption.

"I think I owe the affection you have for me, the poor recompense not to hide from you any of my thoughts, and to let you see them such as they really are ; this in all probability will be the only time I shall allow myself the freedom to discover them to you ; and I cannot confess without a blush, that the certainty of not being loved by you, as I am, appears to me so dreadful a misfortune, that if I had not invincible reasons grounded on my duty, I could not resolve to subject myself to it ; I know that you are free, that I am so too, and that circumstances are such, that the public perhaps would have no reason to blame either you or me, should we unite ourselves forever ; but do men continue to love, when under engagements for life ? Ought I to expect a miracle in my favour ? And shall I place myself in a condition of seeing certainly that passion come to an end, in which I should place all my felicity ? Monsieur de Cleves was perhaps the only man in the world capable of continuing to love after marriage ; it was my ill fate that I was not able to enjoy that happiness, and perhaps his passion had not lasted but that he found none in me ; but I should not have the same way of preserving yours; I even think your constancy is owing to the obstacles you have met with; you have met with enough to animate you to conquer them; and my unguarded actions, or what you learned by chance, gave you hopes enough not to be discouraged." "Ah! Madam," replied Monsieur de Nemours, "I cannot keep the silence you enjoined me; you do me too much injustice, and make it appear too clearly that you are far from being prepossessed in my favour." "I confess," answered she, "that my passions may lead me, but they cannot blind me; nothing can hinder me from knowing that you are born with a disposition for gallantry, and have all the qualities proper to give success; you have already had a great many amours, and you will have more; I should no longer be she you placed your happiness in; I should see you as warm for another as you had been for me; this would grievously vex me, and I am not sure I should not have the torment of jealousy; I have said too much to conceal from you that you have already made me know what jealousy is, and that I suffered such cruel inquietudes the evening the Queen gave me Madam de Themines's letter, which it was said was addressed to you, that to this moment I retain an idea of it, which makes me believe it is the worst of all ills.

"There is scarce a woman but out of vanity or inclination desires to engage you; there are very few whom you do not please, and my own experience would make me believe, that there are none whom it is not in your power to please; I should think you always in love and beloved, nor should I be often mistaken; and yet in this case I should have no remedy but patience, nay I question if I should dare to complain: a lover may be reproached; but can a husband be so, when one has nothing to urge, but that he loves one no longer? But admit I could accustom myself to bear a misfortune of this nature, yet how could I bear that of imagining I constantly saw Monsieur de Cleves, accusing you of his death, reproaching me with having loved you, with having married you, and showing me the difference betwixt his affection and yours? It is impossible to over-rule such strong reasons as these; I must continue in the condition I am in, and in the resolution I have taken never to alter it." "Do you believe you have the power to do it, Madam?" cried the Duke de Nemours. "Do you think your resolution can hold out against a man who adores, and who has the happiness to please you? It is more difficult than you imagine, Madam, to resist a person who pleases and loves one at the same time; you have done it by an austerity of virtue, which is almost without example; but that virtue no longer opposes your inclinations, and I hope you will follow them in spite of yourself." "I know nothing can be more difficult than what I undertake," replied Madam de Cleves; "I distrust my strength in the midst of my reasons; what I think I owe to the memory of Monsieur de Cleves would be a weak consideration, if not supported by the interest of my ease and repose; and the reasons of my repose have need to be supported by those of my duty; but though I distrust myself,

I believe I shall never overcome my scruples, nor do I so much as hope to overcome the inclination I have for you; that inclination will make me unhappy, and I will deny myself the sight of you, whatever violence it is to me: I conjure you, by all the power I have over you, to seek no occasion of seeing me; I am in a condition which makes that criminal which might be lawful at another time; decency forbids all commerce between us." Monsieur de Nemours threw himself at her feet, and gave a loose to all the violent motions with which he was agitated; he expressed both by his words and tears the liveliest and most tender passion that ever heart was touched with; nor was the heart of Madam de Cleves insensible; she looked upon him with eyes swelled with tears: "Why was it," cries she, "that I can charge you with Monsieur de Cleves's death? Why did not my first acquaintance with you begin since I have been at liberty, or why did not I know you before I was engaged? Why does fate separate us by such invincible obstacles?" "There are no obstacles, Madam," replied Monsieur de Nemours; "it is you alone oppose my happiness; you impose on yourself a law which virtue and reason do not require you to obey." "'Tis true," says she, "I sacrifice a great deal to a duty which does not subsist but in my imagination; have patience, and expect what time may produce; Monsieur de Cleves is but just expired, and that mournful object is too near to leave me clear and distinct views; in the meantime enjoy the satisfaction to know you have gained the heart of a person, who would never have loved anyone, had she not seen you: believe the inclination I have for you will last forever, and that it will be uniform and the same, whatever becomes of me: Adieu," said she; "this is a conversation I ought to blush for; however, give an account of it to the Viscount; I agree to it, and desire you to do it."

With these words she went away, nor could Monsieur de Nemours detain her. In the next room she met with the Viscount, who seeing her under so much concern would not speak to her, but led her to her coach without saying a word; he returned to Monsieur de Nemours, who was so full of joy, grief, admiration, and of all those affections that attend a passion full of hope and fear, that he had not the use of his reason. It was a long time ere the Viscount could get from him an account of the conversation; at last the Duke related it to him, and Monsieur de Chartres, without being in love, no less admired the virtue, wit and merit of Madam de Cleves, than did Monsieur de Nemours himself; they began to examine what issue could reasonably be hoped for in this affair; and however fearful the Duke de Nemours was from his love, he agreed with the Viscount, that it was impossible Madam de Cleves should continue in the resolution she was in; they were of opinion nevertheless that it was necessary to follow her orders, for fear, upon the public's perceiving the inclination he had for her, she should make declarations and enter into engagements with respect to the world, that she would afterwards abide by, lest it should be thought she loved him in her husband's lifetime.

Monsieur de Nemours determined to follow the King; it was a journey he could not well excuse himself from, and so he resolved to go without endeavouring to see Madam de Cleves again from the window out of which he had sometimes seen her; he begged the Viscount to speak to her; and what did he not desire him to say in his behalf? What an infinite number of reasons did he furnish him with, to persuade her to conquer her scruples? In short, great part of the night was spent before he thought of going away.

As for Madam de Cleves, she was in no condition to rest; it was a thing so new to her to have broke loose from the restraints she had laid on herself, to have endured the first declarations of love that ever were made to her, and to have confessed that she herself was in love with him that made them, all this was so new to her, that she seemed quite another person; she was surprised at what she had done; she repented of it; she was glad of it; all her thoughts were full of anxiety and passion; she examined again the reasons of her duty, which obstructed her happiness; she was grieved to find them so strong, and was sorry that she had made them out so clear to Monsieur de Nemours: though she had entertained thoughts of marrying him, as soon as she beheld him in the garden of the suburbs, yet her late conversation with him made a much greater impression on her mind; at some moments she could not comprehend how she could be unhappy by marrying him, and she was ready to say in her heart, that her scruples as to what was past, and her fears for the future, were equally groundless: at other times, reason and her duty prevailed in her thoughts, and violently hurried her into a resolution not to marry again, and never to see Monsieur de Nemours; but this was a resolution hard to be established in a heart so softened as hers, and so lately abandoned to the charms of love. At last, to give herself a little ease, she concluded that it was not yet necessary to do herself the violence of coming to any resolution, and decency allowed her a considerable time to determine what to do: however she resolved to continue firm in having no commerce with Monsieur de Nemours. The Viscount came to see her, and pleaded his friend's cause with all the wit and application imaginable, but could not make her alter her conduct, or recall the severe orders she had given to Monsieur de Nemours; she told him her design was not to change her condition; that she knew how difficult it was to stand to that design, but that she hoped she should be able to do it; she made him so sensible how far she was affected with the opinion that Monsieur de Nemours was the cause of her husband's death, and how much she was convinced that it would be contrary to her duty to marry him, that the Viscount was afraid it would be very difficult to take away those impressions; he did not, however, tell the Duke what he thought, when he gave him an account of his conversation with her, but left him as much hope as a man who is loved may reasonably have.

They set out the next day, and went after the King; the Viscount wrote to Madam de Cleves at Monsieur de Nemours's request, and in a second letter, which soon followed the first, the Duke wrote a line or two in his own hand ; but Madam de Cleves determined not to depart from the rules she had prescribed herself, and fearing the accidents that might happen from letters, informed the Viscount that she would receive his letters no more, if he continued to speak of Monsieur de Nemours, and did it in so peremptory a manner, that the Duke desired him not to mention him.

During the absence of the Court, which was gone to conduct the Queen of Spain as far as Poitou, Madam de Cleves continued at home ; and the more distant she was from Monsieur de Nemours, and from everything that could put her in mind of him, the more she recalled the memory of the Prince of Cleves, which she made it her glory to preserve ; the reasons she had not to marry the Duke de Nemours appeared strong with respect to her duty, but invincible with respect to her quiet ; the opinion she had, that marriage would put an end to his love, and the torments of jealousy, which she thought the infallible consequences of marriage, gave her the prospect of a certain unhappiness if she consented to his desires ; on the other hand, she thought it impossible, if he were present, to refuse the most amiable man in the world, the man who loved her, and whom she loved, and to oppose him in a thing that was neither inconsistent with virtue nor decency : she thought that nothing but absence and distance could give her the power to do it ; and she found she stood in need of them, not only to support her resolution not to marry, but even to keep her from seeing Monsieur de Nemours ; she resolved therefore to take a long journey, in order to pass away the time which decency obliged her to spend in retirement ; the fine estate she had near the Pyrenees seemed the most proper place she could make choice of ; she set out a few days before the Court returned, and wrote at parting to the Viscount to conjure him not to think of once enquiring after her, or of writing to her.

Monsieur de Nemours was as much troubled at this journey, as another would have been for the death of his mistress ; the thought of being deprived so long a time of the sight of Madam de Cleves grieved him to the soul, especially as it happened at a time when he had lately enjoyed the pleasure of seeing her, and of seeing her moved by his passion ; however he could do nothing but afflict himself, and his affliction increased every day. Madam de Cleves, whose spirits had been so much agitated, was no sooner arrived at her country seat, but she fell desperately ill ; the news of it was brought to Court ; Monsieur de Nemours was inconsolable ; his grief proceeded even to despair and extravagance ; the Viscount had much a-do to hinder him from discovering his passion in public, and as much a-do to keep him from going in person to know how she did ; the relation and friendship between her and the Viscount served as an excuse for sending frequent messengers ; at last they heard she was out of the extremity of danger she had been in, but continued in a languishing malady that left but little hopes of life.

The nature of her disease gave her a prospect of death both near, and at a distance, and showed her the things of this life in a very different view from that in which they are seen by people in health ; the necessity of dying, to which she saw herself so near, taught her to wean herself from the world, and the lingeringness of her distemper brought her to a habit in it ; yet when she was a little recovered, she found that Monsieur de Nemours was not effaced from her heart ; but to defend herself against him, she called to her aid all the reasons which she thought she had never to marry him ; after a long conflict in herself, she subdued the relics of that passion which had been weakened by the sentiments her illness had given her ; the thoughts of death had reproached her with the memory of Monsieur de Cleves, and this remembrance was so agreeable to her duty, that it made deep impressions in her heart ; the passions and engagements of the world appeared to her in the light, in which they appear to persons who have more great and more distant views. The weakness of her body, which was brought very low, aided her in preserving these sentiments ; but as she knew what power opportunities have over the wisest resolutions, she would not hazard the breach of those she had taken, by returning into any place where she might see him she loved ; she retired, under pretence of change of air, into a convent, but without declaring a settled resolution of quitting the Court.

Upon the first news of it, Monsieur de Nemours felt the weight of this retreat, and saw the importance of it ; he presently thought he had nothing more to hope, but omitted not anything that might oblige her to return ; he prevailed with the Queen to write ; he made the Viscount not only write, but go to her, but all to no purpose ; the Viscount saw her, but she did not tell him she had fixed her resolution ; and yet he judged, she would never return to Court ; at last Monsieur de Nemours himself went to her, under pretence of using the waters ; she was extremely grieved and surprised to hear he was come, and sent him word by a person of merit about her, that she desired him not to take it ill, if she did not expose herself to the danger of seeing him, and of destroying by his presence those sentiments she was obliged to preserve ; that she desired he should know, that having found it both against her duty and peace of mind to yield to the inclination she had to be his, all things else were become so indifferent to her, that she had renounced them for ever ; that she thought only of another life, and had no sentiment remaining as to this, but the desire of seeing him in the same dispositions she was in.

Monsieur de Nemours was like to have expired in the presence of the lady who told him this ; he begged her a thousand times to return to Madam de Cleves, and to get leave for him to see her ; but she told him the Princess had not only forbidden her to come back with any message from him, but even to report the conversation that should pass between them. At length Monsieur de Nemours was obliged to go back, oppressed with the heaviest grief a man is capable of, who has lost all hopes of ever seeing again a person, whom he loved not only with the most violent, but most natural and sincere passion that ever was ; yet still he was not utterly discouraged, but used all imaginable methods to make her alter her resolution ; at last, after several years, time and absence abated his grief, and extinguished his passion. Madam de Cleves lived in a manner that left no probability of her ever returning to Court ; she spent one part of the year in that religious house, and the other at her own, but still continued the austerity of retirement, and constantly employed herself in exercises more holy than the severest convents can pretend to ; and her life, though it was short, left examples of inimitable virtues.

# MANON LESCAUT

# MANON LESCAUT

## I

> **Why did he love her ? Curious fool, be still !**
> **Is human love the fruit of human will ?**
>
> BYRON.

JUST about six months before my departure for Spain, I first met the Chevalier des Grieux. Though I rarely quitted my retreat, still the interest I felt in my child's welfare induced me occasionally to undertake short journeys, which, however, I took good care to abridge as much as possible.

I was one day returning from Rouen, where I had been, at her request, to attend a cause then pending before the Parliament of Normandy, respecting an inheritance to which I had claims derived from my maternal grandfather. Having taken the road by Evreux, where I slept the first night, I on the following day, about dinner-time, reached Passy, a distance of five or six leagues. I was amazed, on entering this quiet town, to see all the inhabitants in commotion. They were pouring from their houses in crowds, towards the gate of a small inn, immediately before which two covered vans were drawn up. Their horses still in harness, and reeking from fatigue and heat, showed that the cortège had only just arrived. I stopped for a moment to learn the cause of the tumult, but could gain little information from the curious mob as they rushed by, heedless of my enquiries, and hastening impatiently towards the inn in the utmost confusion. At length an archer of the civic guard, wearing his bandolier, and carrying a carbine on his shoulder, appeared at the gate ; so, beckoning him towards me, I begged to know the cause of the uproar. " Nothing, sir," said he, " but a dozen of the frail sisterhood, that I and my comrades are conducting to Havre-de-Grace, whence we are to ship them for America. There are one or two of them pretty enough ; and it is that, apparently, which attracts the curiosity of these good people."

I should have passed on, satisfied with this explanation, if my attention had not been arrested by the cries of an old woman, who was coming out of the inn with her hands clasped, and exclaiming : " A downright barbarity !—A scene to excite horror and compassion ! " " What may this mean ? " I enquired. " Oh ! sir ; go into the house yourself," said the woman, and see if it is not a sight to rend your heart ! " Curiosity made me dismount ; and leaving my horse to the care of the ostler, I made my way with some difficulty through the crowd, and did indeed behold a scene sufficiently touching.

Among the twelve girls, who were chained together by the waist in two rows, there was one, whose whole air and figure seemed so ill-suited to her present condition, that under other circumstances I should not have hesitated to pronounce her a person of high birth. Her excessive grief, and even the wretchedness of her attire, detracted so little from her surpassing beauty, that at first sight of her I was inspired with a mingled feeling of respect and pity. She tried, as well as the chain would permit her, to turn herself away, and hide her face from the rude gaze of the spectators. There was something so unaffected in the effort she made to escape observation, that it could but have sprung from natural and innate modesty alone.

As the six men who escorted the unhappy train were together in the room, I took the chief one aside and asked for information respecting this beautiful girl. All that he could supply was of the most vague kind. "We brought her," he said, "from the Hospital, by order of the lieutenant-general of police. There is no reason to suppose that she was shut up there for good conduct. I have questioned her often upon the road; but she persists in refusing even to answer me. Yet, although I received no orders to make any distinction between her and the others, I cannot help treating her differently, for she seems to me somewhat superior to her companions. Yonder is a young man," continued the archer, "who can tell you, better than I can, the cause of her misfortunes. He has followed her from Paris, and has scarcely dried his tears for a single moment. He must be either her brother or her lover."

I turned towards the corner of the room, where this young man was seated. He seemed buried in a profound reverie. Never did I behold a more affecting picture of grief. He was plainly dressed; but one may discover at the first glance a man of birth and education. As I approached him he rose, and there was so refined and noble an expression in his eyes, in his whole countenance, in his every movement, that I felt an involuntary impulse to render him any service in my power. "I am unwilling to intrude upon your sorrows," said I, taking a seat beside him, "but you will, perhaps, gratify the desire I feel to learn something about that beautiful girl, who seems little formed by nature for the miserable condition in which she is placed."

He answered me candidly, that he could not communicate her history without making himself known, and that he had urgent reasons for preserving his own incognito. "I may, however, tell you this much, for it is no longer a secret to these wretches," he continued, pointing to the guards,—"that I adore her with a passion so ardent and absorbing as to render me the most unhappy of human beings. I tried every means at Paris to effect her liberty. Petitions, artifice, force—all failed. Go where she may, I have resolved to follow her—to the extremity of the world. I shall embark with her and cross to America.

"But think of the brutal inhumanity of these cowardly ruffians," he added, speaking of the guards; "they will not allow me to approach her! I had planned an open attack upon them some leagues from Paris;

having secured, as I thought, the aid of four men, who for a considerable sum hired me their services. The traitors, however, left me to execute my scheme single-handed, and decamped with my money. The impossibility of success made me of course abandon the attempt. I then implored of the guards permission to follow in their train, promising them a recompense. The love of money procured their consent; but as they required payment every time I was allowed to speak to her, my purse was speedily emptied; and now that I am utterly penniless, they are barbarous enough to repulse me brutally, whenever I make the slightest attempt to approach her. It is but a moment since, that venturing to do so, in spite of their threats, one of the fellows raised the butt-end of his musket. I am now driven by their exactions to dispose of the miserable horse that has brought me hither, and am preparing to continue the journey on foot."

Although he seemed to recite this story tranquilly enough, I observed the tears start to his eyes as he concluded. This adventure struck me as being not less singular than it was affecting. "I do not press you," said I to him, to make me the confidant of your secrets; but if I can be of use to you in any way, I gladly tender you my services." "Alas!" replied he, "I see not the slightest ray of hope. I must reconcile myself to my destiny in all its rigour. I shall go to America: there, at least, I may be free to live with her I love. I have written to a friend, who will send me money to Havre-de-Grace. My only difficulty is to get so far, and to supply that poor creature," added he, as he cast a look of sorrow at his mistress, "with some few comforts upon the way." "Well!" said I to him, "I shall relieve you from that difficulty. Here is some money, of which I entreat your acceptance: I am only sorry that I can be of no greater service to you."

I gave him four louis-d'ors without being perceived by the guards; for I thought that if they knew he had this money, they might have raised the price of their concessions. It occurred to me, even, to come to an understanding with them, in order to secure for the young man the privilege of conversing with his mistress, during the rest of the journey to Havre, without hindrance. I beckoned the chief to approach, and made the proposition to him. It seemed to abash the ruffian, in spite of his habitual effrontery. "It is not, sir," said he, in an embarrassed tone, "that we refuse to let him speak to the girl, but he wishes to be always near her, which puts us to inconvenience; and it is just that we should be paid for the trouble he occasions." "Let us see!" said I to him, "what would suffice to prevent you from feeling the inconvenience?" He had the audacity to demand two louis. I gave them to him on the spot. "But have a care," said I to him, "that we have no foul play: for I shall give the young man my address, in order that he may write to me on his arrival; and be assured that I am not without the power to punish you." It cost me altogether six louis-d'ors.

The graceful manner and heartfelt gratitude with which the young unknown thanked me, confirmed my notion that he was of good birth and merited my kindness. I addressed a few words to his mistress before I left the room. She replied to me with a modesty so gentle and so charming that I could not help making, as I went out, a thousand reflections upon the incomprehensible character of women.

Returned to my retreat, I remained in ignorance of the result of this adventure; and ere two years had passed, it was completely blotted from my recollection, when chance brought me an opportunity of learning all the circumstances from beginning to end.

I arrived at Calais, from London, with my pupil, the Marquis of ——. We lodged, if I remember rightly, at the "Golden Lion," where, for some reason, we were obliged to spend the following day and night. Walking along the streets in the afternoon, I fancied I saw the same young man whom I had formerly met at Passy. He was miserably dressed, and much paler than when I first saw him. He carried on his arm an old portmanteau, having only just arrived in the town. However, there was an expression in his countenance too amiable not to be easily recognised, and which immediately brought his features to my recollection. "Observe that young man," said I to the Marquis; "we must accost him."

His joy was beyond expression when, in his turn, he recognised me. "Ah, sir!" he cried, kissing my hand, "I have then once again an opportunity of testifying my eternal gratitude to you!" I enquired of him whence he came. He replied, that he had just arrived, by sea, from Havre, where he had lately landed from America. "You do not seem to be too well off for money," said I to him; "go on to the 'Golden Lion,' where I am lodging; I will join you in a moment."

I returned, in fact, full of impatience to learn the details of his misfortunes, and the circumstances of his voyage to America. I gave him a thousand welcomes, and ordered that they should supply him with everything he wanted. He did not wait to be solicited for the history of his life. "Sir," said he to me, "your conduct is so generous, that I should consider it base ingratitude to maintain any reserve towards you. You shall learn not only my misfortunes and sufferings, but my faults and most culpable weaknesses. I am sure that, even while you blame me, you will not refuse me your sympathy."

I should here inform the reader that I wrote down the story almost immediately after hearing it; and he may, therefore, be assured of the correctness and fidelity of the narrative. I use the word fidelity with reference to the substance of reflections and sentiments, which the young man conveyed in the most graceful language. Here, then, is his story, which in its progress I shall not encumber with a single observation that was not his own.

## II

I loved Ophelia! forty thousand brothers
Could not, with all their quantity of love,
Make up my sum.
SHAKESPEARE.

"I WAS seventeen years old, and was finishing my studies at Amiens, whither my parents, who belonged to one of the first families in Picardy, had sent me. I led a life so studious and well regulated, that my masters pointed to me as a model of conduct for the other scholars. Not that I made any extraordinary efforts to acquire this reputation, but my disposition was naturally tractable and tranquil; my inclinations led me to apply to study; and even the natural dislike I felt for vice was placed to my credit as positive proof of virtue. The successful progress of my studies, my birth, and some external advantages of person, made me a general favourite with the inhabitants of the town.

"I completed my public exercises with such general approbation, that the bishop of the diocese, who was present, proposed to me to enter the church, where I could not fail, he said, to acquire more distinction than in the Order of Malta, for which my parents had destined me. I was already decorated with the Cross, and called the Chevalier des Grieux. The vacation having arrived, I was preparing to return to my father, who had promised to send me soon to the Academy.

"My only regret on quitting Amiens arose from parting with a friend, some years older than myself, to whom I had always been tenderly attached. We had been brought up together; but from the straitened circumstances of his family, he was intended to take orders, and was to remain after me at Amiens to complete the requisite studies for his sacred calling. He had a thousand good qualities. You will recognise in him the very best during the course of my history, and above all, a zeal and fervour of friendship which surpass the most illustrious examples of antiquity. If I had at that time followed his advice, I should have always continued a discreet and happy man. If I had even taken counsel from his reproaches, when on the brink of that gulf into which my passions afterwards plunged me, I should have been spared the melancholy wreck of both fortune and reputation. But he was doomed to see his friendly admonitions disregarded; nay, even at times repaid by contempt from an ungrateful wretch, who often dared to treat his fraternal conduct as offensive and officious.

"I had fixed the day for my departure from Amiens. Alas! that I had not fixed it one day sooner! I should then have carried to my father's house my innocence untarnished.

"The very evening before my expected departure, as I was walking with my friend, whose name was Tiberge, we saw the Arras diligence arrive, and sauntered after it to the inn, at which these coaches stop.

We had no other motive than curiosity. Some women alighted, and immediately retired into the inn. One remained behind : she was very young, and stood by herself in the court, while a man of advanced age who appeared to have charge of her, was busy in getting her luggage from the vehicle. She struck me as being so extremely beautiful, that I who had never before thought of the difference between the sexes, or looked on woman with the slightest attention—I, whose conduct had been hitherto the theme of universal admiration, felt myself, on the instant, deprived of my reason and self-control. I had been always excessively timid, and easily disconcerted ; but now, instead of meeting with any impediment from this weakness, I advanced without the slightest reserve towards her, who had thus become, in a moment, the mistress of my heart.

" Although younger than myself, she received my civilities without embarrassment. I asked the cause of her journey to Amiens, and whether she had any acquaintances in the town. She ingenuously told me that she had been sent there by her parents, to commence her novitiate for taking the veil. Love had so quickened my perception, even in the short moment it had been enthroned, that I saw in this announcement a death-blow to my hopes. I spoke to her in a way that made her at once understand what was passing in my mind ; for she had more experience than myself. It was against her consent that she was consigned to a convent, doubtless to repress that inclination for pleasure which had already become too manifest, and which caused, in the sequel, all her misfortunes and mine. I combated the cruel intention of her parents with all the arguments that my new-born passion and schoolboy eloquence could suggest. She affected neither austerity nor reserve. She told me, after a moment's silence, that she foresaw, too clearly, what her unhappy fate must be ; but that it was, apparently, the will of Heaven, since there were no means left her to avert it. The sweetness of her look, the air of sorrow with which she pronounced these words, or rather perhaps the controlling destiny which led me on to ruin, allowed me not an instant to weigh my answer. I assured her that if she would place reliance on my honour, and on the tender interest with which she had already inspired me, I would sacrifice my life to deliver her from the tyranny of her parents, and to render her happy. I have since been a thousand times astonished in reflecting upon it, to think how I could have expressed myself with so much boldness and facility ; but love could never have become a divinity, if he had not often worked miracles.

"I made many other pressing and tender speeches ; and my unknown fair one was perfectly aware that mine was not the age for deceit. She confessed to me that if I could see but a reasonable hope of being able to effect her enfranchisement, she should deem herself indebted for my kindness in more than life itself could pay. I repeated that I was ready to attempt anything in her behalf ; but, not having sufficient experience at once to imagine any reasonable plan of serving her, I did not go beyond this general assurance, from which indeed little good could arise either to her or to myself. Her old guardian having by this time joined us, my hopes would have been blighted, but that she had tact enough to make amends for my stupidity. I was surprised, on his approaching us, to hear her call me her cousin, and say, without being in the slightest degree disconcerted, that as she had been so fortunate as to fall in with me at Amiens, she would not go into the convent until the next morning, in order to have the pleasure of meeting me at supper. Innocent as I was, I at once comprehended the meaning of this ruse; and proposed that she should lodge for the night at the house of an innkeeper, who, after being many years my father's coachman, had lately established himself at Amiens, and who was sincerely attached to me.

"I conducted her there myself, at which the old Argus appeared to grumble a little; and my friend Tiberge, who was puzzled by the whole scene, followed, without uttering a word. He had not heard our conversation, having walked up and down the court while I was talking of love to my angelic mistress. As I had some doubts of his discretion, I got rid of him, by begging that he would execute a commission for me. I had thus the happiness, on arriving at the inn, of entertaining alone the sovereign of my heart.

"I soon learned that I was less a child than I had before imagined. My heart expanded to a thousand sentiments of pleasure, of which I had not before the remotest idea. A delicious consciousness of enjoyment diffused itself through my whole mind and soul. I sank into a kind of ecstasy, which deprived me for a time of the power of utterance, and which found vent only in a flood of tears.

"Manon Lescaut (this she told me was her name) seemed gratified by the visible effect of her own charms. She appeared to me not less excited than myself. She acknowledged that she was greatly pleased with me, and that she should be enchanted to owe to me her freedom and future happiness. She would insist on hearing who I was, and the knowledge only augmented her affection; for, being herself of humble birth, she was flattered by securing for her lover a man of family.

"After many reflections, we could discover no other resource than in flight. To effect this it would be requisite to cheat the vigilance of Manon's guardian, who required management, although he was but a servant. We determined, therefore, that, during the night, I should procure a post-chaise, and return with it at break of day to the inn, before he was awake; that we should steal away quietly, and go straight to Paris, where we might be married on our arrival. I had about fifty crowns in my pocket, the fruit of my little savings at school; and she had about twice as much. We imagined, like inexperienced children, that such a sum could never be exhausted, and we counted, with equal confidence, upon the success of our other schemes.

"After having supped, with certainly more satisfaction than I had ever before experienced, I retired to prepare for our project. All my arrangements were the more easy, because, for the purpose of returning on the morrow to my father's, my luggage had been already packed. I had, therefore, no difficulty in removing my trunk, and having a chaise prepared for five o'clock in the morning, at which hour the gates of the town would be opened ; but I encountered an obstacle which I was little prepared for, and which nearly upset all my plans.

" Tiberge, although only three years older than myself, was a youth of unusually strong mind, and of the best regulated conduct. He loved me with singular affection. The sight of so lovely a girl as Manon, my ill-disguised impatience to conduct her to the inn, and the anxiety I betrayed to get rid of him, had excited in his mind some suspicions of my passion. He had not ventured to return to the inn where he had left me, for fear of my being annoyed at his doing so ; but went to wait for me at my lodgings, where, although it was ten o'clock at night, I found him on my arrival. His presence annoyed me, and he soon perceived the restraint which it imposed. ' I am certain,' he said to me, without any disguise, ' that you have some plan in contemplation which you will not confide to me ; I see it by your manner.' I answered him rather abruptly, that I was not bound to render him an account of all my movements. ' Certainly not ! ' he replied ; ' but you have always, hitherto, treated me as a friend, and that appellation implies a certain degree of confidence and candour.' He pressed me so much and so earnestly to discover my secret, that, having never up to that moment felt the slightest reserve towards him, I confided to him now the whole history of my passion. He heard it with an appearance of disapprobation, which made me tremble ; and I immediately repented of my indiscretion, in telling him of my intended elopement. He told me he was too sincerely my friend not to oppose every obstacle in his power to such a scheme ; that he would first try all other means of turning me from such a purpose, but that if I refused to renounce so fatal a resolution, he assuredly would inform some persons of my intention, who would be able to defeat it. He held forth upon the subject for a full quarter of an hour, in the most serious tone, and ended by again threatening to inform against me, if I did not pledge him my word that I would return to the paths of discretion and reason.

" I was in despair at having so awkwardly betrayed myself. However, love having wonderfully sharpened my intellect during the last two or three hours, I recollected that I had not yet told him of its being my intention to execute my project on the following morning, and I at once determined to deceive him by a little equivocation.

" ' Tiberge,' said I to him, ' up to the present moment I thought you were my friend ; and I wished to prove it by the test of confidence. It is true, I am in love ; I have not deceived you : but with regard to my flight, that is a project not to be undertaken without deliberation. Call for me tomorrow at nine o'clock : you shall see my mistress, if it be possible, and then judge whether she is not worthy of any risk or sacrifice on my part.' He left me, with a thousand protestations of friendship.

"I employed the night in preparing for the journey, and on repairing to the inn at early dawn, I found Manon waiting my arrival. She was at her window, which looked upon the street, and perceiving my approach, she came down and opened the door herself. We took our departure silently, and without creating the least alarm. She merely brought away a small portion of her apparel, of which I took charge. The chaise was in readiness, and we were soon at a distance from the town.

"You will learn in the sequel what was the conduct of Tiberge when he discovered that I had deceived him; that his zeal to serve me suffered no diminution; and you will observe to what lengths his devotion carried him. How ought I to grieve, when I reflect on the base ingratitude with which his affection was always repaid!

"We made such speed on our journey that before night we reached St. Denis. I rode alongside of the chaise, which gave us little opportunity for conversation, except while changing horses; but when we found ourselves so near Paris, and out of the reach of danger, we allowed ourselves time for refreshment, not having tasted food since we quitted Amiens. Passionately in love as I felt with Manon, she knew how to convince me that she was equally so with me. So little did we restrain our fondness, that we had not even patience to reserve our caresses till we were alone. The postilions and innkeepers stared at us with wonder, and I remarked that they appeared surprised at such uncontrollable love in children of our age.

"Our project of marriage was forgotten at St. Denis; we defrauded the Church of her rights; and found ourselves united as man and wife without reflecting on the consequences. It is certain that with my easy and constant disposition, I should have been happy for my whole life, if Manon had remained faithful to me. The more I saw of her, the more I discovered in her new perfections. Her mind, her heart, her gentleness and beauty, formed a chain at once so binding and so agreeable, that I could have found perfect happiness in its enduring influence. Terrible fatality? that which has been the source of my despair, might, under a slight change of circumstances, have constituted my happiness. I find myself the most wretched of mankind, by the force of that very constancy from which I might have fairly expected to derive the most serene of human blisses, and the most perfect recompense of love.

"We took a furnished apartment at Paris, in the Rue V——, and, as it afterwards turned out, to my sorrow, close to the house of M. de B——, the famous Fermier-général. Three weeks passed, during which I was so absorbed in my passion, that I never gave a thought to my family, nor dreamed of the distress which my father probably felt at my absence. However, as there was yet nothing of profligacy about me, and as Manon conducted herself with the strictest propriety, the tranquil life we led served to restore me by degrees to a sense of duty.

"I resolved to effect, if possible, a reconciliation with my parent. My mistress was to me so perfectly lovable, that I could not doubt her power of captivating my father, if I could only find the means of making him acquainted with her good conduct and merit. In a word, I relied on obtaining his consent to our marriage, having given up all idea of accomplishing it without his approval. I mentioned the project to Manon, and explained to her that, besides every motive of filial love and duty, the weightier one of necessity should also have some influence; for our finances were sadly reduced, and I began to see the folly of thinking them, as I once did, inexhaustible.

"Manon received the proposition with considerable coldness. However, the difficulties she made, being apparently the suggestions of tenderness alone, or as arising from the natural fear of losing me, if my father, after learning our address, should refuse his assent to our union, I had not the smallest suspicion of the cruel blow she was at the very time preparing to inflict. As to the argument of necessity, she replied that we had still abundant means of living for some weeks longer, and that she would then find a resource in the kindness of some relations in the country, to whom she should write. She tempered her opposition by caresses so tender and impassioned, that I, who lived only for her, and who never had the slightest misgiving as to her love, applauded at once her arguments and her resolutions.

"To Manon I had committed the care of our finances, and the household arrangements. In a short time, I observed that our style of living was improved, and that she had treated herself to more expensive dresses. As I calculated that we could hardly have at this period more than fifteen or twenty crowns remaining, I did not conceal my surprise at this mysterious augmentation of our wealth. She begged of me, with a smile, to give myself no trouble on that head. 'Did I not promise you,' said she, 'that I would find resources?' I loved her too purely to experience the slightest suspicion.

"One day, having gone out in the afternoon, and told her that I should not be at home so early as usual, I was astonished, on my return, at being detained several minutes at the door. Our only servant was a young girl about our own age. On her letting me in at last, I asked why she had detained me so long? She replied in an embarrassed tone, that she did not hear me knock. 'I only knocked once,' said I; 'so if you did not hear me, why come to open the door at all?' This query disconcerted her so visibly, that losing her presence of mind, she began to cry, assuring me that it was not her fault; and that her mistress had desired her not to open the door until M. de B—— had had time to go down by the back staircase. I was so confounded by this information as to be utterly unable to proceed to our apartment; and was obliged to leave the house, under the pretext of an appointment. I desired the girl, therefore, to let her mistress know that I should return in a few minutes, but on no account to say that she had spoken to me of M. de B——.

"My horror was so great, that I shed tears as I went along, hardly knowing from what feeling they flowed. I entered a coffee-house close by, and placing myself at a table, I buried my face between my hands, as though I would turn my eyes inward to ascertain what was passing in my heart. Still, I dared not recall what I had heard the moment before. I strove to look upon it as a dream ; and was more than once on the point of returning to my lodgings, determined to attach no importance to what I had heard. It appeared to me so impossible that Manon could have been unfaithful, that I feared even to wrong her by a suspicion. I adored her—that was too certain ; I had not on my part given her more proofs of my love than I had received of hers ; why then should I charge her with being less sincere and constant than myself ? What reason could she have to deceive me ? Not three hours before, she had lavished upon me the most tender caresses, and had received mine with transport : I knew her heart as thoroughly as my own. 'No, no !' I said, 'it is not possible that Manon can have deceived me. She well knows that I live but for her ; that I adore her : upon that point I can have no reason to be unhappy.'

"Notwithstanding these reflections, the visit of M. de B——, and his sectret departure, gave me some uneasiness. I remembered, too, the little purchases she had lately made, which seemed beyond our present means. This looked like the liberality of a new lover. And the confidence with which she had foretold resources which were to me unknown ? I had some difficulty in solving these mysteries in as favourable a manner as my heart desired.

"On the other hand, she had been hardly out of my sight since we entered Paris. However occupied, in our walks, in all our amusements, she was ever at my side. Heavens ! even a momentary separation would have been too painful. I could not therefore imagine how Manon could, to any other person, have devoted a single instant.

"At last I thought I had discovered a clue to the mystery. 'M. de B——,' said I to myself, 'is a man extensively engaged in commercial affairs ; and Manon's relations have no doubt remitted her money through his house. She has probably already received some from him, and he is come today to bring her more. She wishes, perhaps, to derive amusement by and by, from an agreeable surprise, by keeping me at present in the dark. She would doubtless have at once told me all, if I had gone in as usual, instead of coming here to distress myself : at all events, she will not conceal it from me when I broach the subject myself.'

"I cherished this idea so willingly, that it considerably lightened my grief. I immediately returned to my lodgings, and embraced Manon as tenderly as ever. She received me as usual. At first I was tempted to mention my conjectures, which I now, more than ever, looked upon as certain ; but I restrained myself in the hope that she might render it unnecessary by informing me of all that had passed.

"Supper was served. Assuming an air of gaiety, I took my seat at table ; but by the light of the candles which were between us, I fancied I perceived an air of melancholy about the eyes and countenance of my beloved mistress. The very thought soon damped my gaiety. I remarked that her looks wore an unusual expression, and although nothing could be more soft or languishing, I was at a loss to discover whether they conveyed more of love than of compassion. I gazed at her with equal earnestness, and she perhaps had no less difficulty in comprehending from my countenance what was passing in my heart.

" We neither spoke nor ate. At length I saw tears starting from her beauteous eyes—perfidious tears! 'Oh heavens!' I cried, 'my dearest Manon, why allow your sorrows to afflict you to this degree without imparting their cause to me?' She answered me only with sighs, which increased my misery. I arose trembling from my seat: I conjured her, with all the urgent earnestness of love, to let me know the cause of her grief: I wept in endeavouring to soothe her sorrows: I was more dead than alive. A barbarian would have pitied my sufferings as I stood trembling with grief and apprehension.

" While my attention was thus confined to her, I heard people coming upstairs. They tapped gently at the door. Manon gave me a kiss, and escaping from my arms, quickly entered the boudoir, turning the key after her. I imagined that, not being dressed to receive strangers, she was unwilling to meet the persons who had knocked; I went to let them in.

" I had hardly opened the door, when I found myself seized by three men, whom I recognised as my father's servants. They offered not the least violence, but two of them taking me by the arms, the third examined my pockets, and took out a small knife, the only weapon I had about me. They begged pardon for the necessity they were under of treating me with apparent disrespect; telling me frankly that they were acting by the orders of my father, and that my eldest brother was in a carriage below waiting to receive me. My feelings were so overpowered, that I allowed myself to be led away without making either reply or resistance. I found my brother waiting for me as they had stated. They placed me by his side, and the coachman immediately drove, by his orders, towards St. Denis. My brother embraced me most affectionately, but during our ride he uttered not a word, so that, as I was not inclined for conversation, I had as much leisure as I could desire to reflect upon my misfortunes.

## III

> That we can call these delicate creatures ours,
> And not their appetites.
>
> SHAKESPEARE.

" THE whole affair was so involved in obscurity that I could not see my way even to a reasonable conjecture. I was cruelly betrayed—that was certain; but by whom? Tiberge first occurred to me. 'Tiberge!' said I, 'it is as much as thy life is worth, if my suspicions turn out to be well founded.' However, I recollected that he could not by possibility know my abode; and therefore, he could not have furnished the information. To accuse Manon was more than my heart was capable of. The unusual melancholy with which she had lately seemed weighed down, her tears, the tender kiss she gave me in parting, made it all as yet a mystery to me. I could only look upon her recent melancholy as a presentiment of our common misfortune; and while I was deploring the event which tore me from her, I was credulous enough to consider her fate as much deserving of pity as my own.

"The result of my reflections was, that I had been seen and followed in the streets of Paris by some persons of my acquaintance, who had conveyed the information to my father. This idea comforted me. I made up my mind to encounter some reproaches, or perhaps harsh treatment, for having outraged the paternal authority. I resolved, however, to suffer with patience, and to promise all that might be required of me, in order to facilitate my speedy return to Paris, that I might restore life and happiness to my dear Manon.

" We soon arrived at St. Denis. My brother, surprised at my long silence, thought it the effect of fear. He assured me that I had nothing to apprehend from my father's severity, provided I showed a disposition to return quietly to the path of duty, and prove myself worthy of his affection. He made me pass the night at St. Denis, merely taking the precaution of putting the three lackeys to sleep in my room. It cost me a pang to find myself in the same inn where I had stopped with Manon on our way from Amiens to Paris. The innkeeper and his servants recognised me, and guessed at once the truth of my history. I overheard them say, 'Ah! that's the handsome young gentleman who travelled this road about a month ago, with the beautiful girl he appeared so much in love with! How pretty she was! The poor young things, how they caressed each other! Pity if they have been separated!' I pretended not to hear, and kept as much out of sight as possible.

" At St. Denis my brother had a chariot waiting for us, in which we started early the next morning, and arrived at home before night. He saw my father first, in order to make a favourable impression by telling him how quietly I had allowed myself to be brought away, so that his reception of me was less austere than I had expected. He merely rebuked me in general terms for the offence I had committed, by absenting myself without his permission. As for my mistress, he said I richly deserved what had happened to me, for abandoning myself to a person utterly unknown; that he had entertained a better opinion of my discretion; but that he hoped this little adventure would make me wiser. I took the whole lecture only in the sense that accorded with my own notions. I thanked my father for his indulgence, and promised that I would in future observe a better regulated and more obedient course of conduct. I felt that I had secured a triumph; for, from the present aspect of affairs, there was no doubt that I should be free to effect my escape from the house even before the night was over.

"We sat down to supper. They rallied me about my Amiens conquest, and my flight with that paragon of fidelity. I took their jokes in good part, glad enough at being permitted to revolve in my mind the plans I had meditated; but some words which fell from my father made me listen with earnest attention. He spoke of perfidy, and the not disinterested kindness he had received at the hands of M. de B——. I was almost paralysed on hearing the name, and begged of my father to explain himself. He turned to my brother, to ask if he had not told me the whole story. My brother answered, that I appeared to him so tranquil upon the road, that he did not suppose I required this remedy to cure me of my folly. I remarked that my father was doubtful whether he should give me the explanation or not. I entreated him so earnestly that he satisfied me, or I should rather say tortured me, with the following most horrible narration.

"He began by asking me whether I was really simple enough to believe that I had been really loved by the girl. I told him confidently that I was perfectly sure of it, and that nothing could make me for a moment doubt it. 'Ha, ha, ha!' said he, with a loud laugh; 'that is excellent! you are a pretty dupe! Admirable idea! 'Twould be a thousand pities, my poor chevalier, to make you a Knight of Malta, with all the requisites you possess for a patient and accommodating husband.' He continued in the same tone to ridicule what he was pleased to call my dullness and credulity.

"He concluded, while I maintained a profound silence, by saying that, according to the nicest calculation he could make of the time since my departure from Amiens, Manon must have been in love with me about twelve days; 'for,' said he, 'I know that you left Amiens on the 28th of last month; this is the 29th of the present; it is eleven days since M. de B—— wrote to me; I suppose he required eight days to establish a perfect understanding with your mistress; so that, take eight and eleven from thirty-one days, the time between the 28th of one month and the 29th of the next, there remains twelve, more or less!' This joke was followed by shouts of laughter.

"I heard it all with a kind of sinking of the heart that I thought I could not bear up against, until he finished. 'You must know then,' continued my father, 'since you appear as yet ignorant of it, that M. de B—— has won the affections of your idol; for he can't be serious in pretending that it is his disinterested regard for me that has induced him to take her from you. It would be absurd to expect such noble sentiments from a man of his description, and one, besides, who is a perfect stranger to me. He knew that you were my son, and in order to get rid of you, he wrote to inform me of your abode, and of the life you led; saying, at the same time, that strong measures would be necessary to secure you. He offered to procure me the means of laying hold of you; and it was by his direction, as well as that of your mistress herself, that your brother hit upon the moment for catching you unawares. Now, you may congratulate yourself upon the duration of your triumph. You know how to conquer, rapid enough ; but you have yet to learn how to secure your conquests.'

"I could no longer endure these remarks, every one of which struck a dagger to my heart. I arose from the table, and had not advanced four steps towards the door, when I fell upon the floor, perfectly senseless. By prompt applications they soon brought me to myself. My eyes opened only to shed a torrent of tears, and my lips to utter the most sorrowful and heartrending complaints. My father, who always loved me most affectionately, tried every means to console me. I listened to him, but his words were without effect. I threw myself at his feet, in the attitude of prayer, conjuring him to let me return to Paris, and destroy the monster B——. 'No !' cried I ; 'he has not gained Manon's heart ; he may have seduced her by charms, or by drugs ; he may have even brutally violated her. Manon loves me. Do I not know that well ? He must have terrified her with a poniard, to induce her to abandon me.' What must he not have done to have robbed me of my angelic mistress ? Oh Heaven ! Heaven ! can it be possible that Manon deceived me, or that she has ceased to love me !

"As I continued to rave about returning at once to Paris, and was perpetually starting up with that purpose, my father clearly saw that while the paroxysm lasted, no arguments could pacify me. He conducted me to one of the upper rooms, and left two servants to keep constant watch over me. I was completely bewildered. I would have given a thousand lives to be but for one quarter of an hour in Paris. I had sense enough, however, to know that having so openly declared my intention, they would not easily allow me to quit my chamber. I looked at the height of the windows. Seeing no possibility of escaping that way, I addressed the servants in the most tranquil tone. I promised, with the most solemn vows, to make at some future day their fortunes, if they would but consent to my escape. I entreated them ; I tried caresses, and lastly threats ; but all were unavailing. I gave myself up to despair. I resolved to die ; and threw myself upon the bed, with a firm determination to quit it only with my life. In this situation I passed the night and the following day. I refused the nourishment that was brought to me next morning.

"My father came to see me in the afternoon. He tried in the most affectionate manner, to soothe my grief. He desired me so urgently to take some refreshment, that, to gratify him, I obeyed his wishes. Several days passed, during which I took nothing but in his presence, and at his special request. He continued to furnish new arguments to restore me to my proper senses, and to inspire me with merited contempt for the faithless Manon. I certainly had lost all esteem for her : how could I esteem the most fickle and perfidious of created beings ! But her image—those exquisite features, which were engraven on my heart's core, were still uneffaced. I understood my own feelings : 'I may die,' said I, 'and I ought to die after so much shame and grief ;

but I might suffer a thousand deaths without being able to forget the ingrate Manon.'

"My father was surprised at my still continuing so powerfully affected. He knew that I was imbued with the principles of honour; and not doubting that her infidelity must make me despise her, fancied that my obstinacy proceeded less from this particular passion, than from a general inclination towards the sex. This idea so took possession of his mind, that, prompted only by his affection for me, he came one day to reveal his thoughts. 'Chevalier,' said he to me, 'it has been hitherto my intention to make you bear the Cross of Malta: I now see that your inclinations do not bend that way. You are an admirer of beauty. I shall be able to find you a wife to your taste. Let me candidly know how you feel upon the subject.'

"I answered that I could never again see the slightest difference amongst women, and that after the misfortune I had experienced, I detested them all equally. 'I will find you one,' replied my father, smiling, 'who shall resemble Manon in beauty, but who shall be more faithful.' 'Ah! if you have any mercy,' said I, 'you will restore my Manon to me. Be assured, my dear father, that she has not betrayed me; she is incapable of such base and cruel treachery. It is the perfidious B—— who deceives both her and me. If you could form an idea of her tenderness and her sincerity—if you only knew her, you yourself would love her!' 'You are absolutely a child,' replied my father. 'How can you so delude yourself, after what I have told you about her? It was she who actually delivered you up to your brother. You ought to obliterate even her name from your memory, and take advantage, if you are wise, of the indulgence I am showing you.'

"I very clearly perceived that my father was right. It was an involuntary emotion that made me thus take part with the traitor. 'Alas!' replied I, after a moment's silence, 'it is but too true that I am the unhappy victim of the vilest perfidy. Yes,' I continued, while shedding tears of anger, 'I too clearly perceive that I am indeed but a child. Credulity like mine was easily gulled; but I shall be at no loss to revenge myself.' My father enquired of me my intentions: 'I will go to Paris,' I said, 'set fire to B——'s house, and immolate him and the perfidious Manon together.' This burst made my father laugh, and had only the effect of causing me to be more vigilantly watched in my cell.

"I thus passed six long months; during the first of which my mind underwent little change. My feelings were in a state of perpetual alternation between hate and love; between hope and despair; according as the tendency of each passing thought brought Manon back to my recollection. At one time, I could see in her the most delightful of women only, and sigh for the pleasure of beholding her once more; at another, I felt she was the most unworthy and perfidious of mistresses, and I would on these occasions swear never again to seek her, but for the purpose of revenge.

"I was supplied with books, which served to restore my peace of mind. I read once again all my favourite authors; and I became acquainted with new ones. All my former taste for study was revived. You will see of what use this was to me in the sequel. The light I had already derived from love, enabled me to comprehend many passages in Horace and Virgil which had before appeared obscure. I wrote an amatory commentary upon the fourth book of the Æneid. I intend one day to publish it, and I flatter myself it will be popular.

" 'Alas!' I used to exclaim, whilst employed on that work, 'it was for a heart like mine the faithful Dido sighed, and sighed in vain!'

## IV

Now, by the strange enchantment that surrounds thee,
There's nothing—nothing thou shalt ask in vain.

Essex.

" While in my confinement Tiberge came one day to see me. I was surprised at the affectionate joy with which he saluted me. I had never, hitherto, observed any peculiar warmth in his friendship that could lead me to look upon it as anything more than the partiality common among boys of the same age. He was so altered, and had grown so manly during the five or six months since I had last seen him, that his expressive features and his manner of addressing me inspired me with a feeling of respect. He spoke more in the character of a mentor than a schoolfellow, lamented the delusion into which I had fallen, congratulated me on my reformation, which he believed was now sincere, and ended by exhorting me to profit by my youthful error, and open my eyes to the vanity of worldly pleasures. I looked at him with some astonishment, which he at once perceived.

" 'My dear chevalier,' said he to me, 'you shall hear nothing but the strict truth, of which I have assured myself by the most serious examination. I had, perhaps, as strong an inclination for pleasure as you, but Heaven had at the same time, in its mercy, blessed me with a taste for virtue. I exercised my reason in comparing the consequences of the one with those of the other, and the divine aid was graciously vouchsafed to my reflections. I conceived for the world a contempt which nothing can equal. Can you guess what it is retains me in it now,' he added, 'and that prevents me from embracing a life of solitude? Simply the sincere friendship I bear towards you. I know the excellent qualities of both your heart and head. There is no good of which you may not render yourself capable. The blandishments of pleasure have momentarily drawn you aside. What detriment to the sacred cause of virtue! Your flight from Amiens gave me such intense sorrow, that I have not since known a moment's happiness. You may judge of this by the steps it induced me to take.' He then told me how, after discovering that

I had deceived him, and gone off with my mistress, he procured horses for the purpose of pursuing me, but having the start of him by four or five hours, he found it impossible to overtake me; that he arrived, however, at St. Denis half an hour after I had left it; that, being very sure that I must have stopped in Paris, he spent six weeks there in a fruitless endeavour to discover me—visiting every place where he thought he should be likely to meet me, and that one evening he at length recognised my mistress at the play, where she was so gorgeously dressed, that he of course set it down to the account of some new lover; that he had followed her equipage to her house, and had there learned from a servant that she was entertained in this style by M. de B——. 'I did not stop here,' continued he; 'I returned next day to the house, to learn from her own lips what had become of you. She turned abruptly away when she heard the mention of your name, and I was obliged to return into the country without further information. I there learned the particulars of your adventure, and the extreme annoyance she had caused you; but I was unwilling to visit you until I could have assurance of your being in a more tranquil state.'

"'You have seen Manon then!' cried I, sighing. 'Alas! you are happier than I, who am doomed never again to behold her.' He rebuked me for this sigh, which still showed my weakness for the perfidious girl. He flattered me so adroitly upon the goodness of my mind and disposition, that he really inspired me, even on this first visit, with a strong inclination to renounce, as he had done, the pleasures of the world, and enter at once into holy orders.

"The idea was so suited to my present frame of mind, that when alone I thought of nothing else. I remembered the words of the Bishop of Amiens, who had given me the same advice, and thought only of the happiness which he predicted would result from my adoption of such a course. Piety itself took part in these suggestions. 'I shall lead a holy and a Christian life,' said I; 'I shall divide my time between study and religion, which will allow me no leisure for the perilous pleasures of love. I shall despise that which men ordinarily admire; and as I am conscious that my heart will desire nothing but what it can esteem, my cares will not be greater or more numerous than my wants and wishes.'

"I thereupon pictured to myself in anticipation a course of life peaceful and retired. I fancied a retreat embosomed in a wood, with a limpid stream of running water bounding my garden; a library, comprising the most select works; a limited circle of friends, virtuous and intellectual; a table neatly served, but frugal and temperate. To all these *agrémens* I added a literary correspondence with a friend whose residence should be in Paris, who should give me occasional information upon public affairs, less for the gratification of my curiosity, than to afford a kind of relaxation by hearing of and lamenting the busy follies of men. 'Shall not I be happy?' added I; 'will not my utmost wishes be thus gratified?' This project flattered my inclinations extremely. But after all the details of this most admirable and prudent plan, I felt that my heart still yearned for something; and that in order to leave nothing to desire in this most enchanting retirement, one ought to be able to share it with Manon.

"However, Tiberge continuing to pay me frequent visits in order to strengthen me in the purpose with which he had inspired me, I took an opportunity of opening the subject to my father. He declared that his intention ever was to leave his children free to choose a profession, and that in whatever manner I should dispose of myself, all he wished to reserve was the right of aiding me with his counsel. On this occasion he gave me some of the wisest, which tended less to divert me from my project, than to convince me of my good father's sound judgment and discretion.

"The recommencement of the scholastic year being at hand, Tiberge and I agreed to enter ourselves together at St. Sulpice, he to pursue his theological studies, and I to begin mine. His merits, which were not unknown to the bishop of the diocese, procured him the promise of a living from that prelate before our departure.

"My father, thinking me quite cured of my passion, made no objection to my taking final leave. We arrived at Paris. The Cross of Malta gave place to the ecclesiastical habit, and the designation of the Abbé de Grieux was substituted for that of chevalier. I applied so diligently to study, that in a few months I had made extraordinary progress. I never lost a moment of the day, and employed even part of the night. I soon acquired such a reputation, that I was already congratulated upon the honours which I was sure of obtaining; and, without solicitation on my part, my name was inscribed on the list for a vacant benefice. Piety was by no means neglected, and I entered with ardent devotion into all the exercises of religion. Tiberge was proud of what he considered the work of his own hands, and many a time have I seen him shed tears of delight in noticing what he styled my perfect conversion.

"It has never been matter of wonder to me that human resolutions are liable to change; one passion gives them birth, another may destroy them; but when I reflect upon the sacredness of those motives that led me to St. Sulpice, and upon the heartfelt satisfaction I enjoyed while obeying their dictation, I shudder at the facility with which I outraged them all. If it be true that the benign succour afforded by Heaven is at all times equal to the strongest of man's passions, I shall be glad to learn the nature of the deplorable ascendancy which causes us suddenly to swerve from the path of duty, without the power of offering the least resistance, and without even the slightest visitation of remorse.

"I now thought myself entirely safe from the dangers of love. I fancied that I could have preferred a single page of St. Augustine, or a quarter of an hour of Christian meditation, to every sensual gratification, not excepting any that I might have derived even from Manon's society. Nevertheless, one unlucky moment plunged me again headlong into the gulf; and my ruin was the more irreparable, because, falling at once to the same depth from whence I had been before rescued, each of the new disorders into which I now lapsed carried me deeper and deeper still down the profound abyss of vice. I had passed nearly a year at Paris without hearing of Manon. It cost me no slight effort to abstain from enquiry; but the unintermitting advice of Tiberge, and my own reflections, secured this victory over my wishes. The last months glided away so tranquilly, that I considered the memory of this charming but treacherous creature about to be consigned to eternal oblivion.

"The time arrived when I was to undergo a public examination in the class of theology: I invited several persons of consideration to honour me with their presence on the occasion. My name was mentioned in every quarter of Paris: it even reached the ears of her who had betrayed me. She had some difficulty in recognising it with the prefix of Abbé; but curiosity, or perhaps remorse for having been faithless to me (I could never after ascertain by which of these feelings she was actuated), made her at once take an interest in a name so like mine; and she came with several other women to the Sorbonne, where she was present at my examination, and had doubtless little trouble in recognising my person.

"I had not the remotest suspicion of her presence. It is well known that in these places there are private seats for ladies, where they remain screened by a curtain. I returned to St. Sulpice covered with honours and congratulations. It was six in the evening. The moment I returned, a lady was announced, who desired to speak with me. I went to meet her. Heavens! what a surprise! It was Manon. It was she indeed, but more bewitching and brilliant than I had ever beheld her. She was now in her eighteenth year. Her beauty beggars all description. The exquisite grace of her form, the mild sweetness of expression that animated her features, and her engaging air, made her seem the very personification of love. The vision was something too perfect for human beauty.

"I stood like one enchanted at beholding her. Unable to divine the object of her visit, I waited trembling and with downcast looks until she explained herself. At first, her embarrassment was equal to mine; but, seeing that I was not disposed to break silence, she raised her hand to her eyes to conceal a starting tear, and then, in a timid tone, said that she well knew she had justly earned my abhorrence by her infidelity; but that if I had ever really felt any love for her, there was not much kindness in allowing two long years to pass without enquiring after her, and as little now in seeing her in the state of mental distress in which she was, without condescending to bestow upon her a single word. I shall not attempt to describe what my feelings were as I listened to this reproof.

"She seated herself. I remained standing, with my face half turned aside, for I could not muster courage to meet her look. I several times commenced a reply without power to conclude it. At length I made an effort, and in a tone of poignant grief exclaimed : ‘ Perfidious Manon ! perfidious, perfidious creature ! ’ She had no wish, she repeated with a flood of tears, to attempt to justify her infidelity. ‘ What is your wish, then ? ’ cried I. ‘ I wish to die,’ she answered, ‘ if you will not give me back that heart, without which it is impossible to endure life.’ ‘ Take my life too, then, faithless girl ! ’ I exclaimed, in vain endeavouring to restrain my tears ; ‘ take my life also ! it is the sole sacrifice that remains for me to make, for my heart has never ceased to be thine.’

“ I had hardly uttered these words, when she rose in a transport of joy, and approached to embrace me. She loaded me with a thousand caresses. She addressed me by all the endearing appellations with which love supplies his votaries, to enable them to express the most passionate fondness. I still answered with affected coldness ; but the sudden transition from a state of quietude, such as that I had up to this moment enjoyed, to the agitation and tumult which were now kindled in my breast and tingled through my veins, thrilled me with a kind of horror, and impressed me with a vague sense that I was about to undergo some great transformation, and to enter upon a new existence.

“ We sat down close by each other. I took her hand within mine. ‘ Ah ! Manon,’ said I, with a look of sorrow, ‘ I little thought that love like mine could have been repaid with treachery ! It was a poor triumph to betray a heart of which you were the absolute mistress—whose sole happiness it was to gratify and obey you. Tell me if among others you have found any so affectionate and so devoted ? No, no ! I believe nature has cast few hearts in the same mould as mine. Tell me at least whether you have ever thought of me with regret ! Can I have any reliance on the duration of the feeling that has brought you back to me today ? I perceive too plainly that you are infinitely lovelier than ever : but I conjure you by all my past sufferings, dearest Manon, to tell me—can you in future be more faithful ? ’

“ She gave me in reply such tender assurances of her repentance, and pledged her fidelity with such solemn protestations and vows, that I was inexpressibly affected. ‘ Beauteous Manon,’ said I, with rather a profane mixture of amorous and theological expressions, ‘ you are too adorable for a created being. I feel my heart transported with triumphant rapture. It is folly to talk of liberty at St. Sulpice. Fortune and reputation are but slight sacrifices at such a shrine ! I plainly foresee it : I can read my destiny in your bright eyes ; but what abundant recompense shall I not find in your affections for any loss I may sustain ! The favours of fortune have no influence over me : fame itself appears to me but a mockery ; all my projects of a holy life were wild absurdities : in fact, any joys but those I may hope for at your side are fit objects of contempt. There are none that would not vanish into worthlessness before one single glance of thine ! ’

“ In promising her, however, a full remission of her past frailties, I enquired how she permitted herself to be led astray by B——. She informed me that having seen her at her window, he became passionately in love with her; that he made his advances in the true style of a mercantile cit;—that is to say, by giving her to understand in his letter, that his payments would be proportioned to her favours; that she had admitted his overtures at first with no other intention than that of getting from him such a sum as might enable us to live without inconvenience; but that he had so bewildered her with splendid promises, that she allowed herself to be misled by degrees. She added, that I ought to have formed some notion of the remorse she experienced, by her grief on the night of our separation; and assured me that, in spite of the splendour in which he maintained her, she had never known a moment's happiness with him, not only, she said, because he was utterly devoid of that delicacy of sentiment and of those agreeable manners which I possessed, but because even in the midst of the amusements which he unceasingly procured her, she could never shake off the recollection of my love, or her own ingratitude. She then spoke of Tiberge, and the extreme embarrassment his visit caused her. 'A dagger's point,' she added, 'could not have struck more terror to my heart. I turned from him, unable to sustain the interview for a moment.'

"She continued to inform me how she had been apprised of my residence at Paris, of the change in my condition, and of her witnessing my examination at the Sorbonne. She told me how agitated she had been during my intellectual conflict with the examiner; what difficulty she felt in restraining her tears as well as her sighs, which were more than once on the point of spurning all control, and bursting forth; that she was the last person to leave the hall of examination, for fear of betraying her distress, and that, following only the instinct of her own heart, and her ardent desires, she came direct to the seminary, with the firm resolution of surrendering life itself, if she found me cruel enough to withhold my forgiveness.

"Could any savage remain unmoved by such proofs of cordial repentance as those I had just witnessed? For my part, I felt at the moment that I could gladly have given up all the bishoprics in Christendom for Manon. I asked what course she would recommend in our present emergency. 'It is requisite,' she replied, 'at all events, to quit the seminary, and settle in some safer place.' I consented to everything she proposed. She got into her carriage to go and wait for me at the corner of the street. I escaped the next moment, without attracting the porter's notice. I entered the carriage, and we drove off to a Jew's. I there resumed my lay-dress and sword. Manon furnished the supplies, for I was without a sou, and fearing that I might meet with some new impediment, she would not consent to my returning to my room at St. Sulpice for my purse. My finances were in truth wretchedly low, and hers more than sufficiently enriched by the liberality of M. de B—— to make her think lightly of my loss. We consulted together at the Jew's as to the course we should now adopt.

"In order to enhance the sacrifice she had made for me of her late lover, she determined to treat him without the least ceremony. 'I shall leave him all his furniture,' she said; 'it belongs to him: but I shall assuredly carry off, as I have a right to do, the jewels, and about sixty thousand francs, which I have had from him in the last two years. I have given him no control over me,' she added, 'so that we may remain without apprehension in Paris, taking a convenient house, where we shall live, oh how happily together!'

"I represented to her that, although there might be no danger for her, there was a great deal for me, who must be sooner or later infallibly recognised, and continually exposed to a repetition of the trials I had before endured. She gave me to understand that she could not quit Paris without regret. I had such a dread of giving her annoyance, that there were no risks I would not have encountered for her sake. However, we compromised matters by resolving to take a house in some village near Paris, from whence it would be easy for us to come into town whenever pleasure or business required it. We fixed on Chaillot, which is at a convenient distance. Manon at once returned to her house, and I went to wait for her at a side-gate of the garden of the Tuileries.

"She returned an hour after, in a hired carriage, with a servant-maid, and several trunks, which contained her dresses, and everything she had of value.

"We were not long on our way to Chaillot. We lodged the first night at the inn, in order to have time to find a suitable house, or at least a commodious lodging. We found one to our taste the next morning.

"My happiness now appeared to be secured beyond the reach of fate. Manon was everything most sweet and amiable. She was so delicate and so unceasing in her attentions to me, that I deemed myself but too bountifully rewarded for all my past troubles. As we had both, by this time, acquired some experience, we discussed rationally the state of our finances. Sixty thousand francs (the amount of our wealth) was not a sum that could be expected to last our whole life; besides, we were neither of us much disposed to control our expenses. Manon's chief virtue assuredly was not economy, any more than it was mine. This was my proposition. 'Sixty thousand francs,' said I, 'may support us for ten years. Two thousand crowns a year will suffice, if we continue to live at Chaillot. We shall keep up appearances, but live frugally. Our only expense will be occasionally a carriage, and the theatres. We shall do everything in moderation. You like the opera; we shall go twice a week, in the season. As for play, we shall limit ourselves; so that our losses must never exceed three crowns. It is impossible but that in the space of ten years some change must occur in my family: my father is even now of an advanced age; he may die; in which event I must inherit a fortune, and we shall then be above all other fears.'

"This arrangement would not have been by any means the most silly act of my life, if we had only been prudent enough to persevere in its execution; but our resolutions hardly lasted longer than a month. Manon's passion was for amusement; she was the only object of mine. New temptations to expense constantly presented themselves, and far from regretting the money which she sometimes prodigally lavished, I was the first to procure for her everything likely to afford her pleasure. Our residence at Chaillot began even to appear tiresome.

" Winter was approaching, and the whole world returning to town ; the country had a deserted look. She proposed to me to take a house in Paris. I did not approve of this ; but, in order partly at least to satisfy her, I said that we might hire furnished apartments, and that we might sleep there whenever we were late in quitting the assembly, whither we often went ; for the inconvenience of returning so late to Chaillot was her excuse for wishing to leave it. We had thus two dwellings, one in town and the other in the country. This change soon threw our affairs into confusion, and led to two adventures, which eventually caused our ruin.

" Manon had a brother in the Guards. He unfortunately lived in the very street in which we had taken lodgings. He one day recognised his sister at the window, and hastened over to us. He was a fellow of the rudest manners, and without the slightest principle of honour. He entered the room swearing in the most horrible way ; and as he knew part of his sister's history, he loaded her with abuse and reproaches.

" I had gone out the moment before, which was doubtless fortunate for either him or me, for I was little disposed to brook an insult. I only returned to the lodgings after he had left them. The low spirits in which I found Manon convinced me at once that something extraordinary had occurred. She told me of the provoking scene she had just gone through, and of the brutal threats of her brother. I felt such indignation, that I wished to proceed at once to avenge her, when she entreated me with tears to desist.

" While we were still talking of the adventure, the guardsman again entered the room in which we sat, without even waiting to be announced. Had I known him, he should not have met from me as civil a reception as he did ; but saluting us with a smile upon his countenance, he addressed himself to Manon, and said, he was come to make excuses for his violence ; that he had supposed her to be living a life of shame and disgrace, and it was this notion that excited his rage ; but having since made enquiry from one of our servants, he had learned such a character of me, that his only wish was now to be on terms with us both.

" Although this admission, of having gone for information to one of my own servants, had in it something ludicrous as well as indelicate, I acknowledged his compliments with civility, I thought by doing so to please Manon, and I was not deceived—she was delighted at the reconciliation. We made him stay to dine with us.

" In a little time he became so familiar, that hearing us speak of our return to Chaillot, he insisted on accompanying us. We were obliged to give him a seat in our carriage. This was in fact putting him into possession, for he soon began to feel so much pleasure in our company, that he made our house his home, and made himself in some measure master of all that belonged to us. He called me his brother, and, under the semblance of fraternal freedom, he put himself on such a footing as to introduce all his friends without ceremony into our house at Chaillot, and there entertain them at our expense. His magnificent uniforms were procured of my tailor and charged to me, and he even contrived to make Manon and me responsible for all his debts. I pretended to be blind to this system of tyranny, rather than annoy Manon, and even to take no notice of the sums of money which from time to time he received from her. No doubt, as he played very deep, he was honest enough to repay her a part sometimes, when luck turned in his favour; but our finances were utterly inadequate to supply, for any length of time, demands of such magnitude and frequency.

"I was on the point of coming to an understanding with him, in order to put an end to the system, when an unfortunate accident saved me that trouble, by involving us in inextricable ruin.

"One night we stopped in Paris to sleep, as it had now indeed become our constant habit. The servant-maid who on such occasions remained alone at Chaillot, came early the next morning to inform me that our house had taken fire in the night, and that the flames had been extinguished with great difficulty. I asked whether the furniture had suffered. She answered, that there had been such confusion, owing to the multitude of strangers who came to offer assistance, that she could hardly ascertain what damage had been done. I was principally uneasy about our money, which had been locked up in a little box. I went off in haste to Chaillot. Vain hope! the box had disappeared!

"I discovered that one could love money without being a miser. This loss afflicted me to such a degree that I was almost out of my mind. I saw at one glance to what new calamities I should be exposed: poverty was the least of them. I knew Manon thoroughly; I had already had abundant proof that, although faithful and attached to me under happier circumstances, she could not be depended upon in want: pleasure and plenty she loved too well to sacrifice them for my sake. 'I shall lose her!' I cried; 'miserable chevalier! you are about then to lose all that you love on earth!' This thought agitated me to such a degree that I actually for some moments considered whether it would not be best for me to end at once all my miseries by death. I however preserved presence of mind enough to reflect whether I was entirely without resource, and an idea occurred to me which quieted my despair. It would not be impossible, I thought, to conceal our loss from Manon; and I might perhaps discover some ways and means of supplying her, so as to ward off the inconveniences of poverty.

"I had calculated in endeavouring to comfort myself, that twenty thousand crowns would support us for ten years. Suppose that these ten years had now elapsed, and that none of the events which I had looked for in my family had occurred. What then would have been my course? I hardly know; but whatever I should then have done, why may I not do now? How many are there in Paris, who have neither my talents, nor the natural advantages I possess, and who, notwithstanding, owe their support to the exercise of their talents, such as they are?

"'Has not Providence,' I added, while reflecting on the different conditions of life, 'arranged things wisely?' The greater number of the powerful and the rich are fools. No one who knows anything of the world can doubt that. How admirable is the compensating justice thereof! If wealth brought with it talent also, the rich would be too happy, and other men too wretched. To these latter are given personal advantages and genius, to help them out of misery and want. Some of them share the riches of the wealthy by administering to their pleasures, or by making them their dupes; others afford them instruction, and endeavour to make them decent members of society; to be sure, they do not always succeed; but that was probably not the intention of the divine wisdom. In every case they derive a benefit from their labours by living at the expense of their pupils; and, in whatever point of view it is considered, the follies of the rich are a bountiful source of revenue to the humbler classes.

"These thoughts restored me a little to my spirits and to my reason. I determined first to consult M. Lescaut, the brother of Manon. He knew Paris perfectly; and I had too many opportunities of learning that it was neither from his own estates, nor from the king's pay, that he derived the principal portion of his income. I had about thirty-three crowns left, which I fortunately happened to have about me. I showed him my purse, and explained to him my misfortune and my fears, and then asked him whether I had any alternative between starvation and blowing out my brains in despair. He coolly replied that suicide was the resource of fools. As to dying of want, there were hundreds of men of genius who found themselves reduced to that state when they would not employ their talents; that it was for myself to discover what I was capable of doing, and he told me to reckon upon his assistance and his advice in any enterprise I might undertake.

"'Vague enough, M. Lescaut!' said I to him: 'my wants demand a more speedy remedy; for what am I to say to Manon?' 'Apropos of Manon,' replied he, 'what is it that annoys you about her? Cannot you always find in her wherewithal to meet your wants, when you wish it? Such a person ought to support us all, you and me as well as herself. He cut short the answer which I was about to give to such unfeeling' and brutal impertinence, by going on to say, that before night he would ensure me a thousand crowns to divide between us, if I would only follow his advice; that he was acquainted with a nobleman, who was so liberal in affairs of the kind, that he was certain he would not hesitate for a moment to give the sum named for the favours of such a girl as Manon.

"I stopped him. 'I had a better opinion of you,' said I; 'I had imagined that your motive for bestowing your friendship upon me was very different indeed from the one you now betray.' With the greatest effrontery he acknowledged that he had been always of the same mind, and that his sister having once sacrificed her virtue, though it might be to the man she most loved, he would never have consented to a reconciliation with her, but with the hope of deriving some advantage from her past misconduct.

"It was easy to see that we had been hitherto his dupes. Notwithstanding the disgust with which his proposition inspired me, still, as I felt that I had occasion for his services, I said, with apparent complacency, that we ought only to entertain such a plan as a last resource. I begged of him to suggest some other.

" He proposed to me to turn my youth and the good looks nature had bestowed upon me to some account, by establishing a liaison with some generous old dame. This was just as little to my taste, for it would necessarily have rendered me unfaithful to Manon.

" I mentioned play as the easiest scheme, and the most suitable to my present situation. He admitted that play certainly was a resource, but that it was necessary to consider the point well. 'Mere play,' said he, 'with its ordinary chances, is the certain road to ruin; and as for attempting, alone and without an ally, to employ the little means an adroit man has for correcting the vagaries of luck, it would be too dangerous an experiment.' There was, he stated, a third course, which was to enter into what he called a partnership; but he feared his confederates would consider my youth an objection to my admittance. He, however, promised to use his influence with them; and, what was more than I expected at his hands, he said that he would supply me with a little money whenever I had pressing occasion for any. The only favour I then asked of him was to say nothing to Manon of the loss I had experienced, nor of the subject of our conversation.

" I certainly derived little comfort from my visit to Lescaut; I felt even sorry for having confided my secret to him: not a single thing had he done for me that I might not just as well have done for myself, without troubling him; and I could not help dreading that he would violate his promise to keep the secret from Manon. I had also reason to apprehend, from his late avowals, that he might form the design of making use of her for his own vile purposes, or at least of advising her to quit me for some happier and more wealthy lover. This idea brought in its train a thousand reflections, which had no other effect than to torment me, and throw me again into the state of despair in which I had passed the morning. It occurred to me, more than once, to write to my father; and to pretend a new reformation, in order to obtain some pecuniary assistance from him; but I could not forget that, notwithstanding all his natural love and affection for me, he had shut me up for six months in a confined room for my first transgression; and I was certain that, after the scandalous sensation caused by my flight from St. Sulpice, he would be sure to treat me with infinitely more rigour now.

" At length, out of this chaos of fancies came an idea that all at once restored ease to my mind, and which I was surprised at not having hit upon sooner; this was, to go again to my friend Tiberge, in whom I might be always sure of finding the same unfailing zeal and friendship. There is nothing more glorious—nothing that does more honour to true virtue, than the confidence with which one approaches a friend of tried integrity; no apprehension, no risk of unkind repulse: if it be not always in his power to afford the required succour, one is sure at least of meeting kindness and compassion. The heart of the poor supplicant, which remains impenetrably closed to the rest of the world, opens in his presence, as a flower expands before the orb of day, from which it instinctively knows it can derive a cheering and benign influence only.

"I consider it a blessing to have thought so apropos of Tiberge, and resolved to take measures to find him before evening. I returned at once to my lodgings to write him a line, and fix a convenient place for our meeting. I requested secrecy and discretion, as the most important service he could render me under present circumstances.

"The pleasure I derived from the prospect of seeing Tiberge dissipated every trace of melancholy, which Manon would not have failed otherwise to detect in my countenance. I described our misfortune at Chaillot as a trifle which ought not to annoy her; and Paris being the spot she liked best in the world, she was not sorry to hear me say that it would be necessary for us to remain there entirely, until the little damage was repaired which had been caused by the fire at Chaillot.

"In an hour I received an answer from Tiberge, who promised to be at the appointed rendezvous. I went there punctually. I certainly felt some shame at encountering a friend whose presence alone ought to be a reproach to my iniquities; but I was supported by the opinion I had of the goodness of his heart, as well as by my anxiety about Manon.

"I had begged of him to meet me in the garden of the Palais Royal. He was there before me. He hastened towards me, the moment he saw me approach and shook me warmly by both hands. I said that I could not help feeling perfectly ashamed to meet him, and that I was weighed down by a sense of my ingratitude; that the first thing I implored of him was to tell me whether I might still consider him my friend, after having so justly incurred the loss of his esteem and affection. He replied, in the kindest possible manner, that it was not in the nature of things to destroy his regard for me; that my misfortunes even, or, if he might so call them, my faults and transgressions, had but increased the interest he felt for me; but that he must confess his affection was not unalloyed by a sentiment of the liveliest sorrow, such as a person may be supposed to feel at seeing a beloved object on the brink of ruin, and beyond the reach of his assistance.

"We sat down upon a bench. 'Alas!' said I with a deep sigh, 'your compassion must be indeed great, my dear Tiberge, if you assure me it is equal to my sufferings. I am almost ashamed to recount them, for I confess they have been brought on by no very creditable course of conduct: the results, however, are so truly melancholy, that a friend even less attached than you would be affected by the recital.'

"He then begged of me, in proof of friendship, to let him know, without any disguise, all that had occurred to me since my departure from St. Sulpice. I gratified him; and so far from concealing anything, or attempting to extenuate my faults, I spoke of my passion with all the ardour with which it still inspired me. I represented it to him as one of those especial visitations of fate, which draw on the devoted victim to his ruin, and which it is as impossible for virtue itself to resist, as for human wisdom to foresee. I painted to him in the most vivid colours, my excitement, my fears, the state of despair in which I had been two hours before I saw him, and into which I should be again plunged, if I found my friends as relentless as fate had been. I at length made such an impression upon poor Tiberge, that I saw he was as much affected by compassion, as I by the recollection of my sufferings.

"He took my hand, and exhorted me to have courage and be comforted; but, as he seemed to consider it settled that Manon and I were to separate, I gave him at once to understand that it was that very separation I considered as the most intolerable of all my misfortunes; and that I was ready to endure not only the last degree of misery, but death itself, of the cruellest kind, rather than seek relief in a remedy worse than the whole accumulation of my woes.

"'Explain yourself, then,' said he to me; 'what assistance can I afford you, if you reject everything I propose?' I had not courage to tell him that it was from his purse I wanted relief. He, however, comprehended it in the end; and acknowledging that he believed he now understood me, he remained for a moment in an attitude of thought, with the air of a person revolving something in his mind. 'Do not imagine,' he presently said, 'that my hesitation arises from any diminution of my zeal and friendship; but to what an alternative do you now reduce me, since I must either refuse you the assistance you ask, or violate my most sacred duty in affording it! For is it not participating in your sin to furnish you with the means of continuing its indulgence?'

"'However,' continued he, after a moment's thought, 'it is perhaps the excited state into which want has thrown you, that denies you now the liberty of choosing the proper path. Man's mind must be at rest, to know the luxury of wisdom and virtue. I can afford to let you have some money; and permit me, my dear chevalier, to impose but one condition; that is, that you let me know the place of your abode, and allow me the opportunity of using my exertions to reclaim you. I know that there is in your heart a love of virtue, and that you have been only led astray by the violence of your passions.'

"I, of course, agreed to everything he asked, and only begged of him to deplore the malign destiny which rendered me callous to the counsels of so virtuous a friend. He then took me to a banker of his acquaintance, who gave one hundred and seventy crowns for his note of hand, which was taken as cash. I have already said that he was not rich. His living was worth about six thousand francs a year, but as this was the first year since his induction, he had as yet touched none of the receipts, and it was out of the future income that he made me this advance.

"I felt the full force of his generosity, even to such a degree as almost to deplore the fatal passion which thus led me to break through all the restraints of duty. Virtue had for a moment the ascendancy in my heart, and made me sensible of my shame and degradation. But this was soon over. For Manon I could have given up my hopes of heaven, and when I again found myself at her side, I wondered how I could for an instant have considered myself degraded by my passion for this enchanting girl.

"Manon was a creature of most extraordinary disposition. Never had mortal a greater contempt for money, and yet she was haunted by perpetual dread of wanting it. Her only desire was for pleasure and amusement. She would never have wished to possess a sou, if pleasure could be procured without money. She never even cared what our purse contained, provided she could pass the day agreeably; so that, being neither fond of play nor at all dazzled by the desire of great wealth, nothing was more easy than to satisfy her, by daily finding out amusements suited to her moderate wishes. But it became by habit a thing so absolutely necessary for her to have her mind thus occupied, that, without it, it was impossible to exercise the smallest influence over her temper or inclinations. Although she loved me tenderly, and I was the only person, as she often declared, in whose society she could ever find the pure enjoyments of love, yet I felt thoroughly convinced that her attachment could not withstand certain apprehensions. She would have preferred me, even with a moderate fortune, to the whole world; but I had no kind of doubt that she would, on the other hand, abandon me for some new M. de B——, when I had nothing more to offer her than fidelity and love.

"I resolved therefore so to curtail my own individual expenses, as to be able always to meet hers, and rather to deprive myself of a thousand necessaries than even to limit her extravagance. The carriage made me more uneasy than anything else, for I saw no chance of being able to maintain either coachman or horses.

"I told M. Lescaut of my difficulties, and did not conceal from him that I had received a thousand francs from a friend. He repeated, that if I wished to try the chances of the gaming-table, he was not without hopes that, by spending a few crowns in entertaining his associates, I might be, on his recommendation, admitted into the association. With all my repugnance to cheating, I yielded to dire necessity.

"Lescaut presented me that night as a relation of his own. He added, that I was the more likely to succeed in my new profession, from wanting the favours of fortune. However, to show them that I was not quite reduced to the lowest ebb, he said it was my intention to treat them with a supper. The offer was accepted, and I entertained them *en prince*. They talked a good deal about my fashionable appearance and the apparent amiability of my disposition; they said that the best hopes might be entertained of me, because there was something in my countenance that bespoke the gentleman, and no one therefore could have a suspicion of my honesty: they voted thanks to Lescaut for having introduced so promising a novice, and deputed one of the members to instruct me for some days in the necessary manœuvres.

"The principal scene of my exploits was the hotel of Transylvania, where there was a faro table in one room, and other games of cards and dice in the gallery. This *academy* was kept by the Prince of R——, who then lived at Clagny, and most of his officers belonged to our society. Shall I mention it to my shame? I profited quickly by my instructor's tuition. I acquired an amazing facility in sleight of hand tricks, and learned in perfection to *sauter le coup*; with the help of a pair of long ruffles, I shuffled so adroitly as to defy the quickest observer, and I ruined several fair players. My unrivalled skill so quickened the progress of my fortunes, that I found myself master, in a few weeks, of very considerable sums, besides what I divided in good faith with my companions.

"I had no longer any fear of communicating to Manon the extent of our loss at Chaillot, and, to console her on the announcement of such disastrous news, I took a furnished house, where we established ourselves in all the pride of opulence and security.

"Tiberge was in the habit, at this period, of paying me frequent visits. He was never tired of his moral lectures. Over and over again did he represent to me the injury I was inflicting upon my conscience, my honour, and my fortune. I received all his advice kindly, and although I had not the smallest inclination to adopt it, I had no doubt of its sincerity, for I knew its source. Sometimes I rallied him good-humouredly, and entreated him not to be more tight-laced than some other priests were, and even bishops, who by no means considered a mistress incompatible with a good and holy life. 'Look,' I said, 'at Manon's eyes, and tell me if there is one in the long catalogue of sins that might not there find a plea of justification.' He bore these sallies patiently, and carried his forbearance almost too far: but when he saw my funds increase, and that I had not only returned him the hundred and seventy crowns, but having hired a new house and trebled my expenses, I had plunged deeper than ever into a life of pleasure, he changed his tone and manner towards me. He lamented my obduracy. He warned me against the chastisement of the Divine wrath, and predicted some of the miseries with which indeed I was shortly afterwards visited. 'It is impossible,' he said, 'that the money which now serves to support your debaucheries can have been acquired honourably. You have come by it unjustly, and in the same way shall it be taken from you. The most awful punishment Heaven could inflict would be to allow you the undisturbed enjoyment of it. All my advice,' he added, 'has been useless; I too plainly perceive that it will shortly become troublesome to you. I now take my leave; you are a weak, as well as an ungrateful friend! May your criminal enjoyments vanish as a shadow! may your ill-gotten wealth leave you without a resource; and may you yourself remain alone and deserted, to learn the vanity of these things, which now divert you from better pursuits! When that time arrives, you will find me disposed to love and to serve you; this day ends our intercourse, and I once for all avow my horror of the life you are leading.'

"It was in my room and in Manon's presence that he delivered this apostolical harangue. He rose to depart. I was about to detain him; but was prevented by Manon, who said it was better to let the madman go.

"What he said, however, did not fail to make some impression upon me. I notice these brief passages of my life when I experienced a returning sentiment of virtue, because it was to those traces, however light, that I was afterwards indebted for whatever of fortitude I displayed under the most trying circumstances.

"Manon's caresses soon dissipated the annoyance this scene had caused me. We continued to lead a life entirely devoted to pleasure and love. The increase of our wealth only redoubled our affection. There were none happier among all the devotees of Venus and Fortune. Heavens! why call this a world of misery, when it can furnish a life of such rapturous enjoyment? But alas, it is too soon over! For what ought man to sigh, could such felicity but last for ever? Ours shared the common fate—in being of short duration, and followed by lasting regrets

"I had realised by play such a considerable sum of money, that I thought of investing a portion of it. My servants were not ignorant of my good luck, particularly my valet and Manon's own maid, before whom we often talked without any reserve. The maid was handsome, and my valet in love with her. They knew they had to deal with a young and inexperienced couple, whom they fancied they could impose upon without much difficulty. They laid a plan, and executed it with so much skill, that they reduced us to a state from which it was never afterwards possible for us to extricate ourselves.

"Having supped one evening at Lescaut's, it was about midnight when we returned home. I asked for my valet, and Manon for her maid; neither one nor the other could be found. They had not been seen in the house since eight o'clock, and had gone out, after having some cases carried before them, according to orders which they pretended to have received from me. I at once foresaw a part of the truth, but my suspicions were infinitely surpassed by what presented itself on going into my room. The lock of my closet had been forced, and my cash as well as my best clothes were gone. While I stood stupefied with amazement, Manon came, in the greatest alarm, to inform me that her apartment had been rifled in the same manner.

"This blow was so perfectly astounding, so cruel, that it was with difficulty I could refrain from tears. The dread of infecting Manon with my despair made me assume a more contented air. I said, smiling, that I should avenge myself upon some unhappy dupe at the hotel of Transylvania. However, she appeared so sensibly affected, that her grief increased my sorrow infinitely more than my attempt succeeded in supporting her spirits. 'We are destroyed!' said she, with tears in her eyes. I endeavoured, in vain, by my entreaties and caresses, to console her. My own lamentations betrayed my distress and despair. In fact, we were so completely ruined, that we were bereft almost of decent covering.

"I determined to send off at once for Lescaut. He advised me to go immediately to the lieutenant of police, and to give information also to the Grand Provost of Paris. I went, but it was to add to my calamities only; for, independently of my visit producing not the smallest good effect, I, by my absence, allowed Lescaut time for discussion with his sister, during which he did not fail to inspire her with the most horrible resolutions. He spoke to her about M. G—— M——, an old voluptuary, who paid prodigally for his pleasures; he so glowingly described the advantages of such a connection, that she entered into all his plans. This discreditable arrangement was all concluded before my return, and the execution of it only postponed till the next morning, after Lescaut should have apprised G—— M——.

"I found him, on my return, waiting for me at my house; but Manon had retired to her own apartment, and she had desired the footman to tell me that, having need of repose, she hoped she should not be disturbed that night. Lescaut left me, after offering me a few crowns which I accepted.

"It was nearly four o'clock when I retired to bed; and having revolved in my mind various schemes for retrieving my fortunes, I fell asleep so late that I did not awake till between eleven and twelve o'clock. I rose at once to enquire after Manon's health; they told me that she had gone out an hour before with her brother, who had come for her in a hired carriage. Although there appeared something mysterious in such a proceeding, I endeavoured to check my rising suspicions. I allowed some hours to pass, during which I amused myself with reading. At length, being unable any longer to stifle my uneasiness, I paced up and down the apartments. A sealed letter upon Manon's table at last caught my eye. It was addressed to me, and in her handwriting. I felt my blood freeze as I opened it; it was in these words:

I protest to you, dearest chevalier, that you are the idol of my heart, and that you are the only being on earth whom I can truly love; but do you not see, my own poor dear chevalier, that in the situation to which we are now reduced, fidelity would be worse than madness? Do you think tenderness possibly compatible with starvation? For my part, hunger would be sure to drive me to some fatal end. Heaving some day a sigh for love, I should find it was my last. I adore you, rely upon that; but leave to me, for a short while, the management of our fortunes. God help the man who falls into my hands. My only wish is to render my chevalier rich and happy. My brother will tell you about me; he can vouch for my grief in yielding to the necessity of parting from you.

"I remained, after reading this, in a state which it would be difficult to describe; for even now I know not the nature of the feelings which then agitated me. It was one of those unique situations of which others can never have experienced anything even approaching to similarity. It is impossible to explain it, because other persons can have no idea of its nature; and one can hardly even analyse it to oneself. Memory furnishes nothing that will connect it with the past, and therefore ordinary language is inadequate to describe it. Whatever was its nature, however, it is certain that grief, hate, jealousy, and shame entered into its composition. Fortunate would it have proved for me if love also had not been a component part!

"'That she loves me,' I exclaimed, 'I can believe; but could she, without being a monster, hate me? What right can man ever have to woman's affections which I had not to Manon's? What is left to me, after all the sacrifices I have made for her sake? Yet she abandons me, and the ungrateful creature thinks to screen herself from my reproaches by professions of love! She pretends to dread starvation! God of love, what grossness of sentiment! What an answer to the refinement of my adoration! I had no dread of that kind; I, who have almost sought starvation for her sake, by renouncing fortune and the comforts of my father's house! I, who denied myself actual necessaries, in order to gratify her little whims and caprices! She adores me, she says. If you adored me, ungrateful creature, I well know what course you would have taken; you would never have quitted me, at least without saying adieu. It is only I who can tell the pangs and torments of being separated from all one loves. I must have taken leave of my senses, to have voluntarily brought all this misery upon myself.'

"My lamentations were interrupted by a visit I little expected; it was from Lescaut. 'Assassin!' cried I, putting my hand upon my sword, 'where is Manon? what have you done with her?' My agitation startled him. He replied, that if this was the reception he was to meet, when he came to offer me the most essential service it was in his power to render me, he should take his leave, and never again cross my threshold. I ran to the door of the apartment, which I shut. 'Do not imagine,' I said, turning towards him, 'that you can once more make a dupe of me with your lies and inventions. Either defend your life, or tell me where I can find Manon.' 'How impatient you are!' replied he; 'that was in reality the object of my visit. I came to announce a piece of good fortune which you little expected, and for which you will probably feel somewhat grateful.' My curiosity was at once excited.

"He informed me that Manon, totally unable to endure the dread of want, and, above all, the certainty of being at once obliged to dispense with her equipage, had begged of him to make her acquainted with M. G—— M——, who had a character for liberality. He carefully avoided telling me that this was the result of his own advice, and that he had prepared the way before he introduced his sister. 'I took her there this morning,' said he, 'and the fellow was so enchanted with her looks that he at once invited her to accompany him to his country seat, where he is gone to pass some days. As I plainly perceived,' said Lescaut, 'the advantage it may be to you, I took care to let him know that she had lately experienced very considerable losses; and I so piqued his generosity that he began by giving her four hundred crowns. I told him that was well enough for a commencement, but that my sister would have, for the future, many demands for money; that she had the charge of a young brother, who had been thrown upon her hands since the death of our parents; and that, if he wished to prove himself worthy of her affections, he would not allow her to suffer uneasiness upon account of this child, whom she regarded as part of herself. This speech produced its effect, he at once promised to take a house for you and Manon, for you must know that you are the poor little orphan. He undertook to set you up in furniture, and to give you four hundred livres a month, which if I calculate rightly, will amount to four thousand eight hundred per annum. He left orders with his steward to look out for a house, and to have it in readiness by the time he returned. You will soon, therefore, again see Manon, who begged of me to give you a thousand tender messages, and to assure you that she loves you more dearly than ever.'

## V

Infected with that leprosy of lust,
Which taints the hoariest years of vicious men
Making them ransack to the very last
The dregs of pleasure for their vanished joys.
BYRON.

"ON sitting down to reflect upon this strange turn of fate, I found myself so perplexed, and consequently so incapable of arriving at any rational conclusion, that I allowed Lescaut to put repeated questions to me without in the slightest degree attending to their purport. It was then that honour and virtue made me feel the most poignant remorse, and that I recalled with bitterness Amiens, my father's house, St. Sulpice, and every spot where I had ever lived in happy innocence. By what a terrific interval was I now separated from that blessed state! I beheld it no longer but as a dim shadow in the distance, still attracting my regrets and desires, but without the power of rousing me to exertion. 'By what fatality,' said I, 'have I become thus degraded? Love is not a guilty passion! why then has it been to me the source of profligacy and distress? Who prevented me from leading a virtuous and tranquil life with Manon? Why did I not marry her before I obtained any concession from her love? Would not my father, who had the tenderest regard for me, have given his consent, if I had taken the fair and candid course of soliciting him? Yes, my father would himself have cherished her as one far too good to be his son's wife! I should have been happy in the love of Manon, in the affection of my father, in the esteem of the world, with a moderate portion of the good things of life, and above all with the consciousness of virtue. Disastrous change! Into what an infamous character is it here proposed that I should sink? To share—— But can I hesitate, if Manon herself suggests it, and if I am to lose her except upon such conditions? 'Lescaut,' said I, putting my hands to my eyes as if to shut out such a horrifying vision, 'if your intention was to render me a service, I give you thanks. You might perhaps have struck out a more reputable course, but it is so settled, is it not? Let us then only think of profiting by your labour, and fulfilling your engagements.'

"Lescaut, who had been considerably embarrassed, not only by my fury, but by the long silence which followed it, was too happy to see me now take a course so different from what he had anticipated. He had not a particle of courage, of which indeed I have, in the sequel of my story, abundant proof. 'Yes, yes,' he quickly answered, 'it is good service I have rendered you, and you will find that we shall derive infinitely more advantage from it than you now expect.' We consulted then as to the best mode of preventing the suspicions which G—— M—— might entertain of our relationship, when he found me older and of riper manhood than he probably imagined. The only plan we could hit upon was to assume in his presence an innocent and provincial air, and to persuade him that it was my intention to enter the Church, and that with that view I was obliged to go every day to the college. We also determined that I should appear as awkward as I possibly could the first time I was admitted to the honour of an introduction.

"He returned to town three or four days after, and at once conducted Manon to the house which his steward had in the meantime prepared. She immediately apprised Lescaut of her return, and he having informed me, we went together to her new abode. The old lover had already gone out.

"In spite of the submission with which I had resigned myself to her wishes, I could not, at our meeting, repress the compunctious visitings of my conscience. I appeared before her grieved and dejected. The joy I felt at seeing her once more could not altogether dispel my sorrow for her infidelity: she, on the contrary, appeared transported with the pleasure of seeing me. She accused me of coldness. I could not help muttering the words perfidious and unfaithful, though they were profusely mixed with sighs.

"At first she laughed at me for my simplicity; but when she found that I continued to look at her with an unchanging expression of melancholy, and that I could not bring myself to enter with alacrity into a scene so repugnant to all my feelings, she went alone into her boudoir. I very soon followed her, and then I found her in a flood of tears. I asked the cause of her sorrow. 'You can easily understand it,' said she; 'how can you wish me to live, if my presence can no longer have any other effect than to give you an air of sadness and chagrin? Not one kiss have you given me during the long hour you have been in the house, while you have received my caresses with the dignified indifference of a Grand Turk, receiving the forced homage of the Sultanas of his harem.'

"'Hearken to me, Manon,' said I, embracing her; 'I cannot conceal from you that my heart is bitterly afflicted. I do not now allude to the uneasiness your sudden flight caused me, nor to the unkindness of quitting me without a word of consolation, after having passed the night away from me. The pleasure of seeing you again would more than compensate for all; but do you imagine that I can reflect without sighs and tears upon the degrading and unhappy life which you now wish me to lead in this house? Say nothing of my birth, or of my feelings of honour; love like mine derives no aid from arguments of that feeble nature; but do you imagine that I can without emotion see my love so badly recompensed, or rather so cruelly treated, by an ungrateful and unfeeling mistress?'

"She interrupted me. 'Stop, chevalier,' said she, 'it is useless to torture me with reproaches, which, coming from you, always pierce my heart. I see what annoys you. I had hoped that you would have agreed to the project which I had devised for mending our shattered fortunes, and it was from a feeling of delicacy to you that I began the execution of it without your assistance; but I give it up since it does not meet your approbation.' She added that she would now merely request a little patient forbearance during the remainder of the day; that she had already received five hundred crowns from the old gentleman, and that he had promised to bring her that evening a magnificent pearl necklace with other jewels, and, in advance, half of the yearly pension he had engaged to allow her. 'Leave me only time enough,' said she to me, to get possession of these presents; I promise you that he will have little to boast of from his connection with me, for in the country I repulsed all his advances, putting him off till our return to town. It is true that he has kissed my hand a thousand times over, and it is but just that he should pay for even this amusement: I am sure that, considering his riches as well as his age, five or six thousand francs is not an unreasonable price!'

"Her determination was of more value in my eyes than twenty thousand crowns. I could feel that I was not yet bereft of every sentiment of honour, by the satisfaction I experienced at escaping thus from infamy. But I was born for brief joys, and miseries of long duration. Fate never rescued me from one precipice, but to lead me to another. When I had expressed my delight to Manon at this change in her intentions, I told her she had better inform Lescaut of it, in order that we might take our measures in concert. At first he murmured, but the money in hand induced him to enter into our views. It was then determined that we should all meet at G——M——'s supper table, and that, for two reasons: first, for the amusement of passing me off as a schoolboy, and brother to Manon ; and secondly, to prevent the old profligate from taking any liberties with his mistress, on the strength of his liberal payments in advance. Lescaut and I were to retire, when he went to the room where he expected to pass the night ; and Manon, instead of following him, promised to come out, and join us. Lescaut undertook to have a coach waiting at the door.

"The supper hour having arrived, M. G—— M—— made his appearance. Already Lescaut was with his sister in the supper room. The moment the lover entered, he presented his fair one with a complete set of pearls, necklaces, ear-rings, and bracelets, which must have cost at least a thousand crowns. He then placed on the table before her, in louis d'or, two thousand four hundred francs, the half of her year's allowance. He seasoned his present with many pretty speeches in the true style of the old court. Manon could not refuse him a few kisses : it was sealing her right to the money which he had just handed to her. I was at the door, and waiting for Lescaut's signal to enter the room.

"He approached to take me by the hand, while Manon was securing the money and jewels, and leading me towards M. G—— M——, he desired me to make my bow. I made two or three most profound ones. 'Pray excuse him, sir,' said Lescaut, 'he is a mere child. He has not yet acquired much of the *ton* of Paris ; but no doubt with a little trouble we shall improve him. You will often have the honour of seeing that gentleman, here,' said he, turning towards me : 'take advantage of it, and endeavour to imitate so good a model.'

"The old libertine appeared to be pleased with me. He patted me on the cheek, saying that I was a fine boy, but that I should be on my guard in Paris, where young men were easily debauched. Lescaut assured him that I was naturally of so grave a character that I thought of nothing but becoming a clergyman, and that, even as a child, my favourite amusement was building little chapels. 'I fancy a likeness to Manon,' said the old gentleman, putting his hand under my chin. I answered him, with the most simple air—'Sir, the fact is, that we are very closely connected, and I love my sister as another portion of myself.' 'Do you hear that,' said he to Lescaut ; 'he is indeed a clever boy ! It is a pity he should not see something of the world.' 'Oh, sir,' I replied, 'I have seen a great deal of it at home, attending church, and I believe I might find in Paris some greater fools than myself.' 'Listen !' said he ; 'it is positively wonderful in a boy from the country.'

"The whole conversation during supper was of the same kind. Manon, with her usual gaiety, was several times on the point of spoiling the joke by her bursts of laughter. I contrived, while eating, to recount his own identical history, and to paint even the fate that awaited him. Lescaut and Manon were in an agony of fear during my recital, especially while I was drawing his portrait to the life : but his own vanity prevented him from recognising it, and I did it so well that he was the first to pronounce it extremely laughable. You will allow that I had reason for dwelling on this ridiculous scene.

" At length it was time to retire. He hinted at the impatience of love. Lescaut and I took our departure. G—— M—— went to his room, and Manon, making some excuse for her absence, came to join us at the gate. The coach, that was waiting for us a few doors off, drove up towards us, and we were out of the street in an instant.

" Although I must confess that this proceeding appeared to me little short of actual robbery, it was not the most dishonest one with which I thought I had to reproach myself. I had more scruples about the money which I had won at play. However, we derived as little advantage from one as from the other ; and Heaven sometimes ordains that the lightest fault shall meet the severest punishment.

" M. G—— M—— was not long in finding out that he had been duped. I am not sure whether he took any steps that night to discover us, but he had influence enough to ensure an effectual pursuit, and we were sufficiently imprudent to rely upon the extent of Paris and the distance between our residence and his. Not only did he discover our abode and our circumstances, but also who I was—the life that I had led in Paris—Manon's former connection with B——,—the manner in which she had deceived him : in a word, all the scandalous facts of our history. He therefore resolved to have us apprehended, and treated less as criminals than as vagabonds. An officer came abruptly one morning into our bedroom, with half a dozen archers of the guard. They first took possession of our money, or I should rather say, of G—— M——'s. They made us quickly get up, and conducted us to the door, where we found two coaches, into one of which they forced poor Manon, without any explanation, and I was taken in the other to St. Lazare.

" One must have experienced this kind of reverse, to understand the despair that is caused by it. The police were savage enough to deny me the consolation of embracing Manon, or of bidding her farewell. I remained for a long time ignorant of her fate. It was perhaps fortunate for me that I was kept in a state of ignorance, for had I known what she suffered, I should have lost my senses, probably my life.

" My unhappy mistress was dragged then from my presence, and taken to a place the very name of which fills me with horror to remember. This to be the lot of a creature the most perfect, who must have shared the most splendid throne on earth, if other men had only seen and felt as I did ! She was not treated harshly there, but was shut up in a narrow prison, and obliged, in solitary confinement, to perform a certain quantity of work each day, as a necessary condition for obtaining the most unpalatable food. I did not learn this till a long time after, when I had myself endured some months of rough and cruel treatment.

" My guards not having told me where it was that they had been ordered to conduct me, it was only on my arrival at St. Lazare that I learned my destination. I would have preferred death, at that moment, to the state into which I believed myself about to be thrown. I had the utmost terror of this place. My misery was increased by the guards on my entrance, examining once more my pockets, to ascertain whether I had about me any arms or weapons of defence.

"The governor appeared. He had been informed of my apprehension. He saluted me with great mildness. 'Do not, my good sir,' said I to him, 'allow me to be treated with indignity. I would suffer a hundred deaths rather than quietly submit to degrading treatment.' 'No, no,' he replied, 'you will act quietly and prudently, and we shall be mutually content with each other.' He begged of me to ascend to one of the highest rooms; I followed him without a murmur. The archers accompanied us to the door, and the governor, entering the room, made a sign for them to depart. 'I am your prisoner, I suppose?' said I; 'well, what do you intend to do with me?' He said, he was delighted to see me adopt so reasonable a tone; that it would be his duty to endeavour to inspire me with a taste for virtue and religion, and mine to profit by his exhortations and advice: that lightly as I might be disposed to rate his attentions to me, I should find nothing but enjoyment in my solitude. 'Ah, enjoyment, indeed!' replied I; "you do not know, my good sir, the only thing on earth that could afford me enjoyment.' 'I know it,' said he, 'but I trust your inclinations will change.' His answer showed that he had heard of my adventures, and perhaps of my name. I begged to know if such were the fact. He told me candidly that they had informed him of every particular.

"This blow was the severest of any I had yet experienced. I literally shed a torrent of tears, in all the bitterness of unmixed despair; I could not reconcile myself to the humiliation which would make me a proverb to all my acquaintances, and the disgrace of my family. I passed a week in the most profound dejection, without being capable of gaining any information, or of occupying myself with anything but my own degradation. The remembrance even of Manon added nothing to my grief; it only occurred to me as a circumstance that had preceded my new sorrow; and the sense of shame and confusion was at present the all-absorbing passion.

"There are few persons who have experienced the force of these special workings of the mind. The generality of men are only sensible of five or six passions, in the limited round of which they pass their lives, and within which all their agitations are confined. Remove them from the influence of love and hate, pleasure and pain, hope and fear, and they have no further feeling. But persons of a finer cast can be affected in a thousand different ways; it would almost seem that they had more than five senses, and that they are accessible to ideas and sensations which far exceed the ordinary faculties of human nature; and, conscious that they possess a capacity which raises them above the common herd, there is nothing of which they are more jealous. Hence springs their impatience under contempt and ridicule; and hence it is that a sense of debasement is perhaps the most violent of all their emotions.

"I had this melancholy advantage at St. Lazare. My grief appeared to the governor so excessive, that, dreading the consequences, he thought he was bound to treat me with more mildness and indulgence. He visited me two or three times a day; he often made me take a turn with him in the garden, and showed his interest for me in his exhortations and good advice. I listened always attentively; and warmly expressed my sense of his kindness, from which he derived hopes of my ultimate conversion.

"'You appear to me,' said he one day, 'of a disposition so mild and tractable, that I cannot comprehend the excesses into which you have fallen. Two things astonish me: one is, how, with your good qualities, you could have ever abandoned yourself to vice; and the other, which amazes me still more, is, how you can receive with such perfect temper my advice and instructions, after having lived so long in a course of debauchery. If it be sincere repentance, you present a singular example of the benign mercy of Heaven; if it proceed from the natural goodness of your disposition, then you certainly have that within you which warrants the hope that a protracted residence in this place will not be required to bring you back to a regular and respectable life.'

"I was delighted to find that he had such an opinion of me. I resolved to strengthen it by a continuance of good conduct, convinced that it was the surest means of abridging the term of my confinement. I begged of him to furnish me with books. He was agreeably surprised to find that when he requested me to say what I should prefer, I mentioned only some religious and instructive works. I pretended to devote myself assiduously to study, and I thus gave him convincing proof of the moral reformation he was so anxious to bring about. It was nothing, however, but rank hypocrisy—I blush to confess it. Instead of studying, when alone I did nothing but curse my destiny. I lavished the bitterest execrations on my prison, and the tyrants who detained me there. If I ceased for a moment from these lamentations, it was only to relapse into the tormenting remembrance of my fatal and unhappy love. Manon's absence—the mystery in which her fate was veiled—the dread of never again beholding her; these formed the subject of my melancholy thoughts. I fancied her in the arms of G—— M——. Far from imagining that he could have been brute enough to subject her to the same treatment to which I was condemned, I felt persuaded that he had only procured my removal, in order that he might possess her in undisturbed enjoyment.

"Oh! how miserable were the days and nights I thus passed! They seemed to be of endless duration. My only hope of escape now, was in hypocrisy; I scrutinised the countenance, and carefully marked every observation that fell from the governor, in order to ascertain what he really thought of me; and looking on him as the sole arbiter of my future fate, I made it my study to win, if possible, his favour. I soon had the satisfaction to find that I was firmly established in his good graces, and no longer doubted his disposition to befriend me.

"I, one day, ventured to ask him whether my liberation depended on him. He replied that it was not altogether in his hands, but that he had no doubt that on his representation M. G—— M——, at whose instance the lieutenant-general of police had ordered me to be confined, would consent to my being set at liberty. 'May I flatter myself,' rejoined I, in the mildest tone, 'that he will consider two months, which I have now spent in this prison, as a sufficient atonement?' He offered to speak to him, if I wished it. I implored him without delay to do me that favour.

"He told me two days afterwards that G—— M—— was so sensibly affected by what he had heard, that he not only was ready to consent to my liberation, but that he had even expressed a strong desire to become better acquainted with me, and that he himself purposed to pay me a visit in prison. Although his presence could not afford me much pleasure, I looked upon it as a certain prelude to my liberation.

"He accordingly came to St. Lazare. I met him with an air more grave and certainly less silly than I had exhibited at his house with Manon. He spoke reasonably enough of my former bad conduct. He added, as if to excuse his own delinquencies, that it was graciously permitted to the weakness of man to indulge in certain pleasures, almost, indeed, prompted by nature, but that dishonesty and such shameful practices ought to be, and always would be, inexorably punished.

"I listened to all he said with an air of submission, which quite charmed him. I betrayed no symptoms of annoyance even at some jokes in which he indulged about my relationship with Manon and Lescaut, and about the little chapels of which he supposed I must have had time to erect a great many in St. Lazare, as I was so fond of that occupation. But he happened, unluckily both for me and for himself, to add, that he hoped Manon had also employed herself in the same edifying manner at the Magdalen. Notwithstanding the thrill of horror I felt at the sound of the name, I had still presence of mind enough to beg, in the gentlest manner, that he would explain himself. 'Oh! yes,' he replied, 'she has been these last two months at the Magdalen learning to be prudent, and I trust she has improved herself as much there, as you have done at St. Lazare!'

"If an eternal imprisonment, or death itself, had been presented to my view, I could not have restrained the excitement into which this afflicting announcement threw me. I flung myself upon him in so violent a rage that half my strength was exhausted by the effort. I had, however, more than enough left to drag him to the ground, and grasp him by the throat. I should infallibly have strangled him, if his fall, and the half-stifled cries which he had still the power to utter, had not attracted the governor and several of the priests to my room. They rescued him from my fury.

"I was, myself, breathless and almost impotent from rage. 'Oh God!' I cried—'Heavenly justice! Must I survive this infamy?' I tried again to seize the barbarian who had thus roused my indignation

—they prevented me. My despair—my cries—my tears, exceeded all belief: I raved in so incoherent a manner that all the bystanders, who were ignorant of the cause, looked at each other with as much dread as surprise.

"G—— M—— in the meantime adjusted his wig and cravat, and in his anger at having been so ill-treated, ordered me to be kept under more severe restraint than before, and to be punished in the manner usual with offenders in St. Lazare. 'No, sir!' said the governor, 'it is not with a person of his birth that we are in the habit of using such means of coercion; besides, he is habitually so mild and well-conducted, that I cannot but think you must have given provocation for such excessive violence.' This reply disconcerted G—— M—— beyond measure and he went away, declaring that he knew how to be revenged on the governor, as well as on me, and everyone else who dared to thwart him.

"The Superior, having ordered some of the brotherhood to escort him out of the prison, remained alone with me. He conjured me to tell him at once what was the cause of the fracas.—'Oh, my good sir!' said I to him, continuing to cry like a child, 'imagine the most horrible cruelty, figure to yourself the most inhuman of atrocities—that is what G—— M—— has had the cowardly baseness to perpetrate: he has pierced my heart. Never shall I recover from this blow! I would gladly tell you the whole circumstance,' added I, sobbing with grief; 'you are kind-hearted, and cannot fail to pity me.'

"I gave him, as briefly as I could, a history of my long-standing and insurmountable passion for Manon, of the flourishing condition of our fortunes previous to the robbery committed by our servants, of the offers which G—— M—— had made to my mistress, of the understanding they had come to, and the manner in which it had been defeated. To be sure, I represented things to him in as favourable a light for us as possible. 'Now you can comprehend,' continued I, 'the source of M. G—— M——'s holy zeal for my conversion. He has had influence enough to have me shut up here, out of mere revenge. That I can pardon; but, my good sir, that is not all. He has taken from me my heart's blood: he has had Manon shamefully incarcerated in the Magdalen; and had the effrontery to announce it to me this day with his own lips. In the Magdalen, good sir! Oh heavens! my adorable mistress, my beloved Manon, a degraded inmate of the Hospital! How shall I command strength of mind enough to survive this grief and shame!'

"The good Father, seeing me in such affliction, endeavoured to console me. He told me that he had never understood my history, as I just now related it; he had of course known that I led a dissolute life, but he had imagined that M. G—— M——'s interest about me was the result of his esteem and friendship for my family; that it was in this sense he had explained the matter to him; that what I had now told him should assuredly produce a change in my treatment, and that he had no doubt but the accurate detail which he should immediately transmit to the lieutenant-general of police would bring about my liberation.

"He then enquired why I had never thought of informing my family of what had taken place, since they had not been instrumental to my incarceration. I satisfactorily answered this by stating my unwillingness to cause my father pain, or to bring upon myself the humiliation of such an exposure. In the end, he promised to go directly to the lieutenant-general of police if it were only, said he, to be beforehand with M. G—— M——, who went off in such a rage, and who had sufficient influence to make himself formidable.

"I looked for the good Father's return with all the suspense of a man expecting sentence of death. It was torture to me to think of Manon at the Magdalen. Besides the infamy of such a prison, I knew not how she might be treated there; and the recollection of some particulars I had formerly heard of this horrible place, incessantly renewed my misery. Cost what it might, I was so bent upon relieving her by some means or other, that I should assuredly have set fire to St. Lazare, if no other mode of escape had presented itself.

"I considered what chances would remain to me if the lieutenant-general still kept me in confinement. I taxed my ingenuity: I scanned every imaginable gleam of hope—I could discover nothing that gave me any prospect of escape, and I feared that I should experience only more rigid confinement, if I made an unsuccessful attempt. I thought of some friends from whom I might hope for aid, but then, how was I to make them aware of my situation? At length I fancied that I had hit upon a plan so ingenious, as to offer a fair probability of success. I postponed the details of its arrangement until after the Superior's return, in case of his having failed in the object of his visit.

"He soon arrived: I did not observe upon his countenance any of those marks of joy that indicate good news. 'I have spoken,' said he, 'to the lieutenant-general of police, but I was too late, M. G—— M—— went straight to him after quitting us, and so prejudiced him against you, that he was on the point of sending me fresh instructions to subject you to closer confinement.

"'However, when I let him know the truth of your story, he reconsidered the matter, and, smiling at the incontinence of old G—— M——, he said it would be necessary to keep you here for six months longer, in order to pacify him; the less to be lamented,' he added, 'because your morals would be sure to benefit by your residence here. He desired that I would show you every kindness and attention, and I need not assure you that you shall have no reason to complain of your treatment.'

"This speech of the Superior's was long enough to afford me time to form a prudent resolution. I saw that by betraying too strong an impatience for my liberty, I should probably be upsetting all my projects. I acknowledged to him, that, as it was necessary to me to remain, it was an infinite comfort to know that I possessed a place in his esteem.

I then requested, and with unaffected sincerity, a favour, which could be of no consequence to others, and which would contribute much to my peace of mind; it was to inform a friend of mine, a devout clergyman, who lived at St. Sulpice, that I was at St. Lazare, and to permit me occasionally to receive his visits.

"This was of course my friend Tiberge; not that I could hope from him the assistance necessary for effecting my liberty; but I wished to make him the unconscious instrument of my designs. In a word, this was my project: I wished to write to Lescaut, and to charge him and our common friends with the task of my deliverance. The first difficulty was to have my letter conveyed to him: this should be Tiberge's office. However, as he knew him to be Manon's brother, I doubted whether he would take charge of this commission. My plan was to enclose my letter to Lescaut in another to some respectable man of my acquaintance, begging of him to transmit the first to its address without delay; and as it was necessary that I should have personal communication with Lescaut, in order to arrange our proceedings, I told him to call on me at St. Lazare, and assume the name of my eldest brother, as if he had come to Paris expressly to see me. I postponed till our meeting all mention of the safest and most expeditious course I intended to suggest for our future conduct. The governor informed Tiberge of my wish to see him. This ever-faithful friend had not so entirely lost sight of me as to be ignorant of my present abode, and it is probable that, in his heart, he did not regret the circumstance, from an idea that it might furnish the means of my moral regeneration. He lost no time in paying me the desired visit.

## VI

It is a strange thing to note the excess of this passion; and how it braves the nature and value of things, by this—that the speaking in a perpetual hyperbole is comely in nothing but in love.—BACON.

"MY interview with Tiberge was of the most friendly description. I saw that his object was to discover the present temper of my mind. I opened my heart to him without any reserve, except as to the mere point of my intention of escaping. 'It is not from such a friend as you,' said I, 'that I can ever wish to dissemble my real feelings. If you flattered yourself with a hope that you were at last about to find me grown prudent and regular in my conduct, a libertine reclaimed by the chastisements of fortune, released alike from the trammels of love, and the dominion that Manon wields over me, I must in candour say, that you deceive yourself. You still behold me, as you left me four months ago, the slave—if you will, the unhappy slave—of a passion, from which I now hope, as fervently and as confidently as I ever did, to derive eventually solid comfort.'

"He answered, that such an acknowledgment rendered me utterly excusable; that it was no uncommon case to meet sinners who llowed themselves to be so dazzled with the glare of vice as to prefer t openly to the true splendour of virtue; they were at least deluded by the false image of happiness, the poor dupes of an empty shadow; but the know and feel as I did, that the object of my attachment was only calculated to render me culpable and unhappy, and to continue thus voluntarily in a career of misery and crime, involved a contradiction of ideas and of conduct little creditable to my reason.

"'Tiberge,' replied I, 'it is easy to triumph when your arguments are unopposed. Allow me to reason for a few moments in my turn. Can you pretend that what you call the happiness of virtue is exempt from troubles, and crosses, and cares? By what name will you designate the dungeon, the rack, the inflictions and tortures of tyrants? Will you say with the Mystics[1] that the soul derives pleasure from the torments of the body? You are not bold enough to hold such a doctrine—a paradox not to be maintained. This happiness, then, that you prize so much, has a thousand drawbacks, or is, more properly speaking, but a tissue of sufferings through which one hopes to attain felicity. If by the power of imagination one can even derive pleasure from these sufferings, hoping that they may lead to a happy end, why, let me ask, do you deem my conduct senseless, when it is directed by precisely the same principle? I love Manon: I wade through sorrow and suffering in order to attain happiness with her. My path is one indeed of difficulties, but the mere hope of reaching the desired goal makes it easy and delightful; and I shall think myself but too bountifully repaid by one moment of her society, for all the troubles I encounter in my course. There appears therefore no difference between us, or, if there be any, it is assuredly in my favour; for the bliss I hope for is near and tangible, yours is far distant, and purely speculative. Mine is of the same kind as my sufferings, that is to say, evident to my senses; yours is of an incomprehensible nature, and only discernible through the dim medium of faith.'

"Tiberge appeared shocked by my remarks. He retired two or three paces from me, while he said, in the most serious tone, that my argument was not only a violation of good sense, but that it was the miserable sophistry of irreligion; 'for the comparison,' he added, 'of the pitiful reward of your sufferings with that held out to us by the divine revelation, is the essence of impiety and absurdity combined.'

"'I acknowledge,' said I, 'that the comparison is not a just one, but my argument does not at all depend upon it. I was about to explain what you consider a contradiction—the persevering in a painful pursuit; and I think I have satisfactorily proved, that if there be any contradiction in that, we shall be both equally obnoxious to the charge. It was in

[1] A favourite tenet of the Mystics, advocated by Madame de Guyon, and adopted by the amiable and eloquent Fénelon, was, that the love of the Supreme Being must be pure and disinterested; that is, exempt from all views of interest, and all hope of reward. See the controversy between Bossuet and Fénelon.

this light, only, that I could observe no difference in our cases, and I cannot as yet perceive any.

" 'You may probably answer, that the proposed end, the promised reward, of virtue, is infinitely superior to that of love? No one disputes it, but that is not the question—we are only discussing the relative aid they both afford in the endurance of affliction. Judge of that by the practical effect: are there not multitudes who abandon a life of strict virtue? how few give up the pursuits of love!

" 'Again, you will reply that if there be difficulties in the exercise of virtue, they are by no means universal and sure; that the good man does not necessarily meet tyrants and tortures, and that, on the contrary, a life of virtue is perfectly compatible with repose and enjoyment. I can say with equal truth, that love is often accompanied by content and happiness; and what makes another distinction of infinite advantage to my argument, I may add that love, though it often deludes, never holds out other than hopes of bliss and joy, whilst religion exacts from her votaries mortification and sorrow.

" 'Do not be alarmed,' said I, perceiving that I had almost offended his zealous feelings of devotion. 'I only wish to say, that there is no more unsuccessful method of weaning man's heart from love, than by endeavouring to decry its enjoyments, and by promising him more pleasure from the exercise of virtue. It is an inherent principle in our nature, that our felicity consists only in pleasure. I defy you to conceive any other notion of it; and it requires little time to arrive at the conviction, that, of all pleasures, those of love are immeasurably the most enchanting. A man quickly discerns the delusion, when he hears the promise made of livelier enjoyment, and the effect of such misrepresentation is only to make him doubt the truth of a more solid promise.

" 'Let the preacher who seeks the reformation of a sinner tell me that virtue is indispensably necessary, but not disguise its difficulty and its attendant denials. Say that the enjoyments of love are fleeting, if you will, that they are rigidly forbidden, that they lead with certainty to eternal suffering; and, what would assuredly make a deeper impression upon me than any other argument, say that the more sweet and delectable they are, the brighter will be the reward of Heaven for giving them up in sacrifice; but do in the name of justice admit, that, constituted as the heart of man is, they form here, on earth, our most perfect happiness.'

"My last sentence restored to Tiberge his good humour. He allowed that my ideas were not altogether so unreasonable. The only point he made, was in asking me why I did not carry my own principle into operation, by sacrificing my passion to the hope of that remuneration of which I had drawn so brilliant a picture. 'Oh! my dear friend,' replied I; 'that it is which makes me conscious of my own misery and weakness: true, alas! it is indeed my duty to act according to my argument; but have I the power of governing my own actions?

What aid will enable me to forget Manon's charms ?' 'God forgive me,' said Tiberge, 'I can almost fancy you a Jansenist.'[1] 'I know not of what sect I am,' replied I, 'nor do I indeed very clearly see to which I ought to belong ; but I cannot help feeling the truth of this at least of their tenets.'

"One effect of our conversation was to revive my friend's pity for me in all its force. He perceived that there was in my errors more of weakness than of vice ; and he was the more disposed in the end to give me assistance ; without which I should infallibly have perished from distress of mind. However, I carefully concealed from him my intention of escaping from St. Lazare. I merely begged of him to take charge of my letter ; I had it ready before he came, and I soon found an excuse for the necessity of writing. He faithfully transmitted it, and Lescaut received before evening the one I had enclosed for him.

"He came to see me next morning, and fortunately was admitted under my brother's name. I was overjoyed at finding him in my room. I carefully closed the door. 'Let us lose no time,' I said. 'First tell me about Manon, and then advise me how I am to shake off these fetters.' He assured me that he had not seen his sister since the day before my arrest, and that it was only by repeated enquiries, and after much trouble, that he had at length been able to discover her fate as well as mine ; and that he had two or three times presented himself at the Magdalen, and been refused admittance. 'Wretch !' muttered I to myself, 'dearly shall G—— M—— pay for this !'

"'As to your escape,' continued Lescaut, 'it will not be so easy as you imagine. Last evening, I and a couple of friends walked round this establishment to reconnoitre it ; and we agreed that, as your windows looked into a court surrounded by buildings, as you yourself mentioned in your letter, there would be vast difficulty in getting you out. Besides, you are on the third story, and it would be impossible to introduce ropes or ladders through the window. I therefore see no means from without—in the house itself we must hit upon some scheme.'

"'No,' replied I ; 'I have examined everything minutely, particularly since, through the governor's indulgence, my confinement has been less rigorous. I am no longer locked into my room ; I have liberty to walk in the gallery ; but there is, upon every landing, a strong door kept closed night and day, so that it is impossible that ingenuity alone, unaided by some violent efforts, can rescue me.

"'Wait,' said I, after turning in my mind for a moment an idea that struck me as excellent ; 'could you bring me a pistol ?' 'Softly,' said Lescaut to me, 'you don't think of committing murder ?' I assured him that I had so little intention of shooting anyone, that it would not be even necessary to have the pistol loaded. 'Bring it to me tomorrow,' I added, 'and do not fail to be exactly opposite the

[1] The first proposition of the Jansenists was, that there are divine precepts which good men, notwithstanding their desire to observe them, are nevertheless absolutely unable to obey : God not having given them such a measure of grace as is essentially necessary to render them capable of obedience.—Mosheim's *Eccles. Hist.*, ii. 397.

great entrance with two or three of your friends at eleven tomorrow night; I think I shall be able to join you there.' He in vain requested me to explain my plan. I told him that such an attempt as I contemplated could only appear rational after it had succeeded. I begged of him to shorten his visit, in order that he might with the less difficulty be admitted next morning. He was accordingly admitted as readily as on his first visit. He had put on so serious an air, moreover, that a stranger would have taken him for a respectable person.

"When I found in my hand the instrument of my liberty, I no longer doubted my success. It was certainly a strange and a bold project; but of what was I not capable, with the motives that inspired me? I had, since I was allowed permission to walk in the galleries, found opportunities of observing that every night the porter brought the keys of all the doors to the governor, and subsequently there always reigned a profound silence in the house, which showed that the inmates had retired to rest. There was an open communication between my room and that of the Superior. My resolution was, if he refused quietly to surrender the keys, to force him, by fear of the pistol, to deliver them up, and then by their help to gain the street. I impatiently awaited the moment for executing my purpose. The porter arrived at his usual time, that is to say, soon after nine o'clock. I allowed an hour to elapse, in order that the priests as well as the servants might be all asleep. I at length proceeded with my pistol and a lighted candle. I first gave a gentle tap at the governor's door to awaken without alarming him. I knocked a second time before he heard me; and supposing of course that it was one of the priests who was taken ill and wanted assistance, he got out of bed, dressed himself, and came to the door. He had, however, the precaution to ask first who it was, and what was wanted? I was obliged to mention my name, but I assumed a plaintive tone, to make him believe that I was indisposed. 'Ah! it is you, my dear boy,' said he on opening the door; 'what can bring you here at this hour?' I stepped inside the door, and leading him to the opposite side of the room, I declared to him that it was absolutely impossible for me to remain longer at St. Lazare; that the night was the most favourable time for going out unobserved, and that I confidently expected, from his tried friendship, that he would consent to open the gates for me, or entrust me with the keys to let myself out.

"This compliment to his friendship seemed to surprise him. He stood for a few moments looking at me without making any reply. Finding that I had no time to lose, I just begged to assure him that I had the most lively sense of all his kindnesses, but that freedom was dearer to man than every other consideration, especially so to me, who had been cruelly and unjustly deprived of it; that I was resolved this night to recover it, cost what it would, and fearing lest he might raise his voice and call for assistance, I let him see the powerful incentive to silence which I had kept concealed in my bosom. 'A pistol!' cried he. 'What! my son? will you take away my life in return for the attentions I have shown you ?' 'God forbid,' replied I; 'you are too reasonable to drive me to that horrible extremity: but I am determined to be free, and so firmly determined, that if you defeat my project, I will put an end to your existence.' 'But, my dear son!' said he, pale and frightened, 'what have I done to you? What reason have you for taking my life?' 'No!' replied I, impatiently, 'I have no design upon your life, if you, yourself, wish to live; open but the doors for me, and you will find me the most attached of friends.' I perceived the keys upon the table. I requested he would take them in his hand and walk before me, making as little noise as he possibly could.

"He saw the necessity of consenting. We proceeded, and as he opened each door, he repeated, always with a sigh, 'Ah! my son, who could have believed it?' 'No noise, good Father, no noise,' I as often answered in my turn. At length we reached a kind of barrier, just inside the great entrance. I already fancied myself free, and kept close behind the governor, with my candle in one hand, and my pistol in the other.

"While he was endeavouring to open the heavy gate, one of the servants, who slept in an adjoining room, hearing the noise of the bolts, jumped out of bed, and peeped forth to see what was passing. The good Father apparently thought him strong enough to overpower me. He commanded him, most imprudently, to come to his assistance. He was a powerful ruffian, and threw himself upon me without an instant's hesitation. There was no time for parleying—I levelled my pistol and lodged the contents in his breast! 'See, Father, of what mischief you have been the cause,' said I to my guide; 'but that must not prevent us from finishing our work,' I added, pushing him on towards the last door. He did not dare refuse to open it. I made my exit in perfect safety, and, a few paces off, found Lescaut with two friends waiting for me, according to his promise.

"We removed at once to a distance. Lescaut enquired whether he had not heard the report of a pistol? 'You are to blame,' said I, 'why did you bring it charged?' I, however, could not help thanking him for having taken this precaution, without which I doubtless must have continued much longer at St. Lazare. We went to pass the night at a tavern, where I made up, in some degree, for the miserable fare which had been doled out to me for nearly three months. I was very far, however, from tasting perfect enjoyment; Manon's sufferings were mine. 'She must be released,' said I to my companions: 'this was my sole object in desiring my own liberty. I rely on your aiding me with all your ingenuity; as for myself, my life shall be devoted to the purpose.'

"Lescaut, who was not deficient in tact, and still less in that better part of valour called discretion, dwelt upon the necessity of acting with extreme caution: he said that my escape from St. Lazare, and the accident that happened on my leaving it, would assuredly create a sensation; that the lieutenant-general of police would cause a strict search to be made for me, and it would be difficult to evade him; in fine, that, unless disposed to encounter something worse, perhaps, than St. Lazare, it would be requisite for me to remain concealed for a few days, in order to give the enemy's zeal time to cool. No doubt this was wise counsel; but, one should have been wise oneself to have followed it. Such calculating slowness little suited my passion. The utmost I could bring myself to promise was, that I would sleep through the whole of the next day. He locked me in my bedroom, where I remained patiently until night.

"I employed great part of the time in devising schemes for relieving Manon. I felt persuaded that her prison was even more inaccessible than mine had been. Force was out of the question. Artifice was the only resource; but the goddess of invention herself could not have told me how to begin. I felt the impossibility of working in the dark, and therefore postponed the further consideration of my schemes until I could acquire some knowledge of the internal arrangements of the Hospital, in which she was confined.

"As soon as night restored to me my liberty, I begged of Lescaut to accompany me. We were not long in drawing one of the porters into conversation; he appeared a reasonable man. I passed for a stranger who had often with admiration heard talk of the Hospital, and of the order that reigned within it. I enquired into the most minute details; and, proceeding from one subject to another, we at length spoke of the managers, and of these I begged to know the names and the respective characters. He gave me such information upon the latter point as at once suggested an idea which flattered my hopes, and I immediately set about carrying it into execution. I asked him (this being a matter essential to my plan) whether any of the gentlemen had children. He said he could not answer me with certainty as to all, but as for M. de T——, one of the principal directors, he knew that he had a son old enough to be married, and who had come several times to the Hospital with his father. This was enough for my purpose.

"I immediately put an end to our interview, and, in returning, I told Lescaut of the plan I had formed. 'I have taken it,' said I, 'into my head, that M. de T——, the son, who is rich and of good family, must have the same taste for pleasure that other young men of his age generally have. He could hardly be so bad a friend to the fair sex, nor so absurd as to refuse his services in an affair of love. I have arranged a plan for interesting him in favour of Manon. If he is a man of feeling and of right mind, he will give us his assistance from generosity. If he is not to be touched by a motive of this kind, he will at least do something for a handsome girl, if it were only with the hope of hereafter sharing her favours. I will not defer seeing him,' added I, 'beyond tomorrow. I really feel so elated by this project, that I derive from it a good omen.'

"Lescaut himself allowed that the idea was not unreasonable, and that we might fairly entertain a hope of turning it to account. I passed the night less sorrowfully.

"Next morning I dressed as well as, in my present state of indigence, I could possibly contrive to do; and went in a hackney coach to the residence of M. de T——. He was surprised at receiving a visit from a perfect stranger. I augured favourably from his countenance and the civility of his manner. I explained my object in the most candid way; and, to excite his feelings as much as possible, I spoke of my ardent passion and of Manon's merit, as of two things that were unequalled, except by each other. He told me, that although he had never seen Manon, he had heard of her; at least, if the person I was talking of was the same who had been the mistress of old G—— M——. I conjectured that he must have heard of the part I had acted in that transaction, and in order to conciliate him more and more by treating him with confidence, I told him everything that had occurred to Manon and myself. 'You see, sir,' said I, 'that all that can interest me in life, all that can command my affections, is in your hands. I have no reserve with you, because I have been informed of your generous and noble character; and, being of the same age, I trust I shall find some resemblance in our dispositions.'

"He seemed flattered by this mark of candour and confidence. He replied in a manner that became a man of the world, and a man of feeling also, for they are not always synonymous terms. He told me that he appreciated my visit as a piece of good fortune; that he considered my friendship as a valuable acquisition, and that he would endeavour to prove himself worthy of it, by the sincerity of his services. He could not absolutely promise to restore Manon to my arms, because, as he said, he himself had very little influence; but he offered to procure me the pleasure of seeing her, and to do everything in his power to effect her release. I was the more satisfied with this frank avowal as to his want of influence, than I should have been by an unqualified promise of fulfilling all my wishes. I found in his moderation a pledge of his sincerity: in a word, I no longer doubted my entire success. The promise alone of enabling me to see Manon filled me with gratitude, and I testified it in so earnest a manner, as to give him a favourable opinion of my heart and disposition; we shook hands warmly, and parted sworn friends, merely from mutual regard, and that natural feeling which prompts a man of kind and generous sentiments to esteem another of congenial mind.

"He, indeed, exceeded me in the proofs of his esteem; for, inferring from my adventures, and especially my late escape from St. Lazare, that I might be in want of money, he offered me his purse, and pressed me to accept it. I refused, but said to him, 'You are too kind, my dear sir! If in addition to such proofs of kindness and friendship, you enable me to see Manon again, rely on my eternal regard and gratitude. If you succeed in restoring altogether this dear creature to my arms, I should think myself happy in spilling the last drop of my blood in your service.'

"Before we parted, we agreed as to the time and place for our meeting. He was so considerate as to appoint the afternoon of the same day.

" I waited for him at a café, where he joined me about four o'clock, and we went together towards the Magdalen ; my knees trembled under me as I crossed the courts. ' Ye heavenly powers ! ' said I, ' then I shall once more behold the idol of my heart—the dear object of so many sighs and lamentations ! All I now ask of Providence is, to vouchsafe me strength enough to reach her presence, and after that, to dispose as it pleaseth of my future fate, and of my life itself. Beyond this, I have no prayer to utter.'

" M. de T—— spoke to some of the porters of the establishment, who appeared all anxious to please him. The quarter in which Manon's room lay was pointed out to us, and our guide carried in his hand the key of her chamber : it was of frightful size. I asked the man who conducted us, and whose duty it was to attend to Manon, how she passed her time ? He said, that she had a temper of the most angelic sweetness ; that even he, disagreeable as his official duties must render him, had never heard from her a single syllable in the nature of rebuke or harshness ; that her tears had never ceased to flow during the first six weeks after her arrival, but that latterly she seemed to bear her misfortunes with more resignation, and that she employed herself from morning till night with her needle, excepting some hours that she, each day, devoted to reading. I asked whether she had been decently provided for. He assured me that at least she had never felt the want of necessaries.

" We now approached her door. My heart beat almost audibly in my bosom. I said to M. de T——, ' Go in alone, and prepare her for my visit ; I fear that she may be overcome by seeing me unexpectedly.' The door was opened. I remained in the passage, and listened to the conversation. He said that he came to bring her consolation ; that he was a friend of mine, and felt deeply interested for the happiness of us both. She asked with the tenderest anxiety, whether he could tell her what had become of me. He promised that she should soon see me at her feet, as affectionate and as faithful as ever. ' When ? ' she asked. ' This very day,' said he ; ' the happy moment shall not be long delayed ; nay, this very instant even, if you wish it.' She at once understood that I was at the door ; as she was rushing towards it, I entered. We embraced each other with that abounding and impassioned tenderness, which an absence of many months makes so delicious to those who truly love. Our sighs, our broken exclamations, the thousand endearing appellations of love, exchanged in languishing rapture, astonished M. de T——, and affected him even to tears.

" ' I cannot help envying you,' said he, as he begged us to be seated ; ' there is no lot, however glorious, that I would hold as comparable to the possession of a mistress at once so tender and impassioned.' ' Nor would I,' I replied, ' give up her love for universal empire ! '

" The remainder of an interview which had been so long and so ardently desired by me, was of course as tender as the commencement. Poor Manon related all her adventures, and I told her mine : we bitterly wept over each other's story. M. de T—— consoled us by his renewed promises to exert himself in our service. He advised us not to make this, our first interview, of too long duration, that he might have the less difficulty in procuring us the same enjoyment again. He at length induced us to follow his advice. Manon especially could not reconcile herself to the separation: she made me a hundred times resume my seat. At one time she held me by my hands, at another by my coat. 'Alas!' she said, 'in what an abode do you leave me! Who will answer for my ever seeing you again?' M. de T—— promised her that he would often come and see her with me. 'As to the abode,' he said, 'it must no longer be called the Magdalen; it is Versailles! now that it contains a person who deserves the empire of all hearts.'

"I made the man who attended a present as I went out, in order to quicken his zeal and attentions. This fellow had a mind less rough and vulgar than the generality of his class. He had witnessed our interview, and was affected by it. The interest he felt was doubtless increased by the louis d'or I gave him. He took me aside as we went down into the courtyard. 'Sir,' said he, 'if you will only take me into your service, or indemnify me in any way for the loss of the situation which I fill here, I think I should not have much difficulty in liberating the beauteous Manon.'

"I caught readily at the suggestion, and, although at the moment I was almost in a state of destitution, I gave him promises far beyond his desires. I considered that it would be at all times easy to recompense a man of his description. 'Be assured, my friend,' said I to him, 'that there is nothing I will not be ready to do for you, and that your fortune is just as certain as my own.' I enquired what means he intended to employ. 'None other,' said he, 'than merely to open the door of her cell for her at night, and to conduct her to the street door, where you, of course, will be to receive her.' I asked whether there was no danger of her being recognised as she traversed the long galleries and the courts. He admitted that there was danger, but that nothing could be done without some slight risk.

"Although I was delighted to find him so determined, I called M. de T——, and informed him of the project, and of the only difficulty in the way. He thought it not so easy of execution. He allowed the possibility of escaping thus: 'But if she be recognised,' continued he, 'if she be stopped in the attempt, all hope will be over with her, perhaps for ever. Besides, you would be obliged to quit Paris instantly, for you could never evade the search that would be made for you: they would redouble their efforts as much on your own account as hers. A single man may easily escape detection, but in company with a handsome woman, it would be utterly impossible to remain undiscovered.'

"However sound this reasoning, it could not, in my mind, outweigh the immediate prospect of restoring Manon to liberty. I said as much to M. de T——, and trusted that he would excuse my imprudence and rashness, on the ground of love. I added that it was already my intention to quit Paris for some neighbouring village, as I had once before done. We then settled with the servant that he should carry his project into execution the following day, and to render our success as certain as he could, we resolved to carry into the prison men's clothes, in order to facilitate her escape. There was a difficulty to be surmounted in carrying them in, but I had ingenuity enough to meet it. I begged of M. de T—— only to put on two light waistcoats the next morning, and I undertook to arrange the rest.

"We returned the following day to the Hospital. I took with me linen, stockings, etc., for Manon, and over my body-coat a surtout, which concealed the bulk I carried in my pockets. We remained but a moment in her room. M. de T—— left her one of his waistcoats; I gave her my short coat, the surtout being sufficient for me. She found nothing wanting for her complete equipment but a pair of pantaloons, which in my hurry I had forgotten.

"The want of so necessary an article might have amused us, if the embarrassment it caused had been of a less serious kind. I was in despair at having our whole scheme foiled by a trifling omission of this nature. However, I soon hit on a remedy, and determined to make my own exit *sans-culotte*, leaving that portion of my dress with Manon. My surtout was long, and I contrived by the help of a few pins to put myself in a decent condition for passing the gate.

"The remainder of the day appeared to me of endless length. When at last night came, we went in a coach to within a few yards of the Hospital. We were not long waiting, when we saw Manon make her appearance with her guide. The door of the coach being opened, they both stepped in without delay. I opened my arms to receive my adored mistress; she trembled like an aspen leaf. The coachman asked where he was to drive? 'To the end of the world!' I exclaimed; 'to some place where I can never again be separated from Manon.'

"This burst, which I could not control, was near bringing me into fresh trouble. The coachman reflected upon what I said, and when I afterwards told him the name of the street to which I wished him to drive, he answered that he feared I was about to implicate him in some bad business; that he saw plainly enough that the good-looking young man whom I called Manon was a girl eloping from the Hospital, and that he was little disposed indeed to ruin himself for love of me.

"Extortion was the source of this scoundrel's delicacy. We were still too near the Hospital to make any noise. 'Silence!' said I to him, 'you shall have a louis d'or for the job': for less than that he would have helped me to burn the Hospital.

"We arrived at Lescaut's house. As it was late, M. de T—— left us on the way, promising to visit us the next morning. The servant alone remained.

"I held Manon in such close embrace in my arms, that we occupied but one place in the coach. She cried for joy, and I could feel her tears trickling down my cheeks.

"When we were about getting out at Lescaut's, I had a new difficulty with the coachman, which was attended with the most unfortunate results. I repented of having promised the fellow a louis d'or, not only because it was extravagant folly, but for another stronger reason, that t was at the moment out of my power to pay him. I called for Lescaut, and he came down to the door. I whispered to him the cause of my present embarrassment. Being naturally rough, and not at all in the habit of treating hackney-coachmen with respect, he answered that I could not be serious. 'A louis!' said he; 'twenty blows of a cane would be the right payment for that rascal!' I entreated him not to destroy us; when he snatched my cane from my hand, and was about to lay it on the coachman. The fellow had probably before experienced the weight of a guardsman's arm, and instantly drove off, crying out, that I had cheated him, and should hear of him again. I in vain endeavoured to stop him.

"His flight caused me, of course, the greatest alarm. I had no doubt that he would immediately give information to the police. 'You have ruined me,' said I to Lescaut; 'I shall be no longer safe at your house; we must go hence at once.' I gave Manon my arm, and as quickly as possible got out of the dangerous neighbourhood. Lescaut accompanied us."

The Chevalier des Grieux having occupied more than an hour with his story, I begged him to give himself a little rest, and meanwhile to share our supper. He saw, by the attention we paid him, that we were amused, and promised that we should hear something of perhaps greater interest in the sequel. When we had finished supper, he continued in the following words.

## VII

. . . How chances mock,
And changes fill the cup of alteration
With divers liquors.

SHAKESPEARE.

"How inscrutably does Providence connect events! We had hardly proceeded for five minutes on our way, when a man, whose face I could not see, recognised Lescaut. He had no doubt been watching for him near his home, with the horrible intention which he now unhappily executed. 'It *is* Lescaut!' said he, snapping a pistol at his head; 'he shall sup tonight with the angels!' He then instantly disappeared. Lescaut fell, without the least sign of life. I pressed Manon to fly, for we could be of no use to a dead man, and I feared being arrested by the police, who would certainly be soon upon the spot. I turned down the first narrow street with her and the servant: she was so overpowered by the scene she had just witnessed, that I could hardly support her. At last, at the end of the street, I perceived a hackney-coach ; we got into it, but when the coachman asked whither he should drive, I was scarcely able to answer him. I had no certain asylum—no confidential friend to whom I could have recourse. I was almost destitute of money, having but one dollar left in my purse. Fright and fatigue had so unnerved Manon, that she was almost fainting at my side. My imagination too was full of the murder of Lescaut, and I was not without strong apprehensions of the patrol. What was to be done ? I luckily remembered the inn at Chaillot, where we first went to reside in that village. I hoped to be not only secure, but to continue there for some time without being pressed for payment. 'Take us to Chaillot,' said I to the coachman. He refused to drive us so far at that late hour for less than twelve francs. A new embarrassment ! At last we agreed for half that sum—all that my purse contained.

"I tried to console Manon as we went along, but despair was rankling in my own heart. I should have destroyed myself a thousand times over, if I had not felt that I held in my arms all that could attach me to life : this reflection reconciled me. 'I possess her at least,' said I ; 'she loves me ! she is mine ! Vainly does Tiberge call this a mere phantom of happiness.' I could, without feeling interest or emotion, see the whole world besides perish around me. Why ? Because I have in it no object of affection beyond her.

"This sentiment was true ; however, while I so lightly esteemed the good things of the world, I felt that there was no doing without some little portion of them, were it only to inspire a more thorough contempt for the remainder. Love is more powerful than wealth—more attractive than grandeur or fame ; but, alas ! it cannot exist without certain artificial aids ; and there is nothing more humiliating to the feelings, of a sensitive lover, than to find himself, by want of means, reduced to the level of the most vulgar minds.

"It was eleven o'clock when we arrived at Chaillot. They received us at the inn as old acquaintances, and expressed no sort of surprise at seeing Manon in male attire, for it was the custom in Paris and the environs to adopt all disguises. I took care to have her served with as much attention as if I had been in prosperous circumstances. She was ignorant of my poverty, and I carefully kept her so, being resolved to return alone the following day to Paris, to seek some cure for this vexatious kind of malady.

"At supper she appeared pale and thin ; I had not observed this at the Hospital, as the room in which I saw her was badly lighted. I asked her if the excessive paleness were not caused by the shock of witnessing her brother's death ? She assured me that, horrified as she naturally was at the event, her paleness was purely the effect of a three months' absence from me. 'You do love me then devotedly ?' I exclaimed.

"'A thousand times more than I can tell !' was her reply.

"'You will never leave me again ?' I added.

"'No ! never, never !' answered she.

"This assurance was confirmed by so many caresses and vows, that it appeared impossible she could, to the end of time, forget them. I have never doubted that she was at that moment sincere. What motive could she have had for dissembling to such a degree? But she became afterwards still more volatile than ever, or rather she was no longer anything, and entirely forgot herself, when, in poverty and want, she saw other women living in abundance. I was now on the point of receiving a new proof of her inconstancy, which threw all that had passed into the shade, and which led to the strangest adventure that ever happened to a man of my birth and prospects.

"As I knew her disposition, I hastened the next day to Paris. The death of her brother, and the necessity of getting linen and clothes for her, were such good reasons, that I had no occasion for any further pretext. I left the inn, with the intention, as I told Manon and the landlord, of going in a hired carriage, but this was a mere flourish; necessity obliged me to travel on foot: I walked very fast as far as Cours-la-Reine, where I intended to rest. A moment of solitude and tranquillity was requisite to compose myself, and to consider what was to be done in Paris.

"I sat down upon the grass. I plunged into a sea of thoughts and considerations, which at length resolved themselves into three principal heads. I had pressing want of an infinite number of absolute necessaries; I had to seek some mode of at least raising a hope for the future; and, though last, not least in importance, I had to gain information, and adopt measures, to secure Manon's safety and my own. After having exhausted myself in devising projects upon these three chief points, I was obliged to put out of view for the moment the two last. We were not ill sheltered from observation in the inn at Chaillot; and as to future wants, I thought it would be time enough to think about them when those of the moment were satisfied.

"The main object now was to replenish my purse. M. de T—— had once offered me his, but I had an extreme repugnance to mention the subject to him again. What a degradation to expose one's misery to a stranger, and to ask for charity: it must be either a man of low mind who would thus demean himself, and that from a baseness which must render him insensible to the degradation, or a humble Christian, from a consciousness of generosity in himself, which must put him above the sense of shame. I would have sacrificed half my life to be spared the humiliation.

"'Tiberge,' said I, 'kind Tiberge, will he refuse me what he has it in his power to grant? No, he will assuredly sympathise in my misery; but he will also torture me with his lectures! One must endure his reproaches, his exhortations, his threats: I shall have to purchase his assistance so dearly, that I would rather make any sacrifice than encounter this distressing scene, which cannot fail to leave me full of sorrow and remorse. Well,' thought I again, 'all hope must be relinquished, since no other course presents itself: so far am I from adopting either of these, that I would sooner shed half my blood than face one of these evils, or the last drop rather than encounter both. Yes, the very last drop,' I repeated after a moment's reflection, 'I would sacrifice willingly rather than submit to such base supplication!

"'But it is not in reality a question of my existence! Manon's life and maintenance, her love and her fidelity, are at stake! What consideration can outweigh that? In her are centred all my glory, happiness, and future fortune! There are doubtless many things that I would gladly give up my life to obtain, or to avoid; but to estimate a thing merely beyond the value of my own life, is not putting it on a par with that of Manon.' This idea soon decided me: I went on my way, resolved to go first to Tiberge, and afterwards to M. de T——.

"On entering Paris I took a hackney-coach, though I had not wherewithal to pay for it; I calculated on the loan I was going to solicit. I drove to the Luxembourg, whence I sent word to Tiberge that I was waiting for him. I had not to stay many minutes. I told him without hesitation the extremity of my wants. He asked if the fifty pounds which I had returned to him would suffice, and he at once went to fetch it with that generous air, that pleasure in bestowing which 'blesseth him that gives, and him that takes,' and which can only be known to love or to true friendship.

"Although I had never entertained a doubt of Tiberge's readiness to grant my request, yet I was surprised at having obtained it on such easy terms, that is to say, without a word of reprimand for my impenitence; but I was premature in fancying myself safe from his reproaches, for when he had counted out the money, and I was on the point of going away, he begged of me to take a walk with him in the garden. I had not mentioned Manon's name; he knew nothing of her escape; so that his lecture was merely upon my own rash flight from St. Lazare, and upon his apprehensions lest, instead of profiting by the lessons of morality which I had received there, I should again relapse into dissipation.

"He told me, that having gone to pay me a visit at St. Lazare, the day after my escape, he had been astonished beyond expression at hearing the mode in which I had effected it; that he had afterwards a conversation with the Superior; that the good Father had not quite recovered the shock; that he had, however, the generosity to conceal the real circumstances from the lieutenant-general of police, and that he had prevented the death of the porter from becoming known outside the walls; that I had, therefore, upon that score, no ground for alarm, but that, if I retained one grain of prudence, I should profit by this happy turn which Providence had given to my affairs, and begin by writing to my father, and reconciling myself to his favour; and finally that, if I would be guided by his advice, I should at once quit Paris, and return to the bosom of my family.

"I listened to him attentively till he had finished. There was much in what he said to gratify me. In the first place, I was delighted to learn that I had nothing to fear on account of St. Lazare—the streets of Paris at least were again open to me. Then I rejoiced to find that Tiberge had no suspicion of Manon's escape, and her return to my arms. I even remarked that he had not mentioned her name, probably from the idea that, by my seeming indifference to her, she had become less dear to my heart. I resolved, if not to return home, at least to write to my father, as he advised me, and to assure him that I was disposed to return to my duty, and consult his wishes. My intention was to urge him to send me money for the purpose of pursuing my ordinary studies at the University, for I should have found it difficult to persuade him that I had any inclination to resume my ecclesiastical habit. I was in truth not at all averse to what I was now going to promise him. On the contrary, I was ready to apply myself to some creditable and rational pursuit, so far as the occupation would be compatible with my love. I reckoned upon being able to live with my mistress, and at the same time continuing my studies. I saw no inconsistency in this plan.

"These thoughts were so satisfactory to my mind, that I promised Tiberge to dispatch a letter by that day's post to my father: in fact, on leaving him, I went into a scrivener's, and wrote in such a submissive and dutiful tone, that, on reading over my own letter, I anticipated the triumph I was going to achieve over my father's heart.

"Although I had money enough to pay for a hackney-coach after my interview with Tiberge, I felt a pleasure in walking independently through the streets to M. de T——'s house. There was great comfort in this unaccustomed exercise of my liberty, as to which my friend had assured me I had nothing now to apprehend. However, it suddenly occurred to me, that he had been only referring to St. Lazare, and that I had the other affair of the Hospital on my hands; being implicated, if not as an accomplice, at all events as a witness. This thought alarmed me so much, that I slipped down the first narrow street, and called a coach. I went at once to M. de T——'s, and he laughed at my apprehensions. I myself thought them ridiculous enough, when he informed me that there was no more danger from Lescaut's affray, than from the Hospital adventure. He told me that, from the fear of their suspecting that he had a hand in Manon's escape, he had gone that morning to the Hospital and asked to see her, pretending not to know anything of what had happened; that they were so far from entertaining the least suspicion of either of us, that they lost no time in relating the adventure as a piece of news to him; and that they wondered how so pretty a girl as Manon Lescaut could have thought of eloping with a servant: that he replied with seeming indifference, that it by no means astonished him, for people would do anything for the sake of liberty.

"He continued to tell me how he then went to Lescaut's apartments, in the hope of finding me there with my dear mistress; that the master of the house, who was a coachmaker, protested he had seen neither me nor Manon; but that it was no wonder that we had not appeared there, if our object was to see Lescaut, for that we must have doubtless heard of his having been assassinated about the very same time; upon which, he related all that he knew of the cause and circumstances of the murder.

"About two hours previously, a guardsman of Lescaut's acquaintance had come to see him, and proposed play. Lescaut had such a rapid and extravagant run of luck, that in an hour the young man was minus twelve hundred francs—all the money he had. Finding himself without a sou, he begged of Lescaut to lend him half the sum he had lost; and there being some difficulty on this point, an angry quarrel arose between them. Lescaut had refused to give him the required satisfaction, and the other swore, on quitting him, that he would take his life; a threat which he carried into execution the same night. M. de T—— was kind enough to add, that he had felt the utmost anxiety on our account, and that, such as they were, he should gladly continue to us his services. I at once told him the place of our retreat. He begged of me to allow him to sup with us.

"As I had nothing more to do than to procure the linen and clothes for Manon, I told him that we might start almost immediately, if he would be so good as to wait for me a moment while I went into one or two shops. I know not whether he suspected that I made this proposition with the view of calling his generosity into play, or whether it was by the mere impulse of a kind heart; but, having consented to start immediately, he took me to a shopkeeper, who had lately furnished his house. He there made me select several articles of a much higher price than I had proposed to myself; and when I was about paying the bill, he desired the man not to take a sou from me. This he did so gracefully, that I felt no shame in accepting his present. We then took the road to Chaillot together, where I arrived much more easy in mind than when I had left it that morning.

"My return and the polite attentions of M. de T—— dispelled all Manon's melancholy. 'Let us forget our past annoyances, my dear soul,' said I to her, 'and endeavour to live a still happier life than before. After all, there are worse masters than love: fate cannot subject us to as much sorrow as love enables us to taste of happiness.' Our supper was a true scene of joy.

"In possession of Manon and of twelve hundred and fifty francs, I was prouder and more contented than the richest voluptuary of Paris with untold treasures. Wealth should be measured by the means it affords us of satisfying our desires. There did not remain to me at this moment a single wish unaccomplished. Even the future gave me little concern. I felt a hope, amounting almost to certainty, that my father would allow me the means of living respectably in Paris, because I had become entitled, on entering upon my twentieth year, to a share of my mother's fortune. I did not conceal from Manon what was the extent of my present wealth; but I added, that it might suffice to support us until our fortune was bettered, either by the inheritance I have just alluded to, or by the resources of the hazard-table.

## VIII

This Passion hath its floods in the very times of weakness, which are great prosperity, and great adversity; both which times kindle Love, and make it more fervent.—Bacon.

" For several weeks I thus continued to think only of enjoying the full luxury of my situation; and being restrained, by a sense of honour, as well as a lurking apprehension of the police, from renewing my intimacy with my former companions at the hotel of Transylvania, I began to play in certain coteries less notorious, where my good luck rendered it unnecessary for me to have recourse to my former accomplishments. I passed a part of the afternoon in town, and returned always to supper at Chaillot, accompanied very often by M. de T——, whose intimacy and friendship for us daily increased.

" Manon soon found resources against ennui. She became acquainted with some young ladies, whom the spring brought into the neighbourhood. They occupied their leisure hours in walking, and the customary amusements of persons of their sex and age. Their little gains at cards (always within innocent limits) were laid out in defraying the expense of a coach, in which they took an airing occasionally in the Bois de Boulogne; and each night when I returned, I was sure of finding Manon more beautiful—more contented—more affectionate than ever.

" There arose, however, certain clouds, which seemed to threaten the continuance of this blissful tranquillity, but they were soon dispelled; and Manon's sprightliness made the affair so excessively comical in its termination, that it is even now pleasing to recur to it, as a proof of the tenderness as well as the cheerfulness of her disposition.

" The only servant we had came to me one day, with great embarrassment, and taking me aside, told me that he had a secret of the utmost importance to communicate to me. I urged him to explain himself without reserve. After some hesitation, he gave me to understand that a foreigner of high rank had apparently fallen in love with Manon. I felt my blood boil at the announcement. 'Has she shown any penchant for him?' I enquired, interrupting my informant with more impatience than was requisite, if I desired to have a full explanation.

" He was alarmed at my excitement; and replied in an undecided tone, that he had not made sufficiently minute observation to satisfy me; but that, having noticed for several days together the regular arrival of the stranger at the Bois de Boulogne, where, quitting his carriage, he walked by himself in the cross-avenues, appearing to seek opportunities of meeting Manon, it had occurred to him to form an acquaintance with the servants, in order to discover the name of their master; that they spoke of him as an Italian prince, and that they also suspected he was upon some adventure of gallantry. He had not been able to learn anything further, he added, trembling as he spoke, because the prince, then on the point of leaving the wood, had approached him, and with the most condescending familiarity asked his name; upon which, as if he at once knew that he was in our service, he congratulated him on having, for his mistress, the most enchanting person upon earth.

"I listened to this recital with the greatest impatience. He ended with the most awkward excuses, which I attributed to the premature and imprudent display of my own agitation. In vain I implored him to continue his history. He protested that he knew nothing more, and that what he had previously told me, having only happened the preceding day, he had not had a second opportunity of seeing the prince's servants. I encouraged him, not only with praises, but with a substantial recompense; and without betraying the slightest distrust of Manon, I requested him, in the mildest manner, to keep strict watch upon all the foreigner's movements.

"In truth, the effect of his fright was to leave me in a state of the cruellest suspense. It was possible that she had ordered him to suppress part of the truth. However, after a little reflection, I recovered sufficiently from my fears to see the manner in which I had exposed my weaknesses. I could hardly consider it a crime in Manon to be loved. Judging from appearances, it was probable that she was not even aware of her conquest. 'And what kind of life shall I in future lead,' thought I, 'if I am capable of letting jealousy so easily take possession of my mind?'

"I returned on the following day to Paris, with no other intention than to hasten the improvement of my fortune, by playing deeper than ever, in order to be in a condition to quit Chaillot on the first real occasion for uneasiness. That night I learned nothing at all calculated to trouble my repose. The foreigner had, as usual, made his appearance in the Bois de Boulogne; and venturing, from what had passed the preceding day, to accost my servant more familiarly, he spoke to him openly of his passion, but in such terms as not to lead to the slightest suspicion of Manon's being aware of it. He put a thousand questions to him, and at last tried to bribe him with large promises; and taking a letter from his pocket, he in vain entreated him, with the promise of some louis d'ors, to convey it to her.

"Two days passed without anything more occurring: the third was of a different character. I learned on my arrival, later than usual, from Paris, that Manon, while in the wood, had left her companions for a moment, and that the foreigner, who had followed her at a short distance, approached, upon her making him a sign, and that she handed him a letter, which he took with a transport of joy. He had only time to express his delight by kissing the *billet-doux*, for she was out of sight in an instant. But she appeared in unusually high spirits the remainder of the day; and even after her return to our lodgings, her gaiety continued. I trembled at every word.

"'Are you perfectly sure,' said I, in an agony of fear, to my servant, 'that your eyes have not deceived you?' He called Heaven to witness the truth of what he had told me.

"I know not to what excess the torments of my mind would have driven me, if Manon, who heard me come in, had not met me with an air of impatience, and complained of my delay. Before I had time to reply, she loaded me with caresses; and when she found we were alone, she reproached me warmly with the habit I was contracting of staying out so late. My silence gave her an opportunity of continuing; and she then said that for the last three weeks I had never spent one entire day in her society; that she could not endure such prolonged absence; that she should at least expect me to give up a day to her from time to time, and that she particularly wished me to be with her on the following day from morning till night.

"'You may be very certain I shall do that,' said I, in rather a sharp tone. She did not appear to notice my annoyance; she seemed to me to have more than her usual cheerfulness; and she described, with infinite pleasantry, the manner in which she had spent the day.

"'Incomprehensible girl!' said I to myself; 'what am I to expect after such a prelude?' The adventures of my first separation occurred to me; nevertheless, I fancied I saw in her cheerfulness, and the affectionate reception she gave me, an air of truth that perfectly accorded with her professions.

"It was an easy matter at supper to account for the low spirits which I could not conceal, by attributing them to a loss I had that day sustained at the gaming-table. I considered it most fortunate that the idea of my remaining all the next day at Chaillot was suggested by herself: I should thus have ample time for deliberation. My presence would prevent any fears for at least the next day; and if nothing should occur to compel me to disclose the discovery I had already made, I was determined on the following day to move my establishment into town, and fix myself in a quarter where I should have nothing to apprehend from the interference of princes. This arrangement made me pass the night more tranquilly, but it by no means put an end to the alarm I felt at the prospect of a new infidelity.

"When I awoke in the morning, Manon said to me, that although we were to pass the day at home, she did not at all wish that I should be less carefully dressed than on other occasions; and that she had a particular fancy for doing the duties of my toilette that morning with her own hands. It was an amusement she often indulged in: but she appeared to take more pains on this occasion than I had ever observed before. To gratify her, I was obliged to sit at her toilette table, and try all the different modes she imagined for dressing my hair. In the course of the operation, she made me often turn my head round towards her, and putting both hands upon my shoulders, she would examine me with most anxious curiosity: then, showing her approbation by one or two kisses, she would make me resume my position before the glass, in order to continue her occupation.

"This amatory trifling engaged us till dinner-time. The pleasure she seemed to derive from it, and her more than usual gaiety, appeared to me so thoroughly natural, that I found it impossible any longer to suspect the treason I had previously conjured up; and I was several times on the point of candidly opening my mind to her, and throwing off a load that had begun to weigh heavily upon my heart: but I flattered myself with the hope that the explanation would every moment come from herself, and I anticipated the delicious triumph this would afford me.

"We returned to her boudoir. She began again to put my hair in order, and I humoured all her whims; when they came to say that the Prince of —— was below, and wished to see her. The name alone almost threw me into a rage.

"'What then,' exclaimed I, as I indignantly pushed her from me, 'who?—what prince?'

"She made no answer to my enquiries.

"'Show him upstairs,' said she coolly to the servant; and then turning towards me, 'Dearest love! you whom I so fervently adore,' she added in the most bewitching tone, 'I only ask of you one moment's patience; one moment, one single moment! I will love you ten thousand times more than ever: your compliance now shall never, during my life, be forgotten.'

"Indignation and astonishment deprived me of the power of utterance. She renewed her entreaties, and I could not find adequate expressions to convey my feelings of anger and contempt. But hearing the door of the ante-chamber open, she grasped with one hand my locks, which were floating over my shoulders, while she took her toilette mirror in the other, and with all her strength led me in this manner to the door of the boudoir, which she opened with her knee, and presented to the foreigner, who had been prevented by the noise he heard inside from advancing beyond the middle of the ante-chamber, a spectacle that must have indeed amazed him. I saw a man extremely well dressed, but with a particularly ill-favoured countenance.

"Notwithstanding his embarrassment, he made her a profound bow. Manon gave him no time for speech-making; she held up the mirror before him: 'Look, sir,' said she to him, 'observe yourself minutely, and I only ask you then to do me justice. You wish me to love you: this is the man whom I love, and whom I have sworn to love during my whole life: make the comparison yourself. If you think you can rival him in my affections, tell me at least upon what pretensions; for I solemnly declare to you, that, in the estimation of your most obedient humble servant, all the princes in Italy are not worth a single one of the hairs I now hold in my hand.'

"During this whimsical harangue, which she had apparently prepared beforehand, I tried in vain to disengage myself, and feeling compassion for a person of such consideration, I was desirous, by my politeness at least, of making some reparation for this little outrage. But recovering his self-possession with the ease of a man accustomed to the world, he put an end to my feelings of pity by his reply, which was, in my opinion, rude enough.

"'Young lady! young lady!' said he to her, with a sardonic smile, 'my eyes in truth are opened, and I perceive that you are much less of a novice than I had pictured to myself.'

"He immediately retired without looking at her again, muttering to himself that the French women were quite as bad as those of Italy. I felt little desire, on this occasion, to change his opinion of the fair sex.

"Manon let go my hand, threw herself into an armchair, and made the room resound with her shouts of laughter. I candidly confess that I was touched most sensibly by this unexpected proof of her affection, and by the sacrifice of her own interest which I had just witnessed, and which she could only have been induced to make by her excessive love for me. Still, however, I could not help thinking she had gone rather too far. I reproached her with what I called her indiscretion. She told me that my rival, after having besieged her for several days in the Bois de Boulogne, and having made her comprehend his object by signs and grimaces, had actually made an open declaration of love; informing her at the same time of his name and all his titles, by means of a letter, which he had sent through the hands of the coachman who drove her and her companions; that he had promised her, on the other side of the Alps, a brilliant fortune and eternal adoration; that she returned to Chaillot, with the intention of relating to me the whole adventure, but that, fancying it might be made a source of amusement to us, she could not help gratifying her whim; that she accordingly invited the Italian prince, by a flattering note, to pay her a visit; and that it had afforded her equal delight to make me an accomplice, without giving me the least suspicion of her plan. I said not a word of the information I had received through another channel; and the intoxication of triumphant love made me applaud all she had done.

## IX

'Twas ever thus;—from childhood's hour
  I've seen my fondest hopes decay;—
I never loved a tree or flower,
  But it was sure to fade away;
I never nursed a dear Gazelle,
  To glad me with its dark-blue eye,
But, when it came to know me well,
  And love me, it was sure to die.

MOORE.

"DURING my life I have remarked that fate has invariably chosen for the time of its severest visitations, those moments when my fortune seemed established on the firmest basis. In the friendship of M. de T——, and the tender affections of Manon, I imagined myself so thoroughly happy, that I could not harbour the slightest apprehension of any new misfortune: there was one, nevertheless, at this very period impending, which reduced me to the state in which you beheld me at Passy, and which eventually brought in its train miseries of so deplorable a nature, that you will have difficulty in believing the simple recital that follows.

"One evening, when M. de T—— remained to sup with us, we heard the sound of a carriage stopping at the door of the inn. Curiosity tempted us to see who it was that arrived at this hour. They told us it was young G—— M——, the son of our most vindictive enemy, of that debauched old sinner who had incarcerated me in St. Lazare, and Manon in the Hospital. His name made the blood mount to my cheeks. 'It is Providence that has led him here,' said I to M. de T——, that I may punish him for the cowardly baseness of his father. He shall not escape without our measuring swords at least.' M. de T——, who knew him, and was even one of his most intimate friends, tried to moderate my feelings of anger towards him. He assured me that he was a most amiable young man, and so little capable of countenancing his father's conduct, that I could not be many minutes in his society without feeling esteem and affection for him. After saying many more things in his praise, he begged my permission to invite him to come and sit in our apartment, as well as to share the remainder of our supper. As to the objection of Manon being exposed by this proceeding to any danger, he pledged his honour and good faith, that when once the young man became acquainted with us, we should find in him a most zealous defender. After such an assurance, I could offer no further opposition.

"M. de T—— did not introduce him without delaying a few moments outside, to let him know who we were. He certainly came in with an air that prepossessed us in his favour: he shook hands with me; we sat down; he admired Manon; he appeared pleased with me, and with everything that belonged to us; and he ate with an appetite that did abundant honour to our hospitality.

"When the table was cleared, our conversation became more serious. He hung down his head while he spoke of his father's conduct towards us. He made, on his own part, the most submissive excuses. 'I say the less upon the subject,' said he, 'because I do not wish to recall a circumstance that fills me with grief and shame.' If he were sincere in the beginning, he became much more so in the end, for the conversation had not lasted half an hour, when I perceived that Manon's charms had made a visible impression upon him. His looks and his manner became by degrees more tender. He, however, allowed no expression to escape him; but, without even the aid of jealousy, I had had experience enough in love affairs to discern what was passing.

"He remained with us till a late hour in the night, and before he took his leave, congratulated himself on having made our acquaintance, and begged permission to call and renew the offer of his services. He went off next morning with M. de T——, who accepted the offer of a seat in his carriage.

"I felt, as I before said, not the slightest symptom of jealousy: I had a more foolish confidence than ever in Manon's vows. This dear creature had so absolute a dominion over my whole soul and affections, that I could give place to no other sentiment towards her than that of admiration and love. Far from considering it a crime that she should have pleased young G—— M——, I was gratified by the effect of her charms, and experienced only a feeling of pride in being loved by a girl whom the whole world found so enchanting. I did not even deem it worth while to mention my suspicions to her. We were for some days occupied in arranging her new wardrobe, and in considering whether we might venture to the theatre without the risk of being recognised. M. de T—— came again to see us before the end of the week, and we consulted him upon this point. He saw clearly that the way to please Manon was to say yes: we resolved to go all together that same evening.

"We were not able, however, to carry this intention into effect; for, having taken me aside, 'I have been in the greatest embarrassment,' said he to me, 'since I saw you, and that is the cause of my visiting you today. G—— M—— is in love with your mistress: he told me so in confidence; I am his intimate friend, and disposed to do him any service in my power; but I am not less devoted to you; his designs appeared to me unjustifiable, and I expressed my disapprobation of them; I should not have divulged his secret, if he had only intended to use fair and ordinary means for gaining Manon's affections; but he is aware of her capricious disposition; he has learned, God knows how, that her ruling passion is for affluence and pleasure; and, as he is already in possession of a considerable fortune, he declared his intention of tempting her at once with a present of great value, and the offer of an annuity of six thousand francs; if I had in all other points considered you both in an equal light, I should have had perhaps to do more violence to my feelings in betraying him: but a sense of justice as well as of friendship was on your side, and the more so from having been myself the imprudent, though unconscious, cause of his passion in introducing him here. I feel it my duty therefore to avert any evil consequences from the mischief I have inadvertently caused.

"I thanked M. de T—— for rendering me so important a service, and confessed to him, in a like spirit of confidence, that Manon's disposition was precisely what G—— M—— had imagined; that is to say, that she was incapable of enduring even the thought of poverty. 'However,' said I to him, 'when it is a mere question of more or less, I do not believe that she would give me up for any other person; I can afford to let her want for nothing, and I have from day to day reason to hope that my fortune will improve; I only dread one thing,' continued I, 'which is, that G—— M—— may take unfair advantage of the knowledge he has of our place of residence, and bring us into trouble by disclosing it.'

"M. de T—— assured me that I might be perfectly easy upon that head; that G—— M—— might be capable of a silly passion, but not of an act of baseness; that if he ever could be villain enough for such a thing, he, de T——, would be the first to punish him, and by that means make reparation for the mischief he had occasioned. 'I feel grateful for what you say,' said I, 'but the mischief will have been all done, and the remedy even seems doubtful; the wisest plan therefore will be to quit Chaillot, and go to reside elsewhere.' 'Very true,' said M. de T——, 'but you will not be able to do it quickly enough, for G—— M—— is to be here at noon; he told me so yesterday, and it was that intelligence that made me come so early this morning to inform you of his intentions. You may expect him every moment."

"The urgency of the occasion made me view this matter in a more serious light. As it seemed to me impossible to escape the visit of G—— M——, and perhaps equally so to prevent him from making his declaration to Manon, I resolved to tell her beforehand of the designs of my new rival. I fancied that when she knew I was aware of the offers that would be made to her, and made probably in my presence, she would be the more likely to reject them. I told M. de T—— of my intention, and he observed that he thought it a matter of extreme delicacy. 'I admit it,' said I, 'but no man ever had more reason for confiding in a mistress, than I have for relying on the affection of mine. The only thing that could possibly for a moment blind her, is the splendour of his offers; no doubt she loves her ease, but she loves me also; and in my present circumstances, I cannot believe that she would abandon me for the son of the man who had incarcerated her in the Magdalen.' In fine, I persisted in my intentions, and taking Manon aside, I candidly told her what I had learned.

"She thanked me for the good opinion I entertained of her, and promised to receive G—— M——'s offers in a way that should prevent a repetition of them. 'No,' said I, 'you must not irritate him by incivility: he has it in his power to injure us. But you know well enough, you little rogue,' continued I, smiling, 'how to rid yourself of a disagreeable or useless lover!' After a moment's pause she said: 'I have just thought of an admirable plan, and I certainly have a fertile invention. G—— M—— is the son of our bitterest enemy: we must avenge ourselves on the father, not through the son's person, but through his purse. My plan is to listen to his proposals, accept his presents, and then laugh at him.'

"'The project is not a bad one,' said I to her; 'but you forget, my dear child, that it is precisely the same course that conducted us formerly to the penitentiary.' I represented to her the danger of such an enterprise; she replied, that the only thing necessary was to take our measures with caution, and she found an answer to every objection I started. 'Show me the lover who does not blindly humour every whim of an adored mistress, and I will then allow that I was wrong in yielding so easily on this occasion.' The resolution was taken to make a dupe of G—— M——, and by an unforeseen and unlucky turn of fortune, I became the victim myself.

"About eleven o'clock his carriage drove up to the door. He made the most complaisant and refined speeches upon the liberty he had taken of coming to dine with us uninvited. He was not surprised at meeting M. de T——, who had the night before promised to meet him there, and who had, under some pretext or other, refused a seat in his carriage. Although there was not a single person in the party who was not at heart meditating treachery, we all sat down with an air of mutual confidence and friendship. G—— M—— easily found an opportunity of declaring his sentiments to Manon. I did not wish to annoy him by appearing vigilant, so I left the room purposely for several minutes.

"I perceived on my return that he had not had to encounter any very discouraging austerity on Manon's part, for he was in the best possible spirits. I affected good humour also. He was laughing in his mind at my simplicity, while I was not less diverted by his own. During the whole evening we were thus supplying to each other an inexhaustible fund of amusement. I contrived, before his departure, to let him have Manon for another moment to himself; so that he had reason to applaud my complaisance, as well as the hospitable reception I had given him.

"As soon as he got into his carriage with M. de T——, Manon ran towards me with extended arms, and embraced me; laughing all the while immoderately. She repeated all his speeches and proposals, without altering a word. This was the substance: He of course adored her; and wished to share with her a large fortune of which he was already in possession, without counting what he was to inherit at his father's death. She should be sole mistress of his heart and fortune; and as an immediate token of his liberality, he was ready at once to supply her with an equipage, a furnished house, a lady's maid, three footmen, and a man-cook.

"'There is indeed a son,' said I, 'very different from his father! But tell me truly, now, does not such an offer tempt you?' 'Me!' she replied, adapting to the idea two verses from Racine—

*Moi! vous me soupçonnez de cette perfidie?*
*Moi! je pourrais souffrir un visage odieux,*
*Qui rappelle toujours l'Hôpital à mes yeux?*

'No!' replied I, continuing the parody—

*J'aurais peine à penser que l'Hôpital, madame,*
*Fut un trait dont l'amour l'eut gravé dans votre àme.*

'But it assuredly is a temptation—a furnished house, a lady's maid, a cook, a carriage, and three servants—gallantry can offer but few more seductive temptations.'

"She protested that her heart was entirely mine, and that it was for the future only open to the impressions I chose to make upon it. 'I look upon his promises,' said she, 'as an instrument for revenge, rather than as a mark of love.' I asked her if she thought of accepting the hotel and the carriage. She replied that his money was all she wanted.

"The difficulty was, how to obtain the one without the other; we resolved to wait for a detailed explanation of the whole project in a letter which G—— M—— promised to write to her, and which in fact she received next morning by a servant out of livery, who, very cleverly, contrived an opportunity of speaking to her alone. She told him to wait for an answer, and immediately brought the letter to me: we opened it together.

"Passing over the usual commonplace expressions of tenderness, it gave a particular detail of my rival's promises. There were no limits to the expense. He engaged to pay her down ten thousand francs on her taking possession of the hotel, and to supply her expenditure in such a way as that she should never have less than that sum at her command. The appointed day for her entering into possession was close at hand. He only required two days for all his preparations, and he mentioned the name of the street and the hotel, where he promised to be in waiting for her in the afternoon of the second day, if she could manage to escape my vigilance. That was the only point upon which he begged of her to relieve his uneasiness; he seemed to be quite satisfied upon every other: but he added that, if she apprehended any difficulty in escaping from me, he could find sure means for facilitating her flight.

"G—— M—— the younger was more cunning than the old gentleman. He wanted to secure his prey before he counted out the cash. We considered what course Manon should adopt. I made another effort to induce her to give up the scheme, and strongly represented all its dangers; nothing, however, could shake her determination.

"Her answer to G—— M—— was brief, merely assuring him that she could be, without the least difficulty, in Paris on the appointed day and that he might expect her with certainty.

"We then resolved, that I should instantly hire lodgings in some village on the other side of Paris, and that I should take our luggage with me; that in the afternoon of the following day, which was the time appointed, she should go to Paris; that, after receiving G—— M——'s presents, she should earnestly entreat him to take her to the theatre; that she should carry with her as large a portion of the money as she could, and charge my servant with the remainder, for it was agreed that he was to accompany her. He was the man who had rescued her from the Magdalen, and he was devotedly attached to us. I was to be with a hackney-coach at the end of the street of St. André-des-arcs, and to leave it there about seven o'clock, while I stole, under cover of the twilight, to the door of the theatre. Manon promised to make some excuse for quitting her box for a moment, when she would come down and join me. The rest could be easily done. We were then to return to my hackney-coach, and quit Paris by the Faubourg St. Antoine, which was the road to our new residence.

"This plan, extravagant as it was, appeared to us satisfactorily arranged. But our greatest folly was in imagining that, succeed as we might in its execution, it would be possible for us to escape the consequences. Nevertheless, we exposed ourselves to all risk with the blindest confidence. Manon took her departure with Marcel—so was the servant called. I could not help feeling a pang as she took leave of me. 'Manon,' said I, 'do not deceive me; will you be faithful to me?' She complained, in the tenderest tone, of my want of confidence, and renewed all her protestations of eternal love.

"She was to be in Paris at three o'clock. I went some time after. I spent the remainder of the afternoon moping in the Café de Fère, near the Pont St. Michel. I remained there till nightfall. I then hired a hackney-coach, which I placed, according to our plan, at the end of the street of St. André-des-arcs, and went on foot to the door of the theatre. I was surprised at not seeing Marcel, who was to have been there waiting for me. I waited patiently for a full hour, standing among a crowd of lackeys, and gazing at every person that passed. At length, seven o'clock having struck, without my being able to discover anything or any person connected with our project, I procured a pit ticket, in order to ascertain if Manon and G—— M—— were in the boxes. Neither one nor the other could I find. I returned to the door, where I again stopped for a quarter of an hour, in an agony of impatience and uneasiness. No person appeared, and I went back to the coach, without knowing what to conjecture. The coachman, seeing me, advanced a few paces towards me, and said, with a mysterious air, that a very handsome young person had been waiting more than an hour for me in the coach; that she described me so exactly that he could not be mistaken, and having learned that I intended to return, she said she would enter the coach and wait with patience.

"I felt confident that it was Manon. I approached. I beheld a very pretty face, certainly, but alas, not hers. The lady asked, in a voice that I had never before heard, whether she had the honour of speaking to the Chevalier des Grieux? I answered, 'That is my name.' 'I have a letter for you,' said she, 'which will tell you what has brought me here, and by what means I learned your name.' I begged she would allow me a few moments to read it in an adjoining café. She proposed to follow me, and advised me to ask for a private room, to which I consented. 'Who is the writer of this letter?' I enquired. She referred me to the letter itself.

"I recognised Manon's hand. This is nearly the substance of the letter: G—— M—— had received her with a politeness and magnificence beyond anything she had previously conceived. He had loaded her with the most gorgeous presents. She had the prospect of almost imperial splendour. She assured me, however, that she could not forget me amidst all this magnificence; but that, not being able to prevail on G—— M—— to take her that evening to the play, she was obliged to defer the pleasure of seeing me; and that, as a slight consolation for the disappointment which she feared this might cause me, she had found a messenger in one of the loveliest girls in all Paris. She signed herself, 'Your loving and constant, MANON LESCAUT.'

"There was something so cruel and so insulting in the letter, that, what between indignation and grief, I resolutely determined to forget eternally my ungrateful and perjured mistress. I looked at the young woman who stood before me: she was exceedingly pretty, and I could have wished that she had been sufficiently so to render me inconstant in my turn. But there were wanting those lovely and languishing eyes, that divine gracefulness, that exquisite complexion, in fine, those innumerable charms which nature had so profusely lavished upon the perfidious Manon. 'No, no,' said I, turning away from her; 'the ungrateful wretch who sent you knew in her heart that she was sending you on a useless errand. Return to her; and tell her from me, to triumph in her crime, and enjoy it, if she can, without remorse. I abandon her in despair, and, at the same time, renounce all women, who, without her fascination, are no doubt her equals in baseness and infidelity.'

"I was then on the point of going away, determined never to bestow another thought on Manon: the mortal jealousy that was racking my heart lay concealed under a dark and sullen melancholy, and I fancied, because I felt none of those violent emotions which I had experienced upon former occasions, that I had shaken off my thraldom. Alas! I was even at that moment infinitely more the dupe of love, than of G—— M—— and Manon.

"The girl who had brought the letter, seeing me about to depart, asked me what I wished her to say to M. G—— M——, and to the lady who was with him? At this question, I stepped back again into the room, and by one of those unaccountable transitions that are only known to the victims of violent passion, I passed in an instant from the state of subdued tranquillity which I have just described, into an ungovernable fury 'Away!' said I to her, 'tell the traitor G—— M—— and his abandoned mistress the state of despair into which your accursed mission has cast me; but warn them that it shall not be long a source of amusement to them, and that my own hands shall be warmed with the heart's blood of both!' I sank back upon a chair; my hat fell on one side, and my cane upon the other: torrents of bitter tears rolled down my cheeks. The paroxysm of rage changed into a profound and silent grief: I did nothing but weep and sigh. 'Approach, my child, approach,' said I to the young girl; 'approach, since it is you they have sent to bring me comfort; tell me whether you have any balm to administer for the pangs of despair and rage—any argument to offer against the crime of self-destruction, which I have resolved upon, after ridding the world of two perfidious monsters. Yes, approach,' continued I, perceiving that she advanced with timid and doubtful steps; 'come and dry my sorrows; come and restore peace to my mind; come and tell me that at least you love me: you are handsome—I may perhaps love you in return.' The poor child, who was only sixteen or seventeen years of age, and who appeared more modest than girls of her class generally are, was thunderstruck at this unusual scene. She however gently approached to caress me, when with uplifted hands

I rudely repulsed her. 'What do you wish with me ?' exclaimed I to her. 'Ah ! you are a woman, and of a sex I abhor, and can no longer tolerate ; the very gentleness of your look threatens me with some new treason. Go, leave me here alone !' She made me a curtsy without uttering a word, and turned to go out. I called to her to stop : 'Tell me at least,' said I, 'wherefore—how—with what design they sent you here ? how did you discover my name, or the place where you could find me ?'

"She told me that she had long known M. G—— M—— ; that he had sent for her that evening about five o'clock ; and that, having followed the servant who had been dispatched to her, she was shown into a large house, where she found him playing at picquet with a beautiful young woman ; and that they both charged her to deliver the letter into my hands, after telling her that she would find me in a hackney-coach at the bottom of the street of St. André. I asked if they had said nothing more. She blushed while she replied, that they had certainly made her believe that I should be glad of her society. 'They have deceived you too,' said I, 'my poor girl—they have deceived you ; you are a woman, and probably wish for a lover ; but you must find one who is rich and happy, and it is not here you will find him. Return, return to M. G—— M—— ; he possesses everything requisite to make a man beloved. He has furnished houses and equipages to bestow, while I, who have nothing but constancy of love to offer, am despised for my poverty, and laughed at for my simplicity.'

"I continued in a tone of sorrow or violence, as these feelings alternately took possession of my mind. However, by the very excess of my agitation, I became gradually so subdued as to be able calmly to reflect upon the situation of affairs. I compared this new misfortune with those which I had already experienced of the same kind, and I could not perceive that there was any more reason for despair now, than upon former occasions. I knew Manon : why then distress myself on account of a calamity which I could not but have plainly foreseen ? Why not rather think of seeking a remedy ? there was yet time ; I at least ought not to spare my own exertions, if I wished to avoid the bitter reproach of having contributed, by my own indolence, to my misery. I thereupon set about considering every means of raising a gleam of hope.

"To attempt to take her by main force from the hands of G—— M—— was too desperate a project, calculated only to ruin me, and without the slightest probability of succeeding. But it seemed to me that if I could ensure a moment's interview with her, I could not fail to regain my influence over her affections. I so well knew how to excite her sensibilities ! I was so confident of her love for me ! The very whim even of sending me a pretty woman by way of consoling me, I would stake my existence, was her idea, and that it was the suggestion of her own sincere sympathy for my sufferings.

"I resolved to exert every nerve to procure an interview. After a multitude of plans which I canvassed one after another, I fixed upon the following : M. de T—— had shown so much sincerity in the services he had rendered me, that I could not entertain a doubt of his zeal and good faith. I proposed to call upon him at once, and make him send for G—— M——, under pretence of some important business. Half an hour would suffice to enable me to see Manon. I thought it would not be difficult to get introduced into her apartment during G—— M——'s absence.

" This determination pacified me, and I gave a liberal present to the girl, who was still with me ; and in order to prevent her from returning to those who had sent her, I took down her address, and half promised to call upon her at a later hour. I then got into the hackney-coach, and drove quickly to M. de T——'s. I was fortunate enough to find him at home. I had been apprehensive upon this point as I went along. A single sentence put him in possession of the whole case, as well of my sufferings, as of the friendly service I had come to supplicate at his hands.

" He was so astonished to learn that G—— M—— had been able to seduce Manon from me, that, not being aware that I had myself lent a hand to my own misfortune, he generously offered to assemble his friends, and evoke their aid for the deliverance of my mistress. I told him that such a proceeding might by its publicity be attended with danger to Manon and to me. ' Let us risk our lives,' said I, ' only as a last resource. My plan is of a more peaceful nature, and promising at least equal success.' He entered without a murmur into all that I proposed ; so again stating that all I required was, that he should send for G—— M——, and contrive to keep him an hour or two from home, we at once set about our operations.

" We first of all considered what expedient we could make use of for keeping him out so long a time. I proposed that he should write a note dated from a café, begging of him to come there as soon as possible upon an affair of too urgent importance to admit of delay. ' I will watch,' added I, ' the moment he quits the house, and introduce myself without any difficulty, being only known to Manon, and my servant Marcel. You can at the same time tell G—— M——, that the important affair upon which you wished to see him was the immediate want of a sum of money ; that you had just emptied your purse at play, and that you had played on, with continued bad luck, upon credit. He will require some time to take you to his father's house, where he keeps his money, and I shall have quite sufficient for the execution of my plan.'

" M. de T—— minutely adhered to these directions. I left him in a café, where he at once wrote his letter. I took my station close by Manon's house. I saw de T——'s messenger arrive, and G—— M—— come out the next moment, followed by a servant. Allowing him barely time to get out of the street, I advanced to my deceiver's door, and notwithstanding the anger I felt, I knocked with as much respect as at the portal of a church. Fortunately it was Marcel who opened for me. Although I had nothing to apprehend from the other servants, I asked him in a low voice if he could conduct me unseen into the room in which Manon was. He said that was easily done, by merely ascending the great staircase. ' Come then at once,' said I to him, ' and endeavour to prevent anyone from coming up while I am there.' I reached the apartment without any difficulty.

" Manon was reading. I had there an opportunity of admiring the singular character of this girl. Instead of being nervous or alarmed at my appearance, she scarcely betrayed a symptom of surprise, which few persons, however indifferent, could restrain, on seeing one whom they imagined to be far distant. ' Ah ! it is you, my dear love,' said she, approaching to embrace me with her usual tenderness. ' Good heavens, how venturesome and foolhardy you are ! Who could have expected to see you in this place ! ' Instead of embracing her in return, I repulsed her with indignation, and retreated two or three paces from her. This evidently disconcerted her. She remained immovable, and fixed her eyes on me, while she changed colour.

" I was in reality so delighted to behold her once more, that, with so much real cause for anger, I could hardly bring my lips to upbraid her. My heart, however, felt the cruel outrage she had inflicted upon me. I endeavoured to revive the recollection of it in my own mind, in order to excite my feelings, and put on a look of stern indignation. I remained silent for a few moments, when I remarked that she observed my agitation, and trembled : apparently the effect of her fears.

" I could not longer endure this spectacle. ' Ah ! Manon,' said I to her in the mildest tone, ' faithless and perjured Manon ! How am I to complain of your conduct ? I see you pale and trembling, and I am still so much alive to your slightest sufferings, that I am unwilling to add to them by my reproaches. But, Manon, I tell you that my heart is pierced with sorrow at your treatment of me—treatment that is seldom inflicted but with the purpose of destroying one's life. This is the third time, Manon ; I have kept a correct account ; it is impossible to forget that. It is now for you to consider what course you will adopt ; for my afflicted heart is no longer capable of sustaining such shocks. I know and feel that it must give way, and it is at this moment ready to burst with grief. I can say no more,' added I, throwing myself into a chair ; 'I have hardly strength to speak, or to support myself.'

" She made me no reply ; but when I was seated, she sank down upon her knees, and rested her head upon my lap, covering her face with her hands. I perceived in a moment that she was shedding floods of tears. Heavens ! with what conflicting sensations was I at that instant agitated ! ' Ah ! Manon, Manon,' said I, sighing, ' it is too late to give me tears after the death-blow you have inflicted. You affect a sorrow which you cannot feel. The greatest of your misfortunes is no doubt my presence, which has been always an obstacle to your happiness. Open your eyes ; look up and see who it is that is here ; you will not throw away tears of tenderness upon an unhappy wretch whom you have betrayed and abandoned.'

"She kissed my hands without changing her position. 'Inconstant Manon,' said I again, 'ungrateful and faithless girl, where now are all your promises and your vows? Capricious and cruel that you are! what has now become of the love that you protested for me this very day? Just Heavens,' added I, 'is it thus you permit a traitor to mock you, after having called you so solemnly to witness her vows! Recompense and reward then are for the perjured! Despair and neglect are the lot of fidelity and truth!'

"These words conveyed even to my own mind a sentiment so bitterly severe, that, in spite of myself, some tears escaped from me. Manon perceived this by the change in my voice. She at length spoke. 'I must have indeed done something most culpable,' said she, sobbing with grief, 'to have excited and annoyed you to this degree; but, I call Heaven to attest my utter unconsciousness of crime, and my innocence of all criminal intention!'

"This speech struck me as so devoid of reason and of truth, that I could not restrain a lively feeling of anger. 'Horrible hypocrisy!' cried I; 'I see more plainly than ever that you are dishonest and treacherous. Now at length I learn your wretched disposition. Adieu, base creature,' said I, rising from my seat; 'I would prefer death a thousand times rather than continue to hold the slightest communication with you. May Heaven punish me, if I ever again waste upon you the smallest regard! Live on with your new lover—renounce all feelings of honour—detest me—your love is now a matter to me of utter insignificance!'

"Manon was so terrified by the violence of my anger, that, remaining on her knees by the chair from which I had just before risen, breathless and trembling, she fixed her eyes upon me. I advanced a little farther towards the door, but, unless I had lost the last spark of humanity, I could not continue longer unmoved by such a spectacle.

"So far, indeed, was I from this kind of stoical indifference, that, rushing at once into the very opposite extreme, I returned, or rather flew back to her without an instant's reflection. I lifted her in my arms; I gave her a thousand tender kisses; I implored her to pardon my ungovernable temper; I confessed that I was an absolute brute, and unworthy of being loved by such an angel.

"I made her sit down, and throwing myself, in my turn, upon my knees, I conjured her to listen to me in that attitude. Then I briefly expressed all that a submissive and impassioned lover could say most tender and respectful. I supplicated her pardon. She let her arms fall over my neck, as she said that it was she who stood in need of forgiveness, and begged of me in mercy to forget all the annoyances she had caused me, and that she began, with reason, to fear that I should not approve of what she had to say in her justification. 'Me!' said I interrupting her impatiently; 'I require no justification; I approve of all you have done. It is not for me to demand excuses for anything you do; I am but too happy, too contented, if my dear Manon will only leave me master of her affections ! But,' continued I, remembering that it was the crisis of my fate, 'may I not, Manon, all-powerful Manon, you who wield at your pleasure my joys and sorrows, may I not be permitted, after having conciliated you by my submission and all the signs of repentance, to speak to you now of my misery and distress ? May I now learn from your own lips what my destiny is to be, and whether you are resolved to sign my death-warrant, by spending even a single night with my rival ?'

"She considered a moment before she replied. 'My good chevalier,' said she, resuming the most tranquil tone, 'if you had only at first explained yourself thus distinctly, you would have spared yourself a world of trouble, and prevented a scene that has really annoyed me. Since your distress is the result of jealousy, I could at first have cured that by offering to accompany you where you pleased. But I imagined it was caused by the letter which I was obliged to write in the presence of G—— M——, and of the girl whom we sent with it. I thought you might have construed that letter into a mockery ; and have fancied that, by sending such a messenger, I meant to announce my abandonment of you for the sake of G—— M——. It was this idea that at once overwhelmed me with grief ; for, innocent as I knew myself to be, I could not but allow that appearances were against me. However,' continued she, 'I will leave you to judge of my conduct, after I shall have explained the whole truth.'

"She then told me all that had occurred to her after joining G—— M——, whom she found punctually awaiting her arrival. He had in fact received her in the most princely style. He showed her through all the apartments, which were fitted up in the neatest and most correct taste. He had counted out to her in her boudoir ten thousand francs, as well as a quantity of jewels, amongst which were the identical pearl necklace and bracelets which she had once before received as a present from his father. He then led her into a splendid room, which she had not before seen, and in which an exquisite collation was served ; she was waited upon by the new servants, whom he had hired purposely for her, and whom he now desired to consider themselves as exclusively her attendants ; the carriage and the horses were afterwards paraded, and he then proposed a game of cards, until supper should be announced.

"'I acknowledge,' continued Manon, 'that I was dazzled by all this magnificence. It struck me that it would be madness to sacrifice at once so many good things for the mere sake of carrying off the money and the jewels already in my possession ; that it was a certain fortune made for both you and me, and that we might pass the remainder of our lives most agreeably and comfortably at the expense of G—— M——.

"'Instead of proposing the theatre, I thought it more prudent to sound his feelings with regard to you, in order to ascertain what facilities we should have for meeting in future, on the supposition that I could carry my project into effect. I found him of a most tractable disposition. He asked me how I felt towards you, and if I had not experienced some compunction at quitting you. I told him that you were so truly amiable, and had ever treated me with such undeviating kindness, that it was impossible I could hate you. He admitted that you were a man of merit, and expressed an ardent desire to gain your friendship.

" 'He was anxious to know how I thought you would take my elopement, particularly when you should learn that I was in his hands. I answered, that our love was of such long standing as to have had time to moderate a little; that, besides, you were not in very easy circumstances, and would probably not consider my departure as any severe misfortune, inasmuch as it would relieve you from a burden of no very insignificant nature. I added that, being perfectly convinced you would take the whole matter rationally, I had not hesitated to tell you that I had some business in Paris; but you had at once consented, and that having accompanied me yourself, you did not seem very uneasy when we separated.

" 'If I thought,' said he to me, 'that he could bring himself to live on good terms with me, I should be too happy to make him a tender of my services and attentions.' I assured him that, from what I knew of your disposition, I had no doubt you would acknowledge his kindness in a congenial spirit: especially, I added, if he could assist you in your affairs, which had become embarrassed since your disagreement with your family. He interrupted me by declaring, that he would gladly render you any service in his power, and that if you were disposed to form a new attachment, he would introduce you to an extremely pretty woman, whom he had just given up for me.

" 'I approved of all he said,' she added, 'for fear of exciting any suspicions; and being more and more satisfied of the feasibility of my scheme, I only longed for an opportunity of letting you into it, lest you should be alarmed at my not keeping my appointment. With this view I suggested the idea of sending this young lady to you, in order to have an opportunity of writing; I was obliged to have recourse to this plan, because I could not see a chance of his leaving me to myself for a moment.'

" 'He was greatly amused with my proposition; he called his valet, and asking him whether he could immediately find his late mistress, he dispatched him at once in search of her. He imagined that she would have to go to Chaillot to meet you, but I told him that, when we parted, I promised to meet you again at the theatre, or that, if anything should prevent me from going there, you were to wait for me in a coach at the, end of the street of St. André; that consequently it would be best to send your new love there, if it were only to save you from the misery of suspense during the whole night. I said it would be also necessary to write you a line of explanation, without which you would probably be puzzled by the whole transaction. He consented; but I was obliged to write in his presence; and I took especial care not to explain matters too palpably in my letter.

" 'This is the history,' said Manon, 'of the entire affair. I conceal nothing from you, of either my conduct or my intentions. The girl arrived; I thought her handsome; and as I doubted not that you would be mortified by my absence, I did most sincerely hope that she would be able to dissipate something of your ennui: for it is the fidelity of the heart alone that I value. I should have been too delighted to have sent Marcel, but I could not for a single instant find an opportunity of telling him what I wished to communicate to you.' She finished her story by describing the embarrassment into which M. de T——'s letter had thrown G—— M——; 'he hesitated,' said she, 'about leaving, and assured me that he should not be long absent; and it is on this account that I am uneasy at seeing you here, and that I betrayed, at your appearance, some slight feeling of surprise.'

" I listened to her with great patience. There were certainly parts of her recital sufficiently cruel and mortifying; for the intention, at least, of the infidelity was so obvious, that she had not even taken the trouble to disguise it. She could never have imagined that G—— M—— meant to venerate her as a vestal. She must therefore clearly have made up her mind to pass at least one night with him. What an avowal for a lover's ears! However, I considered myself as partly the cause of her guilt, by having been the first to let her know G—— M——'s sentiments towards her, and by the silly readiness with which I entered into this rash project. Besides, by a natural bent of my mind, peculiar I believe to myself, I was duped by the ingenuousness of her story—by that open and winning manner with which she related even the circumstances most calculated to annoy me. 'There is nothing of wanton vice,' said I to myself, 'in her transgressions; she is volatile and imprudent, but she is sincere and affectionate.' My love alone rendered me blind to all her faults. I was enchanted at the prospect of rescuing her that very night from my rival. I said to her: 'With whom do you mean to pass the night?' She was evidently disconcerted by the question, and answered me in an embarrassed manner with *buts* and *ifs*.

" I felt for her, and interrupted her by saying that I at once expected her to accompany me.

" 'Nothing can give me more pleasure,' said she; 'but you don't approve then of my project?'

" 'Is it not enough,' replied I, 'that I approve of all that you have, up to this moment, done?'

" 'What,' said she, 'are we not even to take the ten thousand francs with us? Why, he gave me the money; it is mine.'

" I advised her to leave everything, and let us think only of escaping; for although I had been hardly half an hour with her, I began to dread the return of G—— M——. However, she so earnestly urged me to consent to our going out with something in our pockets, that I thought myself bound to make her, on my part, some concession, in return for all she yielded to me.

"While we were getting ready for our departure, I heard someone knock at the street door. I felt convinced that it must be G—— M——; and in the heat of the moment, I told Manon, that as sure as he appeared I would take his life. In truth, I felt that I was not sufficiently recovered from my late excitement to be able to restrain my fury if I met him. Marcel put an end to my uneasiness, by handing me a letter which he had received for me at the door; it was from M. de T——.

"He told me that, as G—— M—— had gone to his father's house for the money which he wanted, he had taken advantage of his absence to communicate to me an amusing idea that had just come into his head; that it appeared to him, I could not possibly take a more agreeable revenge upon my rival, than by eating his supper, and spending the night in the very bed which he had hoped to share with my mistress; all this seemed to him easy enough, if I could only find two or three men upon whom I could depend, of courage sufficient to stop him in the street, and detain him in custody until next morning; that he would undertake to keep him occupied for another hour at least, under some pretext, which he could devise before G—— M——'s return.

"I showed the note to Manon; I told her at the same time of the manner in which I had procured the interview with her. My scheme, as well as the new one of M. de T——'s, delighted her: we laughed heartily at it for some minutes; but when I treated it as a mere joke, I was surprised at her insisting seriously upon it, as a thing perfectly practicable, and too delightful to be neglected. In vain I enquired where she thought I could possibly find, on a sudden, men fit for such an adventure? and on whom I could rely for keeping G—— M—— in strict custody? She said that I should at least try, as M. de T—— ensured us yet a full hour; and as to my other objections, she said that I was playing the tyrant, and did not show the slightest indulgence to her fancies. She said that it was impossible there could be a more enchanting project. 'You will have his place at supper; you will sleep in his bed; and tomorrow, as early as you like, you can walk off with both his mistress and his money. You may thus, at one blow, be amply revenged upon father and son.'

"I yielded to her entreaties, in spite of the secret misgivings of my own mind, which seemed to forebode the unhappy catastrophe that afterwards befell me. I went out with the intention of asking two or three guardsmen, with whom Lescaut had made me acquainted, to undertake the arrest of G—— M——. I found only one of them at home, but he was a fellow ripe for any adventure; and he no sooner heard our plan, than he assured me of certain success: all he required were six pistoles, to reward the three private soldiers whom he determined to employ in the business. I begged of him to lose no time. He got them together in less than a quarter of an hour. I waited at his lodgings till he returned with them, and then conducted him to the corner of a street through which I knew G—— M—— must pass on going back to Manon's house. I requested him not to treat G——

M—— roughly, but to keep him confined, and so strictly watched, until seven o'clock next morning, that I might be free from all apprehension of his escape. He told me his intention was to bring him a prisoner to his own room, and make him undress and sleep in his bed, while he and his gallant comrades should spend the night in drinking and playing.

"I remained with them until we saw G—— M—— returning homewards; and I then withdrew a few steps into a dark recess in the street, to enjoy so entertaining and extraordinary a scene. The officer challenged him with a pistol to his breast, and then told him, in a civil tone, that he did not want either his money or his life; but that if he hesitated to follow him, or if he gave the slightest alarm, he would blow his brains out. G—— M——, seeing that his assailant was supported by three soldiers, and perhaps not uninfluenced by a dread of the pistol, yielded without further resistance. I saw him led away like a lamb.

## X

What lost a world, and bade a hero fly?
The timid tear in Cleopatra's eye.
Yet be the soft triumvir's fault forgiven,
By this, how many lose—not earth—but heaven!
Consign their souls to man's eternal foe,
And seal their own, to spare some wanton's, woe!

BYRON.

"I SOON returned to Manon; and to prevent the servants from having any suspicion, I told her in their hearing, that she need not expect M. G—— M—— to supper; that he was most reluctantly occupied with business which detained him, and that he had commissioned me to come and make his excuses, and to fill his place at the supper table; which, in the company of so beautiful a lady, I could not but consider a very high honour. She seconded me with her usual adroitness. We sat down to supper. I put on the most serious air I could assume, while the servants were in the room, and at length having got rid of them, we passed, beyond all comparison, the most agreeable evening of my life. I gave Marcel orders to find a hackney-coach, and engage it to be at the gate on the following morning a little before six o'clock. I pretended to take leave of Manon about midnight, but easily gaining admission again, through Marcel, I proceeded to occupy G—— M——'s bed, as I had filled his place at the supper table.

"In the meantime our evil genius was at work for our destruction. We were like children enjoying the success of our silly scheme, while the sword hung suspended over our heads. The thread which upheld it was just about to break; but the better to understand all the circumstances of our ruin, it is necessary to know the immediate cause.

"G—— M—— was followed by a servant, when he was stopped by my friend the guardsman. Alarmed by what he saw, this fellow retraced his steps, and the first thing he did was to go and inform old G—— M—— of what had just happened.

"Such a piece of news, of course, excited him greatly. This was his only son; and considering the old gentleman's advanced age, he was extremely active and ardent. He first enquired of the servant what his son had been doing that afternoon; whether he had had any quarrel on his own account, or interfered in any other; whether he had been in any suspicious house. The lackey, who fancied his master in imminent danger, and thought he ought not to have any reserve in such an emergency, disclosed at once all that he knew of his connection with Manon, and of the expense he had gone to on her account; the manner in which he had passed the afternoon with her until about nine o'clock, the circumstance of his leaving her, and the outrage he encountered on his return. This was enough to convince him that his son's affair was a love quarrel. Although it was then at least half-past ten at night, he determined at once to call on the lieutenant of police. He begged of him to issue immediate orders to all the detachments that were out on duty, and he himself, taking some men with him, hastened to the street where his son had been stopped: he visited every place where he thought he might have a chance of finding him; and not being able to discover the slightest trace of him, he went off to the house of his mistress, to which he thought he probably might by this time have returned.

"I was stepping into bed when he arrived. The door of the chamber being closed, I did not hear the knock at the gate, but he rushed into the house, accompanied by two archers of the guard, and after fruitless enquiries of the servants about his son, he resolved to try whether he could get any information from their mistress. He came up to the apartment, still accompanied by the guard. We were just on the point of lying down when he burst open the door, and electrified us by his appearance. 'Heavens!' said I to Manon, 'it is old G—— M——.' I attempted to get possession of my sword; but it was fortunately entangled in my belt. The archers, who saw my object, advanced to lay hold of me. Stript to my shirt, I could, of course, offer no resistance, and they speedily deprived me of all means of defence.

"G—— M——, although a good deal embarrassed by the whole scene, soon recognised me; and Manon still more easily. 'Is this a dream?' said he, in the most serious tone—'do I not see before me the Chevalier des Grieux and Manon Lescaut?' I was so overcome with shame and disappointment, that I could make him no reply. He appeared for some minutes revolving different thoughts in his mind; and as if they had suddenly excited his anger, he exclaimed, addressing himself to me: 'Wretch! I am confident that you have murdered my son!'

"I felt indignant at so insulting a charge. 'You hoary and lecherous villain!' I exclaimed, 'if I had been inclined to kill any of your worthless family, it is with you I should most assuredly have commenced.'

" 'Hold him fast,' cried he to the archers; 'he must give me some tidings of my son; I shall have him hanged tomorrow, if he does not presently let me know how he has disposed of him.'

" 'You will have me hanged,' said I, 'will you? Infamous scoundrel! it is for such as you that the gibbet is erected. Know that the blood which flows in my veins is noble, and purer in every sense than yours. Yes,' I added, 'I do know what has happened to your son; and if you irritate me further, I will have him strangled before morning; and I promise you the consolation of meeting in your own person the same fate, after he is disposed of.'

"I was imprudent in acknowledging that I knew where his son was, but excess of anger made me commit this indiscretion. He immediately called in five or six other archers, who were waiting at the gate, and ordered them to take all the servants into custody. 'Ah! ah! Chevalier,' said he, in a tone of sardonic raillery,—'so you do know where my son is, and you will have him strangled, you say? We will try to set that matter to rights.'

"I now saw the folly I had committed.

"He approached Manon, who was sitting upon the bed, bathed in a flood of tears. He said something, with the most cruel irony, of the despotic power she wielded over old and young, father and son—her edifying dominion over her empire. This superannuated monster of incontinence actually attempted to take liberties with her.

" 'Take care,' exclaimed I, 'how you lay a finger upon her!—neither divine nor human law will be able, should your folly arouse it, to shield you from my vengeance!'

"He quitted the room, desiring the archers to make us dress as quickly as possible.

"I know not what were his intentions at that moment with regard to us; we might perhaps have regained our liberty if we had told him where his son was. As I dressed, I considered whether this would not be the wisest course. But if, on quitting the room, such had been the disposition of his mind, it was very different when he returned. He had first gone to question Manon's servants, who were in the custody of the guard. From those who had been expressly hired for her service by his son, he could learn nothing; but when he found that Marcel had been previously our servant, he determined to extract some information from him, by means of intimidation, threats, or bribes.

"This lad was faithful, but weak and unsophisticated. The remembrance of what he had done at the penitentiary for Manon's release, joined to the terror with which G—— M—— now inspired him, so subdued his mind, that he thought they were about leading him to the gallows, or the rack. He promised that, if they would spare his life, he would disclose everything he knew. This speech made G—— M—— imagine that there was something more serious in the affair than he had before supposed; he not only gave Marcel a promise of his life, but a handsome reward in hand for his intended confession.

"The booby then told him the leading features of our plot, of which we had made no secret before him, as he was himself to have borne a part in it. True, he knew nothing of the alterations we had made at Paris in our original design; but he had been informed, before quitting Chaillot, of our projected adventure, and of the part he was to perform. He therefore told him that the object was to make a dupe of his son; and that Manon was to receive, if she had not already received, ten thousand francs, which, according to our project, would be effectually lost to G—— M——, his heirs and assigns for ever.

"Having acquired this information, the old gentleman hastened back in a rage to the apartment. Without uttering a word, he passed into the boudoir, where he easily put his hand upon the money and the jewels. He then accosted us, bursting with rage; and holding up what he was pleased to call our plunder, he loaded us with the most indignant reproaches. He placed close to Manon's eye the pearl necklace and bracelets. 'Do you recognise them?' said he, in a tone of mockery; 'it is not, perhaps, the first time you may have seen them. The identical pearls, by my faith! They were selected by your own exquisite taste! The poor innocents!' added he; 'they really are most amiable creatures, both one and the other; but they are perhaps a little too much inclined to roguery.'

"I could hardly contain my indignation at this speech. I would have given for one moment's liberty—Heavens! what would I not have given? At length, I suppressed my feelings sufficiently to say in a tone of moderation, which was but the refinement of rage: 'Put an end, sir, to this insolent mockery! What is your object? What do you purpose doing with us?'

"'M. Chevalier,' he answered, 'my object is to see you quietly lodged in the prison of Le Châtelet. Tomorrow will bring daylight with it, and we shall then be able to take a clearer view of matters; and I hope you will at last do me the favour to let me know where my son is.'

"It did not require much consideration to feel convinced that our incarceration in Le Châtelet would be a serious calamity. I foresaw all the dangers that would ensue. In spite of my pride, I plainly saw the necessity of bending before my fate, and conciliating my most implacable enemy by submission. I begged of him, in the quietest manner, to listen to me. 'I wish to do myself but common justice, sir,' said I to him; 'I admit that my youth has led me into egregious follies; and that you have had fair reason to complain: but if you have ever felt the resistless power of love, if you can enter into the sufferings of an unhappy young man, from whom all that he most loved was ravished. you may think me perhaps not so culpable in seeking the gratification of an innocent revenge; or at least, you may consider me sufficiently punished, by the exposure and degradation I have just now endured. Neither pains nor imprisonment will be requisite to make me tell you where your son now is. He is in perfect safety. It was never my intention to injure him, nor to give you just cause for offence. I am ready to let you know the place where he is safely passing the night, if, in return, you will set us at liberty.'

"The old tiger, far from being softened by my prayer, turned his back upon me and laughed. A few words escaped him, which showed that he perfectly well knew our whole plan from the commencement. As for his son, the brute said that he would easily find him, since I had not assassinated him. 'Conduct them to the Petit-Châtelet,' said he to the archers; 'and take especial care that the chevalier does not escape you: he is a scamp that once before escaped from St. Lazare.'

"He went out, and left me in a condition that you may picture to yourself. 'O Heavens!' cried I to myself, 'I receive with humble submission all your visitations; but that a wretched scoundrel should thus have the power to tyrannise over me! this it is that plunges me into the depths of despair!' The archers begged that we would not detain them any longer. They had a coach at the door. 'Come, my dear angel,' said I to Manon, as we went down, 'come, let us submit to our destiny in all its rigour: it may one day please Heaven to render us more happy.'

"We went in the same coach. I supported her in my arms. I had not heard her utter a single word since G—— M——'s first appearance: but now, finding herself alone with me, she addressed me in the tenderest manner, and accused herself of being the cause of all my troubles. I assured her that I never could complain, while she continued to love me. 'It is not I that have reason to complain,' I added; 'imprisonment for a few months has no terrors for me, and I would infinitely prefer Le Châtelet to St. Lazare; but it is for you, my dearest soul, that my heart bleeds. What a lot for such an angel! How can you, gracious Heaven! subject to such rigour the most perfect work of your own hands? Why are we not both of us born with qualities conformable to our wretched condition? We are endowed with spirit, with taste, with feeling; while the vilest of God's creatures—brutes, alone worthy of our unhappy fate, are revelling in all the favours of fortune.'

"These feelings filled me with grief; but it was bliss compared with my prospects for the future. My fear, on account of Manon, knew no bounds. She had already been an inmate of the Magdalen; and even if she had left it by fair means, I knew that a relapse of this nature would be attended with disastrous consequences. I wished to let her know my fears: I was apprehensive of exciting hers. I trembled for her, without daring to put her on her guard against the danger; and I embraced her tenderly, to satisfy her, at least, of my love, which was almost the only sentiment to which I dared to give expression. 'Manon,' said I, 'tell me sincerely, will you ever cease to love me?'

"She answered, that it made her unhappy to think that I could doubt it.

"'Very well,' replied I, 'I do so no longer; and with this conviction, I may well defy all my enemies. Through the influence of my family, I can ensure my own liberation from the Châtelet; and my life will be of little use, and of short duration, if I do not succeed in rescuing you.'

"We arrived at the prison, where they put us into separate cells. This blow was the less severe, because I was prepared for it. I recommended Manon to the attention of the porter, telling him that I was a person of some distinction, and promising him a considerable recompense. I embraced my dearest mistress before we parted; I implored her not to distress herself too much, and to fear nothing while I lived. I had money with me: I gave her some; and I paid the porter, out of what remained, the amount of a month's expenses for both of us in advance. This had an excellent effect, for I found myself placed in an apartment comfortably furnished, and they assured me that Manon was in one equally good.

"I immediately set about devising the means of procuring my liberty. There certainly had been nothing actually criminal in my conduct; and supposing even that our felonious intention was established by the evidence of Marcel, I knew that criminal intentions alone were not punishable. I resolved to write immediately to my father, and beg of him to come himself to Paris. I felt much less humiliation, as I have already said, in being in Le Châtelet than in St. Lazare. Besides, although I preserved all proper respect for the paternal authority, age and experience had considerably lessened my timidity. I wrote, and they made no difficulty in the prison about forwarding my letter; but it was a trouble I should have spared myself, had I known that my father was about to arrive on the following day in Paris. He had received the letter I had written to him a week before; it gave him extreme delight; but, notwithstanding the flattering hopes I had held out of my conversion, he could not implicitly rely on my statements. He determined therefore to satisfy himself of my reformation by the evidence of his own senses, and to regulate his conduct towards me according to his conviction of my sincerity. He arrived the day after my imprisonment.

"His first visit was to Tiberge, to whose care I begged that he would address his answer. He could not learn from him either my present abode or condition: Tiberge merely told him of my principal adventures since I had escaped from St. Lazare. Tiberge spoke warmly of the disposition to virtue which I had evinced at our last interview. He added, that he considered me as having quite got rid of Manon; but that he was nevertheless surprised at my not having given him any intelligence about myself for a week. My father was not to be duped. He fully comprehended that there was something in the silence of which Tiberge complained, which had escaped my poor friend's penetration; and he took such pains to find me out, that in two days after his arrival he learned that I was in Le Châtelet.

"Before I received this visit, which I little expected so soon, I had the honour of one from the lieutenant-general of police, or, to call things by their right names, I was subjected to an official examination. He upbraided me certainly, but not in any harsh or annoying manner. He told me, in the kindest tone, that he bitterly lamented my bad conduct; that I had committed a gross indiscretion in making an enemy of such a man as M. G—— M——; that in truth it was easy to see that there was, in the affair, more of imprudence and folly than of malice; but that still it was the second time I had been brought as a culprit under his cognisance; and that he had hoped I should have become more sedate, after the experience of two or three months in St. Lazare.

"Delighted at finding that I had a rational judge to deal with, I explained the affair to him in a manner at once so respectful and so moderate, that he seemed exceedingly satisfied with my answers to all the queries he put. He desired me not to abandon myself to grief, and assured me that he felt every disposition to serve me, as well on account of my birth as my inexperience. I ventured to bespeak his attentions in favour of Manon, and I dwelt upon her gentle and excellent disposition. He replied, with a smile, that he had not yet seen her, but that she had been represented to him as a most dangerous person. This expression so excited my sympathy, that I urged a thousand anxious arguments in favour of my poor mistress, and I could not restrain even from shedding tears. He desired them to conduct me back to my chamber. 'Love! love!' cried this grave magistrate as I went out, 'thou art never to be reconciled with discretion!'

"I had been occupied with the most melancholy reflections, and was thinking of the conversation I had had with the lieutenant-general of police, when I heard my door open. It was my father. Although I ought to have been half prepared for seeing him, and had reasons to expect his arrival within a day or two, yet I was so thunderstruck, that I could willingly have sunk into the earth, if it had been open at my feet. I embraced him in the greatest possible state of confusion. He took a seat, without either one or other of us having uttered a word.

"As I remained standing, with my head uncovered, and my eyes cast on the ground, 'Be seated, sir,' said he in a solemn voice; 'be seated. I have to thank the notoriety of your debaucheries for learning the place of your abode. It is the privilege of such fame as yours, that it cannot lie concealed. You are acquiring celebrity by an unerring path. Doubtless it will lead you to the Grève,[1] and you will then have the unfading glory of being held up to the admiration of the world.'

"I made no reply. He continued: 'What an unhappy lot is that of a father, who having tenderly loved a child, and strained every nerve to bring him up a virtuous and respectable man, finds him turn out in the end a worthless profligate, who dishonours him. To an ordinary reverse of fortune one may be reconciled; time softens the affliction,

[1]Who has e'er been at Paris must needs know the Grève,
The fatal retreat of th' unfortunate brave,
Where honour and justice most oddly contribute,
To ease heroes' pains by the halter and gibbet.—PRIOR.

and even the indulgence of sorrow itself is not unavailing; but what remedy is there for an evil that is perpetually augmenting, such as the profligacy of a vicious son, who has deserted every principle of honour, and is ever plunging from deep into deeper vice? You are silent,' added he: 'look at this counterfeit modesty, this hypocritical air of gentleness!—might he not pass for the most respectable member of his family?'

"Although I could not but feel that I deserved, in some degree, these reproaches, yet he appeared to me to carry them beyond all reason. I thought I might be permitted to explain my feelings.

"'I assure you, sir,' said I to him, 'that the modesty which you ridicule is by no means affected; it is the natural feeling of a son who entertains sincere respect for his father, and above all, a father irritated as you justly are by his faults. Neither have I, sir, the slightest wish to pass for the most respectable member of my family. I know that I have merited your reproaches, but I conjure you to temper them with mercy, and not to look upon me as the most infamous of mankind. I do not deserve such harsh names. It is love, you know it, that has caused all my errors. Fatal passion! Have you yourself never felt its force? Is it possible that you, with the same blood in your veins that flows in mine, should have passed through life unscathed by the same excitements? Love has rendered me perhaps foolishly tender—too easily excited—too impassioned—too faithful, and probably too indulgent to the desires and caprices, or, if you will, the faults of an adored mistress. These are my crimes; are they such as to reflect dishonour upon you? Come, my dear father,' said I tenderly, 'show some pity for a son, who has never ceased to feel respect and affection for you—who has not renounced, as you say, all feelings of honour and of duty, and who is himself a thousand times more an object of pity than you imagine.' I could not help shedding a tear as I concluded this appeal.

"A father's heart is a chef-d'œuvre of creation. There nature rules in undisturbed dominion, and regulates at will its most secret springs. He was a man of high feeling and good taste, and was so sensibly affected by the turn I had given to my defence, that he could no longer hide from me the change I had wrought.

"'Come to me, my poor chevalier,' said he; 'come and embrace me. I do pity you!'

"I embraced him: he pressed me to him in such a manner, that I guessed what was passing in his heart.

"'But how are we,' said he, 'to extricate you from this place? Explain to me the real situation of your affairs.'

"As there really was not anything in my conduct so grossly improper as to reflect dishonour upon me; at least, in comparison with the conduct of other young men of a certain station in the world; and as a mistress is not considered a disgrace, any more than a little dexterity in drawing some advantage from play, I gave my father a candid detail of the life I had been leading. As I recounted each transgression, I took care to cite some illustrious example in my justification, in order to palliate my own faults.

" 'I lived,' said I, 'with a mistress without the solemnity of marriage. The Duke of —— keeps two before the eyes of all Paris. M—— D—— has had one now for ten years, and loves her with a fidelity which he has never shown to his wife. Two-thirds of the men of fashion in Paris keep mistresses.

" 'I certainly have on one or two occasions cheated at play. Well, the Marquis of —— and the Count —— have no other source of revenue. The Prince of —— and the Duke of —— are at the head of a gang of the same industrious order.' As for the designs I had upon the pockets of the two G—— M——s, I might just as easily have proved that I had abundant models for that also ; but I had too much pride to plead guilty to this charge, and rest on the justification of example ; so that I begged of my father to ascribe my weakness on this occasion to the violence of the two passions which agitated me—Revenge and Love.

" He asked me whether I could suggest any means of obtaining my liberty, and in such a way as to avoid publicity as much as possible. I told him of the kind feelings which the lieutenant-general of police had expressed towards me. 'If you encounter any obstacles,' said I, 'they will be offered only by the two G—— M——s ; so that I think it would be advisable to call upon them.' He promised to do so.

" I did not dare ask him to solicit Manon's liberation ; this was not from want of courage, but from the apprehension of exasperating him by such a proposition, and perhaps driving him to form some design fatal to the future happiness of us both. It remains to this hour a problem whether this fear on my part was not the immediate cause of all my most terrible misfortunes, by preventing me from ascertaining my father's disposition, and endeavouring to inspire him with favourable feelings towards my poor mistress : I might have perhaps once more succeeded in exciting his commiseration ; I might have put him on his guard against the impression which he was sure of receiving from a visit to old G—— M——. But how can I tell what the consequences would have been ! My unhappy fate would have most probably counteracted all my efforts ; but it would have been a consolation to have had nothing else but that, and the cruelty of my enemies, to blame for my afflictions.

" On quitting me, my father went to pay a visit to M. G—— M——. He found him with his son, whom the guardsman had safely restored to liberty. I never learned the particulars of their conversation ; but I could easily infer them from the disastrous results. They went together (the two old gentlemen) to the lieutenant-general of police, from whom they requested one favour each : the first was to have me at once liberated from Le Châtelet ; the second to condemn Manon to perpetual imprisonment, or to transport her for life to America. They happened, at that very period, to be sending out a number of convicts to the Mississippi. The lieutenant-general promised to have her embarked on board the first vessel that sailed.

"M. G—— M—— and my father came together to bring me the news of my liberation. M. G—— M—— said something civil with reference to what had passed; and having congratulated me upon my happiness in having such a father, he exhorted me to profit henceforward by his instruction and example. My father desired me to express my sorrow for the injustice I had even contemplated against his family, and my gratitude for his having assisted in procuring my liberation.

"We all left the prison together, without the mention of Manon's name. I dared not in their presence speak of her to the turnkeys. Alas! all my entreaties in her favour would have been useless. The cruel sentence upon Manon had arrived at the same time as the warrant for my discharge. The unfortunate girl was conducted in an hour after to the Hospital, to be there classed with some other wretched women, who had been condemned to the same punishment.

"My father having forced me to accompany him to the house where he was residing, it was near six o'clock before I had an opportunity of escaping his vigilance. In returning to Le Châtelet, my only wish was to convey some refreshments to Manon, and to recommend her to the attention of the porter; for I had no hope of being permitted to see her; nor had I, as yet, had time to reflect on the best means of rescuing her.

"I asked for the porter. I had won his heart, as much by my liberality to him, as by the mildness of my manner; so that, having a disposition to serve me, he spoke of Manon's sentence as a calamity which he sincerely regretted, since it was calculated to mortify me. I was at first unable to comprehend his meaning. We conversed for some minutes without my understanding him. At length perceiving that an explanation was necessary, he gave me such a one, as on a former occasion I wanted courage to relate to you, and which, even now, makes my blood curdle in my veins to remember.

## XI

**Alack! it is not when we sleep soft and wake merrily that we think on other people's sufferings; but when the hour of trouble comes, said Jeanie Deans.—Walter Scott.**

"Never did apoplexy produce on mortal a more sudden or terrific effect than did the announcement of Manon's sentence upon me. I fell prostrate, with so intense a palpitation of the heart, that as I swooned I thought that death itself was come upon me. This idea continued even after I had been restored to my senses. I gazed around me upon every part of the room, then upon my own paralysed limbs, doubting, in my delirium, whether I still bore about me the attributes of a living man. It is quite certain that, in obedience to the desire I felt of terminating my sufferings, even by my own hand, nothing could have been to me more welcome than death at that moment of anguish and despair. Religion itself could depict nothing more insupportable after death than the racking agony with which I was then convulsed. Yet, by a miracle, only within the power of omnipotent love, I soon regained strength enough to express my gratitude to Heaven for restoring me to sense and reason. My death could have only been a relief and blessing to myself; whereas Manon had occasion for my prolonged existence, in order to deliver her—to succour her—to avenge her wrongs: I swore to devote that existence unremittingly to these objects.

"The porter gave me every assistance that I could have expected at the hands of my oldest friend: I accepted his services with the liveliest gratitude. 'Alas!' said I to him, 'you then are affected by my sufferings! The whole world abandons me; my own father proves one of the very cruellest of my persecutors; no person feels pity for me! You alone, in this abode of suffering and shame—you alone exhibit compassion for the most wretched of mankind!' He advised me not to appear in the street until I had recovered a little from my affliction. 'Do not stop me,' said I, as I went out; 'we shall meet again sooner than you imagine: get ready your darkest dungeon, for I shall shortly become its tenant.'

"In fact, my first idea was nothing less than to make away with the two G—— M——s, and the lieutenant-general of police; and then to attack the Hospital, sword in hand, assisted by all whom I could enlist in my cause. Even my father's life was hardly respected, so just appeared my feelings of vengeance; for the porter had informed me that he and G—— M—— were jointly the authors of my ruin.

"But when I had advanced some paces into the street, and the fresh air had cooled my excitement, I gradually viewed matters in a more rational mood. The death of our enemies could be of little use to Manon; and the obvious effect of such violence would be to deprive me of all other chance of serving her. Besides, could I ever bring myself to be a cowardly assassin? By what other means could I accomplish my revenge? I set all my ingenuity and all my efforts at work to procure the deliverance of Manon, leaving everything else to be considered hereafter when I had succeeded in this first and paramount object.

"I had very little money left; money, however, was an indispensable basis for all my operations. I only knew three persons from whom I had any right to ask pecuniary assistance—M. de T——, Tiberge, and my father. There appeared little chance of obtaining any from the two latter, and I was really ashamed again to importune M. de T——. But it is not in desperate emergencies that one stands upon points of ceremony. I went first to the seminary of St. Sulpice, without considering whether I should be recognised. I asked for Tiberge. His first words showed me that he knew nothing of my latest adventure: this made me change the design I had originally formed of appealing at once to his compassion. I spoke generally of the pleasure it had given me to see my father again; and I then begged of him to lend me some money, under the pretext of being anxious before I left Paris to pay a few little debts, which I wished to keep secret. He handed me his purse, without a single remark. I took twenty or twenty-five pounds, which it contained. I offered him my note of hand, but he was too generous to accept it.

" I then went to M. de T——: I had no reserve with him. I plainly told him my misfortunes and distress: he already knew everything, and had informed himself even of the most trifling circumstance, on account of the interest he naturally took in young G—— M——'s adventure. He, however, listened to me, and seemed sincerely to lament what had occurred. When I consulted him as to the best means of rescuing Manon, he answered that he saw such little ground for hope, that, without some extraordinary interposition of Providence, it would be folly to expect relief; that he had paid a visit expressly to the Hospital since Manon had been transferred from the Châtelet, but that he could not even obtain permission to see her, as the lieutenant-general of police had given the strictest orders to the contrary; and that, to complete the catastrophe, the unfortunate train of convicts, in which she was to be included, was to take its departure from Paris the day but one after.

" I was so confounded by what he said, that if he had gone on speaking for another hour, I should not have interrupted him. He continued to tell me, that the reason of his not calling to see me at the Châtelet was, that he hoped to be of more use by appearing to be unknown to me; that for the last few hours, since I had been set at liberty, he had in vain looked for me, in order to suggest the only plan through which he could see a hope of averting Manon's fate. He told me it was dangerous counsel to give, and implored me never to mention the part he took in it; it was to find some enterprising fellows gallant enough to attack Manon's guard on getting outside the barrière. Nor did he wait for me to urge a plea of poverty. 'Here is fifty pounds,' he said, presenting me his purse; 'it may be of use to you; you can repay me when you are in better circumstances.' He added, that if the fear of losing his character did not prevent him from embarking in such an enterprise, he would have willingly put his sword and his life at my service.

" This unlooked-for generosity affected me to tears. I expressed my gratitude with as much warmth as my depressed spirits left at my command. I asked him if there were nothing to be expected from interceding with the lieutenant-general of police: he said that he had considered that point; but that he looked upon it as a hopeless attempt, because a favour of that nature was never accorded without some strong motive, and he did not see what inducement could be held out for engaging the intercession of any person of power on her behalf; that if any hope could possibly be entertained upon the point, it must be by working a change in the feelings of old G—— M—— and my father, and by prevailing on them to solicit from the lieutenant-general of police the revocation of Manon's sentence. He offered to do everything in his power to gain over the younger G—— M——, although he fancied a coldness in that gentleman's manner towards him, probably from some suspicions he might entertain of his being concerned in the late affair; and he entreated me to lose no opportunity of effecting the desired change in my father's mind.

"This was no easy undertaking for me; not only on account of the difficulty I should naturally meet in overcoming his opinion, but for another reason which made me fear even to approach him; I had quitted his lodgings contrary to his express orders, and was resolved, since I had learned the sad fate of my poor Manon, never again to return thither. I was not without apprehensions indeed of his now retaining me against my will, and perhaps taking me at once back with him into the country. My elder brother had formerly had recourse to this violent measure. True, I was now somewhat older; but age is a feeble argument against force. I hit upon a mode, however, of avoiding this danger, which was to get him by contrivance to some public place, and there announce myself to him under an assumed name: I immediately resolved on this method. M. de T—— went to G—— M——'s, and I to the Luxembourg, whence I sent my father word, that a gentleman waited there to speak with him. I hardly thought he would come, as the night was advancing. He, however, soon made his appearance, followed by a servant: I begged of him to choose a walk where we could be alone. We walked at least a hundred paces without speaking. He doubtless imagined that so much precaution could not be taken without some important object. He waited for my opening speech, and I was meditating how to commence it.

"At length I began.

"'Sir,' said I, trembling, 'you are a good and affectionate parent; you have loaded me with favours, and have forgiven me an infinite number of faults; I also, in my turn, call Heaven to witness the sincere, and tender, and respectful sentiments I entertain towards you. But it does seem to me, that your inexorable severity——'

"'Well, sir, my severity!' interrupted my father, who no doubt found my hesitation little suited to his impatience.

"'Ah, sir,' I replied, 'it does seem to me that your severity is excessive in the penalty you inflict upon the unfortunate Manon. You have taken only M. G—— M——'s report of her. His hatred has made him represent her to you in the most odious colours: you have formed a frightful idea of her. She is, on the contrary, the mildest and most amiable of living creatures; would that Heaven had but inspired you at any one moment with the desire of seeing her! I am convinced that you would be not less sensible of her perfections than your unhappy son. You would then have been her advocate; you would have abhorred the foul artifices of G—— M——; you would have had pity on both her and me. Alas ! I am persuaded of it ; your heart is not insensible ; it must ere now have melted with compassion.'

" He interrupted me again, perceiving that I spoke with a warmth which would not allow me to finish very briefly. He begged to know with what request I intended to wind up so fervent an harangue.

" 'To ask my life at your hands,' said I, ' which I never can retain if Manon once embark for America.'

" 'No ! no !' replied he, in the severest tone ; ' I would rather see you lifeless, than infamous and depraved.'

" 'We have gone far enough, then,' said I, catching hold of his arm ; ' take from me, in common mercy, my life ! weary and odious and insupportable as it henceforward must be ; for in the state of despair into which you now plunge me, death would be the greatest favour you could bestow—a favour worthy of a father's hand.'

" 'I should only give you what you deserve,' replied he ; ' I know fathers who would not have shown as much patience as I have, but would themselves have executed speedy justice ; but it is my foolish and excessive forbearance that has been your ruin.'

" I threw myself at his feet : ' Ah !' exclaimed I, ' if you have still any remains of mercy, do not harden your heart against my distress and sorrow. Remember that I am your child ! Alas ! think of my poor mother ! you loved her tenderly ! would you have suffered her to be torn from your arms ? You would have defended her to the death ! May not the same feeling then be pardoned in others ? Can persons become barbarous and cruel, after having themselves experienced the softening influence of tenderness and grief ?'

" 'Breathe not again the sacred name of your mother,' he exclaimed, in a voice of thunder ; ' the very allusion to her memory rouses my indignation. Had she lived to witness the unredeemed profligacy of your life, it would have brought her in pain and sorrow to her grave.— Let us put an end to this discussion' he added ; ' it distresses me, and makes not the slightest change in my determination : I am going back to my lodgings, and I desire you to follow me.'

" The cool and resolute tone in which he uttered this command, convinced me that he was inexorable. I stepped some paces aside, for fear he should think fit to lay hands upon me.

" 'Do not increase my misery and despair,' said I to him, ' by forcing me to disobey you. It is impossible for me to follow you ; and equally so that I should continue to live, after the unkind treatment I have experienced from you. I, therefore, bid you an eternal adieu. When you know that I am dead, as I shall soon be, the paternal affection which you once entertained for me may be perhaps revived.'

" As I was about to turn away from him : ' You refuse then to follow me,' cried he, in a tone of excessive anger. ' Go ! go on to your ruin. Adieu ! ungrateful and disobedient boy.'

" 'Adieu !' exclaimed I to him, in a burst of grief, ' adieu, cruel and unnatural father !'

"I left the Luxembourg, and rushed like a madman through the streets to M. de T——'s house. I raised my hands and eyes as I went along, invoking the Almighty Powers: 'O Heaven,' cried I, 'will you not prove more merciful than man! The only hope that remains to me is from above!'

"M. de T—— had not yet returned home; but he arrived before many minutes had elapsed. His negotiation had been as unsuccessful as my own. He told me so with the most sorrowful countenance. Young G—— M——, although less irritated than his father against Manon and me, would not undertake to petition in our favour. He was, in great measure, deterred by the fear which he himself had of the vindictive old lecher, who had already vented his anger against him for his design of forming a connection with Manon.

"There only remained to me, therefore, the violent measures which M. de T—— had suggested. I now confined all my hopes to them. They were questionless most uncertain; but they held out to me, at least, a substantial consolation, in the certainty of meeting death in the attempt, if unsuccessful. I left him, begging that he would offer up his best wishes for my triumph; and I thought only of finding some companions, to whom I might communicate a portion of my own courage and determination.

"The first that occurred to me was the same guardsman whom I had employed to arrest G—— M——. I had intended indeed to pass the night at his rooms, not having had a moment of leisure during the afternoon to procure myself a lodging. I found him alone. He was glad to see me out of the Châtelet. He made me an offer of his services. I explained to him in what way he might now do me the greatest kindness. He had good sense enough to perceive all the difficulties; but he was also generous enough to undertake to surmount them.

"We spent part of the night in considering how the plot was to be executed. He spoke of the three soldiers whom he had made use of on the last occasion, as men whose courage had been proved. M. de T—— had told me the exact number of archers that would escort Manon; they were but six. Five strong and determined men could not fail to strike terror into these fellows, who would never think of defending themselves bravely, when they were to be allowed the alternative of avoiding danger by surrendering; and of that they would no doubt avail themselves. As I was not without money, the guardsman advised me to spare no pains or expense to ensure success. 'We must be mounted,' he said, 'and each man must have his carbine and pistols; I will take care to prepare everything requisite by tomorrow. We shall also want three new suits of regimentals for the soldiers, who dare not appear in an affray of this kind in the uniform of their regiment. I handed him the hundred pistoles which I had got from M. de T——; it was all expended the next morning, to the very last sou. I inspected the three soldiers; I animated them with the most liberal promises;

and to confirm their confidence in me, I began by making each man a present of ten pistoles.

" The momentous day having arrived, I sent one of them at an early hour to the Hospital, to ascertain the exact time when the police were to start with their prisoners. Although I merely took this precaution from my excessive anxiety, it turned out to have been a prudent step. I had formed my plans upon false information, which I had received as to their destination ; and believing that it was at Rochelle this unhappy group was to embark, all my trouble would have been thrown away in waiting for them on the Orleans road. However, I learned, by the soldier's report, that they would go out towards Rouen, and that it was from Havre-de-Grace they were to sail for America.

" We at once went to the gate of St. Honoré, taking care to go by different streets. We assembled at the end of the faubourg. Our horses were fresh. In a little time we observed before us the six archers and the two wretched caravans, which you saw at Passy two years ago. The sight alone almost deprived me of my strength and senses. ' Oh fate ! ' said I to myself, ' cruel fate ! grant me now either death or victory.'

" We hastily consulted as to the mode of making the attack. The cavalcade was only four hundred paces in advance, and we might intercept them by cutting across a small field, round which the high road led. The guardsman was for this course, in order to fall suddenly upon them while unprepared. I approved of the plan, and was the first to spur my horse forward—but fate once again relentlessly blasted all my hopes.

" The escort, seeing five horsemen riding towards them, inferred that it was for the purpose of attacking them. They put themselves in a position of defence, preparing their bayonets and guns with an air of resolution.

" This demonstration, which in the guardsman and myself only inspired fresh courage, had a very different effect upon our three cowardly companions. They stopped simultaneously, and having muttered to each other some words which I could not hear, they turned their horses' heads, threw the bridles on their necks, and galloped back towards Paris.

" ' Good heavens ! ' said the guardsman, who appeared as much annoyed as I was by this infamous desertion, ' what is to be done ? we are but two now.'

" From rage and consternation I had lost all power of speech. I doubted whether my first revenge should not be in pursuing the cowards who had abandoned me. I saw them flying, and looked in the other direction at the escort : if it had been possible to divide myself, I should at once have fallen upon both these objects of my fury ; I should have destroyed all at the same moment.

" The guardsman, who saw my irresolution by my wandering gaze, begged of me to hear his advice. ' Being but two,' he said, 'it would be madness to attack six men as well armed as ourselves, and who seem determined to receive us firmly. Let us return to Paris, and endeavour to succeed better in the choice of our comrades. The police cannot make very rapid progress with two heavy vans ; we may overtake them tomorrow without difficulty.'

"I reflected a moment on this suggestion ; but seeing nothing around me but despair, I took a final and indeed desperate resolution : this was to thank my companion for his services, and, far from attacking the police, to go up with submission and implore them to receive me among them, that I might accompany Manon to Havre-de-Grace, and afterwards, if possible, cross the Atlantic with her. 'The whole world is either persecuting or betraying me,' said I to the guardsman ; 'I have no longer the power of interesting anyone in my favour ; I expect nothing more either from fortune or the friendship of man ; my misery is at its height ; it only remains for me to submit, so that I close my eyes henceforward against every gleam of hope. May Heaven,' I continued, 'reward you for your generosity ! Adieu ! I shall go and aid my wretched destiny in filling up the full measure of my ruin !' He, in vain, endeavoured to persuade me to return with him to Paris. I entreated him to leave me at once, lest the police should still suspect us of an intention to attack them.

## XII

**The pauses and intermissions of pain become positive pleasures ; and have thus a power of shedding a satisfaction over the intervals of ease, which few enjoyments exceed.—PALEY.**

"RIDING towards the cortège at a slow pace, and with a sorrowful countenance, the guards could hardly see anything very terrific in my approach. They seemed, however, to expect an attack. 'Be persuaded, gentlemen,' said I to them, 'that I come not to wage war, but rather to ask favours.' I then begged of them to continue their progress without any distrust, and as we went along I made my solicitations. They consulted together to ascertain in what way they should entertain my request. The chief of them spoke for the rest. He said that the orders they had received to watch the prisoners vigilantly were of the strictest kind ; that, however, I seemed so interesting a young man, that they might be induced to relax a little in their duty ; but that I must know, of course, that this would cost me something. I had about sixteen pistoles left, and candidly told them what my purse contained. 'Well,' said the gendarme, 'we will act generously. It shall only cost you a crown an hour for conversing with any of our girls that you may prefer—that is the ordinary price in Paris.'

"I said not a word of Manon, because I did not wish to let them know of my passion. They at first supposed it was merely a boyish whim, that made me think of amusing myself with these creatures but when they discovered that I was in love, they increased their demands in such a way, that my purse was completely empty on leaving Mantes, where we had slept the night before our arrival at Passy.

" Shall I describe to you my heart-rending interviews with Manon during this journey, and what my sensations were when I obtained from the guards permission to approach her caravan ? Oh ! language never can adequately express the sentiments of the heart ; but picture to yourself my poor mistress, with a chain round her waist, seated upon a handful of straw, her head resting languidly against the panel of the carriage, her face pale and bathed with tears, which forced a passage between her eyelids, although she kept them continually closed. She had not even the curiosity to open her eyes on hearing the bustle of the guards when they expected our attack. Her clothes were soiled, and in disorder ; her delicate hands exposed to the rough air ; in fine, her whole angelic form, that face, lovely enough to carry back the world to idolatry, presented a spectacle of distress and anguish utterly indescribable.

" I spent some moments gazing at her as I rode alongside the carriage. I had so lost my self-possession, that I was several times on the point of falling from my horse. My sighs and frequent exclamations at length attracted her attention. She looked at and recognised me, and I remarked that on the first impulse, she unconsciously tried to leap from the carriage towards me, but being checked by her chain, she fell into her former attitude.

" I begged of the guards to stop one moment for the sake of mercy ; they consented for the sake of avarice. I dismounted to go and sit near her. She was so languid and feeble, that she was for some time without the power of speech, and could not raise her hands : I bathed them with my tears ; and being myself unable to utter a word, we formed together as deplorable a picture of distress as could well be seen. When at length we were able to speak, our conversation was not less sorrowful. Manon said little : shame and grief appeared to have altered the character of her voice ; its tone was feeble and tremulous.

" She thanked me for not having forgotten her, and for the comfort I gave her in allowing her to see me once more, and she then bade me a long and last farewell. But when I assured her that no power on earth could ever separate me from her, and that I was resolved to follow her to the extremity of the world—to watch over her—to guard her—to love her—and inseparably to unite my wretched destiny with hers, the poor girl gave way to such feelings of tenderness and grief, that I almost dreaded danger to her life from the violence of her emotion : the agitation of her whole soul seemed intensely concentrated in her eyes ; she fixed them steadfastly upon me. She more than once opened her lips without the power of giving utterance to her thoughts. I could, however, catch some expressions that dropped from her, of admiration and wonder at my excessive love—of doubt that she could have been fortunate enough to inspire me with a passion so perfect—of earnest entreaty that I would abandon my intention of following her, and seek elsewhere a lot more worthy of me, and which, she said, I could never hope to find with her.

"In spite of the cruellest inflictions of Fate, I derived comfort from her looks, and from the conviction that I now possessed her undivided affection. I had in truth lost all that other men value; but I was the master of Manon's heart, the only possession that I prized. Whether in Europe or in America, of what moment to me was the place of my abode, provided I might live happy in the society of my mistress? Is not the universe the residence of two fond and faithful lovers? Does not each find in the other, father, mother, friends, relations, riches, felicity?

"If anything caused me uneasiness, it was the fear of seeing Manon exposed to want. I fancied myself already with her in a barbarous country, inhabited by savages. 'I am quite certain,' said I, 'there will be none there more cruel than G—— M—— and my father. They will, at least, allow us to live in peace. If the accounts we read of savages be true, they obey the laws of nature: they neither know the mean rapacity of avarice, nor the false and fantastic notions of dignity, which have raised me up an enemy in my own father. They will not harass and persecute two lovers, when they see us adopt their own simple habits.' I was therefore at ease upon that point.

"But my romantic ideas were not formed with a proper view to the ordinary wants of life. I had too often found that there were necessaries which could not be dispensed with, particularly by a young and delicate woman, accustomed to comfort and abundance. I was in despair at having so fruitlessly emptied my purse, and the little money that now remained was about being forced from me by the rascally imposition of the gendarmes. I imagined that a very trifling sum would suffice for our support for some time in America, where money was scarce, and might also enable me to form some undertaking there for our permanent establishment.

"This idea made me resolve on writing to Tiberge, whom I had ever found ready to hold out the generous hand of friendship. I wrote from the first town we passed through. I only alluded to the destitute condition in which I foresaw that I should find myself on arriving at Havre-de-Grace, to which place I acknowledged that I was accompanying Manon. I asked him for only fifty pistoles. 'You can remit it to me,' said I to him, 'through the hands of the postmaster. You must perceive that it is the last time I can by possibility trespass on your friendly kindness; and my poor unhappy mistress being about to be exiled from her country for ever, I cannot let her depart without supplying her with some few comforts, to soften the sufferings of her lot, as well as to assuage my own sorrows.'

"The gendarmes became so rapacious when they saw the violence of my passion, continually increasing their demands for the slightest favours, that they soon left me penniless. Love did not permit me to put any bounds to my liberality. At Manon's side I was not master of myself; and it was no longer by the hour that time was measured; rather by the duration of whole days. At length, my funds being completely exhausted, I found myself exposed to the brutal caprice of these six wretches who treated me with intolerable rudeness—you yourself witnessed it at Passy. My meeting with you was a momentary relaxation accorded me by fate. Your compassion at the sight of my sufferings was my only recommendation to your generous nature. The assistance which you so liberally extended, enabled me to reach Havre, and the guards kept their promise more faithfully than I had ventured to hope.

"We arrived at Havre. I went to the post-office: Tiberge had not yet had time to answer my letter. I ascertained the earliest day I might reckon upon his answer: it could not possibly arrive for two days longer; and by an extraordinary fatality, our vessel was to sail on the very morning of the day when the letter might be expected. I cannot give you an idea of my despair. 'Alas!' cried I, 'even amongst the unfortunate, I am to be ever the most wretched!'

"Manon replied: 'Alas! does a life so thoroughly miserable deserve the care we bestow on ours? Let us die at Havre, dearest chevalier! Let death at once put an end to our afflictions! Shall we persevere, and go to drag on this hopeless existence in an unknown land, where we shall, no doubt, have to encounter the most horrible pains, since it has been their object to punish me by exile? Let us die,' she repeated, 'or do at least in mercy rid me of life, and then you can seek another lot in the arms of some happier lover.'

"'No, no, Manon,' said I; 'it is but too enviable a lot, in my estimation, to be allowed to share your misfortunes.'

"Her observations made me tremble. I saw that she was overpowered by her afflictions. I tried to assume a more tranquil air, in order to dissipate such melancholy thoughts of death and despair. I resolved to adopt the same course in future; and I learned by the results, that nothing is more calculated to inspire a woman with courage than the demonstration of intrepidity in the man she loves.

"When I lost all hope of receiving the expected assistance from Tiberge, I sold my horse; the money it brought, joined to what remained of your generous gift, amounted to the small sum of forty pistoles; I expended eight in the purchase of some necessary articles for Manon; and I put the remainder by, as the capital upon which we were to rest our hopes and raise our fortunes in America. I had no difficulty in getting admitted on board the vessel. They were at the time looking for young men as voluntary emigrants to the colony. The passage and provisions were supplied gratis. I left a letter for Tiberge, which was to go by the post next morning to Paris. It was no doubt written in a tone calculated to affect him deeply, since it induced him to form a resolution, which could only be carried into execution by the tenderest and most generous sympathy for his unhappy friend.

## XIII

*Sunt hic etiam sua præmia laudi,*
*Sunt lachrymæ rerum, et mentem mortalia tangunt.*
VIRGIL.

E'en the mute walls relate the victim's fame.
And sinner's tears the good man's pity claim.
DRYDEN.

" WE set sail; the wind continued favourable during the entire passage. I obtained from the captain's kindness a separate cabin for the use of Manon and myself. He was so good as to distinguish us from the herd of our miserable associates. I took an opportunity, on the second day, of conciliating his attentions, by telling him part of our unfortunate history. I did not feel that I was guilty of any very culpable falsehood in saying that I was the husband of Manon. He appeared to believe it, and promised me his protection; and indeed we experienced, during the whole passage, the most flattering evidences of his sincerity. He took care that our table was comfortably provided; and his attentions procured us the marked respect of our companions in misery. The unwearied object of my solicitude was to save Manon from every inconvenience. She felt this, and her gratitude, together with a lively sense of the singular position in which I had placed myself solely for her sake, rendered the dear creature so tender and impassioned, so attentive also to my most trifling wants, that it was between us a continual emulation of attentions and of love. I felt no regret at quitting Europe; on the contrary, the nearer we approached America, the more did I feel my heart expand and become tranquil. If I had not felt a dread of our perhaps wanting, by and by, the absolute necessaries of life, I should have been grateful to fate for having at length given so favourable a turn to our affairs.

"After a passage of two months, we at length reached the banks of the desired river. The country offered at first sight nothing agreeable. We saw only sterile and uninhabited plains, covered with rushes, and some trees rooted up by the wind. No trace either of men or animals. However, the captain having discharged some pieces of artillery, we presently observed a group of the inhabitants of New Orleans, who approached us with evident signs of joy. We had not perceived the town: it is concealed upon the side on which we approached it by a hill. We were received as persons dropped from the clouds.

" The poor inhabitants hastened to put a thousand questions to us upon the state of France, and of the different provinces in which they were born. They embraced us as brothers, and as beloved companions, who had come to share their pains and their solitude. We turned towards the town with them; but we were astonished to perceive, as we advanced, that what we had hitherto heard spoken of as a respectable town, was nothing more than a collection of miserable huts. They were inhabited by five or six hundred persons. The governor's house was a little distinguished from the rest by its height and its position. It was surrounded by some earthen ramparts, and a deep ditch.

"We were first presented to him. He continued for some time in conversation with the captain; and then advancing towards us, he looked attentively at the women one after another: there were thirty of them, for another troop of convicts had joined us at Havre. After having thus inspected them, he sent for several young men of the colony who were desirous to marry. He assigned the handsomest women to the principal of these, and the remainder were disposed of by lot. He had not yet addressed Manon; but having ordered the others to depart, he made us remain. 'I learn from the captain,' said he, 'that you are married, and he is convinced by your conduct on the passage that you are both persons of merit and of education. I have nothing to do with the cause of your misfortunes; but if it be true that you are as conversant with the world and society as your appearance would indicate, I shall spare no pains to soften the severity of your lot, and you may on your part contribute towards rendering this savage and desert abode less disagreeable to me.' I replied in the manner which I thought best calculated to confirm the opinion he had formed of us. He gave orders to have a habitation prepared for us in the town, and detained us to supper. I was really surprised to find so much politeness in a governor of transported convicts. In the presence of others he abstained from enquiring about our past adventures. The conversation was general; and in spite of our degradation, Manon and I exerted ourselves to make it lively and agreeable.

"At night we were conducted to the lodging prepared for us. We found a wretched hovel composed of planks and mud, containing three rooms on the ground, and a loft overhead. He had sent there six chairs, and some few necessaries of life.

"Manon appeared frightened by the first view of this melancholy dwelling. It was on my account much more than upon her own, that she distressed herself. When we were left to ourselves, she sat down and wept bitterly. I attempted at first to console her; but when she enabled me to understand that it was for my sake she deplored our privations, and that in our common afflictions she only considered me as the sufferer, I put on an air of resolution, and even of content, sufficient to encourage her.

"'What is there in my lot to lament?' said I; 'I possess all that I have ever desired. You love me, Manon, do you not? What happiness beyond this have I ever longed for? Let us leave to Providence the direction of our destiny; it by no means appears to me so desperate. The governor is civil and obliging; he has already given us marks of his consideration; he will not allow us to want for necessaries. As to our rude hut and the squalidness of our furniture, you might have noticed that there are few persons in the colony better lodged or more comfortably furnished than we are: and then you are an admirable chemist,' added I, embracing her; 'you transform everything into gold.'

"'In that case,' she answered, 'you shall be the richest man in the universe; for, as there never was love surpassing yours, so it is impossible for man to be loved more tenderly than you are by me. I well know,' she continued, 'that I have never merited the almost incredible fidelity and attachment which you have shown for me. I have often caused you annoyances, which nothing but excessive fondness could have induced you to pardon. I have been thoughtless and volatile; and even while loving you as I have always done to distraction, I was never free from a consciousness of ingratitude. But you cannot believe how much my nature is altered; those tears which you have so frequently seen me shed since quitting the French shore, have not been caused by my own misfortunes. Since you began to share them with me, I have been a stranger to selfishness: I only wept from tenderness and compassion for you. I am inconsolable at the thought of having given you one instant's pain during my past life. I never cease upbraiding myself with my former inconstancy, and wondering at the sacrifices which love has induced you to make for a miserable and unworthy wretch, who could not, with the last drop of her blood, compensate for half the torments she has caused you.'

"Her grief, the language, and the tone in which she expressed herself, made such an impression, that I felt my heart ready to break within me. 'Take care,' said I to her, 'take care, dear Manon; I have not strength to endure such exciting marks of your affection; I am little accustomed to the rapturous sensations which you now kindle in my heart. Oh Heaven!' cried I, 'I have now nothing further to ask of you. I am sure of Manon's love. That has been alone wanting to complete my happiness; I can now never cease to be happy: my felicity is well secured.'

"'It is indeed,' she replied, 'if it depends upon me, and I well know where I can be ever certain of finding my own happiness centred.'

"With these ideas, capable of turning my hut into a palace worthy of earth's proudest monarch, I lay down to rest. America appeared to my view the true land of milk and honey, the abode of contentment and delight. 'People should come to New Orleans,' I often said to Manon, 'who wish to enjoy the real rapture of love! It is here that love is divested of all selfishness, all jealousy, all inconstancy. Our countrymen come here in search of gold; they little think that we have discovered treasures of inestimably greater value.'

"We carefully cultivated the governor's friendship. He bestowed upon me, a few weeks after our arrival, a small appointment which became vacant in the fort. Although not one of any distinction, I gratefully accepted it as a gift of Providence, as it enabled me to live independently of others' aid. I took a servant for myself, and a woman for Manon. Our little establishment became settled: nothing could surpass the regularity of my conduct, or that of Manon; we lost no opportunity of serving or doing an act of kindness to our neighbours. This friendly disposition, and the mildness of our manners, secured us the confidence and affection of the whole colony. We soon became so respected, that we ranked as the principal persons in the town after the governor.

"The simplicity of our habits and occupations, and the perfect innocence in which we lived, revived insensibly our early feelings of devotion. Manon had never been an irreligious girl, and I was far from being one of those reckless libertines who delight in adding impiety and sacrilege to moral depravity: all the disorders of our lives might be fairly ascribed to the natural influences of youth and love. Experience had now begun with us to do the office of age; it produced the same effect upon us as years must have done. Our conversation, which was generally of a serious turn, by degrees engendered a longing for virtuous love. I first proposed this change to Manon. I knew the principles of her heart; she was frank and natural in all her sentiments, qualities which invariably predispose to virtue. I said to her that there was but one thing wanting to complete our happiness: 'it is,' said I, 'to invoke upon our union the benediction of Heaven. We have both of us hearts too sensitive and minds too refined, to continue voluntarily in the wilful violation of so sacred a duty. It signifies nothing our having lived while in France in such a manner, because there it was as impossible for us not to love, as to be united by a legitimate tie: but in America, where we are under no restraint, where we owe no allegiance to the arbitrary distinctions of birth and aristocratic prejudice, where besides we are already supposed to be married, why should we not actually become so—why should we not sanctify our love by the holy ordinances of religion? As for me,' I added, 'I offer nothing new in offering you my hand and my heart; but I am ready to ratify it at the foot of the altar.'

"This speech seemed to inspire her with joy. 'Would you believe it,' she replied, 'I have thought of this a thousand times since our arrival in America? The fear of annoying you has kept it shut up in my breast. I felt that I had no pretensions to aspire to the character of your wife.'

"'Ah! Manon,' said I, 'you should very soon be a sovereign's consort, if I had been born to the inheritance of a crown. Let us not hesitate; we have no obstacle to impede us: I will this day speak to the governor on the subject, and acknowledge that we have in this particular hitherto deceived him. Let us leave,' added I, 'to vulgar lovers the dread of the indissoluble bonds of marriage;[1] they would not fear them if they were assured, as we are, of the continuance of those of love.' I left Manon enchanted by this resolution.

[1]Some say that Love, at sight of human ties,
Spreads his light wings, and in a moment flies.

"I am persuaded that no honest man could disapprove of this intention in my present situation; that is to say, fatally enslaved as I was by a passion which I could not subdue, and visited by compunction and remorse which I ought not to stifle. But will any man charge me with injustice or impiety if I complain of the rigour of Heaven in defeating a design that I could only have formed with the view of conciliating its favour and complying with its decrees? Alas! do I say defeated? nay punished as a new crime. I was patiently permitted to go blindly along the high road of vice; and the cruellest chastisements were reserved for the period when I was returning to the paths of virtue. I now fear that I shall have hardly fortitude enough left to recount the most disastrous circumstances that ever occurred to any man.

"I waited upon the governor, as I had settled with Manon, to procure his consent to the ceremony of our marriage. I should have avoided speaking to him or to any other person upon the subject, if I had imagined that his chaplain, who was the only minister in the town, would have performed the office for me without his knowledge; but not daring to hope that he would do so privately, I determined to act ingenuously in the matter.

"The governor had a nephew named Synnelet, of whom he was particularly fond. He was about thirty; brave, but of a headstrong and violent disposition. He was not married. Manon's beauty had struck him on the first day of our arrival; and the numberless opportunities he had of seeing her during the last nine or ten months, had so inflamed his passion, that he was absolutely pining for her in secret. However, as he was convinced in common with his uncle and the whole colony that I was married, he put such a restraint upon his feelings, that they remained generally unnoticed; and he lost no opportunity of showing the most disinterested friendship for me.

"He happened to be with his uncle when I arrived at the government house. I had no reason for keeping my intention a secret from him, so that I explained myself without hesitation in his presence. The governor heard me with his usual kindness. I related to him a part of my history, to which he listened with evident interest; and when I requested his presence at the intended ceremony, he was so generous as to say, that he must be permitted to defray the expenses of the succeeding entertainment. I retired perfectly satisfied.

"In an hour after, the chaplain paid me a visit. I thought he was come to prepare me by religious instruction for the sacred ceremony; but, after a cold salutation, he announced to me in two words, that the governor desired I would relinquish all thoughts of such a thing, for that he had other views for Manon.

"'Other views for Manon!' said I, as I felt my heart sink within me; 'what views then can they be, chaplain?'

"He replied, that I must be, of course, aware that the governor was absolute master here; that Manon, having been transported from

France to the colony, was entirely at his disposal; that, hitherto he had not exercised his right, believing that she was a married woman; but that now, having learned from my own lips that it was not so, he had resolved to assign her to M. Synnelet, who was passionately in love with her.

"My indignation overcame my prudence. Irritated as I was, I desired the chaplain instantly to quit my house, swearing at the same time that neither governor, Synnelet, nor the whole colony together, should lay hands upon my wife, or mistress, if they chose so to call her.

"I immediately told Manon of the distressing message I had just received. We conjectured that Synnelet had warped his uncle's mind after my departure, and that it was all the effect of a premeditated design. They were, questionless, the stronger party. We found ourselves in New Orleans, as in the midst of the ocean, separated from the rest of the world by an immense interval of space. In a country perfectly unknown, a desert, or inhabited, if not by brutes, at least by savages quite as ferocious, to what corner could we fly? I was respected in the town, but I could not hope to excite the people in my favour to such a degree as to derive assistance from them proportioned to the impending danger: money was requisite for that purpose, and I was poor. Besides, the success of a popular commotion was uncertain; and if we failed in the attempt, our doom would be inevitably sealed.

"I revolved these thoughts in my mind; I mentioned them in part to Manon; I found new ones, without waiting for her replies; I determined upon one course, and then abandoned that to adopt another; I talked to myself, and answered my own thoughts aloud; at length I sank into a kind of hysterical stupor that I can compare to nothing, because nothing ever equalled it. Manon observed my emotion, and from its violence, judged how imminent was our danger; and, apprehensive more on my account than on her own, the dear girl could not even venture to give expression to her fears.

"After a multitude of reflections, I resolved to call upon the governor, and appeal to his feelings of honour, to the recollection of my unvarying respect for him, and the marks he had given of his own affection for us both. Manon endeavoured to dissuade me from this attempt: she said, with tears in her eyes, 'You are rushing into the jaws of death; they will murder you—I shall never again see you—I am determined to die before you.' I had great difficulty in persuading her that it was absolutely necessary that I should go, and that she should remain at home. I promised that she should see me again in a few moments. She did not foresee, nor did I, that it was against herself the whole anger of Heaven, and the rabid fury of our enemies, was about to be concentrated.

"I went to the fort: the governor was there with his chaplain. I supplicated him in a tone of humble submission that I could have ill brooked under other circumstances. I invoked his clemency by every argument calculated to soften any heart less ferocious and cruel than a tiger's.

"The barbarian made to all my prayers but two short answers, which he repeated over and over again. 'Manon,' he said, 'was at his disposal: and he had given a promise to his nephew.' I was resolved to command my feelings to the last: I merely replied, that I had imagined he was too sincerely my friend to desire my death, to which I would infinitely rather consent than to the loss of my mistress.

"I felt persuaded, on quitting him, that it was folly to expect anything from the obstinate tyrant, who would have damned himself a hundred times over to please his nephew. However, I persevered in restraining my temper to the end; deeply resolved, if they persisted in such flagrant injustice, to make America the scene of one of the most horrible and bloody murders that even love had ever led to.

"I was, on my return home, meditating upon this design, when fate, as if impatient to expedite my ruin, threw Synnelet in my way. He read in my countenance a portion of my thoughts. I before said, he was brave. He approached me.

"'Are you not seeking me?' he enquired. 'I know that my intentions have given you mortal offence, and that the death of one of us is indispensable: let us see who is to be the happy man.'

"I replied, that such was unquestionably the fact, and that nothing but death could end the difference between us.

"We retired about one hundred paces out of the town. We drew: I wounded and disarmed him at the first onset. He was so enraged, that he peremptorily refused either to ask his life or renounce his claims to Manon. I might have been perhaps justified in ending both by a single blow; but noble blood ever vindicates its origin. I threw him back his sword. 'Let us renew the struggle,' said I to him, 'and remember that there shall be now no quarter.' He attacked me with redoubled fury. I must confess that I was not an accomplished swordsman, having had but three months' tuition in Paris. Love, however, guided my weapon. Synnelet pierced me through and through the left arm; but I caught him whilst thus engaged, and made so vigorous a thrust that I stretched him senseless at my feet.

"In spite of the triumphant feeling that victory, after a mortal conflict, inspires, I was immediately horrified by the certain consequences of his death. There could not be the slightest hope of either pardon or respite from the vengeance I had thus incurred. Aware, as I was, of the affection of the governor for his nephew, I felt perfectly sure that my death would not be delayed a single hour after his should become known. Urgent as this apprehension was, it still was by no means the principal source of my uneasiness. Manon, the welfare of Manon, the peril that impended over her, and the certainty of my being now at length separated from her, afflicted me to such a degree, that I was incapable of recognising the place in which I stood. I regretted Synnelet's death: instant suicide seemed the only remedy for my woes.

"However, it was this very thought that quickly restored me to my reason, and enabled me to form a resolution. 'What,' said I to myself, 'die, in order to end my pain! Then there is something I dread more than the loss of all I love! No, let me suffer the cruellest extremities in order to aid her; and when these prove of no avail, fly to death as a last resource!'

"I returned towards the town; on my arrival at home, I found Manon half dead with fright and anxiety: my presence restored her. I could not conceal from her the terrible accident that had happened. On my mentioning the death of Synnelet and my own wound, she fell in a state of insensibility into my arms. It was a quarter of an hour before I could bring her again to her senses.

"I was myself in a most deplorable state of mind; I could not discern the slightest prospect of safety for either of us. 'Manon,' said I to her, when she had recovered a little, 'what shall we do? Alas, what hope remains to us? I must necessarily fly. Will you remain in the town? Yes dearest Manon, do remain; you may possibly still be happy here; while I, far away from you, may seek death and find it amongst the savages, or the wild beasts.'

"She raised herself in spite of her weakness, and taking hold of my hand to lead me towards the door: 'Let us,' said she, 'fly together, we have not a moment to lose; Synnelet's body may be found by chance, and we shall then have no time to escape.' 'But, dear Manon,' replied I, 'to what place can we fly? Do you perceive any resource? Would it not be better that you should endeavour to live on without me; and that I should go and voluntarily place my life in the governor's hands?'

"This proposal had only the effect of making her more impatient for our departure. I had presence of mind enough, on going out, to take with me some strong liquors which I had in my chamber, and as much food as I could carry in my pockets. We told our servants, who were in the adjoining room, that we were going to take our evening walk, as was our invariable habit; and we left the town behind us more rapidly than I had thought possible from Manon's delicate state of health.

"Although I had not formed any resolve as to our future destination, I still cherished a hope, without which I should have infinitely preferred death to my suspense about Manon's safety. I had acquired a sufficient knowledge of the country, during nearly ten months which I had now passed in America, to know in what manner the natives should be approached. Death was not the necessary consequence of falling into their hands. I had learned a few words of their language, and some of their customs, having had many opportunities of seeing them.

"Besides this sad resource, I derived some hopes from the fact, that the English had, like ourselves, established colonies in this part of the New World. But the distance was terrific. In order to reach them, we should have to traverse deserts of many days' journey, and more than one range of mountains so steep and vast as to seem almost impassable to the strongest man. I nevertheless flattered myself that we might derive partial relief from one or other of these sources: the savages might serve us as guides, and the English receive us in their settlements.

" We journeyed on as long as Manon's strength would permit, that is to say, about six miles; for this incomparable creature, with her usual absence of selfishness, refused my repeated entreaties to stop. Overpowered at length by fatigue, she acknowledged the utter impossibility of proceeding farther. It was already night: we sat down in the midst of an extensive plain, where we could not even find a tree to shelter us. Her first care was to dress my wound, which she had bandaged before our departure. I, in vain, entreated her to desist from exertion: it would have only added to her distress if I had refused her the satisfaction of seeing me at ease and out of danger, before her own wants were attended to. I allowed her therefore to gratify herself, and in shame and silence submitted to her delicate attentions.

" But when she had completed her tender task, with what ardour did I not enter upon mine! I took off my clothes and stretched them under her, to render more endurable the hard and rugged ground on which she lay. I protected her delicate hands from the cold by my burning kisses and the warmth of my sighs. I passed the livelong night in watching over her as she slept, and praying Heaven to refresh her with soft and undisturbed repose. 'You can bear witness, just and all-seeing God! to the fervour and sincerity of those prayers, and Thou alone knowest with what awful rigour they were rejected.'

" You will excuse me, if I now cut short a story which it distresses me beyond endurance to relate. It is, I believe, a calamity without parallel. I can never cease to deplore it. But although it continues, of course, deeply and indelibly impressed on my memory, yet my heart seems to shrink within me each time that I attempt the recital.

" We had thus tranquilly passed the night. I had fondly imagined that my beloved mistress was in a profound sleep, and I hardly dared to breathe lest I should disturb her. As day broke, I observed that her hands were cold and trembling; I pressed them to my bosom in the hope of restoring animation. This movement roused her attention, and making an effort to grasp my hand, she said, in a feeble voice, that she thought her last moments had arrived.

" I, at first, took this for a passing weakness, or the ordinary language of distress; and I answered with the usual consolations that love prompted. But her incessant sighs, her silence, and inattention to my enquiries, the convulsed grasp of her hands, in which she retained mine, soon convinced me that the crowning end of all my miseries was approaching.

" Do not now expect me to attempt a description of my feelings, or to repeat her dying expressions. I lost her—I received the purest assurances of her love even at the very instant that her spirit fled. I have not nerve to say more upon this fatal and disastrous event.

"My spirit was not destined to accompany Manon's. Doubtless, Heaven did not as yet consider me sufficiently punished, and therefore ordained that I should continue to drag on a languid and joyless existence. I willingly renounced every hope of leading a happy one.

"I remained for twenty-four hours without taking my lips from the still beauteous countenance and hands of my adored Manon. My intention was to await my own death in that position; but at the beginning of the second day, I reflected that, after I was gone, she must of necessity become the prey of wild beasts. I then determined to bury her, and wait my own doom upon her grave. I was already, indeed, so near my end from the combined effect of long fasting and grief, that it was with the greatest difficulty I could support myself standing. I was obliged to have recourse to the liquors which I had brought with me, and these restored sufficient strength to enable me to set about my last sad office. From the sandy nature of the soil there was little trouble in opening the ground. I broke my sword and used it for the purpose; but my bare hands were of greater service. I dug a deep grave, and there deposited the idol of my heart, after having wrapt around her my clothes to prevent the sand from touching her. I kissed her ten thousand times with all the ardour of the most glowing love, before I laid her in this melancholy bed. I sat for some time upon the bank intently gazing on her, and could not command fortitude enough to close the grave over her. At length, feeling that my strength was giving way, and apprehensive of its being entirely exhausted before the completion of my task, I committed to the earth all that it had ever contained most perfect and peerless. I then lay myself with my face down upon the grave, and closing my eyes with the determination never again to open them, I invoked the mercy of Heaven, and ardently prayed for death.

"You will find it difficult to believe that, during the whole time of this protracted and distressing ceremony, not a tear or a sigh escaped to relieve my agony. The state of profound affliction in which I was, and the deep settled resolution I had taken to die, had silenced the sighs of despair, and effectually dried up the ordinary channels of grief. It was thus impossible for me, in this posture upon the grave, to continue for any time in possession of my faculties.

"After what you have listened to, the remainder of my own history would ill repay the attention you seem inclined to bestow upon it. Synnelet having been carried into the town and skilfully examined, it was found that, so far from being dead, he was not even dangerously wounded. He informed his uncle of the manner in which the affray had occurred between us, and he generously did justice to my conduct on the occasion. I was sent for; and as neither of us could be found, our flight was immediately suspected. It was then too late to attempt to trace me, but the next day and the following one were employed in the pursuit.

"I was found, without any appearance of life, upon the grave of Manon: and the persons who discovered me in this situation, seeing that I was almost naked and bleeding from my wounds, naturally supposed that I had been robbed and assassinated. They carried me into the town. The motion restored me to my senses. The sighs I heaved on opening my eyes and finding myself still amongst the living, showed that I was not beyond the reach of art: they were but too successful in its application.

"I was immediately confined as a close prisoner. My trial was ordered; and as Manon was not forthcoming, I was accused of having murdered her from rage and jealousy. I naturally related all that had occurred. Synnelet, though bitterly grieved and disappointed by what he heard, had the generosity to solicit my pardon: he obtained it.

"I was so reduced, that they were obliged to carry me from the prison to my bed, and there I suffered for three long months under severe illness. My aversion from life knew no diminution. I continually prayed for death, and obstinately for some time refused every remedy. But Providence, after having punished me with atoning rigour, saw fit to turn to my own use its chastisements and the memory of my multiplied sorrows. It at length deigned to shed upon me its redeeming light, and revived in my mind ideas worthy of my birth and my early education.

"My tranquillity of mind being again restored, my cure speedily followed. I began only to feel the highest aspirations of honour, and diligently performed the duties of my appointment, whilst expecting the arrival of the vessels from France, which were always due at this period of the year. I resolved to return to my native country, there to expiate the scandal of my former life by my future good conduct. Synnelet had the remains of my dear mistress removed into a more hallowed spot.

"It was six weeks after my recovery that, one day walking alone upon the banks of the river, I saw a vessel arrive, which some mercantile speculation had directed to New Orleans. I stood by whilst the passengers landed. Judge my surprise on recognising Tiberge amongst those who proceeded towards the town. This ever-faithful friend knew me at a distance, in spite of the ravages which care and sorrow had worked upon my countenance. He told me that the sole object of his voyage had been to see me once more, and to induce me to return with him to France; that on receipt of the last letter which I had written to him from Havre, he started for that place, and was himself the bearer of the succour which I solicited; that he had been sensibly affected on learning my departure, and that he would have instantly followed me, if there had been a vessel bound for the same destination; that he had been for several months endeavouring to hear of one in the various seaport towns, and that, having at length found one at St. Malo which was weighing anchor for Martinique, he embarked, in the expectation of easily passing from thence to New Orleans; that the St. Malo vessel having been captured by Spanish pirates and taken to one of their islands, he had contrived to escape; and that, in short, after many adventures, he had got on board the vessel which had just arrived, and at length happily attained his object.

"I was totally unable adequately to express my feelings of gratitude to this generous and unshaken friend. I conducted him to my house, and placed all I possessed at his service. I related to him every circumstance that had occurred to me since I left France: and in order to gladden him with tidings which I knew he did not expect, I assured him that the seeds of virtue which he had in former days implanted in my heart, were now about to produce fruit, of which even he should be proud. He declared to me, that this gladdening announcement more than repaid him for all the fatigue and trouble he had endured.

"We passed two months together at New Orleans whilst waiting the departure of a vessel direct to France; and having at length sailed, we landed only a fortnight since at Havre-de-Grace. On my arrival I wrote to my family. By a letter from my elder brother, I there learned my father's death, which, I dread to think, the disorders of my youth might have hastened. The wind being favourable for Calais, I embarked for this port, and am now going to the house of one of my relations who lives a few miles off, where my brother said that he should anxiously await my arrival."

adventures, he had got on board the vessel which had just arrived, and at length happily attained his object.

"I was quite unable adequately to express my feelings of gratitude to this generous and unshaken friend. I conducted him to my house, and placed all I possessed at his service. I related to him every circumstance that had occurred to me since I left France; and in order to also inform him with tidings which I knew he did not expect, I assured him that the seeds of virtue which he had in former days implanted in my heart, were now about to produce fruit, of which even he should be proud. He declared to me, that this gladdening announcement more than repaid him for all the fatigue and trouble he had endured.

"We passed two months together at New Orleans whilst waiting the departure of a vessel direct to France; and having at length sailed, we landed only a fortnight since at Havre-de-Grace. On my arrival I wrote to my family. By a letter from my elder brother, I there learned my father's death, which I dread to think, the disasters of my youth might have hastened. The wind being favourable for Calais, I embarked for this port, and am now going to the house of one of my relations, who lives a few miles off, where my brother said that he should anxiously await my arrival."

# DANGEROUS ACQUAINTANCES

# DANGEROUS ACQUAINTANCES

## PART I

### LETTER I

*Cécile Volanges to Sophie Carnay at the Ursuline Convent of . .*

You will see, my dear, that I have kept my word and that bonnets and pom-poms do not take up all my time—there will always be some left over for you. Yet I have seen more clothes in this single day than in the four years we spent together; and I think the haughty Tanville[1] will be more angered by my first visit (when I intend to ask for her), than she thought we were when she came to see us *in fiocchi.*[2] Mamma asks my opinion in everything and treats me much less like a school-girl than she used to do. I have my own maid; I have a room and a study at my disposal and I am writing this to you at a very pretty writing-table whose key was given to me so that I can shut up anything I want in it. Mamma says I am to see her every day when she gets up; that I need not arrange my hair[3] until dinner time because we shall always be alone, and that she will tell me every day when I am to join her in the afternoon. The rest of my time is at my disposal and I have my harp, my drawing and my books just as in the convent, except that Mother Perpetue is not here to scold me and that I need do nothing unless I wish; but since my Sophie is not here to talk and laugh with me, I may just as well occupy myself.

It is not yet five o'clock; I do not see Mamma until seven; plenty of time, if I had anything to say to you! but so far nothing has been said and except for the preparations I see being made and the numbers of sewing-women who all come for me I should think there is no intention of marrying me and that it was one more delusion on the part of the good Josephine.[4] Yet Mamma has told me so often that a young lady should remain at the convent until she is married that Josephine must be right, since Mamma has taken me away.

A carriage has just stopped at the door and Mamma sends me a message to come to her at once. Suppose it were *he?* I am not dressed; my hand trembles and my heart beats. I asked my maid if she knew who was with my mother. "Why," said she, "it is M. C. . . ." And she laughed. Oh! I think it *is* he! I shall surely return to tell you what has happened. This, at all events, is his name. I must not keep them waiting. Adieu, for a moment. . . .

[1] Pupil in the same convent. (C. de L.) [2] In her best clothes.
[3] This refers to the elaborate head-dress of the eighteenth century lady.
[4] Attendant at the convent turning-box. (C. de L.)

How you will laugh at your poor Cécile! Oh! I was very much ashamed, but you would have been as helpless as I was. When I entered Mamma's room I saw a gentleman in black standing beside her. I saluted him as well as I could and remained rooted to the spot. You can imagine how I looked at him! "Madame," said he to my mother, as he bowed to me, "This is a charming young lady and I feel more than ever the value of your favour." At this plain remark I began to tremble, to such an extent that I could not stand up; I found an armchair and sat down in it, blushing deeply and very disconcerted. I had scarcely sat down when this man was at my knees! Your poor Cécile then lost her head; as Mamma said, I was thoroughly scared. I sprang up with a piercing cry . . . just like the day of the thunder-storm. Mamma burst out laughing and said: "Why! What is the matter with you? Sit down and give Monsieur your foot." My dear, "Monsieur" was a shoemaker! I cannot tell you how ashamed I was; fortunately no one was there but Mamma. I think that when I am married I shall never employ this shoemaker.

You must admit we are well informed! Good-bye. It is nearly six o'clock and my maid says I must dress. Good-bye, dear Sophie; I love you as if I were still at the convent.

P.S. I do not know by whom to send this letter, so I shall wait until Josephine comes.

Paris, 3rd August, 17—.

## LETTER II

*The Marquise de Merteuil to the Vicomte de Valmont at the Château de . . .*

Come back, my dear Vicomte, come back; what are you doing, what *can* you be doing with an old aunt whose property is entailed on you? Come at once; I need you. I have a wonderful idea and you must carry it out. These few words should be enough for you and, but too honoured by my choice, you should come eagerly to take my orders on your knees; but you abuse my favours even since you have ceased to make use of them; and in the alternative of an eternal hatred or an excessive indulgence your good luck decides that my kindness should win the day. I shall therefore tell you my plan; but swear to me like a faithful knight that you will engage yourself in no other adventure until you have accomplished this. She is worthy of a hero; you will serve both love and vengeance; and it will be a *rouerie*[1] the more to put in your *mémoires*; yes, in your *mémoires*, for I wish them to be printed one day and I undertake to write them. But let us leave this and return to what concerns us.

Madame de Volanges is marrying her daughter; it is still a secret, but she told me about it yesterday. And whom do you think she has

[1] The words *roué* and *rouerie*, which are happily falling out of use in good company, were very fashionable at the time these letters were written. (C. de L.)

chosen for her son-in-law ? The Comte de Gercourt. Who would have thought that I should become Gercourt's cousin ? I am in a rage. . . . Have you not guessed why ? Dullard ! Have *you* forgiven him the adventure with the *Intendante ?* And have *I* not even more reason to complain of him, monster that you are ?[1] But I calm myself and the hope of vengeance soothes my mind.

You have been a hundred times annoyed, as I have myself, by the consequence Gercourt attaches to the wife he is to have and by the silly presumption which makes him think he will avoid the inevitable fate. You know his ridiculous prejudices in favour of a cloistered education and his still more ridiculous preconception of the modesty of fair-haired women. Indeed I would wager that, in spite of the income of sixty thousand *livres* which goes with the Volanges girl, he would never have consented to the marriage if she had been dark or if she had not been to a convent. Let us prove to him that he is a mere fool ; no doubt he will be one day—that is not what troubles me—but it would be amusing to have him begin by being one. How it will delight us to hear him boasting on the morning after (for he will boast) ; and then, if you once mould this girl, it would be very unlucky if Gercourt, like anybody else, does not become the talk of Paris.

Moreover, the heroine of this new adventure is worthy of all your attention ; she is really pretty, she is only fifteen ; a rosebud ; ignorant to a degree and entirely unaffected, but you men are not afraid of that ; in addition, a certain languid gaze seems to promise a great deal. Add to this that I recommend her to you ; you have no more to do than to thank and obey me.

You will receive this letter tomorrow morning. I insist on your being with me tomorrow evening at seven o'clock. I shall receive nobody until eight, not even the reigning Chevalier ; his mind is not equal to so important an affair. You see that love does not blind me. At eight o'clock I will grant you your liberty and you will return at ten to sup with the fair creature ; for she and her mother are taking supper with me. Good-bye, it is after midday ; very soon I shall cease to take an interest in you.

Paris, 4th August, 17—.

## LETTER III

*Cécile Volanges to Sophie Carnay*

I am still kept in ignorance, my dear. Yesterday Mamma invited a number of people to supper. In spite of the fact that it was to my interest to observe them, especially the men, I was very bored. Men

[1] To understand this passage, the reader must know that the Comte de Gercourt had left the Marquise de Merteuil for the *Intendante de* ——, who had sacrificed to him the Vicomte de Valmont and that it was then the Marquise and the Vicomte became attached to one another. Since this adventure is much earlier than the events dealt with in these letters the whole correspondence about it has been suppressed. (C. de L.)

and women, everybody, looked closely at me and then whispered in each other's ears. I saw they were talking about me; this made me blush; I could not prevent it. I wish I could have, for I noticed that when people looked at the other women they did not blush; or else the rouge they put on prevents one seeing the colour caused them by embarrassment; for it must be very difficult not to blush when a man looks steadily at you.

What made me most uneasy was that I did not know what they thought about me. I think I heard two or three times the word "Pretty"; but I very distinctly heard "Awkward"; and the latter must be true because the woman who said it is my mother's relative and friend; she even seemed to have a sudden friendship for me. She is the only person who talked to me at all during the evening. Tomorrow we go to supper at her house.

After supper I heard a man who, I am sure, was speaking of me, say to another: "We must let her ripen; we shall see, this winter." Perhaps it is he who is to marry me; but then it will not be for four months! I wish I knew what is to be.

Here is Josephine, who tells me she is in a hurry. Yet I must tell you another *awkwardness* of mine. Oh! I am afraid the lady was right!

After supper gambling began. I was beside Mamma; I do not know how it happened, but I went to sleep almost at once. I was awakened by a loud burst of laughter. I do not know if they were laughing at me, but I think they were. Mamma gave me permission to go, which gave me great pleasure. Imagine! It was after eleven o'clock! Good-bye, my dear Sophie; always love your Cécile. I assure you the world is not as amusing as we imagined.

Paris, 4th August, 17—.

## LETTER IV

*The Vicomte de Valmont to the Marquise de Merteuil at Paris*

Your orders are charming; your manner of giving them is still more amiable; you would make despotism attractive. As you know, this is not the first time that I regret I am no longer your slave; and however much of a *monster* you say I am I never think but with pleasure of the time you honoured me with softer names. Quite often I even hope to deserve them again and to end up with you by giving the world an example of constancy. But more important interests must occupy us; to conquer is our fate, and fate must be obeyed; perhaps we shall meet again at the end of our career; for be it said without offence, most fair Marquise, you follow me step by step; and since, after separating for the happiness of the world, we preach the faith separately, it seems to me that you make as many proselytes as I, in this mission of love. I know your zeal, your ardent fervour; and if this God estimated us by our works, you would one day be the patroness of some large town, while your friend at best would be a village saint. This form of expression surprises you, does it not ? But for the last eight days I have heard and spoken none other ; and in order to grow perfect in it I am forced to disobey you.

Do not be angry ; and listen to me. You have shared all the secrets of my heart and I am about to confide to you the greatest project I have ever formed. What was it you proposed to me ? To seduce a girl who has seen and knows nothing, who (so to speak) would be handed over to me defenceless, who could not fail to be intoxicated by a first attention and whom curiosity would probably lead more rapidly than love. There are twenty others who could succeed as well as I. But this is not the case with the enterprise which now occupies me ; its success assures me as much fame as pleasure. The Love who is preparing my crown himself hesitates between myrtle and laurel, or rather he will unite them to honour my triumph. You yourself, my fair friend, will be seized by a holy respect and you will say enthusiastically : " Here is a man after my own heart."

You know Madame de Tourvel, her religious devotion, her conjugal love, her austere principles. That is what I am attacking ; that is the enemy worthy of me ; that is the end I mean to reach ;

" And if I do not carry off the prize of obtaining her,
At least I shall have the honour of having attempted it."

Bad verses may be quoted when they are by a great poet.[1]

You must know that her husband is in Burgundy on account of some big law-suit (I hope to make him lose a still more important one). His inconsolable spouse is compelled to spend here the whole time of her distressing widowhood. A mass every day, a few visits to the poor in the district, morning and evening prayers, solitary walks, pious conversations with my old aunt, and sometimes a dismal rubber of whist, are her only distractions. I am preparing more effectual ones for her. My good angel led me here for her happiness and for my own. Madman that I was ! I regretted the twenty-four hours I sacrificed to the demands of convention. How I should be punished were I forced to return to Paris ! Luckily, four people are needed for a hand of whist, and since there is no one here but the local *curé* my eternal aunt pressed me to sacrifice a few days to her. You may guess that I consented. You cannot imagine how much she has flattered me since then and above all how edified she is to see me regularly at prayer and at mass. She does not realise who is the divinity I adore.

For the last four days I have given myself up to this powerful passion. You know I always desire keenly and sweep away obstacles ; but what you cannot know is how much solitude adds to the ardour of desire. I have but one idea ; I think of it by day and dream of it by night. I must have this woman, to save myself from the ridiculous position of being in love with her—for how far may not one be led by

[1] La Fontaine.

a thwarted desire? O delicious possession! I need you for my happiness and still more for my peace of mind. It is fortunate for us that women are so weak in their own defence! Otherwise we should be nothing but their timid slaves. At this very moment I have a feeling of gratitude for facile women which quite naturally brings me to your feet. I cast myself before them to obtain forgiveness and I conclude this long letter. Good-bye, fair lady—all in good part.

From the Château de . . ., 5th August, 17—.

## LETTER V

*The Marquise de Merteuil to the Vicomte de Valmont*

Do you realise, Vicomte, that your letter is extremely insolent and that I ought to be angry with you? But it shows me you have lost your head and that fact alone saves you from my indignation. I am a generous and compassionate friend and forget my own injury to concern myself with your danger; and, however tiresome it may be to argue, I must yield to your present need of it.

You possess Madame de Tourvel! What a ridiculous caprice! I see it is your usual obstinacy which never wants except what seems impossible to obtain. What sort of a woman is she? Regular feature, if you like, but a complete lack of expression; fairly well-made but entirely without grace; always ridiculously dressed with her bunches of neckerchief on her breast and her bodice up to her chin! I warn you as a friend, two women like her will ruin your reputation for you. Think of that day when she made the collection in Saint Roch, when you thanked me so often for having procured you such a spectacle! I can still see her, giving her hand to that hop-pole of a man with long hair ready to sink down at every step, with her four yards of hoop-skir continually on someone's head, and blushing at every bow. Who would have said then that you would desire such a woman? Come, Vicomte, blush, and recover your senses. I promise you secrecy.

And then, think of the annoyances awaiting you. Who is the rival you must combat? A husband! Do you not feel humiliated by the mere word? What a disgrace if you fail! And how little glory if you succeed! I will go further—you must not expect any pleasure. Can there be any with prudes? I mean with those who are really so. They are reserved in the very midst of pleasure and can offer you nothing more than a half-enjoyment. That complete abandonment of self, that delirium of delight wherein pleasure is purified by its excess, those treasures of love are unknown to them. I warn you—supposing the best, your Madame de Tourvel will think she has done everything for you if she treats you like a husband, and in the tenderest conjugal interview the parties always remain two. Here it is still worse; your prude is religious with the sort of religion which condemns a woman to perpetual childishness. Perhaps you will surmount this obstacle, but do not flatter yourself with the idea that you can destroy it ; you may conquer the love of God, but not the fear of the devil ; when you hold your mistress in your arms and feel her heart beating, it will be from terror, not from love. Perhaps if you had known this woman sooner you might have made something of her ; but she is twenty-two and has been married nearly two years. Believe me, Vicomte, when a woman is *encrusted* to that extent she must be left to her fate ; she will never be anything but a poor creature.

Yet it is for this fair object that you refuse to obey me, that you bury yourself in your aunt's tomb, that you give up a most delicious adventure which would do you the utmost honour ! How does it happen that Gercourt always has the advantage over you ? Come, I am talking to you good-humouredly ; but at the moment I really am tempted to think you do not deserve your reputation, I am tempted to withdraw my confidence from you. I could never grow accustomed to confiding my secrets to Madame de Tourvel's lover.

You are to know that the Volanges girl has already turned one head. Young Danceny is madly in love with her. He has sung with her ; and indeed she sings better than a girl just from a convent should. They are to go through a number of duets and I feel sure she will gladly be in unison ; but Danceny is a mere child who will lose his time in making love and will never complete anything. The girl herself is quite shy and, in any event, it will be much less amusing than you could have made it ; it puts me out of humour and I shall certainly quarrel with the Chevalier when he arrives. I advise him to be gentle ; for, at the moment, I could break with him without reluctance. I am sure that if I had the good sense to leave him now he would be in despair ; and nothing amuses me like a lover in despair. He would call me false, and the word " false " always gives me pleasure ; after " cruel " it is the sweetest in a woman's ear and the least difficult to deserve. Seriously I must think about breaking off this affair. See what you are the cause of ! I lay it on your conscience. Good-bye. Recommend me to Madame de Tourvel's prayers.

**Paris, 7th August, 17—.**

## LETTER VI

*The Vicomte de Valmont to the Marquise de Merteuil*

So there is no woman in the world who does not abuse her power ! Even you, whom I so often called " an indulgent friend," cease to be so ; you do not shrink from attacking me through the object of my affection ! With what strokes you dared to paint Madame de Tourvel ! A man would have paid for such insolence with his life and any woman but you would have been repaid at least by some revenge. I beg you will not subject me to such harsh tests ; I cannot promise to endure them. In the name of friendship, wait until I have had the woman if you want to disparage her. Do you not know that pleasure alone has the right of loosening the bandage from Love's eyes?

But what am I saying? Does Madame de Tourvel need illusion? No, she needs but to be herself and she is adorable. You censure her for dressing badly and I agree with you; all clothes do her injustice, whatever hides her disfigures her. In the unconstraint of her morning-dress she is indeed delightful. Thanks to the extremely hot weather we are having, a morning-dress of simple linen allows me to see her round supple figure. Her breasts are hidden by a single fold of muslin and my furtive but keen glances have already spied out their enchanting shape. Her face, you say, lacks expression. And what should it express at a time when nothing speaks to her heart? No doubt, unlike our coquettes, she has not that delusive gaze which sometimes seduces and always deceives. She cannot cover the emptiness of a phrase by a false smile, and although she has the finest teeth imaginable she only laughs at what amuses her. But you should see her in her playful moments—what an image of frank, natural gaiety! What pure joy and pitying kindness are in her gaze when she hastens to help the unfortunate! Above all you should see her when at the least word of praise or flattery her divine face is coloured by the touching embarrassment of an unfeigned modesty! She is chaste and religious and therefore you think her cold and lifeless? I think very differently. What an amazing sensibility she must possess to be able to shed it even on her husband and to love continually a person who is continually absent! What stronger proof could you desire? Yet I have been able to obtain another.

I arranged a walk so that we came upon a ditch which had to be crossed; and although she is very active, she is even more timid; you may imagine that a prude is afraid to take a leap.[1] She was compelled to accept my help. I have clasped this modest woman in my arms! Our preparations and the crossing of my old aunt sent our gay devotee into peals of laughter; but as soon as I took hold of her, by an intentional awkwardness of my part our arms become mutually entwined. I held her breast against my own and, in that brief moment, I felt her heart beat faster. Her face was suffused by a charming blush and her modest embarrassment showed me *that her heart had beaten with love and not with fear*. And yet my aunt was as mistaken as you and said: "The child was afraid"; but the *child's* charming candour does not permit her a lie and she answered naïvely: "O no but. . . ." That single word enlightened me. From that moment my cruel uneasiness gave way to a pleasing hope. I shall have this woman; I shall carry her away from the husband who profanes her; I shall even dare to ravish her from the God she adores. What a delicious pleasure to be alternately the cause and the conqueror of her remorse! Far be it from me to wish to destroy the prejudices which torture her! They

[1] The reader will perceive here that bad taste for puns which was beginning then and is now so popular. (C. de L.) "*Sauter le fossé*" means "to jump a ditch" and "to take a leap," "to cross the Rubicon."

will add to my happiness and my fame. Let her believe in virtue, but let her sacrifice it to me; let her slips terrify her without restraining her; let her be agitated by a thousand terrors and not be able to forget and to crush them save in my arms. Then I agree, she may say: "I adore you"—and she alone among all women will be worthy to say so. I shall indeed be the God she has preferred.

Let us be frank; in our arrangements, as frigid as they are facile, that which we call happiness is scarcely a pleasure. Shall I confess it to you? I thought my heart withered up and, finding I had nothing left but my senses, I pitied myself for a premature old age. Madame de Tourvel has given me back the charming illusions of youth. Near her I do not need to enjoy her to be happy. The only thing which terrifies me is the time this adventure will take; for I can leave nothing to chance. However much I remind myself of my lucky audacities I cannot resolve to put them into practice. For me to be really happy she must give herself—that is no small matter. I am sure you will admire my prudence. The word "love" I have not yet spoken; but already we have got to "confidence" and "interest." To deceive her as little as possible and especially to forestall any gossip which might reach her I have myself told her, as if accusing myself, some of my best known exploits. You would laugh to see the candour with which she reproves me. She says she wishes to convert me. She does not guess the price she would have to pay for attempting it. She is far from thinking that "by pleading (as she puts it) for the unfortunate women I have ruined," that she is pleading beforehand on her own behalf. The idea came to me yesterday in the middle of one of her sermons and I could not refuse myself the pleasure of interrupting her, in order to tell her she spoke like a prophet. Good-bye, fairest lady! You see I am not irrecoverably lost.

P.S. By the way, has the poor Chevalier committed suicide in despair? Really, you are a hundred times worse than I am and you would humiliate me, were I conceited.

From the Château of . . ., 9th August, 17—.

## LETTER VII

*Cécile Volanges to Sophie Carnay*[1]

If I have told you nothing about my marriage, the reason is that I know no more about it than I did the first day. I am growing used to not thinking about it and I find this kind of life quite suits me. I spend a good deal of time working at my singing and my harp; I seem to like them more now that I have no master, or rather now that

[1] In order not to weary the reader's patience, a large number of letters from this daily correspondence have been suppressed; those only have been given which appeared necessary to a complete understanding of the events in this group. For the same reason all Sophie Carnay's letters have been suppressed as well as several others from the actors in these events. (C. de L.)

I have a better one. The Chevalier Danceny, the gentleman of whom I spoke, and with whom I sang at Madame de Merteuil's house, is kind enough to come here every day and to sing with me for hours on end. He is extremely agreeable. He sings like an angel and composes most elegant airs to which he writes the words. What a pity he is a Knight of Malta! It seems to me that if he married, his wife would be very happy. . . . His gentleness is charming. He never seems to be paying one a compliment and yet everything he says is flattering. He corrects me continually, as much in music as in anything else; but he mingles such interest and such gaiety with his criticism that it is impossible not to feel grateful to him. Only, when he looks at you, he seems to be saying something agreeable. And in addition, he is very unselfish. For example, yesterday, he was invited to an important concert—and he preferred to stay the whole evening here. It gave me a great deal of pleasure; for when he is not here, nobody speaks to me and I grow languid; but when he is here, we sing and converse together. He has always something new to tell me. He and Madame de Merteuil are the only two people I think agreeable. But good-bye, my dear, I have promised to learn for today an arietta with a very difficult accompaniment and I do not want to break my word; I shall practise it until he comes.

**From . . ., 7th of August, 17—.**

## LETTER VIII

*Madame de Tourvel to Madame de Volanges*

No one could be more touched than I am, Madame, by the confidence you show me, nor take more interest than I in the future of Mademoiselle de Volanges. With all my heart I wish her the happiness of which I am sure she is worthy and I rely upon your prudence to obtain it. I do not know the Comte de Gercourt; but, since he is honoured by your choice, I cannot but esteem him highly. I limit myself, Madame, to the wish that this marriage may be as happy as my own, which was likewise your work, and for which I am every day more grateful. May your daughter's happiness be your reward for the happiness you procured me; and may the best of friends be also the happiest of mothers!

I am indeed distressed that I cannot convey to you these sincere wishes in person and make the acquaintance of Mademoiselle de Volanges as soon as I should desire. Since I have received from you marks of kindness that were indeed maternal, I have the right to hope from her the tender friendship of a sister. I beg, Madame, you will be good enough to ask it of her on my behalf until I am in a position to merit it.

I have arranged to stay in the country for the whole time of Monsieur de Tourvel's absence. I have made use of this time to enjoy and profit by the society of the respectable Madame de Rosemonde. She is a woman who has remained charming ; her great age has robbed her of nothing ; she keeps her memory and her gaiety intact. Her body alone is eighty-eight ; her spirit is only twenty.

Our solitude is enlivened by her nephew the Vicomte de Valmont, who has been kind enough to spare us a few days. I only knew him by hearsay and what I heard made me little desirous to know more of him ; but I think him better than rumour pretends. Here, where he is not spoiled by the whirl of society, he talks of Reason with astonishing facility and confesses his faults with rare candour. He speaks to me with great confidence and I lecture him with great severity. You, who know him, will admit that his conversion would be a great achievement ; but in spite of his promises I have no doubt that a week of Paris will make him forget all my sermons. His stay here will at least be that much time taken from his ordinary conduct ; and I really think after the way he has lived that the best thing he can do is to do nothing at all. He knows I am writing to you and asks me to convey to you his respectful regards. Accept mine also with your usual kindness and never doubt the sincere feelings with which I have the honour to be, etc.

From the Château of . . ., 9th August, 17—.

## LETTER IX

*Madame de Volanges to Madame de Tourvel*

I have never doubted, my fair young friend, either your friendship for me or your sincere interest in my affairs. It is not for the purpose of clearing up this point—which I hope is forever settled between us—that I reply to your reply ; but I cannot avoid discussing with you the subject of the Vicomte de Valmont.

I must admit I never expected to find that name in your letters. What can there be in common between you and him ? You do not know this man ; where could you have acquired the notion of a libertine's soul ? You speak of his *rare candour ;* ah yes ! Valmont's candour must indeed be vary rare. The more false and dangerous in that he is amiable and seductive, he has never from his earliest youth taken one step or said one word without a purpose, and he has never had a purpose but was wicked or criminal. My dear, you know me ; you know that among the virtues I have tried to acquire, forbearance is the one I most prize. And so, if Valmont were carried away by impetuous passions ; if, like a thousand others, he were seduced by the errors of his age ; while I blamed his conduct, I should pity his person and should await in silence the time when some fortunate change would acquire him the esteem of virtuous people. But Valmont is not that kind of man ; his conduct is the result of his principles. He calculated all that a man may permit himself in wickedness without compromising himself ; and, in order to be cruel and wicked without danger, he chose women for his victims. I will not stop to count those he has seduced; but how many has he not ruined?

In the quiet, retired life which you lead, such scandalous adventures do not reach you. I could tell you some which would make you shudder; but your gaze, as pure as your soul, would be sullied by such pictures; with the certainty that Valmont will never be dangerous to you, you do not need such weapons for your defence. The only thing I have to tell you is that among all the women to whom he has paid attentions, whether successful or no, there is not one but has had reason to complain of him. The Marquise de Merteuil is the single exception to this general rule; she alone was able to resist him and to restrain his wickedness. I must confess that this episode in her life is that which sets her highest in my estimation; and it suffices in the world's eyes as a full justification for certain imprudences she was reproached with when she was first a widow.[1]

At all events, my dear, I am authorised by my age, my experience and above all by my friendship, to point out to you that people in society are beginning to notice Valmont's absence; if it is known that he has spent some time alone with you and his aunt your reputation will be in his hands—the greatest misfortune which can happen to a woman. I advise you to persuade his aunt not to detain him any longer; and if he persists in remaining I think you ought not to hesitate to leave. Why should he remain? What is he doing in that part of the country? If you watch his movements I am sure you will find out that he has simply chosen a convenient place for some evil purpose he is meditating in the neighbourhood. But, since it is impossible to remedy the evil, let us rest satisfied with preserving ourselves from it.

Good-bye, my dear; my daughter's marriage is postponed for a little while. The Comte de Gercourt, whom we were expecting every day, writes me that his regiment is ordered for Corsica; and since the war still drags on, it will be impossible for him to get away before the winter. It is vexatious; but still it lets me hope that we shall have the pleasure of seeing you at the wedding, and I was sorry it should take place without you. Good-bye: without compliment and without reserve I am entirely yours.

P.S. Mention me to Madame de Rosemonde, whom I love as much as she deserves.

From . . ., 11th of August, 17—.

## LETTER X

*The Marquise de Merteuil to the Vicomte de Valmont*

Are you sulking with me, Vicomte? Or are you dead? Or, which would be much the same thing, do you live only for your Madame de

[1] Madame de Volanges's error allows us to see that Valmont like other scoundrels did not reveal his accomplices. (C. de L.)

Tourvel? That woman, who has given you back *the illusions of youth*, will soon give you back its ridiculous prejudices. You are already timid and slavish; you might as well be in love. You have given up your fortunate audacities. You are acting without principles, leaving everything to chance, or rather to caprice. Have you forgotten that love, like medicine, is *simply* the art of aiding nature? You see I am beating you with your own weapons; but I feel no pride in it; it is beating a fallen man. *She must give herself*, you say; doubtless she must! And she will give herself like the others, with this difference: It will be with a bad grace. But in order that she may end up by giving herself, the best means is to begin by taking her. This ridiculous distinction is the merest raving in love! I say "love" because you are in love. To speak to you otherwise would be deceiving you; it would be hiding your disease from yourself. But tell me, O languishing lover, do you suppose you raped the other women you have had? But, however much a woman wants to give herself, however much of a hurry she may be in, some sort of pretext is necessary; and what could be more convenient for us than a pretext which makes us appear to yield to force? For my own part, I must confess that one of the things which most flatters me is a sharp and well conducted attack, where everything is carried out with order but with rapidity; which never puts us to the painful embarrassment of having ourselves to repair an awkwardness by which we ought to have profited; which preserves an air of violence even in those things we grant, and cunningly flatters our two favourite passions—the glory of defence and the pleasure of defeat. I confess that this talent, which is much rarer than is generally believed, has always given me pleasure even when it has not attracted me; sometimes I have yielded myself simply as a recompense. As in our ancient tournaments, Beauty awarded the prize of valour and skill.

But as to you, you are no longer yourself, and you act as if you were afraid of succeeding. How long is it since you began to travel by short stages and side-tracks? My friend, when you want to get somewhere—post-horses and the main-road! But let us leave this subject, which gives me the more annoyance since it deprives me of the pleasure of seeing you. At least you might write to me more often than you do and give me news of your progress. Do you know that for more than a fortnight you have been occupied by this ridiculous adventure and have neglected everyone?

A propos negligence; you are like those people who send regularly for news of their sick friends and never ask what the reply was. You ended your last letter by asking me if the Chevalier is dead. I did not reply and you troubled no more about it. Have you forgotten that my lover is your sworn friend? Don't be uneasy, he is not dead; or if he were, it would be from excess of joy. Poor Chevalier, how tender he is! What a lover he is! How keenly he is affected! My head is in a whirl. Seriously, the perfect happiness he enjoys in being loved by me really attaches me to him.

The very day I wrote you that I was preparing to break with him, how happy I made him! I was actually thinking of the means to reduce him to despair when he was announced. Either from caprice or good sense, he never had appeared so well. However, I received him in a bad humour. He hoped to pass two hours with me before my door opened for the rest of the company. I told him that I was going out; he asked where I was going; I refused to tell him. He insisted. "Where you will not be," I replied tartly. Happily for him he was petrified by this reply; for if he had said a word there would have inevitably followed a scene which would have brought about the rupture I had planned. Astonished by his silence, I turned my eyes on him with no other purpose, I swear, than to see what countenance he was keeping. I perceived on his charming face that profound and tender sadness which you yourself admit is so difficult to resist. The same cause produced the same effect; I was conquered a second time. From that moment I only thought of how to avoid his thinking I had been disagreeable. "I am going out on business," said I, with a slightly more gentle air, "and this business partly concerns you; but don't ask me any questions. I shall dine at home; come back and you shall know all about it." He then regained the use of speech; but I did not allow him to use it. "I am in a great hurry," I continued, "go away until this evening." He kissed my hand and left.

Immediately, to compensate him, perhaps to compensate myself, I decided to show him my little house[1] about which he knew nothing. I called my faithful Victoire, I had my usual headache; the servants were told I was in bed; and, at last when I was alone with "the faithful servant," I dressed myself as a waiting-woman while she disguised herself as a lackey. She then brought a cab to my garden gate and off we went. When we reached the Temple of Love, I chose the most seductive *déshabille*. It was really delicious; it is my own invention; it lets nothing be seen and yet allows everything to be guessed at. I promise you a pattern for your Madame de Tourvel—when you have rendered her worthy of wearing it.

After these preparations, while Victoire was occupied with the other details I read a chapter of the "Sopha," a letter of "Héloïse" and two tales of La Fontaine, to rehearse the different tones I desired to take. Meanwhile my Chevalier comes to my door with his usual eagerness. My door-keeper stops him and tells him I am ill—the first incident. At the same time he gives him a letter from me, but not in my handwriting, according to my prudent rule. He opens it and finds in Victoire's handwriting: "At nine o'clock precisely, on the Boulevard in front of the cafés." He goes there; and a young lackey whom he does not know (at least whom he thinks he does not know, for it was Victoire) comes and tells him to send away his carriage and follow him.

[1] "*Petite-maison*," a house kept secretly for lovers' rendezvous, equivalent to the modern "*garçonnière*." I am informed that such refuges are not unknown in England, but my informant could not tell me by what name they are distinguished.

This whole romantic walk over-excites his brain and that never does any harm. He arrives at last; and surprise and love positively enchant him. To give him time to recover we take a turn in the shrubbery; then I bring him back to the house. He sees a table laid for two and a bed made up; we then go into the boudoir, which has all its decorations displayed. There, half out of premeditation, half from sentiment, I threw my arms around him and fell at his knees. "To prepare you the surprise of this moment," I said, "I reproach myself for having troubled you with an appearance of ill-humour, with having veiled for an instant my heart from your gaze. Forgive these faults, I will expiate them by my love." You may imagine the effect of that sentimental discourse. The happy Chevalier raised me and my pardon was sealed on the same ottoman upon which you and I so gaily and in the same way sealed our eternal separation.

Since we had six hours to spend together and I had determined that the whole time should be equally delicious to him, I moderated his transports, and my tenderness was replaced by amiable coquetry. I do not think I ever took so much trouble to please or that I was ever so satisfied with myself. After supper I was successively youthful and rational, playful and emotional, sometimes even wanton, and I pleased myself by considering him as a sultan in the midst of a harem in which I was successively the different favourites. Indeed, although his reiterated regards were always received by the same woman, it was always by a new mistress.

At last at daybreak we had to separate; and in spite of what he said and did even to prove to me the contrary, he needed it as much as he desired it little. At the moment when we left and as a last farewell, I took the key of this happy dwelling and put it into his hands. "I only acquired it for you," said I, "it is but right that you should be its master; the sacrificing priest should have the disposal of the temple." By this manœuvre I forestalled any reflections which might have occurred to him from my ownership of this little house—which is always a suspicious thing. I know him well enough to be sure that he will only use it for me; and if I take a fancy to go there without him, I still have another key. At all costs he wished to fix another day there; but I still like him too much to want to use him up so quickly. One should only permit excess with those one intends to leave soon. He does not know that; but, for his happiness, I know it for two.

I see that it is three o'clock in the morning and that I have written a volume when I meant only to write a line. Such is the charm of confiding friendship; it is that which makes you still the person I like best, but to tell you the truth the Chevalier gives me more pleasure.

From . . ., 12th of August, 17—.

## LETTER XI

*Madame de Tourvel to Madame de Volanges*

Your severe letter would have terrified me, Madame, if I had not fortunately more grounds for confidence than you find for fear. This dangerous Monsieur de Valmont, who must be the terror of all women, appears to have laid down his murderous arms before entering this *Château.* Far from forming plans here he has not even brought any affectations; and the quality of charm which even his enemies allow him has almost disappeared here, leaving him only good nature. Apparently, the country air has caused this miracle. I can assure you that, although he is constantly with me and even appears to take pleasure in it, he has never let slip a word resembling love, not one of those phrases which all men indulge in, without having—as he has—something to justify it. He never forces one into that reserve which every respectable woman nowadays is compelled to adopt towards the men by whom she is surrounded. He knows how to refrain from misusing the gaiety he creates. Perhaps he overpraises a little; but it is done with such delicacy that he would accustom modesty itself to panegyric. Indeed, if I had a brother, I should wish him to be such as Monsieur de Valmont shows himself here. Many women perhaps would wish him to pay them more marked attentions; I must confess I am infinitely grateful to him for having realised that I am not to be confounded with them.

Certainly this portrait is very different from the one you made me; and yet both may be likenesses at different periods. He himself admits he has had many faults and that he has been credited with more. But I have met few men who speak of virtuous women with so much respect, I might almost say, enthusiasm. What you tell me shows that at least in this matter he is not deceitful. His conduct with regard to Madame de Merteuil proves it. He often speaks of her, and always with so much praise and the appearance of so genuine an attachment that, until I received your letter, I thought that what he called the friendship between them was really love. I plead guilty to a hasty judgment here, and I was the more to blame since he himself has often taken the trouble to justify her. I confess that I thought this artifice when it was really honest sincerity on his part. I don't know; but it seems to me that a man who is capable of so constant a friendship for so estimable a woman cannot be an abandoned libertine. I cannot say if we owe his good conduct here to certain intrigues in the neighbourhood, as you suppose. There are indeed several charming women round about; but he seldom goes out, except in the morning, and then he says he goes shooting. It is true he rarely brings back any game; but he assures me he is unskilful in that exercise. In any case, what he does out of doors does not concern me much; and if I did wish to know, it would only be to have one more reason for sharing your view or bringing you to mine.

As to your proposal that I should take measures to shorten Monsieur de Valmont's stay here, it appears to me very difficult to presume to ask his aunt not to have her nephew in her house, the more so since she is very attached to him. Yet I promise you, merely from deference and not from necessity, to take the first opportunity of making this request either to her or to him. As to myself, Monsieur de Tourvel knows I have arranged to stay here until he returns and he will rightly enough be surprised at my inconsistency if I change my plans.

This is a very long explanation, Madame, but I thought I owed it to truth to give a favourable account of Monsieur de Valmont, which he appears to stand in great need of with you. I am none the less sensible of the friendship which dictated your advice. I owe to it also the obliging things you say to me about the postponement of your daughter's marriage. I thank you sincerely ; but, however great my pleasure would be in passing that time with you, I would gladly sacrifice it to my desire to see Mademoiselle de Volanges sooner happy, if she can ever be happier than at the side of a mother so worthy of all her tenderness and respect. I share with her these two sentiments which attach me to you and I beg you to receive kindly this assurance of them.

I have the honour to be, etc.

From . . ., 13th of August, 17—.

## LETTER XII

*Cécile Volanges to the Marquise de Merteuil*

Mamma is indisposed, Madame ; she will not go out and I must keep her company ; so I shall not have the honour of going to the Opera with you. I assure you that I far more regret not being with you than missing the performance. I beg you will believe me. I like you so much ! Would you be so kind as to tell Monsieur le Chevalier Danceny that I do not possess the album of which he spoke and that it would give me great pleasure if he would bring it to me tomorrow ? If he comes today he will be told we are not at home ; but that is because Mamma does not wish to receive anybody. I hope she will be better tomorrow.

I have the honour to be, etc.

From . . ., 13th of August, 17—.

## LETTER XIII

*The Marquise de Merteuil to Cécile Volanges*

I am very sorry, my dear, to be deprived of the pleasure of seeing you, and for the cause of this deprivation. I hope the opportunity will occur again. I will deliver your message to the Chevalier Danceny, who will certainly be very sorry to know that your Mamma is unwell. If she will receive me tomorrow, I will come and keep her company. She and I will attack the Chevalier de Belleroche[1] at piquet; and while we win his money we shall have as an extra pleasure that of hearing you sing with your charming master, to whom I shall propose it. If this suits your Mamma and you, I will answer for myself and my two Chevaliers. Good-bye, my dear; my regards to dear Madame de Volanges. I kiss you tenderly.

From . . ., 13th of August, 17—.

## LETTER XIV

*Cécile Volanges to Sophie Carnay*

I did not write to you yesterday, my dear Sophie, but it was not on account of my pleasures; I assure you. Mamma was ill and I did not leave her all day. At night when I left her I had no heart for anything; and I went to bed as quickly as I could, to be certain the day was over; I have never spent such a long one. It is not that I don't love Mamma—I don't know what it was. I was to go to the Opera with Madame de Merteuil; the Chevalier Danceny was to have been there. You know they are the two persons I like best. When the time came that I should have been there too, my heart shrank in spite of myself. I felt disgusted with everything and I cried and cried without being able to stop myself. Fortunately, Mamma was in bed and could not see me. I am sure the Chevalier Danceny was sorry too; but he had the distraction of the performance and everybody who was there—it was a very different thing.

Happily Mamma is better today, and Madame de Merteuil is coming with someone else and the Chevalier Danceny; but Madame de Merteuil always comes very late; and it is very tiresome to be all alone so long. It is only eleven o'clock. It is true that I must play on my harp; and then it will take me a little time to dress, for I want to have my hair well done today. I think Mère Perpetue was right and that we become coquettish as soon as we are in the world. I have never wanted so much to be pretty as in the last few days and it seems to me I am not so pretty as I thought; and then one is at a disadvantage beside women who are rouged. Madame de Merteuil, for example—I can see that all the men think she is prettier than I am; that does not annoy me very much because she likes me and then she assures me that the Chevalier Danceny thinks I am prettier than she is. It was very kind of her to have told me! She even seemed to be pleased by it. I can't understand how she could be. It is because she really loves me! And he! . . . Oh! How it pleased me! It seems to me that just to look at him would be enough to make one handsome. I could look at him forever if I were not afraid of meeting his eyes; for every time

[1] The Chevalier mentioned in Madame de Merteuil's letters. (C. de L.)

that happens it puts me out of countenance and hurts me, as it were ; but it doesn't matter.

Good-bye, my dear ; I must begin to dress. I love you as ever.

Paris, the 14th of August, 17—.

## LETTER XV

*The Vicomte de Valmont to the Marquise de Merteuil*

It is very kind of you not to abandon me to my sad fate. The life I lead here is truly fatiguing, with the excess of its repose and its insipid uniformity. When I read your letter and the details of your charming day, I was twenty times tempted to invent an excuse, fly to your feet and ask of you in my favour an infidelity to your Chevalier, who after all does not deserve his happiness. Do you know you have made me jealous of him ? What do you mean by speaking of our " eternal separation ? " I deny the oath, spoken in delirium ; we should not have been worthy to make it if we were to keep it. Ah ! May I one day avenge myself in your arms for the involuntary vexation caused me by the Chevalier's happiness ! I confess I am indignant when I think that this man, without thought, without giving himself the least trouble, by stupidly following the instinct of his heart, should find a felicity to which I cannot attain. Oh ! I shall disturb it. . . . Promise me I shall disturb it. Are you not humiliated yourself ? You take the trouble to deceive him and he is happier than you are. You think he is in your chains ! It is you who are in his. He sleeps calmly while you are awake for his pleasures. What more could his slave do ?

Come, my fair friend, as long as you share yourself between several, I am not in the least jealous ; I simply see your lovers as the successors of Alexander, incapable of holding among them all that Empire where I reigned alone. But that you should give yourself entirely to one of them ! That there should exist another man as happy as I ! I will not endure it ; do not think that I will endure it. Either take me back or at least take someone else as well ; and do not let an exclusive caprice betray the inviolable friendship we have sworn each other.

No doubt it is quite enough that I should have to complain of love. You see that I agree with your ideas and admit my faults. Indeed, if to be in love is not to be able to live without possessing that person one desires, to sacrifice to her one's time, one's pleasures, one's life ; then I am really in love. I am no nearer success ; I should not have anything at all to tell you about the matter, but for an occurrence which makes me reflect a good deal and from which I do not know yet whether I should fear or hope.

You know my man, a treasure for intrigue and a real comedy-valet ; as you may suppose, my instructions included his falling in love with the waiting-woman and making the serving men drunk. The rascal is luckier than I am ; he has succeeded already. He has just discovered that Madame de Tourvel has ordered one of her serving-men to obtain information about my conduct and even to follow my morning walks as much as he can without being perceived. What does the woman mean ? And so the most modest of them all yet dares to risk things we should scarcely dare allow ourselves ! I swear. . . . But, before I think of avenging myself for this feminine ruse, let me think how to turn it to my own advantage. Hitherto these suspected walks have had no purpose ; I must give them one. It deserves all my attention, and I must leave you and reflect on it. Good-bye, my dear friend.

Still from the Château de . . ., 15th of August, 17—.

## LETTER XVI

*Cécile Volanges to Sophie Carnay*

Ah ! my Sophie, here is news ! Perhaps I ought not to tell you ; but I must speak to someone ; it is stronger than I am. The Chevalier Danceny. . . . I am so upset that I cannot write ; I don't know where to begin. After I had told you about the pleasant evening[1] I spent here with him and Madame de Merteuil, I did not speak of him to you again ; it was because I did not wish to speak of him to anyone ; but I kept thinking about him. After that evening he became sad, so sad, so very sad, that it hurt me ; and when I asked him why he said he was not sad, but I could see he was. Yesterday he was worse than ever. I did not prevent his having the kindness to sing with me as usual ; but every time he looked at me, my heart was wrung. After we had finished singing he went to put my harp in its case ; and when he brought me back the key he begged me play on it again this evening as soon as I was alone. I did not suspect anything ; I did not even want to play but he begged me so hard that I said yes. He had his reason. When I went to my own room and my maid had left me I went and got my harp. In the strings I found a letter, folded only and not sealed, from him. Ah ! if you knew all that he wrote to me ! Since I have read his letter I have been so delighted that I could not think of anything else. I read it over again four times in succession and then locked it in my writing-desk. I knew it by heart ; and when I was in bed I said it over so often that I did not think of going to sleep. As soon as I closed my eyes, I saw him there saying to me himself everything I had just read. I did not go to sleep until very late and as soon as I woke up (it was still very early) I went and got his letter to read it over again. I took it into bed and kissed it as if. . . . Perhaps it is wrong to kiss a letter like that but I could not help it.

And now, my dear, although I am very glad, I am also in a great difficulty ; for surely I ought not to reply to this letter. I know I ought not and yet he asks me to ; and if I don't answer I am sure he will go

[1] The letter which speaks of this evening cannot be found. It may be surmised that it was the evening mentioned in Madame de Merteuil's note and is also spoken of in the preceding letter from Cécile Volanges. (C. de L.)

on being sad. It is very unlucky for him ! What do you advise me to do ? But you know no more than I do. I am very much tempted to speak about it to Madame de Merteuil who is very fond of me. I should like to console him but I do not want to do anything wrong. We are always being told to be kind-hearted ! And then we are forbidden to carry out what a kind heart inspires in us when it is for a man ! It is unjust. Is not a man our neighbour as much as a woman, and even more ? For, after all, have we not a father as well as a mother, a brother as well as a sister ? And then there is always the husband, in addition. And yet if I did something which was not right perhaps Monsieur Danceny himself would not think well of me ! Oh ! I would rather he were still sad ; and then, after all, I have plenty of time. Because he wrote yesterday, I am not obliged to write today ; and then I shall see Madame de Merteuil this evening and if I can pluck up courage I shall tell her all about it. If I do what she tells me I shall have nothing to reproach myself with. And then perhaps she will tell me that I may reply to him just a little, so that he will not be so sad ! Oh ! I am very unhappy.

Good-bye, my dear. Tell me what you think.

From . . ., 19th of August, 17—.

## LETTER XVII

*The Chevalier Danceny to Cécile Volanges*

Mademoiselle, before I yield to the pleasure (shall I say ?) or to the necessity of writing to you, I begin by begging you to listen to me. I feel I need your indulgence to dare the declaration of my sentiments ; if I wished merely to justify them, indulgence would not be necessary. For, after all, what am I about to do but to show you your own work ? And what have I to say to you which has not been said before by my looks, my embarrassment, my behaviour and even my silence ? And why should you be angry at a sentiment you alone caused to exist ? It arose from you and doubtless is worthy of being offered to you ; though it be burning as my soul, it is as pure as yours. Can it be a crime to have appreciated your charming features, your seductive talents, your enchanting graces and that touching candour which adds an inestimable value to qualities of themselves so precious ? No, without doubt ; but one may be unhappy without being guilty, and unhappiness will be my fate if you refuse to accept my regard. It is the first my heart has offered. But for you I should still be—not happy—but at peace. I saw you ; repose fled far from me and my happiness is uncertain. Yet you are surprised by my sadness ; you ask me the reason ; sometimes I have even thought that it grieved you. Ah ! Say but one word and my felicity will be your handiwork ! But, before you speak, remember that a word can also overwhelm me with misery. Be the arbitress of my destiny. Because of you I shall be eternally happy or unhappy. To what dearer hands could I confide a greater trust ?

I shall end, as I began, by imploring your indulgence. I asked you to listen to me; I will dare more, I will beg you to answer me. To refuse, would be to let me think that you feel yourself offended and my heart reassures me that my respect is equal to my love.

P.S. To answer, you can use the same means by which I conveyed this letter to you; it seems to me both certain and convenient.

From . . ., 19th of August, 17—.

## LETTER XVIII

*Cécile Volanges to Sophie Carnay*

What, Sophie! You condemn beforehand what I am going to do! I had already enough anxieties, and now you add to them. It is clear, you say, that I ought not to reply. It is very easy for you to talk; and besides, you don't understand the whole situation; you are not here to see. I am sure if you were in my place, you would do what I am doing. Of course, as a general rule, one ought not to reply; and you must have seen from my yesterday's letter that I did not want to; but I think nobody was ever in the position I am in now.

And then to be forced to decide all by myself! Madame de Merteuil, whom I counted on seeing yesterday evening, did not come. Everything combines against me; it was she who was the cause of my knowing him. It is almost always with her that I have seen and spoken to him. Not that I bear her any malice for it; but she leaves me at the very moment of difficulty. Oh! I am very much to be pitied!

You must know that he came yesterday as usual. I was so upset that I dared not look at him. He could not speak to me because Mamma was there. I was very much afraid he would be distressed when he saw I had not written to him. I did not know which way to look. A moment afterwards he asked me if I wanted him to get my harp. My heart beat so hard that it was all I could do to answer yes. When he returned, it was much worse. I only glanced at him for a moment. And he did not look at me; but he really appeared as if he were ill. It really hurt me to see him. He began to tune my harp and then, when he brought it to me, he said: "Ah! Mademoiselle! . . ." He only said those two words, but it was in a tone which completely distracted me. I played a prelude on my harp without knowing what I was doing. Mamma asked if we were not going to sing. He made an excuse and said he was a little unwell; and I, who had no excuse, was forced to sing. I wished I had never had a voice. I expressly chose an air I did not know; for I was quite sure I could not sing any one and I should have aroused suspicion. Fortunately, there came a visitor; and, as soon as I heard the carriage arrive, I stopped and asked him to take back my harp. I was very much afraid he would leave then and there; but he came back.

While Mamma and the lady who had just come were talking together, I wanted to glance at him again only for a moment. A second later I saw his tears falling, and he was obliged to turn aside in order not to be seen. This time I could endure it no longer; I felt I was going to cry too. I went out and immediately wrote in pencil on a scrap of paper: "Do not be so sad, I beg you; I promise to reply." Surely, you cannot say there was anything wrong in that; and then it was stronger than I am. I put the piece of paper in my harp-strings, as his letter was, and returned to the drawing-room. I felt calmer. I was very anxious for the lady to go away. Fortunately, she was only making a call and left soon afterwards. As soon as she had gone, I said I wanted my harp again and I asked him to go and get it. I could see, from his expression, that he suspected nothing. But when he came back, oh! how happy he was! As he put my harp in front of me, he placed himself in such a way that Mamma could not see, and he took my hand and pressed it . . . but in such a way! . . . it was only a moment, but I cannot tell you what pleasure it gave me. However, I withdrew it; so I have nothing to reproach myself with.

And so, my dear, you see I cannot help writing to him, since I promised him; and then, I can't bear to make him unhappy again; for I suffer from it more than he does. If it were for something wrong, of course I should not do it. But what wrong can there be in writing, expecially if it is to prevent someone from being unhappy? What troubles me is that I cannot turn my letter well; but he will feel that it is not my fault; and then I am sure that the mere fact it is from me will please him.

Good-bye, my dear. If you think I am wrong, tell me; but I do not believe I am. As the moment approaches when I am to write to him, my heart beats inconceivably. And yet I must do it, since I promised. Good-bye.

**From . . ., 20th of August, 17—..**

## LETTER XIX

*Cécile Volanges to the Chevalier Danceny*

You were so sad yesterday, Monsieur, and I was so grieved by it, that I allowed myself to promise you I would reply to the letter you wrote me. Today I feel just as much that I ought not to; but, since I promised, I do not want to break my word, and that ought to prove to you the friendship I have for you. Now that you know it, I hope you will not ask me to write to you again. I also hope you will not tell anyone I have written to you; because I should certainly be blamed for it and it might cause me much distress. Above all, I hope you will not think badly of me for doing it; for that would distress me more than anything. I can assure you that I should not have done this favour for anyone but you. I wish you would do me the favour of not being sad as you have been ; it takes away all the pleasure I have in seeing you. You see, Monsieur, I speak to you sincerely. I ask nothing better than that our friendship should last forever ; but, I beg you, do not write to me again.

I have the honour to be,

Cécile Volanges.

From . . ., 20th of August, 17—.

## LETTER XX

*The Marquise de Merteuil to the Vicomte de Valmont*

Ah ! You rogue, so you are coaxing me for fear I shall mock you ? Come, I must pardon you ; you write me so many follies that I am forced to forgive you the sobriety in which you are kept by your Madame de Tourvel. I do not think my Chevalier would be as indulgent as I am ; he is the kind of man who might not approve the renewal of our lease and who would find nothing amusing in your wild idea. Yet I laughed at it and was really sorry I was forced to laugh at it alone. If you had been there I do not know how far this gaiety might have led me ; but I have had time to reflect and I have armed myself with severity. I do not refuse for always ; but I delay, and rightly. Perhaps I should bring vanity into it and, once I became interested in the game, there is no knowing where it might stop. I might enchain you again and make you forget your Madame de Tourvel ; and suppose I, the unworthy, should disgust you with virtue—what a scandal ! To avoid this danger, these are my conditions.

As soon as you have had your fair devotee, and can furnish me with a proof, come, and I am yours. But you know that in important matters only written proofs are accepted. By this arrangement, on the one hand I shall become a recompense instead of being a consolation—an idea which pleases me better—and on the other hand, your success will be the more piquant by becoming itself a means of infidelity. Come, come as soon as you can and bring me the proof of your triumph—like our noble knights of old who laid at their ladies' feet the brilliant fruits of their victory. Seriously, I am curious to know what a prude would write after such a moment and what veil she will throw over her words after having left none upon her person. It is for you to see whether I rate myself at too high a price ; but I warn you it will not be reduced. Until then, my dear Vicomte, you must allow me to remain faithful to my Chevalier and to amuse myself by making him happy, in spite of the little distress it causes you.

And yet, if I were less moral, I believe he would have at this moment a dangerous rival—little Cécile Volanges. I am passionately fond of the child ; it is a real passion. If I am not deceived she will become one of our most fashionable women. I can see her little heart developing, and it is a delightful sight. She is already madly in love with her Danceny, but does not yet know it herself. He himself, though very much in love, still has the timidity of his age and dares not declare himself too plainly. Both adore me. The little girl especially is very anxious to tell me her secret; particularly in the last few days I have noticed she is really oppressed by it and I should have done her a great service by helping her a little; but I do not forget that she is only a child and I do not want to compromise myself. Danceny has spoken to me a little more plainly; but I have made up my mind not to listen to him. As for the girl, I am often tempted to make her my pupil; it is a service I should like to render Gercourt. He leaves me plenty of time since he is in Corsica until October. It occurs to me that I might make use of this time and that we will give him a fully formed woman instead of his innocent convent-girl. What insolent confidence on the part of this man, to dare to sleep tranquilly while a woman who has reason to complain of him has not yet avenged herself! Ah! if the girl were here now I do not know what I might not say to her.

Good-bye, Vicomte; good-night and good luck; but, for Heaven's sake, make some progress. Remember, if you do not have this woman, that others will blush at having had you.

**From . . ., 21st of August 17—. 4 o'clock in the morning.**

## LETTER XXI

*The Vicomte de Valmont to the Marquise de Merteuil*

At last, my fair friend, I have made a step for ward, a large step which, although it has not led me to the goal, has allo wed me to see tha I am on the road and has banished my fear that I had missed the way I have at last declared my love; and although she kept the most obstinate silence I obtained perhaps the least equivocal and most flattering reply possible; let us not anticipate, but go back to the beginning.

You remember that my walks were being watched. Well! I wanted to turn this scandalous circumstance to public edification, and this is what I did. I ordered my man to find in the neighbourhood some unfortunate person in need of help. It was not a difficult task to accomplish. Yesterday afternoon he informed me that this morning there would be a destraint on the furniture of a whole family which could not pay its taxes. I made certain that the family contained no girl or woman whose age or features might render my action suspicious; and, when I was certain of this, I announced at dinner my intention of going shooting the next day. Here I must render justice to my Madame de Tourvel; no doubt she regretted the order she had given and, not having the strength to conquer her curiosity, she had at least enough to oppose my desire. It would be excessively hot; I ran the risk of getting ill; I should kill nothing and tire myself in vain; and during this dialogue, her eyes, which perhaps spoke more than she wished, showed me that she desired I should take her bad reasons as good ones. I was careful not to yield to them, as you may suppose, and in the same way I resisted a little diatribe against shooting and sportsmen and also a small cloud of ill-humour which darkened that heavenly face the whole evening. For a moment I feared she might countermand her orders and that her delicacy might harm me. I reckoned without the curiosity of a woman—and so I was wrong. My man reassured me the same evening and I went to bed satisfied.

At dawn I rose and set out. I was scarcely fifty yards from the Château when I saw my spy following me. I set out across the field as though I were shooting, in the direction of the village I wished to reach ; my only pleasure on the way was to set the pace to the fellow who was following me and since he dared not leave the roads he often had to cover at top speed triple the distance I went. I exercised him so much that I became very hot myself and sat down at the foot of a tree. And did he not have the insolence to slip behind a bush about twenty yards from me and sit down too ? For a moment I was tempted to take a shot at him, for although my gun was only loaded with pellets it would have given him enough of a lesson on the dangers of curiosity ;[1] luckily for him I recollected that he was useful to me and positively necessary to my plans and this reflection saved him.

When I reached the village I saw there was a disturbance ; I went forward ; I asked questions ; I was told what was happening ; I called the Tax-Collector ; and, yielding to my generous compassion, I nobly paid fifty-six *livres*, for which five persons were to be reduced to straw and despair. After so simple an action you cannot imagine what a chorus of benedictions echoed round me from the spectators ! What tears of gratitude flowed from the eyes of the aged head of the family and embellished this patriarchal face which a moment before was rendered truly hideous by the wild imprint of despair ! I was watching this spectacle when another younger peasant, leading a woman and two children by the hand, rushed towards me, saying to them : " Let us all fall at the feet of this Image of God " ; and at the same moment I was surrounded by the family prostrate at my knees. I must admit my weakness ; my eyes filled with tears and I felt an involuntary but delicious emotion. I was astonished at the pleasure there is in doing good ; and I should be tempted to believe that those whom we call virtuous people are not so virtuous as they are pleased to tell us. However that may be, I thought it only just to pay these poor people for the pleasure they had just given me. I had brought ten *louis* with me ; which I gave to them. Their thanks recommenced but without the same degree of pathos ; necessity had produced the great, the true effect ; the rest was only a simple expression of gratitude and astonishment for superfluous gifts.

[1] In 1723, the Comte de Charolais, passing through the village of Anet, saw a " *bourgeois*," in a night-cap, standing at his door ; the Comte shot the *bourgeois* as an amusement. The next day he went to the Regent for a formal pardon and received it, with the remark that the pardon was due to his rank, but would more willingly be granted to anyone who did the same to the Comte. See Carré *Noblesse de France*, p. 293.

However, in the midst of the wordy benedictions of this family I was not unlike the hero of a play in the last scene. You are to know that my faithful spy was in the forefront of the crowd. My object was fulfilled; I got free from them and returned to the Château. Taking it all round, I congratulate myself on my invention. This woman is certainly worth all the trouble I have taken; one day it will form my claim upon her; and having, as it were, thus paid for her beforehand I shall have the right to dispose of her as I fancy, without reproaching myself.

I forgot to tell you that, to turn everything to my profit, I asked these good people to pray to God for the success of my plans. You will see that their prayers have already been partly recompensed. . . . But I am told that dinner is served and it will be too late for this letter to go if I finish it after dinner. And so—the rest by the next post. I am sorry, for the rest is the finest part. Good-bye, my fair friend. You steal from me a moment of the pleasure of seeing her.

From . . . 20th of August 17—.

## LETTER XXII

*Madame de Tourvel to Madame de Volanges*

No doubt you will be glad, Madame, to hear of an act of Monsieur de Valmont which, it seems to me, is in strong contrast to all the traits by which he has been represented to you. It is so painful to think disadvantageously of anyone, so grieving to find nothing but vices in those who should have all the qualities needed to make virtue beloved! And then you are so glad to be indulgent, that it is doing you a favour to furnish you with motives for reversing too harsh a judgment. It seems to me that Monsieur de Valmont has a right to hope for this favour. I might almost say this justice; and this is why I think so.

This morning he went on one of those walks which might lead one to suspect some intrigue on his part in the neighbourhood, as you thought; a thought which I blame myself for having accepted too quickly. Fortunately for him, and above all fortunately for us, since it preserves us from being unjust, one of my men-servants had to go the same way as he did[1]; and in this way my reprehensible but fortunate curiosity was satisfied. He related to us that Monsieur de Valmont found in the village of . . . an unhappy family whose goods were being sold because they could not pay their taxes; Monsieur de Valmont not only hastened to discharge the debt of these poor people but even gave them a considerable sum of money. My servant was a witness of this virtuous action; and moreover he tells me that the peasants, talking among themselves and with him, said that a servant, whom they described, and whom my servant thinks is Monsieur de Valmont's, yesterday made enquiries about such inhabitants of the

[1] Does Madame de Tourvel not dare to say it was by her orders? (C. de L.)

village as might be in need of help. If this is true, it is not merely a passing compassion provoked by accident ; it is a pre-conceived plan of doing good ; it is the solicitude of charity ; it is the fairest virtue of the fairest souls ; but whether it was chance or method, it is still a good and praiseworthy action, the mere relation of which moved me to tears. In addition I must say, still from a sense of justice, that when I spoke to him about this action, of which he did not say a word, he began by denying it, and, when he did admit it, seemed to set so little value upon it that his modesty doubled its merit.

And now, my respectable friend, tell me if Monsieur de Valmont is indeed an abandoned libertine ? If this is all he is and if he acts in this way, what is there left for the virtuous ? What ! Should the wicked share with the good the sacred pleasure of charity ?[1] Would God permit a virtuous family to receive from a wicked man's hand that aid for which it returned thanks to His divine providence ? And could He be pleased to hear pure mouths shed their benedictions upon a reprobate ? No. I prefer to believe that his faults, though long continued, are not eternal ; and I cannot think that he who does good is the enemy of virtue. Monsieur de Valmont is perhaps only one more example of the danger of acquaintances. I dwell on this idea, which pleases me. If, on the one hand, it may serve to justify him in your mind, on the other, it renders more and more precious to me that tender friendship which unites me to you for life.

I have the honour to be, etc.

P.S. Madame de Rosemonde and I are just going to see this honest and unfortunate family and to add our tardy succour to that of Monsieur de Valmont. We are taking him with us. At least we shall give these good people the pleasure of seeing their benefactor again ; I am afraid it is all he has left us to do.

From . . ., 21st of August 17—.

## LETTER XXIII

*The Vicomte de Valmont to the Marquise de Merteuil*

We broke off at my return to the Château ; I continue my story.

I had only time for a brief toilet ; I went into the drawing-room where my fair one was embroidering, while the local Curé was reading the Gazette to my old aunt. I went and sat down beside the frame. Glances, softer than usual, and almost caressing, soon allowed me to guess that the servant had already given an account of his mission. Indeed my amiable Inquisitive was unable to keep for long the secret she had stolen from me ; and she was not afraid to interrupt a venerable

[1] The eighteenth century, the age of privilege and sensibility, considered charity the greatest and most amiable of virtues. The twentieth century, the age of democracy and commerce, considers charity an insult or at best the poor man's " claim " to the rich man's money : the emotions of compassion and gratitude are scarcely involved.

pastor whose utterance closely resembled that of a sermon, by saying : " And I too, have news to tell you " ; and she immediately related my adventure with a precision which did honour to the intelligence of her historian. You may imagine how I displayed all my modesty ; but who could stop a woman when she is praising what she loves, although she does not yet know it ? I decided to let her proceed. It was as if she were preaching the panegyric of a saint. During this time I observed not without hope, all that was promised to love by her animated looks, her freer gestures, and above all by the tone of her voice which by its perceptible alteration betrayed the emotion of her soul. She had scarcely finished speaking when Madame de Rosemonde said : " Come, nephew, come, let me embrace you." I felt immediately that the pretty preacher could not prevent herself from being embraced in turn. However, she tried to escape ; but she was soon in my arms ; and far from having the strength to resist she had scarcely enough to stand upright. The more I observe this woman the more desirable she seems to me. She hastened back to her frame and seemed to the others to recommence her embroidery ; but I could easily perceive that her trembling hand would not permit her to continue her work.

After dinner the ladies desired to visit the unfortunate persons I had so piously succoured. I accompanied them. I spare you the boredom of this second scene of gratitude and praise. My heart, urged by a delicious memory, hastens the moment of the return to the Château. On the way, my fair lady, more preoccupied than usual, did not say a word. I was busy trying to find means to profit from the effect produced by the event of the day and kept equally silent. Madame de Rosemonde alone spoke and received only short and rare answers from us. We must have bored her ; that was my plan and it succeeded. So, when we got out of the carriage, she went to her room and left my fair lady and me alone together in a dimly lighted drawing-room ; soft obscurity, which emboldens timid love !

I did not have the trouble of turning the conversation in the direction I wished it to go. The amiable lady's fervour served me better than my skill could have done. " When a person is so worthy of doing good," said she, fixing her gentle gaze on me, " how can he pass his life in doing ill ? " " I do not deserve either this praise or this censure," I replied, " and I cannot understand that with your intelligence you have not understood me. Even though my confidence should do me harm with you, you are too worthy of it for me to be able to refuse it to you. You will find the key to my conduct in a character which is unfortunately too compliant. Surrounded by the immoral, I have imitated their vices ; I may even have gratified my vanity by surpassing them. Seduced in the same way here by the example of virtues, without hoping to attain to your level, I have at least tried to follow you. Ah ! Perhaps the action for which you praise me today would lose all its value in your eyes, if you knew its real motive ! " (You see, my fair friend, how near the truth I was.) " It is not to me," I continued, " that these unfortunates owe my succour. Where you think you see praiseworthy action, I only sought a means of pleasing. I was only (since I must say it), the weak agent of the divinity I adore." (Here she tried to interrupt me; but I did not give her time.) "At this very moment," I added, "my secret only escaped me through my weakness. I had promised myself to withhold it from you; I held it a happiness to render to your virtues as to your charms a pure regard of which you would forever remain ignorant; but, incapable of deceiving, when I have the example of candour beneath my eyes, I shall not have to reproach myself with culpable dissimulation towards you. Do not suppose that I insult you by a criminal hope. I shall be unhappy, I know it; but my sufferings will be dear to me; they will prove to me the excess of my love; it is at your feet, and in your bosom that I shall lay my troubles. There I shall gather strength to suffer anew; there I shall find compassionate kindness, and I shall think myself consoled because you have pitied me. O you whom I adore, hear me, pity me, help me!" I was now at her knees and clasped her hands in mine; but she suddenly snatched them away and pressed them over her eyes with an expression of despair. "Ah! unhappy woman!" she exclaimed and then burst into tears. Fortunately I had worked myself up to such an extent that I was weeping too; and taking her hands again, I bathed them in tears. This was a very necessary precaution; for she was so occupied by her own grief that she would not have perceived mine, had I not thought of this method of advertising her. In addition I had the advantage of gazing at leisure upon that charming face, still more embellished by the powerful attraction of tears. I grew warm, and was so little master of myself that I was tempted to profit by this moment.

How great is our weakness; how great is the Power of circumstances, if I myself, forgetting my plans, risked losing by a premature triumph the charm of long struggles and the details of a painful defeat; if, seduced by desires worthy only of a young man, I almost exposed the conqueror of Madame de Tourvel to the fate of gathering as the fruit of his labours nothing but the insipid advantage of having had one woman more! Ah! Let her yield herself, but let her struggle! Let her have the strength to resist without having enough to conquer; let her fully taste the feeling of her weakness and be forced to admit her defeat. Let the obscure poacher kill the deer he has surprised from a hiding place; the real sportsman must hunt it down. A sublime plan, is it not? But perhaps I should now be regretting I had not followed it, if chance had not come to the aid of my prudence.

We heard a noise. Somebody was coming into the drawing-room. Madame de Tourvel rose precipitately in terror, seized one of the candlesticks and left the room. I had to let her go. It was only a servant. As soon as I was certain of this, I followed her. Scarcely had I taken a few steps when either because she recognised me or from a vague feeling of fear, I heard her increase her pace and throw herself rather than enter into her apartment whose door she closed behind her. I went up to it ; but the key was in the inside. I was careful not to knock ; for that would have given her the opportunity for too facile a resistance. I had the happy and simple idea of attempting to look through the key-hole and I saw this adorable woman on her knees, bathed in tears and praying fervently. What God did she dare to invoke ? Is there any sufficiently powerful against love ? In vain does she now seek outside aid ; it is I who control her fate.

Thinking I had done enough for one day, I also retired into my apartment and began to write to you. I hoped to see her again at supper ; but she sent a message that she felt unwell and had gone to bed. Madame de Rosemonde wished to go up to her bedroom ; but the cunning invalid pretended a headache which did not allow her to see anybody. You may imagine that I did not sit up late after supper and that I too had my headache. Having retired to my room, I wrote a long letter to complain of this harshness and I went to bed with the idea of delivering it this morning. I slept badly, as you may perceive by the date of this letter. I got up and re-read my epistle. I saw that I had not watched myself enough ; that I showed more ardour than love in it and more ill-humour than sadness. I ought to re-write it ; but then, I should have to be calmer to do so.

I see it is dawn, and I hope its accompanying freshness will bring me sleep. I am going back to bed ; and, whatever may be this woman's domination, I promise you not to be so absorbed with her that I have not plenty of time left to think of you. Good-bye, my fair friend.

From . . . 21st of August, 17—. 4 o'clock in the morning.

## LETTER XXIV

*The Vicomte de Valmont to Madame de Tourvel.*

Ah ! For pity's sake, Madame, deign to calm the distemper of my soul ; deign to inform me what I am to hope or fear. Placed between an excess of happiness or of misfortune, uncertainty is a cruel torture. Why did I speak to you ? Why could I not resist the dominating charm which delivered up my thoughts to you ? Content to adore you in silence, I at least enjoyed my love ; that pure sentiment, which was not then troubled by the image of your grief, sufficed for my felicity ; but that source of happiness has become a source of despair since I saw your tears flow, since I heard that cruel "*Ah ! unhappy woman !*" Those words will long continue to re-echo in my heart. Through what fatality is it that the softest of sentiments is only able to inspire you with fear ? But what is this apprehension ? Ah ! not that of sharing it ; I have misunderstood your heart, it is not made for love ; mine, which you constantly depreciate, is alone sensitive, yours does not even feel pity. If it were not so, you would not have refused a word of consolation to a wretch who confessed to you his sufferings ; you would not have avoided his gaze when he has no pleasure but to look at you ; you would not have played cruelly with his uneasiness by announcing that you were ill, without allowing him to enquire after your state of health; you would have felt that this very night, which for you was merely twelve hours of repose, would be a century of pain for him.

Tell me, how have I deserved this cruel harshness? I am not afraid to refer to you as judge; what have I done, but yield to an involuntary sentiment, inspired by beauty and justified by virtue, always restrained by respect, the innocent admission of which was the result of confidence and not of hope; will you betray the confidence which you yourself seem to allow me and to which I yielded myself unreservedly? No, I cannot believe it; that would be imputing a fault to you, and my heart revolts at the mere idea of finding one in you; I disavow my complaints; I may have written, but would not have thought them. Ah! let me think you perfect—it is the sole pleasure left me. Prove to me that you are so by granting me your generous aid. What wretch have you succoured who needed it as much as I? Do not abandon me in the delirium into which you have plunged me; lend me your good sense since you have stolen my own; when you have corrected me, enlighten me in order to finish your work.

I do not wish to deceive you, you will not succeed in extinguishing my love; but you will teach me to control it; by guiding my steps, by dictating my speech, you will at least save me from the terrible misfortune of displeasing you. I beg you to dissipate this despairing thought; tell me that you forgive me, that you pity me; assure me of your indulgence. You will never grant me all I desire; but I ask for what I need—will you refuse it?

Farewell, Madame; receive graciously the homage of my feelings; it does not diminish my respect.

From . . ., 20th of August, 17—.

## LETTER XXV

*The Vicomte de Valmont to the Marquise de Merteuil*

Here is today's bulletin.

At eleven o'clock I went to Madame de Rosemonde's apartment; and, under her protection, I was taken to see the feigned invalid, who was still in bed. Her eyes were very tired; I hope she slept as badly as I did. I seized a moment, when Madame de Rosemonde had turned away, to deliver my letter; she refused to take it; but I left it on the bed and very virtuously went over to my old aunt's armchair for she wanted to be near her dear child—the letter had to be concealed to avoid a scandal. The invalid said awkwardly that she thought she was a little feverish. Madame de Rosemonde called on me to feel her pulse and boasted of my medical knowledge. My fair one therefore had the double disappointment of being obliged to give me her arm, and of feeling that her little lie would be discovered. I took her hand and clasped it in one of mine, while with the other I wandered over her cool dimpled arm; the malicious creature made no response whatever which made me say as I let her go: "There is not even the least excitement." I guessed her looks must be severe and, to punish her, I did not seek them; a moment after, she said she wished to rise and we left her alone. She appeared at dinner, which was a gloomy meal; she announced she would not go walking, which was to tell me I should not have a chance of speaking to her. I felt that was the moment for a sigh and a pained glance; no doubt she expected it, for it was the only moment in the day when I succeeded in catching her eye. Modest as she is, she has her little wiles like the rest. I found an opportunity to ask her if she would have the goodness to tell me what was my fate, and I was a little astonished to hear her reply: "Yes Monsieur, I have written to you." I was very anxious to have this letter; but either from wiles again, or from clumsiness or from timidity, she only handed it to me this evening just before she went to bed. I send you her letter as well as the rough draft of my own; read them and judge; notice with what obvious falsity she asserts she is not in love, when I am sure of the contrary; and then she will complain if I am unfaithful to her afterwards, when she is not afraid to be faithless to me beforehand! My fair friend, the most skilful man can do no more than keep himself on a level with the most sincere woman; and yet I must feign to believe all this nonsense, and weary myself out with despairing, because it pleases the lady to play at cruelty! How can one avoid being avenged on such baseness! Ah! patience . . . but good-bye, I have still a lot to write.

Apropos, you will send me back the cruel one's letter; it may be that later she will want to set a value on these trifles, and I must be prepared.

I have not said anything about the Volanges girl; we will talk about her at the first opportunity.

From the Château, 22nd of August, 17—.

## LETTER XXVI

*Madame de Tourvel to the Vicomte de Valmont*

Indeed, Monsieur, you would have had no letter from me if my foolish conduct of yesterday evening did not compel me to enter into explanations with you. Yes, I wept, I admit it; and perhaps those two words which you are so careful to quote to me did escape me. Tears and words, you noticed them all; and therefore all must be explained to you.

I am accustomed to inspire none but virtuous sentiments, to hear no speech save that which can be listened to without blushing; consequently to enjoy a feeling of confidence which I dare to say I deserve and therefore I do not know how to dissimulate or to combat the impressions I feel. The astonishment and embarrassment into which I was thrown by your behaviour, a certain fear inspired by a situation which ought never to have occurred to me, perhaps the revolting idea of seeing myself confounded with women you despised and treated as lightly as they—all these causes provoked my tears and may have made me say (rightly, I think) that I was unhappy. This expression, which you thought so strong, would be far too weak if my tears and words had had another motive; if instead of disapproving sentiments which must offend me I could have feared I might share them.

No, Monsieur, I do not have this fear; if I had, I should fly a hundred miles from you; I should bewail in a desert the misfortune of having known you. Perhaps, in spite of my certainty that I do not love you, that I shall never love you, perhaps I should have done better to follow the advice of my friends and not allow you to come near me.

I thought—and this is my one error—I thought you would respect a virtuous woman who asked no more than to find you so and to do you justice; who was defending you while you outraged her by your criminal desires. You do not know me; no, Monsieur, you do not know me. If you did, you would not have supposed you could make your errors into a right; because you said to me words I ought not to have heard, you would not have thought yourself authorised to write me a letter I ought not to have read—and you ask me to "guide your steps, to dictate your speech!" Monsieur, silence and oblivion, that is the advice I must give you, which you must follow; then indeed you will have a right to my indulgence and it will depend upon you to obtain even my gratitude. . . . And yet, no, I will ask nothing of him who has not respected me; I will not give a mark of confidence to one who has abused my frankness.

You compel me to fear you, perhaps to hate you; I did not wish to; I wished to see in you only the nephew of my most respectable friend; I opposed the voice of friendship to the accusations of public fame. You have destroyed everything; and, I foresee, you will not wish to repair anything.

I must tell you, Monsieur, that your feelings are an offence to me, that the admission of them is an outrage, and above all that, far from my coming one day to share them, you would force me never to see you again, if you did not keep a silence in this matter such as I feel I have a right to expect and even to demand from you. I enclose with this letter the one you wrote me and I hope you will be good enough to return me this one; I should indeed be pained if there existed any trace of an event which ought never to have taken place.

I have the honour to be, etc.

From . . ., 21st of August, 17—.

## LETTER XXVII

*Cécile Volanges to the Marquise de Merteuil*

Ah! How kind you are, Madame! How well you realised that it would be easier for me to write than to speak to you! And then, what I have to say to you is very difficult; but you are my friend, are you not? Oh! yes, my most kind friend! I will try not to be afraid; and then I need so much both you and your advice! I am in great trouble, it seems to me that everyone guesses what I am thinking; and especially when *he* is there, I blush as soon as I am looked at. Yesterday, when you saw me crying, I wanted to speak to you, and then something or other prevented me; and when you asked me what was the matter, the tears came in spite of me. I could not have said a word. But for you Mamma would have noticed it and then what would have happened to me? And this is how I spend my life, especially the last four days!

That was the day, Madame, yes, I am going to tell you about it, that was the day the Chevalier Danceny wrote to me. Oh! I assure you that when I found his letter I did not know at all what it could be; but, to tell you the truth, I cannot say that I had no pleasure in reading it; I would rather be unhappy all my life than that he should not have written to me. But I knew very well that I ought not to write to him and I can assure you that I told him I was very angry about it; but he said it was stronger than he was, and I can believe him; for I had made up my mind not to answer him and yet I could not prevent myself Oh! I only wrote to him once and even then it was partly to tell him not to write to me again; but in spite of that he keeps on writing; and as I do not answer, I can see he is sad, and that grieves me still more; and so I don't know what to do or what will become of me and I am very much to be pitied.

Tell me, Madame, I beg you, would it be very wrong to answer him from time to time? Only until he can manage not to write to me any more himself and to be as we were before; because for my part if this goes on I do not know what will happen to me. Why, when I read his last letter, I cried as if I would never stop; and I am quite sure if I do not answer him again, it will be very sad for us both.

I send you his letter too, or rather a copy, and you can judge; you will see he does not ask for anything wrong. However, if you think it ought not to be, I promise you not to do it; but I believe you will think as I do, that there is nothing wrong in it.

And while I am about it, Madame, allow me to ask you another question; I have been told that it is wrong to love anybody—but why is that? What makes me ask you is that the Chevalier Danceny says that it is not wrong at all and that almost everybody loves; if that is true, I do not see why I should be the only one not to; or is it only wrong for girls? Because I heard Mamma herself say that Madame D . . . loved M . . . and she did not speak of it as a thing which was so very bad; and yet I am sure she would be angry with me if she even suspected my friendship for Monsieur Danceny. Mamma still treats me like a child; and she tells me nothing. When she took me out of the convent, I thought it was to marry me; but now I don't think so; not that I care, I assure you; but you, who are so much her friend, perhaps know about it and if you know, I hope you will tell me.

This is a very long letter, Madame, but since you have allowed me to write to you I have taken advantage of it to tell you everything and I rely on your friendship.

I have the honour to be, etc.

Paris, 23rd of August, 17—.

## LETTER XXVIII

*The Chevalier Danceny to Cécile Volanges*

And so, Mademoiselle, you still refuse to answer me! Nothing can bend you; and each day carries away with it the hopes it brought! What is the friendship you consented should exist between us if it is not even powerful enough to make you sensible of my suffering; if it leaves you calm and cold while I endure the torments of a fire I cannot extinguish; if, so far from inspiring you with confidence, it does not even suffice to awaken your pity? What! your friend suffers, and you do nothing to help him! He asks only a word from you and you refuse it to him! And you want him to be contented with a sentiment so weak that you are afraid to repeat your assurance of it!

Yesterday you said you wished not to be ungrateful; ah! believe me, Mademoiselle, to wish to repay love with friendship is not to fear ingratitude, it is only fearing to seem ungrateful. But I dare no longer occupy you with feelings which can only be troublesome to you if they do not affect you; I must shut them up in my own heart until I learn to overcome them. I know how painful this task will be; I do not conceal from myself the fact that I shall need all my strength; I shall try every means—there is one which will wound my heart deepest, and that will be to remind myself frequently that yours is insensible. I shall even try to see you less often and I am already considering how to find a plausible excuse.

What! Must I abandon the sweet custom of seeing you each day! Ah! at least I shall never cease to regret it. An endless misery will be the reward of a most tender love; and you will have willed it so, it will be your work! Never—I see it—shall I recapture the happiness I lose today; you only were made for my heart; with what pleasure would I swear to live only for you! But you do not desire to accept that oath; your silence shows me plainly that your heart makes no plea for me; it is at once the clearest proof of your indifference and the cruellest manner of telling me. Farewell, Mademoiselle.

I dare not flatter myself with hopes of an answer; love would have written eagerly, friendship with pleasure, even pity with indulgence; but pity, friendship and love are alike strangers to your heart.

Paris . . ., 23rd of August, 17—.

## LETTER XXIX

*Cécile Volanges to Sophie Carnay*

I told you, Sophie, that there are cases when one can write; and I assure you I greatly regret having followed your advice, because it gave so much pain to the Chevalier Danceny and to me. The proof that I was right is that Madame de Merteuil, a woman who must surely know, ended by agreeing with me. I told her everything. At first she said what you did; but when I explained everything to her she admitted it was quite a different matter; she only demands that I show her all my letters and all those from the Chevalier Danceny, to be certain I only say what is proper; and so for the present I am content. Ah! how much I love Madame de Merteuil! She is so kind! And such a respectable woman. So nothing can be said.

How I shall write to Monsieur Danceny and how pleased he will be! He will be more pleased than he imagines; for up to now I have only spoken to him of my "friendship" and he always wanted me to say my "love." I think it came to the same thing; but still I was afraid to, and he wanted it. I spoke of it to Madame de Merteuil; she said I was right and that one should never admit loving someone until it was impossible to prevent it any longer. I am sure I shall not be able to prevent myself much longer; after all it is the same thing, and will please him more.

Madame de Merteuil said too that she would lend me books which speak about all this and will teach me how to conduct myself and how to write better than I do; for, you see, she tells me all my faults, which is a proof of how much she loves me; she only advised me not to say anything to Mamma about these books because it would look as if she had neglected my education and that might make her angry. Oh! I shall say nothing to her about them.

But it is very extraordinary that a woman who is scarcely related to me should take more care of me than my mother! It is very fortunate for me that I know her!

She also asked Mamma to allow her to take me tomorrow to her box at the Opera; she says we shall be all alone there, and we will talk the whole time without any fear of being overheard; I shall like that much more than the Opera. We shall also talk about my marriage; for she tells me that it was quite true I was to be married; but we have not been able to say any more about it. Now, is it not really very surprising that Mamma says nothing at all about it?

Good-bye, dear Sophie, I am going to write to the Chevalier Danceny. Oh! I am so glad!

From . . ., 24th of August, 17—.

## LETTER XXX

*Cécile Volanges to the Chevalier Danceny*

At last I agree to write to you, Monsieur, to assure you of my friendship, of my *love*, since otherwise you would be unhappy. You say I am not kind-hearted ; I assure you that you are wrong and I hope you will not think so any more. If you were hurt because I did not write to you, do you think I was not pained too ? But the reason was that nothing in the world could make me do something I thought was wrong ; and I would not even have admitted my love, if I could have prevented myself ; but your sadness hurt me too much. I hope now you will not be sad any more and that we shall be very happy.

I expect to have the pleasure of seeing you this evening and that you will come early ; it will never be as early as I desire. Mamma dines at home and I think she will invite you to stay ; I hope you will not be engaged as you were the day before yesterday. Was it very pleasant, the dinner you went to ? For you left very early. But we will not speak of that any more ; now you know I love you, I hope you will stay with me as much as you can ; for I am only happy when I am with you and I should like you to be the same.

I am very sorry you are still sad, but it is not my fault. I shall ask for my harp as soon as you arrive so that you get my letter at once. I cannot do any more.

Good-bye, Monsieur. I love you with all my heart ; the oftener I tell you so, the happier I am ; I hope you will be so too.

From . . ., 24th of August, 17—.

## LETTER XXXI

*The Chevalier Danceny to Cécile Volanges*

Yes, we shall indeed be happy. My happiness is certain, since I am loved by you ; your happiness will never end if it lasts as long as the love you have inspired in me. Ah ! you love me, you are no longer afraid to assure me of your *love !* " the oftener you tell me so, the happier you are ! " After I had read that charming " I love you," written by your hand, I heard the same admission from your lovely mouth. I saw those charming eyes gaze upon me, embellished by an expression of tenderness. I received your vow to live only for me. Ah ! accept my vow to devote my whole life to your happiness ; accept it and be sure I shall never betray it.

What a happy day we spent yesterday ! Ah ! Why is it that Madame de Merteuil has not secrets to tell your Mamma every day ? Why must the idea of the constraint which awaits us mingle with the delicious memory which possesses me ? Why can I not forever hold that pretty hand which wrote to me " I love you ! " cover it with kisses, and thus avenge myself for the refusal of a greater favour !

Tell me, my Cécile, when your Mamma came back ; when we were forced by her presence to exchange only indifferent looks ; when you could no longer console me by the assurance of your love for your refusal to give me proofs of it ; did you feel no regret ? Did you not say to yourself : " A kiss would have made him happier and I have denied him this happiness ? " Promise me, my dearest, that you will be less severe next time. With the aid of this promise I shall find courage to endure the difficulties which circumstances are preparing for us ; and cruel privations will at least be softened by the certainty that you share my affliction.

Good-bye, my charming Cécile ; the hour has come when I am to visit you. It would be impossible for me to leave you if it were not to go and see you again. Good-bye, you whom I love so much ! You whom I shall ever love more !

From . . ., 24th of August, 17—.

## LETTER XXXII

*Madame de Volanges to Madame de Tourvel*

You wish me, Madame, to believe in the virtues of Monsieur de Valmont ? I confess I cannot bring myself to do so, and it would be as difficult for me to consider him virtuous from the one fact which you tell me, as it would be to consider as vicious a man of recognised virtue about whom I learned one lapse. Humanity is not perfect in any type, no more in evil than in good. The wicked man has his virtues, as the good man has his weaknesses. It seems to me the more necessary to believe this truth since from it arises the necessity of indulgence for the wicked as well as for the good ; since it saves the latter from pride and the former from discouragement. No doubt you will think I am now practising very ill the indulgence I preached ; but I see in indulgence only a dangerous weakness when it leads us to treat the good and the wicked man in the same way.

I will not allow myself to scrutinise the motives for Monsieur de Valmont's action ; I like to think they were as praiseworthy as it ; but has he any the less spent his life in bringing into families confusion, disorder and scandal ? Hearken, if you will, to the voice of the wretch he has succoured ; but do not let it prevent you from hearing the cries of a hundred victims he has sacrificed. Even if he were, as you say, merely an example of the danger of acquaintance, would he himself be any the less a dangerous acquaintance ? You suppose him capable of reformation ? Let us go further ; let us suppose this miracle had happened. Would not public opinion against him still remain, and does not that suffice to govern your conduct ? God alone can absolve at the moment of repentance ; He reads our hearts : but men can only judge of thoughts by actions, and no one who has lost the esteem of others has a right to complain of necessary suspicion, which renders this loss so difficult to repair. Above all, remember, my young friend, that sometimes, to lose this esteem, one need only appear to attach too little value to it; and do not call this severity injustice; for, beside the fact that we have a right to think people do not renounce this valuable advantage when they have a right to it, those who are no longer withheld by this powerful curb are indeed the nearer to acting ill. Such, however, would be the aspect in which you would appear through an intimate acquaintance with Monsieur de Valmont, however innocent it might be.

Alarmed by the warmth with which you defend him, I hasten to forestall the objections I foresee. You will adduce Madame de Merteuil, to whom this acquaintance has been pardoned; you will ask me why I receive him in my house; you will tell me that far from being rejected by virtuous people, he is admitted into, even sought by, what is called good company. I think I can answer everything.

First of all, Madame de Merteuil, who is indeed most estimable, has perhaps no fault but too great a confidence in her own strength; she is a skilful driver who enjoys guiding her chariot among rocks and precipices, and only her success is her justification; it is right to praise her, it would be imprudent to follow her; she herself admits it and reproaches herself. The more she has seen, the more severe her principles have become; and I am bold to assure you that she would think as I do.

As to what concerns me, I will not justify myself any more than others. No doubt I receive Monsieur de Valmont and he is received everywhere; it is one more inconsistency to add to the thousand others which govern society. You know as well as I do that we spend our lives in noticing them, in complaining of them and submitting to them. Monsieur de Valmont, with his ancient name, his wealth, and many amiable qualities, early recognised that to dominate society all he needed was to wield praise and ridicule with equal skill. No one possesses this double talent to the extent he does; with the one he seduces, with the other he makes himself feared. He is not esteemed; but he is flattered. Such is his existence in the midst of a world which, with more prudence than courage, prefers to treat him with deference rather than to combat him.

But neither Madame de Merteuil nor any other woman would dare to shut herself up in the country almost alone with such a man. It was reserved for the most prudent and most modest of women to set the example of this inconsistency—forgive the word, it slipped out from friendship. My dear friend, your very virtue betrays you, through the confidence it inspires in you. Remember that your judges on the one hand will be frivolous people who will not believe in a virtue whose model they do not find in themselves, and, on the other, malignant people who will feign not to believe in it to punish you for having had it. Consider that at this moment you are doing what several men would not dare to risk. Indeed, I see that among the young men (of whom Monsieur de Valmont is but too much the oracle) the most prudent are afraid to appear too intimate with him ; and you are not afraid ! Ah ! recover yourself, I beg you. . . . If my reasons do not suffice to persuade you, yield to my friendship ; it is that which causes me to renew my entreaties, which justifies them. You will think it severe, and I hope it may be unnecessary ; but I prefer that you should have to complain rather of its solicitude than of its negligence.

From . . .,24th of August, 17—.

## LETTER XXXIII

*The Marquise de Merteuil to the Vicomte de Valmont*

As soon as you are afraid of succeeding, my dear Vicomte, as soon as your object is to furnish arms against yourself, and you are less anxious to triumph than to combat, I have nothing more to say. Your conduct is a masterpiece of prudence. It would be a masterpiece of folly on the contrary assumption ; and to tell you the truth, I am afraid you are deluding yourself.

I do not reproach you for not having profited by the moment. On the one hand, I do not quite see that it had arrived ; and on the other I know too well—whatever they may say—that an occasion lost may be found again, while there is no recovery from too hasty a step.

But your real blunder is to have allowed yourself to start writing. I defy you now to foresee where that may lead you. Do you hope perhaps to prove to this woman that she ought to yield herself ? It seems to me that could only be a truth of sentiment, not of demonstration ; and to make her accept it you must move her and not reason with her ; but how can it help you to move her by letter, since you will not be at hand to profit by it ? Suppose your fine phrases should produce the intoxication of love, do you flatter yourself it will last so long that reflection will not have time to prevent her from admitting it ? Remember what is needed for writing a letter, what takes place before it is delivered ; and then see if a woman with principles like your devotee can desire for so long what she tries never to desire at all. This course may succeed with children who, when they write " I love you," do not know they are saying " I yield myself." But the rationalising virtue of Madame de Tourvel seems to me to understand perfectly the value of phrases. So, in spite of the advantage you obtained over her in conversation, she beats you in her letter. And then, do you realise what is happening ? The mere fact of debating makes her unwilling to yield. By dint of looking for good reasons she finds them ; she expresses them ; and then she will hold to them not so much because they are good as not to contradict herself.

And then, I am surprised you have not noticed that there is nothing so difficult in love as to write what one does not feel. I mean, to write it in a credible way. It is not that the same words are not employed ;

but they are not arranged in the same way, or rather they are arranged—and that is enough. Re-read your letter ; there is an order in it which betrays you at every phrase. I am ready to believe that your Madame de Tourvel is sufficiently inexperienced not to notice it ; but what does that matter ? The effect fails none the less. That is the defect of novels ; the author lashes his sides to warm himself up, and the reader remains cold. *Héloïse* is the one exception ; and in spite of the author's talents this observation has always made me think that its subject was true. It is not the same in speaking. Practice in exerting one's speech gives it feeling ; facility of tears adds to it ; the expression of desire in the eyes may be mistaken for that of tenderness ; and then a less coherent language more easily introduces that air of uncertainty and disorder which is the real eloquence of love ; above all the presence of the loved person prevents reflection and makes us women wish to be overcome.

Take my advice, Vicomte ; you are asked not to write again ; take advantage of it to repair your mistake and wait for an opportunity to speak. Do you know, this woman has more strength than I thought ? Her defence holds out well ; and but for the length of her letter and the pretext she gives you to resume by her phrase of gratitude, she would not have betrayed herself at all.

What seems to me still to promise you success is that she uses too many influences at once ; I foresee she will exhaust them all in defending the word and will have none left to defend the thing.

I send you back your two letters ; if you are wise they will be the last until after the happy moment. If it were not so late, I should speak to you of the Volanges girl who is advancing rapidly ; I am very pleased with her. I think I shall have finished before you, and you ought to be very glad of it. Good-bye for today.

From . . ., 24th of August, 17—.

## LETTER XXXIV

*The Vicomte de Valmont to the Marquise de Merteuil.*

You speak admirably, my fair friend ; but why take so much trouble to prove what everyone knows ? To advance rapidly in love it is better to speak than to write ; that, I think, is the whole of your letter. Why ? These are the simplest elements in the art of seduction. I will only point out that you make but one exception to this principle, and there are two. To children who follow this course from timidity and yield from ignorance, must be added the blue-stockings who start on it from conceit and who are led into the snare by vanity. For instance, I am quite sure that the Comtesse de B . . . who readily answered my first letter was no more in love with me then than I was with her ; she only saw an opportunity of writing on a subject which would show her wit to good advantage.

However that may be, a lawyer would tell you that in this case the principle does not apply. You suppose I have a choice between writing and speaking, and I have not. Since the occurrence of the nineteenth my cruel one, who is on the defensive, has avoided any meeting with a skill which outwits my own. It has reached a point where if it continues she will force me to think seriously of means to regain this advantage; for assuredly I do not mean to be beaten by her in any way. Even my letters are the subject of a little war; not content with leaving them unanswered, she refuses to take them. Each one needs a new ruse which is not always successful.

You remember in what a simple way I delivered the first one; the second was just as easy. She had asked me to return her letter; I gave her mine instead, without her having the least suspicion of it. But either from annoyance at having been caught, or from caprice, or perhaps even from virtue—for she will at last force me to believe in it—she obstinately refused the third. However I hope that the embarrassment which nearly involved her as a result of this refusal will correct her for the future.

I was not very surprised when she refused to take this letter, which I merely offered her; that would have been granting something and I expect a longer defence. After this attempt, which was simply an experiment made by the way, I put my letter in an envelope and, choosing the moment of her toilet, when Madame de Rosemonde and the waiting-woman were present, I sent it to her by my man-servant with orders to say to her that this was the paper she had asked for. I had foreseen that she would shrink from the scandal of explanation which would be necessitated by a refusal; she took the letter, and my ambassador, who had been told to watch her face and is no bad observer, only noticed a slight blush and more embarrassment than anger.

I was congratulating myself, you may be sure, on the idea that she would either keep my letter or that if she wished to return it she would be compelled to be alone with me; which would give me an opportunity to speak to her. About an hour afterwards one of her servants came to my room and delivered to me, from his mistress, a packet shaped differently from mine, on whose envelope I recognised the much-desired handwriting. I opened it hastily. . . . It was my own letter unopened and merely folded in two. I suspect that her fear lest I should be not so scrupulous as she in the matter of scandal made her employ this diabolical ruse.

You know me; there is no need for me to describe my rage. However, it was necessary to be calm and to think of some new method. This is the only one I could devise.

Every morning someone goes from here to get the letters at the post office which is about threequarters of a mile away; a closed box rather like a trunk is used for this purpose, and the postmaster has one key and Madame de Rosemonde the other. Everyone puts his letters in at any time during the day; in the evening they are taken to the post office and the next morning someone goes for the letters which have come in. All the servants, visitors' or others, discharge this task. It was not my man's turn ; but he undertook to go on the pretext that he had something to do in the neighbourhood.

Meanwhile I wrote my letter. I disguised my handwriting for the address and imitated fairly well on the envelope the postmark of Dijon. I chose this town because, since I was asking for the same rights as the husband, I thought it more amusing to write from the same place, and also because my fair one had talked all day of her desire to receive letters from Dijon. I thought it only just to procure her that pleasure.

These precautions once taken, it was easy to add my letter to the others. By this expedient I had the advantage of being able to watch its reception ; for the custom here is to meet for breakfast and to await the arrival of the letters before separating. At last they arrived.

Madame de Rosemonde opened the box. " From Dijon," said she, giving the letter to Madame de Tourvel. " It is not my husband's handwriting," said she in an anxious voice, as she broke the seal quickly ; the first glance showed her what it was ; she changed countenance to such an extent that Madame de Rosemonde noticed it and said to her : " What is the matter ? " I went up to her too, saying : " Is this letter so very terrible then ? " The timid devotee dared not raise her eyes, said not a word, and to hide her embarrassment, pretended to run over the letter, although she was in no state to read. I was enjoying her distress and, not being sorry to tease her a little, I added : " Your calmer looks make me hope that this letter gives you more astonishment than pain." Her anger then inspired her better than her prudence had done. " It contains," she replied, " things which offend me and which I am astounded anyone should have dared to write to me." " And who is it ? " interrupted Madame de Rosemonde. " It is not signed," replied the enraged fair one, " but both the letter and its writer inspire me with the same contempt. I shall be obliged if you will not mention it to me again." So saying, she tore up the audacious letter, put the pieces in her pocket, rose, and left the room.

In spite of her anger, she has none the less had my letter ; and I rely on her curiosity at least to read it in full.

The details of the day would take me too far. I add to this the rough draft of my two letters ; you will know as much as I do. If you wish to keep informed of this correspondence you must get used to deciphering my notes ; nothing in the world would induce me to endure the boredom of re-copying them. Good-bye, my fair friend.

From . . ., 25th of August, 17—.

## LETTER XXXV

*Vicomte de Valmont to Madame de Tourvel*

I must obey you, Madame, I must prove to you that in spite of all the faults you are pleased to credit me with I still retain sufficient delicacy not to permit myself a complaint and sufficient courage to burden myself with the most painful of sacrifices. You impose upon me silence and oblivion ! Well ! I will force my love to be silent and I will forget, if it is possible, the cruel manner in which you received it. Of course my wish to please you did not give me the right to do so and I admit that my need for your indulgence constituted no claim to obtaining it ; but you consider my love an outrage and you forget that if it were a fault you are at once its cause and its excuse. You forget also that I was accustomed to show you my soul even when such confidence might harm me and that it was no longer possible to hide from you the emotions which move me ; and so that which was the result of my good faith you consider the fruit of presumption. As a reward for the most tender, the most respectful, the most sincere love, you cast me far from you. You even speak of your hatred. . . . Who else would not complain of such treatment ? I alone am submissive ; I endure everything without a murmur ; you strike and I adore. The inconceivable power you have over me makes you the absolute mistress of my feelings ; and if my love alone resists you, if you cannot destroy it, that is because it is your work and not mine.

I do not ask a return which I never flattered myself I should obtain. I do not expect even that pity which I might have hoped from the interest you have sometimes shown in me. But I confess I think I may appeal to your justice.

You inform me, Madame, that an attempt has been made to harm me in your estimation. If you had followed the advice of your friends you would not even have allowed me to approach you—those are your words. And who are these officious friends ? No doubt such severe people, of so rigid a virtue, will consent to be named ; no doubt they would not hide themselves in an obscurity which would make them resemble vile calumniators ; and I shall learn both their names and their censures. Remember, Madame, I have a right to know both since by them you have judged me. A criminal is not condemned without being told his crimes and the names of his accusers. I ask no other favour and I undertake beforehand to justify myself, to force them to withdraw their statements.

If I have been perhaps too contemptuous of the vain clamour of a public for which I care little, it is different with your esteem ; and when I am consecrating my life to the task of meriting it, I shall not allow myself to be deprived of it with impunity. It becomes the more precious to me since I must owe to it the request you are afraid to ask of me, which would give me, you say, "a right to your gratitude." Ah ! far from claiming your gratitude I should think I owed it to you if you would grant me an opportunity to be agreeable to you. Begin by doing me greater justice, and do not leave me ignorant of what you desire from me. If I could guess it, I would spare you the trouble of saying it. To the pleasure of seeing you, add the happiness of serving you and I shall congratulate myself upon your indulgence. What then can restrain you? Not, I hope, the fear of a refusal? I feel I could not pardon you that. There was no refusal in my not returning your letter. More than you, I desire that it should not be necessary to me; but I was accustomed to believe your spirit was so gentle and it is only in that letter that I can find you such as you would wish to appear. While I form the hope that you will be moved, I see you would fly a hundred miles from me rather than consent; when everything in you increases and justifies my love, it is your letter which repeats to me that my love outrages you; when I look at you and that love seems to me the supreme good, I need to read you to feel it is only a dreadful torment. You can now perceive that my greatest happiness would be to be able to return you that fatal letter; to ask me for it again would be authorising me to cease to believe what it contains; I hope you do not doubt my eagerness to return it to you.

From . . ., 21st of August, 17—.

## LETTER XXXVI

*The Vicomte de Valmont to Madame de Tourvel*

(Postmark of Dijon)

Your severity increases every day, Madame, and if I may be bold to say so, you seem to be more afraid of being indulgent than of being unjust. After having condemned me without hearing me, you must have felt indeed that it would be easier for you not to read my arguments than to reply to them. You refuse my letters with obstinacy; you send them back to me with contempt. And you finally force me to a trick at the very moment when my sole object is to convince you of my good faith. The necessity of defending myself which you have forced upon me no doubt will suffice to excuse the means. Convinced moreover by the sincerity of my feelings that it would suffice to explain to you in order to justify them in your eyes, I felt I might allow myself this slight subterfuge. I even dare to think that you will forgive me for it and that you will not be very surprised that love is more ingenious in putting itself forward than indifference is in putting it aside.

Madame, allow my heart to reveal itself completely to you. It belongs to you and you have a right to know it.

When I came to Madame de Rosemonde's house I was very far from foreseeing the fate which awaited me there. I did not know you were there; and I will add, with my accustomed sincerity, that if I had known it my self-confidence would not have been disturbed—not that I do not render your beauty the justice it cannot be refused, but as I was accustomed to experience nothing but desires and to yield only to those encouraged by hope, I was ignorant of the tortures of love.

You yourself witnessed the entreaties of Madame de Rosemonde to retain me here for some time. I had already passed a day with you; yet I only yielded—or at least I only thought I yielded—to the natural and legitimate pleasure of showing my regard for a respectable relative. The kind of life led here was certainly very different from that to which I was accustomed. It was easy for me to conform to it ; and, without seeking to discover the cause of the change which was taking place in me, I still attributed it solely to that facility of character of which I think I have already spoken to you.

Unfortunately (and why must it be a misfortune ?) as I came to know you better I soon recognised that the enchanting face, which alone had struck me, was the least of your advantages ; your heavenly soul surprised, seduced mine. I admired beauty, I adored virtue. Without hoping that I might possess you I pondered on the means to deserve you. By asking your indulgence for the past, I aspired to your approbation in the future ; I sought for it in your speech, I watched for it in your looks ; in those looks which darted a poison all the more dangerous in that it was cast out undesignedly, and received without suspicion.

And then I knew love. But how far I was from complaining ! Resolved to bury it in eternal silence I gave myself up without fear, as without reserve, to that delicious emotion. Each day increased its power. Soon the pleasure of seeing you became a necessity. Were you absent for a moment ? My heart shrank with sadness ; at the sound which announced your return, it palpitated with joy. I existed only through you and for you. And yet, I call you to witness, never in the gaiety of playful games or in the interest of a serious conversation did there escape from me a word which might betray the secret of my heart.

At last there came a day from which my misfortune was to begin ; and through some inscrutable destiny a good action was the beginning. Yes, Madame, it was in the midst of the wretches I had succoured that, yielding yourself to that precious sensibility which embellishes beauty itself and adds a value to virtue, you completely unsettled a heart which was already intoxicated by an excess of love. You remember perhaps how preoccupied I was during our return ! Alas ! I was trying to overcome an inclination which I felt was becoming stronger than I.

It was when I had exhausted my strength in this unequal struggle that a chance I could not have foreseen left us alone together. There I succumbed, I admit it. My overwrought heart could not restrain its words or its tears. But is that a crime ? And if it is one, is it not sufficiently punished by the frightful torments to which I am abandoned ?

Devoured by a hopeless love, I implore your pity and find nothing but your hatred ; with no other happiness than that of seeing you my eyes seek you out in spite of myself and I tremble to meet your looks. In the cruel condition to which you have reduced me, I spend the days in hiding my pain and the nights in abandoning myself to it ; while you in your peace and tranquillity know nothing of these torments except that you caused them and congratulate yourself on doing so. Yet it is you who complain and I who make excuses.

Here, Madame, is a faithful account of what you call my faults, which might more justly perhaps be called my misfortunes. A pure and sincere love, a respect which has never failed, a perfect submission, such are the feelings you have inspired in me. I should not have been afraid to offer them to the divinity itself. O you, you who are its fairest work, imitate it in its indulgence! Think of my cruel distress; think above all that since you have placed me between despair and supreme happiness, the first word you pronounce will decide my fate forever.

From . . ., 23rd of August, 17—.

## LETTER XXXVII

*Madame de Tourvel to Madame de Volanges*

I submit myself, Madame, to the advice your friendship gives me. Accustomed to defer to your opinion in everything I have come to think it is always founded upon reason. I will even admit that Monsieur de Valmont must indeed be infinitely dangerous if he can at the same time feign to be what he appears here and remain as you describe him. However this may be, since you demand it, I will send him away from me; at least I will do my best; for often those things which in essence should be the most simple, become difficult in form.

It still seems to me impractical to make this request of his aunt; it would be equally impolite to her and to him. On the other hand I should feel some repugnance if I took the decision to go away myself; for in addition to the reasons I have already mentioned relative to Monsieur de Tourvel, if my departure provoked Monsieur de Valmont (as is possible), would it not be easy for him to follow me to Paris? And his return, of which I should be, or at least appear to be, the cause, might seem stranger than a meeting in the country at the house of a person who is known to be his relative and my friend.

My only resource then is to persuade him to leave of his own accord. I feel this is a difficult proposition to make; but since he seems to desire to prove to me that he is more virtuous than is supposed, I do not despair of success. I shall not even be sorry to attempt it and to have an opportunity of judging whether, as he says so often, really virtuous women never have and never will have reason to complain of his actions. If he goes, as I desire, it will indeed be out of regard for me; for I cannot doubt but that he intends to pass a large part of the autumn here. If he refuses my request and persists in remaining, I shall still have time to go myself and I promise you I will.

That, I think, Madame, is all your friendship exacted of me; I hasten to satisfy it, and to prove to you that in spite of the *warmth* I may have showed in defending Monsieur de Valmont, I am none the less disposed, not only to listen to, but to follow, the advice of my friends.

I have the honour to be, etc.

From . . ., 25th of August, 17—.

## LETTER XXXVIII

*The Marquise de Merteuil to the Vicomte de Valmont*

Your enormous packet has just arrived, my dear Vicomte. If its date is correct, I ought to have received it twenty-four hours sooner; however that may be, if I took the time to read it I should have none left in which to answer it. So I prefer to acknowledge receipt of it—and to talk of something else. It is not that I have anything to tell you on my own account; the autumn hardly leaves in Paris one man with a human visage; and so for the last month I have been desperately sober and anyone but my Chevalier would be wearied by the proofs of my constancy. Having nothing to do, I amuse myself with the Volanges girl; and it is about her that I wish to speak to you.

Do you know you have lost more than you thought by not undertaking this child? She is really delicious! She has neither character nor principles; so you may judge how charming and facile her company would be. I do not think that she would ever shine by sentiment but everything about her presages the keenest sensations. Without wit and without finesse, she has yet a certain natural duplicity (if I may say so) which sometimes surprises even me and which will be all the more successful since her face is the image of candour and ingenuousness. She is naturally very caressing, and I sometimes amuse myself with her; she grows excited with incredible facility; and she is all the more amusing because she knows nothing, absolutely, nothing, of what she so much wishes to know. She has the most diverting fits of impatience; she laughs, is piqued, weeps, and then begs me to tell her with a truly seductive good faith. Really, I am almost jealous of the man for whom this pleasure is reserved.

I do not know if I told you that for four or five days I have had the honour to be her confidant. You can guess that at first I pretended to be severe; but as soon as I saw that she thought she had convinced me with her bad reasons, I pretended to accept them as good, and she is intimately persuaded that she owes this success to her eloquence; this precaution was necessary to avoid compromising myself. I have allowed her to write and say "I love"; and the same day, without her guessing it, I arranged her an interview alone with Danceny. But imagine, he is still such a fool that he did not even get a kiss from her. Yet the lad writes very pretty verses! Heavens! How silly these wits are! He is silly to an extent which embarrasses me; for after all I cannot be his guide.

You would be very useful to me at this juncture. You know Danceny sufficiently well to obtain his confidence, and if he once gave it to you, we should progress rapidly. Hurry on with your Madame de Tourvel, for I do not want Gercourt to escape; I spoke of him yesterday to the little girl and painted him in such colours that she could not hate him more if she had been married to him for ten years. I gave her a long lecture on conjugal fidelity ; nothing could equal my severity on this point. Thus, on the one hand, I re-established in her eyes my reputation for virtue which might be destroyed by too much condescension ; and on the other hand I increased in her the hatred with which I desire to gratify her husband. And finally I hope that by making her think that it is not permitted to yield to love except in the little time she has left before marriage, she will decide the quicker not to lose any of it. Good-bye, Vicomte ; I must go to my toilet and will read your volume.

From . . ., 27th of August, 17—.

## LETTER XXXIX

*Cécile Volanges to Sophie Carnay*

I am sad and uneasy, my dear Sophie, I cried almost all night. It is not that I am not very happy at the moment, but I foresee that it will not last.

Yesterday I went to the Opera with Madame de Merteuil ; we talked a lot about my marriage and what I found out about it was not at all nice. It is M. le Comte de Gercourt I am to marry and it is to be in October. He is rich, he is a man of quality, he is colonel of the . . . Regiment. So far so good. But first of all he is old ; consider, he is at least thirty-six ! And then Madame de Merteuil says he is melancholy and severe and that she is afraid I shall not be happy with him. I could see quite well she was sure I should not be, and that she did not wish to say so, in order not to distress me. She talked to me almost all the evening about the duties of wives to husbands ; she admits that M. de Gercourt is not in the least agreeable, and yet she says I must love him. Did she not tell me also that once I am married I must no longer love the Chevalier Danceny ? As if that were possible ! Oh ! I assure you I shall always love him. Let M. de Gercourt look after himself, he was none of my seeking. At present he is in Corsica, far away from here ; I wish he would stay there ten years. If I were not afraid of going back to the convent I should tell Mamma this is not the husband I want ; but that would be even worse. I am very perplexed. I feel I have never loved M. Danceny so much as I do now ; and when I think that I have only one month left to be as I am, the tears come into my eyes at once ; my only consolation is the friendship of Madame de Merteuil—she is so kind-hearted ! She shares all my griefs with me and then she is so agreeable that when I am with her I hardly think about them. Besides she is very useful to me ; for the little I know I have learnt from her ; and she is so kind that I tell her everything I think without being at all bashful. When she thinks it is not right, she scolds me sometimes ; but it is very gently, and then I kiss her with all my heart until she is no longer vexed. At least I can love her as much as I like without there being anything wrong in it, and it gives me a great deal of pleasure. However, we have agreed that I am to appear not to love her so much in front of other people, especially in front of Mamma, so that she will not suspect anything about the Chevalier Danceny. I assure you that if I could always live as I do now, I think I should be very happy. There is only that horrid M. de Gercourt. . . . But I will not speak of him again ; for it would make me sad once more. Instead of that I shall write to the Chevalier Danceny ; I shall only speak to him about my love but not about my griefs, for I do not wish to distress him.

Good-bye, my dear. You see it would be wrong for you to complain and that although I am so *busy*, as you put it, I still have time to love you and to write to you.[1]

From . . ., 17th of August, 17—.

## LETTER XL

*The Vicomte de Valmont to the Marquise de Merteuil*

It is not enough for my cruel one that she does not answer my letters, that she refuses to receive them ; she wants to deprive me of the sight of her, she insists that I go away. What will surprise you more is that I am submitting to such harshness. You will find fault with me. But I did not think I ought to lose an opportunity of allowing myself to be given an order ; being convinced on the one hand that she who commands commits herself, and on the other hand that the illusory authority we appear to let women take is one of the snares they avoid with the most difficulty. Moreover the skill she has shown in avoiding being alone with me placed me in a dangerous situation, which I felt I ought to get out of at any cost ; for as I was continually near her without being able to occupy her with my love I had reason to fear that at last she would grow used to seeing me without disquiet—a state of mind which you know is difficult to alter.

For the rest you can guess I did not yield without conditions. I was even careful enough to make one it was impossible to grant ; so that I can either keep my word or break it, and at the same time begin a discussion either by word of mouth or by letter at a time when my fair one is better pleased with me and when she needs me to be so with her—without reckoning that I should be very clumsy if I found no means of obtaining some satisfaction for desisting from this claim, however indefensible it may be.

After having explained my reasons in this long preamble, I begin the history of the last two days. As corroborating documents I shall add my fair one's letter and my reply. You will admit that few historians are so precise as I am.

You will remember the effect produced by my letter from Dijon the day before yesterday ; the rest of the day was very stormy. The pretty prude only appeared at dinner time and announced a bad headache—a

[1] The letters from Cécile Volanges and the Chevalier Danceny are omitted since they are not interesting and relate no event. (C. de L.)

pretext by which she tried to conceal one of the most violent fits of ill humour a woman could have. Her face was positively changed by it; the expression of gentleness you are familiar with in her was changed into a rebellious look which gave it a new beauty. I have promised myself to make use of this discovery later and sometimes to replace the tender mistress by the rebellious mistress.

I foresaw that the time after dinner would be dull and, to avoid the boredom of it, I pretended I had letters to write and went to my room. I returned to the drawing-room about six o'clock; Madame de Rosemonde proposed that we should go out, which was agreed upon. But at the moment when she was getting into the carriage, the pretended invalid by an infernal piece of malice pretended in her turn (and perhaps to avenge herself for my absence) that she had an increase of pain, and without any pity forced me to endure a *tête a tête* with my old aunt. I do not know if my imprecations against this female demon were heard, but when we got back we found she had gone to bed.

Next morning at breakfast she was a different woman. Her natural gentleness had returned and I had good reason to think I was forgiven. Breakfast was scarcely over when the gentle creature rose with an indolent air and went out into the park; I followed her, as you may suppose. "What has caused this desire for walking?" said I as I met her. "I have done a lot of writing this morning," she replied, "and my head is a little weary." "I am not so fortunate," I replied, "as to have to reproach myself with this fatigue?" "I have indeed written to you," she answered again, "but I hesitate to give you my letter. It contains a request and you have not accustomed me to hope for its success." "Ah! I swear that if it is possible. . . ." "Nothing is easier," she interrupted, "and although you ought perhaps to grant it as a matter of justice, I consent to take it as a grace." Saying these words, she handed me her letter; as I took it I took her hand too, which she withdrew but without anger and with more embarrassment than vivacity. "It is hotter than I thought," she said, "I must go back." And she took the path to the Château. I made vain efforts to persuade her to continue her walk and I was forced to remind myself that we might be seen in order to use nothing more than eloquence. She returned without speaking a word and I saw plainly that this pretended walk had no other purpose than that of giving me her letter. She went to her room as soon as we got back and I went to mine to read the epistle, which you will do well to read also, as well as my reply before going any further. . . .

## LETTER XLI

*Madame de Tourvel to the Vicomte de Valmont*

It seems from your conduct towards me, Monsieur, that you are every day seeking to increase the reasons I have to complain of you. Your obstinacy in wishing to occupy me ceaselessly with a sentiment which I ought not and do not wish to listen to ; the way in which you have dared to abuse my good faith or my timidity in order to send me your letters ; above all the method, which I dare to say was indelicate, you made use of to send me the last, without even fearing the effect of a surprise which might have compromised me ; all these ought to have given rise on my part to reproaches as sharp as they are justly deserved. However, instead of dwelling upon these injuries, I merely make a request as simple as it is just ; and if I obtain it from you, I agree that all shall be forgiven.

You have said yourself, Monsieur, that I need not fear a refusal ; and although, by an inconsistency which is peculiar to you, this very phrase was followed by the only refusal you could give me,[1] I am ready to believe that today you will none the less keep the word formally given so short a time ago.

It is my desire than that you will be good enough to go away from me ; to leave this Château, where a longer stay on your part could only expose me further to the judgment of a public always quick to think ill of others, a public whom you have but too much accustomed to fix their eyes on the women who admit you into their society.

Although I had long been warned of this danger by my friends, I neglected, I even opposed their advice as long as your conduct towards me led me to believe that you did not wish to confound me with that crowd of women who all have reason to complain of you. Now that you treat me like them, that I can no longer remain ignorant of it, I owe to the public, to my friends, to myself to follow this imperative course. I might add here that you will gain nothing by refusing my request, for I am determined to leave myself if you persist in remaining ; but I do not wish to lessen my obligation to you for this complaisance and I wish you to know that by forcing me to leave here you would disorganise my plans. Prove to me, as you have so often told me, Monsieur, that virtuous women will never have reason to complain of you ; prove to me at least that when you have done them an injury you can repair it.

If I thought there was any need to justify my request to you, it would be enough to say to you that you have passed your life in making it necessary and that nevertheless it is not my fault if I have to make it. But do not let us recall events I wish to forget, which force me to judge you sternly at a moment when I give you an opportunity to deserve my gratitude. Good-bye, Monsieur. Your conduct will show me with what sentiments I should be, for life, your most humble, etc.

From . . ., 25th of August, 17—.

## LETTER XLII

*The Vicomte de Valmont to Madame de Tourvel*

However harsh the conditions you impose upon me, Madame, I do not refuse to carry them out. I feel it would be impossible for me to

[1] See *LETTER XXXV*. (C. de L.)

thwart any of your desires. Once agreed on this point, I dare to flatter myself that in my turn you will allow me to make a few requests, much more easy to grant than yours, which I only desire to obtain by my perfect submission to your will.

One, which I hope will be pleaded for by your justice, is to be good enough to tell me the names of those who have accused me to you ; it seems to me they have done me enough wrong for me to have a right to know them ; the other, which I expect from your indulgence, is to be good enough to allow me sometimes to renew the homage of a love which more than ever now will deserve your pity.

Remember, Madame, that I hasten to obey you even when I can only do so at the expense of my own happiness ; I will say more, in spite of my persuasion that you only desire my departure to save yourself from the sight (which is always painful) of the object of your injustice.

Acknowledge, Madame, that you do not so much fear a public which is too much accustomed to respect you to dare to form a disadvantageous judgment of you, as you are inconvenienced by the presence of a man whom it is easier to punish than to blame. You send me away from you as people avert their gaze from an unfortunate they do not wish to aid.

But when absence is about to increase my anguish, to whom but to you can I address my complaints ? From whom else can I expect the consolations which will be so necessary to me ? Will you refuse them to me, when you alone are the cause of my sufferings ?

No doubt you will not be surprised that before I go I should desire to justify to you the sentiments you have inspired in me ; and also that I lack the courage to go away if I do not receive the order from your mouth.

This double reason makes me ask you for a brief interview. It is useless for us to try to replace it by letters ; we write volumes and explain badly what could be perfectly understood in a quarter of an hour's conversation. You will easily find time to grant it to me ; for, however anxious I am to obey you, you know that Madame de Rosemonde is aware of my plan to spend part of the autumn with her and I must at least wait for a letter to be able to form a pretext for leaving.

Good-bye, Madame ; never has it been so difficult for me to write this word as now when it calls to my mind the idea of our separation. If you could imagine how it makes me suffer I dare to think that you would feel some gratitude to me for my docility. At least accept, with more indulgence, the assurance and homage of the tenderest and most respectful love.

From . . ., 26th of August, 17—.

## CONTINUATION OF LETTER XL

*The Vicomte de Valmont to the Marquise de Merteuil.*

And now let us discuss matters, my fair friend. You will agree with me that the scrupulous, the honest Madame de Tourvel, cannot grant me the first of my requests and betray the confidence of her friends, by telling me the names of my accusers ; so by promising everything on this condition, I commit myself to nothing. But you will agree also that her refusal of this will become a claim to obtaining all the rest ; and that, by going away, I then gain the advantage of starting a regular correspondence with her by her own permission ; I make little account of the meeting I have asked from her which has practically no other object but to accustom her beforehand not to refuse me others when they will be really necessary to me.

The only thing remaining for me to do before I leave is to find out who are the people who have busied themselves in harming me in her opinion. I presume it is her pedant of a husband ; I wish it were ; in addition to the fact that a conjugal interdiction is a spur to desire, I should be certain that from the moment my fair one consents to write to me I shall have nothing more to fear from her husband, since she will already be compelled to deceive him.

But if she has a woman friend sufficiently intimate to possess her confidence, and if this friend is against me, it seems to me necessary to set them at variance, and I expect to succeed in this ; but first of all I must know who it is.

I thought yesterday I should find it out ; but this woman does nothing like other women. We were in her room at the moment when she was informed that dinner was served. She was just finishing her toilet and as she hurried and made apologies, I noticed she had left the key in her writing-table ; and I knew it was her habit not to remove the key of her apartment. I was thinking of it during dinner when I heard her maid come down ; I decided what to do at once ; I pretended my nose was bleeding and left the room. I rushed to the writing-table ; but I found all the drawers open and not a piece of written paper. Yet there is no need to burn them at this time of the year. What does she do with the letters she receives ? For she often receives them. I neglected nothing ; everything was open and I looked everywhere ; but I found nothing except that I convinced myself that this precious hoard remains in her pocket.

How am I to get them out ? Ever since yesterday I have been trying in vain to find the way ; yet I cannot overcome my desire for them. I regret I do not possess the talents of a pickpocket. Ought it not indeed to make part of the education of a man who dabbles in intrigues ?[1] Would it not be amusing to steal a rival's letter or portrait, or to take from a prude's pocket the evidence to unmask her ? But our parents never foresee anything ; and though I foresee everything I only perceive that I am clumsy, without being able to remedy it.

In any case I came back to table very much out of humour. However, my fair one calmed my ill humour a little by the air of interest which my

[1] After this insult to the *petit-maitres*, it hardly seems possible that anyone can deny the political-moral motives of Laclos ; still less possible that he could be supposed to identify himself with Valmont.

feigned indisposition gave her; and I did not fail to assure her that for some time I had undergone violent agitations which had harmed my health. Persuaded as she is that she is the cause of them, ought she not in conscience to labour to calm them? But, although she is pious, she is not very charitable; she refuses all amorous alms and it seems to me that this refusal suffices to justify my stealing them. But good-bye; the whole time I am talking to you I am thinking of nothing but those accursed letters.

From . . ., 27th of August, 17—.

## LETTER XLIII

*Madame de Tourvel to the Vicomte de Valmont*

Why do you attempt, Monsieur, to lessen my gratitude? Why do you wish to obey me only by half and as it were to haggle over a right proceeding? It is not sufficient for you, then, that I should feel its cost? You not only ask a great deal; you ask impossible things. If indeed my friends have spoken to me of you, they can only have done so out of interest in me; even if they were wrong, their intention was none the less good and you propose to me to acknowledge this mark of attachment on their part by giving you their secret! I was wrong to speak to you of it and you make me feel so at this moment. What would have been merely candour with anyone else becomes thoughtlessness with you, and would lead me to a base action if I yielded to your request, I appeal to you, to your honour; did you believe me capable of this action? Ought you to have suggested it to me? Certainly not; and I am sure that when you have thought it over you will not repeat this request.

The request you make me that you shall write to me is no easier to grant; and if you have any wish to be just you will not blame me. I do not wish to offend you; but with the reputation you have acquired (which, by your own admission, you deserve at least in part), what woman could admit she was in correspondence with you! And what virtuous woman can make up her mind to do what she feels she will be compelled to hide?

Still, if I were assured that your letters would be such that I should never have to complain of them, that I could always justify myself in my own eyes for having received them, perhaps then the desire of proving to you that I am guided by reason and not by hatred would make me pass over these powerful considerations and do far more than I ought to do, by allowing you to write to me sometimes. If indeed you desire it as much as you tell me, you will willingly submit to the one condition which could make me consent to it; and if you have any gratitude for what I am doing for you now you will delay your departure no further.

Allow me to point out to you in this connection that you received a letter this morning and did not make use of it to announce your departure to Madame de Rosemonde, as you had promised me. I hope that now nothing will prevent you from keeping your word. Above all I desire you will not expect from me, in exchange, the meeting you ask for, to which I absolutely will not lend myself; and that, instead of the order which you pretend is necessary to you, you will content yourself with the entreaty I make you again.

Farewell, Monsieur.

From . . ., 27th of August, 17—.

## LETTER XLIV

*The Vicomte de Valmont to the Marquise de Merteuil*

Share my joy, my fair friend; I am loved; I have triumphed over this rebellious heart. It is in vain for it to dissimulate longer; my fortunate skill has surprised its secret. Thanks to my active exertions, I know everything I want to know; since night, the happy night of yesterday, I am back in my element; I have resumed my whole existence; I have unveiled a double mystery of love and iniquity; I shall enjoy the one, I shall avenge myself upon the other; I shall fly from pleasures to pleasures. The mere idea of it so transports me that I have some difficulty in recalling my prudence, that I find it difficult perhaps to put any order into the account I have to give you. However, let me try.

Yesterday, after I had written you my letter, I received one from the charming devotee. I send it to you; you will see that she gives me, as adroitly as she can, the permission to write to her; but she urges me to leave and I felt I could not put off going much longer without doing myself harm.

Tormented, however, with the desire to know who could have written against me, I was still uncertain what course to take. I tried to win over the waiting-maid and I desired her to let me have her mistress's pockets, which she could easily get hold of at night and replace in the morning, without creating the least suspicion. I offered ten louis for this slight service; but I found only a scrupulous or timid prude, who was moved neither by my money nor my eloquence. I was still lecturing her when the supper bell rang. I had to leave her, only too happy that she consented to promise secrecy, upon which as you may suppose I did not rely.

I was never more out of humour. I felt I had compromised myself; and the whole evening I reproached myself for this imprudent step.

I went to my apartment, not without uneasiness, and spoke to my man who, in his character of the successful lover, ought to have some influence. I wished him either to get this girl to do what I had asked of her or at least to make certain of her discretion; but he who is usually uncertain of nothing seemed uncertain of the success of this negotiation, and made me an observation on this subject which astonished me by its profundity.

"You know better than I, Monsieur," said he, "that to lie with a girl is only to make her do what pleases her; there is often a great distance between that and making her do what we want."

The rascal's good sense sometimes terrifies me.[1]

"I can rely on her the less," he added, "since I have reason to believe that she has a lover and that I only owe her to the inactivity of the country. So, were it not for my zeal in your service, Monsieur, I should only have had her once." (This fellow is a real treasure!) "As to secrecy," he went on, "of what use will it be to make her promise since she will risk nothing by betraying us? To speak of it to her again would only better show her that it is important and so make her more anxious to please her mistress."

The more true these remarks were, the more my embarrassment was increased. Luckily the fellow was in a mood to chatter; and since I needed him I let him talk. As he related his affair with this girl, he informed me that since the room she occupies is only separated from her mistress's by a thin partition, which might allow a suspicious noise to be heard, they came together each night in his room. Immediately I formed my plan, communicated it to him, and we carried it out with success.

I waited until two o'clock in the morning; then, as we had agreed I went to the room where their meeting took place, carrying a light with me under the pretext that I had rung several times without getting an answer. My confidant, who plays his parts perfectly, gave a little scene of surprise, despair and excuses which I closed by sending him to heat me some water I feigned to need; while the scrupulous chamber-maid was the more shamefaced because the rascal, who had wanted to improve upon my plan, had persuaded her to a lack of costume which the season admitted of but did not excuse.

Since I felt that the more this girl was humiliated the more easily I could make use of her, I did not allow her to alter either her posture or her dress; and after I had bade my valet wait for me in my room, I sat down beside her on the bed which was in great disorder and began my conversation. I needed to preserve all the domination over her which the occasion gave me; I therefore maintained a calm which would have done honour to the continence of Scipio; and without taking the slightest liberty with her, which her freshness and the opportunity appeared to give her a right to hope for, I talked to her about business as calmly as I could have done with a solicitor.

My conditions were that I would faithfully keep her secret provided that the next day at about the same hour she would submit to me her mistress's pockets. "Moreover," I added, "I offered you ten louis yesterday; I promise them to you again today. I do not wish to abuse your situation." Everything was granted, as you may believe; then I retired and permitted the happy couple to make up for lost time.

[1] Piron, *Métromanie*. (C. de L.)

I spent my own time in sleeping; and on awaking, since I wished to have an excuse for not replying to my fair one's letter before I had gone through her papers (which I could not do until the following night), I decided to go shooting, where I remained almost all day.

At my return I was received rather coldly. I have reason to think that she was a little piqued by my lack of anxiety to make use of the time which remained; especially after the kinder letter she had written me. I suppose this, because when Madame de Rosemonde reproached me a little for this long absence, my fair one replied rather tartly: "Ah! Do not let us reproach Monsieur de Valmont for giving himself up to the sole pleasure he can find here." I complained of this injustice, and I made use of it to assert that I enjoyed the company of these ladies so much I sacrificed to it a very interesting letter I had to write. I added that, not having been able to sleep for several nights, I had wished to try whether weariness would give it me; and my looks explained sufficiently both the subject of my letter and the cause of my insomnia. I was careful to be gently melancholy all evening which seemed to me to succeed quite well; and under this I hid the impatience I was in for the arrival of the hour which would yield me the secret she persisted in hiding from me. At last we separated and some time after the faithful waiting-woman came to bring me the price agreed upon for my discretion.

Once master of this treasure, I proceeded to go through it with my accustomed prudence; for it was important to put everything in its place. I came first of all upon two letters from the husband, a confused mixture of law-suit details and tirades of conjugal love, which I had the patience to read right through without finding a word referring to myself. I put them back with annoyance; but this was mollified by my finding under my hand the pieces of my famous letter from Dijon carefully put together. Fortunately I took it into my head to run over it. Imagine my joy at perceiving very distinct traces of my adorable devotee's tears! I confess it, I yielded to the sentiment of a young man, and kissed this letter with a rapture of which I thought myself incapable. I continued my happy search; I found all my letters arranged in the order of their date; and what surprised me still more agreeably, was to find the first of all, which I thought had been returned to me by an ingrate, faithfully copied by her hand and in a changed trembling handwriting which sufficiently showed the soft agitation of her heart during this occupation.

Up till then I was entirely given over to love; but soon it gave place to fury. Who do you think it is tries to ruin me with the woman I adore? What fury do you suppose is so malicious as to contrive such a perfidy? You know her; she is your friend, your relative; it is Madame de Volanges. You cannot imagine what a tissue of horrors that infernal shrew has written her about me. It is she and she alone who has disturbed the confidence of this angelic woman; it is by her designs, her pernicious warnings, that I am forced to go away; it is to her I am sacrificed. Ah! Her daughter must certainly be seduced, but that is not enough, I must ruin her; and since the age of this accursed woman protects her from my attacks, I must strike her through the object of her affection.

She wishes me to return to Paris! She forces me to do so. So be it, I will return, but she shall groan for my return. I am sorry Danceny is the hero of this adventure; he has a foundation of virtue which will impede us; however he is in love and I often see him; perhaps some use can be made of this. But I am forgetting myself in my anger and that I owe you an account of what happened today. Let us go back to it.

This morning I saw my delicate prude. Never had I thought her so beautiful. That was inevitable: a woman's fairest moment, the only one in which she can produce that intoxication of the soul, which is always talked of and so rarely experienced, is the moment when we are certain of her love but not of her favours; and that is precisely the position in which I am. Perhaps also the idea that I was about to be deprived of the pleasure of seeing her served to embellish her. At length, when the post arrived I was handed your letter of the twenty-seventh; and while I read it I still hesitated as to whether I should keep my word; but I met my fair one's eyes and it would have been impossible for me to refuse her anything.

I therefore announced my departure. A minute later Madame de Rosemonde left us alone; but I was still four paces from the timid person when she rose with an air of terror, saying: "Leave me, leave me, Monsieur, in the name of God, leave me." This fervent prayer which revealed her emotion could not but animate me the more. Already I was beside her, I held her hand which she clasped in a most touching way; I was beginning a series of tender complaints when some hostile demon brought back Madame de Rosemonde. The timid devotee, who indeed had some reason to be fearful, took advantage of it and retired.

Nevertheless, I offered her my hand and she accepted it; and auguring well from this mildness, which she had not showed me for a long time, I attempted to press her hand as I recommenced my complaints. First of all she tried to withdraw it; but at my warmer entreaty she yielded with a comparatively good grace, but without replying either to this gesture or to my speeches. When we reached the door of her apartment I tried to kiss her hand before leaving her. The defence was at first thorough; but a "remember I am going" spoken very tenderly made it awkward and inadequate. Scarcely was the kiss given when the hand recovered enough strength to escape and the fair one entered her apartment, where her waiting-woman was. Here ends my story.

Since I presume you will be at the house of the Maréchale de . . . tomorrow, where assuredly I shall not go to find you; since I suppose also that at our first interview we shall have more than one matter to discuss, notably that of the Volanges girl which I have not lost sight of;

I am sending this letter on ahead of me, and long as it is, I shall only close it at the moment it goes to post; but in my present condition everything may depend upon an opportunity; and I leave you, to go and watch for it.

P.S. Eight o'clock in the evening.

Nothing new; not the smallest moment of freedom; care even to avoid it. However, as much sadness as decency permitted, at least. Another event which cannot be unimportant, is that I am entrusted with an invitation from Madame de Rosemonde to Madame de Volanges to come and spend some time with her in the country.

Good-bye, my fair friend; tomorrow or the day after at latest.

From . . ., 28th of August, 17—.

## LETTER XLV

*Madame de Tourvel to Madame de Volanges*

Monsieur de Valmont left this morning, Madame; you seemed to desire this departure so much that I felt I ought to inform you. Madame de Rosemonde misses her nephew very much and it must be admitted that his society is agreeable; she passed the whole morning talking to me with her accustomed sensibility; she never ceased praising him. I felt I owed her the gratification of listening without contradicting her, the more so since it must be admitted she is right in many respects. I felt moreover that I had to reproach myself with being the cause of the separation and I do not hope to be able to make up to her for the pleasure of which I have deprived her. You know I am not naturally gay and the kind of life we shall lead here will not increase my gaiety.

If I had not been led by your advice, I should fear I had acted somewhat inconsiderately; for I was really hurt by the grief of my respectable friend; it touched me so much that I would gladly have mingled my tears with hers.

We now live in the hope that you will accept the invitation which Monsieur de Valmont brings you from Madame de Rosemonde, to come and spend some time with her. I hope you have no doubt of the pleasure I shall have in seeing you again; and indeed you owe us this compensation. I shall be very happy to have this opportunity of making an earlier acquaintance with Mademoiselle de Volanges and of being in a position to convince you more and more of my respectful sentiments, etc.

From . . ., 29th of August, 17—.

## LETTER XLVI

*The Chevalier Danceny to Cécile Volanges*

What has happened to you, my adorable Cécile? What can have caused so sudden and so cruel a change in you? What has become of your vows that you would never change? But yesterday, you repeated them with so much pleasure! What can have made you forget them today? However much I scrutinise myself I cannot find the cause in me and it is dreadful to me to have to look for it in you. Ah! You cannot be either fickle or deceitful; and even in this moment of despair my soul shall not be withered by an insulting suspicion. And yet by what fatality is it that you are no longer the same? No, cruel one, you are no longer the same! The tender Cécile, the Cécile I adore, whose vows I have received, would not have avoided my glances, would not have thwarted the lucky chance which placed me beside her; or if some reason which I cannot conceive had forced her to treat me so harshly she would at least not have disdained to tell me of it.

Ah! You do not know, you will never know, my Cécile, how much you have made me suffer today, how much I suffer at this moment. Do you think I can live if I am not loved by you? And yet, when I begged a word from you, one word, to dissipate my fears, instead of replying you pretended a fear that we should be overheard; and you created that obstacle, which up till then did not exist, by the place you chose in the company. When forced to leave you I asked you at what hour I might see you tomorrow, and you feigned not to know, so that Madame de Volanges had to tell me. And so the moment I always desire so much, the moment which brings me back to you, tomorrow will create nothing but uneasiness for me; and the pleasure of seeing you, hitherto so dear to my heart, will be replaced by the fear of being wearisome to you.

Already this fear checks me, I feel it, and I dare not speak to you of my love. That "I love you" which I delighted to repeat when I could hear it in my turn, that sweet phrase which sufficed for my felicity, now offers me, if you are changed, nothing but the image of an eternal despair. Yet I cannot believe that this talisman of love has lost all its power and I still attempt to use it.[1] Yes, my Cécile, I love you. Repeat with me that expression of my happiness, remember that you have accustomed me to hear it and that by depriving me of it you condemn me to a torment which, like my love, will end only with my life.

From . . ., 29th of August, 17—.

## LETTER XLVII

*The Vicomte de Valmont to the Marquise de Merteuil*

I shall not be able to see you today, my fair friend, for the following reasons which I beg you to accept with indulgence.

Instead of returning directly yesterday I stopped with the Comtesse de . . ., whose Château was almost on my road, and from whom I asked a dinner. I did not reach Paris until seven o'clock and I went to the Opera where I hoped I might find you.

[1] Those who have never had occasion to feel sometimes the value of a word, of an expression, consecrated by love, will find no sense in this phrase. (C. de L.)

After the Opera I went to see my ladies of the green-room; there I found my former love, Emilie, surrounded by a retinue of admirers, women as well as men, whom she had invited to supper that evening at P . . . I had no sooner entered the circle than I was invited to the supper by general acclamation. I was also invited by a short, fat, little creature who jabbered an invitation in Dutch French, whom I perceived to be the true hero of the feast. I accepted.

I learned on the way that the house to which we were going was the price agreed upon for Emilie's favours to this grotesque creature and that the supper was a positive wedding-feast. The little man could not contain himself with joy in expectation of the happiness he was about to receive; he seemed to me to feel so much satisfaction that he made me wish to disturb it; which I did accordingly.

The only difficulty I met with was in persuading Emilie who was made a little scrupulous by the Burgomaster's wealth. However, after some demurring, she consented to my plan, which was to fill up this little beer-tub with wine and thus put him out of action for the whole night.

The sublime conception we had of a Dutch drinker caused us to employ all the known methods. We succeeded so well that at dessert he had not even the strength to hold his glass; but the charitable Emilie and I vied with each other in filling him up. At last he fell under the table in such a state of intoxication that it will last at least a week. We then decided to send him back to Paris; and since he had not kept his carriage I had him put into mine and remained in his place. I then received the congratulations of the company who retired soon after, leaving me master of the battlefield. This freak, and possibly my long retirement, made me think Emilie so desirable that I have promised to remain with her until the Dutchman's resurrection.

This complaisance on my part is the reward for one she has just granted me, that of acting as a desk for me to write to my fair devotee; I thought it amusing to send her a letter written from the bed and almost in the arms of a girl, interrupted even for a complete infidelity, in which letter I give her an exact description of my situation and my conduct. Emilie, to whom I read the epistle, laughed extravagantly, and I hope you too will laugh.

Since my letter must have the Paris postmark I am sending it to you; I have left it open. Be good enough to read it, to seal it, and to send it to the post. Be careful not to use your own seal nor any amorous emblem, simply a head. Good-bye, my fair friend.

P.S. I re-open my letter; I have persuaded Emilie to go to the Italiens. . . . I shall make use of this time to come to see you. I shall be with you at six o'clock at the latest; and if it suits you, we will go together to Madame de Volanges at seven. It will be decent not to delay the invitation I have to give her from Madame de Rosemonde; moreover I shall be very glad to see the Volanges girl. Good-bye, most fair lady. I hope to have so much pleasure in embracing you that the Chevalier may be jealous of it !

From P . . ., 30th August, 17—.

## LETTER XLVIII

*The Vicomte de Valmont to Madame de Tourvel*
(Postmark of Paris)

After a restless night, during which I have not closed my eyes ; after having been ceaselessly either in the agitation of a devouring ardour or in the complete annihilation of all the faculties of my soul ; I seek from you, Madame, the calm I need but do not hope to enjoy yet. Indeed the position I am in as I write to you makes me understand more than ever the irresistible power of love ; I can scarcely preserve sufficient control over myself to put my ideas into some order ; and already I perceive that I shall not finish this letter without being forced to interrupt it. Ah ! May I not hope that some day you will share the perturbation I feel at this moment ? Yet I dare to think that if you really knew it you would not be entirely insensible to it. Believe me, Madame, cold tranquillity, the soul's sleep, the image of death, do not lead to happiness ; only the active passions can lead to it ; and, in spite of the torments you make me endure, I think I may boldly assure you that at this moment I am happier than you. In vain do you overwhelm me with your discouraging severities ; they do not prevent me from abandoning myself wholly to love and from forgetting in the delirium it causes me the despair to which you surrender me. It is thus I mean to avenge myself for the exile to which you condemn me. Never did I have so much pleasure in writing to you ; never in that occupation did I feel so soft and yet so keen an emotion. Everything seems to increase my raptures ; the air I breathe is filled with voluptuousness ; the very table upon which I write to you, which for the first time is devoted to that use, becomes for me the sacred altar of love ; how much it will be embellished in my eyes ! I shall have traced upon it the vow to love you forever ! I beg you to pardon the disorder of my senses. Perhaps I ought to abandon myself less to raptures you do not share ; I must leave you a moment to dispel an ecstasy which increases every instant, which becomes stronger than I am.

I return to you, Madame, and without doubt I shall always return with the same eagerness. Yet the feeling of happiness has fled far from me ; it has given place to that of cruel privations. Of what use is it for me to speak to you of my sentiments if I seek vainly the means to convince you ? After so many repeated efforts, confidence and strength abandon me together. If I recall once more the pleasures of love it is but to feel more keenly the regret at being deprived of them. I see no resource save in your indulgence and at this moment I feel but too well how much I need that indulgence to hope to obtain it. However, never was my love more respectful, never ought it to offend you less; it is such, I dare to say, that the most austere virtue need not fear it; but I fear myself that I am occupying you too long with the distress I feel. Although I know that the object which causes it does not share that distress, I must not abuse its favours; and it would be doing so to employ more time in recalling this painful image to you. I shall only beg you to reply to me and never to doubt the truth of my sentiments.

Written from P . . ., dated from Paris, 30th of August, 17—.

## LETTER XLIX

*Cécile Volanges to the Chevalier Danceny*

Without being either fickle or deceitful, Monsieur, it is sufficient for me to be enlightened as to my conduct, to feel the necessity of altering it; I have promised this sacrifice to God, until I can offer Him also that of my sentiments to you which your religious condition renders still more criminal. I feel indeed that this will give me great pain and I will not hide from you the fact that since the day before yesterday I have cried every time I have thought of you. But I hope that God will grant me the grace of sufficient strength to forget you, as I pray Him morning and evening. I expect from your friendship and from your honour that you will not seek to disturb me in the good resolution which has been inspired in me and in which I am trying to remain. Consequently I beg you will be kind enough to write to me no more, especially as I warn you that I shall not answer you again and that you would force me to inform Mamma of all that has happened; which would entirely deprive me of the pleasure of seeing you.

None the less I still have all the attachment for you that may be without there being anything wrong in it; and it is indeed with all my soul that I wish you every kind of happiness. I feel that you will not love me so much now and that perhaps you will soon love another more than me. But that will be one penance the more for the fault I have committed by giving you my heart, which I ought to give only to God and to my husband, when I have one. I hope that the divine mercy will have pity on my weakness and send me no grief that I cannot endure.

Farewell, Monsieur; I can assure you that if I were permitted to love anyone I should never love anybody but you. But that is all I can say to you and perhaps even that is more than I should say.

From . . ., 31st of August, 17—.

## LETTER L

*Madame de Tourvel to the Vicomte de Valmont*

Is it thus, Monsieur, that you carry out the conditions under which I have consented sometimes to receive your letters? And can I "have no reason to complain" when you speak to me of nothing but a sentiment to which I should fear to yield myself even if I could do so without failing in all my duties ?

Moreover, did I need fresh reasons for retaining this salutary fear, it seems to me that I could find them in your last letter. Indeed, at the very moment when you seem to make love's apology, what do you do but show its dreadful storms ? Who can wish for happiness that is bought at the price of reason, whose fleeting pleasures are at least followed by regret, if not remorse ?

And you, upon whom the effect of this dangerous delirium must be lessened by habit, are yet obliged to admit that it often becomes stronger than you ; and are you not the first to complain of the involuntary distress it causes you ? What fearful ravages would it not make upon a fresh and sensitive heart, which would yet increase its power by the extent of the sacrifices such a heart would be compelled to make it ?

You believe, Monsieur, or you feign to believe, that love leads to happiness ; and I am so convinced it would render me unhappy that I wish never to hear its name mentioned. It seems to me that one's tranquillity is disturbed merely by speaking of it ; and it is as much from choice as from a sense of duty that I beg you to keep silent upon this point.

After all, this request must now be very easy for you to grant me. Now you are back in Paris you will find plenty of opportunities to forget a sentiment whose origin was perhaps only due to your habit of occupying yourself with such objects, and whose strength was merely due to the inactivity of the country. Are you not in the very place where you formerly saw me with so much indifference ? Can you make a step without meeting an instance of your facility in changing ? And are you not surrounded by women who are all more amiable than I and have more rights to your homage ? I do not possess the vanity of which my sex is accused ; still less have I that false modesty which is only a refinement of pride ; and it is in good faith that I tell you I know I have very few means of pleasing ; did I possess them all, I should not think them sufficient to secure your constancy. To request you to concern yourself with me no more is therefore only to beg you to do today what you have already done and what you will surely do again in a little time, even if I should beg you to do the contrary.

This truth, which I do not lose sight of, would of itself be a sufficiently strong reason for my not wishing to listen to you. I have a thousand other ; but without entering upon a long discussion I limit myself to asking you (as I have done already) to occupy me no longer with a sentiment I ought not to listen to and to which I ought still less to respond.

From . . ., 1st of September, 17—.

## END OF PART ONE

# PART II

## LETTER LI

*The Marquise de Merteuil to the Vicomte de Valmont*

Really, Vicomte, you are insupportable. You treat me as carelessly as if I were your mistress. Do you know, I shall grow angry, and that I am now in a frightful temper? What! You are to see Danceny tomorrow morning; you know how important it is that I should speak to you before this interview; and without troubling yourself any further, you let me wait for you all day long and run off I know not where. Owing to you I was *indecently* late in reaching Madame de Volanges's and all the old women said I was *wonderful*. I had to flatter them the whole evening to appease them; for old women must not be angered—they make young women's reputations.

It is now one o'clock in the morning and instead of going to bed, as I am dying to do, I must write you a long letter which will increase my drowsiness by the boredom it will cause me. It is very lucky for you that I have no time to scold you more. And do not let that make you believe I have forgiven you; I am simply in a hurry. Now listen to me; I must hurry.

If you are at all skilful, you ought to secure Danceny's confidence tomorrow. This is a favourable moment for confidence; he is unhappy. The little girl has been to confession; she told everything, like a child; and since then she has been so tormented by fear of the devil that she wishes to break off altogether. She told me all her little scruples with a vehemence which showed me how excited she was. She let me see the letter breaking things off, and it is a positive sermon. She prattled a whole hour to me without speaking one word of common sense. None the less she embarrassed me; for as you may suppose I could not risk confiding myself to such a reckless creature.

Nevertheless, I saw through all her chatter that she does not love Danceny any the less; I even noticed one of those expedients (which never fail in love), by which the little girl rather amusingly deceives herself. Tormented by the desire to think about her lover and by the fear of damning herself by thinking about him, she has devised the plan of praying God to make her forget him; and since she renews this prayer at every moment of the day she finds a way of constantly thinking about him.

With someone more *accustomed* than Danceny this little event might perhaps be more favourable than hurtful; but the young man is such a Céladon that, if we do not help him, he will take so much time in overcoming the slightest obstacles that he will not leave us enough to carry out our plan.

You are quite right; it is a pity, and I am as annoyed about it as you, that he should be the hero of this adventure. But what would you have? What is done is done; and it is your fault. I asked to see his reply;[1] it was pitiful. He argued with her interminably to prove that an involuntary sentiment cannot be a crime; as if it did not cease to be involuntary, the moment one ceases to oppose it! It is such a simple idea that it even occurred to the little girl. He complains of his unhappiness in a rather touching way; but his grief is so gentle and seems so great and so sincere that I think it is impossible that a woman who has the opportunity to distress a man to this extent, with so little danger, should not be tempted to gratify the whim. Finally he explains he is not a monk as the little girl believed and undoubtedly this is what he does the best; for, if one went so far as to yield to monastic love, the Knights of Malta would certainly not deserve the preference.

In any case, instead of wasting my time in arguments which would have compromised me and perhaps not have persuaded her, I approved the plan of breaking things off; but I said that in such a case it was more polite to explain one's reasons than to write them, that it was also the custom to return the letters and any other trifles one might have received; and thus appearing to agree with the little creature's ideas I decided her to grant Danceny an interview. We made the arrangements there and then and I undertook to persuade the mother to go out without her daughter; tomorrow afternoon will be the decisive instant. Danceny is already informed; but, for God's sake, if you find an opportunity, persuade this fair shepherd to be a little less languishing; and inform him, since he must be told everything, that the real way of vanquishing scruples is to leave those who have them nothing to lose.

In addition, to prevent a repetition of this ridiculous scene, I did not omit to raise some doubts in the little girl's mind concerning the discretion of confessors; and I can assure you she is now atoning for the fright she gave me by her own fright lest her confessor should tell her mother everything. I hope that when I have talked with her once or twice she will cease telling all her follies to the first person who comes along.[2]

Farewell, Vicomte; gain possession of Danceny and direct him. It would be shameful if we could not do what we chose with two children. If we find it more difficult than we had thought at first, you must stimulate your zeal by remembering that she is Madame de Volanges's daughter; and I, that she is to become Gercourt's wife. Good-bye.

From . . ., 2nd of September, 17—.

[1] This letter could not be found. (C. de L.)

[2] The reader must long have guessed from Mme de Merteuil's morals, how little she respected religion. This whole paragraph would have been suppressed, but it was felt that in showing effects one should not fail to make known the causes. (C. de L.)

## LETTER LII

*The Vicomte de Valmont to Madame de Tourvel*

You forbid me, Madame, to speak to you of my love ; but where shall I find the courage requisite to obey you ? Occupied solely by a sentiment which should be so soft and which you render so cruel ; languishing in the exile to which you have condemned me ; living only upon privations and regrets ; a prey to torments, the more painful in that they continually remind me of your indifference ; must I be compelled to lose the one consolation that is left me, and can I have any other than sometimes to open to you a soul which you fill with distress and bitterness ? Will you avert your gaze, in order not to see the tears which are shed owing to you ? Will you refuse even the homage of the sacrifices you exact ? Would it not be more worthy of you, more worthy of your virtuous and gentle soul, to pity a wretch who is only such because of you, than to wish to aggravate his sufferings still more by a prohibition which is both unjust and harsh ?

You pretend to fear love and you will not see that you alone cause the evils of which you accuse it. Ah ! No doubt, this is a painful sentiment when the person who inspires it does not share it ; but where shall happiness be found if a reciprocal love does not procure it ? Tender friendship, a soft confidence, the only confidence which is without reserve, softened griefs, augmented pleasures, enchanted hope, delicious memories—where shall they be found save in love ? You calumniate love, you who need but to cease to withstand it in order to enjoy all the good it offers you ; and I forget the grief I feel, to undertake its defence.

You force me to defend myself as well ; for while I consecrate my life to adoring you, you spend yours in finding fault with me ; you already suppose me fickle and deceitful ; and by a misuse of certain of my faults—which I myself confessed to you—you take pleasure in confounding what I once was with what I now am. Not content with having abandoned me to the torment of living far from you, you add to it a cruel persiflage about pleasures to which you know how completely you have rendered me insensible. You believe neither my promises nor my vows ; well, I have one guarantee to offer you which you at least will not suspect ; it is yourself. I only ask you to question yourself in good faith ; if you do not believe in my love, if you doubt one moment that you alone reign over my soul, if you are not certain that you have attached this heart, which indeed has hitherto been but too fickle, I consent to bear the pain of this error ; I shall groan for it, but I shall not appeal ; but if on the contrary, doing justice to us both, you are forced to admit to yourself that you have not, that you will never, have a rival, do not force me, I beg you, to struggle with idle fancies, and at least leave me the consolation of seeing you no longer doubt a sentiment which will, which can only, end with my life. Allow me, Madame, to beg you to reply positively to this part of my letter.

Yet if I abandon that period of my life which seems to harm me so cruelly in your eyes, it is not because I lack reasons to defend it, if needed.

After all, what have I done except not to resist the whirlpool into which I was thrown ? Entering the world young and without experience; passed, as it were, from hand to hand by a crowd of women who all hastened to anticipate by their facility a reflection which they felt must be unfavourable to them ; was it for me to show the example of a resistance which was not opposed to me ? Or should I have punished myself for a momentary error which was often provoked, by a useless constancy which would have only appeared ridiculous ? Ah ! What save a quick breaking off can justify a shameful choice !

But, I can assert, that intoxication of the senses, perhaps even that delirium of vanity, never reached my heart. Born for love, it might be distracted by intrigue but could not be occupied by intrigue ; surrounded with seductive but contemptible objects, my soul was reached by none of them ; pleasures were offered me, I sought virtues ; and at last I myself believed I was inconstant only because I was delicate and sensitive.

When I saw you I was enlightened ; I soon recognised that the charm of love was derived from the qualities of the soul ; that they alone could cause its excess and justify it. I felt that it was equally impossible for me not to love you and to love any other but you.

Such, Madame, is the heart to which you fear to confide yourself, upon whose fate you have to pass sentence ; but whatever may be the destiny you reserve for it, you will change nothing in the sentiments which attach it to you ; they are as unalterable as the virtues which gave birth to them.

From . . ., 3rd of September, 17—.

## LETTER LIII

*The Vicomte de Valmont to the Marquise de Merteuil*

I have seen Danceny, but I have only obtained a half-confidence ; he was especially obstinate in concealing the name of the Volanges girl, whom he only spoke of as a very modest woman who was rather pious ; except for that he told me his story and especially the last episode fairly accurately. I inflamed him as much as I could and bantered him on his delicacy and scruples ; but he appears to set a value upon them and I cannot answer for him ; but I shall be able to tell you more after tomorrow. Tomorrow I am taking him to Versailles and on the way I shall occupy myself by investigating him.

The meeting which was to take place today also gave me some hope ; it may be that everything went off as we should desire ; and perhaps all we have to do now is to wrench an admission of it and to assemble proofs. This will be an easier task for you than for me; for the little girl is more confiding or, which comes to the same thing, more of a chatterer, than her discreet lover. However, I will do my best.

Good-bye, my fair friend, I am in a great hurry; I shall not see you tonight nor tomorrow; if you learn anything on your part write me a note for my return. I intend to sleep in Paris.

From . . ., 3rd of September, 17—. In the evening.

## LETTER LIV

*The Marquise de Merteuil to the Vicomte de Valmont*

O yes! Indeed it is from Danceny that something is to be learned! If he told you anything, he was boasting. I never knew such a fool in matters of love and more and more I regret our kindness to him. Do you know I was afraid I should be compromised on account of him! And that it was in pure waste! Oh! I shall be revenged, I promise him.

When I arrived yesterday for Madame de Volanges she did not want to go out; she felt unwell; it needed all my eloquence to persuade her and I saw Danceny arriving before we could get away, which would have been the more awkward because Madame de Volanges had told him the night before she would not be at home. Her daughter and I were on thorns. At last we went; and the little girl pressed my hand so affectionately as we said good-bye that, in spite of her determination to break off—which she really believed she meant to do—I augured wonders from the evening.

I was not at the end of my apprehensions. We had scarcely been half an hour with Madame . . . when Madame de Volanges felt ill, seriously ill; and reasonably enough she wanted to go home, which I quite as much did not want, because I was afraid if we surprised the young people (as you might have wagered we should) that my entreaties to the mother to come out might appear suspicious. I adopted the plan of frightening her about her health, which fortunately is not difficult; and I kept her an hour and a half without consenting to take her home, from the fear I pretended to have that the motion of the carriage would be dangerous. We did not get back finally until the time agreed upon. From the shamefaced air I observed on arriving, I must admit I hoped that at least my trouble had not been wasted.

My desire to learn what had happened made me remain with Madame de Volanges, who went to bed immediately; and after having taken supper at her bedside, we left her very soon, under the pretext that she needed rest; and we went into her daughter's room. She on her part had done everything I expected of her; banished scruples, new vows to love forever, etc., etc., in short she carried things out well; but the fool Danceny did not pass one inch beyond the point he was at before. Oh! He is a person one can quarrel with; reconciliations are not dangerous with him!

However, the little girl asserts that he wanted more, but that she was able to defend herself. I would wager that she is boasting or making an excuse; I practically made sure of it. In fact, the fancy came to me to find out what kind of a defence she was capable of. And I, a mere woman, from one remark to another, excited her to a degree. In short, you may believe me, never was a person so liable to an attack on the senses. She is really delightful, dear little thing! She deserves another lover! At least she will have a good woman friend, for I am sincerely attached to her. I have promised her I will train her, and I believe I shall keep my word. I have often felt the need of having a woman in my confidence, and I should prefer her to any other; but I can do nothing with her until she is . . . what she must be; and that is one more reason for being angry with Danceny.

Good-bye, Vicomte; do not call on me tomorrow, unless in the morning. I have yielded to the entreaties of the Chevalier for an evening in my little house.[1]

From . . ., 4th of September, 17—.

## LETTER LV

*Cécile Volanges to Sophie Carnay*

You are right, my dear Sophie, your prophecies are more successfu than your advice. As you predicted, Danceny has been stronger than the confessor, than you, than myself; we are now exactly as we were. Ah! I do not regret it; and if you scold me, it will be because you do not know the pleasure there is in loving Danceny. It is very easy for you to say what I ought to do, there is nothing to prevent you; but if you had felt how much it hurts to see the grief of a person one loves, how his joy becomes yours, and how difficult it is to say *No* when you want to say *Yes*, you would not be surprised at anything; I felt it myself, I felt it very keenly, I do not yet understand it. Do you suppose I can see Danceny cry without crying myself? I assure you it is impossible for me; and when he is pleased, I am as happy as he is. You may talk as you like; what we say does not change what is, and I am quite sure that this is how it is.

I should like to see you in my place. . . . No, that is not what I mean, for I certainly would not yield my place to anyone, but I should like you to love someone as well; it is not only because you would understand me better and would scold me less, but because you would be happier or, to speak more accurately, you would only then begin to be happy.

Our amusements, our laughter, all of it, you see were only child's-play; when they are gone they leave nothing behind. But love, ah! love. . . . A word, a look, only to know that he is there, that is happiness. When I see Danceny I want nothing else; when I do not see him I want nothing but him. I do not know how it happens; but it is as if

[1] "Petite maison."

everything that pleases me is like him. When he is not with me I think about him ; and when I can think about him completely, without being distracted, when I am quite alone for instance, I am still happy ; I close my eyes and immediately I think I see him ; I remember what he said ; and I think I hear him ; that makes me sigh ; and then I feel a fire, an agitation. . . . I cannot keep still. It is like torture and the torture is an inexpressible pleasure.

I even think that when one is in love once it extends to friendship as well. Yet my friendship for you is not changed ; it is just as it was at the convent ; but the friendship I am speaking about I feel for Madame de Merteuil. It seems to me that I love her more like Danceny than like you, and sometimes I wish she were he. Perhaps the reason for it is that this is not a childish friendship like ours ; or perhaps because I see them so often together, which makes me mistake one for the other. In any case, the truth is that between them they make me very happy ; and after all I do not think there is anything very wrong in what I am doing. So I ask nothing more than to go on as I am ; and the only thing that troubles me is the idea of my marriage ; for if Monsieur de Gercourt is like what I am told he is—and I have no doubt of it—I do not know what will become of me. Good-bye, dear Sophie ; I still love you very tenderly.

From . . ., 4th of September, 17—.

## LETTER LVI

*Madame de Tourvel to the Vicomte de Valmont*

How could the reply you ask from me, Monsieur, be of service to you ? If I believed in your sentiments would that not be still another reason to fear them ? And without attacking or defending their sincerity, does it not suffice me, and should it not suffice you, to know that I neither wish nor ought to reply to them ?

Suppose you really loved me (and it is only to have done with the matter, that I entertain the supposition) would the obstacles which separate us be any the more surmountable ? And should I have anything to do save to wish that you might speedily conquer this love, and above all to aid you to do so to the best of my power by hastening to deprive you of all hope ? You admit yourself that " this is a painful sentiment when the person who inspires it does not share it." Well, you are quite aware that it is impossible for me to share it ; and even if this misfortune happened to me I should be the more to be pitied without your being the happier. I hope you respect me enough not to doubt it for an instant. Desist then, I beg you, desist from attempting to trouble a heart to which tranquillity is so necessary ; do not compel me to regret having known you.

Cherished and respected by a husband whom I love and respect, my duty and my pleasure meet in the same person ; I am happy, I ought to be so. If keener pleasures exist, I do not desire them ; I do not wish to experience them. Is there anything better than to be at peace with oneself, to spend none but tranquil days, to fall asleep without uneasiness and to wake without remorse? What you call happiness is a mere tumult of the senses, a storm of passion, the sight of which is terrifying even looked at from the shore. Ah! How can one dare these tempests? How dare to embark upon a sea covered with the remains of thousands and thousands of shipwrecks? And with whom? No, Monsieur, I shall remain on land; I cherish the bonds which attach me to it. Even if I could break them, I should not wish to do so; if I did not possess them, I should hasten to acquire them.

Why do you attach yourself to my steps? Why do you persist in following me? Your letters, which should be occasional, follow each other with rapidity. They ought to be sober, and you speak to me of nothing but your mad love. You surround me with the idea of you, more than you did in person. Separated from me in one shape, you reappear in another way. You enjoy embarrassing me by specious reasoning; you elude my own. I do not wish to reply to you again, I shall not reply again. . . . How you treat the women you have seduced! With what contempt you speak of them! I am willing to believe that some deserve it; but are all so contemptible? Ah! Doubtless they are, since they betrayed their duty to yield to a criminal love. And that moment they lost everything, even to the respect of him for whom they sacrificed everything. It is a just punishment, but the very idea makes me shudder. But after all what does it matter to me? Why should I concern myself with them or with you? By what right do you trouble my tranquillity? Leave me, do not see me again; write to me no more, I beg you; I insist on it. This letter is the last you will receive from me.

From . . ., 5th of September, 17—.

## LETTER LVII

*The Vicomte de Valmont to the Marquise de Merteuil*

I found your letter yesterday on my arrival. Your anger altogether delighted me. You could not have felt Danceny's mistakes more keenly if they had been directed towards yourself. No doubt it is from vengeance that you are accustoming his mistress to make little infidelities; indeed you are incorrigible! Yes, you are charming and I am not surprised she could resist you less easily than Danceny.

At last I know that fine novel-hero by heart! He has no more secrets! I have told him so often that virtuous love was the supreme good, that one sentiment was worth ten intrigues, that I am myself at the moment both in love and timid—in short he found my way of thinking so conformable to his own that in his enchantment at my candour he told me everything and vowed to me an unreserved friendship. This does not help us on with our plan. First of all, it appeared to me his idea was that an unmarried girl deserves much more deference than a woman, since she has more to lose. He thinks especially that a man cannot be justified in placing a girl in the necessity of marrying him or living dishonoured, when the girl is infinitely richer than the man, as she is in his case. The mother's confidence, the girl's candour, everything intimidates and restrains him. The difficulty would not be to combat his reasonings, however true they may be. With a little skill and the help of passion, they could soon be destroyed ; the more so, since they lend themselves to ridicule and the authority of custom is on our side. But what prevents my having any influence over him, is that he is happy as he is. Indeed, if first loves appear in general more virtuous and, as they say, more chaste ; if they are at least slower in their progress ; it is not, as people think, from delicacy or timidity, but because the heart, surprised by an unknown sentiment, hesitates as it were at every step to enjoy the charm it feels, and because this charm is so powerful upon a fresh heart that it forgets every other pleasure. This is so true, that a libertine in love —if a libertine can be in love—becomes at that very moment less eager to enjoy. In short there is only the difference of more and less between Danceny's conduct with the Volanges girl and mine with the chaste Madame de Tourvel.

To inflame our young man he needs more obstacles than he has met with. Above all he needs more mystery, for mystery leads to boldness. I am not far from thinking that you have harmed us by serving him so well ; your conduct would have been excellent with *an accustomed* man who would merely have had desires ; but you might have foreseen that to a young man, virtuous and in love, the great value of favours is that they are the proof of love ; and consequently that the more certain he was of being loved the less enterprising he would be. What is to be done now ? I do not know ; but I have ceased to hope that the little girl will be taken before her marriage ; we shall have had our trouble for nothing ; I am sorry, but I see no help for it.

While I am discoursing here, you are doing something better with your Chevalier. This reminds me that you have promised an infidelity in my favour ; I have your promise in writing and I do not mean to make it a *La Chârtre.*[1] I admit that it has not yet fallen due ; but it would be generous on your part not to wait until then ; and for my part I will account to you for the interest. What do you say to this, my fair friend ? Are you not wearied by your constancy ? Is this Chevalier so very wonderful ? Oh ! Let me do what I want ; I hope to compel you to admit that if you have found some merit in him, it is because you have forgotten me.

Good-bye, my fair friend ; I embrace you as I desire you ; I defy all the Chevalier's kisses to have as much ardour.

From . . ., 5th of September, 17—.

[1] This refers to an anecdote about Ninon de Lanclos. A man named La Chârtre was wildly in love with her, and had to go away. He made Ninon give him a written promise of fidelity. She was, of course, unfaithful and, suddenly recollecting her written promise in the arms of another lover, exclaimed " Ah ! What a promise La Chârtre has ! "

## LETTER LVIII

*The Vicomte de Valmont to Madame de Tourvel*

How have I deserved, Madame, the reproaches you make me and the anger you display towards me ? The liveliest but yet the most respectful attachment, the most complete submission to your slightest wishes ; there in two phrases is the history of my sentiments and of my conduct. Overwhelmed by the distress of an unhappy love, I had no consolation but that of seeing you ; you ordered me to deny myself that ; I obeyed without a murmur. As a reward for this sacrifice you gave me permission to write to you, and now you wish to deprive me of this one pleasure. Shall I let it be taken from me without attempting to defend it ? No, certainly not. Ah ! how could it fail to be dear to my heart ? It is the one thing which is left me, and I hold it from you.

My letters, you say, are too frequent ! Remember, I beg you, that during the ten days my exile has lasted I have not passed a moment without thinking of you, and yet you have only received two letters from me. " I speak to you of nothing but my love ! " Ah ! What am I to say, if not what I think ? All I could do was to weaken the expression of it ; and you can believe me, I only allowed you to see what it has been impossible for me to hide. You end up by threatening not to answer me again. And so you are not content with treating harshly a man who prefers you to all else and who respects you even more than he loves you ; you wish to add scorn to it ! And why these threats and this anger ? Why should you need them ? Are you not certain to be obeyed, even when your orders are unjust ? Is it possible for me to thwart any of your desires—have I not already given you a proof ? Will you abuse the power you have over me ? After you have rendered me unhappy, after you have become unjust, will it be so easy for you to enjoy that tranquillity which you assert is so necessary to you ? Will you never say to yourself : " He made me the mistress of his fate and I made him miserable ; he implored my aid and I watched him without pity." Do you know how far my despair may go ? No.

To calculate my misery, you would have to know how much I love you and you do not know my heart.

You are sacrificing me to what ? To imaginary fears. And who creates them in you ? A man who adores you, a trustworthy man over whom you will never cease to have complete power. What do you fear, what can you fear, from a sentiment which you will always be able to control as you please, but your imagination creates monsters for itself and you attribute the terror they cause you to love. A little confidence and these phantoms will disappear.

A wise man has said that fears can almost always be dissipated by discovering their cause.[1] This truth is especially applicable to love.

[1] It is thought that this is Rousseau in *Emile*, but the quotation is not exact and Valmont's application is a false one ; and then, had Madame de Tourvel read *Emile* ? (C. de L.)

Love, and your fears will vanish. Instead of the objects which terrify you, you will find a delicious sentiment, a tender and submissive lover; and all your days, impressed by happiness, will leave you no regret except that you have wasted some in indifference. Since I have recognised my errors, and exist only for love, I myself regret a time which I thought was passed in pleasures; and I feel that it is for you alone to make me happy. But, I beg you, do not let the pleasure I have in writing to you be disturbed by the fear of displeasing you. I do not wish to disobey you; but I am at your knees, I implore the happiness you would deprive me of, the only happiness you have left me; I cry to you, hear my prayers and see my tears; ah! Madame, will you refuse me?

From . . ., 7th of September, 17—.

## LETTER LIX

*The Vicomte de Valmont to the Marquise de Merteuil*

Tell me, if you know, what is meant by this raving of Danceny's? What has happened and what has he lost? Perhaps his fair one is annoyed by his eternal respect? One must be just; anybody would be annoyed by less. What shall I say to him this evening, at the meeting he asks of me, which I have given him at hazard? Assuredly I shall not waste my time in listening to his lamentations, if this is not to lead us anywhere. Amorous complaints are not good to listen to except in recitatives or in ariettas. Tell me what has happened and what I am to do; otherwise I shall desert, to avoid the boredom I foresee. Can I have a talk with you this morning? If you are *engaged*, at least write me a word and give me the cues for my part.

Where were you yesterday? I never succeed in seeing you now. Really, it was not worth keeping me in Paris in September. Make up your mind, for I have just received a very pressing invitation from the Comtesse de B . . . to go and see her in the country; and, as she writes me amusingly enough, "her husband has a splendid wood which he carefully preserves for the pleasures of his friends." Well, you know I have some rights over that wood; and I shall go and re-visit it if I am not useful to you. Good-bye, remember Danceny will be with me at four o'clock.

From . . ., 8th of September, 17—.

## LETTER LX

*The Chevalier Danceny to the Vicomte de Valmont*
(Enclosed with the preceding)

Ah! Monsieur, I am in despair, I have lost everything. I dare not confide to paper the secret of my distress; but I need to pour it out into the bosom of a faithful and trustworthy friend. At what hour can I see you and ask consolation and advice? I was so happy the day I opened my soul to you! And now what a difference! Everything has changed for me. What I suffer on my own account is the least part of my torture; my anxiety on behalf of a far dearer object is what I cannot endure. More fortunate than I, you can see her, and I expect of your friendship that you will not refuse me this step; but I must see you, I must tell you about it. You will pity me, you will help me; I have no hope but in you. You are sensitive, you know what love is, and you are the only person in whom I can confide; do not refuse me your assistance.

Farewell, Monsieur, the only consolation I feel in my grief is to remember I have a friend like you. Let me know, I beg you, at what hour I shall find you in. If it is not this morning, I should wish it to be early in the afternoon.

From . . ., 7th of September, 17—.

## LETTER LXI

*Cécile Volanges to Sophie Carnay*

My dear Sophie, pity your Cécile, your poor Cécile; she is very miserable. Mamma knows everything; I cannot conceive how she can have suspected anything and yet she has discovered everything. Yesterday evening, Mamma indeed seemed to me a little out of humour but I did not pay much attention to it; and while we waited for the end of her game, I even chatted very gaily with Madame de Merteuil who had supped here, and we talked much of Danceny. Yet I do not think we could have been overheard. She went away and I retired to my apartment.

I was undressing, when Mamma came in and sent my waiting-woman away; she asked me for the key of my writing-table, and the tone in which she made this demand caused me to shake so much that I could scarcely stand up. I pretended not to be able to find it; but at last I had to obey. The first drawer she opened was precisely that which contained the Chevalier Danceny's letters. I was so upset that when she asked me what they were, I could make no answer except that they were nothing; but when I saw her begin to read the first letter which came to hand I had only time to reach an armchair before I felt so ill that I lost consciousness. As soon as I came to myself, my mother, who had called my waiting-woman, told me to go to bed and left the room. She took all Danceny's letters with her. I shudder every time I think that I must appear before her again. I have done nothing but cry all night.

I am writing to you at dawn, in the hope that Josephine will come. If I can speak to her alone, I shall beg her to deliver a little note which I am going to write to Madame de Merteuil. If not, I shall put it into your letter and you will be kind enough to send it as if it were from you. She is the only person from whom I can receive any consolation. At least we will speak of him for I do not hope ever to see him again. I am very unhappy! Perhaps she will be kind enough to take charge of a letter for Danceny. I dare not confide in Josephine for this purpose, and still less in my waiting-woman; for perhaps it was she who told my mother I had letters in my writing-desk.

I shall not write to you at more length, because I want to have time to write to Madame de Merteuil, and also to Danceny in order to have my letter quite ready if she will take charge of it. After that I shall go to bed again so that they will find me there when they come to my room. I shall say I am ill to avoid going to see Mamma. It will not be much of a lie; indeed I suffer more than if I were feverish. My eyes burn from having cried so long, and I have a weight on my stomach which prevents me from breathing. When I think that I shall never see Danceny again, I wish I were dead. Good-bye, my dear Sophie. I cannot talk to you any further; I am suffocated by tears.

From . . ., 9th of September, 17—.

## LETTER LXII

*Madame de Volanges to the Chevalier Danceny*

Monsieur, after having abused a mother's confidence and the innocence of a child, you will doubtless not be surprised if you are received no longer in a house where you have repaid the proofs of a most sincere friendship by a complete forgetfulness of all good behaviour. I prefer to ask you not to come to my house again, instead of giving orders at my door, which would compromise us all through the remarks the footman could not fail to make. I have a right to hope that you will not force me to make use of this method. I warn you also that if in the future you make the slightest attempt to continue my daughter in the aberration you have plunged her, an austere and eternal retirement will remove her from your solicitation. It is for you to see, Monsieur, whether you will have as little scruple in causing her misfortune as you have had in attempting her dishonour. For my part, I have made my choice and she knows it.

You will find enclosed a packet of your letters. I expect you to send me in exchange all my daughter's letters; and that you will assist in leaving no trace of an event whose memory cannot be recalled by me without indignation, by her without shame, and by you without remorse. I have the honour to be, etc.

From . . ., 7th of September, 17—.

(NOTE.—Cécile Volanges's letter to the Marquise has been suppressed, because it only contained the same facts as the preceding letter and with less details. The Chevalier Danceny's letter could not be found. The reason for this will be seen in *Letter LXIII*, from Madame to the Vicomte C. de L.)

## LETTER LXIII

*The Marquise de Merteuil to the Vicomte de Valmont*

Yes, indeed, I will explain Danceny's note to you. The event which made him write it, is my work and is, I think, my masterpiece. I have not wasted my time since your last letter and I said like the Athenian architect: " What he has said I will do."

This fine novel-hero needs obstacles, he is drowsing in his felicity! Oh! Let him apply to me, I will find work for him; and if I am not mistaken his sleep will not be so tranquil. He had to be taught the value of time and I flatter myself that he now regrets the time he has wasted. He needed more mystery, you said too; well, he will not lack that necessity. I have one good point; I need only to be showed my mistakes and I never rest until I have retrieved them. Learn then what I have done.

When I returned home two mornings, ago, I read your letter and thought it enlightening. Convinced that you had very plainly pointed out the cause of the trouble, I employed myself entirely in thinking how to remove it. However, I began by going to bed; for the indefatigable Chevalier had not allowed me a moment's sleep and I thought I was drowsy; but not at all; I was entirely occupied with Danceny, and my desire to drag him out of his indolence or to punish him for it prevented me from shutting my eyes, and it was not until I had thoroughly worked out my plans that I obtained a couple of hours' rest.

The same evening, I called on Madame de Volanges and, in accordance with my plan, I told her in confidence that I was sure there existed a dangerous acquaintance between her daughter and Danceny. This woman, so clear-sighted against you, was so blinded that she replied to me at first that I must be wrong; that her daughter was a child, etc., etc. I could not tell her all I knew; but mentioned glances, remarks, " which had alarmed my virtue and my friendship." Finally I talked almost as well as a devotee would have done; and, to strike the decisive blow, I went so far as to say that I thought I had seen a letter given and received. That reminds me, I added, that one day she opened a drawer of her writing-table in my presence, and I saw in it a lot of papers, which no doubt she is keeping. Do you know whether she has any frequent correspondence? Here Madame de Volanges's face changed and I saw a few tears swim in her eyes. " I thank you, my real friend," she said, pressing my hand, " I shall look into this."

After this conversation, which was too short to be suspicious, I went up to the young person. I left her soon after, to ask the mother not to compromise me with her daughter; which she promised the more willingly, since I pointed out to her how convenient it would be if the child should attain enough confidence in me to open her heart to me and put me in a position to give her " my careful advice." What convinces me that she will keep her promise, is that I have no doubt but that she wishes to impress her daughter with her own acuteness. In this way I shall be able to keep up my tone of friendship with the girl, without appearing deceitful in Madame de Volanges's eyes; which I desired to avoid. Moreover, in the future I shall have the advantage of remaining as long and as secretly with the girl as I wish, without the mother ever taking offence.

I profited by it that very evening; and when my card game was over I took the child aside into a corner and started her on the subject of Danceny, about whom she is inexhaustible. I amused myself by exciting her with the pleasure she would have in seeing him the next day; there was no kind of folly I did not make her express. I had to give her back in hope what I took from her in reality; and then all this will make her feel the blow more acutely and I am convinced that the more she suffers the more eager she will be to console herself for it on the first occasion. Moreover it is good to accustom to such events someone whom one destines to great adventures.

After all, can she not pay with a few tears for the pleasure of having her Danceny? She is wild about him! Well, I promise her she shall have him and that but for this storm she would never have had him. It is a bad dream, the awakening from which will be delicious; and looking at it all round, it seems to me she ought to be grateful to me; and if I have mixed a little malice with it, one must be amused:

> "Fools are here below for our minor pleasures."[1]

I left at last, very pleased with myself. Either Danceny, I said to myself, animated by obstacles, will redouble his love, and then I shall have served him to the best of my power; or if he is a mere fool, as I have sometimes been tempted to think, he will be in despair and will consider himself beaten; in this case, at least I shall be avenged on him, as far as it was in my power, and so doing I shall have increased the mother's esteem, the daughter's friendship, and the confidence of both. As to Gercourt, who is the primary object of my attention, I shall be very unlucky if, mistress of his wife's mind as I am and shall be even more, I do not find a thousand ways of making him what I wish him to be. I went to bed with these pleasant ideas; I therefore slept well and woke up very late.

At my waking, I found two notes, one from the mother and one from the daughter; I could not keep from laughing when I found literally the same phrase in both: "it is from you alone I expect any consolation." Is it not indeed amusing to console for and against, and to be the only agent of two directly opposite interests? Here I am like the Divinity, receiving the contrary prayers of blind mortals and changing nothing in my immutable decrees. However I quitted this august rôle to take on that of the consoling angel; and in accordance with the precept, I have visited my friends in their affliction.

[1] Gresset, *Le Méchant.* (C. de L.)

I began by the mother; I found her in a state of grief which already partly avenges me for the annoyances she made you undergo with your fair prude. Everything has succeeded perfectly; my one fear was lest Madame de Volanges might profit by the moment to gain her daughter's confidence, which would have been very easy if the language of gentleness and kindness had been employed towards her, and if the advice of reason had been given with the air and tone of indulgent tenderness. Fortunately, she armed herself with severity; she arranged it all so badly indeed that I had nothing to do but to applaud. It is true she nearly spoiled all our plans by her determination to send her daughter back to the convent, but I parried this thrust; and I have persuaded her merely to threaten it in case Danceny should continue his attentions; this was to force them both to a circumspection I think necessary for success.

I then went to the daughter. You will not believe how grief has improved her! If she becomes even a little coquettish I warrant you she will often cry; but this time she was crying without malice aforethought. Struck by this new charm which I had not observed in her before and which I was very glad to notice, I gave her only clumsy consolations at first which increased rather than allayed her grief; and in this way I brought her to a state where she was really choking. She ceased crying and for a moment I was afraid of convulsions. I advised her to go to bed which she agreed to; I acted as her waiting-woman; she had not made her toilet and soon her scattered hair fell on her shoulders and breasts which were entirely uncovered. I kissed her; she let me take her in my arms and her tears began to flow again without effort. Heavens! How beautiful she was! Ah! if Magdalene was like this she must have been far more dangerous as a penitent than as a sinner.

When the disconsolate fair one was in bed I began to console her in earnest. First of all I reassured her about her fear of the convent. I awoke the hope in her of seeing Danceny secretly; and sitting on the bed I said to her: "If he were here"; and then embroidering on that theme I led her from one diversion to another until she forgot she was afflicted. We should have separated perfectly pleased with each other if she had not wished to entrust me with a letter for Danceny, which I consistently refused. Here are my reasons, which no doubt you will approve.

First of all it was compromising me with Danceny; and though this was the only reason I could give the little girl, there are nevertheless many other reasons between ourselves. Would it not be risking the fruit of my labours if I gave our young people so soon such an easy way of soothing their distress? And then, I should not be sorry to compel them to entangle a few servants in this adventure; for if it turns out well, as I hope it will, it must be known immediately after the marriage; and there are few more certain methods of spreading it about; or, if by some miracle they did not talk, we would talk, and it will be more convenient to lay the indiscretion upon them.

You must put this idea into Danceny's head today; and since I am not certain of the Volanges's waiting-woman (whom she seems not to trust) tell him of mine, my faithful Victoire. I shall take care that the application succeeds. This idea pleases me all the more because the confidence will only be useful to us and not to them; for I have not reached the end of my story.

While I was refusing to take charge of the little girl's letter, I feared every moment that she would ask me to put it in the post-box; which I could not have refused. Happily, either from agitation, or from ignorance, or because she thinks less of the letter than of the reply (which she could not receive in this way) she did not speak of it; but to prevent this idea coming to her or at least to prevent her making use of it, I made up my mind immediately; and returning to her mother I persuaded her to take her daughter away for some time, to take her to the country . . . and where? Does not your heart beat with joy? . . . To your aunt, to the old Rosemonde woman. She is to let her know about it today; and thus you have a pretext to return to your devotee who will not be able to reproach you with the scandal of a *tête à tête*: and thanks to my care, Madame de Volanges herself will repair the harm she has done you.

But listen to me, and do not busy yourself so eagerly with your own affairs that you lose sight of this; remember I am interested in it.

I want you to become the correspondent and adviser of the two young people. Inform Danceny of this journey and offer him your services. Do not allow any difficulty except that of delivering your letter of credit to the fair one's hands; and immediately overcome the obstacle by telling him that my waiting-woman is the way. There can be no doubt that he will accept; and as a reward for your trouble you will have the confidence of an unspoiled heart, which is always an interesting thing. Poor little girl! How she will blush when she hands you her first letter! Really, the part of confidant, against which prejudices exist, seems to me a very pleasant relaxation when one is occupied elsewhere; which will be the case with you.

The result of this intrigue will depend upon your care. You must decide on the time when the actors must be brought together. The country offers a thousand means; and Danceny will assuredly be ready to go there at your first signal. A night, a disguise, a window . . . anything. But if the little girl returns here in the same state she goes away I shall blame you. If you think she needs any encouragement from me, let me know. I think I have given her a good enough lesson on the danger of keeping letters to dare to write to her now; and I still mean to make her my pupil.

I think I have forgotten to tell you that her suspicions about the betrayal of her correspondence fell first of all upon her waiting-woman, and that I directed them against the confessor. It is killing two birds with one stone.

Good-bye, Vicomte; I have been writing to you a long time and it has delayed my dinner; but my letter was dictated by self-esteem and friendship; both are chatterers. However, it will reach you at three o'clock and that is all you need.

Complain of me now if you dare; and if you are tempted, go and have another look at the Comte de B . . .'s wood. You say he keeps it for his friends' pleasure! And is the man everybody's friend? But good-bye, I am hungry.

From . . ., 9th of September, 17—.

## LETTER LXIV

*The Chevalier Danceny to Madame de Volanges*

(Sent with *Letter LXVI* from the Vicomte to the Marquise)

Without seeking to justify my conduct, Madame, and without complaining of yours, I cannot but be afflicted by an event which makes three persons miserable, all three of whom are worthy of a happier fate. I am more grieved that I am its cause than that I am its victim, and ever since yesterday I have been trying to reply to you without finding strength to do so. Yet I have so many things to tell you that I must make an effort; and if this letter lacks order and continuity you will be sufficiently conscious of the painfulness of my situation to grant me some indulgence.

Permit me first to protest against the first phrase in your letter. I dare to assert that I abused neither the confidence nor the innocence of Mademoiselle de Volanges; I respected both in my actions. My actions alone were within my control; and if you should make me responsible for an involuntary sentiment I am not afraid to add that the feelings inspired in me by your daughter were such as might displease you but could not offend you. On this matter, which moves me more than I can say I ask none but yourself as judge and my letters as witnesses.

You forbid me to enter your house in the future and I shall certainly submit to everything you are pleased to order in this matter; but will not this sudden and total absence give as much occasion to the observations you wish to avoid as the order which, for that very reason, you did not wish to give at your door? I insist the more on this point, since it is far more important for Mademoiselle de Volanges than for me. I beg you then to weigh everything carefully and not to allow your severity to warp your prudence. I am convinced that nothing but your daughter's interests will determine your resolve and shall await new orders on your part.

But in case you should permit me to call upon you sometimes, I promise you, Madame (and you can count upon my promise), not to abuse these occasions by attempting to speak privately to Mademoiselle de Volanges or to convey any letter to her. The fear of what might compromise her reputation binds me to this sacrifice ; and the happiness of seeing her sometimes will console me. This part of my letter is also the sole reply I can make to what you say about the fate to which you destine Mademoiselle de Volanges, a fate which you wish to make dependent upon my conduct. To promise you more would be to deceive you. A vile seductor can suit his plans to circumstances and calculate according to events ; but the love which animates me permits me only two sentiments—courage and constancy.

What ! Shall I consent to be forgotten by Mademoiselle de Volanges, to forget her myself ? No, no, never. I shall be faithful to her ; she has received my oath and I renew it today. Pardon me, Madame, I digress ; I must return.

There remains one other matter for me to discuss with you ; that of the letters you ask from me. I am truly pained to add a refusal to the harm you think I have committed ; but I beg you will listen to my reasons and will deign to remember, in order to appreciate them, that the sole consolation for the misfortune of having lost your friendship is the hope of retaining your esteem.

Mademoiselle de Volanges's letters which were always so precious have become much more so at this moment. They are the one treasure left to me ; they alone still recall to me a sentiment which creates the whole charm of my life ; yet, you may believe me, I should not hesitate a moment to sacrifice them, and my regret at being deprived of them would yield to the desire to prove my respectful deference to you ; but powerful considerations restrain me and I am sure that you yourself will not be able to condemn them.

It is true you have Mademoiselle de Volanges's secret. But allow me to tell you I have every reason to believe that this was the result of a surprisal and not of confidence. I do not presume to blame a proceeding which was authorised, perhaps, by maternal solicitude. I respect your rights but they do not go so far as to relieve me of my duties. The most sacred of all is never to betray the confidence placed in us. I should be failing in my duty if I exposed to the eyes of another the secrets of a heart which desired only to unveil them to mine. If your daughter consents to confide them to you, let her speak ; her letters are useless to you. If on the contrary she wishes to keep her secret to herself, doubtless you will not expect that I should make them known to you.

As to the silence in which you desire this event to remain buried, be at rest, Madame ; in all that concerns Mademoiselle de Volanges, I can defy even the heart of a mother. To relieve you completely of all uneasiness, I have foreseen everything. The precious packet which hitherto has been inscribed " Papers to be burned " ; is now inscribed : " Papers belonging to Madame de Volanges." The course I am taking will also prove to you that my refusal is not based on the fear that you would find in these letters a single sentiment of which you personally might have reason to complain.

This is a very long letter, Madame. Yet it will not be sufficiently long if it leaves you the least doubt of the honesty of my sentiments, of my very sincere regret at having displeased you and of the profound respect with which I have the honour to be, etc.

From . . ., 9th of September, 17—.

## LETTER LXV

*The Chevalier Danceny to Cécile Volanges*

(Sent open to the Marquise de Merteuil in *Letter LXVI* from the Vicomte)

O, my Cécile, what will become of us ? What god will save us from the misfortunes which threaten us ? May love at least give us courage to endure them ! How can I describe to you my astonishment, my despair, at the sight of my letters, at reading Madame de Volanges's note ? Who can have betrayed us ? Whom do your suspicions fall upon ? Did you do something imprudent ? What are you doing now ? What has been said to you ? I want to know all about it and I know nothing. But perhaps you yourself know nothing more than I do.

I send you your Mamma's note and a copy of my reply. I hope that you will approve of what I say to her. I want you to approve also the steps I have taken since this fatal event ; the purpose of them all is to have news from you and to give you news of me ; and, who knows ? perhaps to see you again, more freely than before.

Can you imagine, my Cécile, what pleasure it would be to be together again, to be able to swear once more an eternal love, and to see in our eyes, to feel in our souls, that this vow will never be broken ? What griefs would not be forgotten in so sweet a moment ? Well, I hope to see it come, and I owe it to the very steps I beg you to approve. What do I say ? I owe it to the consoling solicitude of the tenderest friend and my one request is that you will permit this friend to be yours also.

Perhaps I ought not to have given your confidence without your permission ? But I have unhappiness and necessity for my excuse. Love it was that guided me ; it is love which claims your indulgence, which begs you to forgive a necessary confidence without which we should remain perhaps separated forever.[1] You know the friend of whom I speak ; he is the friend of the woman you love most. It is the Vicomte de Valmont.

My design, in going to him, was first of all to ask him to persuade Madame de Merteuil to take charge of a letter to you. He did not think this method would succeed ; but in default of the mistress he answers for the waiting-woman, who has obligations to him. She will hand you this letter and you can give her your reply.

This assistance will be of no use to us if, as Monsieur de Valmont believes, you are going to the country immediately. But in that case he

[1] Monsieur Danceny does not state the matter accurately. He had given his confidence to Monsieur de Valmont before this event. See *Letter LVII*. (C. de L.)

himself will help us. The woman to whose house you are going is his relative. He will take advantage of this pretext to go there at the same time as you do ; and our correspondence will pass through his hands. He even promises that if you will allow yourself to be guided he will arrange for us to see each other without any risk of compromising you at all.

And now, my Cécile, if you love me, if you pity my misfortune, if, as I hope, you share my regrets, will you refuse your confidence to a man who will be our guardian angel ? But for him I should be reduced to the despair of being unable even to soften the sorrows I cause you. They will end, I hope ; but, my dear one, promise me not to abandon yourself to sorrow too much, do not let yourself be prostrated. The idea of your pain is unendurable torture to me. I would give my life to make you happy ! You know it. May the certainty that you are adored bring some consolation to your soul ! Mine needs your assurance that you forgive Love the ills he makes you suffer.

Good-bye, my Cécile ; good-bye, my dear one.

From . . ., 9th of September, 17—.

## LETTER LXVI

*Vicomte de Valmont to the Marquise de Merteuil*

You will see, my fair friend, when you read the two enclosed letters that I have carried out your plan well. Although they are both dated today, they were written yesterday in my house and under my eyes ; that to the little girl says everything we could wish. I can only bow before the profundity of your insight, if I may judge of it by the success of your proceedings. Danceny is all on fire ; and assuredly at the first occasion you will have nothing more to reproach him with. If his fair *ingénue* is docile all will be over soon after his arrival in the country ; I have a hundred methods ready. Thanks to your care I am now positively *Danceny's friend ;* the only thing he needs now is to be a *Prince.*[1]

Danceny is still very young ! Would you believe I could not persuade him to promise the mother that he would give up his love ; as if it were very difficult to make a promise when you have decided not to keep it ! It would be deceitful, he kept repeating ; an edifying scruple, is it not, especially as he wants to seduce the daughter ; but that is what men are ! They are all equally base in their designs and their weakness in carrying them out they call probity.

It will be your business to prevent Madame de Volanges's being scared at the little pranks our young man has allowed himself in his letter ; preserve us from the convent ; and try to make her give up her request for the little girl's letters. First of all he will not give them up, he does not want to, and I agree with him ; here love and reason tally. I have read these letters, I have devoured their boredom. They may become useful. I will explain.

[1] An expression referring to a passage in a poem by M. de Voltaire. (C. de L.)

In spite of all our prudence, there might be a scandal ; it would prevent the marriage, would it not, and destroy all our plans for Gercourt. But since I want to avenge myself on the mother, in this case I intend to dishonour the girl. By choosing carefully from this correspondence and only producing part of it, the little Volanges girl could be made to appear as if she had taken all the first steps and absolutely thrown herself at his head. Some of the letters might even compromise her mother, and would at least *stain* her with an unpardonable negligence. I quite realise that the scrupulous Danceny would refuse at first but since he would be personally attacked, I think he could be persuaded. It is a thousand to one against the luck turning this way ; but we must foresee everything.

Farewell, my fair friend ; it would be very agreeable of you to come and sup tomorrow with the Maréchale de . . . ; I was unable to refuse. I suppose there is no need to recommend secrecy towards Madame de Volanges about my country projects ; she would soon decide to stay in town ; while, once she arrives there, she will not leave the next day ; and if she gives us only a week I will answer for everything.

From . . ., 9th September, 17—.

## LETTER LXVII

*Madame de Tourvel to the Vicomte de Valmont*

I did not desire to answer you again, Monsieur, and perhaps the embarrassment I feel at this moment is itself a proof that indeed I ought not to do so. However I do not wish to leave you any subject for complaint against me ; I wish to convince you that I have done everything for you I could do.

I gave you permission to write to me, you say ? I admit it ; but when you remind me of this permission do you think I forget on what conditions it was given to you ? If I had kept to them as much as you have departed from them, would you have received a single reply from me ? Yet this is the third ; while you are doing everything that must force me to break off this correspondence, it is I who am employed in trying to continue it. There is one way of doing so, but only one ; and if you refuse to take it, it will be, whatever you may say, a proof to me of how little value you set upon it.

Abandon a language which I cannot and will not listen to ; renounce a sentiment which offends and frightens me, to which perhaps you ought to be less attached by remembering that it is the object which separates us. Is this sentiment the only one you are able to feel, and shall love have one fault the more in my eyes by excluding friendship ? And will you yourself commit the fault of not desiring to have as a friend her in whom you have wished for more tender sentiments ? I am unwilling to think so ; this humiliating idea would revolt me, would estrange me from you forever.

In offering you my friendship, Monsieur, I give you all I have, all that I can bestow. What more can you desire ? To yield to this gentle sentiment, so well suited to my heart, I await only your consent and the promise I exact from you that this friendship shall suffice for your happiness. I shall forget everything which may have been said to me ; I shall rely on you to justify my choice.

You see my frankness ; it should prove to you my confidence ; it depends entirely on you to increase it further ; but I warn you that the first word of love destroys it forever and brings back all my fears, above all that it will become for me the signal for an eternal silence towards you.

If, as you say, you have abandoned your errors, would you not prefer to be the object of a virtuous woman's friendship than of a guilty woman's remorse ? Good-bye, Monsieur ; you will realise that after having spoken thus I can say nothing more until you have replied to me.

From . . ., 9th September, 17—.

## LETTER LXVIII

*The Vicomte de Valmont to Madame de Tourvel*

How can I reply to your last letter, Madame ? How can I dare to be outspoken, when my sincerity may ruin me with you ? No matter, it must be so ; I shall have the courage to do it. I tell myself, I repeat to myself, that it is better to deserve you than to obtain you ; and though you should refuse me forever a happiness I shall ceaselessly desire, I must at least prove to you that my heart is worthy of it.

What a pity it is that, as you put it, I have abandoned my errors. With what transports of joy I should then have read this very letter to which I fear to reply today ! In it you speak to me " frankly," you express your " confidence " in me, you finally offer me your " friendship." What treasures, Madame, and how I regret I cannot profit by them ! Why am I no longer what I was ?

If I were so ; if I felt only an ordinary inclination for you, that light desire, the child of seduction and pleasure, which is called love nowadays, I should hasten to take advantage of all I could obtain. With little delicacy concerning means so long as they procured the success, I should encourage your frankness in order to discover your thoughts ; I should want your confidence with the purpose of betraying it ; I should accept your friendship in the hope of deluding it. . . . What ! This picture frightens you, Madame ? . . . Well ! It would be my portrait if I told you that I consent to be nothing but your friend. . . .

Shall I consent to share with anyone else a sentiment that comes from your soul ? If ever I should say so, do not believe me. From that moment I should be seeking to deceive you ; I might still desire you, but I should certainly have ceased to love you.

It is not that amiable frankness, soft confidence, tender friendship are valueless in my eyes. . . . But love, true love, the love you inspire, uniting all these feelings, giving them more energy, could not lend itself like them to that tranquillity, to that coldness of soul which allows comparisons, which even endures preferences. No, Madame, I shall not be your friend; I shall love you with the tenderest, the most ardent and yet the most respectful love; you may bring it to despair, but you cannot destroy it.

By what right do you presume to dispose of a heart whose homage you refuse? From what refinement of cruelty is it that you envy me even the happiness of loving you? That is mine, it is independent of you. I shall take care to defend it. Though it is the source of my woes, it is also their remedy.

No, once again, no. Persist in your cruel denials, but leave me my love. You delight in rendering me unhappy! Well, so be it; try to weary my courage; I shall at least be able to compel you to decide my fate and perhaps some day you will do me more justice. It is not that I hope ever to make you feel this emotionally: but without being persuaded, you will be convinced, you will say to yourself: I misjudged him.

Let us put it more plainly, you do yourself an injustice. To know you without loving you, to love you without being constant to you, are both equally impossible; and in spite of the modesty which embellishes you, it must be easier for you to complain of, than to be surprised by, the feelings you create. As for me, whose sole merit is that of having appreciated you, I desire not to lose you; and far from agreeing to your insidious offers, I renew at your feet my oath to love you forever.

From . . ., 10th of September, 17—.

## LETTER LXIX

*Cécile Volanges to the Chevalier Danceny*

(Note written in pencil and copied out by Danceny)

You ask me what I am doing; I love you, and I weep. My mother does not speak to me; she has taken away my paper, pens and ink; I am using a pencil which luckily was left me and I write to you on a piece of your letter. I must approve all you have done; I love you too much not to take any means of getting news of you and giving you my news. Although I did not like Monsieur de Valmont and did not believe him to be your friend, I shall try to accustom myself to him and I shall love him for your sake. I do not know who betrayed us; it can only have been my waiting-woman or my confessor. I am very miserable; tomorrow we are going to the country; I do not know for how long. Great Heaven! Never to see you again! I have no more space. Good-bye; try to read this. These pencilled words will perhaps be effaced, but never the sentiment engraved in my heart.

From . . ., 10th of September, 17—.

## LETTER LXX

*The Vicomte de Valmont to the Marquise de Merteuil*

I have something important to tell you, my dear friend. Yesterday, as you know, I supped with the Maréchale de . . . ; you were mentioned and I expressed, not all the good I think of you, but all the good I do not think. Everybody appeared to be of my opinion and the conversation was languishing as always happens, when we say nothing but good of our neighbour, when a contradictor arose ; it was Prévan.

"Heaven forbid," said he as he got up, "that I should doubt Madame de Merteuil's virtue ; but I dare to think she owes more to her levity than to her principles. It is perhaps more difficult to pursue her than to please her ; since in running after a woman one never fails to meet others on the way, since, all things considered, these other women may be as good or better than she is, some men are distracted by a new inclination, others desist from lassitude ; and perhaps she has had to defend herself less than any woman in Paris. For my part," he added (encouraged by the smiles of several women), "I shall only believe in Madame de Merteuil's virtue after I have killed six horses in paying court to her."

This mockery succeeded like all those which arise from malice ; and during the laughter it excited, Prévan sat down and the general conversation changed. But the two Comtesses de B. . . ., who were beside our unbeliever, continued the subject with him in their private conversation, which happily I was in a position to overhear.

The challenge to move your tenderness was accepted. The promise to tell everything was given ; and of all the promises which might be given in this adventure that would assuredly be the most religiously kept. But you are forewarned, and you know the proverb. . . .

It remains for me to tell you this Prévan, whom you do not know, is infinitely agreeable and still more dextrous. If you have sometimes heard me say the contrary, it is only because I do not like him, that I enjoy thwarting his successes and that I know what power my opinion has with some thirty of our most fashionable women.

Indeed, by this means I prevented him for a long time from appearing on what we call the theatre of fashion ; and he performed prodigies without acquiring any reputation. But the noise of his triple adventure, by turning all eyes upon him, has given him the confidence he lacked hitherto and has made him really formidable. In short he is perhaps the only man I should now be afraid of meeting on my path ; and apart from your own interests, you would do me a real service by making him a little ridiculous on the way. I leave him in good hands and I hope that when I return he will be a lost man.

In return I promise you to conduct successfully your pupil's adventure and to pay as much attention to her as to my fair prude.

The latter has just sent me a plan of capitulation. Her whole letter shows her desire to be deluded. It is impossible to offer a more convenient and more usual method. She wants me to be her friend. But I, who like new and difficult methods, do not intend to let her off so easily; and I shall certainly not have taken so much trouble with her in order to end up with an ordinary seduction.

On the contrary, my plan is that she shall feel, and feel thoroughly, the value and extent of each sacrifice she makes me; not to lead her so fast that remorse cannot follow her; to make her virtue expire in a slow agony; to hold her attention continually upon this painful spectacle; and not to grant her the happiness of having me in her arms until I have forced her to admit her desire for it. After all, I am not worth much if I am not worth the trouble of being asked for. And can I take a less vengeance on a lofty woman who appears to blush to admit that she adores?

I have therefore refused this precious friendship and have held to my title of lover. Since I am aware that this title, which at first appears merely a dispute about words, is really an important thing to obtain, I took great care with my letter and tried to put into it that disorder which alone can render sentiment. In short I talked as much nonsense as I could; for without talking nonsense, there is no tenderness; and I think that is the reason why women are so much our superiors in love-letters.

I ended up mine with a piece of flattery and that is another result of my profound observation. When a woman's heart has been exercised for some time, it needs rest; and I have noticed that flattery is the softest pillow one can offer any of them. Good-bye, my fair friend; I leave tomorrow. If you have any orders to give me for the Comtesse de . . ., I shall stay at her house at least for dinner. I am sorry to go without seeing you. Send me your sublime instructions and help me with your wise counsels at this decisive moment.

Above all things resist Prévan; and may I one day compensate you for this sacrifice! Good-bye.

From . . ., 11th of September, 17—.

## LETTER LXXI

*The Vicomte de Valmont to the Marquise de Merteuil*

My rattle-headed servant has left my portfolio in Paris! My fair one's letters, those of Danceny to the Volanges girl, were all left behind and I need them all. He is just leaving to make amends for his stupidity; and while he is saddling his horse, I will give you an account of last night; for I beg you to believe I do not waste my time.

The adventure of itself is a very small thing; it was only a revival with the Vicomtesse de M. . . . But it interested me in its details. Moreover I am glad to let you see that if I have a talent for misleading women I have none the less, when I wish, that of excusing them. I always take the most difficult or the most amusing course ; and I do not blame myself for a good action, so long as it gives me exertion or amusement.

I found the Vicomtesse here, and when she added her requests to the entreaties of the others that I should spend the night in the Château : " Well ! I consent," I said to her, " on condition that I spend it with you." " Impossible," she replied, " Vressac is here." Till that moment I had merely meant to say something polite ; but that word " impossible " roused me, as it always does. I felt humiliated at being sacrificed to Vressac and I resolved not to endure it ; so I insisted.

The circumstances were not favourable. Vressac has been clumsy enough to arouse the Vicomte's suspicions ; so that the Vicomtesse cannot receive him in her own house ; and this visit to the good Comtesse had been arranged between them with the purpose of snatching a few nights. At first the Vicomte even showed his annoyance at meeting Vressac there ; but since he is even more a sportsman than a jealous husband he stayed none the less ; and the Comtesse, who is still the same as she was when you knew her, after putting the wife in the main corridor, lodged the husband on one side and the lover on the other and left them to arrange it between them. The evil genius of both of them caused me to be lodged opposite.

That very day (that is to say yesterday), Vressac who, as you may suppose, is flattering the Vicomte, went shooting with him in spite of his dislike for sport, and intended to console himself at night in the wife's arms for the boredom the husband caused him all day ; but I considered he would need a rest and devoted my attention to the means of persuading his mistress to give him time for it.

I succeeded and made her agree to quarrel with him over this day's shooting, to which obviously he had only consented for her sake. A worse pretext could not have been found ; but no woman possesses to a higher degree than the Vicomtesse that talent common to them all of putting caprice in the place of common sense and of being never so difficult to soothe as when she is in the wrong. Moreover it was not a convenient time for explanation ; and, as I only wanted one night I agreed that they should patch matters up the next day.

Vressac then was sulked with when he came back. He tried to ask the reason ; she started a quarrel with him. He attempted to justify himself ; the husband, who was present, served as a pretext for breaking off the conversation ; finally he tried to profit by a moment when the husband was out of the room to request that he might be given a hearing at night. It was then that the Vicomtesse was sublime. She grew indignant with the audacity of men who, because they have received favours from a woman, think they have the right to abuse her even when she has reason to complain of them ; and having changed the topic thus skilfully, she talked delicacy and sentiment so well that Vressac was rendered mute and confused and I myself was tempted to think she was right; for you must know that as a friend of them both I was present at the conversation.

She finally declared positively that she would not add the fatigues of love to those of shooting and that she would blame herself for disturbing such soft pleasures. The husband came back; the wretched Vressac, who thereby lost the opportunity of replying, addressed himself to me; and after he had told me his grievances at great length (which I knew as well as he did) he begged me to speak to the Vicomtesse and I promised him to do so. I did indeed speak to her; but it was to thank her and to arrange with her the hour and means of our meeting.

She told me that since she was lodged between her husband and her lover, she had thought it more prudent to go to Vressac than to receive him in her apartment; and that since I was opposite her she thought it safer also to come to me; that she would arrive as soon as her waiting-woman had left her alone; and that I had only to leave my door ajar and to wait for her.

Everything was carried out as we had agreed; she came to my room about one o'clock in the morning.

. . . . . in the simple attire
Of a beauty just snatched from sleep.[1]

Since I am without vanity, I will not dwell upon the details of the night; but you know me, and I was satisfied with myself.

At dawn we had to separate. And here the interest begins. The scatterbrain thought she had left her door ajar; we found it closed with the key inside; you can have no idea of the expression of despair with which the Vicomtesse said to me at once: "Ah! I am ruined." It must be admitted that it would have been amusing to leave her in this situation, but could I allow a woman to be ruined *for* without being ruined *by* me? And ought I, like the majority of men, to let myself be dominated by events? A way out had to be found. What would you have done, my fair friend? This is what I did, and it succeeded.

I soon found out that the door in question could be broken in by making a great deal of noise. I therefore persuaded the Vicomtesse, not without difficulty, to give piercing cries of terror, such as "Thieves!" "Murder!" etc., etc. And we agreed that at the first cry I should break down the door while she rushed into bed. You cannot think how much time was needed to bring her to the point even after she had agreed to do it. However it was the only thing to do and at the first kick the door gave way.

It was fortunate for the Vicomtesse that she did not waste any time. For at the same moment the Vicomte and Vressac were in the corridor and the waiting-woman rushed to her mistress's room.

I alone kept my head and I made use of it to extinguish a night-light which was still burning and to throw it on the ground; for you will realise how ridiculous it would have been to feign this panic terror with a light in the room. I then abused the husband and the

[1] Racine, *Tragedy of Britannicus*. (C. de L.)

lover for their heavy sleeping, assuring them that the cries, at which I had run out and my efforts to break down the door had lasted at least five minutes.

The Vicomtesse, who had recovered her courage in her bed, seconded me well enough and vowed by all the gods that there was a thief in her apartment. She protested with more sincerity that she had never been so afraid in her life. We looked everywhere and found nothing, when I pointed out the overturned night-light and concluded that no doubt a rat had caused the damage and the terror ; my opinion was accepted unanimously and after a few hackneyed pleasantries about rats the Vicomte was the first to return to his room and his bed, begging his wife to have quieter rats in future.

Vressac remained alone with us and went up to the Vicomtesse to tell her that this was a vengeance of Love ; upon which she looked at me and replied : " He must have been angry for he has avenged himself amply ; but," she added, " I am quite exhausted, I must go to sleep."

I was in an expansive mood ; consequently, before we separated I pleaded Vressac's cause and brought about a reconciliation. The two lovers embraced and I in my turn was embraced by them both. I had no more interest in the Vicomtesse's kisses ; but I admit that Vressac's gave me pleasure. We went out together, and after I had received his lengthy thanks we each went back to bed.

If you think this story amusing, I do not ask you to keep it secret. Now that I have had my amusement it is just that the public should have its turn. At the moment I am only speaking of the story ; perhaps we shall very soon say as much of the heroine.

Good-bye ; my servant has been waiting an hour ; I delay only long enough to embrace you and to warn you above everything to beware of Prévan.

From the Château of . . ., 13th of September, 17—.

## LETTER LXXII

*The Chevalier Danceny to Cécile Volanges*

(Not delivered till the fourteenth)

O my Cécile ! How I envy Valmont's lot ! Tomorrow he will see you. He will deliver this letter to you and I, languishing far from you, shall drag out my weary existence between regrets and misery. My love, my tender love, pity me for my misfortune ; above all pity me for yours ; it is against them that courage abandons me.

How dreadful it is for me to be the cause of your misery ! But for me, you would be happy and tranquil. Can you forgive me ? Tell me, ah ! tell me that you forgive me ; tell me also that you love me, that you will love me forever. I must have you repeat it to me. It is not that I doubt it ; but it seems to me that the more certain I am of it the sweeter it is to hear it said. You love me, do you not ? Yes, you love me with all your soul. I do not forget that this was the last word I heard you speak! How I gathered it to my heart! How profoundly it is engraved there! And with what delight mine responded to it!

Alas! In that moment of happiness I was far from foreseeing the dreadful fate which awaited us. Let us think, my Cécile, of how to mitigate it. If I am to believe my friend, you have only to give him the confidence he deserves and we shall achieve it.

I admit I was pained by the unfavourable idea you seem to have of him. In that I recognised your mother's prejudices; it was from deference to them that for some time I neglected this truly amiable man who today is doing everything for me, who, in short, is working to re-unite us when your Mamma has separated us. I beg you, my dear, to look upon him with a more favourable eye. Remember he is my friend, that he wishes to be yours, that he can procure me the happiness of seeing you. If these reasons do not convince you, my Cécile, you do not love me as much as I love you, you do not love me as much as you did love me. Ah! If ever you should love me less. . . . But no, my Cécile's heart is mine; it is mine for life; and if I have to dread the grief of an unhappy love, her constancy at least will save me from the tortures of a betrayed love.

Good-bye, my charming love; do not forget that I am suffering and that it only depends upon you to render me happy, perfectly happy. Listen to my heart's prayer, and receive the tenderest kisses of love.

Paris, 11th of September, 17—.

## LETTER LXXIII

*The Vicomte de Valmont to Cécile Volanges*

(Enclosed with the preceding letter)

The friend who assists you has learned that you have no means of writing and has already provided for it. In the ante-chamber of the apartment you occupy, under the large wardrobe on the left, you will find a stock of paper, pens and ink, which he will renew when wished, and which he thinks you can leave in the same place if you do not find a safer one.

He asks you not to be offended if he seems to pay no attention to you in company and only to look upon you as a child. This behaviour seems to him necessary in order to create the confidence he needs to be able to work more efficaciously for his friend's happiness and your own. He will try to create opportunities of speaking to you when he has something to tell you or to hand to you; and he hopes to succeed if you are zealous in assisting him.

He also advises you to return to him one by one the letters you receive, so that there may be less risk of compromising you.

He ends by assuring you that if you will give him your confidence he will use all his energy to soften the persecution inflicted by a too cruel mother upon two persons, one of whom is already his best friend while the other appears to him to deserve the tenderest interest.

From the Château de . . ., 14th of September, 17—.

## LETTER LXXIV

*The Marquise de Merteuil to the Vicomte de Valmont.*

How long is it, my friend, that you have been so easily terrified? Is this Prévan so very formidable? See how simple and modest I am! I have often met this proud conqueror; and I have scarcely looked at him! It needed no less an event than your letter to make me pay attention to him. Yesterday I repaired my injustice. He was at the Opera, almost opposite me, and I took note of him. He is certainly handsome, very handsome; fine and delicate features! He must improve when seen at close quarters! And you say that he wants to have me! Assuredly, he will do me both honour and pleasure! Seriously, I have a caprice for him, and I here confide to you that I have taken the first steps.

As we left the Opera, he was two steps from me, and in a loud voice, I arranged with the Marquise de . . . to sup on Thursday with the Maréchale. I think this is the only house where I can meet him. I have no doubt he heard me. . . . Suppose the ungrateful wretch does not come? Tell me, do you think he will come? Do you know that if he does not come I shall be out of humour all the evening? You see, he will not find so much difficulty in following me, and, which will surprise you more, he will find still less in pleasing me. He says he wishes to kill six horses in paying court to me! Oh! I will save the lives of those horses. I shall never have the patience to wait so long as that. You know it is not one of my principles to make a man languish when once I have made up my mind, and I have made it up for him.

Admit now that it is a pleasure to talk reason to me. Has not your important advice had a great success? But what do you expect; I have been vegetating so long; it is more than six weeks since I allowed myself a frolic. This one comes along; can I deny myself this? Is not the motive of it worth the trouble? Is there anyone more acceptable, in whatever sense you take the word?

You yourself are compelled to do him justice; you do more than praise him, you are jealous of him. Well! I make myself judge between you; but first of all I must have information and that is what I want to obtain. I shall be a just judge and you shall both be weighed in the same balance. I have your records, and your affair is completely investigated. Is it not just that I should now busy myself with your adversary? Come, submit yourself with a good grace, and to begin with, tell me, I beg you, what is the triple adventure of which he is the hero? You speak of it as if I had never known anything else and this is the first I have heard of it. Apparently it happened while I was away at Geneva and your jealousy must have prevented you from writing it to me. Atone for this fault at once; remember that nothing which concerns him is indifferent to me. It seems to me that when I returned people were still talking about it; but I was busy with other matters and I rarely listen to anything of this kind which is not a topic of the day.

Even if what I ask of you should annoy you a little, is it not the least return you can make for the trouble I have taken on your behalf? Was it not I who brought you in touch with your Madame de Tourvel again, when your stupidities had separated you from her? Was it not I again who put into your hands the means of avenging yourself on the intense zeal of Madame de Volanges? You have complained so often of the time you wasted in seeking your adventures! Now you have them under your hand. Love, hatred, you have only to choose; they all sleep under the same roof; you can double your existence, caress with one hand and strike with the other.

Again it is to me that you owe the adventure of the Vicomtesse. I am very pleased with it; but, as you say, it must be talked about; for if the occasion led you, as I can well understand, to prefer mystery to scandal for the moment, it must yet be admitted that the woman did not deserve such good treatment.

Moreover, I have reason to complain of her. The Chevalier de Belleroche thinks her prettier than I like; and for many reasons I should be glad to have a pretext for breaking with her; well, there is no more convenient pretext than to be able to say "It is impossible to meet that woman."

Good-bye, Vicomte; remember that in your position, time is precious; I shall spend mine in procuring Prévan's happiness.

Paris, 15th of September, 17—.

## LETTER LXXV

*Cécile Volanges to Sophie Carnay*

(Note.—In this letter Cécile Volanges relates in the fullest detail everything relative to her in the events which the reader has seen at the end of the first part, *Letter XLI*, and those following. This repetition has been suppressed. She speaks at last of the Vicomte de Valmont and expresses herself as follows.) C. de L.

. . . I assure you he is a very extraordinary man. Mamma speaks very ill of him; but the Chevalier Danceny speaks very well of him and I think he is in the right. I have never seen such an able man. When he gave me Danceny's letter, it was before everybody, and nobody saw anything; it is true I was very frightened because I had not been warned of anything; but after this I shall be in readiness. I already understand what he wants me to do to convey him my reply. It is very easy to arrange with him, for his looks say anything he wants. I do not know how he does it; he told me in the note I mentioned to you that he would appear not to pay any attention to me in Mamma's presence;

and indeed you would say he never thinks of me; and yet every time I seek his eyes, I am certain to meet them at once.

There is a close friend of Mamma's here whom I did not know, who also seems not to like Monsieur de Valmont at all, although he is very attentive to her. I am afraid he will soon grow weary of the life we lead here and that he will return to Paris; it would be a great pity. He must have a good heart to have come here on purpose to help his friend and me! I should like to show him my gratitude, but I do not know what to do to get an opportunity to speak to him; and if I did find one, I should be so bashful that perhaps I should not know what to say to him.

I can only speak freely to Madame de Merteuil, when I speak of my love; perhaps I should be embarrassed even with you, whom I tell everything, if it was in conversation. I have often felt with Danceny himself, as if in spite of myself, a certain fear which prevented me from saying everything I was thinking. Now I blame myself for it, and I would give everything in the world to find a moment to tell him once, only once, how much I love him. Monsieur de Valmont has promised him that if I allow myself to be guided, he will procure us an opportunity of seeing each other. I shall do whatever he wishes; but I cannot imagine that it is possible.

Good-bye, my dear, I have no more space.[1]

From the Château de . . ., 14th of September, 17—.

## LETTER LXXVI

*The Vicomte de Valmont to the Marquise de Merteuil*

Either your letter is a joke which I have not understood; or when you wrote to me you were in a very dangerous delirium. If I knew you less, my fair friend, I should really be very frightened; and whatever you may say, I am not easily frightened.

However much I read and re-read you I get no further; for your letter cannot be taken in the obvious sense it presents. What did you mean?

Was it only that it is unnecessary to take such precautions against an enemy so little dangerous? But in this case you may be wrong. Prévan is really amiable; he is more so than you think; above all he has the very useful talent of interesting a woman in his love by his skill of speaking of it in company and before everyone, by making use of the first conversation he finds. There are few women who avoid the snare of replying to him because they all have pretentions to subtlety and none of them likes to miss an opportunity of showing it. Now, you know well enough that a woman who consents to speak of love very soon ends by accepting it, or at least by acting as if she had done so. By this method, which he has really perfected, he has the further advantage of

[1] Mlle. de Volanges changed her confidant shortly after this, as will be seen in the following letters; this collection will not contain any of those she continued to write to her convent friend; they would tell the reader nothing. (C. de L.)

often calling women themselves as witness to their own defeat; and what I tell you I have seen myself.

I was only in the affair at second hand; I have never been intimate with Prévan; but there were six of us; and the Comtesse de P . . ., while she thought herself very sly, and indeed appeared, to everybody who was not in the secret, to be carrying on a general conversation, told us everything in the greatest detail, both how she had yielded to Prévan and all that had passed between them. She related this so confidently that she was not even disturbed by a smile which came to all six of us at the same time; and I shall always remember that when one of us tried to excuse himself by feigning to doubt what she was saying, or rather what she appeared to be saying, she replied gravely that assuredly none of us knew so much about it as she; and she was not afraid even to address Prévan and to ask him if she had been mistaken in a single word.

I had reason to believe then that this man was dangerous for everybody; but is it not enough for you, Marquise, that he is handsome, very handsome, as you say yourself? Or that he should make upon you "One of those attacks which you are pleased sometimes to reward for no reason except that you think them well made?" Or that you should have thought it amusing to yield for any other reason? Or. . . . How can I tell? How can I divine the thousands and thousands of caprices which govern a woman's mind, by which alone you are still related to your sex? Now that you are warned of the danger I have no doubt you will easily escape it; but still you had to be warned of it; I return then to my text—what did you mean?

If it is only a joke about Prévan, in addition to its being a very long one, it was not of any use with me; it is in society that you must fasten some ridicule upon him, and I repeat my request to you in this matter.

Ah! I think I have the key to the enigma! Your letter is a prophecy, not of what you will do, but of what he will believe you ready to do at the moment of the fall you are preparing for him. I quite approve of this plan, but it demands very great caution. You know as well as I that for public effect, to have a man or to receive his attentions is absolutely the same thing, unless the man is a fool; and Prévan is far from being that. If he obtains nothing but an appearance, he will boast of it and that will be enough. The fools will believe in it, the malicious will appear to believe in it; what resource will you have? I am really afraid. It is not that I doubt your skill; but it is the best swimmers who get drowned.

I do not think I am more stupid than others. I have found a hundred, I have found a thousand ways of dishonouring a woman; but when I have tried to find a way to save her from dishonour, I have never found the possibility of it. Even with you, my fair friend, whose conduct is a masterpiece, I have thought a hundred times that you had more luck than skill.

But after all perhaps I am seeking a reason where there is none. I wonder that for an hour I have been seriously considering what is assuredly only a jest on your part. You will banter me! Well! So be it; but hurry up and let us speak of something else. Of something else! I am wrong, it is always the same thing; always women to have or to ruin, and often both together.

Here, as you have very well pointed out, I have the means of exercising myself in both sorts, but not with the same facility. I foresee that vengeance will be swifter than love. The Volanges girl has surrendered, I will answer for it; she is dependent simply on the opportunity, and I shall take care to provide one. But it is not the same with Madame de Tourvel; she is an annoying woman, I do not understand her; I have a hundred proofs of her love, but a thousand of her resistance; and indeed I am afraid she will escape me.

The first effect produced by my return made me hope for something better. You may suppose that I wanted to judge of it for myself; and to be sure of seeing her first impulses, I sent no one on ahead of me and calculated my journey to arrive while they were at table. In fact, I dropped from the sky like a Divinity at the Opera, who comes to wind up the plot.

Having made enough noise on entering to turn their looks upon me, I could see at one glance the joy of my old aunt, the annoyance of Madame de Volanges and the disconcerted pleasure of her daughter. My fair one was in a seat where her back was turned to the door; at that moment she was engaged in cutting something and did not even turn her head; I spoke to Madame de Rosemonde and at the first word, the tender devotee recognised my voice and gave a cry in which I thought I noticed more love than surprise and fear. By this time I was far enough into the room to see her face; the tumult of her soul, the combat of her thoughts and sentiments, were painted on it in twenty different ways. I sat down at table beside her; she did not know what she was doing or what she was saying. She tried to continue eating; and could not; at last, less than a quarter of an hour afterwards, her embarrassment and her pleasure became stronger than she, and she could think of nothing better than to ask permission to leave the table; she escaped into the park, under the pretext that she needed the air. Madame de Volanges wished to go with her; the tender prude would not allow it; no doubt she was but too happy to find a pretext for being alone and yielding without constraint to the soft emotions of her heart!

I cut the dinner as short as I could Desert had scarcely been served when that infernal Volanges woman, urged apparently by the necessity of injuring me, rose from her place to go and find my charming invalid; but I had foreseen this plan and I thwarted it. I feigned to take this one rising for the general rising. And as I stood up at the same time the Volanges girl and the local *curé* allowed themselves to be led by this double example; so that Madame de Rosemonde found herself sitting alone at table with the old Knight-Commander T . . . and they both decided to leave too. We all went then to rejoin my fair one whom we found in a grove near the Château; and since she wanted solitude and not a walk she was just as glad to return with us as to make us stay with her.

As soon as I was certain that Madame de Volanges would have no opportunity of speaking to her alone, I thought of carrying out your orders, and busied myself with your pupil's interests. Immediately after the coffee, I went up to my room and entered the others', to reconnoitre the ground; I made my dispositions to provide for the little girl's correspondence; and after this first kindness, I wrote a note to inform her of it and to ask for her confidence; I put my note in with Danceny's letter. I returned to the drawing-room. There I found my fair one stretched out on a sofa in a delicious lassitude.

This spectacle by awakening my desires animated my glances; I felt they must be tender and pressing, and I placed myself in such a way that I could make use of them. Their first effect was to make my heavenly prude lower her large, modest eyes. For some time I looked at this angelic face; then wandering over all her person I amused myself by guessing at the curves and forms through a light but always troublesome garment. After I had descended from the head to her feet, I returned from the feet to her head. My fair friend, that soft gaze was fixed upon me; immediately it was lowered again; but, desirous of favouring its return, I turned away my eyes. Then there was established between us that tacit convention, the first treaty of timid love, which to satisfy the mutual need for looking at each other allows glances to follow each other until it is time for them to mingle.

I was so sure that my fair one was completely absorbed in this new pleasure that I took it upon myself to watch over our common safety; but after I had assured myself that a fairly brisk conversation prevented our being noticed by the company, I tried to persuade her eyes to speak their language frankly. With that purpose I first of all surprised a few glances but with so much reserve that her modesty could not be alarmed by it; and to put the timid creature more at her ease I appeared myself as embarrassed as she. Little by little our eyes grew accustomed to meeting each other and remained steady for a longer time; finally they ceased to relinquish each other and I perceived in hers that soft languor which is the happy signal of love and desire; but it was only for a moment; she soon recovered herself and, not without some shamefacedness, changed her attitude and her gaze.

Not wishing to leave her any doubt that I had noticed her different movements, I got up quickly and asked her with an air of anxiety if she felt ill. Immediately everyone surrounded her. I let them all pass in front of me; and as the little Volanges girl who was working at her embroidery near the window, needed a little time to leave her frame, I seized this opportunity to give her Danceny's letter.

I was a little way from her; I threw the epistle on her knee. She did not at all know what to do with it. You would have laughed at her look of surprise and embarrassment; however I did not laugh, for I was afraid so much clumsiness would betray us. But a strongly marked glance and gesture at length made her understand that she had to put the letter in her pocket.

The rest of the day brought nothing interesting. What has happened since may perhaps lead to events which will please you, at least in the matter of your pupil; but it is better to spend one's time in carrying out plans than in relating them. Besides this is the eighth page I have written and I am tired; so, good-bye.

You will realise without my telling you that the little girl has replied to Danceny.[1] I have also had a reply from my fair one, to whom I wrote the day after my arrival. I send you the two letters. You will read them or you will not read them; for this perpetual repetition, which already is ceasing to amuse me, must be very insipid for any one not directly concerned.

Once more, good-bye. I still love you very much; but I beg your if you speak to me of Prévan again, do it in such a way that I understand, you.

From the Château de . . ., 17th of September, 17—.

## LETTER LXXVII

*The Vicomte de Valmont to Madame de Tourvel*

What can be the reason, Madame, for your cruel pertinacity in avoiding me? How can it be that the most tender eagerness on my part should only obtain from you a behaviour which would scarcely be legitimate towards a man of whom you had the greatest reason to complain? What! I am brought back to your feet by love; and when a fortunate chance places me beside you, you prefer to feign an indisposition and to alarm your friends rather than consent to remain near me! How often yesterday did you not turn away your eyes to deprive me of the favour of a look? And if for one instant I was able to see less severity in it, the moment was so short that it seemed as if you desired less to let me enjoy it than to make me feel what I lost by being deprived of it.

That, I dare to say, is not the treatment love deserves nor the treatment friendship would tolerate; and yet you know I am animated by one of these sentiments and I think I have reason to believe that you did not decline the other. What have I done to lose that precious friendship, of which no doubt you thought me worthy since you offered it to me? Have I harmed myself by confiding in you, and will you punish me for my frankness? Are you not afraid at least of abusing them both? Indeed was it not in your bosom, my friend, that I laid the secret of my heart? Was it not with you alone that I felt obliged to refuse conditions which I had only to accept to procure myself the means of not keeping and perhaps of exploiting to my advantage? Would you, by so undeserved a harshness, force me to believe that I had only to deceive you in order to obtain more indulgence?

[1] This letter could not be found. (C. de L.)

I do not regret a line of conduct which I owed you, which I owed myself; but by what fatality is it that each praiseworthy action becomes the signal of a new misfortune for me! It was after I had given rise to the only praise you have yet deigned to give my conduct, that for the first time I had to deplore the misfortune of having displeased you. It was after I had proved to you my complete submission by depriving myself of the happiness of seeing you, solely to reassure your delicacy, that you wished to break off all correspondence with me, to take from me that poor compensation for the sacrifice you had exacted and to deprive me even of the love which alone could have given you a right to it. Finally it is after I spoke to you with a sincerity which even the interests of my love could not weaken that you now fly me as if I were a dangerous seducer whose perfidy you had detected.

Will you never grow weary of being unjust? At least tell me what new faults can have brought you to such severity and do not refuse to give me the orders you wish me to follow; when I promise to carry them out is it claiming too much to ask to know what they are?

From . . ., 15th of September, 17—.

## LETTER LXXVIII

*From Madame de Tourvel to the Vicomte de Valmont*

You appear surprised by my conduct, Monsieur, and you are not far from demanding an explanation of it, as if you had the right to blame it. I confess I should have thought I had more reason than you to be surprised and to complain; but since the refusal contained in your last reply I have adopted the course of enclosing myself in an indifference which leaves no occasion for observations or for reproaches. However, since you ask for explanations, and since, thanks be to Heaven, I feel nothing in myself which can prevent me from giving them, I am willing once more to come to an explanation with you.

Anyone who read your letters would think me unjust or capricious. I think I deserve that no one should think that of me; it seems to me that you especially are least of all in a position to think so. No doubt you felt that by compelling my justification you would force me to recall all that has passed between us. Apparently you thought you had only to gain by this examination; since, for my part, I do not think I have anything to lose by it, at least in your eyes, I am not afraid to undertake it. Indeed it is perhaps the only means of knowing which of us two has the right to complain of the other.

From the first day of your arrival at this Château, Monsieur, I think you will admit that at least your reputation gave me the right to be reserved with you; and without being taxed with an excess of prudery I think I might have limited myself merely to expressions of the coldest politeness. You yourself would have treated me with indulgence and would have thought it quite simple for so inexperienced a woman to have not even the merit necessary to appreciate your own.

Assuredly that would have been the prudent course ; and it would have been the less difficult for me to follow because (I will not conceal it from you) when Madame de Rosemonde came to inform me of your arrival I was compelled to recollect my friendship for her, and her friendship for you, in order not to let her see how much I was annoyed by this news.

I willingly admit that you showed yourself at first under a more favourable aspect than I had imagined ; but you will admit in your turn that it did not last long and that you soon grew weary of a constraint for which you apparently did not think yourself sufficiently recompensed by the favourable opinion it gave me of you.

It was then that you took an unfair advantage of my good faith and confidence ; you did not shrink from speaking to me about a sentiment which you must have known would offend me ; and, while you did nothing save aggravate your faults by multiplying them, I was seeking an opportunity to forget them by offering you a chance to atone for them, at least in part. My request was so just that you yourself did not feel you could refuse it ; but you made a right out of my indulgence and profited by it to ask me for a permission which, no doubt, I ought not to have granted, yet which you obtained. Certain conditions were attached to it, none of which you have observed ; and your correspondence has been such that every one of your letters made it a duty for me not to reply. It was at the moment when your obstinacy compelled me to send you away from me that, perhaps from a blameworthy condescension, I tried the one means which could permit me to bring you back ; but of what value is a virtuous sentiment in your eyes ? You scorn friendship ; and in your mad intoxication you count miseries and shame as nothing, you seek only pleasures and victims.

You are as inconsiderate in your proceedings as you are inconsequential in your reproaches ; you forget your promises, or rather you make it an amusement to break them ; after having consented to go away from me, you return here without being recalled ; without any regard for my requests and reasons, without having even the politeness to inform me beforehand, you did not shrink from exposing me to a surprise whose effect (although it was assuredly a very simple matter) might have been interpreted in a sense unfavourable to me by the other persons present. You did not try to distract attention from, or to dissipate, the embarrassment you had caused ; you appeared to devote all your attention to increasing it still more. At table you chose a place exactly beside mine ; a slight indisposition forced me to leave before the others and instead of respecting my solitude you persuaded everyone to come and disturb it. Returned to the drawing-room, I found you beside me if I took a step ; if I said a word it was always you who replied. The most insignificant word served you as a pretext for returning to a conversation I did not wish to hear, which might even have compromised me ; for indeed, Monsieur, however skilful you may be, I think others are able to understand what I understand.

Thus I am forced by you into immobility and silence, and none the less you continue to pursue me ; I cannot raise my eyes without meeting yours. I am continually obliged to look away ; and from a most incomprehensible thoughtlessness you fixed the eyes of the company upon me at a moment when I should have liked to be able even to avoid my own.

And you complain of my conduct ! And you are surprised at my eagerness to avoid you ! Ah ! Rather blame my indulgence, rather be surprised that I did not leave at the moment you arrived. I ought perhaps to have done so ; and you will compel me to this violent but necessary course if you do not cease your offensive pursuit. No, I do not forget, I shall never forget what I owe to myself, what I owe to the bonds I have formed, bonds I respect and cherish ; and I beg you to believe that if ever I found myself reduced to the unhappy dilemma of having to sacrifice them or sacrifice myself, I should not hesitate for an instant. Good-bye, Monsieur.

From . . ., 16th of September, 17—.

## LETTER LXXIX

*The Vicomte de Valmont to the Marquise de Merteuil*

I meant to go shooting this morning ; but the weather is detestable. I have nothing to read but a new novel, which would bore even a school-girl. It will be at least two hours until luncheon ; so in spite of my long letter yesterday I shall chat to you again. I am quite sure not to weary you, for I shall talk to you about the "very handsome Prévan." How is it you have not heard of his famous adventure which separated "the inseparables ?" I wager the first word will bring it back to your mind. However, here it is, since you want it.

Yo u remember that all Paris was surprised that three women, all three of them pretty, all three of them with the same talents, and able to advance the same claims, should remain in intimate friendship from the moment of their entry into society. At first the reason was thought to be their extreme timidity ; but soon they were surrounded by a numerous group whose attentions they shared, and were made aware of their worth by the eagerness and regards of which they were the objects ; yet their union became all the closer ; and you would have said that the triumph of one was always the triumph of the two others. It was hoped that the moment of love at least would create some rivalry. Our charming ladies vied with each other for the honour of being the apple of discord ; I should myself have entered the ranks if the great vogue of the Comtesse de . . . at that time had allowed me to be unfaithful to her before I obtained the favour I sought.

However our three beauties made their choice at the same carnival, as if in concert ; and far from exciting the storms which had been expected it only rendered their friendship more interesting through the charm of mutual confidences.

The crowd of rejected suitors then joined the crowd of jealous women and this scandalous constancy was submitted to public censure. Some asserted that in this society of "inseparables" (so they were called then) the fundamental law was community of property and that it applied even to love; others maintained that if the three lovers were exempt from male rivals, they had female rivals; some went so far as to say that the lovers had only been received from decency and had merely obtained a title with no functions.

These rumours, true or false, did not have the expected effect. On the contrary the three couples felt they would be lost if they separated at this moment; they adopted the course of weathering out the storm; the public, which wearies of everything, soon wearied of a fruitless satire. Carried away by its natural frivolity, it turned to other things; and then, coming back to this with its usual inconsistency, it changed censure into praise. Since everything here is a matter of fashion, the enthusiasm gained ground; it was becoming a positive delirium when Prévan undertook to verify these prodigies and to settle public opinion and his own about them.

He therefore sought out these models of perfection. He was easily admitted into their society and considered this a favourable omen. He knew very well that happy people are not so easily accessible. He very soon saw, in fact, that this boasted happiness was like the happiness of kings—more envied than desirable. He noticed that these supposed inseparables began to look for outside pleasures and even to seek distractions; and from this he concluded that the bonds of love or friendship were already slackened or broken and that only the ties of vanity and habit retained some strength.

However, the women, united by the emergency, preserved among themselves the appearance of the same intimacy; but the men, who were freer in their proceedings, discovered they had duties to fulfil or other affairs to follow; they still complained of them but had ceased to avoid them and their evenings were rarely complete.

This behaviour on their part was useful to the assiduous Prévan who, naturally placed beside the neglected lady of the day, took occasion to offer alternately, as circumstance permitted, the same attentions, to each of the three friends. He easily perceived that to make a choice among them would be his ruin; that the false shame of finding herself the first to be unfaithful would frighten whichever woman he preferred; that the wounded vanity of the two others would make them enemies of the new lover and that they would not fail to oppose him with all the severity of high principles; and finally that jealousy would certainly revive the attentions of a rival who might still be formidable. Everything would have become an obstacle; but in his triple project everything became easy; each woman was indulgent because she was concerned in it and each man because he thought he was not.

Prévan, who at that time had only one woman to victimise, was so fortunate as to have her become conspicuous. Her position as a foreigner and her adroit refusal of a great prince's attentions had fixed upon her the observation of the court and the town; her lover shared the honour of it and made use of it with his new mistresses. The one difficulty was to carry on the three intrigues at the same time, for their progress was necessarily regulated by the slowest; indeed I had it from one of his confidants that his greatest difficulty was to delay one of them who was ready to begin nearly a fortnight before the others.

At last the great day arrived. Prévan, who had obtained the consent of all three, was now master of the proceedings and arranged them as you will see. One of the three husbands was away, the other was going at dawn the next day, the third was in Paris. The inseparable women were to sup with the future widow; but the new Master had not allowed the old Servants to be invited. The morning of the same day he made three packets from the letters of his mistress; he accompanied one with a portrait he had received from her, the second with a true lover's knot she had painted herself, the third with a lock of her hair; each one took this third of a sacrifice as a complete sacrifice and consented in exchange to send a letter, breaking off relations, to the disgraced lover.

That was a good deal; but it was not enough. She whose husband was in Paris had only the daytime at her disposal; it was agreed that a feigned indisposition should excuse her from supping with her friend and that the whole evening should be Prévan's; she whose husband was away granted the night; and dawn, the moment of the third husband's departure, was marked down by the last for the rendezvous.[1]

Prévan, who neglected nothing, then ran to the fair foreigner, carried and created there the ill-humour he needed and only left after having made a quarrel which assured him twenty-four hours of liberty. Having thus made his dispositions, he went home with the purpose of taking some rest; but other affairs were waiting for him.

The letters breaking off relations had been a flash of light to the disgraced lovers; each one of them could have no doubt but that he was sacrificed to Prévan; and their annoyance at being trifled with was added to the ill-humour which is almost always created by the little humiliation of being left; all three, without communicating with each other, but as if in concert, resolved to have satisfaction and took the course of demanding it from their favoured rival.

He therefore found three challenges waiting for him; he accepted them honourably; but not wishing to lose either the pleasures or the fame of this adventure he fixed the meetings for the morning of the next day and assigned them all three to the same place and the same hour. This was at one of the gates of the Bois de Boulogne.

When evening came he ran his triple career with equal success, at least he afterwards boasted that each of his new mistresses thrice received the gage and oath of his love. Here, as you may suppose, the

[1] "*L'heure du berger*" literally "the shepherd's hour," the common phrase for a lover's rendezvous.

story lacks proof ; all the impartial historian can do is to point out to the incredulous reader that excited vanity and imagination can achieve prodigies, and moreover that the morning that was to follow so brilliant a night might be held to excuse him from consideration of the future. In any case the following facts are more certain.

Prévan arrived punctually at his rendezvous ; there he found his three rivals, a little surprised at meeting each other ; and perhaps each of them already partly consoled by finding he had companions in misfortune. He addressed them in an affable and sprightly way and made them the following speech which has been faithfully reported to me :

" Gentlemen," said he, " by finding yourselves met together here you have doubtless guessed that all three of you have the same reason for complaint against me. I am ready to give you satisfaction. Decide by lot among yourselves which of the three shall first attempt a vengeance to which you have all an equal right. I have brought no second and no witnesses. I had none for the offence ; I ask none for the reparation." Then, giving way to his gambling propensities, he added : " I know one rarely wins ' seven and the go '[1] ; but whatever be the fate which is in store for me, a man has always lived long enough when he has had time to acquire the love of women and the esteem of men ! "

While his astonished adversaries gazed at each other in silence and their delicacy was perhaps calculating that this triple combat was not an equal match, Prévan went on : " I will not conceal from you that the night I have just passed has fatigued me cruelly. It would be generous on your part to allow me to recruit my strength. I have given orders for a breakfast to be prepared near here. Do me the honour of accepting it. Let us breakfast together and above all let us breakfast gaily. We may fight for such trifles but I think they should not be allowed to spoil our temper."

The breakfast was accepted. Prévan, they say, had never been so amiable. He had the skill to humiliate none of his rivals ; to persuade them that they would all easily have had the same successes, and above all to make them admit they would not have missed the opportunity any more than he had. Once these facts were admitted the rest arranged itself. And so before the breakfast was over they had already repeated ten times that such women did not deserve that honest men should fight for them. This idea brought cordiality with it, wine fortified the cordiality ; so that a few moments afterwards, it was not sufficient to bear no ill will, and they swore an unreserved friendship.

Prévan no doubt was as glad of this result as of the other, but he was unwilling to lose any of his celebrity. Consequently he adroitly altered his plans to fit the circumstances. " After all," said he to the three offended lovers, " you should avenge yourselves not upon me but upon your faithless mistresses. I offer you the opportunity. Like yourselves, I feel already an injury which I shall soon share ; for if each of you has been unable to hold one of them, can I hope to hold all three of them ?

[1] " *Sept et le va,*" a gambling term.

Your quarrel becomes mine. Come and sup this evening in my house, and I hope to delay your vengeance no longer." They wanted him to explain, but he replied in the tone of superiority which the circumstances authorised him to take : " Gentlemen, I think I have proved to you that I have some ability in managing ; rely on me." They all consented ; and after having embraced their new friend, separated until the evening to await the result of his promises.

Without wasting any time Prévan returned to Paris, and, in accordance with custom, visited his new conquests. He persuaded all three of them to come that evening and sup privately with him at his house. Two of them indeed made some difficulties, but what is there left to refuse on the morning after ? He arranged the meetings with an hour between each, the time needed for his plan. After these preparations, he went away, informed the three other conspirators and all four went off gaily to wait for their victims.

They heard the first one arrive. Prévan appeared alone, received her with an air of alacrity, and led her to the sanctuary of which she thought herself the divinity ; then, disappearing on some slight pretext, he immediately sent the outraged lover in his stead.

As you may suppose, the confusion of a woman who is not yet accustomed to adventures rendered the triumph very easy, at this moment ; every reproach which was not made was counted as a grace ; and the fugitive slave, delivered up again to her former master, was only too glad to hope for pardon by returning to her first chains. The treaty of peace was ratified in a more solitary place, and the empty stage was filled in turn by the other actors practically in the same way, and assuredly with the same ending.

However, each of the women still thought herself the only one concerned. Their astonishment and embarrassment increased when the three couples met for supper ; but their confusion was at its height when Prévan reappeared among them and had the cruelty to make excuses to the three faithless ladies—excuses which gave away their secret and showed them plainly to what extent they had been duped.

However they sat down to table and soon regained countenance ; the men accepted the situation, the women submitted to it. All had hatred in their hearts ; but their words were none the less tender ; gaiety awakened desire which in turn lent new charms to their merriment. This astounding orgy lasted until morning ; and when they separated the women had every reason to think themselves forgiven but the men had kept their resentment and the next day broke matters off without the possibility of a reconciliation ; and not content with leaving their light mistresses they completed their vengeance by making the adventure public. Since that time one of the women is in a convent and the other two are languishing in exile in their country estates.[1]

[1] This end to this edifying adventure was occasionally a fact in eighteenth century life, in spite of the general tolerance. It will be noticed that the women pay the price. Here again we find Laclos's " feminist thesis " and incidentally a justification for the perfidy of the Madame de Merteuil.

This is the story of Prévan ; it is for you to see whether you wish to add to his fame and harness yourself to his triumphal chariot. Your letter really made me uneasy and I am impatiently waiting a wiser and clearer answer to the last letter I wrote you.

Good-bye, my fair friend ; beware of the amusing or capricious ideas which always seduce you too easily. Remember that in the career you are following, intelligence is not enough and that a single imprudence may become an irreparable misfortune. And finally sometimes allow prudent friendship to guide your pleasures.

Good-bye, I still love you as much as if you were reasonable.

From . . ., 18th of September, 17—.

## LETTER LXXX

*The Chevalier Danceny to Cécile Volanges*

Cécile, my dearest Cécile, when will the day come for us to meet again ? Who will teach me to live so far from you ? What will give me the needful strength and courage ? Never, no, never, can I endure this fatal absence. Every day adds to my misery and I see no end to it ! Valmont who promised me help and consolation, Valmont neglects and perhaps has forgotten me. He is near her whom I love ; he knows not what one suffers when far from her. He did not write to me when sending me your last letter. Yet it is he who should inform me when and how I am to see you. Has he then nothing to tell me ? You yourself do not speak to me of it ; can it be that you have ceased to share my longing for it ? Ah ! Cécile, Cécile, I am very unhappy. I love you more than ever ; but this love which is the charm of my life is becoming its torment.

No, I cannot continue to live thus, I must see you, I must, if only for a moment. When I get up I say to myself : I shall not see her. I go to bed saying : I have not seen her. These long, long days bring not a moment of happiness. All is privation, all is regret, all is despair ; and all these misfortunes come to me from her whence I expected all my pleasure ! Add to these killing griefs my uneasiness about yours and you will have an idea of my situation. I think of you continually, yet never think of you without uneasiness. If I see you grieved and unhappy, I suffer for all your griefs ; if I see you tranquil and consoled, my own griefs are redoubled. Everywhere I find unhappiness.

Ah ! It was not thus when you dwelt in the same place as I ! Then all was pleasure. The certainty of seeing you embellished even the moments of absence ; the time I was compelled to pass far from you brought me nearer to you as it glided away. The use I made of it was always concerned with you. If I carried out my duties, they rendered me more worthy of you ; if I cultivated some talent, I hoped I should please you more. Even when the distractions of society took me away from you I was not separated from you. At the theatre I tried to guess what would have pleased you ; a concert reminded me of your talents and our sweet occupation. In company and on walks I seized upon the slightest resemblance to you. I compared you with everyone ; you had the advantage everywhere. Each moment of the day was marked by a new homage and each evening I brought them as a tribute to your feet.

And now, what have I left ? Painful regrets, eternal privations, and a faint hope which is diminished by Valmont's silence and changed into uneasiness by yours ! We are separated only by ten leagues and this distance, so easily traversed, becomes an insurmountable obstacle ! And when I implore my friend and my mistress to help me overcome it. both remain cold and calm ! Far from helping me, they do not even answer me.

What has happened to Valmont's active friendship ? Above all what has happened to those tender feelings of yours which rendered you so ingenious in discovering means for us to see each other every day ? I remember that sometimes, though I still desired it, I was forced to sacrifice it to prudence or to duties ; what did you not say to me then ? By how many pretexts did you combat my reasons ! And recollect, my Cécile, my reasons always yielded to your wishes. I do not make that a merit ; I had not even the merit of sacrifice. What you desired to obtain, I burned to grant. But now I ask in my turn ; and what is my request ? To see you for a moment, to give and receive once more the vow of an eternal love. Is it no longer your happiness as it is mine ? I repel this disheartening idea which would put the finishing touch to my misfortunes. You love me, you will always love me ; I believe it, I am sure of it, I will never doubt it ; but my situation is terrible and I cannot endure it much longer. Good-bye, Cécile.

Paris, 18th of September, 17—.

## LETTER LXXXI

*The Marquise de Merteuil to the Vicomte de Valmont*

How much I pity you for your fears ! How they prove my superiority over you ! And you think to teach me, to lead me ? Ah ! My poor Valmont, what a distance there still is from you to me ! No, not all the pride of your sex will suffice to fill up the interval which separates us. Because you could not carry out my plans, you think them impossible ! Proud, weak creature ! It well befits you to try to gauge my methods and to judge of my resources ! Really, Vicomte, your advice put me out of humour and I cannot conceal it from you. That you should mask your incredible clumsiness towards your Madame de Tourvel by displaying to me as a triumph the fact that for a moment you disconcerted this timid woman—that I allow. When you boast of obtaining a look, a single look, I smile and grant it you. And when, feeling in spite of yourself the unimportance of your action, you try to hide it from my notice by flattering me with your sublime effort in bringing together two children, who are both of them burning to see each other, and who, let me observe in parenthesis, owe the ardour of that desire to me alone—that too I will admit. And when finally you make use of these brilliant actions to tell me in a doctoral tone that " it is better to spend one's time in carrying out plans than in talking about them "—well, such vanity does not harm me and I forgive it. But that you should think I need your prudence, that I should go astray if I did not defer to your opinion, that I ought to sacrifice to it a pleasure, a fantasy—really, Vicomte, you are becoming too proud of the confidence I have in you!

And what then have you done that I have not surpassed a thousand times? You have seduced, ruined even, a number of women; but what difficulties did you have to overcome? What obstacles to surmount? Where is there in that any merit which is really yours? A handsome face, the result of mere chance; grace, which is almost always given by experience; wit indeed, but mere chatter would take its place if needed; a quite praiseworthy impudence, but probably due solely to the facility of your first successes; if I am not wrong, those are all your methods; for, as for the celebrity you have been able to acquire, I think you will not expect me to rank very high the art of creating or seizing the opportunity of a scandal.

As to prudence and shrewdness, I do not mention myself—but where is the woman who would not possess more than you? Why! Your Madame de Tourvel leads you like a child.

Believe me, Vicomte, people rarely acquire the qualities they can dispense with. You fought without risk and necessarily acted without wariness. For you men defeats are simply so many victories the less. In this unequal struggle our fortune is not to lose and your misfortune not to win. If I granted you as many talents as we have, still how much we should surpass you from the continual necessity we have of using them!

Let us suppose, if you like, that you display as much skill in conquering us as we do in defending ourselves or in yielding; yet you will admit this skill becomes useless to you after success. You are wholly occupied with your new inclination and you give yourselves up to it without fear and without reserve; its duration does not matter to you.

Indeed, these ties reciprocally given and received (I speak the jargon of love) can be drawn tighter or broken by you alone as you choose; we are but too happy if in your inconsistencies you prefer mystery to publicity and content yourselves with a humiliating abandonment without making the idol of one day a victim of the next!

But if an unfortunate woman is the first to feel the weight of her chain, what risks she runs if she tries to escape it, if she even dares to raise it. It is with trembling that she attempts to send away the man whom her heart repels with an effort. If he persists in staying, she has to yield from fear what she granted to love:

> Her arms still open though her heart is closed.

She must unloose with prudent skill the very ties you would have broken. She is at the mercy of her enemy and is without resource if he is without generosity ; and how can she hope it of him, when, though he is sometimes praised for having it, he is never blamed for lacking it ?

Doubtless you will not deny these truths which are so obvious they are commonplaces. But if you have seen me directing events and opinions and making these formidable men the toy of my caprices or my fantasies ; depriving some of will, others of the power of harming me ; if in accordance with my changing tastes I have turn by turn attached to my train or cast far from me

Those unthroned tyrants now become my slaves[1] ;

if through these frequent revolutions I have kept my reputation intact ; ought you not to have concluded that, since I was born to avenge my sex and to dominate yours, I must have created methods unknown to anybody but myself ?

Ah ! Keep your advice and your fears for those unbalanced women who rave of their " sentiment," whose excited imagination would make one think nature had placed their senses in their heads ; who, having never reflected, always confuse love with the lover ; who, in their foolish illusion, think that the one man with whom they have sought pleasure is the sole depository of it ; who, being truly superstitious, give the priest the respect and faith which is due only to the divinity.

Fear also for those who are more vain than prudent and who will not allow themselves to be abandoned when necessary.

Tremble above all for those women, active in their idleness, whom you call " tender," of whom love takes possession so easily and with such power ; women who feel the need to occupy themselves with it even when they do not enjoy it and who, abandoning themselves unreservedly to the ebullition of their ideas, give birth through them to those sweet letters which are so dangerous to write ; women who are not afraid to confide these proofs of their weakness to the person who causes them, imprudent women, who cannot see their future enemy in their present lover.

But what have I in common with these incautious women ? When have you seen me depart from the rules I have prescribed for myself or lose my principles ? I say my principles and I say it advisedly ; for they are not, like other women's principles, given at hazard, accepted without reflection and followed from habit ; they are the result of my profound meditations ; I created them and I can say that I am my own work.

[1] It is not known whether this verse and the one before it, " Her arms still open though her heart is closed " are quotations from little known works or whether they are part of Mme de Merteuil's prose. What makes it probable is the multitude of faults of this kind in all the letters of this correspondence. Only those of the Chevalier Dançeny are free from them, perhaps because he sometimes occupied himself with poetry and therefore his more practised ear enabled him to avoid this defect more easily. (C. de L.)

I entered society, an unmarried girl, at a time when my condition compelled me to silence and inaction ; I made use of it to observe and to reflect. While I was thought light-headed or inattentive because I paid little attention to the conversations they were careful to hold with me, I carefully gathered those they tried to hide from me.

That useful curiosity which served to instruct me, also taught me to dissimulate ; I was often forced to conceal the objects of my attention from the eyes of those about me and I tried to direct my own eyes at will ; from this I gained that ability to simulate when I chose that preoccupied gaze you have praised so often. Encouraged by this first success, I tried to govern the different expressions of my face in the same way. Did I experience some grief, I studied to show an air of serenity, even one of joy ; I carried my zeal so far as to cause myself voluntary pain and to seek for an expression of pleasure at the same time. I worked over myself with the same care and more trouble to repress the symptoms of an unexpected joy. In this way I acquired that power over my features by which I have sometimes seen you astonished.

I was still very young and practically without any interest ; but I only possessed my thoughts and I felt indignant that they might be snatched from me or surprised in me against my will. Furnished with these first arms, I made trial of them. I was not content with not allowing people to see through me, I amused myself by showing myself under various aspects ; certain of my movements, I now watched over what I said ; I regulated both according to circumstances or even only according to my fancy. From that moment on, my way of thinking was for myself alone and I only showed what it was useful for me to render visible.

This labour upon myself fixed my attention on the expression and character of faces ; from that I obtained a penetrating glance which experience however, has taught me not to rely upon entirely, but which in general has rarely deceived me.

I was not yet fifteen and already I possessed the talents to which the greater part of our politicians owe their reputation ; and I considered myself still in the first elements of the science I wished to acquire.

As you may suppose, I was like all young girls and tried to guess at love and its pleasures. But I had never been to a convent, I had no intimate friend, and I was watched by a vigilant mother ; I had only vague ideas which I could not settle ; even nature which I have subsequently had every reason to be grateful to, had not given me any indication. It was as if she was silently working to perfect her labour. My head alone was in a ferment ; I did not desire to enjoy, I wanted to know ; my desire to learn suggested the means to me.

I realised that the only man with whom I could discuss this topic without compromising myself was my confessor. I made up my mind at once ; I overcame my little bashfulness ; and boasting of a fault I had not committed, I accused myself of having done " everything that women do." That was my expression ; but when I spoke in this way I did not know at all what idea I was expressing. My hope was not entirely disappointed or entirely fulfilled ; the fear of betraying myself prevented me from obtaining information ; but the good father made it out to be so wicked that I concluded the pleasure must be extreme ; and the desire to enjoy it succeeded the desire to know what it was.

I do not know where this desire might have led me and as I was then quite without experience a single occasion might perhaps have ruined me ; fortunately for me my mother informed me a few days later that I was to be married and immediately the certainty of knowing extinguished my curiosity and I reached Monsieur de Merteuil's arms a virgin.

I awaited with confidence the moment which would enlighten me and I needed premeditation to show embarrassment and fear. This first night, which is generally thought to be so cruel or so sweet, was for me simply an opportunity for experience ; I noticed very carefully both pain and pleasure and in these different sensations I saw nothing but facts to collect and to meditate upon.

This kind of study very soon began to please me ; but faithful to my principles, and feeling perhaps instinctively that no one should be further from my confidence than my husband, I resolved from the mere fact that I was moved by it to appear unmoved to my husband. This apparent coldness was afterwards the unshakable foundation of his blind confidence ; on further reflection I added to this the air of heedlessness which my years sanctioned ; and he never thought me so childish as in the moments when I praised him with most boldness. However, I must confess I allowed myself at first to be carried away in the whirlpool of society and I gave myself up entirely to its futile distractions. But when after some months Monsieur de Merteuil took me to his gloomy country estate, the fear of boredom brought back the taste for study ; and finding myself surrounded by people whose difference of rank placed me above all suspicion, I made use of this to give my experiments a wider field. It was there that I made certain that love which they tell us is the cause of our pleasures, is at most only the pretext for them.

Monsieur de Merteuil's illness interrupted these soft occupations ; I had to follow him to town whither he went for medical aid. He died, as you know, shortly afterwards ; and although, taking it all round, I had no reason to complain of him, I felt none the less keenly the value of the liberty my widowhood would give me and I promised myself to make good use of it.

My mother expected I should go into a convent or return to live with her. I refused both courses ; all I granted to decency was to return to the country again, where I still had a few observations to make.

I supported them with the assistance of reading ; but do not think that it was all of the kind you suppose. I studied our manners in novels, our opinions in philosophers ; I even sought in the severest moralists what it was they exacted of us and in this way I learned what one could do, what one ought to think and what one ought to appear. Once I was certain on these three points, the last alone presented some difficulties in practice ; I hoped to conquer them and I meditated the means.

I began to grow weary of my rustic pleasures which were too monotonous for my active head ; I felt a need for coquetry to reconcile me with love, not to feel it veritably but to inspire and to feign it. In vain I had been told and had read that this sentiment could not be feigned ; I saw that to do so successfully one had only to join the talent of a comedian to the mind of an author. I practised myself in both arts and perhaps with some success ; but instead of seeking the vain applause of the theatre, I resolved to employ for my happiness what others sacrifice to vanity.

A year passed away in these different occupations. My period of mourning allowed me to reappear and I returned to town with my plans ; I had not foreseen the first obstacle I met with.

My long solitude, my austere retirement had given me a veneer of prudery which frightened all our most charming men ; they kept away and left me at the mercy of a crowd of wearisome creatures who all wanted to marry me. The difficulty was not in refusing them ; but several of these refusals displeased my family and I wasted on these private annoyances a time which I had promised myself to employ so charmingly. I was therefore obliged, in order to recall the one party and to get rid of the other, to display a few imprudences and to employ the care I had meant to use for the preservation of my reputation in harming it. I succeeded easily, as you may believe. But not being carried away by any passion, I only did what I considered necessary and measured the doses of my heedlessness with prudence.

As soon as I obtained the objective I wished to reach, I returned on my steps and gave the honour of my amendment to those women who claim merit and virtue since they can have no pretention to charm. This was a master stroke which was of more value to me than I had hoped. These grateful Duennas constituted themselves my defenders ; and their blind zeal for what they called their work was carried to such an extent that at the slightest remark anyone dared to make about me, the whole band of prudes exclaimed that it was a scandal and an insult. The same method secured me also the support of our women with pretentions, who, persuaded that I had given up the idea of following the same course as themselves, chose me as the object of their praises every time they wished to prove that they did not talk scandal about everybody.

However my preceding conduct had brought back the lovers ; and to steer cautiously between them and my faithless female protectors I gave myself out to be a tender-hearted but fastidious woman, whose excessive delicacy supplied her with weapons against love.

Then I began to display on the great stage the talents I had procured myself. My first care was to acquire the reputation of being invincible.

To attain this I always pretended to accept the attentions of those men only who did not please me. I employed them usefully in gaining me the honours of resistance, while I yielded myself fearlessly to the accepted lover. But my feigned timidity never allowed him to accompany me into society ; and thus the gaze of the company was always fixed upon the rejected lover.

You know how quickly I make up my mind ; that is because I have observed a woman's secret is almost always betrayed by the preliminary attentions. Whatever one may do the tone is never the same after as before the success. This difference does not escape an attentive observer; and I have found it less dangerous to be mistaken in my choice than to allow myself to be fathomed. In this way I have the further advantage of removing the appearances by which alone we are judged.

These precautions and the further ones of never writing and never giving up any proof of my defeat may appear excessive, but have never seemed to me sufficient. I had descended into my own heart and I studied in it the heart of others. There I saw that everybody keeps a secret in it which he must not allow to be revealed—a truth which antiquity appears to have known better than we and of which the story of Samson may be only an ingenious parable. Like a new Delilah I always used my power as she did to surprise this important secret. Ah ! How many of our modern Samsons are there whose hair I keep under my scissors ! I have ceased to be afraid of them ; they are the only men I have sometimes let myself humiliate. With the others I was more pliant ; the art of making them unfaithful to avoid appearing fickle, a feigned friendship, an apparent confidence, a few generous actions, the flattering idea each of them had that he was my only lover, these procured me their discretion. Finally, when these methods failed me I have foreseen the time of breaking things off and I have smothered with ridicule or calumny any credence these dangerous men might have obtained.

You see me constantly practise what I tell you here ; and you doubt my prudence ! Well ! Think of the time when you paid your first attentions to me ; none ever flattered me so much ; I desired you before I had seen you. Seduced by your reputation, I felt you were lacking to my glory ; I burned to wrestle with you hand to hand. This was the only one of my inclinations which ever had a moment's power over me. And yet if you had wished to ruin me, what means could you have found ? Vain talk which leaves no trace behind it, which your very reputation would have helped to make suspicious, and a train of improbable facts, the accurate relation of which would have sounded like a badly written novel.

Since then I have indeed given up to you all my secrets ; but you know the interests which unite us and whether, of us two, it is I who should be charged with imprudence.[1]

[1] It will be seen later, in *Letter CLII*, not what M. de Valmont's secret was, but practically of what kind it was ; and the reader will understand that further enlightenment on this subject could not be given. (C. de L.)

Since I am in the way of giving you information, I will do so exactly. I can hear you telling me that at least I am at the mercy of my waiting-woman ; indeed, although she has not the secret of my feelings, she has the secret of my actions. When you spoke to me of her before, I simply answered that I was sure of her ; and the proof that this reply was sufficient for your tranquillity is that you have since on your own account confided dangerous secrets to her. But now that you are offended about Prévan and have lost your head I suppose you will not believe me any more on my bare word. You must therefore be instructed.

First of all, this girl is my foster-sister, and that tie which to us does not appear to be one is not without strength for people of her class ; moreover I have her secret and better still ; she was the victim of a love-folly which would have ruined her if I had not saved her. Her parents, bristling up with honour, wanted nothing less than to have her shut up. They applied to me. I saw at a glance how useful their anger might be to me. I supported them and asked for the order, which I obtained. Then, suddenly going over to the side of clemency to which I brought her parents also, and making use of my credit with the old Minister, I made them all consent to leave the order in my hands, and to give me the power of withholding it or demanding its execution according as I should determine from the girl's future conduct. She knows therefore that her fate is in my hands ; and if, which is impossible, these powerful methods should not stop her, is it not obvious that her conduct made public and her authentic punishment would soon deprive her words of all credence ? To these precautions which I call fundamental, are added a thousand others, either local or casual, which are suggested to me by reflection and habit ; to give them in detail would be circumstantial but the use of them is important and you must take the trouble to collect them from my whole conduct if you wish to understand them.

But to suppose that I have taken so much trouble and shall not enjoy the fruits of it ; that after I have raised myself above other women by painful labour, I should consent to crawl like them between impudence and timidity ; that above all I should fear a man to the extent of seeing my safety nowhere but in flight—no, Vicomte, never. I must conquer or perish. As to Prévan, I want to have him and I will have him ; he wants to tell it and he shall not tell it ; that is our romance in a phrase. Good-bye.

From . . ., 20th of September, 17—.

## LETTER LXXXII

*Cécile Volanges to the Chevalier Danceny*

Heavens, how your letter distressed me ! I did well to be so impatient to receive it ! I hoped to find consolation in it and now I am more upset than before I received it. I cried a lot in reading it ; I do not blame you for that; I have already cried many times on account of you without that distressing me. But this time it is not the same thing.

What do you mean when you say your love becomes a torment to you, that you cannot live any longer in this way, nor endure your situation any more? Are you going to stop loving me because it is not so agreeable as it was before? It seems to me that I am no happier than you are, on the contrary; and yet I only love you the more. If Monsieur de Valmont has not written to you, it is not my fault; I could not ask him to do so, because I have not been alone with him and we have arranged never to speak to each other in other people's presence; and that is on your account too, so that he can sooner do what you desire. I do not say that I do not desire it also, and you ought to be certain of this; but what do you expect me to do? If you think it is so easy, find the way, I ask nothing better.

Do you think it is very pleasant for me to be scolded every day by Mamma, who never said anything harsh to me before; but on the contrary? It is worse now than if I were at the convent.

But I consoled myself by remembering that it was for your sake; there were even moments when I felt I was glad of it; but when I see that you are angry as well and that without it being my fault at all, I am more upset than by anything that has happened to me up to now.

It is difficult even to receive your letters and if Monsieur de Valmont were not so kind and so clever I should not know what to do, and it is still more difficult to write to you. All the morning I dare not, because Mamma is close at hand and keeps coming into my room. Sometimes I can in the afternoon, under the pretext of singing or playing on my harp; and even then I must break off at every line so that they can hear I am working. Luckily my waiting-woman sometimes goes to sleep in the evening and I tell her I can easily go to bed myself, to make her go away and leave me the light. And then I must get under my bed-curtains so that no light can be seen, and then I must listen for the slightest noise so that I can hide everything in my bed if anyone comes. I wish you were here to see! You would see that one has to be very much in love to do all this. Indeed it is true I do all I can and I wish I could do more.

Certainly I do not refuse to tell you that I love you and that I shall always love you; I never said it with a better heart; and you are angry! Yet you assured me before I had said it to you that it was enough to make you happy. You cannot deny it; it is in your letters. Although I have them no longer, I remember it as well as when I read them every day. And because we are absent from each other, you do not think in the same way! But this absence will not last forever, perhaps? Heavens! How unhappy I am! And you are the cause of it!

About your letters—I hope you have kept those that Mamma took from me and sent back to you; there must come a time when I shall not be so oppressed as I am now, and you will give them all back to me. How happy I shall be when I can keep them all without anybody being able to object! Now I give them all back to Monsieur de Valmont, because it would be too risky; in spite of that I never give them back to him without feeling very distressed.

Good-bye, my dear. I love you with all my heart. I shall love you all my life. I hope you are not grieved any more now; if I were sure of it I should cease to be grieved myself. Write me as soon as you can, for I feel I shall be sad until then.

From the Château de ——, 23rd of September, 17—.

## LETTER LXXXIII

### *The Vicomte de Valmont to Madame de Tourvel*

Pray, Madame, let us continue the intercourse so unhappily interrupted! How can I finally prove to you how much I differ from the odious portrait of me which has been made to you; above all how can I enjoy again that charming confidence you began to show me! What charms you lent to virtue! How you embellished all virtuous sentiments and forced one to cherish them! Ah! That is where you seduce; that is the most powerful seduction; it is the only one which is both powerful and respectable.

Doubtless it is enough to see you, to have the desire of pleasing you; to listen to you in company, to have this desire increased; but he who has the happiness to know you better, who can sometimes read in your soul, soon yields to a more noble enthusiasm and, touched by veneration as well as by love, adores in you the image of all virtues. I was perhaps created to love them and follow them more than others, and, after being carried away from them by a few errors, I was brought back to them by you; through you I felt all their charm again. Will you make this new love a crime in me? Will you condemn your own work? Would you reproach yourself even for the interest you might take in it? What evil can you fear from so pure a sentiment, what sweetness might you not taste in it?

My love frightens you, you think it violent, extreme? Temper it by a gentler love; do not refuse the power I offer you, which I swear never to escape from, which I dare to think would not be entirely a loss for virtue. What sacrifice could appear difficult to me were I sure your heart would reward me for it! What man is so unhappy as to be unable to enjoy the privations he imposes on himself; as not to prefer a word or a look that is granted to all the enjoyments he might ravish or surprise! And you thought I was that man! And you feared me! Ah! Why does your happiness not depend upon me! How I would avenge myself upon you, by making you happy! But that soft power is not produced by sterile friendship; it is granted only to love.

That word intimidates you! And why? A more tender attachment, a closer union, a single thought, the same happiness and the same griefs —what in these is foreign to your soul? Yet such is love! Such at least is the love you inspire and I feel! Above all it is that love which calculates without interest and can appreciate actions on their merits, not from their value; the inexhaustible treasure of tender minds, everything becomes precious when it is done by love or for love.

What is there frightening in these truths which are so easy to grasp, so sweet to practise? What fears can be caused you by a tender man whom love allows no happiness but yours? That is today the only wish I have; I would sacrifice everything to carry it out except the sentiment which inspires it; and, if you but consent to share that sentiment itself, you shall govern it yourself. But do not let us allow it to divide us any longer when it ought to unite us. If the friendship you have offered me is not a vain word, if, as you said to me yesterday, it is the softest feeling known to your soul; I do not refuse to allow friendship to bargain between us; but if friendship becomes the judge of love she must consent to listen to it, refusal to hear it would become an injustice and friendship is not unjust. A second interview will have no more disadvantages than the first; chance may again furnish the opportunity; you yourself can appoint the time. I am willing to believe that I am wrong; would you not rather amend me than combat me, and have you any doubts of my docility? If that annoying third person had not interrupted us, perhaps I should already be entirely of your opinion; who knows how far your power might go?

Shall I confess it? Sometimes I am afraid of this invincible power to which I yield myself without daring to calculate, of that irresistible charm which renders you the sovereign of my thoughts as of my actions. Alas! Perhaps it is I who should dread this interview I ask for! When it is over perhaps I shall find myself changed by my promises and doomed to burn with a love which I feel can never be extinguished, without daring even to implore your aid! Ah! Madame, for pity's sake, do not abuse your power! Ah! But if they would make you happier, if by them I should appear more worthy of you—what pains would not be softened by these consoling ideas! Yes, I feel it; to speak to you again is to give you more powerful weapons against me, is to yield myself more completely to your will. It is easier to defend oneself against your letters; they are indeed your very words, but you are not there to lend them strength. Nevertheless, the pleasure of listening to you makes me brave the danger; at least I shall have the happiness of having done everything for you even against myself; and my sacrifices will become a homage. I am but too happy to prove to you in a thousand ways, as I feel it in a thousand shapes, that, not even excepting myself, you are, you always will be the dearest object of my heart.

From the Château de . . ., 23rd September, 17—.

## LETTER LXXXIV

*The Vicomte de Valmont to Cécile Volanges*

You saw how we were thwarted yesterday. All day long I was unable to hand you the letter I had for you; I do not know if I shall find more opportunity today. I am afraid of compromising you by showing more zeal than skill; and I should not forgive myself an imprudence which would be so fatal to you and would cause my friend's despair by making you eternally unhappy. However I know love's impatiences. I feel how irksome it must be for you in your position to experience any delay in the only consolation you can enjoy at this time. I have been considering means of putting aside these obstacles and I have discovered one which will be easy to carry out, if you take some trouble.

I think I have noticed that the key to your bedroom door which opens on to the corridor, is always on your Mamma's mantelpiece. With that key everything would be easy, as you will realise; but in default of it I will procure you one like it, which will do instead. To carry this out it will be enough if I have it for one or two hours. You ought easily to find an opportunity to take it, and in order that it shall not be missed I enclose one of my own, which is rather like it, so that the difference cannot be seen unless it is tried; which they will not do. You must merely be careful to put a faded blue ribbon on it like the ribbon on yours.

You must try to have this key at breakfast-time tomorrow or the day after; because it will be easier to give it me then and can be returned to its place for evening, when your Mamma is more likely to look closely at it. I could return it to you at dinner-time if we have a proper understanding.

You know that when we go from the drawing-room to the dining-room, Madame de Rosemonde always comes last. I will give her my arm. You have only to leave your tapestry frame slowly or to let something drop, so that you stay behind; you will then be able to take the key which I shall be careful to hold behind me. Immediately after you have taken it you must not neglect to rejoin my old aunt and to caress her. If by chance you let the key drop, do not be disconcerted; I will pretend I did it and I answer for everything.

Your Mamma's lack of confidence in you and her harsh treatment of you justify this little deceit. Moreover it is the only way for you to continue to receive Danceny's letters and to transmit yours to him; any other is really too dangerous and might completely ruin you both; my prudent friendship would blame me if I continued to employ that method.

Once master of the key we shall still have to take some precautions against the noise of the door and the lock; but they are very easy. Under the same wardrobe where I hid your paper you will find oil and a feather. You sometimes go to your room when you are alone; you must make use of this time to oil the lock and the hinges. The only thing to beware of is to take care of oil-stains which would be evidence against you. You must also wait until it is night-time because if this is done with the intelligence of which you are capable, no trace of it will remain the next morning.

However, if it is noticed do not hesitate to say that it was the floor-polisher of the Château. In this case you must specify the time and even what he said to you ; as, for example, that he takes this precaution against rust for all locks which are not used. For you will realise it is not probable that you should be a witness of this without asking the reason. It is the small details which give probability, and probability renders lies without consequence by taking away the desire to verify it.

After you have read this letter, I beg you to re-read it and to pay attention to it ; first, because you must know well anything you wish to do well ; and then in order to assure yourself that I have omitted nothing. I am unaccustomed to employ artifice on my own account and have not great practice in it ; nothing less than my keen friendship for Danceny and the interest I have in you could have persuaded me to make use of these methods, however innocent they may be. I hate anything which looks like deceit ; that is my character. But I am so moved by your misfortunes that I would attempt anything to soften them.

You will realise that when this communication is once established between us it will be much easier for me to procure you the interview with Danceny which he desires. However do not speak to him yet about all this ; you would only increase his impatience, and the moment to satisfy it has not yet come. I think you ought to calm his impatience rather than to irritate it. I rely on your delicacy in this. Good-bye, my fair pupil ; for you are my pupil. Love your tutor a little and above all be docile with him ; you will find it to your advantage. I am busying myself with your happiness and you may rest assured I shall find my own in it.

From . . ., 24th of September, 17—.

## LETTER LXXXV

*The Marquise de Merteuil to the Vicomte de Valmont*

At last you will be tranquillised, and above all you will do me justice. Listen, and never again confound me with other women. My adventure with Prévan is ended ; ended ! Do you understand what that means ? You shall now judge whether he or I should boast. The relation will not be so amusing as the action ; but it would not be just that you who have done nothing but argue well or ill about this affair should receive as much pleasure from it as I, who gave my time and my trouble.

However, if you have some grand stroke to make, if you have some enterprise to attempt in which this dangerous rival seems to you to be feared, come here. He leaves the field free to you, at least for some time ; perhaps he will never rise again after the blow I have dealt him.

How fortunate you are to have me as your friend ! I am your good fairy. You languish far from the beauty who attracts you ; I say a word and you find yourself near her. You wish to avenge yourself on a woman who does you harm ; I show you the place where you can strike her and hand her over to your discretion. Finally it is I whom you invoke to remove a dangerous competitor from the lists, and I grant your prayer. Indeed if you do not pass your life in thanking me you are an ingrate. I return to my adventure and go back to the beginning.

The rendezvous made in such a loud voice as I left the Opera was overheard as I had hoped. Prévan was there ; and when the Maréchale told him politely that she was happy to see him twice in succession at her days, he was careful to reply that since Monday evening he had altered a thousand arrangements to be able to come that evening. " A word to the wise ! " However as I wished to know with more certainty whether or not I was the real object of this flattering eagerness, I wanted to compel the new wooer to choose between me and his ruling passion. I declared I should not gamble ; and he on his part discovered a thousand pretexts for not gambling ; so my first triumph was over *lansquenet*.

I took possession of the Bishop of . . . for my conversation ; I chose him because of his acquaintance with the hero of the day, to whom I wished to give every opportunity of addressing me. I was also very glad to have a respectable witness who, if needed, could depose to my conduct and to my speech. This arrangement succeeded.

After the usual vague remarks, Prévan soon made himself master of the conversation and assumed different tones in turn to try which would please me. I refused that of sentiment, as not believing in it ; by being serious I stopped his gaiety which seemed to me too airy for a beginning; he fell back on delicate friendship and it was under that commonplace flag that we began our mutual attack.

The Bishop did not go down to supper ; Prévan therefore gave me his arm and was naturally placed beside me at table. I must be just and admit he showed great skill in keeping up our private conversation while appearing only to concern himself with the general conversation, the whole weight of which seemed to fall on him. At dessert he spoke of a new play to be given on Monday next at the Français. I expressed some regret at not having my box ; he offered me his which I first refused, as is customary ; to which he replied wittily enough that I did not understand him, that he would certainly not sacrifice his box to someone he did not know, but that he simply informed me the Maréchale had the use of it. She lent herself to the jest and I accepted.

When we had returned to the drawing-room, he asked for a place in the box, as you may suppose, and when the Maréchale, who treats him very kindly, promised it to him " if he were good," he made it the occasion for one of those conversations with a double meaning, in which you boasted his talents. He knelt down like an obedient child (as he said) under the pretext of asking her advice and imploring her judgment, and said many flattering and quite tender things which it was easy for me to apply to myself. After supper several people gave up gambling and the conversation was more general and less interesting, but our eyes were very eloquent. I say our eyes ; I ought to have said his eyes, for mine had only one expression, that of surprise. He must have thought I was astonished and excessively preoccupied by the prodigious effect he was making on me. I think I left him very well satisfied ; I was just as pleased.

The following Monday I went to the Français as we had agreed. In spite of your literary curiosity I can tell you nothing of the play except that Prévan has a marvellous talent for flattery and that the play was a failure ; that is all I learnt. It was with regret I saw the evening ending, for really it gave me great pleasure ; and to prolong it I invited the Maréchale to come and sup with me ; this gave me a pretext to invite the amiable Flatterer who only asked for time to run and postpone an engagement with the Comtesses de P . . .[1] This name brought back all my anger ; I saw clearly that he was going to begin his confidences ; I recollected your wise advice and promised myself . . . to pursue the adventure, feeling sure I should cure him of this dangerous indiscretion.

As he was a stranger among my guests, who were not numerous that evening, he owed me the customary attentions ; and so when we went to supper he offered me his hand. When I took it I was malicious enough to make mine tremble slightly and to walk with lowered eyes and more rapid breathing. I appeared to foresee my defeat and to fear my conqueror. He noticed it perfectly ; and the traitor immediately changed his tone and behaviour. He had been gallant, he became tender. Circumstances compelled him to much the same remarks, but his gaze became less sprightly and more caressing, the inflection of his voice softer and his smile was no longer that of artifice but of contentment. In his talk he gradually subdued the fire of his sallies, and delicacy replaced wit. I ask you, would you have done better ?

On my part I became absent-minded, to such an extent that the company was forced to notice it ; and when I was reproached with it, I was skilful enough to defend myself awkwardly and to cast at Prévan a quick but timid and disconcerted glance, such as would make him think that my one fear was lest he should guess the cause of my confusion.

After supper I took advantage of the time when the good Maréchale was telling one of those stories she always tells, to place myself on my ottoman in the languid attitude caused by a tender reverie. I was not sorry that Prévan should see me thus, and indeed he honoured me with a very particular attention. As you may suppose, my timid glances did not dare to seek my conqueror's eyes ; but when directed towards him in a more humble way they soon informed me that I had obtained the effect I wished to produce. It was then necessary to convince him that I shared it ; and so, when the Maréchale announced that she was leaving, I exclaimed in a soft and tender voice : " Ah ! I was so comfortable there ! " However, I got up ; but before taking leave of her, I asked her plans, to have a pretext to tell mine and to let it be known I should be at home on the day after the morrow. After which everyone left.

[1] See *Letter LXX*. (C. de L.)

I then began to reflect. I had no doubt that Prévan would make use of the sort of rendezvous I had given him; that he would come early enough to find me alone and that the attack would be sharp; but I was also very sure that with my reputation he would not treat me with that brusqueness which men of any experience only employ with women who have had intrigues or with those who have had no experience; and I saw my success was certain if he uttered the word "love"; above all if he tried to obtain it from me.

How convenient it is to have to deal with you "men of principles!" Sometimes a bungling lover disconcerts one by his timidity or embarrasses one by his passionate raptures; it is a fever which, like others, has its cold shiverings and its burning, and sometimes varies in its symptoms. But it is so easy to guess your prearranged advance! The arrival, the bearing, the tone, the remarks—I knew what they would all be the evening before. I shall therefore not tell you our conversation which you will easily supply. You will only observe that in my feigned defence I gave him all the help in my power; embarrassment, to give him time to speak; poor arguments, for him to combat; fear and suspicion, to encourage his protestations; and the perpetual refrain on his part, "I only ask one word of you"; and the silence on my part, which only seemed to let him wait in order to make him desire it more; and through all this, a hand taken a hundred times, always withdrawn and never quite refused. One could spend all day in this way; we spent a mortal hour; we should perhaps be there still if we had not heard a carriage come into my court-yard. This fortunate occurrence naturally made his entreaties more pressing; and I, seeing that the moment had come when I was safe from any sudden attack on his part, prepared myself by a long sigh and granted the precious word. Someone was announced and soon after there was a numerous company.

Prévan asked if he might come the next morning and I consented; but, careful of my defence, I ordered my waiting-woman to remain in my bedroom during the whole of this visit, and you know that from there you can see everything that is going on in my dressing-room, which was where I received him. Free in our conversation, and both having the same desire, we were soon in agreement; but it was necessary to get rid of this importunate spectator, which was what I expected.

Then, I gave him my own version of my private life and easily convinced him that we should never find a moment of liberty; that he must consider as a miracle the opportunity we had enjoyed the day before and that even this was far too dangerous for me to risk, since at any moment someone might come into my drawing-room. I did not fail to add that all these customs had grown up because hitherto they had never been an impediment to me; and at the same time I insisted upon the impossibility of altering them without compromising myself in the eyes of my servants. He tried to look sad, to be out of humour, to tell me my love was slight; and you can guess how much that touched me!

but to strike the decisive blow, I called in tears to my help. It was precisely the situation of "Zaïre, you are weeping."[1] The power he thought he had over me, and the hope it gave him that he could take me as he wished, stood him in stead of all the love of Orosmane.

After this theatrical incident, we returned to our arrangements. As the daytime was impossible, we considered the night; but my porter became an insurmountable obstacle and I would not allow Prévan to try to bribe him. He then proposed the small door into my garden; but I had foreseen that and I invented a dog which was tranquil and silent by day but a real demon at night. The facility with which I entered into all these details naturally emboldened him; and so at last he proposed the most ridiculous expedient, which was the one I accepted.

First of all, his servant was as trustworthy as he was; in this he did not deceive me, for one was as little trustworthy as the other. I was to give a big supper in my house; he would be there and would arrange to leave alone. The skilful confidant would call the carriage, open the door, and Prévan, instead of getting in, would nimbly slip away. His coachman would not be able to perceive it; and so everyone would think he had gone and yet he would be in my house; it remained to be seen if he could get to my room. I admit that at first my difficulty was to allege against this project reasons sufficiently weak for him to be able to destroy them; he replied by instances. According to him, nothing was more usual than this way; he had often made use of it himself; it was even the method he usually adopted, as being the least dangerous.

Subjugated by this irrefutable authority, I candidly admitted that there was a concealed stairway which led up to my boudoir; that I could leave the key in it and he could lock himself in and wait without much risk until my women had left; and then, to make my consent more probable, a moment afterwards I would not allow it, I was only brought to consent on condition of his perfect submission, his restraint. . . . Ah! What restraint! In short I was willing to prove my love to him, but not to satisfy his.

I forgot to tell you that he was to leave by the small garden door; he had only to wait until dawn; the Cerberus would then say not a word. Not a soul passes at that hour and the servants are in their deepest sleep. If you are surprised at this heap of silly arguments, it is because you have forgotten our mutual situation. Where was the necessity for better ones? He asked nothing better than that everything should be known and I was quite sure it would not be known. The appointment was fixed for two days afterwards.

Notice that the affair had been arranged and that nobody had yet seen Prévan alone with me. I meet him at supper at a friend's house; he offers her his box for a new play and I accept a seat in it. I invite this woman to supper during the play and in Prévan's presence. It is

[1] Reference to Voltaire's tragedy *Zaïre*.

almost impossible for me not to ask him too. He accepts and two days afterwards pays me the visit demanded by custom. It is true he comes to see me the next morning ; but, apart from the fact that morning visits no longer count, it was in my power to consider this improper ; and in fact I put him in the class of my less intimate friends by a written invitation to a formal supper. I can say like Anette : " But that is all, after all ! "

When the fatal day came, the day on which I was to lose my virtue and my reputation, I gave my instructions to my faithful Victoire and she carried them out as you will soon see.

The evening came. There were already a number of people with me when Prévan was announced. I received him with a marked politeness, which showed how little intimate I was with him ; and I put him in the Maréchale's party, as being that through which I had made his acquaintance. The evening produced nothing but a very short note, which the discreet lover found a way to hand me and which I burned in accordance with my custom. He announced in it that I could count upon him ; and this essential word was surrounded by all the parasitic words about love, happiness, etc., which are never found missing on such an occasion.

At midnight when the card parties were finished, I proposed a short *macédoine*.[1] I had the double intention of giving Prévan his opportunity to leave and at the same time rendering it noticeable ; which could not fail to happen from his reputation as a gambler. I was also glad that, if necessary, people could remember I had not been in a hurry to remain alone.

The play lasted longer than I had thought. The devil tempted me and I yielded to the desire to go and tempt the impatient prisoner. I was proceeding towards my ruin when I reflected that once I had surrendered to him it would no longer be in my power to keep him in the costume of decency necessary to my plans. I had the strength to resist. I turned back and, not without ill humour, returned to my place at the eternal game. At last it ended and everyone went away. I rang for my women, undressed very quickly and sent them away at once.

Can you see me, Vicomte, in my light toilette, walking timidly and carefully, and opening the door to my conqueror with a trembling hand ? He saw me—a flash is not quicker. How shall I tell you ? I was overcome, completely overcome, before I could say a word to stop him or to defend myself. He then wished to put himself into a more comfortable situation, more suitable to the circumstances. He cursed his clothes which, he said, kept him at a distance from me ; he wished to combat me with equal weapons, but my extreme timidity opposed this plan and my tender caresses did not leave him time for it. He busied himself with other matters.

[1] Some persons may not know perhaps that a " macédoine " is a mixture of several games of chance among which each dealer has the right to choose when it is his turn. This is one of the inventions of the age. (C. de L.)

His privileges were doubled and his pretentions returned ; and then : " Listen to me," I said, " Up till now you will have a very agreeable story to tell the two Comtesses de P . . . and a thousand others ; but I am curious to know how you will relate the end of the adventure." So saying, I rang the bell with all my strength. This time it was my turn, and my action was quicker than his speech. He had only begun to stammer when I heard Victoire running and calling the men-servants whom she had kept in her room as I had ordered. Then taking a lofty tone and raising my voice, I continued : " Go, Monsieur, and never appear before me again." Thereupon a crowd of my servants rushed in.

Poor Prévan lost his head and thought he saw an ambush in what at bottom was only a pleasantry, and rushed for his sword. It turned out badly for him ; for my footman who is brave and strong, seized him round the body and threw him on the ground. I admit I was in mortal terror. I called to them to stop and ordered them to let him go free, merely making sure that he left my house. My servants obeyed me ; but there was a great clamour among them and they were indignant that anyone should have dared to insult " their virtuous mistress." They all went out with the unhappy Chevalier, with noise and scandal as I had wished. Victoire alone remained and during this time we occupied ourselves in repairing the disorder of my bed.

My servants came back still in a tumult ; and I, " still thoroughly upset," asked them by what good fortune it was that they were still up ; and Victoire told me that she had given a supper to two of her friends, that they had sat up in her room ; in short, everything we had agreed on together. I thanked them all and sent them away, but ordered one of them to go for my doctor. It appeared to me that I had a right to fear the effects of " my profound shock " ; and this was a certain means of giving circulation and celebrity to the news.

The doctor came, pitied me very much and only ordered me rest. I ordered Victoire to go out early in the morning and gossip about it in the neighbourhood.

Everything succeeded so well that before midday and as soon as it was daylight with me, my devout neighbour was at my bedside to know the truth and the details of this horrible adventure. For an hour I was forced to lament with her over the corruption of the age. Shortly afterwards, I received the enclosed note from the Maréchale. Finally just before five to my great astonishment M. . . .[1] arrived. He said he came to apologise to me for the fact that an officer in his corps could have insulted me to such an extent. He had only learned it when dining with the Maréchale and had immediately sent orders to Prévan to consider himself under arrest. I asked pardon for him and it was refused. I then thought that as an accomplice I ought to comply with the order myself and at least keep myself under close arrest. I ordered my door to be closed and said I was unwell.

[1] The Commander of the corps in which M. de Prévan was serving. (C. de L.)

You owe this long letter to my solitude. I shall write one to Madame de Volanges, who will surely read it in public, and you will see how the story ought to be told.

I forgot to tell you that Belleroche is in a rage and is determined to call Prévan out. Poor boy! Fortunately I shall have time to calm him down. Meanwhile I shall rest myself for my head is weary with writing. Good-bye, Vicomte.

From the Château de . . ., 25th of September, 17—. (In the evening.)

## LETTER LXXXVI

*The Maréchale de . . . to the Marquise de Merteuil*
(Note enclosed in the preceding letter)

Heavens! What is this I hear, my dear Madame? Is it possible that little Prévan should attempt such abominations? And upon you too! What one is liable to! And so we shall not be safe in our own houses! Really, such happenings are a consolation for being old. But what I shall never feel consoled for, is that I was partly the cause of your having received such a monster in your house. I promise you that if what I am told is true, he shall never set foot in my house again; all decent people will adopt the same course with him, if they act as they ought.

I am told that it made you ill, and I am anxious about your health. Pray, give me news of your dear self; or let me hear by one of your women, if you cannot do it yourself. I should have hastened to you this morning, but for the baths which the doctor will not allow me to interrupt; and this afternoon I must go to Versailles about that affair of my nephew's.

Farewell, dear Madame; count upon my sincere and lifelong friendship.

Paris, 25th of September, 17—.

## LETTER LXXXVII

*The Marquise de Merteuil to Madame de Volanges*

I am writing to you from my bed, my good, dear friend. A most disagreeable event, the most impossible to foresee has made me ill with shock and grief. Assuredly I have nothing to reproach myself with; but for a virtuous woman who preserves the modesty befitting her sex, it is always so painful to have public attention directed upon her, and I would give anything in the world to have been able to avoid this unfortunate adventure; I am not yet certain whether I shall not go to the country to wait for it to be forgotten. This is what happened.

At the Maréchale de . . .'s house I met a Monsieur de Prévan whom you will certainly know by name and whom I did not know otherwise. But as I met him in this house I think I had every reason to believe him an honourable man. In his person he is quite handsome, and he seemed to me not to be lacking in intelligence. Chance and the tedium of gambling left me the only woman between him and the Bishop of . . ., while everyone else was occupied with *lansquenet*. We all three conversed until supper-time. At table a new play was spoken of, which gave him the opportunity to offer his box to the Maréchale, who accepted it ; and it was agreed that I should have a place in it. It was for last Monday, at the Français. As the Maréchale was coming to sup with me after the play, I invited this gentleman to accompany her, and he came. Two days later he paid me a call which was spent with the usual talk and without anything noticeable occurring. The next day he came to see me in the morning, which appeared to me a little improper ; but I thought that instead of letting him feel it by my manner of receiving him, it would be better to warn him by some act of politeness that we were not as intimately known to each other as he seemed to think. For that reason I sent him the same day a very dry and very ceremonious invitation for a supper I gave the day before yesterday. I did not speak four times to him the whole evening ; and he, on his part, left as soon as he had finished his game of cards. You will admit that hitherto nothing could appear less likely to lead to an adventure ; after the card parties there was a " *macédoine* " which kept us up until nearly two o'clock ; and then I went to bed.

At least a mortal half hour after my women had gone, I heard a noise in my room. I opened my curtains in great terror and saw a man come in by the door which leads to my boudoir. I gave a piercing cry ; and by the glimmer of my night-light I recognised this Monsieur de Prévan who, with incredible effrontery, told me not to be alarmed, that he would enlighten me upon the mystery of his behaviour and that he begged me to make no noise. So saying, he lighted a candle ; I was so startled I could not speak. His tranquil and easy air petrified me I think even more. But he had not spoken two words when I saw what this pretended mystery was ; and, as you may suppose, my only answer was to ring as hard as I could.

By an incredible good fortune all the servants on duty had remained up with one of my women and had not yet gone to bed. As my waiting-woman was coming up to me she heard me speaking with great warmth, was frightened, and called them all up. You may imagine what a scene it was ! My servants were furious ; at one moment I thought my footman would kill Prévan. I confess that at that time I was very glad to be in force ; but when reflecting on it today I should have preferred that only my waiting-woman had come. She would have sufficed and perhaps I should have avoided the scandal which so distresses me.

Instead of that, the noise awoke the neighbours, the servants gossiped about it, and ever since yesterday all Paris is talking about it. Monsieur de Prévan is under arrest by the orders of his commanding officer who had the politeness to call upon me ; to apologise, he said. This imprisonment will increase the talk ; but I was unable to get it changed. The

Town and the Court have enquired at my door which I have closed to everybody. The few persons I have seen tell me that people do me justice, and that the public indignation against Monsieur de Prévan is intense ; certainly he deserves it, but that does not remove the unpleasantness of this adventure.

Moreover this man must surely have some friends and his friends must be evil ; who knows, who can know what they will invent to harm me ? Heavens, how unfortunate a young woman is ! She has done nothing when she has preserved herself from scandal, she must overcome even calumny.

Pray tell me what you would have done and what you would do in my place ; in brief, all you think. I have always received from you the kindest consolation and the wisest advice ; and it is from you I most like to receive them.

Farewell, my dear and good friend ; you know the sentiments which will forever attach me to you. I kiss your amiable daughter.

Paris, 26th of September, 17—.

## END OF PART TWO

# PART III

## LETTER LXXXVIII

*Cécile Volanges to the Vicomte de Valmont*

In spite of all my pleasure, Monsieur, in receiving letters from M. le Chevalier Danceny, and although I desire no less than he does that we should see each other again without our being prevented, yet I dare not do what you propose. First of all, it is too dangerous ; the key you wish me to put in place of the other does indeed resemble it ; but still there is a difference between them, and Mamma looks at everything and notices everything. Moreover, although it has not been used since we have been here, by some misfortune it might be ; and if it were noticed, I should be ruined for ever. And then it seems to me it would be very wrong ; to make a double key in that way—it is too much ! It is true that you would be the person who would be kind enough to take charge of it ; but in spite of that, if it were known, the blame and the fault would none the less be laid on me, because you would have done it for me. Lastly, I twice tried to take it and certainly it would be very easy if it were anything else ; but I do not know why, I always began to tremble and had not the courage to do it. I think it is better to remain as we are.

If you still have the kindness to be as complaisant as you have been, you will always find means of giving me a letter. Even with the last one, but for the accident which made you turn round quickly at the wrong moment, we should have done it easily. I know that you cannot always be thinking about this, as I do; but I prefer to have more patience and not to take such risks. I am sure Monsieur Danceny would say as I do; for everytime he wanted something which was too hard for me to do, he always agreed that it should not be done. I shall hand you at the same time as this letter, Monsieur, your own letter, Monsieur Danceny's and your key. I am none the less grateful to you for all your kindnesses and I beg you will continue them. It is true I am very unhappy, and but for you I should be much more so; but after all, it is my mother; we must be patient. And so long as Monsieur Danceny loves me and you do not abandon me, perhaps there will come a happier time.

I have the honour to be, Monsieur, with much gratitude, your most humble and most obedient servant.

From ——, 26th September, 17—.

## LETTER LXXXIX

*The Vicomte de Valmont to the Chevalier Danceny*

If your affairs do not always progress as fast as you would like, my friend, you must not blame me alone. I have more than one obstacle to overcome here. Madame de Volanges's vigilance and severity are not the only ones; your young friend herself hinders me with some. Either from coldness or timidity, she does not always do what I advise her and yet I think I know what ought to be done better than she.

I had found a simple, convenient and certain way of delivering your letters to her and even of facilitating later the interviews you desire; but I cannot persuade her to make use of it. I am the more distressed by this since I see no other way to bring you together; and even with your correspondence I am continually in fear of compromising all three of us. Well, you will realise that I desire neither to run that risk myself nor to expose either of you to it.

Yet I should be really pained if your little friend's lack of confidence should prevent me from being useful to you; perhaps you would do well to write to her about it. Consider what you wish to do, it is for you alone to decide; for it is not enough to serve one's friends, they must be served in the manner they wish. This might also be a further means of making sure of her feelings for you; for the woman who keeps a will of her own does not love as much as she says.

It is not that I suspect your mistress of inconstancy; but she is very young; she is very much afraid of her Mamma who, as you know, seeks only to harm you; and perhaps it would be dangerous to remain too long without occupying her with you. But do not grow too uneasy about what I tell you. I have really no reason for suspicion; it is merely the solicitude of friendship. I do not write you at more length because

I too have some affairs on my own account. I am not so far forward as you ; but I love as much and that is consoling ; and even if I do not succeed on my own account, I shall think I have employed my time well if I can be useful to you. Good-bye, my friend.

From the Château de . . ., 26th of September, 17—.

## LETTER XC

*Madame de Tourvel to the Vicomte de Valmont*

I very much hope, Monsieur, that this letter will give you no pain ; or, if it must give you pain, that at least it may be softened by that I feel in writing to you. You ought to know me enough now to be quite sure I would not willingly distress you ; but doubtless you yourself would be just as unwilling to plunge me into an eternal despair. I call upon you then, in the name of the tender friendship I promised you, in the name even of those sentiments, perhaps keener but certainly not more sincere, which you have for me, not to let us see each other again ; leave me ; and, until then, let us especially avoid those private and too dangerous interviews in which through some inconceivable power I pass my time in listening to what I ought not to hear, without being able to tell you what I wish to say.

Even yesterday, when you came and joined me in the park, my sole object was to tell you what I am writing to you today ; and yet what did I do except occupy myself with your love . . . with your love, to which I ought never to reply ! Ah ! I beseech you, leave me.

Do not fear that my absence should ever alter my feelings for you ; how should I succeed in conquering them, when I have no longer the courage to combat them ? You can see it, I confess everything ; I am less afraid of admitting my weakness than of yielding to it ; but the power I have lost over my feelings, I have kept over my actions ; yes, I shall keep it, I am resolved upon it, were it at the cost of my life.

Alas ! It was not long ago that I felt certain I should never have to engage in such struggles. I felt glad of it and perhaps glorified myself on it too much. Heaven has punished, cruelly punished my pride ; but full of pity at the moment even when it strikes us, it warns me again before I fall ; and I should be doubly guilty if I continued to be lacking in prudence when I am already made aware that I have no more strength.

You have said a hundred times that you would not want a happiness bought by my tears. Ah ! Let us talk no more of happiness, but allow me to regain some tranquillity.

By granting my request, what new rights will you not acquire over my heart ? And as they will be founded upon virtue, I shall not need to defend myself from them. What delight I shall take in my gratitude ! I shall owe to you the pleasure of enjoying a delicious sentiment without remorse. But now, on the contrary, I am frightened by my feelings, by my thoughts, and dread equally to occupy myself with you or with myself; even the very idea of you terrifies me; when I cannot fly from it, I combat it; I do not drive it away, but repel it.

Is it not better for us both to end this state of uneasiness and anxiety? O you, whose ever tender soul remained the friend of virtue even in the midst of its errors, you will respect my painful situation, you will not reject my prayer! A softer but not less tender interest will take the place of these violent agitations; then, breathing by your favours, I shall cherish my existence, and I shall say in the joy of my heart: "The joy I feel is owing to my friend."

In submitting to a few slight privations, which I do not impose upon you but which I ask of you, shall you think you are buying too dearly the cessation of my torments? Ah! If I could make you happy by only consenting to be unhappy myself, believe me, I should not hesitate a moment . . . but to become guilty! . . . No, my friend, no, rather death a thousand times.

Already I am assailed by shame, I am on the eve of remorse, and I shrink from others and myself; I blush in company and shiver in solitude; I have nothing but a life of grief; I shall have no tranquillity unless you consent. My most praiseworthy resolutions are insufficient to reassure me; I made this resolution yesterday and yet I passed the night in tears.

Behold your friend, she whom you love, confused and supplicating, begging you for rest and innocence. Ah God! But for you would she ever have been reduced to this humiliating request? I do not blame you at all; I feel too much myself how difficult it is to resist an imperious sentiment. A wail is not a murmur. Do from generosity what I am doing from duty, and to all the sentiments you have inspired in me I shall add that of an eternal gratitude. Good-bye, good-bye, Monsieur.

From . . ., 27th of September, 17—.

## LETTER XCI

*The Vicomte de Valmont to Madame de Tourvel*

I am in consternation at your letter, Madame and still do not know how to reply to it. Doubtless if there must be a choice between your unhappiness and mine, it is for me to sacrifice myself, and I do not hesitate; but it seems to me that things of this importance ought above all to be discussed and made clear; and how can that be done, if we are never to speak to each other nor see each other again?

What! When we are united by the softest feelings, shall a vain terror suffice to separate us, perhaps for ever! In vain will tender friendship and ardent love claim their rights; their voices will not be heard. And why? What is this pressing danger which threatens you? Ah! Believe me; such fears, so lightly conceived, are already, it seems to me, sufficiently powerful reasons for confidence.

Permit me to tell you that I find in this a trace of the unfavourable impressions you have been given about me. A woman does not tremble in the presence of the man she esteems ; above all she does not send away the man she has thought worthy of a certain friendship ; it is the dangerous man who is feared and shunned.

And yet who was ever more respectful and more submissive than I ? Already, as you see, I am watching what I say ; I no longer allow myself those names which are so soft, so dear to my heart, and which my heart does not cease to give you in secret. I am no longer the faithful and unhappy lover receiving advice and consolations from a tender and sensitive friend ; I am the prisoner before his judge, the slave before his master. No doubt these new titles imply new duties ; I promise to carry them all out. Hear me and if you condemn me, I will accept the sentence and go. I promise more ; do you prefer the despotism which judges without hearing ? Do you feel in yourself the courage to be unjust ? Command and I will still obey.

But let me hear this judgment or this order from your mouth. And why ? you will say in your turn. Ah ! If you put that question, you little know love and my heart ! Is it then nothing to see you once more ? Ah ! Even if you carry despair into my soul perhaps a consoling look will prevent me from succumbing to it. And then if I must renounce love, renounce friendship, for which alone I exist, at least you will see your work and your pity will be left me ; even if I did not deserve that slight favour I think I am ready to pay dearly enough for it to hope to obtain it.

What ! You are about to send me away from you ! You agree that we shall become strangers to each other ! What do I say ? You desire it ; and while you assure me that my absence will not alter your sentiments, you only hasten my departure to labour more easily at their destruction.

You already speak to me of replacing them by gratitude. And so you offer me the sentiment which a stranger would obtain from you for the slightest service, which even your enemy would obtain by ceasing to do you harm ! And you wish my heart to be content with that ! Question your own ; if your lover, if your friend, should one day speak to you of their gratitude, would you not say to them indignantly : " Leave me, you are ungrateful."

I pause here and call upon your indulgence. Forgive the expression of a grief which you have created ; it will do no harm to my complete submission. But in my turn I call upon you, in the name of those soft sentiments, which you call upon yourself, not to refuse to hear me ; and at least from pity for the utter distress into which you have plunged me, do not put off the moment. Good-bye, Madame.

From . . ., 27th of September, 17—, in the evening.

## LETTER XCII

*The Chevalier Danceny to the Vicomte de Valmont*

O my friend ! Your letter froze me with terror. Cécile . . . . Oh God ! Is it possible ? Cécile no longer loves me. Yes, I see that dreadful truth through the veil your friendship throws over it. You wish to prepare me to receive a mortal blow ; I thank you for your pains, but can Love be imposed upon ? It anticipates what concerns it ; it does not hear its fate, but divines it. I have no longer any doubt of mine ; speak to me plainly, you can do so, and I beg you to. Tell me everything ; what gave birth to your suspicions, what confirmed them ? The slightest details are precious. Above all try to recollect her words. One word for another may change a whole phrase ; the same word has sometimes two meanings . . . you may have been deceived. Alas ! I am still trying to flatter myself. What did she say to you ? Does she blame me for anything ? Does she not at least excuse herself for her faults ? I ought to have foreseen this change from the difficulties which for some time she has found in everything. Love does not admit so many obstacles.

What ought I to do ? What do you advise me ? Should I try to see her ? Is that impossible ? Absence is so cruel, so disastrous . . . and she has refused a way to see me ! You do not tell me what it was ! If it was indeed too dangerous, she well knows I should not wish her to risk too much, But then I know your prudence ; and, to my misfortune, cannot but believe it.

What am I to do now ? How shall I write to her ? If I let her see my suspicions they may perhaps grieve her ; and if they are unjust, should I ever forgive myself for having distressed her ? If I hide them from her, it is deceiving her, and I cannot use dissimulation with her.

Oh ! If she could know what I suffer, my pain would touch her. I know she is tender, her heart is excellent and I have a thousand proofs of her love. Too much timidity, some embarrassment, she is so young ! And her mother treats her with such severity ! I shall write to her ; I shall restrain myself ; I shall only ask her to rely implicitly upon me. Even if she refuses again, at least she cannot be angry at your request ; and perhaps she will consent.

I send you a thousand apologies, both for her and for myself. I assure you that she feels the value of the pains you are taking and that she is grateful for them. This is not suspicion on her part, it is timidity. Be indulgent ; it is the fairest trait of friendship. Yours is very precious to me and I do not know how to acknowledge all you are doing for me. Good-bye, I am going to write to her at once.

I feel all my fears return ; who could have believed it would ever be difficult for me to write to her ! Alas ! But yesterday it was my dearest pleasure.

Good-bye, my friend ; continue your exertions and pity me.

Paris, 27th of September, 17—.

## LETTER XCIII

*The Chevalier Danceny to Cécile Volanges*

(Enclosed with the preceding)

I cannot conceal from you how distressed I was to learn from Valmont of the small confidence you continue to have in him. You know he is my friend, that he is the only person who can bring us together again; I thought these claims would have been sufficient for you; I see with pain that I was wrong. Can I hope at least that you will tell me your reasons? Will you still find certain difficulties to prevent your doing so? Yet without your aid I cannot guess the mystery of this conduct. I dare not suspect your love, and doubtless you would not dare to betray mine. Ah! Cécile! . . .

Is it then true that you have refused a way of seeing me? A way which is "simple, convenient and certain?"[1] And this is how you love me! So short an absence has greatly altered your sentiments. But why deceive me? Why tell me that you still love me, that you love me more than ever? Has your Mamma destroyed your candour as well as your love? If at least she has left you some pity you will not hear without pain of the dreadful torments you cause me. Ah! I should suffer less in dying.

Tell me, is your heart closed to me for ever? Have you entirely forgotten me? Thanks to your refusal, I do not know when you will hear my complaints nor when you will reply to them. Valmont's friendship had made our correspondence certain; but you did not want it; you thought it difficult, you preferred that it should be seldom. No, I no longer believe in love, in good faith. Ah! Who is to be believed if Cécile has deceived me?

Answer me. Is it true you love me no more? No, that is impossible; you delude yourself; you calumniate your own heart. A passing fear, a moment of discouragement, which love has soon banished; is it not so, my Cécile? Ah! Doubtless it is, and I am wrong to accuse you. How happy I should be to be wrong! How glad I should be to make you tender apologies, to repair this moment of injustice by an eternity of love!

Cécile, Cécile, have pity on me! Consent to see me, take any way of doing it! See what is the result of absence! Fears, suspicions, perhaps coldness! One look, one word, and we shall be happy, But what! Can I still speak of happiness? Perhaps it is lost for me, lost for ever. Tormented by fear, urged cruelly between unjust suspicions and more cruel truth, I cannot fix upon any thought; I retain only sufficient existence to suffer and to love you. Ah! Cécile! You alone have the right to render existence dear to me; and I expect from the first word

[1] Danceny does not know what this way is; he simply repeats Valmont's expression. (C. de L.)

you pronounce the return of happiness or the certainty of an eternal despair.

Paris, 27th of September, 17—.

## LETTER XCIV

*Cécile Volanges to the Chevalier Danceny*

I understand nothing of your letter, except the pain it causes me. What has Monsieur de Valmont told you, what can have made you believe I do not love you? Perhaps it would be very fortunate for me, for assuredly I should be less tortured; and it is very hard, when I love you as I do, to see that you always think I am wrong, and that instead of consoling me, it is you who always cause me the pains which grieve me most. You think that I am deceiving you and that I tell you things which do not exist! You have a pretty idea of me! But even if I were as untruthful as you reproach me with being, what interest should I have in being so? Assuredly, if I did not love you any more I should only have to say so and everyone would praise me for it; but unluckily it is stronger than I am; and then it must needs be for someone who has no gratitude at all to me for it!

What have I done to make you so angry? I did not dare take the key because I was afraid Mamma would notice it and that it would cause me more trouble and you too on my account; and then too, because it seemed wrong to me. But only Monsieur de Valmont had spoken to me about it; I could not know whether you wanted it or not since you knew nothing about it. Now I know that you want it, do I refuse to take the key? I shall take it tomorrow; and then we shall see what you will have to say. Monsieur de Valmont may well be your friend; I think I love you quite as much as he can like you, at least; and yet he is always right and I am always wrong. I assure you I am very angry. That is all the same to you, because you know I am pacified at once; but when I have the key I can see you when I want; and I assure you I shall not want to, if you act like this. I would rather suffer the grief which comes from myself than from you; consider what you wish to do.

If you would allow it, we should love each other so much! And at least we should have no troubles except those inflicted on us by other people! I assure you that if it were in my control you would never have to complain of me; but if you do not believe me, we shall always be very unhappy and it will not be my fault. I hope we shall soon be able to see each other, and that then we shall have no more reasons to hurt each other as we do now.

If I could have foreseen this, I should have taken the key at once; but, truly, I thought I was doing right. Do not be angry with me, I beg you. Do not be sad any more, and always love me as much as I love you; then I shall be quite content. Good-bye, my dear.

From the Château de . . ., 28th of September, 17—.

## LETTER XCV

*Cécile Volanges to the Vicomte de Valmont*

I beg you, Monsieur, to be good enough to return me the key you gave me to put in place of the other ; since everybody desires it, I too must agree to it.

I do not know why you told Monsieur Danceny I did not love him any more ; I do not think I have ever given you any reason to think so ; and it has pained him very much and me too. I know you are his friend ; but that is not a reason for grieving him, nor me either. You would do me a great pleasure to tell him the contrary the next time you write to him and that you are sure of it ; for he has more confidence in you ; and when I have said a thing and I am not believed, I do not know what else to do. You can be at rest about the key ; I remember perfectly everything you told me in your letter. However, if you still have it and would give it to me at the same time as the key, I promise you to pay great attention to it. If it could be tomorrow when we are going in to dinner, I could give you the other key at breakfast the next day and you would return it to me in the same way as the first. I should prefer it not to be a long time, because there would be less risk of Mamma noticing it.

And then, once you have this key, will you have the kindness to make use of it to get my letters ; in this way Monsieur Danceny will have news of me more often. It is true that this will be more convenient than it is now ; but at first it frightened me too much ; I beg you to excuse me and I hope you will continue to be as complaisant as in the past. I shall always be very grateful for it.

I have the honour to be, Monsieur, your most humble and most obedient servant.

From . . ., 28th of September, 17—.

## LETTER XCVI

*The Vicomte de Valmont to the Marquise de Merteuil*

I wager that ever since your adventure you have every day been expecting my compliments and praise ; I have no doubt but that my long silence has put you a little out of temper ; but what do you expect ? I have always thought that when one had nothing but praise to give a woman one can be at rest about her and occupy oneself with something else. However, I thank you on my own account and congratulate you on yours. To make you perfectly happy, I am even willing to admit that this time you have surpassed my expectations. After that, let us see if on my side I have at least partly fulfilled yours.

I do not want to talk to you about Madame de Tourvel ; her slow advance displeases you. You only like completed affairs. Drawn-out scenes weary you ; but I have never tasted the pleasure I now enjoy in this supposed tardiness.

Yes, I like to see, to watch this prudent woman impelled, without her perceiving it, upon a path which allows no return, and whose steep and dangerous incline carries her on in spite of herself, and forces her to follow me. There, terrified by the peril she runs, she would like to halt and cannot check herself. Her exertions and her skill may render her steps shorter ; but they must follow one upon the other. Sometimes, not daring to look the danger in the face, she shuts her eyes, lets herself go, and abandons herself to my charge. More often her efforts are revived by a new fear ; in her mortal terror she would like to try to turn back once again ; she exhausts her strength in painfully climbing back a short distance and very soon a magic power replaces her nearer the danger from which she had vainly tried to fly. Then having no one but me for guide and for support, without thinking of reproaching me for the inevitable fall, she implores me to retard it. Fervent prayers, humble supplications, all that mortals in their fear offer to the divinity, I receive from her ; and you expect me to be deaf to her prayers, to destroy myself the worship she gives me, and to use in casting her down that power she invokes for her support ! Ah ! At least leave me the time to watch these touching struggles between love and virtue.

What ! Do you think that very spectacle which makes you rush eagerly to the theatre, which you applaud there wildly, is less interesting in reality ? You listen with enthusiasm to the sentiments of a pure and tender soul, which dreads the happiness it desires and does not cease to defend itself even when it ceases to resist ; should they only be valueless for him who gives birth to them ? But these, these are the delicious enjoyments this heavenly woman offers me every day ; and you reproach me for lingering over their sweetness ! Ah ! The time will come only too soon when, degraded by her fall, she will be nothing but an ordinary woman to me.

But in speaking to you of her I forget that I did not wish to speak of her. I do not know what power attaches me to her, ceaselessly brings me back to her, even when I insult it. Let me put aside the dangerous thought of her ; let me become myself again to deal with a more amusing subject. It concerns your pupil, now become mine, and I hope you will recognise me here.

For some days I had been better treated by my tender devotee and in consequence, being less preoccupied with her, I noticed that the Volanges girl is indeed very pretty ; and that if it was silly to be in love with her like Danceny, perhaps it was none the less silly on my part not to seek with her a distraction rendered necessary by my solitude. I also thought it just to pay myself for the trouble I am giving myself for her ; I remembered too that you had offered it to me before Danceny had any claims to it ; and I thought myself authorised to claim some rights in a property he only possessed through my refusal and rejection. The little person's pretty look, her fresh mouth, her childish air, even her awkwardness fortified these sage reflections ; I resolved to act upon them and the enterprise was crowned by success.

You are wondering already by what means I have so soon supplanted the cherished lover ; what seduction is suitable to this age, this inexperience ? Spare yourself the trouble, I used none. While you skilfully handled the arms of your sex and triumphed by subtlety ; I returned to man his imprescriptible rights and overcame by authority. I was sure of seizing my prey if I could come at it ; I needed no ruse except to approach her and that I made use of hardly deserves the name.

I profited by the first letter I received from Danceny for his fair one, and after having notified her of it by the signal agreed upon between us, instead of using my skill to give it her I used it to find means not to give it ; I feigned to share the impatience I had created, and after having caused the difficulty I pointed out the remedy for it.

The young person's room has a door opening on the corridor ; but naturally the mother had taken the key. It was only a question of getting possession of it. Nothing could have been easier to carry out ; I only asked to have it at my disposition for a couple of hours and I guaranteed to have one like it. Then correspondence, interviews, nocturnal rendezvous, all became convenient and certain. However, would you believe it ? the timid child was afraid and refused. Another would have been nonplussed by this ; but I only saw in it an opportunity for a more piquant pleasure. I wrote to Danceny to complain of this refusal and I acted so well that our scatterbrain had no rest until he had obtained, exacted even, from his timorous mistress her consent to grant my request and to yield wholly to my discretion.

I confess I was very pleased to have changed parts in this way and to have the young man do for me what he thought I should do for him. This idea doubled the value of the adventure in my eyes ; therefore as soon as I had the precious key, I hastened to make use of it ; this was last night.

After making sure that everything was quiet in the Château, I armed myself with a dark lantern, made the toilet which suited the hour and was demanded by the situation, and paid my first visit to your pupil. I had caused everything to be prepared (and by herself) to be able to enter noiselessly. She was in her first sleep and in the sleep of her age ; so that I came up to her bedside without awakening her. At first I was tempted to go further and to try to pass as a dream ; but fearing the effect of surprise and the noise it brings with it, I preferred to arouse the pretty sleeper cautiously, and in fact I succeeded in preventing the cry I feared.

After having calmed her first fears, I risked a few liberties since I had not come there to talk. Doubtless she had not been well informed at her convent as to how many different perils timid innocence is exposed, and all it has to guard to avoid a surprisal ; for giving all her attention and all her strength to defending herself from a kiss, which was only a false attack, she left all the rest without defence. How could

I not profit by it! I therefore changed my movement and immediately took post. Here we were both very nearly lost; the little girl was terrified and tried to scream in good faith; fortunately her voice was quenched in tears. She also threw herself towards her bell-rope, but my skill restrained her arm in time.

"What are you doing," I then said to her, "you will ruin yourself forever. Suppose someone comes; what does it matter to me? Whom will you convince that I am not here by your wish? Who but you could have given me the means of coming in? And will you be able to explain the use of this key I hold from you, which I could only have had through you?"

This short harangue calmed neither her grief nor her anger; but it brought about submission. I do not know if I achieved the tone of eloquence; it is at least true that I did not have its gestures. With one hand occupied by force and the other by love what orator could pretend to grace in such a situation? If you imagine it correctly, you will at least admit it was favourable to attack; but I do not understand anything and, as you say, the simplest woman, a mere schoolgirl, leads me like a child.

For all her distress she felt she had to adopt some course and come to terms. Since prayers found me inexorable she had to come to offers. You will suppose that I sold this important post very dearly; no, I promised everything for a kiss. It is true that, having taken the kiss, I did not keep my promise; but I had good reasons. Had we agreed that it should be taken or given? After much bargaining, we agreed on a second; and it was said that this should be received. Then I guided the timid arms around my body, I held her more amorously in one of mine, and the soft kiss was indeed received, well received, perfectly received, in short, love himself could not have done better.

Such good faith deserved a reward; and so I immediately granted the request. The hand was withdrawn; but I do not know by what chance I found myself in its place. You suppose that there I was very eager, very active, do you not? Not at all. I have begun to like slow methods, I tell you. Once certain of arriving, why hurry on the journey so fast?

Seriously, I was very glad to observe for once the power of opportunity, and here I found it divested of all other aid. Yet she had to combat love, and love supported by modesty or shame, fortified above all by the annoyance I had given, which was considerable. Opportunity was alone; but it was there, all was offered, all was present, and love was absent.

To make certain of my observations I was cunning enough to use no more force than she could combat. Only if my charming enemy abused my facility, and was ready to escape me, I restrained her by the same fear whose happy effects I had already made proof of. Well, without my taking any other exertion, the tender mistress, forgetting her oaths, yielded at first and ended up by consenting; not but that after the first moment reproaches and tears returned in concert ; I do not know whether they were true or feigned ; but, as always happens, they ceased as soon as I busied myself with giving reason for others. In short, from frailty to reproaches and from reproaches to frailty, we did not separate until we were satisfied with each other and had both agreed on the rendezvous for this evening.

I did not go back to my room until dawn. And I was worn out with fatigue and lack of sleep ; however I sacrificed both to the desire of being at breakfast in the morning ; I have a passion for observing behaviours the morning after. You can have no idea of what this was. There was embarrassment in her countenance ! Difficulty in walking ! Eyes continually lowered, and so large and so tired ! That round face had grown so much longer ! Nothing could be more amusing. And for the first time, her mother (alarmed by this extreme change) showed quite a tender interest in her ! And Madame de Tourvel too was very attentive about her Oh ! Her attentions are only lent ; a day will come when they can be returned to her and that day is not far off. Good-bye, my fair friend.

From the Château, 1st of October, 17—.

## LETTER XCVII

*Cécile Volanges to the Marquise de Merteuil*

Ah Heaven ! Madame, how distressed I am ! How miserable I am ! Who will console me in my grief ? Who will advise me in my present state of embarrassment ? This Monsieur de Valmont . . . and Danceny ! No, the idea of Danceny fills me with despair. . . . How can I relate it to you ? How can I tell you ? . . . I do not know what to do. Yet my heart is full. . . . I must speak to someone and you are the only person in whom I can, in whom I dare confide. You are so kind to me ! But do not be so now ; I am not worthy of it ; how shall I put it ? I do not desire your kindness. Everyone here has showed an interest in me today ; they all increased my pain. I felt so much that I did not deserve it ! Scold me, rather ; scold me well, for I deserve it ; but afterwards save me ; if you do not have the kindness to advise me I shall die of grief.

You must know then . . . my hand trembles, as you see, I can hardly write, my face feels on fire. . . . Ah ! it is indeed the red of shame. Well, I will endure it ; it will be the first punishment for my fault. Yes, I will tell you everything.

You must know then that Monsieur de Valmont, who hitherto had been handing me Monsieur Danceny's letters, suddenly found that it was too difficult and wanted to have the key of my room. I can assure you I did not want to do it ; but he went to the extent of writing to Danceny and Danceny wanted it too ; and it hurts me so much when I refuse him anything, especially since my absence which makes him so unhappy, that I ended by consenting to it. I did not foresee the misfortune which would occur from it.

Yesterday Monsieur de Valmont made use of this key to come into my room when I was asleep ; I expected it so little that he frightened me very much when he woke me up ; but as he spoke to me at once, I recognised him and did not scream ; and then my first idea was that he had perhaps come to bring me a letter from Danceny. It was far from that. A moment afterwards he wanted to kiss me ; and while I defended myself, as was natural, he did what I would not have him do for anything in the world . . . but, he wanted a kiss first. I had to, for what could I do ? I had tried to call, but I could not and then he told me that if somebody came he could throw all the blame on me ; and indeed that was very easy on account of the key. After it he did not withdraw at all. He wanted a second ; and I don't know what there was about this one but it completely disturbed me ; and after, it was still worse than before. Oh ! This is very wrong. Afterwards . . . you will exempt me from telling you the rest ; but I am as unhappy as one can be.

What I blame myself the most for, and yet must speak to you about, is that I am afraid I did not defend myself as much as I could have ; I do not know how this could have happened ; assuredly I do not love Monsieur de Valmont, on the contrary ; and there were moments when I was as if I loved him. . . . You may well suppose that did not prevent me from continuing to say no to him ; but I felt I was not doing what I said ; and it was as if in spite of myself ; and then I was very much upset ! If it is always as difficult as that to defend oneself, one must need a lot of practice ! It is true that Monsieur de Valmont has a way of talking that one does not know how to answer ; and will you believe it ? when he went away it was as if I was sorry, and I was weak enough to consent that he should come again this evening ; that troubles me even more than all the rest.

Oh ! In spite of this, I promise you I shall prevent him from coming. He had scarcely gone when I felt how wrong I had been to promise it him. And I cried all the rest of the time. Above all Danceny grieved me ! Every time I thought of him my tears increased until they stifled me, and still I thought of him . . . and even now you see what happens ; my paper is all wet. No, I shall never be consoled were it only for his sake. . . . At last I could cry no more, and yet I could not sleep a minute. This morning when I got up and looked at myself in the mirror, it frightened me to see how changed I was.

Mamma noticed it as soon as she saw me and asked me what was the matter. I began to cry at once. I thought she was going to scold me, and perhaps that would have hurt me less ; but, no, she spoke gently to me ! I did not deserve it. She told me not to grieve like that ! She did not know the reason for my grief. That I should make myself ill. There are moments when I wish I were dead. I could not endure it. I threw myself sobbing into her arms, saying : " Ah Mamma ! your little girl is very unhappy ! " Mamma could not prevent herself from crying a little and that only increased my grief ; fortunately she did not ask me why I was so unhappy, for I should not have known what to say to her.

I beg you, Madame, to write to me as soon as you can and tell me what I ought to do, for I have not the courage to think of anything and can do nothing but grieve. Please send me your letter by Monsieur de Valmont; but pray, if you write to him at the same time, do not mention to him what I have told you.

I have the honour to be, Madame, always with great friendship, your most humble and most obedient servant . . .

I dare not sign this letter.

From the Château de . . ., 1st of October, 17—.

## LETTER XCVIII

*Madame de Volanges to the Marquise de Merteuil*

A few days ago, my charming friend, you asked me for consolation and advice ; today it is my turn ; and I make the same request on my own behalf which you made on yours. I am really very distressed, and I fear I have not taken the best way to avoid the grief I feel.

My daughter is the cause of my uneasiness. Since my departure, I had indeed seen that she remained sad and wretched ; but I expected it and had armed my heart with the severity I considered necessary. I hoped that absence and distractions would soon destroy a love which I looked upon rather as a childish error, than as a real passion. Yet far from having improved since my sojourn here, I notice the child is more and more giving way to a dangerous melancholy ; and I seriously fear her health will be affected. Particularly in the last few days she has changed visibly. Yesterday above all I was struck by her appearance and everyone here was truly alarmed by it.

What proves to me still further the extent to which she is affected, is that I see her at the point of overcoming the timidity she has always showed me. Yesterday morning when I simply asked her if she was ill, she threw herself into my arms, telling me she was very unhappy ; and she cried until she sobbed. I cannot tell you how much it pained me ; the tears came into my eyes at once and I had only time to turn away to prevent her from seeing them. Fortunately I had the prudence not to ask her any questions and she did not dare to say anything else to me. But it is none the less clear that she is tormented by this unfortunate passion.

What course am I to take if this continues ? Shall I create my daughter's unhappiness ? Shall I turn against her the most precious qualities of the soul—sensibility and constancy ? Is it for this I am her mother ? And even if I stifled the natural sentiment which makes us desire the happiness of our children ; even if I considered as a weakness what I think, on the contrary, to be the first, the most sacred of our duties; yet should I force her choice, shall I not have to answer for the disastrous results which might follow? What a use for maternal authority, to place one's daughter between crime and misery!

My friend, I shall not imitate what I have so often condemned. Doubtless I might attempt to choose a husband for my daughter; in that all I did was to help her by my experience; I was not exercising a right, I was fulfilling a duty. I should betray a duty on the contrary, if I bestowed her in defiance of an inclination I could not prevent from existing, the extent and duration of which neither she nor I can know. No, I will not allow her to marry one man and love another and I prefer to forfeit my authority rather than her virtue.

I think then that the wisest thing I can do is to withdraw from the arrangement I have made with Monsieur de Gercourt. You see the reasons for it; they seem to me more important than my promises. I go further; in the state things are now, to fulfil my engagement would be really to break it. For if I owe it to my daughter not to reveal her secret to Monsieur de Gercourt, at least I owe it to him not to abuse the ignorance in which I leave him and to do for him everything I think he would do himself, if he were informed of the situation. Shall I, on the contrary, betray him unworthily when he relies upon my faith and while he honours me by choosing me as his second mother, shall I deceive him in the choice he makes of the mother of his children? These undeniable reflections which I cannot escape, alarm me more than I can tell you.

With the misfortunes they make me dread I compare my daughter, happy with a husband her heart has chosen, only knowing her duties by the pleasure she finds in carrying them out; my son-in-law equally satisfied and congratulating himself every day upon his choice; each of them finding happiness in the other's happiness, and that of both uniting to increase mine. Should the hope of so delightful a future be sacrificed to vain considerations of prudence? And what are those which restrain me? Solely the views of interest. What advantage would it be for my daughter to have been born rich if she must none the less be the slave of wealth?

I admit that Monsieur de Gercourt is perhaps a more distinguished husband than I could have hoped for my daughter; I will even admit that I was extremely flattered by his choosing her. But after all, Danceny is as well born as he is; in personal qualities he yields to him in nothing; he has the advantage over Monsieur de Gercourt of loving and of being loved; he is not rich, it is true, but is not my daughter rich enough for them both? Ah why should I deprive her of the delightful satisfaction of enriching the man she loves!

These marriages which are calculated instead of being matched, which are called "marriages of convenience," where everything indeed is convenient except their tastes and characters, are the most fertile source of those scandalous discords which become more frequent every day.[1]

[1] This states in a sentence one of the principal themes of this novel.

I prefer to delay; at least I shall have the time to observe my daughter whom I do not know. I have the courage to cause her a transitory grief if she will acquire through it a more solid happiness; but it is not in my heart to risk giving her up to an eternal despair.

Those are the ideas, my dear friend, which torment me, and on which I require your advice. These severe matters contrast greatly with your amiable gaiety and do not at all appear suitable to your age; but your reason is so far in advance of it! Moreover your friendship will aid your prudence; and I do not fear that either will be refused to the maternal solicitude which implores them.

Good-bye, my charming friend; never doubt the sincerity of my sentiments.

From the Château de . . ., 2nd of October, 17—.

## LETTER XCIX

*Vicomte de Valmont to the Marquise de Merteuil*

More little events, my fair friend; but only scenes, no actions, so arm yourself with patience; take a lot of it; for while my Madame de Tourvel advances with such slow steps, your pupil retreats, and that is much worse. Well, I have the wit to amuse myself with these trifles. I am positively growing accustomed to my stay here; and I can say that I have not passed a boring moment in my old aunt's dull Château. Indeed, have I not enjoyment, deprivation, hope, uncertainty? What more can one have on a wider stage? Spectators? Eh! Let things go, spectators will not be lacking. Though they do not see me at work, I will show them my completed task; they will have nothing to do but admire and applaud; Yes, they will applaud; for I can at last predict with certainty the moment when my austere devotee will fall. This evening I was present at the death-agony of her virtue. Soft frailty will reign in its place. I fix the time no later than our next interview. But I hear you already crying out upon pride. To announce a victory, to boast of it beforehand! Ah well, calm yourself! To prove my modesty to you, I will begin with the story of my defeat.

Your pupil is indeed a very ridiculous little person! She is indeed a child who should be treated as such, and one would do her a favour by only giving her a child's punishment! Would you believe that after what passed between her and me the day before yesterday, after the friendly way we parted yesterday morning, when I went to her again in the evening, as she had agreed, I found the door closed from the inside? What do you say to that? We endure such puerilities sometimes on the eve, but on the day after! Is it not amusing?

Yet I did not laugh at it at first; I had never felt so much the ascendency of my character. Assuredly I went to this rendezvous without pleasure and solely as a matter of procedure. My own bed, which I greatly needed, seemed to me at the moment preferable to anyone else's and I only left it with regret. Yet I had no sooner found an obstacle, than I burned to overcome it; I was especially humiliated to be outwitted by a child. I retired therefore in a very ill humour; and with the idea of concerning myself no further with this silly child and her affairs, I wrote her at once a note, which I meant to give to her today, in which I rated her at her true value. But, as people say, night brings wisdom; this morning I realised that, having no choice of distractions here, I should have to keep this one; so I suppressed the severe note. Since I have reflected upon it, I cannot get over my having had the idea of ending an adventure before having in my hands the evidence to ruin its heroine. How far we are led astray by first thoughts! Happy is he, my fair friend, who, like you, has grown accustomed never to yield to them! In short, I put off my vengeance; I made this sacrifice to your designs on Gercourt.

Now that I am no longer angry, I only see the ridiculous side of your pupil's conduct. Indeed, I should like to know what she hopes to gain by it! For my part, I have no idea; if it were only to defend herself, you must admit that she was a little late. One day she must tell me the answer to this enigma! I very much want to know it. Perhaps it was only because she was tired? Frankly, it might be so; for doubtless she is still ignorant that the shafts of love, like the lance of Achilles, carry with them the remedy to the wounds they make. But no, from her little grimace all that day, I would wager there entered into it repentance . . . there . . . something . . . like virtue. . . . Virtue! . . . Does it beseem her to have it? Ah! Let her leave virtue to the woman truly born for it, the only one who knows how to embellish it, who would make it beloved! . . . Pardon, my fair friend, but this very evening there took place between Madame de Tourvel and me the scene I am to relate to you, from which I still feel some emotion. I need to make an effort over myself to distract myself from the impression it made on me; it was as an assistance to this that I began to write to you. You must pardon something to this first moment.

For some days Madame de Tourvel and I have been in agreement upon our sentiments; we were only disputing about words. It was indeed always *her friendship* which responded to *my love;* but this conventional language did not alter the root of things; and even if we had remained there, I should perhaps have advanced less quickly, but none the less surely. Already there was no longer any question of sending me away, as she wished at first; and as to our daily interviews, if I give my attention to offering her the opportunity, she gives hers to seizing it.

As our little rendezvous usually take place out of doors today's horrible weather left me no hope; I was even positively annoyed; I did not foresee how much I should profit by this mishap.

As they were unable to go out, they began to play cards after leaving the table; and as I play very little and am no longer necessary, I went up to my room with no other project but to wait there until about the end of the game.

I was returning to join the company when I met the charming woman going into her room and she, either from imprudence or frailty, said to me in her soft voice : "Where are you going ? There is no one in the drawing-room." I needed nothing more, as you may believe, to make an attempt to enter her room ; and I found less resistance than I expected. It is true that I took the precaution to begin the conversation at the door and to start it on indifferent topics ; but we were scarcely settled when I brought in the real topic and spoke of *my love to my friend.* Although her first reply was simple, it seemed to me expressive : "Oh !" she said, "Do not let us speak of that here" ; and she trembled. Poor woman ! She saw herself dying.

However she was wrong to be in fear. For some time I have been certain of success one day or another, and, as I watched her use so much strength in useless combats, I resolved to spare my own and to await without effort the time when she would yield herself from very weariness. You will realise that I want a complete triumph with her and that I wish to owe nothing to opportunity. It was in accordance with this plan, and with the purpose of being pressing without engaging myself too far, that I returned to this word "love," which was so obstinately refused ; since I was certain she believed me to be sufficiently ardent, I tried a more tender tone. This refusal had ceased to annoy me, it distressed me ; did not my tender friend owe me some consolation ?

While she was consoling me, a hand remained in mine ; the pretty body leant upon my arm, and we were extremely close together. You have surely noticed in this situation how, as the defence weakens, demands and refusals take place at closer quarter ; how the head turns away and the looks are lowered, while the sentences, all enunciated in a weak voice, become infrequent and broken. These valuable symptoms announce the consent of the mind in an unmistakable manner ; but it has barely touched the senses at that time ; I even think that it is always dangerous to attempt any too conspicuous enterprise then, because this state of abandonment never exists without a very delightful pleasure and a woman cannot be forced out of it without an ill humour on her part which infallibly turns to the profit of the defence.

But in the present case prudence was all the more necessary since I had especially to apprehend the terror which this forgetfulness of herself would not fail to cause my tender dreamer. And so I did not even exact that the admission I asked for should be put into words ; a look would suffice me, a single look, and I was happy.

My fair friend, those beautiful eyes were indeed lifted to mine, that heavenly mouth even said : "Yes, I . . ." But suddenly the gaze was obscured, the voice failed, and this adorable woman fell into my arms. Scarcely had I the time to receive her when, tearing herself away with convulsive force, her eyes wandering and her hands lifted to Heaven . . . "God. . . . Oh ! my God, save me," she cried ; and suddenly swifter than lightning, she was on her knees ten paces from me. I could hear that she was almost suffocating. I went to help her; but she, taking my hand which she bathed in tears, sometimes even embracing my knees, exclaimed: "Yes, it will be you, it will be you, who will save me! You do not wish my death, leave me; save me; leave me; in the name of God, leave me!" And these broken sentences were barely audible through her redoubled sobs. However, she held me with such strength, that I could not have gone away; then, collecting my own strength, I lifted her in my arms. At the same instant the tears ceased; she spoke no more; all her limbs stiffened and violent convulsions succeeded to this storm.

I must admit I was deeply moved and I think I should have consented to her request, even if the circumstances had not compelled me. The truth is, after I had given her some assistance, I left her as she begged me and I congratulate myself upon having done so. Already I have almost received the reward for it.

I expected that, as on the day of my first declaration, she would not show herself during the evening. But about eight o'clock she came down to the drawing-room and simply announced to the company that she had been very indisposed. Her face was dejected, her voice weak, and her behaviour composed; but her gaze was gentle and often fixed itself upon me. Her refusal to play cards having obliged me to take her place, she sat down at my side. During supper, she remained alone in the drawing-room. When we returned, I thought I noticed that she had been crying; to find out, I said to her it seemed to me she was still suffering from her indisposition; to which she obligingly replied: "This illness does not go as quickly as it comes!" Finally, when we retired, I gave her my hand; and at the door of her apartment she pressed my hand hard. It is true that this movement seemed to be almost involuntary; but so much the better, it is one more proof of my domination.

I would wager that now she is enchanted to be where she is; all the price is paid; nothing remains but to enjoy. Perhaps while I am writing to you she is already occupied with that soft idea! And even if she is occupied, on the contrary, with a new plan of defence, do we not know what becomes of all such plans? I ask you, can it be later than our next interview? I quite expect she will make some difficulties in granting it; but there! When the first step is made, do these austere prudes know how to stop? Their love is a positive explosion; their resistance gives it more strength. My shy devotee would run after me if I ceased to run after her.

In short, my fair friend, I shall very soon be with you to demand the execution of your word. Doubtless you have not forgotten what you promised me after this success—an infidelity to your Chevalier? Are you ready? For my part, I desire it as if we had never known each other; for the rest, to have known you is perhaps a reason for desiring it the more:

"I am just, I am not being gallant."[1]

[1] Voltaire, comedy of *Nanine*. (C. de L.)

So this shall be the first infidelity I shall make my demure conquest; and I promise you to make use of the first pretext to absent myself from her for twenty-four hours. That shall be her punishment for having kept me so long away from you. Do you know that this adventure has occupied me for more than two months? Yes, two months and three days; it is true that I am including tomorrow, since it will only be really consummated then. This reminds me that Mademoiselle de B . . . resisted for three whole months. I am very glad to see that frank coquetry has more defences than austere virtue.

Good-bye, my fair friend; I must leave you, for it is very late; this letter has led me further than I reckoned; but as I am sending to Paris tomorrow, I wanted to profit by it to allow you to share your friend's joy a day sooner.

From the Château de . . ., 2nd of October, 17—. (In the evening.)

## LETTER C

*The Vicomte de Valmont to the Marquise de Merteuil*

My friend, I am outwitted, betrayed, lost; I am in despair: Madame de Tourvel has gone. She has gone, and I did not know it! And I was not there to oppose her departure, to reproach her with her unworthy betrayal. Ah! Do not think I should have let her go; she would have remained; yes, she would have remained, even if I had been compelled to employ violence. But in my credulous confidence, I was sleeping calmly; I was sleeping and the thunderbolt fell on me. No, I simply cannot understand this departure; I must give up trying to understand women.

When I recollect yesterday afternoon! What am I saying? The very evening! That gentle look, that tender voice! And that pressure of the hand! And during this time she was planning to run away from me! O women, women! Complain after this, if you are deceived! Yes, every perfidy we employ is a theft from you.

What pleasure I shall have in avenging myself! I shall find this perfidious woman again, I shall reassert my power over her. If love sufficed me to find means for it, what will it not be, aided by vengeance? I shall see her again at my knees, trembling and bathed in tears, crying to me for mercy in her deceitful voice; and I shall be without pity.

What is she doing now? What is she thinking? Perhaps she congratulates herself on having deceived me; and, faithful to the tastes of her sex, finds this the most agreeable pleasure. What this boasted virtue could not achieve, the spirit of deceit obtained without effort. Fool that I was! I dreaded her modesty; I ought to have feared her bad faith.

And to be obliged to swallow down my resentment! Only to dare to show a tender pain, when my heart is filled with rage? To see myself reduced to imploring a rebellious woman, who has escaped my domination! Ought I to be humiliated to this point? And by whom? By a timid woman, who has never had any practice in defending herself. Of what use is it to me to have established myself in her heart, to have inflamed her with all the fires of love, to have brought the disturbance of her senses to the point of delirium if she is tranquil in her retirement and can take more pride in her flight today than I in my victories? And shall I endure this? My friend, you will not think so; you have not this humiliating idea of me.

But what fate attaches me to this woman? Are there not a hundred others who desire my attentions? Will they not be eager to reply to them? Even if none of them was worth her, do not the attractions of variety, the charm of new conquests, the splendour of their number, offer delightful enough pleasures? Why run after her who flies from us and neglect those who offer themselves? Ah! why? . . . I do not know, but I feel it strongly.

For me there is no happiness, no rest, until I possess this woman whom I hate and whom I love with equal fury. I shall only endure my fate from the moment I am master of hers. Then I shall be calm and satisfied and I, in my turn, shall see her given up to the storms I feel at this moment; I shall create in her a thousand others as well. Hope and fear, suspicion and confidence, all the ills invented by hatred, all the good allowed by love—I want them to fill her heart, to succeed each other at my will. This time will come. . . . But what work still remains! How near I was to it yesterday, and how far I am from it today! How am I to draw near it once more? I dare not attempt any measures; I feel that I must be calmer to adopt any course, and my blood boils in my veins.

What redoubles my torture is the calm with which everybody here replies to my questions about this event, about its cause, about all its extraordinary side. . . . Nobody knows, nobody desires to know; they would scarcely have spoken of it, if I had allowed them to speak of anything else. Madame de Rosemonde, to whom I rushed this morning when I learned the news, replied with the coldness of her age, that it was the natural result of the indisposition Madame de Tourvel felt yesterday; that she had feared an illness and had preferred to be in her own home. She thinks it quite simple; she would have done the same, she told me; as if there could be anything in common between them! Between her, who has nothing left but to die and the other, who is the charm and torment of my life!

Madame de Volanges, whom I suspected at first of being an accomplice, only appeared moved by the fact that she had not been consulted upon this step. I confess I am very glad that she has not had the pleasure of doing me harm. This proves to me that she does not possess the woman's confidence as much as I feared; it is one enemy the less. How glad she would be, if she knew that it was from me Madame de Tourvel fled! How puffed up with pride she would have been if it had been by her advice! How her self-importance would have redoubled! Heavens! How I hate her! Oh! I shall renew the affair with her daughter; I want to work upon her as I fancy; so I think I shall stay here some time; at least, the few reflections I have made lead me to that course.

Do you not think that after so obvious a step, my ungrateful lady must dread my presence? If the idea has occurred to her that I might follow her, she will not have failed to close her doors to me; and I no more wish to accustom her to this method than to suffer the humiliation of it myself. On the contrary, I prefer to announce to her that I am staying here; and I shall even beg her to return here; and when she is fully persuaded of my absence I shall arrive at her house; we shall see how she will sustain that adventure. But to increase its effect, it must be postponed, and I do not know yet if I shall have the patience; twenty times today I have had my mouth open to call for my horses. However I will control myself; I promise to wait for your reply here; I only ask you, my fair friend, not to keep me waiting.

What would annoy me most would be not to know what is happening; but my servant, who is in Paris, has the right to some access to the waiting-woman; he will be able to help me. I am sending him instructions and money. I beg you will allow me to enclose both in this letter and that you will send them to him by one of your servants, with orders to give them to him in person. I take this precaution because the rascal has a habit of never receiving the letters I write him when they order him to do something which gives him trouble, and because he does not appear to me at present to be as interested in his conquest as I should like him to be.

Good-bye, my fair friend; if you have some happy idea, some way of hastening my advance, let me know. More than once I have proved how useful your friendship can be; I feel it again now; for since I have written to you I feel calmer; at least I am speaking to someone who understands me and not to the automata near whom I have vegetated since this morning. Really, the further I go the more I am tempted to believe that you and I are the only people in the world who are worth anything.

From the Château de——, 3rd of October, 17—.

## LETTER CI

*The Vicomte de Valmont to Azolan, his servant*
(Enclosed in the preceding letter)

You must be an imbecile, not to have known when you left here this morning that Madame de Tourvel was going too; or, if you knew it, not to have come to tell me. What use is it your spending my money getting drunk with the footmen and passing the time you ought to give to my service in playing the agreeable with waiting-women, if I am not better informed of what is taking place? But this is one of your negligencies. I warn you that if there is one more in this affair, it be will your last in my service.

You must find out for me everything that is happening at Madame de Tourvel's ; her health ; if she sleeps ; if she is sad or gay ; if she often goes out and where she goes ; if she receives company in her house and who comes to it ; how she spends her time, if she is bad-tempered with her women, particularly with the woman she brought here ; what she does when she is alone ; if when she reads, she reads continuously or interrupts her reading to meditate ; and similarly when she writes. Remember to become friendly with the servant who takes her letters to the post. Offer frequently to perform this duty in his place ; and when he accepts, only post those letters which seem to you unimportant and send the others to me, especially those to Madame de Volanges, if you come across any.

Make your plans to remain for some time yet the favoured lover of your Julie. If she has another, as you thought, make her agree to share herself ; and do not pique yourself upon ridiculous delicacy ; you will be in the position of many others who are worth far more than you are. However, if your second becomes too importunate, if you notice, for example, that he occupies Julie too much during the day and that she is consequently less often near her mistress, get rid of him in some way ; or pick a quarrel with him ; do not fear for the consequences, I will support you. Above all do not leave that house. It is by assiduity that everything is seen and seen clearly. If by chance one of the servants is sent away, present yourself to take his place, as if you were no longer in my service. In this event, say that you have left me to look for a quieter and more orderly house. Try to get yourself accepted. I will continue you in my service during this time ; it will be the same as it was with the Duchesse de . . . ; and in the end Madame de Tourvel will reward you in the same way.

If you have enough adroitness and zeal these instructions ought to suffice you ; but to make up for both I am sending you some money. The enclosed note authorises you, as you will see, to draw twenty-five *louis* from my agent ; for I have no doubt you are penniless. Out of this sum you will use so much as may be necessary to persuade Julie to establish a correspondence with me. The rest will serve to buy drinks for the servants. Take care as much as possible to let this happen in the porter's lodge, so that he will be glad to see you come. But do not forget that I am not paying for your pleasures but your services.

Accustom Julie to observe everything and to report everything, even what appear to her to be details. It is better that she should write ten useless phrases than omit one important ; and often what seems to be unimportant is not so. Since I must be informed at once if anything happens which appears to you to deserve attention, as soon as you receive this letter you will send Philippe on the errands horse to wait at . . .[1] ; he will remain there until he receives fresh orders ; he will

[1]A village half-way between Paris and Madame de Rosemonde's Château. (C. de L.)

be a relay in case of necessity. For ordinary correspondence the Post will suffice.

Be careful not to lose this letter. Read it over every day, both to make certain that you have forgotten nothing and to make certain you have not lost it. In short, do everything a man ought to do when he is honoured by my confidence. You know that if I am pleased with you, you will be so with me.

From the Château de . . ., 3rd of October, 17—.

## LETTER CII

*Madame de Tourvel to Madame de Rosemonde*

You will be very surprised, Madame, when you learn I have left your house so suddenly. This step will appear very extraordinary to you; but how greatly your surprise will be increased when you know the reasons for it! Perhaps you will think that in confiding them to you I am not sufficiently respectful of the tranquillity necessary to your age; that I am even departing from those sentiments of veneration which are your due upon so many accounts? Ah! Madame, forgive me; but my heart is over-laden; it needs to pour out its grief upon the bosom of a friend who is both gentle and prudent; what other but you could it choose? Look upon me as your child. Show me the kindness of a mother; I implore it. Perhaps I have some right to it through my feelings for you.

Where is that time when, occupied solely with laudable sentiments, I was ignorant of those which bear into the soul the mortal disturbance I feel and take away the strength to combat them at the same time that they impose the duty of doing so? Ah! This fatal visit has ruined me. . . .

How shall I tell you? I love, yes, I love wildly. Alas! that word which I write for the first time, that word so often asked for and never granted—I would give my life for the sweetness of being able once only to say it to him who inspires it; and yet it must be refused forever! He will still doubt my feelings; he will think he has reason to complain of them. I am very unfortunate! Why is it not as easy for him to read in my heart as it is for him to reign over it? Yes, I should suffer less, if he knew all that I am suffering; but you, to whom I tell this, can have but a feeble idea of it.

In a few moments I am about to fly from him and to hurt him. While he still thinks me near him I shall already be far away; at the hour when I was accustomed to see him each day, I shall be in places where he has never been, where I must not permit him to come. All my preparations are made; everything is here before my eyes; I cannot rest them on anything which does not tell me of this cruel departure. Everything is ready, except me! . . . And the more my heart refuses it, the more it proves to me the necessity for submitting.

Without doubt I shall submit, it is better to die than to live guilty. Already I feel I am too much so ; I have only saved my modesty, my virtue has vanished. Must I confess it ? What virtue I have left I owe to his generosity. Intoxicated with the pleasure of seeing him, of hearing him, with the sweetness of feeling him near me, with the greater happiness of being able to make him happy, I was without power and without strength ; I had scarcely enough to combat, not enough to resist ; I shuddered at my danger without being able to escape it. Well ! He saw my anguish and he pitied me. How can I not cherish him ? I owe him more than life itself.

Ah ! If by remaining near him I had only to tremble for my life, do not think that I should ever consent to go away. What is life to me without him ; should I not be but too happy to lose it ? Condemned to make him and myself unhappy forever ; to dare neither to complain nor to console him ; to defend myself every day against him, against myself ; to give my attention to causing his pain when I wish to consecrate it all to his happiness—to live thus, is it not to die a thousand times ? Yet that will be my fate. Yet I will endure it, I shall have the courage. O you, whom I choose as my mother, receive my oath !

Receive also the oath I make you never to hide from you any of my actions ; receive it, I beg you ; I ask it of you as an aid I sorely need ; thus, having promised to tell you everything, I shall grow accustomed to thinking myself always in your presence. Your virtue shall replace mine. Never indeed will I consent to blush at your gaze ; and, restrained by this powerful curb, I shall cherish in you the indulgent friend, the confidant of my frailty, and I shall still honour in you the guardian Angel who will save me from shame.

It is indeed sufficient shame to have to make this request. Fatal effect of a presumptuous self-confidence ! Why did I not sooner dread this feeling which I felt growing ? Why did I flatter myself that I could dominate or overcome it at will ? Ah ! If I had combatted it with more attention, perhaps it would have gained less power over me ! Perhaps this departure would not then have been necessary ; or even, in submitting to this painful course, I should have been able not to break off entirely an acquaintance which it would have sufficed to render less frequent ! But to lose everything at once ! And forever ! O my friend ! . . . But, even as I write to you, am I not wandering into criminal wishes ? Ah ! Let me go, let me go, and at least let these involuntary errors be expiated by my sacrifices.

Farewell, my respected friend ; love me as your daughter, adopt me as such ; and be certain that, in spite of my weakness, I would rather die than render myself unworthy of your choice.

From . . ., 3rd, of October, at one o'clock in the morning.

## LETTER CIII

*Madame de Rosemonde to Madame de Tourvel*

I was more distressed, my dear Beauty, by your departure than surprised at its cause ; a long experience and the interest I take in you were sufficient to enlighten me as to the state of your heart ; and if I must tell you everything, your letter told me little or nothing I did not know. If I had had no information but your letter I should still not know who it is you love ; for in speaking of *him* the whole time you have not written his name once. But I notice it because I recollect that was always the style of love. I see it is now as it used to be.

I did not think I should ever again be in a situation to have to return to memories so distant from me and so foreign to my years. Yet, since yesterday I have truly thought much upon them, from my desire to find something in them which might be of use to you. But what can I do except admire and pity you ? I praise the wise course you have taken ; but it frightens me, because I conclude you felt it necessary ; and when you have reached that point it is very difficult to remain always distant from him to whom your heart always draws you near.

Yet do not be discouraged. Nothing should be impossible to your fine soul ; and even if you should one day have the misfortune to succumb (which God forbid !) believe me, my dear Beauty, keep for yourself at least the consolation of having fought with all your strength. And then, what human wisdom cannot do, Divine grace operates when it pleases. Perhaps you are on the eve of receiving this aid and your virtue, tried in these terrible struggles, will emerge purer and more brilliant. Hope that you will receive tomorrow the strength you do not possess today. Do not expect it as a matter of course, but as an encouragement to use all your own strength.

When I leave to Providence the care of aiding you in a danger against which I can do nothing, I reserve for myself the task of supporting and consoling you as much as I am able. I shall not relieve your anguish, but I shall share it. On this basis I will gladly receive your confidences. I feel your heart must need to pour itself out. I open mine to you ; age has not yet chilled it to the point of being insensible to friendship. You will find it always ready to receive you. It will be a poor relief to your pain, but at least you will not weep alone ; and when this unhappy love gains too much power over you and forces you to speak of it, it is better that it should be with me than with *him*. You see I am talking as you did ; and I believe that the two of us will never succeed in naming him ; however, we understand each other.

I do not know if I am doing right to tell you that he appeared to be keenly affected by your departure ; it would perhaps be wiser not to tell you this ; but I do not like that wisdom which distresses its friends. Yet I am compelled not to speak of him much longer. My failing sight and my trembling hand do not permit me long letters when I have to write them myself.

Good-bye then, my dear Beauty, good-bye, my sweet child ; yes, I gladly adopt you as my daughter, and you indeed possess all that is needed to make the pride and pleasure of a mother.

From the Château de . . ., 3rd of October, 17—.

## LETTER CIV

### *The Marquise de Merteuil to Madame de Volanges*

Indeed, my dear and good friend, I found it hard to avoid a feeling of pride when I read your letter. What ! You honour me with your complete confidence ! You even go so far as to ask my advice ! Ah ! I am very happy if I deserve this favourable opinion on your part ; if I do not owe it only to the favour of friendship. But whatever the motive, it is none the less precious to my heart ; and to have obtained it is in my eyes but one more reason for labouring to deserve it. I shall then (but without pretending to give you advice) tell you freely what I think. I am mistrustful of it because it differs from yours ; but when I have given you my reasons you will form your judgment ; and if you condemn them I accept your judgment beforehand. At least I shall have the wisdom not to think myself wiser than you.

But if on this single occasion my opinion appears preferable, the cause must be sought in the illusions of maternal love. Since this is a laudable sentiment, you must possess it. How well it can be perceived in the course you are tempted to take ! It is thus, that if you ever err, it is in the choice of virtues.

It seems to me that prudence is the preferable virtue when we are disposing of the fate of others, especially when it is a matter of binding it with an indissoluble and sacred tie like that of marriage. It is then that a mother, equally wise and tender, ought, as you say so well " to help her daughter with her experience." Now, I ask you, what has she to do to achieve that ? To distinguish for herself between what is pleasing and what is expedient.

Would it not be debasing maternal authority, would it not be annihilating it, to subordinate it to a frivolous inclination whose illusory power is only felt by those who dread it, which disappears as soon as it is treated with contempt ? For my part, I confess I have never believed in these overpowering and irresistible passions, which by general agreement seem to have been made the excuse for our licentiousness. I cannot conceive how an inclination, which is born one moment and dies the next, can have more strength than the inalterable principles of decency, honour, and modesty ; and I do not understand how a woman who betrays them can be justified by a pretended passion, any more than a thief would be by the passion for money or a murderer by that of vengeance.

Ah ! Who can say she has never had to struggle ? But I have always tried to convince myself that it was sufficient to want to resist in order to be able to do so ; and hitherto at least my experience has confirmed my opinion. What would virtue be without the duties it imposes ? Its cult is in our sacrifices, its reward in our hearts. These truths can only be denied by those whose interest it is to disregard them and who, being already depraved, hope to create a moment of illusion by trying to justify their bad conduct with bad reasons.

But can one fear this from a simple and timid child, from a child born of you, whose modest pure education can only have fortified her natural good character ? Yet to this fear, which I dare to call humiliating to your daughter, you wish to sacrifice the advantageous marriage your prudence had arranged for her ! I like Danceny very much ; and for a long time, as you know, I have seen little of M. de Gercourt ; but my friendship for the one, my indifference to the other, do not prevent me from feeling the enormous difference between them as husbands.

Their birth is equal, I admit ; but one has no fortune and the other's wealth is such that even without good birth it would have sufficed to lead him anywhere. I admit that money does not make happiness ; but it must be admitted also that it greatly facilitates happiness. As you say, Mademoiselle de Volanges is wealthy enough for two ; and yet, the income of sixty thousand *livres* she will enjoy is already not much when she bears the name of Danceny, when she must display and keep up an establishment worthy of it. We are no longer in the times of Madame de Sévigné. Luxury absorbs everything ; we deplore it, but we must imitate it ; and superfluities end up by absorbing necessities.

As to the personal qualities which you consider so important, and with such good reason ; assuredly M. de Gercourt is irreproachable in that respect ; he has given proofs of it. I like to think, and I do indeed think that Danceny yields to him in nothing ; but are we as sure of this ? It is true that hitherto he has appeared free from the faults of his age and that, in spite of the current tone, he shows a taste for good company which allows one to augur well of him ; but who knows if he does not owe this apparent virtue to the mediocrity of his fortune ? Even if a man fears to be a rogue or debauched, he needs money to be a gambler and a libertine and he may like the faults whose excess he fears. In short, he would not be the thousandth who has kept good company solely because he could afford nothing worse.

I do not say (God forbid !) that I think all this of him ; but still there is always a risk of it ; and how you would blame yourself if the result were unhappy ! What would you reply to your daughter if she said to you : " Mother, I was young and inexperienced ; I was carried away by an error pardonable at my age ; but Heaven, which had foreseen my frailty, had given me a wise mother to redress it and to preserve me. Why then, forgetting your prudence, did you consent to my misfortune ? Was it for me to choose a husband when I knew nothing of the condition of marriage ? Even if I wished to do so, was it not for you to oppose it? But I never had that foolish presumption. I had decided to obey you and awaited your choice with respectful obedience; I never departed from the submission which I owed you and yet today I endure the pain which is the lot of rebellious children. Ah! Your weakness has ruined me. . . ." Perhaps her respect would stifle these complaints; but maternal love would guess them; and though your daughter's tears were concealed they would none the less flow upon your heart. Where then will you seek for consolation? Will it be in this foolish love, against which you ought to have fore-armed her and by which, on the contrary, you will have allowed yourself to be seduced?

I do not know, my dear friend, if I have too strong a prejudice against this passion; but I think it is to be dreaded, even in marriage. It is not that I have any disapproval of a soft and virtuous sentiment which should embellish the conjugal tie and soften, as it were, the duties imposed by it; but the sentiment should not form the tie; the illusion of a moment should not govern our choice for life. After all, to choose, we must compare; and how can we compare when one person occupies us entirely, when we cannot even comprehend him since we are plunged in ecstasy and blindness?

As you may suppose I have met several women infected with this dangerous disorder; and I have received the confidences of some of them. To listen to them you would think every lover was a perfect being; but these illusory perfections only exist in their imaginations. Their excited minds dream of nothing but attractions and virtues; they invest the man they prefer with them at pleasure; it is the drapery of a god, often worn by an abject model; but in any case, they have scarcely dressed him up in them when they are duped by their own handiwork and prostrate themselves to adore it.

Either your daughter does not love Danceny or she is undergoing this illusion; it is common to them both, if their love is mutual. Thus your reason for uniting them forever comes down to the certainty that they do not know each other, that they cannot know each other. But, you will say, do M. de Gercourt and your daughter know each other any better? No, doubtless they do not; but at least they do not delude themselves, they are merely ignorant of each other. What happens in such a case between two married people, whom I suppose to be virtuous? Each of them studies the other, observes the other, seeks for and soon perceives what must be yielded to the other's tastes and wishes for their mutual tranquillity. These slight sacrifices are made without pain because they are mutual and because they have been foreseen; soon they create a mutual good-will; and habit which strengthens all inclinations it does not destroy little by little brings with it that gentle friendship, that tender confidence which, added to esteem, form in my opinion the real, the solid happiness of marriage.

The illusions of love may be sweeter; but who does not know that they are less durable? And what dangers are brought by the moment which destroys those illusions! It is then that the slightest faults appear offensive and unendurable from their contrast with the idea of perfection which had seduced us. Yet each one thinks that the other alone has changed and that he or she still possesses the worth a moment of error won for them. They are surprised at not creating the charm they no longer feel; they are humiliated; wounded vanity embitters their minds, increases their errors, produces ill-temper, gives birth to hatred; and idle pleasures are paid for by long misfortunes.

That, my dear friend, is how I think of the subject which now occupies us; I do not defend it, I merely express it; it is for you to decide. But if you persist in your opinion I ask you to let me know the reasons which overcome mine; I shall be very glad to be enlightened by you and above all to be reassured as to the fate of your charming child, whose happiness I desire most ardently, both from my friendship with her and from that which unites me to you for life.

Paris, 4th of October, 17—.

## LETTER CV

*The Marquise de Merteuil to Cécile Volanges*

Well, little one, you are very angry and very much ashamed, and this M. de Valmont is a wicked man, is he not? Why! He dares to treat you as the woman he loves best. He teaches you what you were dying to know! Indeed, such proceedings are unpardonable. And you, for your part, wished to keep your modesty for your lover (who does not abuse it); you only cherish the pains of love, not its pleasures! Nothing could be better, and you would make an excellent figure in a novel. Passion, misfortune, above all virtue, what excellent things! In the midst of this brilliant throng one is bored sometimes, it is true, but then it is in turn boring.

Come, poor child, how she is to be pitied! She had rings under her eyes the next morning! And what will you say when they are caused by your lover? Ah! my angel, you will not always have them so; all men are not Valmonts. And then; not to dare to lift those eyes! Ah! you were quite right there; everyone would have read your adventure in them! Believe me, if that were so, our women and even our girls would have a more modest gaze.

In spite of the praises I am compelled to give you, as you see, it must still be admitted that you missed your master stroke—that was to tell your Mamma everything. You began so well! You had already thrown yourself into her arms, you were sobbing and she was crying too; what a pathetic scene! And what a pity you did not complete it! Your tender mother would have been delighted and, to aid your virtue, would have shut you up for the rest of your life; and there you could have loved as much as you liked, without rivals and without sin; you could have despaired at leisure, and Valmont assuredly would not have come to trouble your grief with annoying pleasures.

Seriously now, can you at over fifteen be as childish as you are? You are right to say you do not deserve my kindness. Yet I should like to be your friend; perhaps you will need one with the mother you have and the husband she wants to give you! But if you do not develop more, what is to be done with you? What can be hoped if that which gives girls understanding takes yours away?

If you could but persuade yourself to reason a little, you would soon find that you ought to be glad rather than to complain. But you are ashamed, and that troubles you! Hey! Calm yourself; the shame love causes is like its pain; we only feel it once. We may feign it afterwards, but we do not feel it. However, the pleasure remains, and that is indeed something. I think I could make out through your chatter that you might count it for a good deal. Come now, a little honesty. That disturbance which prevented you from "doing what you said," which made you find it so "difficult to defend" yourself, which made you "as if sorry" when Valmont went away—was it caused by shame? Or was it pleasure? "And his way of saying things which one does not know how to answer"—does that not come from "his way of pleasing"? Ah, little girl, you tell an untruth, and to your friend too. That is not right. But let us have no more of this.

What would be a pleasure for anyone, and be only a pleasure, in your situation becomes positive happiness. Indeed, placed as you are between a mother whose love is important to you and a lover by whom you desire to be loved always, how can you fail to see that the only way to obtain these opposite ends is to occupy yourself with a third? Entertained by this new adventure, you will appear to your Mamma to sacrifice to your submission to her an inclination which displeases her, while with your lover you will acquire the honour of a long resistance. While you continually assure him of your love, you will not grant him the last proofs of it. These refusals, which are not difficult in your present situation, he will place to the credit of your virtue; he will complain perhaps but he will love the more, and, to secure the double merit, in the eyes of the one of sacrificing love, in the eyes of the other of resisting it, you have to do nothing but enjoy its pleasures. O, how many women have lost their reputation who would have preserved it with care if they could have supported it by such means!

Does not the course I propose to you seem the most reasonable, as it is the pleasantest? Do you know what you have gained by your present course? Your Mamma attributes your increase of sadness to an increase of love; she is angered by it and she is only waiting to be more certain to punish you. She has just written to me; she will try everything to obtain this admission from you. She will perhaps go so far, she tells me, as to propose Danceny to you as a husband; and that to get you to speak! If you let yourself be deceived by this false tenderness, if you reply as your heart wishes, you will soon be shut up for a long time, perhaps forever, where you can cry at pleasure over your blind credulity.

You must combat this ruse she is going to make use of against you by another. Begin by showing less sadness, by making her believe that you are thinking less of Danceny. She will be the more readily convinced of it, since it is the usual effect of absence ; and she will be all the more pleased with you because it gives her an opportunity to congratulate herself on her prudence, which suggested this way. But if she retains some doubt and persists in testing you, if she speaks to you of marriage, show yourself, as a well-born girl should, completely submissive. After all, what do you risk ? One husband is as good as another; and the most inconvenient is less so than a mother.

Once she is more pleased with you, your Mamma will marry you ; and you will be freer in your movements and you will be able to leave Valmont for Danceny as you choose, or even to keep them both. For, notice this, your Danceny is agreeable, but he is one of those men one can have when and as long as one wishes ; you can therefore be easy about him. It is not the same with Valmont ; it is difficult to keep him ; and it is dangerous to leave him. With him you need a lot of skill, or, if you do not possess it, great docility. But if you can succeed in attaching him to you as a friend, that would be good fortune ! He would put you at once in the first rank of our fashionable women. That is the way to acquire a position in the world, not by blushing and crying as you did when the nuns made you eat your dinner kneeling.

If you are wise you will try to patch matters up with Valmont, who must be very angry with you ; and since we must make up for our silly mistakes, do not be afraid to make some advances to him ; you will soon learn that if men make the first advances to us, we are almost always obliged to make the second. You have a pretext for this ; for you must not keep this letter and I insist that you give it to Valmont as soon as you have read it. But do not forget to re-seal it first. You must be left the merit of the measure you are going to take with him and it must not seem to have been suggested to you ; and then you are the only person in the world with whom I am friendly enough to speak as I am doing.

Good-bye, my angel, follow my advice and tell me if it turns out well.

P.S. By the way, I forgot. . . . One word more. Try to take more care with your style. You still write like a child. I see why that is ; it is because you say everything you think and nothing you do not think. That is all very well between you and me who have nothing to hide from each other, but with everyone else ! Above all with your lover ! You will always seem like a little fool. You can see that when you write to someone it is for him and not for yourself ; you ought then to try less to say what you are thinking than to say what will please him more.

Good-bye, my heart ; I kiss you instead of scolding you in the hope that you will be more reasonable.

Paris, 4th of October, 17—.

## LETTER CVI

*The Marquise de Merteuil to the Vicomte de Valmont*

Wonderful! Vicomte, and this time I love you madly! For the rest, after the first of your two letters the second might have been expected; so it did not surprise me; and while you were so proud of your success, while you solicited your reward and asked me if I were ready, I saw I had no such need to hurry. Yes, on my word of honour; when I read the fine account of that tender scene and that you had been so "profoundly moved"; when I saw that restraint, worthy of the best ages of our chivalry, I said twenty times: That affair will be a failure!

But it could not have been otherwise. What do you expect a poor woman to do when she yields herself and is not taken? Faith, in such cases, honour at least must be saved; and that is what your Madame de Tourvel has done. For my part I know that the course she took is really not ineffective and I propose to make use of it on my own account, at the first serious opportunity which occurs; but I promise that if the man for whom I go to the trouble does not profit by it better than you, he may certainly renounce me forever.

There you are, absolutely reduced to nothingness, and that between two women, one of whom was already at the day after and the other was asking nothing better than to be there! Well! You will think I am boasting and that it is easy to prophesy after the event; but I swear to you that I expected it. The fact is, you have not the genius of your condition; you only know what you have learned, and you invent nothing. Thus, as soon as circumstances do not fit your usual formulas and you have to leave the beaten path, you are as taken aback as a schoolboy. So, on the one side a puerility, on the other side a return of prudery, are sufficient to disconcert you because they are not to be met with every day, and you can neither avoid nor remedy them. Ah! Vicomte, Vicomte, you teach me not to judge of men by their successes, very soon we shall have to say of you: He *was* brave on such a day. And when you have piled stupidities on stupidities, you come to me. It appears I have nothing else to do but to retrieve them. I shall soon have plenty of work, it is plain.

In any case, one of these two adventures was undertaken against my will and I shall not meddle with it; as to the other, since it was partly out of consideration for me, I make it my business. The letter I enclose, which you will read and then give to the Volanges girl, is more than sufficient to bring her back to you; but I beg you to give some attention to the child and let us together make her the despair of her mother and of Gercourt. There is no need to fear increasing the doses. I see clearly that the little person will not be frightened by it; and once we have carried out our intentions she will become what she can.

I take no further interest in her. I had some idea of making her at least a subsidiary intriguer and to take her on to play second parts under me ; but I see she has not the material in her ; she has a silly ingenuousness which has not even yielded to the specific you employed, which is hardly ever unsuccessful ; and in my opinion, it is the most dangerous malady a woman can have. It shows especially a weakness of character, almost always incurable, which thwarts everything ; so that while we are trying to fit this girl for intrigue we shall make nothing of her but a facile woman. Now, I know nothing so flat as the facility of stupidity which yields without knowing how or why, solely because it is attached and does not know how to resist. These sorts of women are absolutely nothing but pleasure machines.

You will tell me that that is the only thing to do and that it suffices for our plans. Well enough ! But do not forget that very soon everybody gets to know the springs and contrivances of these machines ; so, to make use of this one without danger, we must hurry, know when to stop, and then break it. After all, we shall have plenty of ways of getting rid of her, and Gercourt will always shut her up when we like to make him. Indeed, when he can no longer doubt his discomfiture, when it is public and notorious, what does it matter to us whether he revenges himself, so long as he has no consolation ? What I say of the husband, you doubtless think of the mother ; so it is as good as done.

The course I consider best, and have fixed on, has decided me to lead the young person rather quickly, as you will see from my letter ; this makes it very important to leave nothing in her hands which might compromise us, and I beg you will give your attention to this. This precaution once taken, I will look after the moral side, the rest concerns you. If we see later that she gets over her ingenuousness, we shall always have time to change our plans. One day or other we should have had to consider what we were going to do ; in any event our trouble will not be wasted.

Do you know my trouble was nearly wasted and that Gercourt's star very nearly overcame my prudence ? Did not Madame de Volanges have a moment of maternal weakness ? And did she not want to give her daughter to Danceny ? That was what was meant by that more tender interest you noticed on " the morning after." It is you again who would have been the cause of this wonderful master stroke. Happily, the tender mother wrote to me, and I hope my reply will disgust her with the idea. I talked so much of virtue and above all I flattered her so much that she is certain to think I am right.

I am sorry I had not time to take a copy of my letter, to edify you with the austerity of my morals. You would have seen what scorn I have for women so depraved as to have a lover ! It is convenient to be a rigorist in words ! It never hurts others and does not hinder us in the least. . . . And then I happen to know that the good lady had weaknesses, like others, in her youth and I was not sorry to humiliate her, at least in her conscience ; that consoled me a little for the praises I gave her against my own conscience. And in the same letter the idea of harming Gercourt gave me the courage to speak well of him.

Good-bye, Vicomte ; I strongly approve your determination to stay where you are for some time. I have no means of hastening your advance ; but I invite you to chase away boredom with our common pupil. As to what concerns me, you will see (in spite of your polite quotation) that you must wait a little longer ; and no doubt you will admit that it is not my fault.

## LETTER CVII

*Azolan to the Vicomte de Valmont*

Monsieur,

In accordance with your orders I went, as soon as I got your letter, to M. Bertrand, who handed me twenty-five *louis*, as you ordered him. I asked him for two more for Philippe, whom I had told to start at once, as Monsieur wrote me, and who had no money ; but your agent would not do it, saying that he had no order for it from you. I was obliged to give them myself and Monsieur will take this into account, if he will be so good.

Philippe started yesterday evening. I warned him not to leave the inn, so that I can be sure to find him if necessary.

Immediately afterwards I went to Madame de Tourvel's house to see Mademoiselle Julie ; but she had gone out, and I only spoke to La Fleur, from whom I learned nothing, because since his return he has only been in the house to meals. The second footman is doing all the waiting, and Monsieur knows that I have no acquaintance with him. But I began today.

I went back this morning to Mademoiselle Julie and she seemed very pleased to see me. I asked her what was the cause of her Mistress's returning ; but she told me she knew nothing about it, and I think she was telling the truth. I reproached her for not having told me she was going and she assured me she only knew it the same evening when she went to help Madame to bed ; so she spent the whole night in packing and the poor girl did not have two hours' sleep. She only left her Mistress's room that evening after one o'clock, and when she went, her Mistress was beginning to write.

In the morning when Madame de Tourvel was leaving she gave a packet to the Concierge of the Château. Mademoiselle Julie does not know who it was for ; she says perhaps it was for Monsieur ; but Monsieur does not say anything about it.

During the whole journey Madame had a large hood over her face, so she could not be seen ; but Mademoiselle Julie thinks she can be sure she often cried. She did not say a word all the way and would not stop at . . .[1], as she did when coming ; which did not please

[1] The same village mentioned before, half-way between Paris and the Château. (C. de L.)

Mademoiselle Julie who had had no breakfast. But, as I told her, Masters are masters.

On arriving, Madame went to bed; but she only stayed there two hours. When she got up she sent for the door-porter and told him to allow no one to come in. She made no toilet at all. She sat down at table to dine; but she only ate a little soup and left at once. Her coffee was taken up to her and Mademoiselle Julie went in at the same time. She found her Mistress arranging papers in her writing-desk and she saw they were letters. I would wager they are Monsieur's; and one of the three which came in the afternoon she kept in front of her all evening! I am sure it was another of Monsieur's again. But why did she go away like that? That surprises me. Monsieur must surely know? But it is not my business.

Madame de Tourvel went to the library in the afternoon and took two books which she brought up to her boudoir; but Mademoiselle Julie assures me she did not read them a quarter of an hour all day, and that she did nothing but read this letter, think, and lean her head on her hand. As I thought Monsieur would be glad to know what these books were, and Mademoiselle Julie did not know, I got myself taken into the library, under the pretext of seeing it. There were empty places for only two books; one is the second volume of *Christian Thoughts* and the other, the first volume of the book, has the title *Clarissa.* I write it just as it was; Monsieur will perhaps know it.

Yesterday evening Madame did not take supper; she only had some tea.

She rang early this morning; she asked for her horses at once and before nine o'clock she went to the Feuillants, where she heard Mass. She wanted to go to confession, but her confessor was away and he will not be back for eight or ten days; I thought it important to tell Monsieur that.

Afterwards, she came back, had breakfast, and began to write, and remained at it until one o'clock. I soon found an opportunity to do what Monsieur most desires; and it was I took the letters to post. There was none for Madame de Volanges; but I send one to Monsieur which was for Monsieur de Tourvel; I thought that would be the most important. There was one for Madame de Rosemonde as well; but I supposed Monsieur could always see it when he wanted, so I let it go. Moreover, Monsieur will soon know everything since Madame de Tourvel writes to him also. In the future I shall have all the letters Monsieur wants, for it is almost always Mademoiselle Julie who gives them to the servants, and she assures me that from friendship to me, and to Monsieur too, she will gladly do what I want.

She even refused the money I offered her; but I think Monsieur would wish to give her some little present; and if it is his wish and he will leave it to me, I shall easily find out what will please her.

I hope that Monsieur will not think I have shown any negligence in his service, and I have it upon my heart to justify myself from his reproaches. If I did not know that Madame de Tourvel was leaving, the reason is my zeal for Monsieur's service, since it is he who made me leave at three o'clock in the morning; and that was why I did not see Mademoiselle Julie the night before, as usual, having gone to sleep at the roadside inn, so as not to wake the Château.

As to what Monsieur says about my being often without money, first it is because I like to keep clean-looking, as Monsieur can see; and then I must keep up the honour of the cloth I wear; I know that I ought to save a little for the future; but I confide entirely in the generosity of Monsieur, who is such a good Master.

As to entering Madame de Tourvel's service, while remaining in Monsieur's, I hope Monsieur will not insist on it. It was very different with Madame la Duchesse; but assuredly I will not wear livery, and a magistrate's livery, after having had the honour to be Monsieur's servant. In anything else Monsieur may dispose of him who has the honour to be with as much respect as affection, his most humble servant.

Roux Azolan, *Chasseur*.

Paris, 5th of October, 17—., at eleven o'clock at night.

## LETTER CVIII

### *Madame de Tourvel to Madame de Rosemonde*

O my indulgent mother! How many thanks I have to give you and what need I had of your letter! I read and re-read it continually; I could not tear myself away from it. I owe to it the only less painful moments I have passed since I left. How good you are! Wisdom and virtue, then, can feel for weakness! You have pity on my misfortunes! Ah! If you knew them! . . . They are terrible. I thought I had endured the pains of love; but the inexpressible torture, the torture which must be felt for one to have any idea of, is to be separated from what one loves, and separated forever! . . . Yes, the pain which overwhelms me today will return tomorrow, the day after tomorrow, all my life! Heaven! How young I am still, and how long I have yet to suffer!

To be oneself the creator of one's misery; to tear one's heart with one's own hands; and, while suffering these unendurable pains, to feel every instant that one could end them with a word and that this word is a sin! Ah! My friend! . . .

When I took this painful step of going away from him, I hoped that absence would increase my courage and my strength; how much I was deceived! On the contrary, it seems to have completed their destruction. It is true I had more to struggle against; but even in resistance everything was not deprivation; at least I saw him sometimes; often, without daring to raise my eyes to his, I felt his gaze fixed upon me; yes, my friend, I felt it, it seemed to warm my soul; and without passing through my eyes it none the less reached my heart. Now, in my painful solitude, isolated from everything that is dear to me, alone with my misfortune, every moment of my sad existence is marked by tears, and nothing softens their bitterness, no consolation mingles with my sacrifices ; those I have made hitherto only serve to make more painful those I have still to make.

Yesterday I felt it very keenly. Among the letters brought to me there was one from him ; I recognised it among the others when the servant was a yard away. Involuntarily I got up ; I trembled, I had difficulty in hiding my emotion ; and this state was not without pleasure. A moment later I was alone and this deceptive pleasure soon vanished and left me only one sacrifice the more to make. Indeed, could I open that letter, which I was burning to read ? Through the fatality which pursues me, the consolations which appear to come to me, only impose new privations ; and these become still more cruel, from the thought that M. de Valmont shares them.

There it is at last, that name which continually occupies me and which I have such difficulty in writing ; the kind of reproach you made me really alarmed me. I beg you to believe that my confidence in you was not lessened by false shame ; and why should I blush to name him ? Ah ! I blush for my feelings, not the person who causes them. Who else is more worthy of inspiring them ! Yet I do not know why that name does not naturally come to my pen ; and this time too, I had to think before putting it down. I come back to him.

You tell me that he seemed keenly affected by my leaving. What has he done ? What has he said ? Has he talked of returning to Paris ? I beg you to dissuade him from it as much as you can. If he has judged me rightly, he ought not to be angry with me for this step ; but he ought to feel too that it is a final determination. One of my greatest tortures is not knowing what he thinks. I still have his letter here . . but you will surely agree with me that I ought not to open it.

It is only through you, my indulgent friend, that I am not entirely separated from him. I do not wish to impose upon your kindness ; I understand perfectly that your letters cannot be long ; but you will not refuse a word to your child ; a word to support her courage, a word to console her. Good-bye, my respected friend.

Paris, 5th of October, 17—.

## LETTER CIX

*Cécile Volanges to the Marquise de Merteuil*

It is only today, Madame, that I returned to M. de Valmont the letter you did me the honour to write me. I kept it four days, in spite of my terror lest someone should find it, but I hid it very carefully ; and when my grief returned I locked myself in to read it.

I see that what I thought a great misfortune is scarcely one at all; and I must admit there is great pleasure in it; so I am scarcely at all unhappy. There is only the idea of Danceny which still torments me sometimes. But already there are many times when I do not think of him at all! And also M. de Valmont is very charming!

I made things up with him two days ago; it was very easy; for I had only said two words when he said that if I had anything to say to him he would come to my room at night, and I had only to say that I agreed. And then, when he came, he seemed no more angry than if I had never done anything to annoy him. He only scolded me afterwards and then very gently and in such a way. . . . Just like you; which proves to me that he was friendly to me too.

I cannot tell you how many funny things he has told me which I should never have thought, especially about Mamma. You would do me a great pleasure if you would tell me whether it is all true. What is certain is that I could not keep from laughing; so that once I laughed out loud, which frightened us very much; for Mamma might have heard it; and if she had come to see what it was, what would have become of me? She would certainly have sent me back to the convent this time!

As we must be prudent and since, as M. de Valmont says, he would not risk compromising me for the world, we have agreed that henceforth he will simply come and open the door and we will go to his room. There is nothing to fear there; I went there yesterday and as I write you now I am waiting for him to come. I hope, Madame, you will not scold me now.

Yet there is one thing in your letter which surprised me; it is what you say about Danceny and M. de Valmont when I am married. I thought that one day at the Opera you said just the opposite, that when I was married I could only love my husband and that I should even have to forget Danceny; perhaps I did not hear properly and I should prefer it to be otherwise, because now I do not feel afraid of my marriage. I even want it, because I shall have more liberty; I hope that I can then arrange things so as not to think of anything but Danceny. I feel I should only be really happy with him; for the idea of him always torments me and I am not happy except when I do not think of him, which is very difficult; and as soon as I think of him, I become unhappy at once.

What consoles me a little is that you assure me Danceny will love me all the more; but are you quite sure? . . . Oh! yes, you would not deceive me. Yet it is amusing that I should love Danceny and that M. de Valmont. . . . But, as you say, perhaps it is a piece of good fortune! We shall see, in any case.

I did not quite understand what you meant about my way of writing. It seems to me that Danceny likes my letters as they are. Yet I do not feel that I should tell him anything of what is going on between M. de Valmont and me; so you have no reason to fear.

Mamma has not yet spoken to me about my marriage ; but let things go ; when she speaks to me, I promise you I shall tell her lies, since she wants to catch me.

Good-bye, my kind friend ; I thank you very much and I promise you I shall never forget all your kindness to me. I must stop now, for it is after one o'clock ; M. de Valmont will be here soon.

From the Château de . . ., 10th of October, 17—.

## LETTER CX

*The Vicomte de Valmont to the Marquise de Merteuil*

"Powers of Heaven, I had a soul for grief : give me one for joy !"[1] I think it is the tender Saint-Preux who expresses himself thus. Better gifted than he, I possess the two existences at once. Yes, my friend, I am at the same time very happy and very unhappy ; and since you have my entire confidence I owe you the double account of my pains and of my pleasures.

Know then that my ungracious devotee is still severe to me. I am at the fourth returned letter. Perhaps I am wrong to say the fourth ; for having guessed at the first return that it would be followed by many others, and not wishing to waste my time, I adopted the course of putting my complaints into commonplaces and adding no date ; and since the second post it is always the same letter which goes to and fro ; I only change the envelope. If my Beauty ends up as Beauties usually do, and softens one day, at least from lassitude, she will at last keep the missive and it will then be time to find out how things are going. You will see that with this new sort of correspondence I cannot be perfectly informed.

Yet I have discovered that the unstable person has changed her confidant ; at least I have made certain that since her departure from the Château no letter has come from her for Madame de Volanges, while there have been two for old Rosemonde ; and as she has said nothing about it to us, as she no longer opens her mouth about "her dear Beauty," whom she used to talk of ceaselessly, I concluded that it was she who now has her confidence. I presume that on the one hand, the need to speak of me, and on the other the little shame of having to make admissions to Madame de Volanges about a sentiment so long disavowed, have produced this great revolution. I am afraid I have lost by the change ; for the older women get, the more harsh and severe they become ; the first would have said worse things about me ; but the other will say them about love ; and the tender prude is much more terrified of the sentiment than of the person.

The only way for me to find out is, as you see, to intercept this clandestine commerce. I have already sent orders about it to my man-servant ; and I await the execution of them daily. Until then I can do

[1] *Nouvelle Heloïse.* (C. de L.)

nothing except at hazard; so for the last week I have been vainly going over all the known methods, all those in novels and in my secret memoirs. I do not find one which suits either the circumstances of the adventure or the character of the heroine. The difficulty would not be to get into her house, even at night, or even to drug her and to make her a new Clarissa; but after more than two months of attentions and trouble, to have recourse to means which are not mine! To crawl servilely in the traces of others, and to triumph without glory! . . . No, she shall not have "the pleasures of vice and the honours of virtue."[1] It is not enough for me to possess her, I want her to yield to me. Now, to achieve that I must not only get into her house but come there by her consent, find her alone and with the intention of listening to me, above all I must close her eyes to the danger, for if she sees it she will either overcome it or die. But the more I know what ought to be done, the more difficulty I find in carrying it out; and even if you should laugh at me again, I must admit to you that my embarrassment increases the more I dwell on it.

I think my head would turn, but for the pleasant distractions given me by our common pupil; I owe it to her that I have done something else except write elegies.

Would you believe that the little girl was so timid that three whole days passed before your letter had produced all its effect? See how a single false idea can spoil the best natures!

It was not until Saturday that she came circling about me and stammered a few words; but spoken in so low a tone and so stifled by shame, that it was impossible for me to hear them. But the blushing they caused allowed me to guess their sense. Up till then I had remained proud; but softened by so amusing a repentance I promised to go to the pretty penitent the same evening; and this grace on my part was received with all the gratitude due to so great a benefit.

As I never lose sight of your plans or of mine, I resolve to profit by this occasion to find out exactly what the child is worth and to accelerate her education. But to carry out this labour with more liberty, I needed to change the place of our rendezvous; for a mere closet, which separated your pupil's room from her mother's, could not inspire her with sufficient confidence to allow her to display herself freely. I had therefore promised myself to make some noise "innocently," which would cause her sufficient fear to persuade her to take a surer refuge in the future; she spared me that trouble too.

The little person laughs easily; and to encourage her gaiety I related to her, during our intervals, all the scandalous adventures which came into my head; and to make them more attractive and the better to hold her attention, I laid them all to the credit of her Mamma; whom I amused myself in this way by covering with vices and ridicule.

It was not without a reason that I made this choice; it encouraged my timid pupil better than anything else and at the same time inspired

[1] *Nouvelle Heloïse.* (C. de L.)

her with a most profound contempt for her mother. I have long noticed that, if this method is not always necessary for seducing a girl, it is indispensable and often the most efficacious way, when you wish to deprave her ; for she who does not respect her mother will not respect herself, a moral truth which I think so useful that I was very glad to furnish an example in support of the precept.

However, your pupil, who was not thinking of morality, was suffocated with laughter every instant ; and at last she once almost laughed out loud. I had no difficulty in making her believe that she had made " a terrible noise." I feigned a great terror which she easily shared. To make her remember it better I did not allow pleasure to reappear, and left her alone three hours earlier than usual; so, on separating, we agreed that from the next day onwards the meeting should be in my room.

I have received her there twice ; and in this short space the scholar has become almost as learned as the master. Yes, truly, I have taught her everything, including the complaisances ! I only excepted the precautions.

Occupied thus all night, I make up for it by sleeping a large part of the day ; and as the present society of the Château has nothing to attract me, I scarcely appear in the drawing-room for an hour during the day. Today I even decided to eat in my room and I only mean to leave it after this for short walks. These fantasies are supposed to be on account of my health. I declared that I was " overcome with vapours " ; I also announced that I was rather feverish. It costs me nothing but the speaking in a slow, colourless voice. As to the change in my face, rely upon your pupil. " Love will see to that."[1] I spend my leisure in thinking of means to regain my ungracious lady, of the advantages I have lost, and also in composing a kind of catechism of sensuality for the use of my scholar. I amuse myself by naming everything by the technical word ; and I laugh in advance at the interesting conversation this will furnish between her and Gercourt on the first night of their marriage. Nothing could be more amusing than the ingeniousness with which she already uses the little she knows of this speech ! She does not imagine that anyone can speak otherwise. The child is really seductive ! The contrast of naïve candour with the language of effrontery makes a great effect ; and, I do not know why, only fantastic things please me now.

Perhaps I am giving myself up too much to this, since I am wasting both my time and my health ; but I hope that my feigned illness, besides saving me from the boredom of the drawing-room, may also be of some use to me with the austere devotee, whose tigress virtue is nevertheless allied with soft sensibility ! I have no doubt that she already knows of this great event, and I should much like to know what she thinks of it ; the more so since I should wager she will not fail to attribute the honour of it to herself. I shall regulate the state of my health according to the impression it makes on her.

[1] Regnard, *Folies Amoureuses*. (C. de L.)

You now know, my fair friend, as much about my affairs as I do. I should like soon to have more important news to tell you; and I beg you to believe that in the pleasure I promise myself, I count for a great deal the reward I expect from you.

From the Château de ——, 11th of October, 17—.

## LETTER CXI

*The Comte de Gercourt to Madame de Volanges*

Everything in this country, Madame, seems as if it will be tranquil; and we are daily expecting permission to return to France. I hope that you will not doubt I have still the same eagerness to return and to form the bonds which will unite me to you and to Mademoiselle de Volanges. But Monsieur le duc de . . . my cousin, to whom as you know, I have so many obligations, has just informed me of his recall from Naples. He tells me that he means to pass through Rome and to see on his way that part of Italy he does not yet know. He invites me to accompany him on this journey, which will last for six weeks or two months. I do not hide from you that it would be agreeable for me to profit by this opportunity, since I feel that once I am married it will be difficult for me to take the time for other absences than those demanded by my service. And perhaps it would be more becoming to wait until the winter for this marriage, since all my relatives will not be gathered in Paris until then, and especially Monsieur le Marquis de . . ., to whom I owe the hope of being related to you. In spite of these considerations, my plans in this matter shall be absolutely subordinated to yours. And should you prefer your first arrangement, I am ready to renounce mine. I only beg you to let me know your intentions in this matter as soon as possible. I shall await your reply here and my conduct will be guided by that alone.

I am with respect, Madame, and with all the sentiments which befit a son, your most humble, etc.

Comte de Gercourt.

Bastia, 10th of October, 17—.

## LETTER CXII

*Madame de Rosemonde to Madame de Tourvel*

(Dictated)

I have only just received, my dear Beauty, your letter of the eleventh,[1] and the gentle reproaches it contains. Confess that you would have liked to reproach me more; and that if you had not remembered you were "my daughter," you would have really scolded me. Yet you would have been very unjust! It was the desire and hope of being able to

[1] This letter could not be found. (C. de L.)

reply to you myself which made me put it off each day, and you see that today I am still obliged to borrow my waiting-woman's hand. My unfortunate rheumatism has come back. It has settled this time in the right arm and I am absolutely one-armed. See what it is, young and fresh as you are, to have so old a friend! We suffer for these inconveniences.

As soon as my pain gives me a little respite I promise to talk to you at length. Meanwhile I can only tell you that I have received your two letters; that they would have increased my tender friendship for you, had that been possible; and that I shall never cease to be keenly interested in everything that touches you.

My nephew is also a little indisposed, but without any danger and without the least cause for uneasiness; it is a slight inconvenience which, in my opinion, affects his temper more than his health. We scarcely see him any more.

His retirement and your departure do not make our little circle any gayer. The Volanges child especially finds great fault with you and all day long yawns incessantly. Particularly in the last few days she has done us the honour of going fast asleep after dinner.

Good-bye, my dear Beauty; I am always your good friend, your Mamma, your sister even, if my great age permitted me that title. In short, I am attached to you by all my tenderest feelings.

(Signed Adelaide, for Madame de Rosemonde.)

From the Château de ——, 14th of October, 17—.

## LETTER CXIII

*The Marquise de Merteuil to the Vicomte de Valmont*

I think I ought to warn you, Vicomte, that people in Paris are beginning to talk about you; that your absence has been noticed and that the cause is already guessed. Yesterday I was at a supper where many people were present; it was positively announced that you were detained in a village by a romantic and unfortunate love; immediately joy was painted on the faces of all the men who envy your successes and of all the women you have neglected. If you will take my advice, you will not allow these dangerous rumours to gain ground, and you will return at once and destroy them by your presence.

Remember that once you allow the idea that you cannot be resisted to be destroyed, you will soon find that in fact you will be resisted more easily; that your rivals will also lose their respect for you and will dare to compete with you; for which among them does not believe himself stronger than virtue? Remember especially that among the multitude of women you have claimed, all those you have not had will try to undeceive the public, while the others will attempt to abuse it. In short, you must expect to be ranked perhaps as far below your value, as you have hitherto been ranked above it.

Come back, Vicomte, and do not sacrifice your reputation to a childish caprice. You have done all we wanted with the Volanges girl ; and as to your Madame de Tourvel, you will not satisfy your whim for her by remaining ten leagues distant from her. Do you think she will come to look for you ? Perhaps she no longer thinks of you or only concerns herself with you to congratulate herself on having humiliated you. Here at least you might find some opportunity of reappearing with effect, and you need it ; and even if you persist in your ridiculous adventure I do not see that your return can make any difference. . . ; on the contrary.

Indeed, if your Madame de Tourvel " adores you " ; as you have told me so often and proved to me so little ; her one consolation, her only pleasure, now must be to talk about you, to know what you are doing, what you are saying, what you are thinking, down to the smallest things which concern you. These trifles gain value according to the privations one undergoes. They are the crumbs of bread falling from the rich man's table ; he despises them ; but the poor man eagerly gathers them and is fed by them. At present poor Madame de Tourvel receives all these crumbs ; and the more of them she has, the less she will be in a hurry to indulge in an appetite for the rest.

Moreover, since you know her confidant you can have no doubt that each letter from her contains at least a little sermon and everything she thinks likely " to strengthen her modesty and fortify her virtue."[1] Then why leave the one resources for defence and the other the opportunities for harming you ?

It is not that I am at all of your opinion about the loss you think you have sustained by the change of confidents. First of all, Madame de Volanges hates you and hatred is always more clear-sighted and more ingenious than friendship. All your old aunt's virtue will never bring her for a single instant to speak ill of her dear nephew ; for virtue also has its weaknesses. And then your fears are founded on an absolutely false observation.

It is not true that " the older women are, the more harsh and severe they become." It is between forty and fifty that the despair of seeing their beauty fade, the rage of feeling themselves obliged to abandon the pretentions and the pleasures to which they still cling, make almost all women disdainfully prudish and crabbed. They need this long interval to make the whole of that great sacrifice ; but as soon as it is consummated, they all fall into two classes.

The more numerous, that of women who have never had to their advantage anything but their face and their youth, fall into an imbecile apathy and never come out of it except to play cards and for a few devotional practices ; this kind is always boring, often grumbling, sometimes a little quarrelsome but rarely spiteful. It cannot be said either that these women are or are not severe ; without ideas and without existence, they repeat with indifference and without

[1] " *On ne s'avise jamais de tout !* " Comedy. (C. de L.)

comprehension everything they hear said, and in themselves remain absolute nullities.

The other class, much more rare but really valuable, is that of women who, having had character and having not failed to nourish their minds, are able to create an existence for themselves when that of nature fails them, and adopt the course of giving to their minds all the ornaments they formerly employed for their faces. They generally have a very clear judgment, and a mind which is at once solid, gay, and gracious. They replace seductive charms by engaging kindness and still more by a cheerfulness whose charm increases in proportion to their age; in this way they succeed to some extent in becoming friends with youth and in making themselves beloved by it. But then, far from being, as you say, "harsh and severe," the habit of indulgence, their long reflections on human weakness, and above all the memories of their youth, by which alone they still hold to life, place them perhaps rather too near laxity.

I can tell you as well that as I have always sought out old women, the usefulness of whose support I early recognised, I have found among them several to whom I returned as much from inclination as from interest. I pause here, for since you now grow inflamed so quickly and so morally I should be afraid lest you might suddenly fall in love with your old aunt and bury yourself with her in the tomb where you have already lived so long. I proceed then.

In spite of the enchantment you appear to find in your little scholar, I cannot believe that she has any influence upon your plans. You found her at hand, you took her; very well! But this cannot be an inclination. To tell you the truth, it is not even a complete enjoyment; you possess absolutely nothing but her person! I do not speak of her heart, about which I have no doubt you hardly concern yourself; but you do not even occupy her head. I do not know if you have noticed it, but I have the proof of it in the last letter she wrote me;[1] I send it to you for you to form your own opinion. Observe that when she speaks of you, it is always "Monsieur de Valmont"; that all her ideas, even those which start from you, always end up in Danceny, and she never calls him Monsieur, it is always "Danceny" alone. By that she distinguishes him from all others; and even as she yields herself to you, she only grows familiar with him. If such a conquest appears "seductive" to you, if the pleasures she gives "captivate you," assuredly you are modest and not hard to please! I am perfectly willing that you should keep her; that is part of my plans. But it seems to me that this is not worth putting oneself out for a quarter of an hour; you ought to have some power over her and, for example, only allow her to come back to Danceny after having made her forget him a little more.

Before I leave you and come to myself, I should still like to tell you that this method of being ill which you announce to me is very well known and quite worn out. Really, Vicomte, you are not inventive!

[1] See *Letter CIX*. (C. de L.)

I repeat myself sometimes also, as you will see; but I try to make up for it in the details and above all I am justified by success. I am going to try one more and to seek a new adventure. I admit it will not have the merit of difficulty; but at least it will be a diversion, and I am bored to death.

I do not know why, but since my adventure with Prévan, Belleroche has become unendurable. He has so redoubled in attentions, in tenderness, in "veneration," that I can stand it no longer. Just at first his anger appeared amusing to me; but I had to calm it, for had I let him go on I should have been compromised; and there was no way of making him listen to reason. So I adopted the plan of showing him more love in order to succeed more easily; but he took it seriously and ever since then he has wearied me with his eternal delight. I have especially noticed the insulting reliance he has upon me and the confidence with which he looks upon me as his forever. I am positively humiliated by it. He cannot value me very highly if he thinks himself good enough to hold me! Did he not tell me recently that I shall never have loved anyone but him? Oh! I needed all my prudence not to undeceive him at once by telling him the truth. Here indeed is an amusing gentleman to have an exclusive right! I admit he is well-made and tolerably handsome; but on the whole he is really only a manual labourer in love. In short the moment has come, we must separate.

I have been trying for the last fortnight and, turn by turn, I have employed coolness, caprice, temper, quarrels; but the tenacious creature does not leave hold so easily; I must therefore adopt a more violent course and consequently I am taking him to my country house. We leave the day after tomorrow. There will only be with us a few uninterested and not very clear-sighted people, and we shall have almost as much liberty there as if we were alone. There, I shall so overburden him with love and caresses, we shall live so uniquely for one another, that I wager that, even more than I, he will desire the end of this visit which he thinks so great a happiness; and if he does not come back more weary of me than I am of him I will allow you to say that I know no more than you.

A pretence for this kind of retirement is to occupy myself seriously with my big law-suit, which will at last come up for judgment at the beginning of the winter. I am very glad of it; for it is really disagreeable to have all one's money in the air.

It is not that I am uneasy about the result; first of all I am right, all my lawyers assure me of it; and even if I were not, I should be very unskilful if I could not win a law-suit when my only adversaries are minors still in the cradle and their old guardian! But since nothing should be neglected in so important a matter, I shall in fact have two lawyers with me. Does not this journey sound gay to you? However, if it makes me win my law-suit and lose Belleroche I shall not regret my time.

And now, Vicomte, guess his successor ; I give you a hundred guesses. But there ! Do I not know you never guess anything ? Well, it is Danceny. You are surprised, are you not ? For after all I am not yet reduced to educating children ! But he deserves to be an exception ; he has only the graces of youth, not its frivolity. His great reserve in company is very useful in keeping away all suspicion, and he is but the more charming when he opens out in private. It is not that I have yet had any such interview with him, I am still only his confidant ; but under this veil of friendship I think he has a very keen inclination for me, and I feel I am acquiring a considerable one for him. It would really be a pity that so much wit and delicacy should be sacrificed and brutalised with that little imbecile of a Volanges ! I hope he deceives himself in thinking he loves her ; she is so far from deserving him ! It is not that I am jealous of her ; but it would be a manslaughter, and I wish to save Danceny from it. I beg you then, Vicomte, to take care that he does not meet " his Cécile " (as he still has the bad habit of calling her). A first inclination has always more power than one thinks, and I should not be sure of anything if he saw her again now, especially during my absence. On my return I will take charge of everything and will answer for it.

I had thought of taking the young man with me ; but I made the sacrifice to my usual prudence ; and then I was afraid he might notice something between Belleroche and me, and I should be in despair if he had the least idea of what is going on. I wish at least to offer myself to his imagination pure and unspotted ; such indeed as one ought to be, to be really worthy of him.

Paris, 15th of October, 17—.

## LETTER CXIV

*Madame de Tourvel to Madame de Rosemonde*

My dear friend, I give way to my deep uneasiness ; and without knowing if you are in a condition to answer me, I cannot prevent myself from questioning you. Your telling me that Monsieur de Valmont's condition is " without danger," does not leave me with as much confidence as you appear to have. It is not rare that melancholy and a disgust with the world are the preliminary symptoms of some serious illness ; the sufferings of the body, like those of the mind, make us desire solitude and often we reproach a person with ill-humour when we should only pity their sickness.

I think he ought at least to consult someone. How is it, that, being ill yourself, you have not a doctor with you ? I saw my doctor this morning and I will not conceal from you that I consulted him indirectly ; his opinion is that with naturally active people this kind of sudden apathy should never be neglected ; and, as he said afterwards, illnesses do not yield to treatment when they are not taken in time. Why do you allow someone who is so dear to you to run this risk ?

My uneasiness is greatly increased since I have had no news of him for four days. Heavens! Are you not deceiving me about his condition? Why has he suddenly ceased to write to me? If it were merely the result of my persistence in sending back his letters, I think he would have adopted this course sooner. And then, without believing in presentiments, for some days I have felt a sadness which frightens me. Ah! Perhaps I am on the eve of the greatest of misfortunes!

You will not believe, and I am ashamed to tell you, how it grieves me not to receive any longer those very letters which I refused to read. At least I was sure that he was thinking of me! And I saw something which came from him. I did not open these letters, but I cried as I looked at them; my tears were sweeter and more easy; and they only partly relieve the continual oppression I have felt since my return. I beg you, my indulgent friend, write to me yourself as soon as you can, and meanwhile, let me receive news of you and of him every day.

I see that I have scarcely said a word about you; you know my sentiments, my unreserved attachments, my tender gratitude for your sympathetic friendship; you will forgive the distress I am in, my extreme pain, the dreadful torture of having to dread ills of which I am perhaps the cause. Great Heaven! That desperate idea pursues me and tears my heart; this was a misfortune I lacked, and I feel I was born to endure them all.

Good-bye, my dear friend; love me, pity me. Shall I have a letter from you today?

Paris, 16th of October, 17—.

## LETTER CXV

*The Vicomte de Valmont to the Marquise de Merteuil*

It is an inconceivable thing, my fair friend, how easily as soon as people are apart, they cease to be in agreement. As long as I was near you, we had always the same perception, the same way of looking at things; and because I have not seen you for nearly three months, we no longer have the same opinion about anything. Which of us two is wrong? You certainly would not hesitate about the answer; but I, who am wiser or more polite, do not decide. I shall only reply to your letter and continue to inform you of what I am doing.

First, I have to thank you for the information you give me of the rumours about me which are circulating; but I am not yet disturbed by them; I think that very soon I am certain to have the means of ending them. Be at rest, I shall reappear in society more celebrated than ever and still more worthy of you.

I hope that I shall even gain some credit for the adventure with the Volanges girl, which you seem to think so little of; as if it were nothing to take a girl away from her beloved lover in an evening, to make use of her afterwards as much as I wanted, absolutely as my own property, and without any more difficulty to obtain from her what one does not even dare to exact from all the women who make their living by it; and that, without in the least upsetting her tender love; without making her inconstant, not even unfaithful; for, indeed, I do not even occupy her head! So that when my whim is past, I shall return her to her lover's arms, so to speak, without her having noticed anything. Is that then so ordinary a course? And then, believe me, once she leaves my hands, the principles I have given her will develop none the less; and I predict that the timid scholar will soon take her flight in a way which will do honour to her master.

But if they prefer the heroic, I shall point to Madame de Tourvel, that often quoted model of all the virtues! Respected even by our greatest libertines! To such an extent that they had even abandoned the mere idea of attacking her! I shall point to her, I say, forgetting her duties and her virtue, sacrificing her reputation and two years of modesty, to run after the happiness of pleasing me, to intoxicate herself with the happiness of loving me, thinking herself sufficiently recompensed for so many sacrifices by a word, by a look, which she even did not always obtain. I shall do more, I shall abandon her; and either I do not know this woman or I shall have no successor. She will resist the need for consolation, the habit of pleasure, even the desire for vengeance. In short, she will have existed only for me and whether her course be more or less long, I alone shall have opened and closed the barrier. Once I have achieved this triumph, I shall say to my rivals: "Behold my work, and seek a second example in the age!"

You will ask me whence comes this excess of confidence today? For the past week I have been in my fair one's confidence; she does not tell me her secrets, but I surprise them. Two letters from her to Madame de Rosemonde have given me sufficient information, and I shall only read the others from curiosity. To succeed I only need to be near her, and I have found the way. I am going to make use of it immediately.

You are curious, I think . . .? But no, to punish you for not believing in my designs, you shall not know this way. Frankly, you deserve that I should withdraw my confidence from you, at least in this adventure; indeed, but for the sweet prize attached by you to this success, I would not speak to you of it again. You see that I am annoyed. However, in the hope that you will reform, I will limit myself to this slight punishment; and, returning to indulgence, I will forget my great projects for a moment to reason with you about yours.

And so you are in the country, which is as wearisome as sentiment and as dull as fidelity! And poor Belleroche! You are not content to make him drink the water of oblivion, you put him to the torture with it! How is he? How well does he endure the nausea of love? I greatly wish that it would only make him more attached to you; I am curious to see what more efficacious remedy you would come to use. Really, I pity you for being obliged to make use of this one. Only once in my life have I made love by procedure. I had certainly good grounds, since it was the Comtesse de . . . ; and twenty times in her arms I have been tempted to say to her: "Madame, I renounce the place I solicited, allow me to leave that which I occupy." So, among all the women I have had, she is the only one whom it gives me pleasure to speak ill of.

As to your grounds, to tell you the truth, I think them very ridiculous; and you were right to think I should not guess the successor. What? You are giving yourself all that trouble for Danceny! Hey! My dear friend, leave him to adore "his virtuous Cécile," do not involve yourself in these children's games. Leave the schoolboys to be improved by "good women,"[1] or to play with schoolgirls at little innocent games. Why are you burdening yourself with a novice who will not know how to take you or when to leave you, and with whom you will have to do everything? I tell you seriously I disapprove of this choice, and however secret it remains it will humiliate you at least in my eyes and in your own consciousness.

You say you have a great inclination for him; come, you are surely wrong, and I think I have found the cause of your error. This wonderful disgust with Belleroche came to you at a time of famine, and as Paris offered you no choice, your fancy, always too keen, fell upon the first object you met with. But remember, when you return you can choose among a thousand; and if you dread the inaction into which you may fall by delaying, I offer myself to amuse your leisure.

Between now and your arrival, my important affairs will be settled in one way or another; and, assuredly, neither the Volanges girl nor Madame de Tourvel herself will then occupy me so much that I cannot be at your service as much as you desire. Perhaps by then I shall have already returned the little girl to the hands of her discreet lover. Without agreeing, whatever you may say, that it is not a "captivating" enjoyment, since my project is that all her life she shall keep an idea of me superior to all other men, I have adopted with her a tone which I cannot sustain for long without damaging my health; and from this moment I am only bound to her by the kind of attention we owe to family affairs. . . .

You do not understand me; the truth is I am waiting for a second period to confirm my hope and to be certain I have fully succeeded in my projects. Yes, my fair friend, I have already a first indication that my scholar's husband will not run the risk of dying without posterity and that the head of the house of Gercourt will in future be only a cadet of the house of Valmont. But let me finish as I fancy an adventure I only undertook at your request. Remember, if you make Danceny unfaithful, you take away all the piquancy of this story. And then consider that when I offer myself to you as his representative I have, I think, some rights to the preference.

I rely upon it so much, that I have not shrunk from acting contrary to your views, by assisting myself in augmenting the tender passion of

[1] "Bonnes," a double entendre; it means "good women," and "maid-servants."

the discreet lover for the first and worthy object of his choice. Yesterday I found your pupil engaged in writing to him, and having first disturbed her in this sweet occupation by another still sweeter, I asked afterwards to see her letter ; and since I thought it cold and constrained I pointed out to her that this was not the way to console her lover and persuaded her to write another at my dictation ; in which, imitating her silly little chatter as best I could, I tried to feed the young man's love with a more certain hope. The little girl was quite delighted, she told me, to find herself speaking so well ; and henceforth I am to take charge of the correspondence. What is there I shall not have done for Danceny ? I shall have been at once his friend, his confidant, his rival, and his mistress ! and again, at this moment, I am doing him the service of saving him from your dangerous bonds ; for to possess you and to lose you, is to buy a moment of happiness with an eternity of regrets.

Good-bye, my fair friend ; have the courage to dispatch Belleroche as soon as you can. Leave Danceny, and prepare yourself to rediscover and to give me again the delicious pleasures of our first acquaintance.

P.S. My compliments upon the near completion of your great law-suit. I shall be very glad if this happy event takes place under my reign.

From the Château de ——, 19th of October, 17—.

## LETTER CXVI

*The Chevalier Danceny to Cécile Volanges*

Madame de Merteuil left this morning for the country ; thus, my charming Cécile, I am deprived of the sole pleasure which was left to me in your absence, that of talking about you to your friend and mine. Recently she has allowed me to give her that title ; and I adopted it the more eagerly in that it seemed to draw me nearer to you. Heaven ! What an amiable woman she is ! And what a flattering charm she gives to friendship ! It seems as if this gentle feeling is embellished and fortified in her by all that she refuses to love. If you knew how she loves you, how it pleases her to hear me talk of you ! . . . Doubtless it is this which so attaches me to her. What happiness to be able to live solely for you two, to pass continually from the delights of love to the sweetness of friendship, to consecrate all my existence to them, to be, as it were, the meeting point of your mutual attachment ; and to feel always that in occupying myself with the happiness of the one I should equally be working for the happiness of the other ! Love this adorable woman, love her very much, my charming friend, give an even greater value to my attachment for her by sharing it. Since I have enjoyed the charm of friendship I wish you to feel it in your turn. It seems to me I only half enjoy the pleasures I do not share with you. Yes, my Cécile, I should like to surround your heart with all the softest sentiments ; I should like each of these emotions to cause you a sensation of happiness and I should still think I could never return you more than a part of the felicity I gained from you.

Why must these charming projects be nothing but a fantasy of my imagination, while reality on the contrary brings me only painful and indefinite privations ? I perceive that I must abandon the hope you gave me of seeing you in the country. My only consolation is to convince myself that this is not possible for you. And you neglect to tell me so, to lament over it with me ! Already my complaints on this subject have twice gone unanswered. Ah ! Cécile, Cécile, I believe you love me with all the faculties of your soul, but your soul does not burn like mine ! Why is it not my part to raise these obstacles ? Why is it not my interest which must be safeguarded instead of yours ? I could soon prove to you that nothing is impossible to love.

You do not tell me either when this cruel absence is to end ; here at least I might see you, your charming glances would reanimate my drooping spirits ; their touching expression would reassure my heart which sometimes needs it so much. Forgive me, Cécile ; this fear is not a suspicion. I believe in your love, in your constancy. Ah ! I should be too wretched if I doubted it. But so many obstacles ! Continually renewed ! My dear, I am sad, very sad. It seems as if Madame de Merteuil's departure has renewed in me the feelings of all my misfortunes.

Good-bye, Cécile ; good-bye, my beloved. Remember that your lover is in distress, and that you alone can give him back happiness.

Paris, 17th of October, 17—.

## LETTER CXVII

*Cécile Volanges to the Chevalier Danceny*

(Dictated by Valmont)

Do you think, my dear, that you have to scold me for me to be sad when I know that you are distressed ? And do you doubt that I suffer as much as you in all your troubles ? I even share those which I cause you voluntarily ; and I suffer more than you when I see that you do not do me justice. Oh ! That is not kind. I can see what it is that annoys you ; it is because I have not replied on the last two occasions when you asked me if you could come here ; but is this such an easy reply to make ? Do you think I do not know that what you want is very wrong ? And yet if it is so hard for me to refuse you at a distance, what would it be if you were here ? And then, I should be unhappy all my life for having wished to console you for a moment.

Come, I have nothing to hide from you ; here are my reasons, judge for yourself. Perhaps I should have done what you wanted, had it not been that (as I told you) this Monsieur de Gercourt who is the cause of all our grief, will not arrive here so soon ; and as Mamma has showed me much more kindness for some time ; and as I am as caressing to her as

I can be for my part; who knows what I might be able to obtain from her? And would it not be much better if we could be happy without my having anything to reproach myself with? If I am to believe what I have often been told, men do not love their wives so much when they have loved them too much before they were their wives. This fear restrains me more than all the rest. My friend, are you not sure of my heart and will there not always be time?

Listen, I promise you that if I cannot avoid the misfortune of marrying Monsieur de Gercourt, whom I hate so much before I know him, nothing will restrain me from being yours as much as I can, and even before everything. As I only care to be loved by you, and as you will see that if I do wrong it will not be my fault, the rest is of no concern to me; provided you promise me to love me always as much as you do now. But, my dear, until then let me go on as I am; and do not ask me any more for a thing I have good reasons for not doing but which it hurts me to refuse you.

I wish also that Monsieur de Valmont were not so pressing on your behalf; it only serves to make me still sadder. Oh! You have a very good friend in him, I assure you! He does everything just as you would do it yourself. But good-bye, my dear; it was very late when I began to write to you and I have spent part of the night on it. I am going to bed to make up for lost time. I kiss you, but do not scold me again.

From the Château de . . ., 18th of October, 17—.

## LETTER CXVIII

*The Chevalier Danceny to the Marquise de Merteuil*

If I am to believe my almanac, my adorable friend, you have only been absent for two days; but if I am to believe my heart it is for two centuries. Now, I have it from you yourself, that we should always believe our hearts; it is therefore quite time for you to return and all your business must be more than finished. How do you expect me to be interested in your law-suit, if, whether lost or gained, I must pay the costs, through the weariness of your absence? Oh! How I should like to quarrel! And how sad it is, with such an excellent reason for ill temper, to have no right to show it!

Yet is it not a real infidelity, a wicked betrayal, to leave your friend far from you, after you have accustomed him to depend upon your presence? However much you consult your lawyers they will not find you any justification for this wrong procedure; and then such people only give reasons, and reasons are not a sufficient response to sentiments.

For my part, you have so often told me that you were making this journey from reason, that you have altogether put me out of temper with reason. I never want to listen to it again; not even when it tells me to forget you. Yet that is a very reasonable reason; and indeed it would not be so difficult as you might believe. It would be enough merely to lose the habit of always thinking about you; and I assure you nothing here would recall you to my mind.

Our prettiest women, those who are said to be the most charming, are still so far from you that they could only give a very weak idea of you. I believe even that with practised eyes, the more one thought at first they resembled you, the more difference one would find afterwards; whatever they may do, and however much they put into it all their knowledge, they will always fail to be you and it is there that the charm lies. Unfortunately, when the days are so long, and I am without occupation, I dream, I make castles in Spain, I create my fantasy; little by little the imagination grows warm; I wish to embellish my work; I bring together everything that can please, and at last I reach perfection; and when I am there the portrait brings me back to the model, and I am amazed to find I have only been thinking of you.

At this very moment I am again the dupe of an almost similar error. Perhaps you think I began to write to you to dwell on you? Not at all; it was to distract myself from you I had a hundred things to say to you, of which you were not the object, and which, as you know, interest me very deeply; and yet it is from these I have been distracted. Since when does the charm of friendship distract from that of love? Ah! If I looked at it very closely, perhaps I should have to blame myself a little! But hush! Let me forget this little fault for fear of falling into it again; and let my friend ignore it.

So why are you not here to reply to me, to bring me back if I wander, to talk to me of my Cécile, to increase—if that is possible—the happiness I feel in loving her by the delightful idea that it is your friend I love? Yes, I confess it, the love she inspires in me has become still more precious to me since you have condescended to receive my confidence. It gives me such pleasure to open my heart to you, to occupy yours with my feelings, to place them there without reserve! It seems to me that I cherish them the more as you deign to receive them; and then I look at you and say to myself: "It is in her that all my happiness is enclosed."

I have nothing new to tell you about my situation. The last letter I received from *her* increases and assures my hope, but still retards it. But her motives are so tender and so virtuous, that I cannot blame her or complain myself. Perhaps you do not quite understand what I am telling you; but why are you not here? Although one says everything to a friend, one dares not write everything. The secrets of love especially are so delicate that one cannot let them go thus on their own good faith. If we sometimes let them go out, we must at least not lose sight of them; we must, as it were, see them enter their new refuge. Ah! Come back, my adorable friend, you see your return is necessary. Forget the "thousand reasons" which detain you where you are, or teach me how to live away from you.

I have the honour to be, etc.

Paris, 19th of October, 17—.

## LETTER CXIX

*Madame de Rosemonde to Madame de Tourvel*

Although I am still suffering a great deal, my dear Beauty, I am trying to write to you myself so that I can speak to you of what interests you. My nephew still retains his misanthropy. He sends very regularly each day to have news of me; but he has not come once to enquire although I sent to ask him to do so and I see no more of him than if he were at Paris. I met him this morning, however, where I hardly expected it. It was in my chapel, to which I went down for the first time since my painful indisposition. I learned today that for the last four days he has gone there regularly to hear Mass. God grant that this lasts!

When I entered, he came to me and congratulated me very affectionately on the better state of my health. As Mass was beginning, I cut short the conversation which I intended to renew afterwards; but he disappeared before I could join him. I will not conceal from you that I found him a little changed. But, my dear Beauty, do not make me repent my confidence in your reason, by too keen an anxiety; and above all be certain that I should rather distress you than deceive you.

If my nephew continues to avoid me, I shall take the course of going to see him in his room, as soon as I am better; and I shall try to find out the cause of this singular proceeding, in which I believe you have some part. I will let you know what I find out. I must leave you now, I cannot move my fingers any longer; and then if Adelaide knew I had been writing she would scold me all the evening. Good-bye, my dear Beauty.

From the Château de . . ., 20th of October, 17—.

## LETTER CXX

*The Vicomte de Valmont to Father Anselme*

(Monk of St. Bernard of the Convent in the rue St. Honoré)

I have not the honour to be known to you, Monsieur; but I know the complete confidence which Madame de Tourvel has in you, and I know moreover how worthily that confidence is placed. I think I can address myself to you without indiscretion, to obtain an essential service, worthy indeed of your holy ministry, in which the interest of Madame de Tourvel is joined with mine.

I have in my hands certain important papers which concern her, which cannot be confided to anyone, which I must not and will not give into any hands but hers. I have no way to inform her of this, from reasons which perhaps you have learned from her but which I do not think myself justified in telling you, and which have caused her to refuse all correspondence from me; a course which I willingly admit today that I cannot blame, since she could not foresee the events I was myself very far from expecting ; events only possible to the more than human power I am forced to recognise in them.

I beg you then, Monsieur, to be good enough to inform her of my new resolutions and to ask her on my behalf for a private interview, when I can at least partly atone for my faults by my excuses ; and, as a last sacrifice, destroy before her eyes the sole existing traces of an error or of a fault which rendered me culpable towards her.

Only after this preliminary expiation shall I dare to lay at your feet the humble admission of my long misconduct ; and to implore your mediation for a still more important reconciliationun, happily even more difficult. Can I hope, Monsieur, that you will not refuse me such necessary and such precious care ? That you will consent to support my weakness and to guide my steps in a new path which I most ardently desire to follow, but blush to admit I do not yet know ?

I await your reply with the impatience of a repentance which desires to make reparation, and I beg you to believe that I am, with as much gratitude as veneration,

Your most humble, Etc.

P.S. I authorise you, Monsieur, if you think fit, to hand this letter to Madame de Tourvel, whom I shall make it a duty all my life long to respect, and in whom I shall never cease to honour her whom Heaven made use of to bring back my soul to virtue through the moving spectacle of hers.

From the Château de . . ., 22nd of October, 17—.

## LETTER CXXI

*The Marquise de Merteuil to the Chevalier Danceny*

I have received your letter, my too young friend ; but before thanking you, I must scold you, and warn you that if you do not correct yourself, you will have no more reply from me. Be ruled by me, and abandon this tone of flattery which is nothing but a mere jargon as soon as it ceases to be the expression of love. Is that the style of friendship ? No, my friend, each sentiment has its befitting language, and to use another is to disguise the thought one is expressing. I know our little women understand nothing of what is said to them unless it is translated, as it were, into this customary jargon ; but I confess I think I deserve to be distinguished from them by you. I am really annoyed, and perhaps more than I should be, that you have judged me so ill.

You will only find in my letter then what is lacking in yours—frankness and simplicity. I will, for example, tell you that it would give me great pleasure to see you and that I am vexed to have near me only such people as weary me, instead of those who please me ; but you translate this phrase thus : " Teach me how to live away from you " ; so, I suppose, that even if you were with your mistress you could not live unless I made a third. What folly! And those women, "who always fail to be me"—perhaps you find that your Cécile fails to be so! But that is where you are carried by a language which, from the abuse that is made of it today, is even beneath the jargon of compliments and becomes nothing more than a mere formula, in which people no more believe than in "your most humble servant"!

My friend, when you write to me, let it be to tell me your manner of thinking and feeling and not to send me phrases which I shall find, without your help, more or less well expressed in the first modern novel. I hope you will not be angry with what I have said to you, even if you should see a little ill humour in it; for I do not deny that I am a little out of temper; but to avoid even the appearance of the fault I reproach you with, I shall not tell you that this ill humour is perhaps a little increased by my absence from you. Taking it all round, it seems to me that you are preferable to a law-suit and two lawyers, and perhaps even more so than the *attentif* Belleroche.

You see that instead of lamenting my absence, you ought to be glad of it; for I have never paid you so fine a compliment. I think that the example is infecting me and that I shall be sending you flatteries too; but no, I prefer to stick to my frankness; that alone then assures you of my tender friendship and of the interest it inspires in me. It is very delightful to have a young friend, whose heart is occupied elsewhere. It is not the habit of most women; but it is mine. It seems to me that we yield with more pleasure to a sentiment from which we can have nothing to fear; so with you I have come to the rôle of confidant, perhaps rather early. But you choose your mistresses so young, that you have made me perceive for the first time that I am beginning to get old! You do well to prepare yourself thus a long career of constancy, and I hope with all my heart that it may be mutual.

You are right to give way "to the tender and virtuous motives" which, you tell me, "retard your happiness." A long defence is the sole merit left to those who do not always resist; and I should think it unpardonable in anyone but a child like the Volanges girl not to have avoided a danger, of which she was sufficiently informed by her admission of her love. You men have no idea what virtue is, and what it costs to sacrifice it! But if a woman reasons a little, she must know that, independently of the wrong she commits, a weakness is for her the greatest of misfortunes; and I cannot imagine how any woman ever allows herself to fall into it, when she has a moment to reflect.

Do not combat this idea, for it is what principally attaches me to you. You will save me from the dangers of love; and although I have hitherto been able to defend myself from them without you, I consent to be grateful for it and I shall like you better.

And now, my dear Chevalier, I pray God to have you in his holy and lofty care.

From the Château de . . . 22nd of October, 17—.

## LETTER CXXII

*Madame de Rosemonde to Madame de Tourvel*

I hoped, my amiable daughter, that at last I should be able to calm your anxieties ; and I see with grief, on the contrary, that I am about to increase them still further. But, be calm ; my nephew is not in danger ; it cannot even be said that he is really ill. But there is surely something extraordinary passing within him. I do not understand it ; but I left his room with a feeling of sadness ; perhaps even of terror, which I reproach myself for sharing with you and about which nevertheless I cannot prevent myself from talking to you. Here is an account of what happened ; you may be sure that it is a faithful one ; for were I to live another eighty years I should not forget the impression made upon me by this sad scene.

This morning, then, I went to my nephew's room ; I found him writing and surrounded with different piles of papers, which appeared to be the object of his labour. He was so absorbed in them that I was in the middle of his room before he had even turned his head to find out who had entered. As soon as he perceived me I noticed as he rose he tried to compose his features, and perhaps it is that which made me pay more attention. He was undressed and unpowdered ; but I thought him pale and wasted, and above all that his physiognomy had changed. His glance which we have seen so lively and so gay, was downcast and sad ; in short, let it be said between ourselves, I should not have wished you to see him thus ; for he looked very touching and very fit, I should think, to inspire that tender pity which is one of the most dangerous snares of love.

Although I was struck by my observations, I began the conversation as if I had noticed nothing. First of all I spoke to him of his health ; and, without saying that it was good, he did not in so many words say that it was bad. Then I complained of his retirement, which seemed a little like an obsession, and I tried to mingle some gaiety with my little reprimand ; but he only replied with an air of conviction : " It is one wrong the more I confess ; but it shall be repaired with the others." His air, even more than what he said, rather disturbed my cheerfulness, and I hastened to tell him that he attached too much importance to a single reproach of friendship.

We then began to converse quietly. He told me, a little afterwards, that perhaps business, " the most important business of his life," would soon recall him to Paris ; but as I was afraid of guessing it, my dear Beauty, and feared this opening might lead me to a confidence I did not desire, I asked him no questions and contented myself by replying that more distraction would be useful to his health. I added that, on this occasion I would trouble him with no entreaties, since I loved my friends for their own sake ; at this very simple phrase he grasped my hands, and, speaking with a vehemence I cannot convey to you, said: "Yes, aunt, love, love a nephew who respects and cherishes you, and as you say, love him for himself. Do not feel distressed for his happiness, and do not disturb by any regret the eternal calm he soon hopes to enjoy. Tell me again that you love me, that you forgive me; yes, you will forgive me; I know your goodness; but how can I hope for the same indulgence from those I have so offended?" Then he leaned over me, to hide, I think, the signs of grief which in spite of himself were revealed to me by the sound of his voice.

More moved than I can tell you, I rose hastily; and doubtless he noticed my terror; for composing himself immediately he went on: "Forgive me, Madame, forgive me, I feel that I am falling into error in spite of myself. I beg you to forget what I have said and to remember only my profound respect. I shall not fail," he added, "to come and renew my expression of it before I go." It seemed to me that this last phrase was a hint to terminate my visit; and so I went away.

But the more I reflect upon it, the less I can guess what he meant. What is this business, "the most important of his life"? Why did he ask my pardon? What was the cause of his involuntary emotion in speaking to me? I have asked myself these questions a thousand times, without being able to reply to them. I see nothing in them which touches you; yet, as the eyes of love are more clearsighted than those of friendship, I was unwilling to leave you in ignorance of what passed between my nephew and me.

I have four times resumed the writing of this long letter, which I would make longer but for the fatigue I feel. . . . Good-bye, my dear Beauty.

From the Château de . . ., 25th October, 17—.

## LETTER CXXIII

*Father Anselme to the Vicomte de Valmont*

I have received, Monsieur le Vicomte, the letter with which you honour me, and yesterday, in accordance with your desire, I went to the person in question. I informed her of the object and the motives of the application you asked me to make to her. However attached I found her to the wise course she had first adopted, upon my pointing out that by her refusal she was perhaps placing an obstacle to your happy conversion, and thus, as it were, opposing the merciful intentions of Providence, she has consented to receive your visit on condition that it is the last, and has charged me to tell you that it will be at her house on Thursday next, the twenty-eighth. If this day does not suit you, will you let her know and appoint another. Your letter will be received.

But, Monsieur le Vicomte, let me ask you not to delay without very good reason, so that you can the sooner and the more entirely give yourself up to the praiseworthy designs of which you inform me.

Remember that he who delays to profit by the moment of grace, runs the risk of its being withdrawn from him ; that if the goodness of God is infinite his use of it is nevertheless regulated by justice ; and that there may come a moment when the God of mercy is changed into a God of vengeance.

If you continue to honour me with your confidence, I beg you to believe that all my exertions are at your command, as soon as you desire ; however considerable my occupations may be, my most important business will always be to carry out the duties of the holy ministry, to which I am particularly devoted ; and the fairest moment of my life is that when I shall see my efforts prosper through the blessing of the Almighty. Weak sinners that we are, we can do nothing of ourselves ! But the God who calls you back to Him can do everything ; and we both owe it equally to His goodness, you the constant desire of uniting yourself to Him, and I the means of guiding you there. It is with His aid, that I hope soon to convince you that only our holy religion can give, even in this world, the solid and durable happiness we vainly search for in the blindness of human passions.

I have the honour to be, with respectful esteem, etc.

Paris, 25th of October, 17—.

## LETTER CXXIV

*Madame de Tourvel to Madame de Rosemonde*

In the midst of the surprise which was caused me, Madame, by the news I learned yesterday, I do not forget the satisfaction it must cause you, and I hasten to give you information of it. Monsieur de Valmont is now concerned neither with me nor with his love ; and only desires to repair by a more edifying life the faults, or rather the errors, of his youth. I was informed of this great event by Father Anselme, to whom he applied for direction in the future, and also to procure him an interview with me, the principal object of which I think is to return me my letters which he has hitherto retained, in spite of the contrary request I had made him.

Doubtless I cannot but applaud this happy change, and congratulate myself upon it, if, as he says, I have furthered it to some extent. But why should I have to be the instrument, and why should it cost me a lifetime's tranquillity ? Could Monsieur de Valmont's happiness only come about through my misfortune ? Oh ! My indulgent friend, forgive me for this complaint. I know it is not for me to fathom the decrees of God ; but while I ceaselessly ask Him, and ask Him always in vain, for strength to overcome my unhappy love, He squanders it upon one who did not ask for it, and leaves me helpless, entirely surrendered to my weakness.

But I must stifle this guilty murmur. Do I not know that the prodigal son on his return obtained more grace from his Father than the son who had never been away? What account have we to demand from Him who owes us nothing? And even if it were possible that we should have some rights with Him, what could mine be? Should I boast a virtue, which already I only owe to Valmont? He saved me, and I dare to complain of suffering for him! No; my sufferings will be dear to me, if his happiness is their reward. Doubtless he had to come back to the common Father in his turn. The God who created him must cherish His work. He did not create that charming being, to make him only a castaway. It is for me to bear the pain of my bold imprudence; should I not have felt that, since it was forbidden me to love him I ought not to have allowed myself to see him?

My sin or my misfortune is that I refused too long to see this truth. You are my witness, my dear and worthy friend, that I submitted to this sacrifice as soon as I recognised its necessity; but the one thing lacking to make it complete was that Monsieur de Valmont should not share it. Shall I confess to you that this idea is now my greatest torment? Unendurable pride, which softens the ills we feel by those we make others suffer! Ah! I will overcome this rebellious heart, I will accustom myself to humiliations.

It is with the especial purpose of achieving this that I have consented to receive the painful visit of Monsieur de Valmont on Thursday next. There, I shall hear him tell me himself that I am nothing to him, that the faint and passing impression I had made upon him is entirely effaced! I shall see his gaze rest upon me without emotion, while the fear of revealing my own will make me keep my eyes lowered. I shall receive from his indifference those very letters which he refused so long to my reiterated request; he will return them to me as useless objects which no longer interest him; and as my trembling hands receive this shameful packet, they will feel that it is given to them by a calm, firm hand! And then, I shall see him go away. Go away for ever, and my gaze will follow him, will not see his turned back upon me!

And I was reserved for such humiliation! Ah! At least let me make it useful to myself, by letting it fill me with the sentiment of my weakness. . . . Yes, I will carefully keep those letters he no longer cares to retain. I will impose upon myself the shame of re-reading them every day, until my tears have washed out the last traces of them; and I shall burn his as being infected with the dangerous poison which has corrupted my soul. Oh! What then is love, if it makes us regret even the danger to which it exposes us; above all if we may dread to feel it still even when we no longer inspire it! Let me fly from this disastrous passion, which leaves no choice between shame and misery, and often unites them both; and at least let prudence replace virtue.

How far off Thursday still is! Why can I not consummate this painful sacrifice at this instant, and forget at once both its cause and its object! This visit troubles me; I regret having promised it. Ah! Why does he need to see me again! What are we to each other now?

If he has offended me, I pardon him. I even congratulate him on the desire to repair his wrongs ; I praise him for it. I will do more, I will imitate him ; and, seduced by the same errors, I will be saved by his example. But when his project is to fly from me, why does he begin by seeking me ! Is not the most urgent matter for each of us to forget the other ? Ah ! Doubtless, and henceforth it shall be my one anxiety.

If you permit it, my amiable friend, I shall come and occupy myself with this difficult labour near you. If I need aid, perhaps even consolation, I wish to receive them only from you. You alone can understand me and can speak to my heart. Your precious friendship will fill my whole existence. Nothing will appear difficult to me to second the solicitude you might give me. I shall owe you my tranquillity, my happiness, my virtue ; and the fruit of your kindnesses to me will be to have made me worthy of them at last.

I think I have wandered a good deal in this letter ; I presume so, at least, from the agitation I have been in all the time I was writing to you. If it contains some sentiments at which I might have to blush, hide them with your indulgent friendship. I commit myself entirely to it. I do not wish to conceal any of the emotions of my heart from you.

Farewell, my respectable friend. In a few days I hope to inform you of the day of my arrival.

Paris, 25th October, 17—.

## END OF PART THREE

# PART IV

## LETTER CXXV

*The Vicomte de Valmont to the Marquise de Merteuil*

She is conquered, that proud woman who dared to think she could resist me ! Yes, my friend, she is mine, entirely mine ; after yesterday she has nothing left to grant me.

I am still too full of my happiness to be able to appreciate it, but I am astonished by the unsuspected charm I felt. Is it true then that virtue increases a woman's value even in her moment of weakness ? But let me put that puerile idea away with old woman's tales. Does one not meet almost everywhere a more or less well-feigned resistance to the first triumph ? And have I not found elsewhere the charm of which I speak ? But yet it is not the charm of love ; for after all, if I have sometimes had surprising moments of weakness with this woman resembling that pusillanimous passion, I have always been able to overcome them and return to my principles. Even if yesterday's scene carried me, as I now think, a little further than I intended; even if I shared for a moment the agitation and ecstasy I created; that passing illusion would now have disappeared, and yet the same charm remains. I confess I should even feel a considerable pleasure in yielding to it, if it did not cause me some anxiety. Shall I, at my age, be mastered like a schoolboy, by an involuntary and unsuspected sentiment? No; before everything else, I must combat and thoroughly examine it.

And perhaps I have already a glimpse of the cause of it! At least the idea pleases me and I should like it to be true.

Among the crowd of women for whom I have hitherto filled the part and functions of a lover, I had never met one who had not at least as much desire to yield to me as I had to bring her to doing so; I had even accustomed myself to call "prudes" those who only came half-way to meet me, in opposition to so many others whose provocative defence never covers but imperfectly the first advances they have made.

Here on the contrary I found a first unfavourable prejudice, supported afterwards by the advice and reports of a woman who hated me but who was clear-sighted; I found a natural and extreme timidity strengthened by an enlightened modesty; I found an attachment to virtue, controlled by religion, able to count two years of triumph already, and then remarkable behaviour inspired by different motives but all with the object of avoiding my pursuit.

It was not then, as in my other adventures, a merely more or less advantageous capitulation which it is more easy to profit by than to feel proud of; it was a complete victory, achieved by a hard campaign and decided by expert manœuvres. It is therefore not surprising that this success, which I owe to myself alone, should become more valuable to me; and the excess of pleasure I feel even yet is only the soft impression of the feeling of glory. I cling to this view which saves me from the humiliation of thinking I might depend in any way upon the very slave I have enslaved myself; that I do not contain the plenitude of my happiness in myself; and that the faculty of enjoying it in all its energy should be reserved to such or such a woman, exclusive of all others.

These sensible reflections shall guide my conduct in this important occasion; and you may be sure I shall not allow myself to be so enchained that I cannot break these new ties at any time, by playing with them, and at my will. But I am already talking to you of breaking off and you still do not know the methods by which I acquired the right to do so; read then, and see what wisdom is exposed to in trying to help folly. I observed my words and the replies I obtained so carefully that I hope to be able to report both with an exactness which will content you.

You will see by the copies of the two enclosed letters[1] who was the mediator I chose to bring me back to my fair one and what zeal the holy person used to unite us. What I must still inform you of—a thing I learned from a letter intercepted as usual—is that the fear and little

[1] Letters *CXX* and *CXXII*. (C. de L.)

humiliation of being abandoned had rather upset the austere devotee's prudence and had filled her heart and head with sentiments and ideas which, though they lacked common sense, were none the less important. It was after these preliminaries, necessary for you to know, that yesterday, Thursday, the 28th, a day fixed beforehand by the ungrateful person herself, that I presented myself before her as a timid and repentant slave, and left a crowned conqueror.

It was six o'clock in the evening when I arrived at the fair recluse's house, for, since her return, her doors have been shut to everyone. She tried to rise when I was announced; but her trembling knees did not allow her to remain in that position: she sat down at once. As the servant who had brought me in had some duty to perform in the room, she seemed to be made impatient by it. We filled up this interval with the customary compliments. But not to lose any time, every moment of which was precious, I carefully examined the locality; and there and then I noted with my eyes the theatre of my victory. I might have chosen a more convenient one, for there was an ottoman in the same room. But I noticed that opposite it there was a portrait of the husband; and I confess I was afraid that with such a singular woman one glance accidentally directed that way might destroy in a moment the work of so many exertions. At last we were left alone and I began.

After having pointed out in a few words that Father Anselme must have informed her of the reasons for my visit, I complained of the rigorous treatment I had received from her; and I particularly dwelt upon the "contempt" which had been shown me. She defended herself, as I expected; and as you would have expected too, I founded the proofs of it on the suspicion and fear I had inspired, on the scandalous flight which had followed upon them, the refusal to answer my letters, and even the refusal to receive them, etc., etc. As she was beginning a justification (which would have been very easy) I thought I had better interrupt; and to obtain forgiveness for this brusque manner I covered it immediately by a flattery: "If so many charms have made an impression on my heart," I went on, "so many virtues have made no less a mark upon my soul. Seduced no doubt by the idea of approaching them I dared to think myself worthy of doing so. I do not reproach you for having thought otherwise; but I am punished for my error." As she remained in an embarrassed silence, I continued: "I desired, Madame, either to justify myself in your eyes or to obtain from you forgiveness for the wrongs you think I have committed, so that at least I can end in some peace the days to which I no longer attach any value since you have refused to embellish them."

Here she tried to reply, however: "My duty did not permit me." And the difficulty of finishing the lie which duty exacted did not permit her to finish the phrase. I therefore went on in the most tender tones: "It is true then that it was from me you fled?" "My departure was necessary." "And what took you away from me?" "It was necessary." "And forever?" "It must be so." I do not need to tell you that during this short dialogue the tender prude was in a state of oppression and her eyes were not raised to me.

I felt I ought to animate this languishing scene a little; so, getting up with an air of pique, I said: "Your firmness restores me all of my own. Yes, Madame, we shall be separated, separated even more than you think; and you shall congratulate yourself upon your handiwork at leisure." She was a little surprised by this tone of reproach and tried to answer. "The resolution you have taken . . ." said she. "Is only the result of my despair," I replied with vehemence. "It is your will that I should be unhappy; I will prove to you that you have succeeded even beyond your wishes." "I desire your happiness," she answered. And the tone of her voice began to show a rather strong emotion. So, throwing myself at her feet, I exclaimed in that dramatic tone of mine you know: "Ah! cruel woman, can there exist any happiness for me which you do not share? Ah! Never! Never!" I confess that at this point I had greatly been relying on the aid of tears; but either from a wrong disposition or perhaps only from the painful and continual attention I was giving to everything, it was impossible for me to weep.

Fortunately I remembered that any method is equally good in subjugating a woman, and that it sufficed to astonish her with a great emotion for the impression to remain both deep and favourable. I made up therefore by terror for the sensibility I found lacking; and with that purpose, only changing the inflection of my voice and remaining in the same position, I continued: "Yes, I make an oath at your feet, to possess you or die." As I spoke the last words our eyes met. I do not know what the timid person saw or thought she saw in mine, but she rose with a terrified air, and escaped from my arms, which I had thrown round her. It is true I did nothing to detain her; for I have several times noticed that scenes of despair carried out too vividly become ridiculous as soon as they become long, or leave nothing but really tragic resources which I was very far from desiring to adopt. However, as she escaped from me, I added in a low and sinister tone, but loud enough for her to hear: "Well, then! Death!"

I then got up; and after a moment of silence I cast wild glances upon her which, however much they seemed to wander, were none the less clear-sighted and observant. Her ill-assured bearing, her quick breathing, the contraction of all her muscles, her trembling half-raised arms, all proved to me that the result was such as I had desired to produce; but, since in love nothing is concluded except at very close quarters, and we were rather far apart, it was above all things necessary to get closer together. To achieve this, I passed as quickly as possible to an apparent tranquillity, likely to calm the effects of this violent state, without weakening its impression.

My transition was: "I am very unfortunate. I wished to live for your happiness, and I have disturbed it. I sacrifice myself for your tranquillity, and I disturb it again." Then in a composed but constrained way: "Forgive me, Madame; I am little accustomed to the storms of passions and can repress their emotions but ill. If I am wrong to yield to them, remember at least that it is for the last time. Ah! Calm yourself, calm yourself, I beseech you." And during this long speech, I came gradually nearer. "If you wish me to be calm," said the startled beauty, "you must yourself be more tranquil." "Well, then, I promise it," said I. And I added in a weaker voice: "If the effort is great, at least it will not be for long. But," I went on immediately in a distraught way, "I came, did I not, to return you your letters? I beg you, deign to receive them back. This painful sacrifice remained for me to accomplish; leave me nothing that can weaken my courage." And taking the precious collection from my pocket, I said: "There it is, that deceitful collection of assurances of your friendship! It attached me to life," I went on. "So give the signal yourself which must separate me from you forever."

Here the frightened Mistress yielded entirely to her tender anxiety. "But, M. de Valmont, what is the matter, and what do you mean? Is not the step you are taking today a voluntary one? Is it not the fruit of your own reflections? And are they not those which have made you yourself approve the necessary course I adopted from a sense of duty?" "Well," I replied, "that course decided mine." "And what is that?" "The only one which, in separating me from you, can put an end to my own." "But tell me, what is it?" Then I clasped her in my arms, without her defending herself in the least; and, judging from this forgetfulness of conventions, how strong and powerful her emotion was, I said, risking a tone of enthusiasm: "Adorable woman, you have no idea of the love you inspire; you will never know to what extent you were adored, and how much this sentiment is dearer to me than my existence! May all your days be fortunate and tranquil; may they be embellished by all the happiness of which you have deprived me! At least reward this sincere wish with a regret, with a tear; and believe that the last of my sacrifices will not be the most difficult for my heart. Farewell."

While I was speaking, I felt her heart beating violently; I observed the change in her face; I saw above all that she was suffocated by tears but that only a few painful ones flowed. It was at that moment only that I feigned to go away; but, detaining me by force, she said quickly: "No, listen to me." "Let me go," I answered. "You will listen to me, I wish it." "I must fly from you, I must." "No," she cried. At this last word she rushed or rather fell into my arms in a swoon. As I still doubted of so lucky a success, I feigned a great terror; but with all my terror I guided, or rather, carried her towards the place designed beforehand as the field of my glory; and indeed she only came to her senses submissive and already yielded to her happy conqueror.

Hitherto, my fair friend, I think you will find I adopted a purity of method which will please you; and you will see that I departed in no respect from the true principles of this war, which we have often remarked is so like the other. Judge me then as you would Frederic or

Turenne. I forced the enemy to fight when she wished only to refuse battle; by clever manœuvres I obtained the choice of battlefield and of dispositions; I inspired the enemy with confidence, to overtake her more easily in her retreat; I was able to make terror succeed confidence before joining battle; I left nothing to chance except from consideration of a great advantage in case of success and from the certainty of other resources in case of defeat; finally, I only joined action when I had an assured retreat by which I could cover and retain all I had conquered before. I think that is everything that can be done; but now I am afraid of growing softened in the delights of Capua, like Hannibal. This is what happened afterwards.

I expected so great an event would not take place without the usual tears and despair; and if I noticed at first a little more confusion, and a kind of interior meditation, I attributed both to her prudishness; so, without troubling about these slight differences which I thought were purely local, I simply followed the high-road of consolations; being well persuaded that, as usually happens, sensations would aid sentiment, and that a single action would do more than all the words in the world, which, however, I did not neglect. But I found a really frightening resistance, less from its excess than from the manner in which it showed itself.

Imagine a woman seated, immovably still and with an unchanging face, appearing neither to think, hear, nor listen; a woman whose fixed eyes flowed with quite continual tears which came without effort. Such was Madame de Tourvel while I was speaking; but if I tried to recall her attention to me by a caress, even by the most innocent gesture, immediately there succeeded to this apparent apathy, terror, suffocation, convulsions, sobs, and at intervals a cry, but all without one word articulated.

These crises returned several times and always with more strength; the last was so violent that I was entirely discouraged and for a moment feared I had gained a useless victory. I fell back on the usual commonplaces, and among them was this: "Are you in despair because you have made me happy?" At these words the adorable woman turned towards me; and her face, although still a little distraught, had yet regained its heavenly expression. "Your happiness!" said she. You can guess my reply. "You are happy then?" I redoubled my protestations. "And happy through me?" I added praises and tender words. While she was speaking, all her limbs relaxed; she fell back limply, resting on her armchair; and abandoning to me a hand which I had dared to take, she said: "I feel that idea console and relieve me."

You may suppose that having found my path thus, I did not leave it again; it was really the right, and perhaps the only, one. So when I wished to attempt a second victory I found some resistance at first, and what had passed before made me circumspect; but having called to my aid that same idea of happiness I soon found its results favourable. "You are right," said the tender creature, "I cannot endure my existence except as it may serve to make you happy. I give myself wholly up to it; from this moment I give myself to you and you will experience neither refusals nor regrets from me."

It was with this naïve or sublime candour that she surrendered to me her person and her charms, and that she increased my happiness by sharing it. The ecstasy was complete and mutual; and, for the first time, my own outlasted the pleasure. I only left her arms to fall at her knees, to swear an eternal love to her; and, I must admit it, I believed what I said. Even when we separated, the idea of her did not leave me and I had to make an effort to distract myself.

Ah! Why are you not here to balance the charm of this action by that of its reward? But I shall lose nothing by waiting, shall I? And I hope I can consider as a thing agreed on between us the pleasant arrangement I proposed to you in my last letter. You see I carry things out and that, as I promised you, my affairs have gone well enough for me to be able to give you part of my time. Make haste then to get rid of your heavy Belleroche, abandon the whining Danceny, and concern yourself with me. What can you be doing in the country that you do not even reply to me? Do you know I should like to scold you for it? But happiness inclines us to indulgence. And then I do not forget that by returning to my place among your numerous suitors I must again submit to your little caprices. But remember, the new lover wishes to lose none of his old rights as a friend.

Good-bye, as of old. . . . Yes, good-bye, my angel! I send you all love's kisses.

P.S. Do you know that Prévan, after a month's imprisonment, has been forced to leave his Corps? It is the news of all Paris today. Really, he is cruelly punished for a fault he did not commit, and your success is complete!

Paris, the 29th of October, 17—.

## LETTER CXXVI

*Madame de Rosemonde to Madame de Tourvel*

I should have answered you sooner, my dear child, if the fatigue of my last letter had not brought back my pains, which have again deprived me of the use of my arm during the past few days. I was very anxious to thank you for the good news you gave me of my nephew, and equally anxious to send you my sincere congratulations on your own account. We cannot help but see in this a stroke of Providence which, by moving the one, has saved the other. Yes, my dear Beauty, God wished only to try you and helped you at the moment when your strength was exhausted; and, in spite of your little murmuring, I think you have some thanks to return Him. It is not that I am unaware that it would have been pleasanter for you if this resolution had come to you first and Valmont's had only been the result of it; it even seems, humanly speaking, that the rights of our sex would have been better preserved, and we are unwilling to lose any of them! But what are these slight matters compared with the important objects which are attained? Do we see a man who escapes from a shipwreck complain that he did not have a choice of ways?

You will soon feel, my dear daughter, that the pain you dread will disappear of itself; and even if it remains always and entire you will none the less feel that it is easier to endure than remorse and self-contempt. It would have been useless for me to speak to you with this apparent severity earlier; love is an independent sentiment, which prudence may enable us to avoid but which she cannot overcome, and, once love is born, it only dies of a natural death or from a complete lack of hope. You are in the latter position and this gives me the courage and the right to tell you my opinion freely. It is cruel to frighten a despairing invalid, who can endure nothing but consolations and palliatives, but it is wise to enlighten a convalescent on the dangers he has run, to give him the prudence he needs and submission to advice which may still be necessary to him.

Since you have chosen me for your doctor, I speak to you as such and tell you that the little discomforts you now feel (which perhaps require a few medicines) are yet nothing in comparison with the alarming illness whose cure is now assured. Then as your friend, as the friend of a reasonable and virtuous woman, I take it upon myself to add that this passion, in itself so unfortunate, became even more so through its object. If I am to believe what I am told, my nephew, whom I confess I love to a point of weakness and who, indeed, possesses many praiseworthy qualities and great charm, is not without danger for women and has wronged many, indeed prizes almost equally the seducing and the ruining of them. I believe you would have converted him. Doubtless no one was ever more worthy of doing so; but so many others have flattered themselves in the same way and their hope has been deceived, that I prefer you should not have been reduced to this resource.

Think now, my dear Beauty, that instead of all the dangers you would have had to run, you will have the quiet of your own conscience, your own tranquillity, as well as the satisfaction of having been the principal cause of Valmont's conversion. For my part, I have no doubt that it was largely due to your courageous resistance, and that a moment of weakness on your part might perhaps have left my nephew in a perpetual state of infidelity. I like to think so and wish to see you think the same; you will find in it your first consolation and I new reasons for loving you still more.

I expect you here in a few days, my charming daughter, as you have promised me. Come and seek calm and happiness in the very place you lost them; above all come and rejoice with your tender mother that you have kept so well the promise you made her, that you would never do anything which was unworthy of her and of you!

**From the Château de . . ., 30th October, 17—.**

## LETTER CXXVII

*The Marquise de Merteuil to the Vicomte de Valmont*

If I did not answer your letter of the 19th, Vicomte, the reason was not that I lacked time ; it is merely that it annoyed me and that I thought it devoid of common sense. I thought I could not do better than leave it in oblivion ; but since you return to it and seem to value the ideas it contained while you take my silence for consent, I must plainly tell you my opinion.

I may sometimes have claimed to take the place of a harem by myself, but it has never suited me to be part of one. I thought you knew that. Now at least, when you know it, you will easily see how ridiculous your proposal seemed to me. What I! I sacrifice an inclination, a new inclination, to concern myself with you ? And concern myself how ? By waiting my turn, like a submissive slave, for the sublime favours of your " Highness ! " When, for example, you wished to distract yourself for a moment from " this unsuspected charm " which you have only experienced with the " adorable, the heavenly " Madame de Tourvel, or when you are afraid of compromising in the eyes of the " delightful Cécile " the superior idea you are very glad to have her retain of you : then, condescending to me, you will come to seek pleasures, less keen indeed, but without consequence ; and your precious favours, although rather rare, will quite suffice for my happiness !

Assuredly, you are rich in your good opinion of yourself ; but apparently I am not so in modesty ; for, however much I examine myself, I cannot think I have fallen so low as that. Very likely I am wrong, but I warn you that I am so in many other matters.

I am especially wrong in thinking that " the schoolboy, the whining " Danceny, entirely occupied with me, sacrificing to me, without even making a merit of it, a first passion, even before it has been satisfied, and loving me as men love at his age, could, in spite of his twenty years, work more effectively than you for my happiness and my pleasures. I take it upon me to add that if I had the caprice to give him a rival, it would not be you, at least at this moment.

And for what reasons ? you will ask. But, in the first place, there might not be any ; for the caprice which might make you preferred, might just as well exclude you. But for politeness' sake I am willing to tell the motives of my decision. It seems to me that you would have too many sacrifices to make me ; and I, instead of feeling grateful as you would not fail to expect, should be capable of thinking that you owed me even more ! You see that our way of thinking keeps us so far apart that we cannot draw near each other in any way ; and I fear it will take a long time, a very long time, before my feelings change. I promise to let you know when I change. Until then, take my advice, make other arrangements, and keep your kisses, you have so many better ways of bestowing them!

"Good-bye, as of old," you say? But of old, it seems to me, you thought more of me; you did not destine me to play third parts; and above all you waited until I said yes before being certain of my consent. Excuse me then if, instead of saying "Good-bye, as of old," I say to you "Good-bye as at present."

Servant, Vicomte.

From the Château de . . ., 31st of October, 17—.

## LETTER CXXVIII

*Madame de Tourvel to Madame de Rosemonde*

It was only yesterday, Madame, that I received your delayed reply. It would have killed me there and then, if my existence were still my own; but it belongs to another; and that other is M. de Valmont. You see I hide nothing from you. Even if you should now think me unworthy of your friendship, I would rather lose it than hold it by deceit. All I can tell you is that I was placed by M. de Valmont between his death or his happiness, and I chose the latter. I neither boast of it nor blame myself for it; I simply say what is.

After that, you will easily imagine what an effect your letter and the severe truths it contained had upon me. Yet do not think it created any regret in me or can ever make me alter my feelings or my conduct. It is not that I do not pass through cruel moments; but when my heart is most torn, when I feel I can no longer endure my torture, I say to myself: Valmont is happy; and everything vanishes before that idea, or rather it changes everything into pleasure.

I have then consecrated myself to your nephew; for his sake I am ruined. He has become the sole centre of my thoughts, of my feelings, of my actions. As long as my life is necessary to his happiness, it will be precious to me, and I shall think it a fortunate one. If some day he should think otherwise . . . he will hear no complaint and no reproach from me. I have dared already to fix my eyes upon that fatal moment and my mind is made up.

You can now see how I must be affected by the fear you seem to have that one day M. de Valmont might ruin me; for before he wishes to do so, he must have ceased to love me; and what effect on me can be made by vain reproaches I shall not even hear? He alone shall be my judge. As I shall only have lived for him, my memory will rest with him; and if he is forced to recognise that I loved him, I shall be sufficiently justified.

You have now read my heart, Madame. I prefer the misfortune of losing your esteem by my frankness to that of rendering myself unworthy of it by the degradation of a lie. I felt I owed this complete confidence to your former kindnesses to me. To add a word more might make you suspect that I have the pride to claim it still when, on the contrary, I do myself justice by abandoning any claim to it. I am with respect, Madame, your most humble and most obedient servant.

Paris, 1st of November, 17—.

## LETTER CXXIX

*The Vicomte de Valmont to the Marquise de Merteuil*

Tell me, my fair friend, what is the reason for the tone of bitterness and banter which reigns in your last letter ? What is this crime I have committed, apparently without knowing it, which makes you so out of humour ? You blame me because I appeared to count upon your consent before I had obtained it ; but I thought that what might appear presumption with other people, could never be taken for anything but confidence between you and me ; and since when has that feeling harmed friendship and love ? By adding hope to desire I only yielded to a natural impulse, which makes us always place the happiness we seek as near as possible ; and you took the result of my eagerness for that of pride. I know very well that custom has introduced a respectful doubt into this matter ; but you know it is only a form, a protocol ; and I think I had every reason to believe that these minute precautions were not necessary between us.

It even seems to me that this frank and free proceeding, when it is founded upon old acquaintance, is very preferable to the insipid flattery which so often makes love tasteless. And perhaps the value I find in this manner only comes from that I attach to the happiness of which it reminds me ; but, for that very reason, it would be still more disagreeable for me to have you think otherwise.

But that is the only fault I know of myself ; for I do not imagine that you can have seriously believed there is a woman in the world whom I should prefer to you ; and still less that I should have rated you as low as you feign to believe. You examined yourself in this matter, you tell me, and you do not think you have fallen so low as that. So I think and that simply proves that your mirror is faithful. But might you not have concluded more easily and with more justice that I certainly never had such an opinion of you ?

I vainly look for a reason for this strange idea. But it seems to me that it comes more or less from the praises I have allowed myself to give other women. At least, so I infer from your affectation in dwelling upon the epithets of " adorable," " heavenly," " delightful," which I used in speaking to you of Madame de Tourvel or the Volanges girl. But do you not know that these words, taken at hazard rather than on reflection, do not so much express one's opinion of the person as the situation one is in when speaking ? And if, at the very moment when I was so keenly affected by one or the other, I still desired you no less ; if I gave you a marked preference over both of them, since I could not renew our first *liaison* except at the expense of both of them; I do not think there is any great reason for blaming me here.

It would not be more difficult for me to justify myself on the "unsuspected charm," by which you also seem to be a little annoyed; for, first of all, it does not follow that it is stronger because it was unsuspected. Ah! Who could surpass you in the delicious pleasures which you alone can make always new and always more intense? I merely wished to say it was of a kind I had not before experienced, but without intending to classify it; and I added, as I repeat today, that, whatever it may be, I shall combat and overcome it. I shall do this with even more zeal, if I can think that this slight labour is a homage I can offer you.

As to little Cécile—I see no use in talking about her to you. You have not forgotten that I took charge of the child at your request, and only await your permission to get rid of her. I may have mentioned her ingenuousness and her freshness; I may even for a moment have thought her "delightful," because one is always more or less pleased with one's own work; but she certainly has not enough consistency in any way to hold one's attention at all.

And now, my fair friend, I appeal to your justice, to your first favours to me; to the long and perfect friendship, to the complete confidence, which have so long bound us to each other: have I deserved the harsh tone you take towards me? But how easy it will be for you to compensate me for it whenever you choose! Say but a word, and you will see if all the charms and all the delights keep me here—not a day, but a minute. I shall fly to your feet and your arms, and I will prove to you a thousand times and in a thousand ways that you are, that you always will be, the true ruler of my heart.

Good-bye, my fair friend; I expect your reply with great eagerness.

Paris, 3rd of November, 17—.

## LETTER CXXX

*Madame de Rosemonde to Madame de Tourvel*

And why, my dear Beauty, do you no longer wish to be my daughter? Why do you seem to declare that all correspondence between us is to be broken off? Is it to punish me for not having guessed something which was contrary to all probability? Or did you suspect me of having voluntarily distressed you? No, I understand your heart too well to believe that it thinks of mine in this way. So the pain your letter caused me is much less relative to myself than to you!

O my friend! It is with pain I say it, but you are far too worthy of being loved, for love ever to make you happy. Ah! What really delicate and sensitive woman has not found misfortune in the very sentiment which promised her so much happiness! Do men know how to appreciate the women they possess?

Many of them are honourable in their behaviour and constant in their affection but, even among those, how few are able to place themselves in unison with our hearts ! Do not think my dear child, that their love is like ours. They feel indeed the same ecstasy ; they often put more vehement emotion into it ; but they do not know that anxious eagerness, that delicate solicitude, which in us produce those tender and continuous attentions whose sole end is always the beloved person. Man enjoys the happiness he feels, woman the happiness she gives. This difference, so essential and so rarely noticed, has a very perceptible influence on the whole of their respective behaviour. The pleasure of one is the satisfaction of desires, the pleasure of the other is above all to create them. To please is for him only a method of success ; but for her it is success itself. And coquetry, for which women are so often blamed, is nothing but the excess of this way of feeling, and by that very fact proves its reality. Finally, that exclusive desire which particularly characterises love is, in man, only a preference which at most serves to increase a pleasure which another object would perhaps weaken but not destroy ; while with women it is a profound sentiment which not only annihilates every other desire but, being stronger than nature itself and out of its control, makes them feel nothing but repugnance and disgust even where it seems pleasure should be created.

And do not think that the more or less numerous objections which may be quoted can be successfully opposed to these general truths ! They are supported by public opinion which in men alone distinguishes infidelity from inconstancy—a distinction which they are proud of when they ought to feel humiliated ; for our sex this distinction has only been adopted by those depraved women who are its shame, women to whom any way seems good if they can hope by it to be saved from the painful feeling of their baseness.

I thought, my dear Beauty, it might be useful for you to have these reflections to oppose to the deceitful ideas of perfect happiness with which love never fails to abuse our imagination ; a fallacious hope to which we still cling even when forced to abandon it, the loss of which irritates and multiplies the griefs, already but too real, inseparable from a strong passion ! This occupation of softening your troubles or diminishing their number is the only one I can and will fulfil at this moment. In ills without remedy, advice can only be directed to the regimen. All I ask of you is to remember that to pity an invalid is not to blame him. Ah ! What are we, to blame one another ? Let us leave the right to judging to Him who reads in our hearts ; and I even dare to think that in his paternal eyes a host of virtues can atone for one weakness.

But, I beg you, dear friend, avoid especially these violent resolutions which are less a sign of strength than of complete discouragement ; do not forget that, by rendering another the possessor of your existence (to use your own expression) you cannot have frustrated your friends of what they possessed before, which they will continue to claim.

Good-bye, my dear daughter; think sometimes of your tender mother and believe that you will always and above everything be the object of her dearest thoughts.

From the Château de . . ., 6th of November, 17—.

## LETTER CXXXI

*The Marquise de Merteuil to the Vicomte de Valmont*

Well and good, Vicomte, I am more pleased with you this time than before; but now let us discuss matters in a friendly way; I hope to convince you that the arrangement you appear to desire would be a real folly for you as well as for me.

Have you not yet noticed that pleasure, which is indeed the sole motive for the union of the two sexes, is not sufficient to form a bond between them? And that, though it is preceded by the desire which brings together, it is none the less followed by the disgust which repels? It is a law of nature that love alone can change; and is one able to feel love at will? Yet it is always necessary, and this would be really a difficulty had people not perceived that it was enough if love existed on one side. In this way the difficulty was halved, and without much loss; indeed, one enjoys the happiness of loving, the other that of pleasing, a little less animated it is true, but I add to it the pleasure of deceiving, which makes a balance; and thus everything goes well.

But tell me, Vicomte, which of us two will undertake to deceive the other! You know the story of the two rogues who recognised each other when gambling: "We shall achieve nothing," they said, "let us each pay half for the cards"[1]; and they gave up the game. Take my advice, let us follow this prudent example, and not lose together a time we could employ so much better elsewhere.

To prove to you that your interest influences this decision as much as my own and that I am not acting from ill humour or caprice, I will not refuse you the reward agreed upon between us; and I am quite certain that for one evening only we shall satisfy each other, and I have no doubt that we shall be able to embellish it in such a way that we shall see it end with regret. But do not forget that this regret is necessary to happiness; and however pleasant our illusion may be, do not let us think it can be durable.

You see that I fulfil my promise in my turn and that before you have carried out your part; for I was to have the first letter from the heavenly prude and yet, either you still value it or you have forgotten the conditions of a bargain, which perhaps interests you less than you would like to persuade me; but I have received nothing, absolutely nothing. Yet either I am wrong or the tender devotee must write often; for what does she do when she is alone? She surely has not the wit to amuse herself. If I wished, then, I might make you a few little reproaches;

[1] Or: "Let us share the stakes."

but I leave them in silence to atone for a little ill-humour I may have had in my last letter.

And now, Vicomte, I have nothing else to say but to make you a request which is as much for your sake as for mine; this is to put off a moment, which perhaps I desire as much as you do but which I think ought to be delayed until my return to town. On the one hand, we shall not have the necessary liberty here, for it would only need a little jealousy to attach to me more firmly than ever this dull Belleroche, who is now only hanging by a thread. He is already in the state of having to lash himself up to the point of loving me; he is in such a state that I put as much malice as prudence into the caresses with which I overwhelm him. But at the same time you will see that this would not be a sacrifice to make you! A mutual infidelity will make the charm much more powerful.

Do you know I sometimes regret that we are reduced to these resources. In the time when we loved each other, for I think it was love, I was happy; and you too, Vicomte! . . . But why trouble about a happiness which can never return? No, whatever you may say, it is impossible. First of all, I should exact sacrifices which you would not or could not make me and which I may not deserve; and then, how is one to retain you? Oh! No, no, I will not even consider the idea; and in spite of the pleasure I feel in writing to you, I prefer to leave you abruptly. Good-bye, Vicomte.

From the Château de . . ., 6th of November, 17—.

## LETTER CXXXII

### *Madame de Tourvel to Madame de Rosemonde*

I am touched by your kindness to me, Madame; I should yield entirely to it were I not restrained to some degree by the fear of profaning it by the acceptance. Why must it be that when I find it so precious I feel at the same time I am not worthy of it? Ah! I shall at least dare to express my gratitude to you; above all I shall admire that indulgence of virtue which only knows our faults to pity them, whose powerful charm keeps so sweet and so strong a domination over our hearts even beside the charm of love.

But can I still deserve a friendship which no longer suffices for my happiness? I say the same of your advice; I feel its value but I cannot follow it. And how could I not believe in perfect happiness when I feel it at this very moment? Yes, if men are as you say, they must be avoided, they are hateful; but how far is Valmont from resembling them! If, like them, he has that violence of passion, which you call vehement emotion, is it not exceeded in him by his delicacy! O, my friend! You speak of sharing my troubles, rejoice at my happiness; I owe it to love and how much more to the object of that love who increases its value! You love your nephew, you say, perhaps to the point of weakness? Ah! If you knew him as I do! I love him with idolatry, and even then much less than he deserves. No doubt he has been carried away into a few errors, he admits it himself; but who has ever known real love as he does? What more can I say to you? He feels it as he inspires it.

You will think that this is "one of the deceitful ideas with which love never fails to deceive our imagination"; but in this case why should he become more tender, more ardent, now he has nothing more to obtain? I will confess I had noticed in him formerly an appearance of reflection and reserve which rarely left him and often brought me back, in spite of myself, to the false and cruel impressions I had been given of him. But since he has been able to yield unconstrainedly to the emotions of his heart he seems to guess all the desires of mine. Who knows whether we were not born for each other! If this happiness were not reserved for me—to be necessary to his! Ah! If it is an illusion, may I die before it ends. But no; I want to live to cherish him, to adore him. Why should he cease to love me? What other woman could make him happier than I do? And I feel it myself; this happiness one creates is the strongest bond, the only one which really binds. Yes, it is this delicious feeling which ennobles love, which, in a way, purifies it, and makes it really worthy of a tender and generous soul, like Valmont's.

Good-bye, my dear, my respectable, my indulgent friend. It would be vain for me to try to write longer to you; this is the time he promised to come and every other idea abandons me. Forgive me! But you desire my happiness and it is so great at this moment that I am scarcely capable of feeling it all.

Paris, 7th of November, 17—.

## LETTER CXXXIII

*The Vicomte de Valmont to the Marquise de Merteuil*

And what, my fair friend, are these sacrifices you think I would not make, the reward of which would be to please you? Only let me know them and if I hesitate to offer them to you, I give you permission to refuse the homage of them. Hey! What have you been thinking of me for some time if, even in a mood of indulgence, you doubt my feelings and my energy? Sacrifices I would not or could not make! So you think me in love, subjugated? And the value I put upon the victory you suspect me of attaching to the person? Ah! Thanks be to Heaven, I am not yet reduced to that and I offer to prove it to you. Yes, I will prove it to you, even if it must be at the expense of Mme de Tourvel. After that you cannot surely have any doubts.

I think I may give some time, without compromising myself, to a woman who at least has the merit of belonging to a class one rarely meets. And perhaps the dead season in which this adventure happened made me give myself up to it more completely; and even now, when the full rush of society has hardly begun, it is not surprising that it absorbs me almost entirely. But remember it is hardly a week ago that I enjoyed the fruit of three months of trouble. I have so often stayed longer with someone who was worth less and had not cost me so much! . . . And you never drew any conclusions from them about me.

And then, would you know the real cause of the ardour I put into it? Here it is. The woman is naturally timid; at first, she continually doubted her happiness, and this doubt was enough to disturb her, so that I am scarcely beginning to be able to notice how far my power extends in this class. Yet it is a thing I was curious to know, and the opportunity is not so easily found as people think.

First, for a great many women pleasure is always pleasure, and is never anything more; whatever title may be given us, to them we are never anything but factors, mere agents whose sole merit is activity, and among whom he who does most, does best.

In another class, perhaps the most numerous today, the celebrity of the lover, the pleasure of taking him away from another woman, the fear of his being taken away in turn, preoccupy women almost entirely; we have a share, to a greater or less extent, in the kind of happiness they enjoy, but it is rather a matter of the circumstances than the person. It comes to them by way of us and not from us.

For my observations I needed to find a delicate and sensitive woman who would make love her sole interest and who in love itself would see only her lover; a woman whose emotion, far from following the ordinary track, would start from the heart and reach the senses; whom I have seen, for example (and I am not speaking of the first day) emerge from pleasure in tears and a moment later regain delight through a word which replied to her soul. And then, it was necessary for her to add to all this the natural candour which has become insurmountable from the habit of yielding to it, which does not allow her to dissimulate any of the feelings of her heart. Now, you will admit that such women are rare; and I am ready to believe that but for her I should never have met with one perhaps.

It would not be surprising then if she should hold me longer than another woman would; and since the experiment I wish to make with her demands that I render her happy, perfectly happy, why should I refuse to do so, especially when it aids and does not hinder me? But because the mind is engaged, does it follow that the heart is enslaved? Certainly not. So the value I do not deny that I set on this adventure will not prevent my seeking others or even my sacrificing it to more agreeable ones.

I am so free that I have not even neglected the Volanges girl, for whom I care so little. Her mother is bringing her back to town in three days' time; yesterday I arranged my communications; some money to the porter, a few compliments to his wife, arranged the whole matter. Can you imagine that Danceny did not find out so simple a way? And yet people say love makes them ingenious! On the contrary those it dominates it makes stupid. And I am unable to protect myself from it! Ah! You need not be uneasy. In a few days I shall weaken, by sharing it elsewhere, the possibly too lively impression I have received; and if sharing it with one only is not enough, I shall share it with several.

I shall be quite ready, however, to hand the schoolgirl over to her discreet lover as soon as you think fitting. It seems to me you have no further reason to prevent it, and I agree to render poor Danceny this signal service. Indeed it is the least I can do for him in exchange for all those he has done me. At the present moment he is in a great state of anxiety to know whether Mme de Volanges will receive him; I calm him as best I can by assuring him I will make him happy on the first opportunity; and meanwhile I continue to take charge of his correspondence which he wishes to continue on the arrival of "his Cécile." I have six letters from him already and I shall have one or two more before the happy day. He must be a very unoccupied young man!

But let us leave this childish couple and come back to ourselves; let me concentrate solely on the delightful hope your letter gave me. Yes, of course, you will hold me and I should not forgive you for doubting it. Our ties were loosened, not broken; and the so-called breaking-off was merely an error of our imagination; our feelings, our interests, remained just as united as ever. Like a traveller who returns home undeceived, I shall realise, like him, that I had left happiness to pursue hope and I shall say with Harcourt:

"The more foreigners I saw, the more I loved my country."[1] Do not oppose any longer the idea, or rather, the sentiment which brings you back to me; and after having tried all pleasures in our different paths, let us enjoy the happiness of feeling that none of them is comparable with that we have experienced, which we shall once more find still more delicious!

Good-bye, my charming friend. I consent to wait until you return; but hasten it, and do not forget how much I desire it.

Paris, 8th of November, 17—.

## LETTER CXXXIV

*The Marquise de Merteuil to the Vicomte de Valmont*

Really, Vicomte, you are like children, in whose presence one must never say anything and to whom one can never show anything without their wanting to get hold of it once! A mere idea comes to me and I warn you I do not intend to dwell on it; and, because I speak of it to you, you take advantage of this to bring back my attention to it, to hold me to it when I wish to be diverted from it and, as it were, to make me share your absurd desires in spite of myself! Is it generous of you to leave me to bear the whole burden of prudence? I tell you again, and I repeat it to myself still more often, the arrangement you propose is really

[1] Du Belloi. Tragedy of *The Siege of Calais*. (C. de L.)

impossible. Even if you put into it all the generosity you show at the moment, do you think I have not any delicacy myself, that I would accept sacrifices which would injure your happiness?

Now, Vicomte, have you really any illusions about the sentiment which attaches you to Madame de Tourvel? It is love, or love never existed; you may deny it in a hundred ways but you prove it in a thousand. For example, what subterfuge is this you make use of against yourself (for I think you are sincere with me) which makes you attribute to a desire for observation the wish to keep this woman, a wish you can neither hide nor combat? Would one not say you had never made another woman happy, perfectly happy? Ah! If you doubt that, you have very little memory! But no, it is not that. Your heart simply abuses your mind and makes it accept bad reasons; but I, who have a great interest in not allowing myself to be deceived, am not so easily contented.

Thus, in noticing your politeness which made you carefully suppress all the words which you thought had displeased me, I yet perceived that you had none the less preserved the same ideas, perhaps without realising it. Indeed, it is no longer the adorable, the heavenly Madame de Tourvel, but "an amazing woman, a delicate and sensitive woman," and that to the exclusion of all others; "a rare woman," such that "a second one like her could never be met with." It is the same with that unsuspected charm which is not "the more powerful." Well! So be it; but since you have never found it until now, it is to be supposed that you would never find it again in the future, and the loss you would make would be just as irreparable. Vicomte, either these are the certain symptoms of love or one must give up ever looking for them.

Rest assured, this time I am speaking to you without ill humour. I have promised myself not to be out of humour again; I have realised but too well that it may become a dangerous snare. Take my advice, let us be friends and remain as we are. Be thankful to me only for my courage in defending myself; yes, my courage, for it is needed sometimes even to avoid taking a course one knows to be the wrong one.

It is therefore not with the purpose of bringing you round to my opinion by persuasion that I reply to the request you make about the sacrifices I should exact, and you could not make. I use the word "exact" on purpose, because I am sure that in a moment you will indeed think me to exacting; but so much the better! Far from being annoyed by your refusal, I shall thank you for it. Come, I will not dissimulate with you, though perhaps I need it

I should exact then—see the cruelty of it!—that this rare, this astonishing Madame de Tourvel be no more to you than an ordinary woman, a woman such as she really is; for we must not deceive ourselves; this charm we think we find in others exists in us, and love alone embellishes so much the beloved person. Perhaps you would make the effort to promise me, to swear to me that you would do what I ask, however impossible it may be; but, I confess, I should not believe mere words, I could only be persuaded by your whole conduct.

That is not all; I should be capricious. I should not pay any attention to the sacrifice of little Cécile which you offer me so graciously. On the contrary I should ask you to continue this painful service until further orders from me; either because I should like to abuse my power or because from indulgence or justice it would suffice me to control your sentiments without thwarting your pleasures. In any case, I should want to be obeyed; and my orders would be very harsh!

It is true that I should then think myself obliged to thank you and—who knows?—perhaps even to reward you. For example, I should certainly cut short an absence which would become unendurable to me. I should see you at last, Vicomte, and I should see you . . . how? . . . But remember this is nothing more than a conversation, a mere account of an impossible project, and I do not want to forget it alone . . . .

Do you know I am a little anxious about my law-suit. I wanted to find out exactly what my rights are; my lawyers quote me a few laws and a great many "precedents" as they call them; but I do not see as much reason and justice in it. I am almost at the point of regretting that I did not agree to a compromise. However, I reassure myself by remembering that the solicitor is sharp, the barrister eloquent, and the client pretty. If these three methods do not succeed, the whole course of affairs would have to be changed, and what would become of respect for ancient customs!

This law-suit is now the only thing which keeps me here. Belleroche's is over; nonsuited, each side to pay its own costs. He is now regretting this evening's ball—it is indeed the regret of an idler! I shall return him complete liberty when I get back to town. I make him this painful sacrifice and console myself for it by the generosity he perceives in it!

Good-bye, Vicomte, write to me often; the recital of your pleasure will compensate me to some extent for the boredom I endure.

From the Château de . . ., 11th of November, 17—.

## LETTER CXXXV

*Madame de Tourvel to Madame de Rosemonde*

I am trying to write to you without knowing if I shall be able to do so. Ah! Heaven, when I think that in my last letter it was the excess of my happiness which prevented my continuing it! And now it is the excess of my despair which overwhelms me, which leaves me no strength except to feel my pain, and takes away from me the strength to express it.

Valmont. . . . Valmont loves me no more, he never loved me. Love does not disappear in this way. He deceives me, he betrays me, he outrages me. I endure all the misfortunes and humiliations which can be gathered together, and they come upon me from him.

And do not think this is a mere suspicion ; I was so far from having any ! I have not the happiness to be able to doubt. I saw him ; what can he say to justify himself ? . . . But what does it matter to him ! He will not even attempt it. . . . Wretch that I am ! What will my tears and reproaches matter to him ? What does he care for me ! . . .

It is true that he has sacrificed me, surrendered me . . . and to whom ? . . . a vile creature. . . . But what am I saying ? Ah ! I have lost even the right to scorn her. She has betrayed fewer duties, she is less guilty than I. Oh ! How painful is grief when it is founded on remorse ! I feel my tortures increase. Farewell, my dear friend ; however unworthy of your pity I have rendered myself, you will yet have some pity for me if you can form any idea of what I am suffering.

I have just re-read my letter, and I see that it tells you nothing ; I will try to have the courage to relate this cruel event. It was yesterday ; for the first time since my return I was to dine out. Valmont came to see me at five ; never had he seemed so tender. He let me know that my plan of going out vexed him, and, as you may suppose, I soon decided to stay at home. However, suddenly, two hours later his manner and tone changed perceptibly. I do not know if anything escaped me which could offend him ; but in any case, a little later he pretended to recollect an engagement which forced him to leave me and he went away ; yet it was not without expressing very keen regrets which seemed to me tender and which I then thought sincere.

Left to myself, I thought it more polite not to avoid my first engagement since I was free to carry it out. I completed my toilet and entered my carriage. Unhappily my coachman took me by the Opera and I found myself in the confusion of the exit ; a few steps in front of me in the next line I saw Valmont's carriage. My heart beat at once, but it was not from fear ; and the one idea which filled me was the desire that my carriage would go forward. Instead of that, his was forced to retire, and stopped opposite mine. I leaned forward at once ; what was my astonishment to see at his side a woman of ill-repute, well known as such ! I leaned back, as you may suppose ; this alone was enough to rend my heart ; but, what you will scarcely believe, this same creature, apparently informed by an odious confidence, did not leave her carriage window, kept looking at me, and laughed so loudly it might have made a scene.

In the state of prostration I was in I allowed myself to be driven to the house where I was to sup, but it was impossible to remain there ; every moment I felt ready to faint and I could not restrain my tears.

When I returned I wrote to M. de Valmont and sent him my letter immediately ; he was not at home. Desirous, at any price, to emerge from this state of death or to have it confirmed for ever, I sent the man back with orders to wait, but my servant returned before midnight and told me that the coachman, who had come back, had said that his master would not be in that night. This morning I thought there was nothing to do but to ask for my letters once more and to request him never to come to my house again. I gave orders to that effect ; but doubtless they were useless. It is nearly midday ; he has not yet arrived and I have not even received a word from him.

And now, my dear friend, I have nothing more to add ; you know all about it and you know my heart. My one hope is that I shall not be here long to distress your tender friendship.

Paris, 15th of November, 17—.

## LETTER CXXXVI

*Madame de Tourvel to the Vicomte de Valmont*

Doubtless, Monsieur, after what happened yesterday you will not expect to be received in my house again and, doubtless, you have no great wish to do so ! The object of this note, then, is not so much to ask you not to come again as to request from you once more those letters which ought never to have existed ; letters which, if they may have amused you for a moment as proofs of the delusion you created, cannot but be indifferent to you now that it is dissipated and now that they express nothing but a sentiment you have destroyed.

I recognise and confess I was wrong to give you a confidence by which so many other women before me have been victimised ; in this I blame myself alone ; but I thought at least I did not deserve from you that I should be abandoned to contempt and insult. I thought that in sacrificing myself to you, in losing for you alone my rights to the esteem of others and of myself, that I might expect not to be judged by you with more severity than by the public, whose opinion still recognises an immense difference between a weak woman and a depraved woman. These wrongs, which would be wrongs to anyone, are the only ones of which I speak. I am silent upon those of love ; your heart would not understand mine. Farewell, Monsieur.

Paris, 15th of November, 17—.

## LETTER CXXXVII

*The Vicomte de Valmont to Madame de Tourvel*

Your letter, Madame, has only just been handed to me ; I shuddered on reading it, and it has left me scarcely strength to reply. What a dreadful idea of me you hold ! Ah ! No doubt I have done wrong, and such wrong that I shall never forgive myself for it in my life, even if you should hide it with your indulgence. But how far from my soul those wrongs you reproach me with have ever been ! What I ! I humiliate you ! I degrade you ! When I respect you as much as I cherish you, when my pride dates from the moment when you thought me worthy of you ! Appearances have deceived you ; and I confess they may have been against me ; but why have you not in your heart that which should combat them? Why was it not revolted at the mere idea that it could have any reason to complain of mine? Yet you believed this! So you not only thought me capable of this atrocious madness, but you even feared you had made yourself liable to it by your favours to me. Ah! Since you feel yourself so degraded by your love I am then very vile in your eyes?

Oppressed by the painful feeling this idea causes me, I am wasting in resenting it the time I should employ in destroying it. I will confess all; but another consideration still restrains me. Must I then relate facts I wish to annihilate and fix your attention and mine upon a moment of error which I should like to atone for by the remainder of my life, whose cause I have yet to comprehend, whose memory must forever bring me humiliation and despair? Ah! If by accusing myself I must excite your anger, you will at least not have to seek far for your vengeance; it will suffice you to leave me to my remorse.

Yet—who would believe it?—the first cause of this event is the all-powerful charm I feel in your presence. It was that which made me forget too long an important engagement which could not be postponed. When I left you it was too late and I did not find the person I was looking for. I hoped to find him at the Opera and this step was equally fruitless. Emilie, whom I found there, whom I knew at a time when I was far from knowing either you or love; Emilie had no carriage and asked me to take her to her home close at hand. I saw no objection and consented. But it was then that I met you and I felt at once that you would be tempted to think me guilty.

The fear of displeasing or distressing you is so powerful in me that it must have been, and was indeed, speedily noticed. I confess even that it made me request the woman not to show herself; this precaution of delicacy turned against my love. Accustomed, like all those of her condition, never to be certain of a power which is always usurped, except through the abuse they allow themselves to make of it, Emilie took care not to allow so striking an opportunity to escape. The more she saw my embarrassment increase the more pains she took to show herself; and her silly mirth—I blush to think that you could have believed for a moment that you were its object—was only caused by the cruel anxiety I felt, which was itself the result of my respect and my love.

So far I am certainly more unfortunate than guilty; and these wrongs "which would be wrongs to anyone and are the only ones of which you speak" cannot be blamed upon me since they do not exist. But it is in vain that you are silent upon the wrongs of love; I shall not keep the same silence about them; too great an interest compels me to break it.

In my shame at this inconceivable aberration I cannot recall its memory without extreme pain. I am deeply convinced of my errors and would consent to bear their punishment or to await their forgiveness from time, from my unending affection, and from my repentance. But how can I be silent when what I have to say is important to your sensibility ?

Do not think I am looking for a roundabout way to excuse or palliate my error ; I confess myself guilty. But I do not confess, I will never confess that this humiliating fault can be regarded as a wrong to love. Ah ! What can there be in common between a surprisal of the senses, between a moment of self-forgetfulness soon followed by shame and regret, and a pure sentiment which can only be born in a delicate soul, can only be sustained there by esteem, and whose fruit is happiness ! Ah ! Do not profane love thus ! Above all, fear to profane yourself by collecting under the same point of view what can never be confounded. Let vile and degraded women dread a rivalry they feel can be established in spite of them, let them endure the torments of a jealousy which is both cruel and humiliating ; but you, turn your eyes away from objects which sully your gaze and, pure as the Divinity itself, punish, like it, the offence without resenting it.

But what punishment can you inflict upon me which could be more painful than that I feel, which can be compared with the regret of having displeased you, to the despair of having distressed you, to the crushing idea of having rendered myself less worthy of you ? You are thinking how to punish me ! And I ask you for consolation ; not that I deserve it, but because it is necessary to me and can only come to me from you.

If, suddenly forgetting my love and yours and setting no value upon my happiness, you wish, on the contrary, to give me over to an eternal pain, you have the right to do so ; strike ; but if, being more indulgent or more tender, you remember still the sweet feelings which united our hearts—that pleasure of the soul, always reborn and always more deeply felt ; those days, so sweet, so happy, which each of us owes to the other ; all those treasures of love which love alone procures—perhaps you may prefer the power of recreating them to that of destroying them. What more shall I say ? I have lost everything, and lost it through my own fault ; but I can regain all by your benefaction. It is for you to decide now. I add only one word. Yesterday you swore to me that my happiness was certain as long as it depended on you ! Ah ! Madame, will you abandon me today to an eternal despair ?

Paris, 15th of November, 17—.

## LETTER CXXXVIII

*The Vicomte de Valmont to the Marquise de Merteuil*

I persist, my fair friend ; no, I am not in love ; and it is not my fault if circumstances force me to play the part. Only consent and come back ; you will soon see for yourself that I am sincere. I gave proofs of it yesterday and they cannot be destroyed by what is happening today.

I went to see the tender prude and went without having any other engagement; for the Volanges girl, in spite of her age, was to spend the whole night at Madame V . . .'s precocious ball. At first, lack of occupation made me desire to prolong this evening with her and I had even, with this purpose, exacted a small sacrifice; but scarcely was it granted when the pleasure I promised myself was disturbed by the idea of this love which you persist in believing of me, or at least in accusing me of; to such an extent that I felt no other desire than that of being able at the same time to assure myself and to convince you that it was a pure calumny on your part.

I therefore adopted a violent course; and on some slight pretext I left my Beauty in great surprise and doubtless even more distress. For myself, I went off calmly to meet Emilie at the Opera; and she can inform you that no regret troubled our pleasures until we separated this morning.

Yet I had a fair enough cause for anxiety if my perfect indifference had not preserved me from it; for you must know that I was barely four houses from the Opera, with Emilie in my carriage, when the austere devotee's carriage came up exactly opposite mine and a block kept us for nearly ten minutes beside one another. We could see each other as plainly as at midday and there was no way to escape.

But that is not all; it occurred to me to confide to Emilie that this was the woman of the letter. (Perhaps you will remember that jest and that Emilie was the writing-table).[1] She had not forgotten it; she is a merry creature; and she had no rest until she had observed at her ease "that virtue," as she called it, and that with peals of laughter outrageous enough to provoke a temper.

That is still not all; did not the jealous creature send to my house that very evening? I was not there; but, in her obstinacy, she sent there a second time with orders to wait for me. As soon as I had decided to remain with Emilie I sent back my carriage with no orders to the coachman except to come for me there next morning; when he got back he found the messenger of love, and thought it quite simple to say that I was not returning that night. You can guess the effect of this news and that when I returned I found my dismissal expressed with all the dignity demanded by the situation.

So this adventure which you think interminable might have been ended this morning, as you see; if it is not ended the reason is not, as you will think, that I set any value on its continuance; the reason is that, on the one hand, I did not think it decent to allow myself to be deserted; and, on the other hand, that I wished to reserve the honour of this sacrifice for you.

I have therefore replied to the severe note by a long sentimental letter; I gave lengthy reasons and I relied on love to get them accepted as good. I have just received a second note, still very rigorous and still confirming the eternal breach, as was to be expected; but its tone was

[1] Letters *XLVI* and *XLVII*. (C. de L.)

not the same. She will above all things not see me; this determination is announced four times in the most irrevocable manner. I concluded I ought not to lose a moment before presenting myself. I have already sent my servant to get hold of the door-porter, and in a moment I shall go myself to have my pardon signed; for in wrongs of this kind there is only one formula which gives a general absolution and that can only be obtained in person.

Good-bye, my charming friend; I am now going to attempt this great event.

Paris, 15th of November, 17—.

## LETTER CXXXIX

*Madame de Tourvel to Madame de Rosemonde*

How I blame myself, my tender friend, for having spoken to you of my passing troubles too much and too soon! It is because of me that you are now in distress; the grief which came to you from me still lasts while I am happy. Yes, all is forgotten, forgiven; let me express it better, all is retrieved. Calm and bliss have succeeded grief and anguish. O joy of my heart, how shall I express you! Valmont is innocent—a man who loves so much cannot be guilty. He had not done me the heavy, offensive injuries for which I blamed him with such bitterness; and if I needed to be indulgent in one point, had I not my own injustices to repair?

I will not tell you in detail the facts or reasons which justify him; perhaps the mind would not thoroughly appreciate them; the heart alone is capable of feeling them. Yet if you suspect me of weakness, I shall appeal to your own judgment in support of mine. For men, you said yourself, infidelity is not inconstancy.

It is not that I do not feel that this distinction, which opinion authorises in vain, wounds my susceptibility; but how can mine complain when Valmont's susceptibility suffers even more? Do not think that he pardons or can console himself for this very fault which I forgive; and yet, how he has retrieved this little error by the excess of his love and of my happiness!

Either my felicity is greater or I am more conscious of its value since I feared I had lost it; in any case I can say that if I felt I had the strength to endure again distress as cruel as that I have just passed through, I should not think I was buying too dearly this increase of happiness I have since enjoyed. O! my tender mother, scold your inconsiderate daughter for having troubled you over-much by her hastiness; scold her for having judged rashly and calumniated him whom she ought never to have ceased to adore; but as you recognise that she is imprudent, see that she is happy, and increase her joy by sharing it.

Paris, 16th of November, 17—, in the evening.

## LETTER CXL

*The Vicomte de Valmont to the Marquise de Merteuil*

How does it happen, my fair friend, that I have had no answer from you ? Yet it seems to me that my last letter deserved a reply and, though I ought to have received it three days ago, I am still waiting for it ! I am vexed, to put it at the lowest ; so I shall not talk to you about my important affairs at all.

That the reconciliation had its full result ; that instead of reproaches and suspicion, it produced only new affection ; that I it was who received excuses and compensation due to my mistrusted candour ; of all this I will not say a word ; and, but for the unforeseen occurrence of last night, I should not write to you at all. But as this concerns your pupil and as she will probably not be in a position herself to inform you of it at least for some time, I have undertaken this task.

For reasons which you will guess, or which you will not guess, Madame de Tourvel has not occupied me so much for the last few days, and as these reasons could not exist with the Volanges girl, I became more assiduous with her. Thanks to the obliging porter, I had no obstacle to overcome ; and your pupil and I were leading a regular and convenient life. But habit leads to carelessness ; the first days we could not take too many precautions for our safety ; we trembled even behind bolts. Yesterday, an incredible carelessness caused the accident I am about to tell you ; and if, for myself, I escaped with nothing but the fright, it cost the little girl more dearly.

We were not asleep, but we were in the repose and abandonment which follow pleasure, when we heard the door of the room suddenly open. I leaped for my sword at once, both for my own defence and for that of our common pupil ; I advanced and saw nobody ; but the door was actually open. Since we had a light I investigated and found no living soul. Then I remembered that we had forgotten our usual precautions ; and doubtless the door had been only pushed to or partly closed and had opened of itself.

I returned to calm my timid companion, but did not find her in the bed ; she had fallen or had hidden herself between it and the wall ; in any case, she was lying there unconscious and with no movement but rather violent convulsions. Imagine my embarrassment ! However, I succeeded in getting her back to bed and in bringing her back to consciousness ; but she had hurt herself in her fall and very soon felt the results of it.

Pains in the loins, violent colics, still less uncertain symptoms soon enlightened me as to her condition ; but to tell her what it was I had first to inform her of the state she was in before, for she did not suspect it. Never perhaps until now has a girl kept so much innocence while doing so effectually everything necessary to get rid of it ! Oh ! She is not one to waste her time in reflection !

But she wasted a lot of time in lamenting and I felt something had to be done. I finally agreed with her that I would go at once to the Physician and the Surgeon of the family, that I would tell them to come to her and at the same time confide everything to them under the seal of secrecy; that she would ring for her waiting-woman; that she would or would not take the woman into her confidence, as she chose; but that she would send for assistance and especially forbid that Madame de Volanges should be awakened—a delicate and natural consideration on the part of a daughter who did not wish to cause her mother anxiety.

I carried out my two errands and two confessions as quickly as I could and then went home and have not since gone out; but the Surgeon, whom I knew before, came to me at midday to give me news of the invalid. I was not wrong; but he hopes that if no accident happens, nothing will be noticed in the house. The waiting-woman is in the secret; the Physician has given some name to the illness; and this affair will be arranged like a hundred others, unless it is afterwards useful to us to have it talked about.

But is there still any common interest between you and me? Your silence might make me think so; I should even have ceased to believe there was, if my desire for it did not make me seek all means of retaining hope of it.

Good-bye, my fair friend; I kiss you, with a grudge.

Paris, 21st of November, 17—.

## LETTER CXLI

*The Marquise de Merteuil to the Vicomte de Valmont*

Heavens, Vicomte, how you worry me with your obstinacy! What does my silence matter to you? Do you think that I keep silence because I lack reasons to defend myself? Ah! How much better it would be! But no, it is only that it is painful to me to tell them to you.

Tell me the truth; are you deluding yourself or are you trying to deceive me? The difference between your words and your actions leaves me no choice except between these two sentiments; which is the true one? What do you expect me to say to you when I do not know what to think myself?

You appear to make a great merit of your last scene with Madame de Tourvel; but what does it prove for your system or against mine? Assuredly I never told you that you loved the woman enough not to be unfaithful to her, not to seize all opportunities which might appear pleasant or easy; I even felt that it would be almost the same to you to satisfy with another woman, the first who came to hand, the very desires which she alone could create; and I am not surprised that, from a libertinage of mind which it would be wrong to deny you, you should have once done from design what you have done on a thousand other occasions from opportunity. Who does not know that it is the mere run of the world and the custom of all of you from the scoundrel to the "creatures[1]"! He who abstains from it today is considered romantic; and I do not think that is the fault I blame you for.

But what I said, what I thought, what I still think, is that you are none the less in love with your Madame de Tourvel; not indeed with a very pure or very tender love, but with the kind of love you can feel; the kind of love, for example, which makes you think a woman possesses the charms or qualities she does not possess, which puts her in a class apart and ranks all others in a second order, which holds you still to her even when you insult her; such a love in fact as I suppose a Sultan might feel for a favourite Sultana, which does not prevent his often preferring a mere odalisque to her. My comparison seems to me all the more accurate because, like a Sultan, you are never a woman's lover or friend, but always her tyrant or her slave. So I am quite sure you humiliated yourself, degraded yourself, to return to this fair creature's good graces! And you were but too happy to have succeeded, so that as soon as you thought the moment had come to obtain your forgiveness, you left me "for this great event."

Even in your last letter, if you do not speak to me wholly of this woman it is because you do not want to tell me anything of "your important affairs"; they seem to you so important that to be silent about them appears to you a kind of punishment to me. And after a thousand proofs of your decided preference for another, you ask me calmly if there is still "a common interest between you and me!" Be careful, Vicomte! If I once reply, my answer will be irrevocable; and to fear to do so now, is perhaps already to say too much. So I absolutely will not speak of it.

All I can do is to tell you a story. Perhaps you will not have time to read it or time to give it enough attention to understand it properly? It is for you to choose. At worse, it will only be a story wasted.

A man I know had entangled himself, like you, with a woman who did him very little honour. At intervals he had indeed the wit to see that sooner or later the adventure would do him harm; but although he blushed for it, he had not the courage to break away. His embarrassment was the greater because he had boasted to his friends that he was entirely free and he realised that one's ridiculousness increases in proportion as one denies it. Thus he passed his life, continually doing foolish things and continually saying afterwards: "It is not my fault." This man had a woman friend who was for a moment tempted to exhibit him to the public in this state of intoxication and thus to make his ridiculousness perpetual; but yet, more generous than malignant, or perhaps from some other motive, she wished to try one last means to be able in any event to say like her friend: "It is not my fault." She therefore sent him without any other remark the following letter, as a remedy whose application might be useful to his disease.

"One grows weary of everything, my angel, it is a law of Nature; it is not my fault.

[1] "Espèces"—eighteenth century polite slang.

" If therefore I am weary today of an adventure which has wholly preoccupied me for four mortal months, it is not my fault.

" If, for example, I had just as much love as you had virtue (and that is surely saying a lot) it is not astonishing that one should end at the same time as the other. It is not my fault

" From this it follows that for some time I have been deceiving you ; but then your pitiless affection forced me, as it were, to do so ! It is not my fault.

" Today, a woman I love madly insists that I sacrifice you to her. It is not my fault.

" I realise that this is a fine opportunity of crying out upon perjury ; but if Nature has only given men assurance, while she gave women obstinacy, it is not my fault.

" Take my advice, choose another lover, as I have chosen another mistress. This is good advice, very good ; if you think it bad, it is not my fault.

" Farewell, my angel, I took you with pleasure, I abandon you without regret ; perhaps I shall come back to you. So goes the world. It is not my fault."

This is not the moment, Vicomte, to tell you the result of this last effort and what followed upon it ; but I promise to tell you in my next letter. You will also find in it my " ultimatum " on the renewal of the treaty which you propose to me. Until then, good-bye and nothing more. . . .

By the way, thank you for your details about the Volanges girl ; it is a matter to reserve until the day after the marriage for the Scandal-monger's Gazette. Meanwhile, I send you my complimentary condolences on the loss of your posterity. Good night, Vicomte.

From the Château de . . ., 24th of November, 17—.

## LETTER CXLII

*The Vicomte de Valmont to Madame de Merteuil*

Faith, my fair friend, I am not sure whether I have mis-read or misunderstood your letter, the story you relate and the little epistolary model which accompanied it. What I can tell you is that the letter seemed to me original and likely to make an effect ; so I simply copied it out, and still more simply I sent it to the heavenly Madame de Tourvel. I did not waste a moment, for the tender missive was sent off yesterday evening. I preferred it thus, because first of all I had promised to write to her yesterday ; and then too because I thought she would not have too much time if she took all night to meditate and consider " this great event," even if you should a second time reproach me for that expression.

I hoped to be able to send you this morning my beloved's answer ; but it is nearly midday and I have not yet received anything. I shall wait until five o'clock ; and if I have no news then I shall go for them in person ; for especially in such proceedings it is only the first step which is troublesome.

As you may suppose, I am now very eager to learn the end of the story of the man you know who is so violently suspected of being unable to sacrifice a woman when necessary. Has he not reformed ? And will his generous woman friend not show him some favour ?

I am not less anxious to receive your " ultimatum," as you call it so politely ! Above all I am curious to know whether you will still see love in this latest step of mine. Ah ! No doubt, there is a great deal ! But for whom ? However, I do not mean to lay stress on anything, and I await everything from your goodness.

Farewell, my charming friend ; I shall not close this letter until two o'clock in the hope that I may be able to enclose the desired reply.

*Two o'clock in the afternoon.*

Still nothing, and I have no time ; I have not time to add a word ; but this time will you still refuse the tenderest kisses of love ?

Paris, 27th of November, 17—.

## LETTER CXLIII

*Madame de Tourvel to Madame de Rosemonde*

The veil is torn, Madame, the veil upon which was painted the illusion of my happiness. The disastrous truth enlightens me and allows me to see nothing but a certain and near death, the path to which is laid between shame and remorse. I shall follow it. . . . I shall cherish my tortures if they shorten my existence. I send you the letter I received yesterday ; I will add no reflections upon it, they are carried in it. It is no longer the time to complain ; there is nothing to do but suffer. It is not pity I need, but strength.

Receive, Madame, the only farewell I shall make and grant my last prayer ; it is to leave me to my fate, to forget me entirely, to feel as if I were no longer on the earth. There is a limit in misery after which friendship itself increases our sufferings and cannot heal them. When wounds are mortal all aid becomes inhuman. Every feeling but that of despair is foreign to me. Nothing now can befit me save the profound night where I go to bury my shame. There I shall weep my errors, if I can still weep ! Since yesterday I have not shed a tear. My broken heart grants me none.

Farewell, Madame. Do not reply to me. I have sworn upon that cruel letter never to receive another.

Paris, 27th of November, 17—.

## LETTER CXLIV

*The Vicomte de Valmont to the Marquise de Merteuil*

Yesterday, at three o'clock in the afternoon, growing impatient at receiving no news, I presented myself at the house of the abandoned fair one; I was told she had gone out. In this phrase I only saw a refusal to receive me which neither vexed nor surprised me; and I left in the hope that this step would at least force so polite a woman to honour me with a word of reply. My desire to receive it made me return home expressly about nine o'clock, and I found nothing. Surprised by this silence, which I did not expect, I ordered my servant to collect information and to find out if the affectionate creature were dead or dying. At length, when I returned, he informed me that Madame de Tourvel had indeed gone out at eleven o'clock in the morning, that she had driven to the Convent of . . ., and that at seven o'clock in the evening she had sent back her carriage and her servants, with the message that she was not to be expected home. Certainly, she is doing the right thing. The convent is the proper refuge for a widow; and if she persists in so praiseworthy a resolution I shall add to all the obligations I already owe her that of the celebrity which will follow this adventure.

Some time ago I told you that, in spite of your anxieties, I should only reappear on the world's stage shining with a new lustre. Now let those malignant critics who accused me of a romantic and unlucky love show themselves, let them break off with more rapidity and brilliance; but no, let them do better, let them present themselves as consolers, the way is marked out for them. Well! Let them only attempt the course I have run through completely, and if one of them obtains the least success, I yield him first place. But they will all find that when I give my attention to it, the impression I leave is ineffaceable. Ah! This one will certainly be so; and I should count all my other triumphs as nothing, if ever I should have a rival preferred by this woman.

The course I have adopted flatters my self-love, I admit; but I am sorry she found sufficient strength to separate herself from me so completely. There will then be obstacles between us other than those I have placed there myself! What! If I wished to return to her, she would be in a position not to allow it; what am I saying? not to desire it, no longer to make it her supreme happiness! Is that the way to love? And do you think, my fair friend, that I ought to endure it? For example, am I not able, and would it not be better, to bring the woman back to the point of foreseeing the possibility of a reconciliation, which people always desire as long as they hope? I might attempt this without attaching any importance to it, and consequently without offending you. On the contrary! It would be a mere attempt which we would make together; and even if I should succeed, it would only be one way more of repeating at your will a sacrifice which seems to be pleasing to you. And now, my fair friend, I still have to receive the reward and all my wishes are for your return. Come back quickly and find once more your lover, your pleasures, your friends, and the regular course of adventures.

The Volanges girl's adventure has turned out excellently. Yesterday, when my anxiety did not allow me to stay anywhere, I went among other expeditions to call on Madame de Volanges. I found your pupil already in the drawing-room, still in her invalid's dress, but in full convalescence, and only the fresher and more attractive for it. In a similar case you women would remain a month on your sofas; faith, long live girls! Really she made me want to find out if her cure is complete.

I have still to tell you that the little girl's accident almost drove your "sentimental" Danceny mad. First, it was with grief; then, it was with joy. "His Cécile" was ill! You can guess how he lost his head in such a misfortune. Three times a day he sent for news and did not let a day pass without calling himself; finally he sent a handsome letter to the Mamma asking permission to come and congratulate her on the convalescence of so dear an object, and Madame de Volanges consented; so that I found the young man installed there as of old, except for a little familiarity which he dared not yet take.

It is from him that I learned these details; for I left at the same time as he did and I made him chatter. You have no idea of the effect this visit made upon him. It is impossible to describe his joy, his desires, his transports. I like these great emotions and made him lose his head entirely by assuring him that in a very few days I would enable him to see his fair one still more intimately.

In fact, I have decided to hand her back to him as soon as I have made my experiment. I want to devote myself entirely to you; and then would it be worth while for your pupil to be mine also if she were to be unfaithful only to her husband? The master-stroke is to be unfaithful to her lover and particularly to her first lover! For I cannot reproach myself with having uttered the word love to her.

Good-bye, my fair friend; return as quickly as possible to enjoy your power over me, to accept my submission, and to give me its reward.

Paris, 28th of November, 17—.

## LETTER CXLV

*The Marquise de Merteuil to the Vicomte de Valmont*

Seriously, Vicomte, you have deserted Madame de Tourvel? You sent her the letter I composed for her! Really, you are charming, and you have surpassed my expectation! I admit freely that this triumph flatters me more than all those I have obtained up till now. You will perhaps think I value this woman very highly after having formerly rated her so low; not at all; I have not obtained this advantage over her, but over you; that is the amusing thing and it is really delicious.

Yes, Vicomte, you loved Madame de Tourvel very much and you still love her; you love her like a madman; but because I amused myself by making you ashamed of it, you have bravely sacrificed her. You would have sacrificed a thousand rather than endure one jest.

Where vanity will take us! The wise man is indeed right when he says that it is the enemy of happiness.

Where would you be now if I had wanted to do more than play you a trick? But I am incapable of deceiving, as you well know; and even if you should reduce me in turn to despair and a convent, I will run the risk and yield to my conqueror.

Yet if I capitulate, it is from the merest weakness; for, if I wanted, how many cavils I should still have to raise! And perhaps you would deserve them? For example, I marvel at the skill or clumsiness with which you calmly propose that I should let you patch things up with Madame de Tourvel. It would suit you very well, would it not, to take the credit for breaking off without losing the pleasures of possession? And as this apparent sacrifice would no longer be one for you, you make me an offer to repeat it at my will! But this arrangement the heavenly devotee would still think herself the one choice of your heart, while I should pride myself upon being the preferred rival; we should both be deceived, but you would be pleased, and what matters the rest?

It is a pity that with so much talent for planning you have so little for execution; and that by one unconsidered step you have placed an invincible obstacle between you and what you most desire.

What! You think of making things up and you could have written that letter I sent! You must have thought me very clumsy in my turn! Ah! Believe me, Vicomte, when a woman strikes at another woman's heart, she rarely fails to find the sensitive place, and the wound is incurable. When I struck her, or rather when I guided your blows, I did not forget that this woman was my rival, that for a moment you had thought her preferable to me and, in short, that you had placed me beneath her. If I am deceived in my vengeance, I consent to put up with the mistake. So, I agree to your trying every means; I even invite you to do so and promise not to be angry at your success, if you manage to obtain any. I am so much at ease upon this matter, that I shall not concern myself with it further. Let us speak of other things.

For example, the Volanges girl's health. You will give me precise news of it on my return, will you not? I shall be very glad to have it. After that, it is for you to judge whether it suits you better to hand the little girl back to her lover, or to try to become a second time the founder of a new branch of the Valmonts, under the name of Gercourt. This idea seemed rather amusing to me and, while I leave the choice to you, I still request you not to make up your mind definitely until we have talked it over together. This is not putting you off for an indefinite time, because I shall be back in Paris immediately. I cannot tell you which day positively, but be certain that you shall be the first to be informed of my arrival.

Good-bye, Vicomte; in spite of my quarrels, my tricks, and my reproaches, I still love you very much and I am preparing to prove it to you. Until we meet, my friend.

From the Château de . . ., 29th of November, 17—.

## LETTER CXLVI

*The Marquise de Merteuil to the Chevalier Danceny*

At last I am leaving here, my young friend, and tomorrow evening I shall be back in Paris. In the midst of all the confusion which a journey brings with it I shall receive no one. However, if you have any very urgent confidence to make me, I will except you from the general rule ; but I shall except no one else ; so I beg you to keep my arrival a secret. Even Valmont will not know it.

If anyone had told me a little time ago that you would soon have my complete confidence, I should not have believed it. But yours has impelled mine. I should be tempted to think that you had put adroitness into it, perhaps even seduction. That would be very wrong, at the least ! But it would not be dangerous now ; you have indeed other things to do ! When the heroine is on the stage nobody cares about the confidant.

So you have had no time to inform me of your new successes ? When your Cécile was away, the days were not long enough to listen to your tender complaints. You would have made them to the echoes, if I had not been there to hear them. When later she was ill, you still even honoured me with an account of your anxieties ; you needed someone to tell them to. But now that she whom you love is in Paris, that she is well, and especially since you see her sometimes, she suffices for everything and your friends are now nothing to you.

I do not blame you ; it is the fault of your youth. Do we not know that from Alcibiades down to you, young people have never wanted friendship except in their troubles ? Happiness sometimes makes them indiscreet but never confiding. I will say with Socrates : " I like my friends to come to me when they are unhappy " ; but as he was a philosopher, he could get on without them when they did not come. In that respect, I am not quite so wise as he, and I felt your silence with all a woman's weakness.

But do not think me exacting ; I am far from being that ! The same feeling which makes me notice these deprivations makes me endure them with courage, when they are the proof or the cause of my friend's happiness. I do not count upon seeing you tomorrow evening then, unless love leaves you free and unoccupied, and I forbid you to make me the least sacrifice.

Good-bye, Chevalier ; it will be a great delight to me to see you again ; will you come ?

From the Château de . . ., 29th of November, 17—.

## LETTER CXLVII

*Madame de Volanges to Madame de Rosemonde*

You will certainly be as distressed as I am, my excellent friend, when you hear of Madame de Tourvel's condition ; she has been ill since yesterday; her illness came upon her suddenly and shows such grave symptoms that I am really alarmed.

A burning fever, a violent and almost continual delirium, a thirst which nothing can quench, are all that can be observed. The doctors say they cannot yet prognosticate anything, and the treatment will be the more difficult because the invalid obstinately refuses any assistance whatever, to such an extent that she had to be held down by main force to be bled; and twice afterwards force has had to be used to replace her bandage which in her delirium she kept wanting to tear off.

You who saw her, as I did, so delicate, so timid, and so gentle, can you imagine that four persons could hardly restrain her and that she becomes inexpressibly furious if one attempts to point anything out to her? For my part, I am afraid it is something more than delirium and that it is a real mental alienation.

What happened yesterday increases my fears in this respect.

On that day she arrived at the Convent of . . . at eleven o'clock in the morning with her waiting-woman. Since she was brought up in that house and has the habit of going to it sometimes, she was received in the usual way, and appeared calm and well to everybody. About two hours later she enquired if the room she occupied as a schoolgirl was vacant, and when she was told it was, she asked to see it again; the Prioress accompanied her with several other nuns. She then declared that she had come back to live in this room which (she said) she ought never to have left; and she added that she would only leave it "for death"; that was her expression.

At first they did not know what to say; but after their first astonishment, they pointed out that as she was a married woman she could not be received there without a special permission. This reason and a thousand others had no effect on her; from that moment she persisted not only that she would not leave the convent but even her room. Finally, growing weary of the discussion, at seven o'clock in the evening they consented that she should spend the night there. They sent away her carriage and her servants and put off taking any steps until the next day.

I am assured that during the whole evening her air and behaviour had nothing disordered about them, both were composed and thoughtful; only, four or five times she fell into a reverie so profound that each time she could not be drawn out of it by being spoken to; and each time, before coming out of it, she lifted both hands to her head which she appeared to clasp tightly; whereupon one of the nuns who were present asked her if she were suffering in her head and she gazed at her a long time before answering, saying at last: "The pain is not there." A moment later she asked to be left alone and requested that she should be asked no more questions.

Everyone retired, except her waiting-woman, who luckily was to sleep in the same room, from lack of other accommodation.

According to the girl's account, her mistress was quite calm until eleven o'clock at night. She then said she wished to go to bed; but, before she was entirely undressed, she began to walk up and down her room with a great deal of motion and frequent gestures. Julie, who had been a witness of what had happened during the day, did not dare say anything to her, and waited in silence for nearly an hour. At last, Madame de Tourvel called twice in quick succession; she had barely time to rush forward when her mistress fell into her arms, saying: "I am exhausted." She let herself be guided to her bed, would not take anything nor allow any assistance to be sent for. She simply had water placed beside her and ordered Julie to go to bed.

Julie declares that she did not go to sleep until two o'clock and that during that time she heard neither movement nor complaints. But she says she was awakened at five o'clock by her mistress' speaking in a loud voice, that she then asked if she needed anything and, obtaining no reply, found a light and took it to Madame de Tourvel's bed but Madame de Tourvel did not recognise her and, suddenly breaking off the incoherent words she was saying, exclaimed: "Let me be left alone, let me be left in darkness; it is darkness which befits me." I have myself noticed today that she often repeats this phrase.

Julie made this apparent order an excuse to go for other people and help, but Madame de Tourvel refused both with the wildness and delirium which have returned to her so often since.

The difficulty in which the whole convent was placed by this determined the Prioress to send for me at seven o'clock in the morning. . . . It was not yet daylight. I hastened thither at once. When I was announced to Madame de Tourvel, she seemed to regain consciousness and replied: "Ah! Yes, let her come in." But when I went up close to her bed, she gazed steadfastly at me, took my hand quickly and pressed it, and said to me in a clear but melancholy voice: "I am dying because I did not trust in you." Immediately afterwards she hid her eyes and returned to her most frequent expression: "Let me be left alone, etc."; and she lost all consciousness.

This remark she made me and some others which escaped her in delirium make me fear this cruel illness has a still more cruel cause. But we must respect our friend's secret and content ourselves with pitying her misfortune.

The whole of yesterday was equally stormy, and was divided between outbursts of terrifying delirium and moments of swooning exhaustion, the only moments when she takes any rest. I did not leave her bed-side until nine o'clock at night and I am returning there this morning to spend the day. I shall assuredly not abandon my unhappy friend; but what is distressing is her persistence in refusing all attention and help.

I send you last night's bulletin which I have just received; as you will see, it is the reverse of consoling. I shall be careful to send them all to you.

Good-bye, my excellent friend, I must now go to the invalid. My daughter, who is happily nearly well again, presents her respects to you.

*Paris, 29th of November, 17—.*

## LETTER CXLVIII

*The Chevalier Danceny to the Marquise de Merteuil*

O you whom I love! O you whom I adore! O you who began my happiness! O you who completed it! Sensitive friend, tender lover, why does the memory of your pain come to trouble the charm I feel? Ah! Madame, compose yourself, it is friendship that asks this of you. O my friend! Be happy, that is the prayer of love.

Ah! What reproaches have you to make yourself? Believe me, your susceptibility misleads you. The regrets it causes you, the faults of which it accuses me, are equally illusory; and I feel in my heart that there has been no other seducer between us but love. Fear no longer to give yourself up to the feelings which you inspire, to let yourself be imbued with all the passions you create. What! Can our hearts be less pure because they were late enlightened? No, indeed. On the contrary, it is seduction, which, never acting except from design, can organise its advance and its methods and foresee events from afar. But true love does not allow us to meditate and reflect thus; it diverts us from our thoughts by our feelings; its power is never stronger than when it is unknown; and it is in silence that love binds us by ties which it is equally impossible to perceive and to break.

Thus, even yesterday, in spite of the keen emotion caused me by the idea of your return, in spite of the extreme pleasure I felt in seeing you again, I still thought I was called and guided by friendship alone; or rather, I was so entirely given up to the soft feelings of my heart that I gave very little attention to distinguishing their origin or cause. Like me, my tender friend, you felt without realising it that despotic charm which delivered up our souls to the sweet influences of affection; and we both only recognised love when we emerged from the ecstasy into which God had plunged us.

But that alone justifies us instead of condemning us. No, you have not betrayed friendship, neither have I abused your trust. It is true we were both in ignorance of our feelings; but we experienced the illusion only, we did not try to create it. Ah! We should not complain of it, we should only think of the happiness it gives us; let us not disturb it by unjust reproaches, let us concern ourselves with increasing it even more by the charm of trust and confidence. O! My friend! How precious that hope is to my heart! Yes, henceforth freed from all fear and entirely given up to love, you will share my desires, my transports, the delirium of my senses, the ecstasy of my soul; and every moment of our happy days will be marked by a new pleasure.

Farewell, you whom I adore! I shall see you this evening, but shall I find you alone? I dare not hope it. Ah! You do not desire it as much as I.

Paris, 1st of December, 17—.

## LETTER CXLIX

*Madame de Volanges to Madame de Rosemonde*

I hoped almost all day yesterday, my excellent friend, that I should be able to give you this morning more favourable news of our dear invalid's health; but after yesterday evening that hope has vanished and I have nothing left but the regret of losing it. An occurrence, quite unimportant in appearance, but very cruel from the results it has had, rendered the invalid's condition at least as unfavourable as it was before, if it has not made it worse.

I should have understood nothing of this sudden change, had I not yesterday received our unhappy friend's complete confidence. Since she did not conceal from me that you are also informed of all her misfortunes, I can speak to you without reserve about her sad situation.

Yesterday morning, when I reached the convent, I was told that the invalid had been asleep for more than three hours, and her sleep was so profound and so calm that for a time they were afraid it was a swoon. Some time later she awoke and herself drew the bed-curtains. She looked at us with an air of surprise, and, as I got up to go to her, she recognised me, called me by name, and asked me to come to her. She left me no time to put any question to her, but asked me where she was, what she was doing there, if she were ill, and why she was not at home. At first I thought this was a new attack of delirium, of a calmer kind than the others; but I noticed that she quite understood my replies. She had indeed recovered her reason, but not her memory.

She questioned me in great detail about everything which had happened to her since she had been at the convent, to which she did not remember coming. I answered her truthfully, only suppressing what I thought might frighten her too much; and when in turn I asked her how she felt, she replied that she was not in any pain at the moment, but that she had been very harassed in her sleep and that she felt tired. I urged her to compose herself and not to speak much; after which, I partly closed the curtains, leaving them a little apart, and sat down at her bed-side. At the same time she was offered some soup, which she accepted and enjoyed.

She remained in this state for about half an hour, during which she only spoke to thank me for the care I had taken of her; and she put into her thanks the charm and grace which you will remember she had. After this, she remained absolutely silent for some time and then broke her silence by saying: "Ah! yes, I remember coming here," and a moment afterwards she exclaimed sorrowfully: "My friend, my friend, pity me; I have recovered all my miseries." As I then went towards her, she seized my hand, leaned her head against it, and went on: "Great Heaven! Why can I not die?" Her look, even more than her words, moved me to tears; she noticed them from my voice and said: "You pity me! Ah! If you knew!" . . . And then she interrupted herself: "Let us be left alone, I will tell you everything."

As I think I hinted to you, I had already some suspicions of what the subject of this confidence might be; and as I feared that this conversation (which I foresaw would be long and sad) might perhaps be harmful to our friend's condition, I refused at first, on the pretext that she needed rest; but she insisted and I yielded to her request. As soon as we were alone, she told me everything which you have heard from her, for which reason I shall not repeat it to you.

At last, when she was speaking to me of the cruel way in which she had been sacrificed, she added: "I thought I was quite certain to die of it, and I had the courage to do so; but what is impossible to me is to survive my misery and my shame." I tried to combat this discouragement or rather this despair with the weapons of religion, hitherto so powerful over her; but I soon felt I had not strength enough for these august functions, and I limited myself to proposing that Father Anselme should be sent for, since I know he has her entire confidence. She consented and even seemed to wish it greatly. He was sent for and came at once. He remained for a very long time with the invalid and, on coming out, said that if the doctors were of the same opinion he thought that the ceremony of the sacraments might be postponed, and that he would return the next day.

It was then about three o'clock in the afternoon, and until five our friend was fairly composed, to such an extent that we had all regained hope. Unfortunately, a letter was then brought to her. When they tried to give it to her, she said at first that she would receive none, and nobody insisted. But from that moment she appeared more agitated. Very soon afterwards she asked where this letter came from. It was not stamped. Who had brought it? Nobody knew. On whose behalf it had been delivered? The door-keepers had not been told. She then remained silent for some time; after which she began to speak, but her disconnected words only showed us that the delirium had returned.

However, there was again an interval of calm, until at length she asked to be given the letter which had been brought for her. As soon as she looked at it, she exclaimed: "From him! Great Heaven!" And then in a weaker voice: "Take it away, take it away." She had the bed-curtains closed at once and forbade anyone to approach; but almost immediately afterwards we were compelled to return to her. The delirium had returned with more violence than ever and it was accompanied by truly frightful convulsions. These symptoms did not cease all evening, and this morning's bulletin informs me that the night has been no less stormy. In short, she is in such a condition that I am surprised she has not already succumbed to it, and I will not conceal from you that I have very little hope remaining.

I suppose this unfortunate letter is from M. de Valmont; but what can he dare say to her now? Forgive me, my dear friend, I restrain myself from any remarks ; but it is very cruel to see perish so cruelly a woman until now so happy and so worthy of being so.

Paris, 2nd of December, 17—.

## LETTER CL

*The Chevalier Danceny to the Marquise de Merteuil*

While awaiting the pleasure of seeing you, my tender friend, I abandon myself to the pleasure of writing to you ; and I charm away the regret of being absent from you by occupying myself with you. It is a true delight to my heart to trace my feelings, to remember yours ; and in this way the very time of deprivation still offers a thousand precious treasures to my love. Yet, if I am to believe you, I shall obtain no reply from you ; this very letter will be the last and we shall deprive ourselves of a familiar intercourse which, in your opinion, is dangerous and " unnecessary to us." Assuredly I shall believe you, if you persist ; for what is there you can wish that I should not also wish for that very reason ? But before you decide finally, will you not allow us to discuss it together ?

You alone must judge the matter of danger ; I can calculate nothing and limit myself to begging you to take care of your safety, for I cannot be calm if you are anxious. In this respect, it is not we two who are one, it is you who are both of us.

It is not the same " about the necessity " ; here we can only have the same thought ; and if we differ in opinion, it can only be from lack of explaining ourselves or of understanding each other. This is what I think I feel.

Doubtless, a letter appears not very necessary when we can see each other freely. What can it say which a word, a look, or even silence do not express a hundred times better ? This seemed so true to me that when you spoke to me of not writing any longer, the idea glided easily over my soul ; perhaps the idea incommoded it, but did not make an effect on it. It was much the same as when I wish to set a kiss upon your heart and meet a ribbon or a gauze—I merely put it aside and yet do not feel there was an obstacle.

But since then, we have separated ; and as soon as you were no longer present, the idea of letters returned to torment me. Why, I asked myself, this additional privation ? What ! Because we are apart, have we nothing more to say to each other ? I will suppose that we are favoured by circumstances and that we spend a whole day together ; must we take time to talk from that of enjoyment ? Yes, of enjoyment, my tender friend ; for beside you even moments of rest still provide delicious enjoyment. But at last, whatever the time may be, we end by separating ; and then one is so lonely ! It is then that a letter is so precious ; if one does not read it, at least one looks at it. . . . Ah ! Certainly, one can look at a letter without reading it, as it seems to me that at night I should still have some pleasure in touching your portrait. . . .

Your portrait, did I say ? But a letter is the soul's portrait. It is not like a cold image, with its stagnation, so remote from love ; it lends itself to all our emotions ; turn by turn it grows animated, it enjoys, it rests. . . . Your feelings are all so precious to me—will you deprive me of the means of collecting them ?

Are you then certain that the necessity for writing will never torment you ? If in solitude your heart dilates or is oppressed, if an emotion of joy passes to your soul, if an involuntary sadness should trouble it for a moment, would you not pour out your happiness or your grief in the bosom of your friend ? Will you have a feeling which he does not share ? Will you then leave him to wander dreamily and in solitude far from you ? My friend . . . my tender friend ! But it is for you to decide. I only wished to argue, not to seduce you ; I have given you only reasons, I dare to think that I should have been more potent by using entreaties. I you persist, I shall try not to be afflicted ; I shall make efforts to say to myself what you would have written me ; but there ! you would say it better than I and I should above all take more pleasure in hearing it.

Good-bye, my charming friend ; the hour at last approaches when I can see you ; I leave you hastily to come to meet you the sooner.

Paris, 3rd of December, 17—.

## LETTER CLI

*The Vicomte de Valmont to the Marquise de Merteuil*

No doubt, Marquise, you do not think me so little experienced as to believe that I could be deceived about the private conversation I found you in, and about "the extraordinary chance" which brought Danceny to your house ! Your practised face was indeed able to take on marvellously the expression of calm and serenity and you betrayed yourself by none of those phrases which sometimes escape owing to disorder or regret. I even agree that your docile looks served you perfectly and that if they could have made themselves believed as easily as they made themselves understood, I should have been far from feeling or retaining the least suspicion and should not have doubted one moment the extreme annoyance caused you by "this importunate third party." But, if you do not want to display such great talents in vain, if you wish to obtain the success you count on, if you wish to produce the illusion you tried to create, you must first of all train your novice of a lover with more care.

Since you are beginning to take charge of educations, teach your pupils not to blush and grow disconcerted at the least pleasantry, not to deny so vehemently about one woman the same things they deny so languidly about all others. Teach them also to be able to hear their mistress praised without thinking themselves obliged to do the honours of it; and, if you allow them to gaze at you in company, let them at least know beforehand how to disguise that look of possession which is so easily recognised and which they so clumsily confuse with the gaze of love. Then you can let them appear in your public exercises without their conduct doing any harm to their modest schoolmistress; and I myself, but too happy to contribute towards your celebrity, promise you to make and publish the programmes of this new college.

But I must admit I am surprised that you should have tried to treat me like a schoolboy. Oh! How soon I should be avenged with any other woman! With what pleasure I should do so! And how easily it would surpass the pleasure she would think she had made me miss! Yes, it is indeed with you alone that I can prefer reparation to vengeance; and do not think I am restrained by the least doubt, by the least uncertainty; I know everything.

You have been four days in Paris; and each day you have seen Danceny and you have seen him alone. Today even, your door was still shut; and to prevent my coming in upon you, your porter only lacked an assurance equal to your own. But you wrote me that I should be the first to be informed of your arrival, of this arrival whose date you could not tell me, though you wrote to me on the eve of your departure. Will you deny these facts or will you try to excuse yourself? Either is equally impossible; and yet I still restrain myself! See then your power; but, take my advice, be content with having tested it and do not abuse it any longer. We both know each other, Marquise; that ought to be enough for you.

You are going out all day tomorrow you said? Very good, if you do really go; and you will realise that I shall know it. But then, you will come back in the evening; and to effect our difficult reconciliation we shall not have too much time between then and the next morning. Let me know if we are to make our numerous and mutual atonements at your house or "at the other." Above all, no more Danceny. Your silly head was filled with the idea of him and it is possible for me not to be jealous of this delirium of your imagination; but remember that from this moment on, what was merely a fancy would become a marked preference. I do not think I was made for that humiliation and I do not expect to receive it from you.

I even hope that this sacrifice will not appear to be one to you. But even if it cost you something, I think I have given you quite a good example! I think a beautiful and sensitive woman, who only lived for me, who at this very moment is perhaps dying of love and regret, is well worth a schoolboy who (if you like) lacks neither face nor wit, but who so far has neither experience nor stability.

Good-bye, Marquise; I say nothing of my feelings for you. All I can do at this moment is not to scrutinise my heart. I await your reply. When you make it, remember, remember carefully that the more easy it is for you to make me forget the offence you have given me, the more a refusal on your part, a mere delay, would engrave it upon my heart in permanent characters.

Paris, 3rd of December, 17—.

## LETTER CLII

*The Marquise de Merteuil to the Vicomte de Valmont*

Pray be careful, Vicomte, and treat my extreme timidity with more caution! How do you expect me to endure the crushing idea of incurring your indignation and, especially, not to succumb to the fear of your vengeance? The more so, since, as you know, if you do anything cruel to me it would be impossible for me to revenge it! Whatever I said, your existence would not be less brilliant or less peaceful. After all, what would you have to fear? To be obliged to leave the country—if you were given time to do so! But do not people live abroad as they do here? After all, provided the Court of France left you in peace at the foreign court you resided at, it would only mean for you that you had changed the scene of your triumphs. After this attempt to make you cool again with these moral considerations, let me come back to our affairs.

Do you know why I never remarried, Vicomte? It was certainly not because I could not find advantageous matches; it was solely because I would not allow anyone the right to criticise my actions. I am not even afraid of being unable to carry out my wishes, for I should always have achieved that at length; but it would have annoyed me if there had been anyone who had the right even to complain of them; in short, I wanted to deceive only for my pleasure, not from necessity. And then you write the most marital letter one could ever behold! You speak to me of nothing but wrongs on my side and forgiveness on yours! But how can one fail a person to whom one owes nothing? I cannot conceive how!

Come, what is it all about? You found Danceny at my house and it displeased you? Very well; but what could you deduce from this? Either that it was the result of chance, as I told you; or the result of my wish, as I did not tell you. In the first case, your letter is unjust; in the second, it is ridiculous; it was not worth the trouble of writing! But you are jealous and jealousy does not reason. Well! I will reason for you.

Either you have a rival or you have not. If you have one, you must please if you wish to be preferred to him; if you have not a rival, you must still please in order to avoid having one. In either case, you have the same line of conduct to follow; so, why torment yourself? Why, especially, torment me? Are you now unable to be the more charming of the two? Are you no longer sure of your successes? Come, Vicomte, you wrong yourself. But, it is not that; for your own sake I do not want you to give yourself so much trouble. You want my favours less than you want to abuse your power. Ah, you are ungrateful! There! I believe that is sentiment! And if I went on a little further this letter might become very tender; but you do not deserve it.

You do not deserve either that I should justify myself. To punish you for your suspicions; you shall keep them; so I shall say nothing about the date of my return or about Danceny's visits. You gave yourself a lot of trouble to obtain information about it, did you not? Well, are you any better off? I hope you found a great deal of pleasure in it; for my part, it did no harm to my pleasure.

All I can say in answer to your threatening letter, then, is that it has neither the gift of pleasing me nor the power of intimidating me; and that at the moment I could not be less disposed to grant your demands.

To accept you as you show yourself today would positively be showing you a real infidelity. It would not be returning to my former lover; it would be taking a new one who is far from being worth the other. I have not so far forgotten the first as to deceive myself thus. The Valmont I loved was charming. I will even admit that I have not met a more delightful man. Ah! I beg you, Vicomte, to bring him to me if you meet him; he will always be well received.

But warn him that in any case it cannot be today or tomorrow. His twin-brother has done him a little harm; and if he pressed me too much I should be afraid of making a mistake; or perhaps I have made arrangements with Danceny for those two days? And your letter informs me that you do not joke when someone breaks his word. So you see what you have to expect.

But what does it matter to you? You can always avenge yourself on your rival. He will do nothing worse to your mistress than you do to his, and, after all, is not one woman worth as much as another? They are your own principles. Even she who is "tender and sensitive, who only lived for you, and who would die at last of love and regret" would none the less be sacrificed to the first fancy, to the fear of being laughed at for a moment; and you expect people to put themselves out for you! Ah! That is not just.

Good-bye, Vicomte; make yourself pleasant once more. Why, I ask nothing better than to think you charming; and as soon as I am sure of it, I promise to prove it to you. Positively I am too good.

Paris, 4th of December, 17—.

## LETTER CLIII

*The Vicomte de Valmont to the Marquise de Merteuil*

I answer your letter at once; I shall try to make myself clear, which is not easy with you when once you have made up your mind to misunderstand.

Long phrases were not necessary to show that, since each of us possesses all that is needed to ruin the other, we have an equal interest in treating each other with mutual consideration; so, that is not the question. But between the violent course of ruining each other and the obviously better course of remaining united as we have been, or becoming still more so by renewing our former affair—between these two courses, I say, there are a thousand others which might be adopted. It was therefore not ridiculous to tell you and is not ridiculous to repeat to you that from this day on I shall be either your lover or your enemy.

I am perfectly aware that this choice incommodes you; that you would much prefer to evade it; and I am not ignorant that you never liked to be placed between yes and no; but you must be aware also that I cannot let you out of this narrow circle, without running the risk of being tricked; and you ought to have foreseen that I would not endure that. It is for you to decide now; I can leave you the choice, but not remain in uncertainty.

I only warn you that you will not impose upon me with your reasons, good or bad; nor will you seduce me any the more by the few flatteries with which you attempt to dress up your refusals; in fact the moment has come to be frank. I ask nothing better than to give you an example of frankness and I tell you gladly that I prefer peace and union, but if one or the other must be broken, I think I have the right and the means.

I add to this that the least obstacle presented on your part will be taken on my part as a real declaration of war; you see that the reply I ask from you needs neither long nor fine phrases. A word will do.

Paris, 4th of December, 17—.

*The Marquise de Merteuil's reply, written at the end of the above letter:*

Very well! War.

## LETTER CLIV

### *Madame de Volanges to Madame de Rosemonde*

The bulletins will inform you better than I can do, my dear friend, of our poor invalid's unhappy condition. I am entirely occupied with the attention I give her and only take time to write to you when there are other events besides those of the illness. Here is one, which I certainly did not expect. It is a letter I received from M. de Valmont, who has been pleased to choose me as a confidant and even as a mediator between himself and Madame de Tourvel, for whom he enclosed a letter in the one to me. I sent back the one when I replied to the other. I send you the latter and I think you will be of my opinion, that I could not do and ought not to do what he asks me. Even if I had wanted to do it, our unfortunate friend is not in a state to understand me. Her delirium is continuous. But what do you say to this despair of M. de Valmont's? Is one to believe in it, or does he only want to deceive everyone and that until the end?[1] If he is sincere this time, he may well

[1] Monsieur de Valmont's letter has been suppressed because nothing could be found in the remainder of their correspondence to settle these questions. (C. de L.)

tell himself that he has made his own happiness. I think he will not be very pleased with my reply; but I confess that everything which fixes my attention on this unhappy adventure makes me more and more indignant with the author of it.

Good-bye, my dear friend; I am now going back to my sad duties, which become far more so from the little hope I have of their proving successful. You know my feelings for you.

Paris, 5th of December, 17—.

## LETTER CLV

### *The Vicomte de Valmont to the Chevalier Danceny*

I have twice been to your house, my dear Chevalier; but since you have abandoned your rôle of lover for that of a ladies' man it has become impossible to find you, as one might expect. Your man-servant tells me, however, that you come home at night; that he had orders to wait for you; but I, who know your projects, know very well that you only return for a moment, to adopt the custom of the thing, and that you immediately start again on your victorious career. Well and good; I can do nothing but applaud; but perhaps this evening you may be tempted to change its direction. You only know half your affairs yet; I must tell you about the other half and then you will decide. But take the time to read my letter. It will not distract you from your pleasures, since on the contrary its only object is to give you a choice between them.

If I had had your complete confidence, if I had learned from you that part of your secrets which you have left me to guess, I should have been informed in time; my zeal would have been less clumsy and would not impede your progress today. But let us start from the point where we are. Whatever course you adopt, the worst you do will make someone else happy.

You have a rendezvous for tonight, have you not? With a charming woman whom you adore? For at your age, what woman does one not adore, at least for the first week! The setting of the scene will add even more to your pleasures. A delicious "little house," "which has only been taken for you" will embellish the pleasure with the charms of liberty and of mystery. All is agreed; you are expected; and you are burning to go! That is what we both know, although you have told me nothing. Now, here is what you do not know, which I must tell you.

Since my return to Paris I have busied myself with the means of bringing you and Mademoiselle de Volanges together; I had promised it to you; and the very last time I spoke to you of it I had reason to think from your replies, I might say from your ecstasies, that I was busying myself with your happiness. I could not succeed unaided in this rather difficult enterprise; but after having prepared the means, I left the rest to the zeal of your young mistress. In her love she has found resources which were lacking to my experience; in short, your misfortune has willed it that she should succeed. She told me this evening that for the last two days all obstacles have been overcome and that your happiness only depends upon yourself.

For the last two days also she has been flattering herself that she would give you this news herself, and, in spite of her Mamma's absence, you would have been received; but you did not even call! And to tell you everything, the little person (either from caprice or reason) seemed to me a little annoyed by this lack of eagerness on your part. At all events, she succeeded in bringing me to her and made me promise to give you as soon as possible the letter I enclose with this. From her eagerness I would wager that it is concerned with a rendezvous for this evening. However that may be, I promised upon honour and friendship that you should have the tender missive today and I cannot and will not break my word.

And now, young man, what are you going to do? You are placed between coquetry and love, between pleasure and happiness; what will your choice be? If I were speaking to the Danceny of three months ago, even to the Danceny of a week ago, I should be certain of his heart and of what he would do; but the Danceny of today is snatched at by women, runs after adventures, and has become, as always happens, something of a scoundrel; will he prefer a very timid girl who has nothing on her side but her beauty, her innocence and her love to the charms of a perfectly "accustomed woman?"

For my part, my dear fellow, it seems to me that even with your new principles (which I confess are also mine to some extent) circumstances would make me decide for the young mistress. First, it is one more, and then there is the novelty and again the fear of losing the fruit of your exertions by neglecting to gather it; for, in this respect, it would really be a lost opportunity, especially for a first weakness; in such a case, it often needs only a moment of ill-humour, a jealous suspicion, even less, to frustrate the fairest triumph. Drowning virtue sometimes clutches at a straw and, once it has escaped, is on its guard and is not easily surprised.

What do you risk on the other side? Not even a breaking off; at most a quarrel where the pleasure of a reconciliation is purchased by a few attentions. What course can be taken by a woman who has already yielded, except that of indulgence? What would she gain by severity? The loss of her pleasures, with no profit to her pride.

If, as I suppose, you adopt the course of love (which also seems to me that of reason) I think it would be prudent not to send excuses about the missed rendezvous; let her simply wait for you; if you try to give a reason, she may be tempted to verify it. Women are curious and obstinate; everything might be discovered; as you know, I have just been an example of this myself. But if you leave hope, which will be supported by vanity, it will not be lost until long after the time for enquiries has past; then tomorrow you can choose the insurmountable obstacle which detained you; you can have been ill, dead if necessary, or anything else which might have reduced you to despair, and everything will be made up.

For the rest, whichever way you decide, I only ask you to let me know; and as I have no interest in the matter, I shall approve whatever you do. Good-bye, my dear friend.

I must just add that I regret Madame de Tourvel; I am in despair at being separated from her; I would pay with one half my life the happiness of devoting the other half to her. Ah! Believe me, we are only happy through love.

Paris, 5th of December, 17—.

## LETTER CLVI

### *Cécile Volanges to the Chevalier Danceny*

(Enclosed with the preceding letter)

How does it happen, my dear, that I have ceased to see you at a time when I have not ceased to desire it? Do you not want it any more as much as I? Ah! Now I am very sad! Sadder then when we were quite separated. The grief which I endured through others now comes to me from you, and that is much worse.

For some days Mamma has been out, as you know; and I hoped you would try to profit by this time of freedom; but you do not even think of me; I am very miserable! You told me so often that I did not love as much as you! I knew to the contrary, and this is the proof of it. If you had come to see me, you would have seen me; for I am not like you, I only think of what will unite us. You do not deserve that I should tell you anything of what I have arranged for it, which I took so much trouble about; but I love you too much and I want to see you too much to be able to prevent myself from telling you. And then, I shall see afterwards if you really love me!

I have so arranged it that the porter is on our side and he has promised me that every time you come, he will let you come in as if he did not see you; and we can rely on him, for he is a very honest man. The only other difficulty is that you must not let yourself be seen in the house; and that will be quite easy if you only come in the evening when there will be nothing at all to fear. For example, since Mamma has been away all day she has been going to bed at eleven o'clock each evening; so we should have plenty of time.

The porter says that when you want to come in this way, instead of knocking at the door, you must just tap on his window and he will let you in at once; you will easily find the little stairway and, as you cannot have any light, I will leave my bedroom door ajar which will give you a little light. You must be very careful not to make a noise, especially when passing the side door into Mamma's room. It does not matter about my waiting-woman's door, because she has promised me she will not wake up; and she is a very good girl! And it will be the same when you leave. Now, we shall see whether you will come.

Heaven, why does my heart beat so fast as I write to you ! Will some misfortune fall on me, or is it the hope of seeing you which so upsets me ! What I do feel is that I never loved you so much and never desired so much to tell you so. Come, my friend, my dear friend ; let me repeat to you a hundred times that I love you, that I adore you, that I shall never love anyone but you.

I found a way to let M. de Valmont know I had something to say to him ; and, as he is a very good friend, he will surely come tomorrow and I shall beg him to give you this letter at once. So I shall expect you tomorrow evening and you will not fail to come unless you want your Cécile to be very miserable.

Good-bye, my dear ; I kiss you with all my heart.

Paris, 4th of December, 17—, in the evening.

## LETTER CLVII

*The Chevalier Danceny to the Vicomte de Valmont*

Do not doubt either my heart or my actions, my dear Vicomte ; how could I resist a desire of my Cécile's ? Ah ! It is she, she only, whom I love, whom I shall love forever ! Her ingenuousness, her affection, have a charm for me, a charm from which I may have been weak enough to allow myself to be distracted, but which nothing will ever efface. I was engaged in another adventure, as it were without realising it, and often the memory of Cécile has troubled me in the most delightful pleasures ; and perhaps my heart never paid her truer tribute than at the very moment when I was unfaithful to her. But let us spare her susceptibility, my friend, and hide my errors from her ; not to deceive her, but to save her from distress. Cécile's happiness is my most ardent desire ; I should never forgive myself for a fault which cost her a tear.

I know I deserved your jest about what you call my new principles ; but you may believe me, I am not guided by them at this moment ; and tomorrow I am determined to prove it. I shall go and confess to her who caused my error and who has shared it ; I shall say to her : " Read in my heart ; it has the most tender friendship for you ; friendship united with desire is so like love ! . . . We have both been deceived ; but though I am liable to error I am incapable of bad faith." I know this woman friend of mine ; she is as honourable as she is indulgent ; she will do more than forgive me, she will approve of what I do. She has often reproached herself for betraying friendship ; her delicacy often frightened her love ; she is wiser than I and she will strengthen in my soul these useful fears which I rashly attempted to suppress in hers. I shall owe it to her that I am better, as I shall owe it to you that I am happier. O ! my friend, share my gratitude ! The idea that I owe my happiness to you increases its value.

Good-bye, my dear Vicomte. The excess of my joy does not prevent me from thinking of your troubles and sharing them. Why can I not be of use to you! Does Madame de Tourvel remain inexorable? I hear too she is very ill. Heavens, how I pity you! May she regain both health and indulgence and make you happy forever! These are the wishes of friendship; I dare to hope they will be granted by love.

I should like to talk longer with you; but time presses and perhaps Cécile is waiting for me already.

Paris, 5th of December, 17—.

## LETTER CLVIII

*The Vicomte de Valmont to the Marquise de Merteuil*

(First thing in the morning)

Well, Marquise, how are you after last night's pleasures? Are you not a little tired? Confess now, Danceny is charming! The young man performs prodigies! You did not expect that of him, did you? Come now, I estimate myself justly, such a rival deserved that I should be sacrificed to him. Seriously, he has many good qualities! But, especially how much love, constancy, delicacy! Ah! If you are ever loved by him as his Cécile is, you will have no rivals to fear; he proved it to you last night. Perhaps another woman by dint of coquetry might take him away from you for a moment—a young man never knows how to resist provocative advances—but, as you see, one word from the beloved person is sufficient to dissipate this illusion; so you have only to become that person to be perfectly happy.

Certainly, you will not make any mistake in the matter; you have too sure a tact for there to be any fear of this. But the friendship which unites us, as sincere on my part as it is well recompensed on yours, made me desire last night's proof for your sake; it is the work of my zeal; it succeeded; but, pray, no thanks, it is not worth the trouble; nothing could have been easier.

After all, what did it cost me? A slight sacrifice and a little skill. I consented to share with the young man his mistress's favours; but then he had quite as much right to them as I, and I cared so little for them! The letter sent him by the young person was dictated by me; but it was only to gain time, since we had a better use for it. As to the letter I sent with it—oh! it was nothing, practically nothing; a few friendly ideas to guide the new lover's choice; but upon honour, they were unnecessary; to tell you the truth, he did not hesitate a moment.

And then, in his candour, he is to come to you today to tell you everything; and that will certainly be a great pleasure for you! He will say to you: "Read in my heart"; he writes me this; and, as you see, that patches everything up. I hope that when you read what he wants in his heart you will perhaps also read that such young lovers have their dangers; and in addition that it is better to have me for a friend than an enemy.

Good-bye, Marquise, until the next occasion.

Paris, 6th of December, 17—.

## LETTER CLIX

*The Marquise de Merteuil to the Vicomte de Valmont*

(A note)

I do not like people who add paltry jokes to paltry proceedings; it is neither my way nor to my taste. When I have reason to complain of someone, I do not jest; I do something better; I avenge myself. However pleased with yourself you may be now, do not forget that this is not the first time you have congratulated yourself too soon and alone in the hope of a triumph which escapes you at the very moment you rejoice over it. Good-bye.

**Paris, 6th of December, 17—.**

## LETTER CLX

*Madame de Volanges to Madame de Rosemonde*

I am writing to you from the bedroom of your unfortunate friend, whose condition is still about the same. This afternoon there is to be a consultation of four doctors. Unhappily, as you know, this is more often a proof of danger than a means of aid.

It appears, however, that she recovered partial consciousness last night. The waiting-woman told me this morning that about midnight her mistress called her, desired to be left alone with her and dictated quite a long letter. Julie added that, while she was making the envelope, Madame de Tourvel's delirium returned, so that the girl did not learn to whom the letter was to be addressed. I was surprised at first that the letter itself was not enough to tell her; but on her replying that she was afraid of making a mistake and that her mistress had ordered her to send it at once, I took it upon myself to open the letter.

I found the enclosed writing, which indeed is not addressed to anyone but to too many. I think, however, that our unhappy friend at first wished to write to M. de Valmont; and that, without realising it, she yielded to the disorder of her ideas. However this may be, I felt that the letter ought not to be sent to anyone. I am forwarding it to you because you will see from it, better than I could tell you, what are the thoughts which occupy our invalid's head. As long as she remains so deeply affected I shall have hardly any hope. It is difficult for the body to regain health when the mind is so disordered.

Good-bye, my dear and excellent friend. I am glad that you are far away from the sad spectacle I have continually before my eyes.

**Paris, 6th of December, 17—.**

## LETTER CLXI

*Madame de Tourvel to . . . .*

(Dictated by her and written by her waiting-woman)

Cruel and malevolent being, will you never grow weary of persecuting me? Is it not enough for you that you have tormented me, degraded me, debased me, that you wish to ravish from me even the peace of the grave? What! In this dwelling place of darkness in which I have been forced by ignominy to bury myself, is pain without cessation, is hope unknown? I do not implore a mercy I do not deserve; I will suffer without complaint if my sufferings do not exceed my strength. But do not make my tortures unendurable. Leave me my grief, but take from me the cruel memory of the treasures I have lost. When it is you who ravished them from me, do not again draw their agonising image before my eyes. I was innocent and at peace; it is because I saw you that I have lost my peace of mind; it is by listening to you that I became criminal. You are the author of my sins; what right have you to punish them?

Where are the friends who cherished me, where are they? My misfortune terrifies them. None dares to approach me. I am crushed and they leave me without aid! I am dying and none weeps for me. All consolation is refused me. Pity stays on the brink of the gulf into which the criminal plunges. He is torn by remorse and his cries are not heard!

And you, whom I have outraged; you, whose esteem adds to my torture; you, who alone have the right to avenge yourself, what are you doing so far from me? Come, punish a faithless wife. Let me suffer deserved torments at last. Already I should have submitted to your vengeance, but courage failed me to confess my shame to you. It was not dissimulation, it was shame. At least may this letter tell you my repentance. Heaven took up your cause and avenges you for an injury you did not know. It is Heaven which bound my tongue and restrained my words; it feared you might have pardoned a fault it wished to punish. It has removed me from your indulgence which would have wounded its justice.

Pitiless in its vengeance, it has delivered me up to him who ruined me. It is at once through him and by him that I suffer. I try to fly him, in vain, he follows me; he is there; he besets me continually. But how different he is from himself! His eyes only express hatred and scorn. His mouth only utters insult and blame. His arms embrace me only to rend me. Who will save me from his barbarous fury?

But what! It is he. . . . I am not deceived; I see him again. O! My charming love! Receive me into your arms; hide me in your bosom; yes, it is you, it is indeed you! What disastrous illusion made me mistake you? How I have suffered in your absence! Let us not separate again, let us never be separated. Let me breathe. Feel my heart, feel how it beats! Ah! It is no longer fear, it is the sweet emotion of love. Why do you refuse my tender caresses? Turn that soft gaze upon me! What are those bonds you try to break? Why do you prepare that equipment of death? What can have so altered those features? What are you doing? Leave me; I shudder! God! It is that monster again! My friends, do not abandon me. You who call upon me to fly, help me to combat him; and you, more indulgent, you who promised to lessen my pain, come nearer to me. Where are you both? If I am not allowed to see you again, at least answer this letter; let me know that you still love me.

Leave me, cruel one! What new frenzy animates you? Are you afraid some gentle sentiment might pierce to my soul? You redouble my tortures; you force me to hate you. Oh! How painful hate is! How it corrodes the heart which distills it! Why do you persecute me? What more can you have to say to me? Have you not made it impossible for me to listen to you, impossible to reply to you? Expect nothing more of me. Farewell, Monsieur.

Paris, 5th of December, 17—.

## LETTER CLXII

*The Chevalier Danceny to the Vicomte de Valmont*

I am informed, Monsieur, of your conduct towards me. I know as well that, not content with basely duping me, you have not feared to boast of it, to congratulate yourself on it. I have seen the proof of your betrayal written by your own hand. I confess it broke my heart and that I felt some shame at having contributed so much myself to your odious abuse of my blind confidence; yet I do not envy you this shameful advantage; I am only curious to know if you will keep all other advantages over me. I shall learn this, if, as I hope, you will be good enough to meet me tomorrow morning, between eight and nine o'clock, at the Bois de Vincennes gate; Village of Saint-Mandé. I shall take care to bring there everything necessary for the explanations I yet have to make with you.

The Chevalier Danceny.

Paris, 6th of December, 17—, in the evening.

## LETTER CLXIII

*M. Bertrand to Madame de Rosemonde*

Madame,

It is with great regret that I carry out the sad duty of announcing to you an event which will cause you such cruel grief. Allow me first of all to exhort you to that pious resignation which everyone has so often admired in you and which alone can enable us to endure the ills which strew our miserable life.

Your nephew. . . . Heaven ! Must I so afflict so respectable a lady ! Your nephew has had the misfortune to die in a duel he had this morning with the Chevalier Danceny. I am entirely ignorant of the cause of the quarrel ; but it appears, from the note I found in the Vicomte's pocket, which I have the honour to send you ; it appears, I say, that he was not the aggressor. And it was he whom Heaven allowed to die !

I was waiting for M. le Vicomte at his house at the very time when he was brought home. Imagine my terror at seeing your nephew carried in by two of his servants, soaked in his own blood. He had two sword wounds in his body and was already very weak. M. Danceny was there too and was even weeping. Ah ! No doubt he must weep ; but it is too late to shed tears when one has caused an irreparable misfortune !

I lost control of myself ; and in spite of my humble rank I told him what I thought of him. But it was there that M. le Vicomte showed himself truly great. He ordered me to be silent ; and he took the hand of his murderer, called him his friend, embraced him in our presence and said to us : " I order you to treat this gentleman with all the respect due to a brave and gallant man." Moreover, in my presence, he handed to him a voluminous mass of papers with which I am not acquainted but to which I know he attached great importance. Then he desired that they should be left alone for a time. Meanwhile I sent for aid, spiritual and temporal ; but alas ! the ill was beyond remedy. Less than half an hour afterwards M. le Vicomte lost consciousness. He could receive nothing but the extreme unction ; and the ceremony was barely over when he breathed his last sigh.

Ah Heavens ! When I received into my arms at his birth this precious support of so illustrious a family, could I foresee that he would die in my arms, and that I should have to weep his death ? A death so early and so unhappy ! My tears flow in spite of me ; I beg your pardon, Madame, for daring thus to mingle my grief with yours ; but in all ranks we have a heart and sensibility ; and I should be very ungrateful if I did not mourn all my life a Lord who was so kind to me, who honoured me with so much confidence.

Tomorrow, after the body is taken away, I shall have seals put on everything and you can rely entirely upon my services. You know, Madame, that this unfortunate event puts an end to the entail and leaves your disposal entirely free. If I can be of any use to you, I beg you will be good enough to send me your orders ; I will give all my attention to carrying them out punctually.

I am with the deepest respect, Madame, your most humble, etc., etc.

Bertrand

**Paris, 7th of December, 17—.**

## LETTER CLXIV

*Madame de Rosemonde to M. Bertrand*

I have just received your letter, my dear Bertrand, and learn from it the terrible event of which my nephew has been the unhappy victim. Yes, certainly I have orders to give you and it is only with them that I concern myself with anything but my mortal grief.

M. Danceny's note, which you sent me, is a very convincing proof that he provoked the duel, and it is my intention that you should lodge a complaint against him in my name. By forgiving his enemy, his murderer, my nephew satisfied his natural generosity; but I must avenge at once his death, humanity, and religion. The severity of the laws cannot be too much excited against this remnant of barbarity which still infects our customs and I do not think that this is a case when we are commanded to forgive injuries. I expect you to carry out this business with all the zeal and activity of which I know you capable and which you owe to the memory of my nephew.

Before everything else, you will be careful to see M. le Président de . . .[1] on my behalf and to confer with him. I am not writing to him, I am in haste to give myself up entirely to my grief. You will make my excuses to him and show him this letter.

Farewell, my dear Bertrand; I praise you and thank you for your right feelings and, for life, I am yours, etc.

From the Château de . . ., 8th of December, 17—.

## LETTER CLXV

*Madame de Volanges to Madame de Rosemonde*

I know you are informed, my dear and excellent friend, of your recent loss; I knew your affection for M. de Valmont and I share very sincerely the affliction you must feel. I am truly pained to have to add new regrets to those you already feel; but alas! there is nothing left but tears for you to give our unfortunate friend. We lost her yesterday at eleven o'clock in the evening. By the fatality attached to her lot which seemed to mock at all human prudence, the short time she survived M. de Valmont was long enough for her to learn of his death; and, as she said herself, to succumb under the weight of her misfortunes only when the measure was filled.

You have already heard that for the last two days she was absolutely unconscious; yesterday morning, when her doctor came, and we both went over to her bed, she recognised neither of us and we could not obtain a word or the least sign from her. Well, we had scarcely returned to the fireplace where the doctor was telling me of the sad happening

[1] A Magistrate.

of M. de Valmont's death, when the unfortunate woman regained her senses, either because nature alone produced this change or because the repetition of the words " M. de Valmont " and " death " may have recalled to the invalid the only ideas which have so long occupied her.

However this may be, she suddenly opened her bed-curtains, exclaiming : " What ! What is it you say ? M. de Valmont is dead ? " I hoped to make her think she was mistaken and I assured her at first that she had misunderstood us ; but far from being convinced thus, she compelled the doctor to repeat the cruel announcement and when I tried once more to dissuade her, she called me to her and said in a low voice : " Why try to deceive me ? Was he not already dead for me ! " I was forced to yield then.

Our unhappy friend listened to the account at first calmly enough, but very soon she interrupted, saying : " Enough, I know enough." She immediately requested that her curtains might be closed ; and when the doctor then tried to give her his professional services, she would never allow him to come near her.

As soon as he had gone, she sent away her nurse and her waiting-woman as well ; and when we were alone together she asked me to help her to get upon her knees in bed and to support her. There she remained for some time in silence with no other expression than that of her tears which flowed abundantly. At last, clasping her hands and lifting them to Heaven, she said in a weak but fervent voice : " Almighty God, I submit myself to your justice ; but pardon Valmont. May my misfortunes, which I know I deserved, not be blamed upon him and I will bless your mercy ! " I have allowed myself, my dear and excellent friend, to dwell upon these details concerning a matter which I know must renew and aggravate your grief, because I have no doubt that Madame de Tourvel's prayer will bring great consolation to your spirit.

After our friend had spoken these few words, she fell back in my arms ; she was scarcely back in bed when she fell into a long swoon, which yielded at length to the usual remedies. As soon as she regained consciousness, she asked me to send for Father Anselme, and added : " He is now the only doctor I need ; I feel that my woes will soon be over." She complained greatly of a feeling of oppression and spoke with difficulty.

A little time after she sent me by her waiting-woman a casket (which I send to you) which she said contained papers of hers, charging me to send them to you immediately after her death.[1] Afterwards she spoke to me of you and of your friendship for her, as much as her condition allowed her and with great tenderness.

Father Anselme arrived about four o'clock and remained nearly an hour alone with her. When we returned, the invalid's face was calm and serene ; but it was easy to see that Father Anselme had wept a great deal. He remained to be present at the last ceremonies of the Church.

[1] This casket contained all the letters relating to her adventure with M. de Valmont. (C. de L.)

This spectacle, always so imposing and painful, became more so from the contrast between the sick person's calm resignation and the profound grief of her venerable confessor, who burst into tears beside her. The emotion became general; and she whom we all wept for was the one person who did not weep.

The remainder of the day was spent in the customary prayers which were only interrupted by the invalid's frequent swoons. Finally, about eleven o'clock at night, she seemed to me more oppressed and in greater pain. I put out my hand to find her arm; she still had strength enough to take it and put it on her heart. I could not feel it beating; and in fact our unhappy friend expired at that very moment.

You remember, my dear friend, that on your last journey here less that a year ago, we were talking of a few persons whose happiness seemed more or less assured and we dwelt with complaisance on the fate of this same woman whose misfortunes and death we weep today! So many virtues, praiseworthy qualities and charms; so gentle and so easy a character; a husband whom she loved and by whom she was adored; a society which pleased her and which she delighted; good looks, youth, wealth; so many advantages united have been lost through a single imprudence! O Providence! Doubtless we must adore your decrees, but how incomprehensible they are! I restrain myself, I am afraid of increasing your sadness by yielding to my own.

I must leave you and go to my daughter who is a little indisposed. When she heard this morning of the sudden death of these two persons of her acquaintance, she became unwell and I sent her to bed. But I hope this slight indisposition will have no evil results. At her age, they are unaccustomed to grief and its impression is sharper and deeper. No doubt this active sensibility is a praiseworthy quality, but how much one learns to dread it after what one sees every day! Good-bye, my dear and excellent friend.

Paris, 9th of December, 17—.

## LETTER CLXVI

*M. Bertrand to Madame de Rosemonde*

Madame,

In consequence of the orders you did me the honour of sending me, I had the honour to see M. le Président de . . ., and I handed him your letter, informing him at the same time that, in accordance with your orders, I should do nothing except upon his advice. That respectable Magistrate commands me to inform you that the complaint you intend to lodge against M. le Chevalier Danceny would equally compromise the memory of your nephew and that his honour would inevitably be stained by the sentence of the Court, which undoubtedly would be a great misfortune. His opinion is that no step whatever should be taken; or, if one must be taken, it should be to try to prevent the Public

Prosecutor from taking notice of this unfortunate adventure, which has already become too public.

These remarks seemed to me full of wisdom and I have determined to await fresh orders from you.

Permit me, Madame, to ask you to be so kind, when you send me your orders, as to add a word on the state of your health, on whose account I dread extremely the result of so many griefs. I hope you will pardon this liberty in consideration of my attachment and my zeal.

I am with respect, Madame, your, etc.

Paris, 10th of December, 17—.

## LETTER CLXVII

*Anonymous to the Chevalier Danceny*

Monsieur,

I have the honour to inform you that this morning, at the Public Prosecutor's office, His Majesty's legal advisers discussed the meeting which took place a few days ago between you and M. le Vicomte de Valmont, and there is reason to fear that the Public Prosecutor may lodge a complaint. I thought this warning might be useful to you, either for you to put in motion your protectors to prevent these unpleasant consequences; or, in case you are unable to achieve this, for you to be in a position to look after your personal safety.

If you will allow me to advise you, I think you would do well for a short time to show yourself less than you have been accustomed to do recently. Although this sort of affair is usually treated with indulgence, yet this form of respect is nevertheless due to the law.

This precaution becomes the more necessary since I have heard that a Madame de Rosemonde, said to be an aunt of M. de Valmont, wishes to lodge a complaint against you, in which case the Public Prosecutor could not refuse her demand. It might be useful if you could find someone to speak to this lady.

Private reasons prevent me from signing this letter. But I hope that, although you do not know from whom it comes, you will not render less justice to the sentiment which dictated it.

I have the honour to be, etc.

Paris, 19th of December, 17—.

## LETTER CLXVIII

*Madame de Volanges to Madame de Rosemonde*

Very surprising and annoying rumours, my dear and excellent friend, are being spread here concerning Madame de Merteuil. I am certainly very far from believing them and I would wager that it is only a dreadful calumny; but I know too well how the least probable spitefulness gains credit and how hard it is to erase the impression it leaves, not to be very alarmed by these, however easily I think they may be destroyed. But it was very late yesterday when I heard of these horrors which are only beginning to be repeated; and this morning, when I sent to Madame de Merteuil's house, she had gone to the country where she is to remain for two days. I could not hear where she had gone. Her second waiting-woman, whom I sent for to speak to me told me that her mistress had simply given her orders to expect her on Thursday, and none of the servants she has left here know more than this. I myself cannot conjecture where she can be; I do not recollect anyone she knows who remains in the country so late in the season.

However that may be, I hope that you will be able to procure me between now and her return certain explanations which may be useful to her, for these odious stories are founded upon the circumstances of M. de Valmont's death, of which you would apparently have been informed if they were true, or at least, it will be easy for you to find out about them, which I beg you to do. This is what people say, or, to express it better, what they are still murmuring; but it cannot be long before it breaks out more openly.

It is said, then, that the quarrel between M. de Valmont and the Chevalier Danceny is the work of Madame de Merteuil, who was unfaithful to both of them; that, as almost always happens, the two rivals began by fighting and did not come to an explanation until afterwards; that this explanation produced a sincere reconciliation; and that, to complete the Chevalier Danceny's knowledge of Madame de Merteuil and also to justify himself completely, M. de Valmont added to his words a whole mass of letters, forming a regular correspondence which he kept up with her, in which she relates about herself the most scandalous anecdotes in the most licentious style.

It is added that Danceny, in his first indignation, showed these letters to anyone who wished to see them and that they are all over Paris now. Two in particular[1] are mentioned; one in which she tells the whole story of her life and principles and which is said to be the height of enormity; the other which entirely justifies M. de Prévan (whose history you will remember) from the proof it gives that he only yielded to the most marked advances on the part of Madame de Merteuil and that the rendezvous was agreed to by her.

Happily, I have the strongest reasons to believe that these imputations are as false as they are odious. First of all, we both know that M. de Valmont was certainly not devoting himself to Madame de Merteuil and I have every reason to think that Danceny was not doing so either; so it seems proved that she could not have been either the reason or the creator of the quarrel. I do not understand either how it could have been to the interest of Madame de Merteuil (who is supposed to have been in agreement with Prévan) to make a scene which could never have been anything but disagreeable by its publicity and might have become

[1] Letters *LXXXI* and *LXXXV*, of this collection. (C. de L.)

very dangerous to her, since she thus made an irreconcilable enemy of a man who was master of part of her secret and who then had many supporters. Yet it is to be observed that since this adventure not a single voice has been raised in favour of Prévan and that there has been no protest even on his part.

These reflections make me suspect him as the author of the rumours today and I regard these base accusations as the work of the hatred and vengeance of a man who, seeing himself ruined, hopes in this way at least to spread doubts and perhaps to cause a useful diversion. But wherever these spiteful rumours come from, the most urgent thing is to destroy them. They would fall of themselves, if, as is probable, M. de Valmont and Danceny did not speak to each other after their unfortunate affair and if no papers were handed over.

In my impatience to verify these facts I sent this morning to M. Danceny; he is no longer in Paris. His servants told my footman that he left last night after a warning he received yesterday and that the place where he is staying is a secret. Apparently he is afraid of the results of this affair. It is therefore only through you, my dear and excellent friend, that I can obtain these details which interest me so much and which may become so necessary to Madame de Merteuil I renew my request that you will let me have them as soon as possible.

P.S. My daughter's indisposition had no bad result; she sends you her respect.

Paris, 11th of December, 17—.

## LETTER CLXIX

*The Chevalier Danceny to Madame de Rosemonde*

Perhaps you will think the step I am taking today a very strange one; but, I beg you, hear me out before you judge me and do not see boldness and temerity where there is only respect and confidence. I do not conceal from myself the wrongs I have done you, and I should not forgive myself for them all my life if I could for a moment think that it would have been possible to avoid them. Be sure, Madame, that though I think myself free from blame I am not free from regrets; and I can say with sincerity that the regrets I have caused you are a considerable part of those I feel myself. To believe these sentiments which I dare to express to you, it will suffice you to do justice to yourself and to know that, without having the honour to be known by you, I have that of knowing you.

Yet, while I groan at a fatality which has caused at once your grief and y misery, I am made to fear that you are given up entirely to thoughts of vengeance, that you are seeking the means of satisfying it even through the severity of the law.

Allow me to point out to you in this respect, that here you are carried away by your grief, since in this point my interest is essentially one with that of M. de Valmont who would himself be involved in the condemnation you provoked against me. I should then think, Madame, that I might rather count upon aid than obstacles on your part in the care I am obliged to take so that this unhappy incident may remain buried in silence.

But this resource of complicity which suits equally the guilty and the innocent is insufficient for my delicacy ; while I desire to remove you as an opponent, I claim you as my judge. The esteem of persons one respects is too precious for me to allow yours to be torn from me without defence, and I think I have the means to do so.

Indeed if you agree that vengeance is allowed, let me rather say is a duty, when one has been betrayed in one's love, in one's friendship, in one's confidence above all ; if you agree to that, my injuries to you will disappear in your eyes. Do not rely on what I say but read, if you have the courage, the correspondence I hereby place in your hands.[1] The number of original letters among them appear to render authentic those which only exist in copy. Moreover, I received these papers just as I have the honour to hand them to you, from M. de Valmont himself. I have added nothing to them and I have only taken from them two letters which I have taken the liberty to publish.

One was necessary to the common vengeance of M. de Valmont and myself, to which we both had a right and which he expressly charged me with. Moreover, I thought it was rendering a service to society to unmask a woman so really dangerous as Madame de Merteuil and who, as you can see, is the only, the real cause of all that passed between M. de Valmont and me.

A sentiment of justice induced me also to publish the second for the justification of M. de Prévan, whom I hardly know, but who by no means deserved the rigorous treatment he has endured nor the still more formidable severity of public condemnation under which he has suffered since that time, without having anything for his defence.

You will therefore only find copies of these two letters whose originals I must retain. As to the remainder, I think I cannot place in surer hands a collection which it is important for me not to have destroyed, but which I should blush to abuse. By confiding these papers to you, Madame, I think I am serving the persons they concern as well as if I handed them over to themselves ; and I save them from the embarrassment of receiving them from me and of knowing that I am informed of their adventures, of which doubtless they wish everybody to be kept in ignorance.

I think I ought to inform you that the enclosed correspondence is only part of a much more voluminous collection from which M. de Valmont took it in my presence ; you will find it, when the seals are

[1] From this correspondence, from that delivered on the death of Madame de Tourvel, from letters confided to Madame de Rosemonde by Madame de Volanges, the present collection has been formed, the originals of which are in the possession of Madame de Rosemonde's heirs. (C. de L.)

broken, under the title, which I saw myself, of "Account opened between the Marquise de Merteuil and the Vicomte de Valmont." You will take in this matter the course which your prudence suggests.

I am with respect, Madame, etc.

P.S. Certain warnings I have received and the advice of my friends have determined me to leave Paris for some time; but the place of my retirement, which is kept secret from everyone else, will not be so kept from you. If you honour me with a reply, I beg you to address it to the Commandery of P. . . ., under cover to M. le Commandeur de . . . . It is from his residence that I have the honour to write to you.

Paris, 12th of December, 17—.

## LETTER CLXX

*Madame de Volanges to Madame de Rosemonde*

I go, my dear friend, from surprise to surprise, from grief to grief. Only a mother can have an idea of what I suffered all yesterday morning; and, though my most cruel anxieties have since been calmed, I still retain a keen affliction, the end of which I cannot foresee.

Yesterday, about ten o'clock in the morning, astonished at not having seen my daughter, I sent my waiting-woman to find what was the reason for this lateness. She returned a moment later in great fear, and frightened me still more by announcing that my daughter was not in her room and that her waiting-woman had not found her there this morning. Imagine my position! I called together all my servants, especially the porter; all swore they knew nothing and could tell me nothing about this event. I then went at once to my daughter's room. The disorder it was in showed me that apparently she had only left that morning; but I found no explanation. I examined her wardrobes and her writing-table; I found everything in its place and all her possessions, except the dress she had gone out in. She had not even taken the little money she had with her.

As it was only yesterday that she heard all that is being said about Madame de Merteuil to whom she is very much attached, to such an extent that she did nothing but weep all evening; as I remembered also that she did not know Madame de Merteuil is in the country; my first idea was that she had wished to see her friend and had been heedless enough to go there alone. But the time which elapsed without her returning brought back all my anxieties. Every moment increased my pain and, while I burned to find out what had happened, I did not dare to make any enquiries in the fear of giving publicity to an event which perhaps I should afterwards wish hidden from everyone. No, I have never suffered so much all my life!

At length, it was not until after two o'clock that I received at once a letter from my daughter and another from the Mother Superior of the Convent of . . . My daughter's letter merely informed me that she had been afraid lest I should thwart the vocation she felt to become a nun and that she had not dared to speak to me about it ; the rest was only excuses for having taken this course without my permission, a course, she added, which I should certainly not disapprove if I knew her motives which, however, she begged me not to ask her.

The Mother Superior informed me that, seeing a young person arrive alone, she had at first refused to receive her ; but, having questioned her and having learnt who she was, she thought she would be doing me a service by giving shelter to my daughter and thereby saving her from other expeditions, which she seemed determined to make. The Mother Superior, while she naturally offers to return me my daughter, exhorts me, as her profession requires, not to thwart a vocation which she calls " so decided " ; she also tells me that she could not give me earlier information of this occurrence owing to the difficulty she had in making my daughter write to me, for her project was to keep everyone in ignorance of her place of retirement. The unreasonableness of children is a cruel thing !

I went to the convent at once ; and after having seen the Mother Superior, I asked to see my daughter ; she only could be made to come with difficulty and she trembled very much. I spoke to her in the presence of the nuns and I spoke to her in private ; all I could obtain from her in the midst of many tears was that she could only be happy in the convent ; I decided to allow her to remain there, but not yet as one of the Novices, as she desired. I fear that the deaths of Madame de Tourvel and M. de Valmont have too much affected her young mind. However much I respect a religious vocation I could not see my daughter embrace that condition without pain, and even without fear. It seems to me that we already have enough duties to fulfil without creating new ones for ourselves ; and, moreover, that at her age we hardly know what is most suitable for us.

My embarrassment is greatly increased by the very near return of M. de Gercourt ; ought I to break off so advantageous a marriage ? How can we make our children happy if it is insufficient to desire their happiness and to give all our attention to it ? You would greatly oblige me if you would tell me what you would do in my place ; I cannot decide upon any course ; I think nothing is so terrifying as to have to decide the fate of others and in this present situation I am equally afraid of showing the severity of a judge or the weakness of a mother.

I keep reproaching myself for increasing your griefs by speaking to you of mine ; but I know your heart ; the consolation you could give others would become for you the greatest you could receive.

Good-bye, my dear and excellent friend ; I await your two replies in great impatience.

Paris, 13th of December, 17—.

## LETTER CLXXI

*Madame de Rosemonde to the Chevalier Danceny*

After the information you have given me, Monsieur, there is nothing left but to weep and to be silent. I regret to be still alive when I learn such horrors ; I blush that I am a woman when I see one capable o such excesses.

In what concerns myself, Monsieur, I will gladly consent to leave in silence and forgetfulness everything connected with these sad events and their consequences. I even hope that they may never cause you any griefs save those inseparable from the unhappy advantage you gained over my nephew. In spite of his faults, which I am compelled to recognise, I feel I shall never be consoled for his loss ; but my eternal affliction will be the only vengeance I shall allow myself to take upon you ; it is for your heart to perceive the extent of it.

If you will allow me, at my age, to make an observation which is never made at yours, I would say that if we understood our true happiness we should never seek it outside the limits prescribed by the Laws and Religion.

You may be sure that I shall faithfully and willingly guard the collection you ave confided to me ; but I ask you to authorise me not to hand it over to anyone, not even to you, Monsieur, unless it becomes necessary for your justification. I dare to think that you will not refuse this request and that you now feel that one often regrets having yielded even to the most just vengeance.

I do not pause in my requests, so persuaded am I of your generosity and your delicacy ; it would be worthy of both if you also placed in my hands Mademoiselle de Volanges' letters which you have apparently preserved and which doubtless are no longer of interest to you. I know that this young person did you great injuries ; but I do not believe you would think of punishing her for them ; if only from self-respect you would not degrade the person you had loved so much. It is not necessary therefore for me to add that the consideration the daughter does not deserve is at least due to her mother, to that respectable woman to whom you have many amends to make ; for, after all, however you try to delude yourself by a pretended delicacy of sentiment, he who first attempts to seduce a still simple and virtuous heart by that very fact renders himself the first instigator of her corruption and must forever be held accountable for the excesses and misconduct which follow it.

Do not be surprised, Monsieur, at so much severity on my part ; it is the greatest proof I can give you of my complete esteem. You will acquire still further rights to it by consenting, as I desire, to the preservation of a secret whose publicity would do harm to yourself and would carry death to a maternal heart which you have already wounded. And then, Monsieur, I wish to do my friend this service; if I could fear that you would refuse me this consolation, I would ask you first to remember that it is the only one you have left me.

From the Château de . . ., 15th of December, 17—.

## LETTER CLXXII

*Madame de Rosemonde to Madame de Volanges*

If I had been obliged, my dear friend, to send to Paris and wait for the explanations you ask concerning Madame de Merteuil, it would not be possible yet for me to give them to you; and I should certainly only have received in this way vague and uncertain ones; but I received explanations I did not expect, which I had no reason to expect; and they are but too precise. O my friend! How that woman deceived you!

It is repugnant to me to enter into any of the details of this mass of enormities; but whatever may be said about her, be assured that it is still less than the truth. I hope, my dear friend, that you know me well enough to believe me on my bare word and that you will not require any proofs from me. Let it suffice you to know that masses of proofs exist and that they are now in my hands.

It is not without extreme pain that I also request you not to force me to give you my reasons for the advice you ask me concerning Mademoiselle de Volanges. I urge you not to oppose yourself to the vocation she shows. Certainly, no reason can authorise one to compel another to adopt that state when the subject is not called to it; but sometimes it is very fortunate that she should be; and you see your daughter herself tells you that you would not disapprove if you knew her motives. He who inspires our feelings knows, far better than our vain wisdom can know, what befits each of us; and often that which appears an act of His severity is on the contrary an act of His clemency.

My advice then, which I know will distress you and which for that very reason you will realise is not given you without deep reflection, is that you leave Mademoiselle de Volanges in the convent, since this determination is her choice; that you encourage rather than oppose the plan she seems to have formed; and that, in expectation of its being carried out, you do not hesitate to break off the marriage you had arranged.

After having fulfilled these painful duties of friendship and in my powerlessness to add any consolation, I have one favour left to ask you; it is that you will not question me any further about these sad events; let us leave them in the oblivion which befits them; and, without seeking for useless and distressing explanations, let us submit ourselves to the decrees of Providence, let us believe in the wisdom of its views, even when it does not permit us to understand them. Good-bye, my dear friend.

From the Château de . . ., 15th of December, 17—.

## LETTER CLXXIII

*Madame de Volanges to Madame de Rosemonde*

Oh ! My friend ! What a fearful veil you wrap about my daughter's fate ! And you seem to fear lest I should attempt to raise it ! What does it conceal which could more distress a mother's heart than the dreadful suspicions to which you abandon me ? The more I know your friendship, your indulgence, the more my tortures increase ; twenty times since yesterday I have wanted to leave these cruel uncertainties and to ask you to inform me without circumspection and without evasion ; and each time I shuddered with fear, remembering your request that I should not question you. At last, I have decided on a course which still leaves me some hope ; and I expect of your friendship that it will not refuse me what I desire—it is to answer me if I have practically understood what you might have to tell me, not to be afraid to tell me everything that maternal indulgence might excuse, that is not impossible to repair. If my misfortunes exceed this measure, I consent to allow you only to explain yourself by your silence. Here then is what I know already and the extent to which my fears go.

My daughter showed some inclination for the Chevalier Danceny and I was informed that she went so far as to receive letters from him and even to answer him ; but I thought I had succeeded in preventing any dangerous consequence from this childish error ; today, when I fear everything, I suppose it was possible that my vigilance may have been deceived and I fear that my daughter has been seduced, has carried her misconduct to its height.

I remember several circumstances which might strengthen this fear. I told you that my daughter was taken unwell at the news of M. de Valmont's misfortune ; perhaps the only cause of this sensibility was the thought of the risks M. Danceny had run in this combat. Later, when she wept so much at learning what was said of Madame de Merteuil, perhaps what I thought was the grief of friendship was only the result of jealousy or regret at finding her lover unfaithful. Her last step, I think, can be explained in the same way. We often feel ourselves called to God merely because we feel in revolt against men. Supposing that these are true facts and that you knew them, no doubt you might have thought them sufficient to authorise the severe advice you give me.

Yet, if this is so, while I blame my daughter I think I should still owe it to her to attempt every means to save her from the tortures and dangers of an illusory and temporary vocation. If M. Danceny is not lost to all sense of honour, he will not refuse to repair a wrong of which he is the sole author, and I dare to think that marriage with my daughter is so advantageous that he might be flattered by it, as well as his family.

That, my dear and excellent friend, is the one hope left me; hasten to confirm it, if it is possible for you to do so. You will understand how much I desire that you should reply to me and what a dreadful blow to me your silence would be.[1]

I was about to close this letter when a man of my acquaintance came to see me and told me of the cruel scene endured by Madame de Merteuil the day before yesterday. As I have seen nobody for the last few days I had heard nothing of this occurrence; here is an account of it, as I received it from an eye-witness.

Madame de Merteuil on returning from the country the day before yesterday, Thursday, was set down at the Comédie Italienne, where she has a box; she was alone and, what must have seemed very extraordinary to her, no man entered it during the whole of the play. When it was over she went, as she was accustomed, to the small drawing-room which was already filled with people; there was at once a murmur, but apparently she did not think she was the cause of it. She noticed an empty place on one of the benches and went to sit down in it; but immediately all the women who were already there rose as if in concert and left her absolutely alone. This marked movement of general indignation was applauded by all the men and increased the murmurs, which, they say, become hooting.

For there to be nothing lacking to her humiliation, her ill-luck would have it that M. de Prévan, who had showed himself nowhere since his adventure, entered the small drawing-room at that moment. As soon as he was observed everyone, men and women, surrounded and applauded him; and he was carried, as it were, before Madame de Merteuil by the public who made a circle around them. I am assured that she preserved an air of seeing and hearing nothing and that she did not even change countenance! But I think that fact exaggerated. However that may be, this situation, so ignominious for her, lasted until her carriage was announced; and at her departure the scandalous hootings were redoubled. It is dreadful to be a relative of this woman. That same evening, M. de Prévan was welcomed by all the officers of his Corps who were present and no one doubts that he will soon regain his post and his rank.

The same person who gave me these details told me that the following night Madame de Merteuil was seized with a strong fever, which was at first thought to be the result of the violent situation in which she had been placed; but since yesterday evening it is known that a confluent smallpox of a very bad kind has shown itself. Really, I think it would be fortunate for her if she died of it. It is also said that this adventure will perhaps do her great harm in her law-suit which will soon be decided and for which they say she needed a great deal of favour.

Good-bye, my dear and excellent friend. In all this I see the wicked are punished, but I find no consolation in it for the unhappy victims.

Paris, 18th of December, 17—.

[1] No answer was sent to this letter. (C. de L.)

## LETTER CLXXIV

*The Chevalier Danceny to Madame de Rosemonde*

You are right, Madame, and I shall certainly not refuse you anything which depends upon me and to which you appear to attach some value. The packet I have the honour to send you contains all Mademoiselle de Volanges's letters. If you read them, you will see perhaps not without astonishment how so much ingenuousness and so much perfidy can be united. At least, that is what most struck me at the last reading I have just given them.

But, especially, can one resist the keenest indignation against Madame de Merteuil when one recollects with what dreadful pleasure she gave all her attention to perverting so much innocence and candour ?

No, I am no longer in love. I retain nothing of a sentiment so unworthily betrayed ; it is not love which makes me seek to justify Mademoiselle de Volanges. But yet, would not that simple heart, that gentle, facile character, have been conducted even more easily towards good than they were led towards evil ! What other girl, coming thus from a convent without experience and almost without ideas, bringing into society (as almost always happens) only an equal ignorance of good and evil—what other girl, I say, would have resisted any better such criminal cunning ? Ah ! To be indulgent it suffices to reflect on how many circumstances, independent of ourselves, depends the dreadful alternative of delicacy or the degradation of our feelings. You did me justice then, Madame, when you thought that the injuries done me by Mademoiselle de Volanges, though I felt them keenly, do not inspire me with any idea of vengeance. It is sufficient to be obliged to give up loving her ! It would cost me too much to hate her.

I needed no reflection to make me desire that everything which concerns her and might harm her should forever remain unknown to the world. If I have seemed to delay for some time my compliance with your wishes in this respect, I think I need not conceal my motive from you ; I wished first of all to be sure that I should not be molested about the consequences of my unhappy affair. At a time when I was asking for your indulgence, when I even dared to think I had some right to it, I should have been unwilling to seem in any way to be buying it by this compliance on my part ; I was certain of the purity of my motives and, I confess it, I was proud enough to desire that you should have no doubt of it. I hope you will pardon this delicacy, perhaps too susceptible to the veneration you inspire in me, to the value I set on your esteem.

The same feeling makes me ask you as a last favour to be good enough to tell me if you think I have fulfilled all the duties imposed upon me by the unfortunate circumstances in which I was placed. Once assured of this, my course is plain ; I shall leave for Malta ; I shall go there to make gladly and to keep religiously the vows which will separate me from the world, of which, while yet so young, I have already so much reason to complain; I shall go and try to forget under a foreign sky the idea of so many accumulated enormities, whose memory can never but sadden and wither my soul.

I am with respect, Madame, your most humble, etc

Paris, 26th of December, 17—.

## LETTER CLXXV

*Madame de Volanges to Madame de Rosemonde*

Madame de Merteuil's destiny seems at last accomplished, my deal and excellent friend; and it is such that her worst enemies are divided between the indignation she merits and the pity she inspires. I was indeed right to say that it would perhaps be fortunate for her if she died of her smallpox. She has recovered, it is true, but horribly disfigured; and particularly by the loss of one eye.[1] You may easily imagine that I have not seen her again; but I am told she is positively hideous.

The Marquis de . . ., who never misses the opportunity of saying a spiteful thing, speaking of her yesterday, said that her disease had turned her round and that now her soul is in her face. Unhappily, everyone thought the expression a very true one.

Another event has increased her disgrace and her errors. Her lawsuit was decided yesterday and she lost it by a unanimous vote. Costs, damages, and interest, restitution of profits—everything was given to the minors; so that the small part of her fortune which was not concerned in this suit is more than absorbed by its expenses.

As soon as she heard this news, although she was still unwell, she made her arrangements and left, alone and by night. Her servants say today that not one of them would follow her. It is thought that she went in the direction of Holland.

This departure has caused even more comment than all the rest because she took with her the very valuable diamonds which ought to have been comprised in her husband's estate, her silver, her jewels, in fact everything she could, while she leaves behind nearly 50,000 *livres* of debts. It is a positive bankruptcy.

The family is to meet today to discuss what arrangements shall be made with the creditors. Although I am a very distant relative, I have offered to assist; but I shall not be at this gathering, for I have to be present at a still sadder ceremony. Tomorrow my daughter takes the veil as a Novice. I hope you will not forget, my dear friend, that my only motive for thinking myself forced to make this great sacrifice is the silence you have kept towards me.

M. Danceny left Paris nearly a fortnight ago. It is said that he is going to Malta and intends to remain there. There might be yet time

[1] This is perhaps the weakest thing in the book; it is perhaps intentionally so. See *Introduction*.

to detain him? . . . My friend! . . . My daughter is very culpable then! . . . You will surely pardon a mother for only yielding with difficulty to this dreadful certainty.

What fatality is that which has spread about me recently and has struck me through my dearest possessions! My daughter and my friend!

Who would not shudder at thinking of the miseries which may be caused by one dangerous acquaintance! And what griefs we should avoid if we reflected more upon this! What woman would not flee from the first words of a seducer! What mother could see, without trembling, anyone but herself talking to her daughter! But these tardy reflections never occur until after the event; and one of the most important truths, which is also perhaps one of the most generally recognised, remains stifled and unregarded in the whirl of our inconsequent morals.

Farewell, my dear and excellent friend; I feel at this moment that our reason, so incapable of foreseeing our misfortunes, is still less capable of consoling us for them.[1]

[1] Private reasons and other consideration which we feel it our duty to respect, force us to stop here.

For the moment we cannot give the reader the continuation of Mademoiselle de Volanges's adventures nor inform him of the sinister event which completed the misfortunes or the punishment of Madame de Merteuil. Perhaps some day we may be allowed to complete this work; but we cannot make any undertaking to do so, and even if we could, we think the public taste ought first to be consulted, since it has not our reasons for taking an interest in reading these matters.

(*Publishers' Note: 1782*)

# THE DUCHESS OF LANGEAIS

# THE DUCHESS OF LANGEAIS

## I

In a Spanish city on an island in the Mediterranean, there stands a convent of the Order of Barefoot Carmelites, where the rule instituted by St. Theresa is still preserved with all the first rigour of the reformation brought about by that illustrious woman. Extraordinary as this may seem, it is none the less true. Almost every religious house in the Peninsula, or in Europe for that matter, was either destroyed or disorganised by the outbreak of the French Revolution and the Napoleonic wars; but as this island was protected through those times by the English fleet, its wealthy convent and peaceable inhabitants were secure from the general trouble and spoliation. The storms of many kinds which shook the first fifteen years of the nineteenth century spent their force before they reached those cliffs at so short a distance from the coast of Andalusia.

If the rumour of the Emperor's name so much as reached the shore of the island, it is doubtful whether the holy women kneeling in the cloisters grasped the reality of his dream-like progress of glory, or the majesty that blazed in flame across kingdom after kingdom during his meteor life.

In the minds of the Roman Catholic world, the convent stood out pre-eminent for a stern discipline which nothing had changed; the purity of its rule had attracted unhappy women from the furthest parts of Europe, women deprived of all human ties, sighing after the long suicide accomplished in the breast of God. No convent, indeed, was so well fitted for that complete detachment of the soul from all earthly things, which is demanded by the religious life, albeit on the continent of Europe there are many convents magnificently adapted to the purpose of their existence. Buried away in the loneliest valleys, hanging in mid-air on the steepest mountainsides, set down on the brink of precipices, in every place man has sought for the poetry of the Infinite, the solemn awe of Silence; in every place man has striven to draw closer to God, seeking Him on mountain peaks, in the depths below the crags, at the cliff's edge; and everywhere man has found God. But nowhere, save on this half-European, half-African ledge of rock could you find so many different harmonies, combining so to raise the soul, that the sharpest pain comes to be like other memories; the strongest impressions are dulled, till the sorrows of life are laid to rest in the depths.

The convent stands on the highest point of the crags at the uttermost end of the island. On the side towards the sea the rock was once rent sheer away in some globe-cataclysm ; it rises up a straight wall from the base where the waves gnaw at the stone below high-water mark. Any assault is made impossible by the dangerous reefs that stretch far out to sea, with the sparkling waves of the Mediterranean playing over them. So, only from the sea can you discern the square mass of the convent built conformably to the minute rules laid down as to the shape, height, doors, and windows of monastic buildings. From the side of the town, the church completely hides the solid structure of the cloisters and their roofs, covered with broad slabs of stone impervious to sun or storm or gales of wind.

The church itself, built by the munificence of a Spanish family, is the crowning edifice of the town. Its fine, bold front gives an imposing and picturesque look to the little city in the sea. The sight of such a city, with its close-huddled roofs, arranged for the most part amphitheatre-wise above a picturesque harbour, and crowned by a glorious cathedral front with triple-arched Gothic doorways, belfry towers, and filigree spires, is a spectacle surely in every way the sublimest on earth. Religion towering above daily life, to put men continually in mind of the End and the way, is in truth a thoroughly Spanish conception. But now surround this picture by the Mediterranean, and a burning sky, imagine a few palms here and there, a few stunted evergreen trees mingling their waving leaves with the motionless flowers and foliage of carved stone ; look out over the reef with its white fringes of foam in contrast to the sapphire sea ; and then turn to the city, with its galleries and terraces whither the townsfolk come to take the air among their flowers of an evening, above the houses and the tops of the trees in their little gardens ; add a few sails down in the harbour ; and lastly, in the stillness of falling night, listen to the organ music, the chanting of the services, the wonderful sound of bells pealing out over the open sea. There is sound and silence everywhere ; oftener still there is silence over all.

The church is divided within into a sombre mysterious nave and narrow aisles. For some reason, probably because the winds are so high, the architect was unable to build the flying buttresses and intervening chapels which adorn almost all cathedrals, nor are there openings of any kind in the walls which support the weight of the roof. Outside there is simply the heavy wall structure, a solid mass ofgrey stone further strengthened by huge piers placed at intervals. Inside, the nave and its little side galleries are lighted entirely by the great stained-glass rose-window suspended by a miracle of art above the centre doorway ; for upon that side the exposure permits of the display of lacework in stone and of other beauties peculiar to the style improperly called Gothic.

The larger part of the nave and aisles was left for the townsfolk, who came and went and heard mass there. The choir was shut off from the rest of the church by a grating and thick folds of brown curtain, left slightly apart in the middle in such a way that nothing of the choir could be seen from the church except the high altar and the officiating priest. The grating itself was divided up by the pillars which supported the organ loft; and this part of the structure, with its carved wooden columns, completed the line of the arcading in the gallery carried by the shafts in the nave. If any inquisitive person, therefore, had been bold enough to climb upon the narrow balustrade in the gallery to look down into the choir, he could have seen nothing but the tall eight-sided windows of stained glass beyond the high altar.

At the time of the French expedition into Spain to establish Ferdinand VII once more on the throne, a French general came to the island after the taking of Cadiz, ostensibly to require the recognition of the King's Government, really to see the convent and to find some means of entering it. The undertaking was certainly a delicate one; but a man of passionate temper, whose life had been, as it were, but one series of poems in action, a man who all his life long had lived romances instead of writing them, a man pre-eminently a Doer, was sure to be tempted by a deed which seemed to be impossible.

To open the doors of a convent of nuns by lawful means! The metropolitan or the Pope would scarcely have permitted it! And as for force or strategem—might not any indiscretion cost him his position, his whole career as a soldier, and the end in view to boot? The Duc d'Angoulême was still in Spain; and of all the crimes which a man in favour with the Commander-in-Chief might commit, this one alone was certain to find him inexorable. The General had asked for the mission to gratify private motives of curiosity, though never was curiosity more hopeless. This final attempt was a matter of conscience. The Carmelite convent on the island was the only nunnery in Spain which had baffled his search.

As he crossed from the mainland, scarcely an hour's distance, he felt a presentiment that his hopes were to be fulfilled; and afterwards, when as yet he had seen nothing of the convent but its walls, and of the nuns not so much as their robes; while he had merely heard the chanting of the service, there were dim auguries under the walls and in the sound of the voices to justify his frail hope. And, indeed, however faint those so unaccountable presentiments might be, never was human passion more vehemently excited than the General's curiosity at that moment. There are no small events for the heart; the heart exaggerates everything; the heart weighs the fall of a fourteen-year-old Empire and the dropping of a woman's glove in the same scales, and the glove is nearly always the heavier of the two. So here are the facts in all their prosaic simplicity. The facts first, the emotions will follow.

An hour after the General landed on the island, the royal authority was re-established there. Some few Constitutional Spaniards who had found their way thither after the fall of Cadiz were allowed to charter a vessel and sail for London. So there was neither resistance nor reaction. But the change of government could not be effected in the little town without a mass, at which the two divisions under the General's command were obliged to be present. Now, it was upon this mass that the General had built his hopes of gaining some information as to the sisters in the convent; he was quite unaware how absolutely the Carmelites were cut off from the world; but he knew that there might be among them one whom he held dearer than life, dearer than honour.

His hopes were cruelly dashed at once. Mass, it is true, was celebrated in state. In honour of such a solemnity, the curtains which always hid the choir were drawn back to display its riches, its valuable paintings and shrines so bright with gems that they eclipsed the glories of the ex-votos of gold and silver hung up by sailors of the port on the columns in the nave. But all the nuns had taken refuge in the organ-loft. And yet, in spite of this first check, during this very mass of thanksgiving, the most intimately thrilling drama that ever set a man's heart beating opened out widely before him.

The sister who played the organ aroused such intense enthusiasm, that not a single man regretted that he had come to the service. Even the men in the ranks were delighted, and the officers were in ecstasy. As for the General, he was seemingly calm and indifferent. The sensations stirred in him as the sister played one piece after another belong to the small number of things which it is not lawful to utter; words are powerless to express them; like death, God, eternity, they can only be realised through their one point of contact with humanity. Strangely enough, the organ music seemed to belong to the school of Rossini, the musician who brings most human passion into his art. Some day his works, by their number and extent, will receive the reverence due to the Homer of music. From among all the scores that we owe to his great genius, the nun seemed to have chosen *Moses in Egypt* for special study, doubtless because the spirit of sacred music finds therein its supreme expression. Perhaps the soul of the great musician, so gloriously known to Europe, and the soul of this unknown executant had met in the intuitive apprehension of the same poetry. So at least thought two dilettanti officers who must have missed the Théâtre Favart in Spain.

At last in the *Te Deum* no one could fail to discern a French soul in the sudden change that came over the music. Joy for the victory of the Most Christian King evidently stirred this nun's heart to the depths. She was a Frenchwoman beyond mistake. Soon the love of country shone out, breaking forth like shafts of light from the fugue, as the sister introduced variations with all a Parisienne's fastidious taste, and blended vague suggestions of our grandest national airs with her music. A Spaniard's fingers would not have brought this warmth into a graceful tribute paid to the victorious arms of France. The musician's nationality was revealed.

"We find France everywhere, it seems," said one of the men.

The General had left the church during the *Te Deum;* he could not listen any longer. The nun's music had been a revelation of a woman loved to frenzy; a woman so carefully hidden from the world's eyes, so deeply buried in the bosom of the Church, that hitherto the most ingenious and persistent efforts made by men who brought great influence and unusual powers to bear upon the search had failed to find her. The suspicion aroused in the General's heart became all but a certainty with the vague reminiscence of a sad, delicious melody, the air of *Fleuve du Tage*. The woman he loved had played the prelude to the ballad in a boudoir in Paris, how often ! and now this nun had chosen the song to express an exile's longing, amid the joy of those that triumphed. Terrible sensation ! To hope for the resurrection of a lost love, to find her only to know that she was lost, to catch a mysterious glimpse of her after five years—five years, in which the pent-up passion, chafing in an empty life, had grown the mightier for every fruitless effort to satisfy it !

Who has not known, at least once in his life, what it is to lose some precious thing ; and after hunting through his papers, ransacking his memory, and turning his house upside down ; after one or two days spent in vain search, and hope, and despair ; after a prodigious expenditure of the liveliest irritation of soul, who has not known the ineffable pleasure of finding that all-important nothing which had come to be a king of monomania ? Very good. Now, spread that fury of search over five years ; put a woman, put a heart, put love in the place of the trifle ; transpose the monomania into the key of high passion ; and, furthermore, let the seeker be a man of ardent temper, with a lion's heart and a leonine head and mane, a man to inspire awe and fear in those who come in contact with him—realise this, and you may, perhaps, understand why the General walked abruptly out of the church when the first notes of a ballad, which he used to hear with a rapture of delight in a gilt-panelled boudoir, began to vibrate along the aisles of the church in the sea.

The General walked away down the steep street which led to the port, and only stopped when he could not hear the deep notes of the organ. Unable to think of anything but the love which broke out in volcanic eruption, filling his heart with fire, he only knew that the *Te Deum* was over when the Spanish congregation came pouring out of the church. Feeling that his behaviour and attitude might seem ridiculous, he went back to head the procession, telling the alcalde and the governor that, feeling suddenly faint, he had gone out into the air. Casting about for a plea for prolonging his stay, it at once occurred to him to make the most of this excuse, framed on the spur of the moment. He declined, on a plea of increasing indisposition, to preside at the banquet given by the town to the French officers, betook himself to his bed, and sent a message to the Major-General, to the effect that temporary illness obliged him to leave the Colonel in command of the troops for the time being. This commonplace but very plausible stratagem relieved him of all responsibility for the time necessary to carry out his plans. The General, nothing if not " catholic and monarchical," took occasion to inform himself of the hours of the services, and manifested the greatest zeal for the performance of his religious duties, piety which caused no remark in Spain.

The very next day, while the division was marching out of the town, the General went to the convent to be present at vespers. He found an empty church. The townsfolk, devout though they were, had all gone down to the quay to watch the embarkation of the troops. He felt glad to be the only man there. He tramped noisily up the nave, clanking his spurs till the vaulted roof rang with the sound; he coughed, he talked aloud to himself to let the nuns know, and more particularly to let the organist know that if the troops were gone, one Frenchman was left behind. Was this singular warning heard and understood? He thought so. It seemed to him that in the *Magnificat* the organ made response which was borne to him on the vibrating air. The nun's spirit found wings in music and fled towards him, throbbing with the rhythmical pulse of the sounds. Then, in all its might, the music burst forth and filled the church with warmth. The Song of Joy set apart in the sublime liturgy of Latin Christianity to express the exaltation of the soul in the presence of the glory of the ever-living God, became the utterance of a heart almost terrified by its gladness in the presence of the glory of a mortal love; a love that yet lived, a love that had risen to trouble her even beyond the grave in which the nun is laid, that she may rise again as the bride of Christ.

The organ is in truth the grandest, the most daring, the most magnificent of all instruments invented by human genius. It is a whole orchestra in itself. It can express anything in response to a skilled touch. Surely it is in some sort a pedestal on which the soul poises for a flight forth into space, essaying on her course to draw picture after picture in an endless series, to paint human life, to cross the Infinite that separates heaven from earth? And the longer a dreamer listens to those giant harmonies, the better he realises that nothing save this hundred-voiced choir on earth can fill all the space between kneeling men, and a God hidden by the blinding light of the Sanctuary. The music is the one interpreter strong enough to bear up the prayers of humanity to heaven, prayer in its omnipotent moods, prayer tinged by the melancholy of many different natures, coloured by meditative ecstasy, upspringing with the impulse of repentance—blended with the myriad fancies of every creed. Yes. In those long vaulted aisles the melodies inspired by the sense of things divine are blent with a grandeur unknown before, are decked with new glory and might. Out of the dim daylight, and the deep silence broken by the chanting of the choir in response to the thunder of the organ, a veil is woven for God, and the brightness of His attributes shines through it.

And this wealth of holy things seemed to be flung down like a grain of incense upon the fragile altar raised to Love beneath the eternal throne of a jealous and avenging God. Indeed, in the joy of the nun there was little of that awe and gravity which should harmonise with the solemnities of the *Magnificat*. She had enriched the music with graceful variations, earthly gladness throbbing through the rhythm of each. In such brilliant quivering notes some great singer might strive to find a voice for her love, her melodies fluttered as a bird flutters about her mate. There were moments when she seemed to leap back into the past, to dally there now with laughter, now with tears. Her changing moods, as it were, ran riot. She was like a woman excited and happy over her lover's return.

But at length, after the swaying fugues of delirium, after the marvellous rendering of a vision of the past, a revulsion swept over the soul that thus found utterance for itself. With a swift transition from the major to the minor, the organist told her hearer of her present lot. She gave the story of long melancholy broodings, of the slow course of her moral malady. How day by day she deadened the senses, how every night cut off one more thought, how her heart was slowly reduced to ashes. The sadness deepened shade after shade through languid modulations, and in a little while the echoes were pouring out a torrent of grief. Then on a sudden, high notes rang out like the voices of angels singing together, as if to tell the lost but not forgotten lover that their spirits now could only meet in heaven. Pathetic hope ! Then followed the *Amen*. No more joy, no more tears in the air, no sadness, no regrets. The *Amen* was the return to God. The final chord was deep, solemn, even terrible ; for the last rumblings of the bass sent a shiver through the audience that raised the hair on their heads ; the nun shook out her veiling of crepe, and seemed to sink again into the grave from which she had risen for a moment. Slowly the reverberations died away ; it seemed as if the church, but now so full of light, had returned to thick darkness.

The General had been caught up and borne swiftly away by this strong-winged spirit ; he had followed the course of its flight from beginning to end. He understood to the fullest extent the imagery of that burning symphony ; for him the chords reached deep and far. For him, as for the sister, the poem meant future, present, and past. Is not music, and even opera music, a sort of text, which a susceptible or poetic temper, or a sore and stricken heart, may expand as memories shall determine ? If a musician must needs have the heart of a poet, must not the listener too be in a manner a poet and a lover to hear all that lies in great music ? Religion, love, and music—what are they but a threefold expression of the same fact, of that craving for expansion which stirs in every noble soul. And these three forms of poetry ascend to God, in whom all passion on earth finds its end. Wherefore the holy human trinity finds a place amid the infinite glories of God ; of God, whom we always represent surrounded with the fires of love and seistrons of gold—music and light and harmony. Is not He the Cause and the End of all our strivings ?

The French General guessed rightly that here in the desert, on this bare rock in the sea, the nun had seized upon music as an outpouring of the passion that still consumed her. Was this her manner of offering up her love as a sacrifice to God? Or was it Love exultant in triumph over God? The questions were hard to answer. But one thing at least the General could not mistake—in this heart, dead to the world, the fire of passion burned as fiercely as in his own.

Vespers over, he went back to the alcalde with whom he was staying. In the all-absorbing joy which comes in such full measure when a satisfaction sought long and painfully is attained at last, he could see nothing beyond this—he was still loved! In her heart love had grown in loneliness, even as his love had grown stronger as he surmounted one barrier after another which this woman had set between them! The glow of soul came to its natural end. There followed a longing to see her again, to contend with God for her, to snatch her away—a rash scheme, which appealed to a daring nature. He went to bed, when the meal was over, to avoid questions; to be alone and think at his ease; and he lay absorbed by deep thought till day broke.

He rose only to go to mass. He went to the church and knelt close to the screen, with his forehead touching the curtain; he would have torn a hole in it if he had been alone, but his host had come with him out of politeness, and the least imprudence might compromise the whole future of his love, and ruin the new hopes.

The organ sounded, but it was another player, and not the nun of the last two days whose hands touched the keys. It was all colourless and cold for the General. Was the woman he loved prostrated by emotion which wellnigh overcame a strong man's heart? Had she so fully realised and shared an unchanged, longed-for love, that now she lay dying on her bed in her cell? While innumerable thoughts of this kind perplexed his mind, the voice of the woman he worshipped rang out close beside him; he knew its clear resonant soprano. It was her voice, with that faint tremor in it which gave it all the charm that shyness and diffidence gives to a young girl; her voice, distinct from the mass of singing as a *prima donna's* in the chorus of a finale. It was like a golden or silver thread in dark frieze.

It was she! There could be no mistake. Parisienne now as ever, she had not laid coquetry aside when she threw off worldly adornments for the veil and the Carmelite's coarse serge. She who had affirmed her love last evening in the praise sent up to God, seemed now to say to her lover, "Yes, it is I. I am here. My love is unchanged, but I am beyond the reach of love. You will hear my voice, my soul shall enfold you, and I shall abide here under the brown shroud in the choir from which no power on earth can tear me. You shall never see me more!"

"It is she indeed!" the General said to himself, raising his head. He had leant his face on his hands, unable at first to bear the intolerable emotion that surged like a whirlpool in his heart, when that well-known voice vibrated under the arcading, with the sound of the sea for accompaniment.

Storm was without, and calm within the sanctuary. Still that rich voice poured out all its caressing notes; it fell like balm on the lover's burning heart; it blossomed upon the air—the air that a man would fain breathe more deeply to receive the effluence of a soul breathed forth with love in the words of the prayer. The alcalde coming to join his guest found him in tears during the elevation, while the nun was singing, and brought him back to his house. Surprised to find so much piety in a French military man, the worthy magistrate invited the confessor of the convent to meet his guest. Never had news given the General more pleasure; he paid the ecclesiastic a good deal of attention at supper, and confirmed his Spanish hosts in the high opinion they had formed of his piety by a not wholly disinterested respect. He enquired with gravity how many sisters there were in the convent, and asked for particulars of its endowment and revenues, as if from courtesy he wished to hear the good priest discourse on the subject most interesting to him. He informed himself as to the manner of life led by the holy women. Were they allowed to go out of the convent, or to see visitors?

"Señor," replied the venerable churchman, "the rule is strict. A woman cannot enter a monastery of the order of St. Bruno without a special permission from His Holiness, and the rule here is equally stringent. No man may enter a convent of Barefoot Carmelites unless he is a priest specially attached to the services of the house by the Archbishop. None of the nuns may leave the convent; though the great Saint, St. Theresa, often left her cell. The Visitor or the Mothers Superior can alone give permission, subject to an authorisation from the Archbishop, for a nun to see a visitor, and then especially in a case of illness. Now we are one of the principal houses, and consequently we have a Mother Superior here. Among other foreign sisters there is one Frenchwoman, Sister Theresa; she it is who directs the music in the chapel."

"Oh!" said the General, with feigned surprise. "She must have rejoiced over the victory of the House of Bourbon."

"I told them the reason of the mass; they are always a little bit inquisitive."

"But Sister Theresa may have interests in France. Perhaps she would like to send some message or to hear news."

"I do not think so. She would have come to ask me."

"As a fellow-countryman, I should be quite curious to see her," said the General. "If it is possible, if the Lady Superior consents, if——"

"Even at the grating and in the Reverend Mother's presence, an interview would be quite impossible for anybody whatsoever; but, strict as the Mother is, for a deliverer of our holy religion and the throne of his Catholic Majesty, the rule might be relaxed for a moment," said the confessor, blinking. "I will speak about it."

"How old is Sister Theresa?" enquired the lover. He dared not ask any questions of the priest as to the nun's beauty.

"She does not reckon years now," the good man answered, with a simplicity that made the General shudder.

Next day before siesta, the confessor came to inform the French General that Sister Theresa and the Mother consented to receive him at the grating in the parlour before vespers. The General spent the siesta in pacing to and fro along the quay in the noonday heat. Thither the priest came to find him, and brought him to the convent by way of the gallery round the cemetery. Fountains, green trees, and rows of arcading maintained a cool freshness in keeping with the place.

At the further end of the long gallery the priest led the way into a large room divided in two by a grating covered with a brown curtain. In the first, and in some sort of public half of the apartment, where the confessor left the newcomer, a wooden bench ran round the wall, and two or three chairs, also of wood, were placed near the grating. The ceiling consisted of bare unornamented joists and cross-beams of ilex wood. As the two windows were both on the inner side of the grating, and the dark surface of the wood was a bad reflector, the light in the place was so dim that you could scarcely see the great black crucifix, the portrait of Saint Theresa, and a picture of the Madonna which adorned the grey parlour walls. Tumultuous as the General's feelings were, they took something of the melancholy of the place. He grew calm in that homely quiet. A sense of something vast as the tomb took possession of him beneath the chill unceiled roof. Here, as in the grave, was there not eternal silence, deep peace—the sense of the Infinite ? And besides this there was the quiet and the fixed thought of the cloister—a thought which you felt like a subtle presence in the air, and in the dim dusk of the room ; an all-pervasive thought nowhere definitely expressed, and looming the larger in the imagination ; for in the cloister the great saying, " Peace in the Lord," enters the least religious soul as a living force.

The monk's life is scarcely comprehensible. A man seems confessed a weakling in a monastery ; he was born to act, to live out a life of work ; he is evading a man's destiny in his cell. But what man's strength, blended with pathetic weakness, is implied by a woman's choice of the convent life ! A man may have any number of motives for burying himself in a monastery ; for him it is the leap over the precipice. A woman has but one motive—she is a woman still ; she betrothes herself to a Heavenly Bridegroom. Of the monk you may ask, " Why did you not fight your battle ? " But if a woman immures herself in the cloister, is there not always a sublime battle fought first ?

At length it seemed to the General that that still room, and the lonely convent in the sea, were full of thoughts of him. Love seldom attains to solemnity ; yet surely a love still faithful in the breast of God was something solemn, something more than a man had a right to look for as things are in this nineteenth century ? The infinite grandeur of the situation might well produce an effect upon the General's mind ; he had precisely enough elevation of soul to forget politics, honours, Spain, and society in Paris, and to rise to the height of this lofty climax. And what in truth could be more tragic ? How much must pass in the souls of these two lovers, brought together in a place of strangers, on a ledge of granite in the sea ; yet held apart by an intangible, unsurmountable barrier ! Try to imagine the man saying within himself, " Shall I triumph over God in her heart ? " when a faint rustling sound made him quiver, and the curtain was drawn aside.

Between him and the light stood a woman. Her face was hidden by the veil that drooped from the folds upon her head ; she was dressed according to the rule of the order in a gown of the colour become proverbial. Her bare feet were hidden ; if the General could have seen them, he would have known how appallingly thin she had grown ; and yet in spite of the thick folds of her coarse gown, a mere covering and no ornament, he could guess how tears, and prayer, and passion, and loneliness had wasted the woman before him.

An ice-cold hand, belonging, no doubt, to the Mother Superior, held back the curtain. The General gave the enforced witness of their interview a searching glance, and met the dark, inscrutable gaze of an aged recluse. The Mother might have been a century old, but the bright, youthful eyes belied the wrinkles that furrowed her pale face.

" Mme la Duchesse," he began, his voice shaken with emotion, " does your companion understand French ? " The veiled figure bowed her head at the sound of his voice.

" There is no duchess here," she replied. " It is Sister Theresa whom you see before you. She whom you call my companion is my mother in God, my superior here on earth."

The words were so meekly spoken by the voice that sounded in other years amid harmonious surroundings of refined luxury, the voice of a queen of fashion in Paris. Such words from the lips that once spoke so lightly and flippantly struck the General dumb with amazement.

" The Holy Mother only speaks Latin and Spanish," she added.

" I understand neither. Dear Antoinette, make my excuses to her."

The light fell full upon the nun's figure ; a thrill of deep emotion betrayed itself in a faint quiver of her veil as she heard her name softly spoken by the man who had been so hard in the past.

" My brother," she said, drawing her sleeve under her veil, perhaps to brush tears away, " I am Sister Theresa."

Then, turning to the Superior, she spoke in Spanish ; the General knew enough of the language to understand what she said perfectly well ; possibly he could have spoken it had he chosen to do so.

" Dear Mother, the gentleman presents his respects to you, and begs you to pardon him if he cannot pay them himself, but he knows neither of the languages which you speak——"

The aged nun bent her head slowly, with an expression of angelic sweetness, enhanced at the same time by the consciousness of her power and dignity.

" Do you know this gentleman ? " she asked, with a keen glance.

" Yes, Mother."

"Go back to your cell, my daughter!" said the Mother imperiously.

The General slipped aside behind the curtain lest the dreadful tumult within him should appear in his face; even in the shadow it seemed to him that he could still see the Superior's piercing eyes. He was afraid of her; she held his little, frail, hardly-won happiness in her hands; and he, who had never quailed under a triple row of guns, now trembled before this nun. The Duchess went towards the door, but she turned back.

"Mother," she said, with dreadful calmness, "the Frenchman is one of my brothers."

"Then stay, my daughter," said the Superior, after a pause.

The piece of admirable Jesuitry told of such love and regret, that a man less strongly constituted might have broken down under the keen delight in the midst of a great and, for him, an entirely novel peril. Oh! how precious words, looks, and gestures became when love must baffle lynx eyes and tiger's claws! Sister Theresa came back.

"You see, my brother, what I have dared to do only to speak to you for a moment of your salvation and of the prayers that my soul puts up for your soul daily. I am committing mortal sin. I have told a lie. How many days of penance must expiate that lie! But I shall endure it for your sake. My brother, you do not know what happiness it is to love in heaven; to feel that you can confess love purified by religion, love transported into the highest heights of all, so that we are permitted to lose sight of all but the soul. If the doctrine and the spirit of the Saint to whom we owe this refuge had not raised me above earth's anguish, and caught me up and set me, far indeed beneath the Sphere wherein she dwells, yet truly above this world, I should not have seen you again. But now I can see you, and hear your voice, and remain calm——"

The General broke in, "But, Antoinette, let me see you, you whom I love passionately, desperately, as you could have wished me to love you."

"Do not call me Antoinette, I implore you. Memories of the past hurt me. You must see no one here but Sister Theresa, a creature who trusts in the Divine mercy." She paused for a little, and then added, "You must control yourself, my brother. Our Mother would separate us without pity if there is any worldly passion in your face, or if you allow the tears to fall from your eyes."

The General bowed his head to regain self-control; when he looked up again he saw her face beyond the grating—the thin, white, but still impassioned face of the nun. All the magic charm of youth that once bloomed there, all the fair contrast of velvet whiteness and the colour of the Bengal rose, had given place to a burning glow, as of a porcelain jar with a faint light shining through it. The wonderful hair in which she took such pride had been shaven; there was a bandage round her forehead and about her face. An ascetic life had left dark traces about the eyes, which still sometimes shot out fevered glances; their ordinary calm expression was but a veil. In a few words, she was but the ghost of her former self.

"Ah! you that have come to be my life, you must come out of this tomb! You were mine; you had no right to give yourself, even to God. Did you not promise me to give up all at the least command from me? You may perhaps think me worthy of that promise now when you hear what I have done for you. I have sought you all through the world. You have been in my thoughts at every moment for five years; my life has been given to you. My friends, very powerful friends, as you know, have helped with all their might to search every convent in France, Italy, Spain, Sicily, and America. Love burned more brightly for every vain search. Again and again I made long journeys with a false hope; I have wasted my life and the heaviest throbbings of my heart in vain under many a dark convent wall. I am not speaking of a faithfulness that knows no bounds, for what is it?—nothing compared with the infinite longings of my love. If your remorse long ago was sincere, you ought not to hesitate to follow me today."

"You forget that I am not free."

"The Duke is dead," he answered quickly.

Sister Theresa flushed red.

"May heaven be open to him!" she cried with a quick rush of feeling. "He was generous to me.—But I did not mean such ties; it was one of my sins that I was ready to break them all without scruple—for you."

"Are you speaking of your vows?" the General asked, frowning. "I did not think that anything weighed heavier with your heart than love. But do not think twice of it, Antoinette; the Holy Father himself shall absolve you of your oath. I will surely go to Rome, I will entreat all the powers of earth; if God could come down from heaven, I would——"

"Do not blaspheme."

"So do not fear the anger of God. Ah! I would far rather hear that you would leave your prison for me; that this very night you would let yourself down into a boat at the foot of the cliffs. And we would go away to be happy somewhere at the world's end, I know not where. And with me at your side, you should come back to life and health under the wings of love."

"You must not talk like this," said Sister Theresa; "you do not know what you are to me now. I love you far better than I ever loved you before. Every day I pray for you; I see you with other eyes. Armand, if you but knew the happiness of giving yourself up, without shame, to a pure friendship which God watches over! You do not know what joy it is to me to pray for heaven's blessing on you. I never pray for myself: God will do with me according to His will; but, at the price of my soul, I wish I could be sure that you are happy here on earth, and that you will be happy hereafter throughout all ages. My eternal life is all that trouble has left me to offer up to you. I am old now with weeping; I am neither young nor fair; and in any case, you could not respect the nun who became a wife; no love, not even motherhood, could give me absolution. . . . What can you say to outweigh the uncounted thoughts that have gathered in my heart during the past five years, thoughts that have changed, and worn, and blighted it ? I ought to have given a heart less sorrowful to God."

"What can I say ? Dear Antoinette, I will say this, that I love you ; that affection, love, a great love, the joy of living in another heart that is ours, utterly and wholly ours, is so rare a thing and so hard to find, that I doubted you, and put you to sharp proof ; but now, today, I love you, Antoinette, with all my soul's strength. . . . If you will follow me into solitude, I will hear no voice but yours, I will see no other face."

"Hush, Armand ! You are shortening the little time that we may be together here on earth."

"Antoinette, will you come with me ?"

"I am never away from you. My life is in your heart, not through the selfish ties of earthly happiness, or vanity, or enjoyment ; pale and withered as I am, I live here for you, in the breast of God. As God is just, you shall be happy——"

"Words, words all of it ! Pale and withered ? How if I want you ? How if I cannot be happy without you ? Do you still think of nothing but duty with your lover before you ? Is he never to come first and above all things else in your heart ? In time past you put social success, yourself, heaven knows what, before him ; now it is God, it is the welfare of my soul ! In Sister Theresa I find the Duchess over again, ignorant of the happiness of love, insensible as ever, beneath the semblance of sensibility. You do not love me ; you have never loved me——"

"Oh, my brother——!"

"You do not wish to leave this tomb. You love my soul, do you say ? Very well, through you it will be lost forever. I shall make away with myself——"

"Mother !" Sister Theresa called aloud in Spanish, "I have lied to you ; this man is my lover !"

The curtain fell at once. The General, in his stupor, scarcely heard the doors within as they clanged.

"Ah ! she loves me still !" he cried, understanding all the sublimity of that cry of hers. "She loves me still. She must be carried off. . . ."

The General left the island, returned to headquarters, pleaded ill-health, asked for leave of absence, and forthwith took his departure for France.

And now for the incidents which brought the two personages in this Scene into their present relation to each other.

The thing known in France as the Faubourg Saint-Germain is neither a Quarter, nor a sect, nor an institution, nor anything else that admits of a precise definition. There are great houses in the Place Royale, the Faubourg Saint-Honoré, and the Chaussée d'Antin, in any one of which you may breathe the same atmosphere of Faubourg Saint-Germain. So, to begin with, the whole Faubourg is not within the Faubourg. There are men and women born far enough away from its influences who respond to them and take their place in the circle; and again there are others, born within its limits, who may yet be driven forth forever. For the last forty years the manners, and customs, and speech, in a word, the tradition of the Faubourg Saint-Germain, has been to Paris what the Court used to be in other times; it is what the Hôtel Saint-Paul was to the fourteenth century; the Louvre to the fifteenth; the Palais, the Hôtel Rambouillet, and the Place Royale to the sixteenth; and lastly, as Versailles was to the seventeenth and the eighteenth.

Just as the ordinary workaday Paris will always centre about some point; so, through all periods of history, the Paris of the nobles and the upper classes converges towards some particular spot. It is a periodically recurrent phenomenon which presents ample matter for reflection to those who are fain to observe or describe the various social zones; and possibly an enquiry into the causes that bring about this centralisation may do more than merely justify the probability of this episode; it may be of service to serious interests which some day will be more deeply rooted in the commonwealth, unless, indeed, experience is as meaningless for political parties as it is for youth.

In every age the great nobles, and the rich who always ape the great nobles, build their houses as far as possible from crowded streets. When the Duc d'Uzés built his splendid hôtel in the Rue Montmartre in the reign of Louis XIV, and set the fountain at his gates—for which beneficent action, to say nothing of his other virtues, he was held in such veneration that the whole quarter turned out in a body to follow his funeral—when the Duke, I say, chose this site for his house, he did so because that part of Paris was almost deserted in those days. But when the fortifications were pulled down, and the market gardens beyond the line of the boulevards began to fill with houses, then the d'Uzés family left their fine mansion, and in our time it was occupied by a banker. Later still, the noblesse began to find themselves out of their element among shopkeepers, left the Place Royale and the centre of Paris for good, and crossed the river to breathe freely in the Faubourg Saint-Germain, where palaces were reared already about the great hôtel built by Louis XIV for the Duc de Maine—the Benjamin among his legitimated offspring. And indeed, for people accustomed to a stately life, can there be more unseemly surroundings than the bustle, the mud, the street cries, the bad smells, and narrow thoroughfares of a populous quarter? The very habits of life in a mercantile or manufacturing district are completely at variance with the lives of nobles. The shopkeeper and artisan are just going to bed when the great world is thinking of dinner; and the noisy stir of life begins among the former when the latter have gone to rest. Their day's calculations never coincide; the one class represents the expenditure, the other the receipts.

Consequently their manners and customs are diametrically opposed.

Nothing contemptuous is intended by this statement. An aristocracy is in a manner the intellect of the social system, as the middle classes and the proletariat may be said to be its organising and working power. It naturally follows that these forces are differently situated ; and of their antagonism there is bred a seeming antipathy produced by the performance of different functions, all of them, however, existing for one common end.

Such social dissonances are so inevitably the outcome of any charter of the constitution, that however much a Liberal may be disposed to complain of them, as of treason against those sublime ideas with which the ambitious plebeian is apt to cover his designs, he would none the less think it a preposterous notion that M. le Prince de Montmorency, for instance, should continue to live in the Rue Saint-Martin at the corner of the street which bears that nobleman's name ; or that M. le Duc de Fitz-James, descendant of the royal house of Scotland, should have his hôtel at the angle of the Rue Marie Stuart and the Rue Montorgueil. *Sint ut sunt*, *aut non sint*, the grand words of the Jesuit, might be taken as a motto by the great in all countries. These social differences are patent in all ages ; the fact is always accepted by the people ; its "reasons of state" are self-evident ; it is at once cause and effect, a principle and a law. The common sense of the masses never deserts them until demagogues stir them up to gain ends of their own ; that common sense is based on the verities of social order ; and the social order is the same everywhere, in Moscow as in London, in Geneva as in Calcutta. Given a certain number of families of unequal fortune in any given space, you will see an aristocracy forming under your eyes ; there will be the patricians, the upper classes, and yet other ranks below them. Equality may be a *right*, but no power on earth can convert it into *fact*. It would be a good thing for France if this idea could be popularised. The benefits of political harmony are obvious to the least intelligent classes. Harmony is, as it were, the poetry of order, and order is a matter of vital importance to the working population. And what is order, reduced to its simplest expression, but the agreement of things among themselves—unity, in short ? Architecture, music, and poetry, everything in France, and in France more than in any other country, is based upon this principle ; it is written upon the very foundations of her clear accurate language, and a language must always be the most infallible index of national character. In the same way you may note that the French popular airs are those most calculated to strike the imagination, the best-modulated melodies are taken over by the people ; clearness of thought, the intellectual simplicity of an idea attracts them ; they like the incisive sayings that hold the greatest number of ideas. France is the one country in the world where a little phrase may bring about a great revolution. Whenever the masses have risen, it has been to bring men, affairs, and principles into agreement. No nation has a clearer conception of that idea of unity which should permeate the life of an aristocracy ; possibly no other nation has so intelligent a comprehension of a political necessity ; history will never find her behind the time. France has been led astray many a time, but she is deluded, woman-like, by generous ideas, by a glow of enthusiasm which at first out-strips sober reason.

So, to begin with, the most striking characteristic of the Faubourg is the splendour of its great mansions, its great gardens, and a surrounding quiet in keeping with princely revenues drawn from great estates. And what is this distance set between a class and a whole metropolis but visible and outward expression of the widely different attitude of mind which must inevitably keep them apart ? The position of the head is well defined in every organism. If by any chance a nation allows its head to fall at its feet, it is pretty sure sooner or later to discover that this is a suicidal measure ; and since nations have no desire to perish, they set to work at once to grow a new head. If they lack the strength for this, they perish as Rome perished, and Venice, and so many other states.

This distinction between the upper and lower spheres of social activity, emphasised by differences in their manner of living, necessarily implies that in the highest aristocracy there is real worth and some distinguishing merit. In any state, no matter what form of " government " is affected, so soon as the patrician class fails to maintain that complete superiority which is the condition of its existence, it ceases to be a force, and is pulled down at once by the populace. The people always wish to see money, power, and initiative in their leaders, hands, hearts, and heads ; they must be the spokesmen, they must represent the intelligence and the glory of the nation. Nations, like women, love strength in those who rule them ; they cannot give love without respect ; they refuse utterly to obey those of whom they do not stand in awe. An aristocracy fallen into contempt is a *roi fainéant*, a husband in petticoats ; first it ceases to be itself, and then it ceases to be.

And in this way the isolation of the great, the sharply marked distinction in their manner of life, or in a word, the general custom of the patrician caste is at once the sign of a real power, and their destruction so soon as that power is lost. The Faubourg Saint-Germain failed to recognise the conditions of its being, while it would still have been easy to perpetuate its existence, and therefore was brought low for a time. The Faubourg should have looked the facts fairly in the face, as the English aristocracy did before them ; they should have seen that every institution has its climacteric periods, when words lose their old meanings, and ideas reappear in a new guise, and the whole conditions of politics wear a changed aspect, while the underlying realities undergo no essential alteration.

These ideas demand further development which form an essential part of this episode ; they are given here both as a succinct statement of the causes, and an explanation of the things which happen in the course of the story.

The stateliness of the castles and palaces where nobles dwell; the luxury of the details; the constantly maintained sumptuousness of the furniture; the "atmosphere" in which the fortunate owner of landed estates (a rich man before he was born) lives and moves easily and without friction; the habit of mind which never descends to calculate the petty workaday gains of existence; the leisure; the higher education attainable at a much earlier age; and lastly, the aristocratic tradition that makes of him a social force, for which his opponents, by dint of study and a strong will and tenacity of vocation, are scarcely a match—all these things should contribute to form a lofty spirit in a man, possessed of such privileges from his youth up; they should stamp his character with that high self-respect, of which the least consequence is a nobleness of heart in harmony with the noble name that he bears. And in some few families all this is realised. There are noble characters here and there in the Faubourg, but they are marked exceptions to a general rule of egoism which has been the ruin of this world within a world. The privileges above enumerated are the birthright of the French noblesse, as of every patrician efflorescence ever formed on the surface of a nation; and will continue to be theirs so long as their existence is based upon real estate, or money; *domaine-sol* and *domaine-argent* alike, the only solid bases of an organised society; but such privileges are held upon the understanding that the patricians must continue to justify their existence. There is a sort of moral *fief* held on a tenure of service rendered to the sovereign, and here in France the people are undoubtedly the sovereigns nowadays. The times are changed, and so are the weapons. The knight-banneret of old wore a coat of chain armour and a hauberk,; he could handle a lance well and display his pennon, and no more was required of him; today he is bound to give proof of his intelligence. A stout heart was enough in the days of old; in our days he is required to have a capacious brain-pan. Skill and knowledge and capital—these three points mark out a social triangle on which the scutcheon of power is blazoned; our modern aristocracy must take its stand on these.

A fine theorem is as good as a great name. The Rothschilds, the Fuggers of the nineteenth century, are princes *de facto*. A great artist is in reality an oligarch; he represents a whole century, and almost always he is a law to others. And the art of words, the high pressure machinery of the writer, the poet's genius, the merchant's steady endurance, the strong will of the statesman who concentrates a thousand dazzling qualities in himself, the general's sword—all these victories, in short, which a single individual will win, that he may tower above the rest of the world, the patrician class is now bound to win and keep exclusively. They must head the new forces as they once headed the material forces; how should they keep the position unless they are worthy of it? How, unless they are the soul and brain of a nation, shall they set its hands moving? How lead a people without the power of command? And what is the marshal's bâton without the innate power of the captain in the man who wields it? The Faubourg Saint-Germain took to playing with bâtons, and fancied that all the power was in its hands. It inverted the terms of the proposition which called it into existence. And instead of flinging away the insignia which offended the people, and quietly grasping the power, it allowed the bourgeoisie to seize the authority, clung with fatal obstinacy to its shadow, and over and over again forgot the laws which a minority must observe if it would live. When an aristocracy is scarce a thousandth part of the body social, it is bound today, as of old, to multiply its points of action, so as to counterbalance the weight of the masses in a great crisis. And in our days those means of action must be living forces, and not historical memories.

In France, unluckily, the noblesse were still so puffed up with the notion of their vanished power, that it was difficult to contend against a kind of innate presumption in themselves. Perhaps this is a national defect. The Frenchman is less given than anyone else to undervalue himself; it comes natural to him to go from his degree to the one above it; and while it is a rare thing for him to pity the unfortunates over whose heads he rises, he always groans in spirit to see so many fortunate people above him. He is very far from heartless, but too often he prefers to listen to his intellect. The national instinct which brings the Frenchman to the front, the vanity that wastes his substance, is as much a dominant passion as thrift in the Dutch. For three centuries it swayed the noblesse, who, in this respect, were certainly pre-eminently French. The scion of the Faubourg Saint-Germain, beholding his material superiority, was fully persuaded of his intellectual superiority. And everything contributed to confirm him in his belief; for ever since the Faubourg Saint-Germain existed at all—which is to say, ever since Versailles ceased to be the royal residence—the Faubourg, with some few gaps in continuity, was always backed up by the central power, which in France seldom fails to support that side. Thence its downfall n 1830.

At that time the party of the Faubourg Saint-Germain was rather like an army without a base of operation. It had utterly failed to take advantage of the peace to plant itself in the heart of the nation. It sinned for want of learning its lesson, and through an utter incapability of regarding its interests as a whole. A future certainty was sacrificed to a doubtful present gain. This blunder in policy may perhaps be attributed to the following cause.

The class-isolation so strenuously kept up by the noblesse brought about fatal results during the last forty years; even caste-patriotism was extinguished by it, and rivalry fostered among themselves. When the French noblesse of other times were rich and powerful, the nobles (*gentilhommes*) could choose their chiefs and obey them in the hour of danger. As their power diminished, they grew less amenable to discipline; and as in the last days of the Byzantine Empire, everyone wished to be emperor. They mistook their uniform weakness for uniform strength.

Each family ruined by the Revolution and the abolition of the law of primogeniture thought only of itself, and not at all of the great family of the noblesse. It seemed to them that as each individual grew rich, the party as a whole would gain in strength. And herein lay their mistake. Money, likewise, is only the outward and visible sign of power. All these families were made up of persons who preserved a high tradition of courtesy, of true graciousness of life, of refined speech, with a family pride, and a squeamish sense of *noblesse oblige* which suited well with the kind of life they led; a life wholly filled with occupations which become contemptible so soon as they cease to be accessories and take the chief place in existence. There was a certain intrinsic merit in all these people, but the merit was on the surface, and none of them were worth their face-value.

Not a single one among those families had courage to ask itself the question, "Are we strong enough for the responsibility of power?" They were cast on the top, like the lawyers of 1830; and instead of taking the patron's place, like a great man, the Faubourg Saint-Germain showed itself greedy as an upstart. The most intelligent nation in the world perceived clearly that the restored nobles were organising everything for their own particular benefit. From that day the noblesse was doomed. The Faubourg Saint-Germain tried to be an aristocracy when it could only be an oligarchy—two very different systems, as any man may see for himself if he gives an intelligent perusal to the list of the patronymics of the House of Peers.

The King's Government certainly meant well; but the maxim that the people must be made to *will* everything, even their own welfare, was pretty constantly forgotten, nor did they bear in mind that La France is a woman and capricious, and must be happy or chastised at her own good pleasure. If there had been many dukes like the Duc de Laval, whose modesty made him worthy of the name he bore, the elder branch would have been as securely seated on the throne as the House of Hanover at this day.

In 1814 the noblesse of France were called upon to assert their superiority over the most aristocratic bourgeoisie in the most feminine of all countries, to take the lead in the most highly educated epoch the world had yet seen. And this was even more notably the case in 1820. The Faubourg Saint-Germain might very easily have led and amused the middle classes in days when people's heads were turned with distinctions, and art and science were all the rage. But the narrow-minded leaders of a time of great intellectual progress all of them detested art and science. They had not even the wit to present religion in attractive colours, though they needed its support. While Lamartine, Lamennais, Montalembert, and other writers were putting new life and elevation into men's ideas of religion, and gilding it with poetry, these bunglers in the Government chose to make the harshness of their creed felt all over the country. Never was nation in a more tractable humour; La France, like a tired woman, was ready to agree to anything;

never was mismanagement so clumsy; and La France, like a woman, would have forgiven wrongs more easily than bungling.

If the noblesse meant to reinstate themselves, the better to found a strong oligarchy, they should have honestly and diligently searched their Houses for men of the stamp that Napoleon used; they should have turned themselves inside out to see if peradventure there was a Constitutionalist Richelieu lurking in the entrails of the Faubourg; and if that genius was not forthcoming from among them, they should have set out to find him, even in the fireless garret where he might happen to be perishing of cold; they should have assimilated him, as the English House of Lords continually assimilates aristocrats made by chance; and finally ordered him to be ruthless, to lop away the old wood, and cut the tree down to the living shoots. But, in the first place, the great system of English Toryism was far too large for narrow minds; the importation required time, and in France a tardy success is no better than a fiasco. So far, moreover, from adopting a policy of redemption, and looking for new forces where God puts them, these petty great folk took a dislike to any capacity that did not issue from their midst; and, lastly, instead of growing young again, the Faubourg Saint-Germain grew positively older.

Etiquette, not an institution of primary necessity, might have been maintained if it had appeared only on state occasions, but as it was, there was a daily wrangle over precedence; it ceased to be a matter of art or court ceremonial, it became a question of power. And if from the outset the Crown lacked an adviser equal to so great a crisis, the aristocracy was still more lacking in a sense of its wider interests, an instinct which might have supplied the deficiency. They stood nice about M. de Talleyrand's marriage, when M. de Talleyrand was the one man among them with the steel-encompassed brains that can forge a new political system and begin a new career of glory for a nation. The Faubourg scoffed at a minister if he was not gently born, and produced no one of gentle birth that was fit to be a minister. There were plenty of nobles fitted to serve their country by raising the dignity of justices of the peace, by improving the land, by opening out roads and canals, and taking an active and leading part as country gentlemen; but these had sold their estates to gamble on the Stock Exchange. Again the Faubourg might have absorbed the energetic men among the bourgeoisie, and opened their ranks to the ambition which was undermining authority; they preferred instead to fight, and to fight unarmed, for of all that they once possessed there was nothing left but tradition. For their misfortune there was just precisely enough of their former wealth left them as a class to keep up their bitter pride. They were content with their past. Not one of them seriously thought of bidding the son of the house take up arms from the pile of weapons which the nineteenth century flings down in the market-place. Young men, shut out from office, were dancing at Madame's balls, while they should have been doing the work done under the Republic and the Empire by young, conscientious, harmlessly employed energies. It was their place to carry out at Paris the programme which their seniors should have been following in the country. The heads of houses might have won back recognition of their titles by unremitting attention to local interests, by falling in with the spirit of the age, by recasting their order to suit the taste of the times.

But, pent up together in the Faubourg Saint-Germain, where the spirit of the ancient court and traditions of bygone feuds between the nobles and the Crown still lingered on, the aristocracy was not whole-hearted in its allegiance to the Tuileries, and so much the more easily defeated because it was concentrated in the Chamber of Peers, and badly organised even there. If the noblesse had woven themselves into a network over the country, they could have held their own ; but cooped up in their Faubourg, with their backs against the Château, or spread at full length over the Budget, a single blow cut the thread of a fast-expiring life, and a petty, smug-faced lawyer came forward with the axe. In spite of M. Royer-Collard's admirable discourse, the hereditary peerage and law of entail fell before the lampoons of a man who made it a boast that he had adroitly argued some few heads out of the executioner's clutches, and now forsooth must clumsily proceed to the slaying of old institutions.

There are examples and lessons for the future in all this. For if there were not still a future before the French aristocracy, there would be no need to do more than find a suitable sarcophagus ; it were something pitilessly cruel to burn the dead body of it with fire of Tophet. But though the surgeon's scalpel is ruthless, it sometimes gives back life to a dying man ; and the Faubourg Saint-Germain may wax more powerful under persecution than in its day of triumph, if it but chooses to organise itself under a leader.

And now it is easy to give a summary of this semi-political survey. The wish to re-establish a large fortune was uppermost in everyone's mind ; a lack of broad views, and a mass of small defects, a real need of religion as a political factor, combined with a thirst for pleasure which damaged the cause of religion and necessitated a good deal of hypocrisy ; a certain attitude of protest on the part of loftier and clearer-sighted men who set their faces against Court jealousies ; and the disaffection of the provincial families, who often came of purer descent than the nobles of the Court which alienated them from itself—all these things combined to bring about a most discordant state of things in the Faubourg Saint-Germain. It was neither compact in its organisation, nor consequent in its action ; neither completely moral, nor frankly dissolute ; it did not corrupt, nor was it corrupted ; it would neither wholly abandon the disputed points which damaged its cause, nor yet adopt the policy that might have saved it. In short, however effete individuals might be, the party as a whole was none the less armed with all the great principles which lie at the roots of national existence. What was there in the Faubourg that it should perish in its strength ?

It was very hard to please in the choice of candidates; the Faubourg had good taste, it was scornfully fastidious, yet there was nothing very glorious nor chivalrous truly about its fall.

In the Emigration of 1789 there were some traces of a loftier feeling; but in the Emigration of 1830 from Paris into the country there was nothing discernible but self-interest. A few famous men of letters, a few oratorical triumphs in the Chambers, M. de Talleyrand's attitude in the Congress, the taking of Algiers, and not a few names that found their way from the battlefield into the pages of history—all these things were so many examples set before the French noblesse to show that it was still open to them to take their part in the national existence, and to win recognition of their claims, if, indeed, they could condescend thus far. In every living organism the work of bringing the whole into harmony within itself is always going on. If a man is indolent, the indolence shows itself in everything that he does; and, in the same manner, the general spirit of a class is pretty plainly manifested in the face it turns on the world, and the soul informs the body.

The women of the Restoration displayed neither the proud disregard of public opinion shown by the court ladies of olden time in their wantonness, nor yet the simple grandeur of the tardy virtues by which they expiated their sins and shed so bright a glory about their names. There was nothing either very frivolous or very serious about the woman of the Restoration. She was hypocritical as a rule in her passion, and compounded, so to speak, with its pleasures. Some few families led the domestic life of the Duchesse d'Orléans, whose connubial couch was exhibited so absurdly to visitors at the Palais Royal. Two or three kept up the traditions of the Regency, filling cleverer women with something like disgust. The great lady of the new school exercised no influence at all over the manners of the time; and yet she might have done much. She might, at worst, have presented as dignified a spectacle as Englishwomen of the same rank. But she hesitated feebly among old precedents, became a bigot by force of circumstances, and allowed nothing of herself to appear, not even her better qualities.

Not one among the Frenchwomen of that day had the ability to create a salon whither leaders of fashion might come to take lessons in taste and elegance. Their voices, which once laid down the law to literature, that living expression of a time, now counted absolutely for nought. Now when a literature lacks a general system, it fails to shape a body for itself, and dies out with its period.

When in a nation at any time there is a people apart thus constituted, the historian is pretty certain to find some representative figure, some central personage who embodies the qualities and the defects of the whole party to which he belongs; there is Coligny, for instance, among the Huguenots, the Coadjuteur in the time of the Fronde, the Maréchal de Richelieu under Louis XV, Danton during the Terror. It is in the nature of things that the man should be identified with the company in which history finds him. How is it possible to lead a party without conforming to its ideas ? or to shine in any epoch unless a man represents the ideas of his time ? The wise and prudent head of a party is continually obliged to bow to the prejudices and follies of its rear ; and this is the cause of actions for which he is afterwards criticised by this or that historian sitting at a safer distance from terrific popular explosions, coolly judging the passion and ferment without which the great struggles of the world could not be carried on at all. And if this is true of the Historical Comedy of the Centuries, it is equally true in a more restricted sphere in the detached scenes of the national drama known as the *Manners of the Age*.

At the beginning of that ephemeral life led by the Faubourg Saint-Germain under the Restoration, to which, if there is any truth in the above reflections, they failed to give stability, the most perfect type of the aristocratic caste in its weakness and strength, its greatness and littleness, might have been found for a brief space in a young married woman who belonged to it. This was a woman artificially educated, but in reality ignorant ; a woman whose instincts and feelings were lofty, while the thought which should have controlled them was wanting. She squandered the wealth of her nature in obedience to social conventions ; she was ready to brave society, yet she hesitated till her scruples degenerated into artifice. With more wilfulness than real force of character, impressionable rather than enthusiastic, gifted with more brain than heart ; she was supremely a woman, supremely a coquette, and above all things a Parisienne, loving a brilliant life and gaiety, reflecting never, or too late ; imprudent to the verge of poetry, and humble in the depths of her heart, in spite of her charming insolence. Like some straight-growing reed, she made a show of independence ; yet, like the reed, she was ready to bend to a strong hand. She talked much of religion, and had it not at heart, though she was prepared to find in it a solution of her life. How explain a creature so complex ? Capable of heroism, yet sinking unconsciously from heroic heights to utter a spiteful word ; young and sweet-natured, not so much old at heart as aged by the maxims of those about her ; versed in a selfish philosophy in which she was all unpractised, she had all the vices of a courtier, all the nobleness of developing womanhood. She trusted nothing and no one, yet there were times when she quitted her sceptical attitude for a submissive credulity.

How should any portrait be anything but incomplete of her, in whom the play of swiftly-changing colour made discord only to produce a poetic confusion ? For in her there shone a divine brightness, a radiance of youth that blended all her bewildering characteristics in a certain completeness and unity informed by her charm. Nothing was feigned. The passion or semi-passion, the ineffectual high aspirations, the actual pettiness, the coolness of sentiment and warmth of impulse, were all spontaneous and unaffected, and as much the outcome of her own position as of the position of the aristocracy to which she belonged. She was wholly self-contained ; she put herself proudly above the world and beneath the shelter of her name. There was something of the egoism of Medea in her life, as in the life of the aristocracy that lay a-dying, and would not so much as raise itself or stretch out a hand to any political physician ; so well aware of its feebleness, or so conscious that it was already dust, that it refused to touch or be touched.

The Duchesse de Langeais (for that was her name) had been married for about four years when the Restoration was finally consummated, which is to say, in 1816. By that time the revolution of the Hundred Days had let in the light on the mind of Louis XVIII. In spite of his surroundings, he comprehended the situation and the age in which he was living ; and it was only later, when this Louis XI, without the axe, lay stricken down by disease, that those about him got the upper hand. The Duchesse de Langeais, a Navarreins by birth, came of a ducal house which had made a point of never marrying below its rank since the reign of Louis XIV. Every daughter of the house must sooner or later take a *tabouret* at Court. So, Antoinette de Navarreins, at the age of eighteen, came out of the profound solitude in which her girlhood had been spent to marry the Duc de Langeais's eldest son. The two families at that time were living quite out of the world ; but after the invasion of France, the return of the Bourbons seemed to every Royalist mind the only possible way of putting an end to the miseries of the war.

The Ducs de Navarreins and de Langeais had been faithful throughout to the exiled Princes, nobly resisting all the temptations of glory under the Empire. Under the circumstances they naturally followed out the old family policy ; and Mlle Antoinette, a beautiful and portionless girl, was married to M. le Marquis de Langeais only a few months before the death of the Duke his father.

After the return of the Bourbons, the families resumed their rank, offices, and dignity at Court ; once more they entered public life, from which hitherto they held aloof, and took their place high on the sunlit summits of the new political world. In that time of general baseness and sham political conversions, the public conscience was glad to recognise the unstained loyalty of the two houses, and a consistency in political and private life for which all parties involuntarily respected them. But, unfortunately, as so often happens in a time of transition, the most disinterested persons, the men whose loftiness of view and wise principles would have gained the confidence of the French nation and led them to believe in the generosity of a novel and spirited policy — these men, to repeat, were taken out of affairs, and public business was allowed to fall into the hands of others, who found it to their interest to push principles to their extreme consequences by way of proving their devotion.

The families of Langeais and Navarreins remained about the Court, condemned to perform the duties required by Court ceremonial amid the reproaches and sneers of the Liberal party. They were accused of gorging themselves with riches and honours, and all the while their family estates were no larger than before, and liberal allowances from the civil list were wholly expended in keeping up the state necessary for any European government, even if it be a Republic.

In 1818, M. le Duc de Langeais commanded a division of the army, and the Duchess held a post about one of the Princesses, in virtue of which she was free to live in Paris and apart from her husband without scandal. The Duke, moreover, besides his military duties, had a place at Court, to which he came during his term of waiting, leaving his major-general in command. The Duke and Duchess were leading lives entirely apart, the world none the wiser. Their marriage of convention shared the fate of nearly all family arrangements of the kind. Two more antipathetic dispositions could not well have been found; they were brought together; they jarred upon each other; there was soreness on either side; then they were divided once for all. Then they went their separate ways, with a due regard for appearances. The Duc de Langeais, by nature as methodical as the Chevalier de Folard himself, gave himself up methodically to his own tastes and amusements, and left his wife at liberty to do as she pleased so soon as he felt sure of her character. He recognised in her a spirit pre-eminently proud, a cold heart, a profound submissiveness to the usages of the world, and a youthful loyalty. Under the eyes of great relations, with the light of a prudish and bigoted Court turned full upon the Duchess, his honour was safe.

So the Duke calmly did as the *grands seigneurs* of the eighteenth century did before him, and left a young wife of two-and-twenty to her own devices. He had deeply offended that wife, and in her nature there was one appalling characteristic—she would never forgive an offence when woman's vanity and self-love, with all that was best in her nature perhaps, had been slighted, wounded in secret. Insult and injury in the face of the world a woman loves to forget; there is a way open to her of showing herself great; she is a woman in her forgiveness; but a secret offence women never pardon; for secret baseness, as for hidden virtues and hidden love, they have no kindness.

This was Mme la Duchesse de Langeais's real position, unknown to the world. She herself did not reflect upon it. It was the time of the rejoicings over the Duc de Berri's marriage. The Court and the Faubourg roused itself from its listlessness and reserve. This was the real beginning of that unheard-of splendour which the Government of the Restoration carried too far. At that time the Duchess, whether for reasons of her own, or from vanity, never appeared in public without a following of women equally distinguished by name and fortune. As queen of fashion she had her *dames d'atours*, her ladies, who modelled their manner and their wit on hers. They had been cleverly chosen. None of her satellites belonged to the inmost Court circle, nor to the highest level of the Faubourg Saint-Germain; but they had set their minds upon admission to those inner sanctuaries. Being as yet simple dominations, they wished to rise to the neighbourhood of the throne, and mingle with the seraphic powers in the high sphere known as *le petit château*. Thus surrounded, the Duchess's position was stronger and more commanding and secure. Her "ladies" defended her character and helped her to play her detestable part of a woman of fashion. She could laugh at men at her ease, play with fire, receive the homage on which the feminine nature is nourished, and remain mistress of herself.

At Paris, in the highest society of all, a woman is a woman still; she lives on incense, adulation, and honours. No beauty, however undoubted, no face, however fair, is anything without admiration. Flattery and a lover are proofs of power. And what is power without recognition? Nothing. If the prettiest of women were left alone in a corner of a drawing-room, she would droop. Put her in the very centre and summit of social grandeur, she will at once aspire to reign over all hearts—often because it is out of her power to be the happy queen of one. Dress and manner and coquetry are all meant to please one of the poorest creatures extant—the brainless coxcomb, whose handsome face is his sole merit; it was for such as these that women threw themselves away. The gilded wooden idols of the Restoration, for they were neither more nor less, had neither the antecedents of the *petits maîtres* of the time of the Fronde, nor the rough sterling worth of Napoleon's heroes, not the wit and fine manners of their grandsires; but something of all three they meant to be without any trouble to themselves. Brave they were, like all young Frenchmen; ability they possessed, no doubt, if they had had a chance of proving it, but their places were filled up by the old worn-out men, who kept them in leading strings. It was a day of small things, a cold prosaic era. Perhaps it takes a long time for a Restoration to become a Monarchy.

For the past eighteen months the Duchesse de Langeais had been leading this empty life, filled with balls and subsequent visits, objectless triumphs, and the transient loves that spring up and die in an evening's space. All eyes were turned on her when she entered a room; she reaped her harvest of flatteries and some few words of warmer admiration, which she encouraged by a gesture or a glance, but never suffered to penetrate deeper than the skin. Her tone and bearing and everything else about her imposed her will upon others. Her life was a sort of fever of vanity and perpetual enjoyment, which turned her head. She was daring enough in conversation; she would listen to anything, corrupting the surface, as it were, of her heart. Yet when she returned home, she often blushed at the story that had made her laugh; at the scandalous tale that supplied the details, on the strength of which she analysed the love that she had never known, and marked the subtle distinctions of modern passion, not with comment on the part of complacent hypocrites. For women know how to say everything among themselves, and more of them are ruined by each other than corrupted by men.

There came a moment when she discerned that not until a woman is loved will the world fully recognise her beauty and her wit. What does a husband prove? Simply that a girl or woman was endowed with wealth, or well brought up; that her mother managed cleverly; that in some way she satisfied a man's ambitions. A lover constantly bears witness to her personal perfections. Then followed the discovery, still in Mme de Langeais's early womanhood, that it was possible to be loved without committing herself, without permission, without vouchsafing any satisfaction beyond the most meagre dues. There was more than one demure feminine hypocrite to instruct her in the art of playing such dangerous comedies.

So the Duchess had her court, and the number of her adorers and courtiers guaranteed her virtue. She was amiable and fascinating; she flirted till the ball or the evening's gaiety was at an end. Then the curtain dropped. She was cold, indifferent, self-contained again, till the next day brought its renewed sensations, superficial as before. Two or three men were completely deceived, and fell in love in earnest. She laughed at them, she was utterly insensible. "I am loved!" she told herself. "He loves me!" The certainty sufficed her. It is enough for the miser to know that his every whim might be fulfilled if he chose; so it was with the Duchess, and perhaps she did not even go so far as to form a wish.

One evening she chanced to be at the house of an intimate friend, Mme la Vicomtesse de Fontaine, one of the humble rivals who cordially detested her, and went with her everywhere. In a "friendship" of this sort both sides are on their guard, and never lay their armour aside; confidences are ingeniously indiscreet, and not unfrequently treacherous. Mme de Langeais had distributed her little patronising, friendly, or freezing bows, with the air natural to a woman who knows the worth of her smiles, when her eyes fell upon a total stranger. Something in the man's large gravity of aspect startled her, and, with a feeling almost like dread, she turned to Mme de Maufrigneuse with, "Who is the newcomer, dear?"

"Someone that you have heard of, no doubt. The Marquis de Montriveau."

"Oh! is it he?"

She took up her eyeglass and submitted him to a very insolent scrutiny, as if he had been a picture meant to receive glances, not to return them.

"Do introduce him; he ought to be interesting."

"Nobody more tiresome and dull, dear. But he is the fashion."

M. Armand de Montriveau, at that moment all unwittingly the object of general curiosity, better deserved attention than any of the idols that Paris needs must set up to worship for a brief space, for the city is vexed by periodical fits of craving, a passion for *engouement* and sham enthusiasm, which must be satisfied. The Marquis was the only son of General de Montriveau, one of the *ci-devants* who served the Republic nobly, and fell by Joubert's side at Novi. Bonaparte had placed his son at the school at Châlons, with the orphans of other generals who fell on the battlefield, leaving their children under the protection of the Republic. Armand de Montriveau left school with his way to make, entered the artillery, and had only reached a major's rank at the time of the Fontainebleau disaster. In his section of the service the chances of advancement were not many. There are fewer officers, in the first place, among the gunners than in any other corps; and in the second place, the feeling in the artillery was decidedly Liberal, not to say Republican; and the Emperor, feeling little confidence in a body of highly educated men who were apt to think for themselves, gave promotion grudgingly in the service. In the artillery, accordingly, the general rule of the army did not apply; the commanding officers were not invariably the most remarkable men in their department, because there was less to be feared from mediocrities. The artillery was a separate corps in those days, and only came under Napoleon in action.

Besides these general causes, other reasons, inherent in Armand de Montriveau's character, were sufficient in themselves to account for his tardy promotion. He was alone in the world. He had been thrown at the age of twenty into the whirlwind of men directed by Napoleon; his interests were bounded by himself, any day he might lose his life; it became a habit of mind with him to live by his own self-respect and the consciousness that he had done his duty. Like all shy men, he was habitually silent; but his shyness sprang by no means from timidity; it was a kind of modesty in him; he found any demonstration of vanity intolerable. There was no sort of swagger about his fearlessness in action; nothing escaped his eyes; he could give sensible advice to his chums with unshaken coolness; he could go under fire, and duck upon occasion to avoid bullets. He was kindly; but his expression was haughty and stern, and his face gained him this character. In everything he was rigorous as arithmetic; he never permitted the slightest deviation from duty on any plausible pretext, nor blinked the consequences of a fact. He would lend himself to nothing of which he was ashamed; he never asked anything for himself; in short, Armand de Montriveau was one of many great men unknown to fame, and philosophical enough to despise it; living without attaching themselves to life, because they have not found their opportunity of developing to the full their power to do and feel.

People were afraid of Montriveau; they respected him, but he was not very popular. Men may indeed allow you to rise above them, but to decline to descend as low as they can do is the one unpardonable sin. In their feeling towards loftier natures, there is a trace of hate and fear. Too much honour with them implies censure of themselves, a thing forgiven neither to the living nor to the dead.

After the Emperor's farewells at Fontainebleau, Montriveau, noble though he was, was put on half-pay. Perhaps the heads of the War Office took fright at uncompromising uprightness worthy of antiquity, or perhaps it was known that he felt bound by his oath to the Imperial Eagle. During the Hundred Days he was made a Colonel of the Guard, and left on the field of Waterloo. His wounds kept him in Belgium; he was not present at the disbanding of the Army of the Loire, but the King's government declined to recognise promotion made during the Hundred Days, and Armand de Montriveau left France.

An adventurous spirit, a loftiness of thought hitherto satisfied by the hazards of war, drove him on an exploring expedition through Upper Egypt; his sanity or impulse directed his enthusiasm to a project of great importance, he turned his attention to that unexplored Central Africa which occupies the learned of today. The scientific expedition was long and unfortunate. He had made a valuable collection of notes bearing on various geographical and commercial problems, of which solutions are still eagerly sought; and succeeded, after surmounting many obstacles, in reaching the heart of the continent, when he was betrayed into the hands of a hostile native tribe. Then, stripped of all that he had, for two years he led a wandering life in the desert, the slave of savages, threatened with death at every moment, and more cruelly treated than a dumb animal in the power of pitiless children. Physical strength, and a mind braced to endurance, enabled him to survive the horrors of that captivity; but his miraculous escape well-nigh exhausted his energies. When he reached the French colony at Senegal, a half-dead fugitive covered with rags, his memories of his former life were dim and shapeless. The great sacrifices made in his travels were all forgotten like his studies of African dialects, his discoveries, and observations. One story will give an idea of all that he passed through. Once for several days the children of the sheikh of the tribe amused themselves by putting him up for a mark and flinging horses' knuckle-bones at his head.

Montriveau came back to Paris in 1818 a ruined man. He had no interest, and wished for none. He would have died twenty times over sooner than ask a favour of anyone; he would not even press the recognition of his claims. Adversity and hardship had developed his energy even in trifles, while the habit of preserving his self-respect before that spiritual self which we call conscience led him to attach consequence to the most apparently trivial actions. His merits and adventures became known, however, through his acquaintances, among the principal men of science in Paris, and some few well-read military men. The incidents of his slavery and subsequent escape bore witness to a courage, intelligence, and coolness which won him celebrity without his knowledge, and that transient fame of which Paris salons are lavish, though the artist that fain would keep it must make untold efforts.

Montriveau's position suddenly changed towards the end of that year. He had been a poor man, he was now rich; or, externally at any rate, he had all the advantages of wealth. The King's government, trying to attach capable men to itself and to strengthen the army, made concessions about that time to Napoleon's old officers if their known loyalty and character offered guarantees of fidelity. M. de Montriveau's name once more appeared in the army list with the rank of colonel ; he received his arrears of pay and passed into the Guards. All these favours, one after another, came to seek the Marquis de Montriveau ; he had asked for nothing however small. Friends had taken the steps for him which he would have refused to take for himself.

After this, his habits were modified all at once ; contrary to his custom, he went into society. He was well received, everywhere he met with great deference and respect. He seemed to have found some end in life ; but everything passed within the man, there were no external signs ; in society he was silent and cold, and wore a grave, reserved face. His social success was great, precisely because he stood out in such strong contrast to the conventional faces which line the walls of Paris salons. He was, indeed, something quite new there. Terse of speech, like a hermit or a savage, his shyness was thought to be haughtiness, and people were greatly taken with it. He was something strange and great. Women generally were so much the more smitten with this original person because he was not to be caught by their flatteries, however adroit, nor by the wiles with which they circumvent the strongest men and corrode the steel temper. Their Parisian's grimaces were lost upon M. de Montriveau ; his nature only responded to the sonorous vibration of lofty thought and feeling. And he would very promptly have been dropped but for the romance that hung about his adventures and his life ; but for the men who cried him up behind his back ; but for a woman who looked for a triumph for her vanity, the woman who was to fill his thoughts.

For these reasons the Duchesse de Langeais's curiosity was no less lively than natural. Chance had so ordered it that her interest in the man before her had been aroused only the day before, when she heard the story of one of M. de Montriveau's adventures, a story calculated to make the strongest impression upon a woman's ever-changing fancy.

During M. de Montriveau's voyage of discovery to the sources of the Nile, he had had an argument with one of his guides, surely the most extraordinary debate in the annals of travel. The district that he wished to explore could only be reached on foot across a tract of desert. Only one of his guides knew the way ; no traveller had penetrated before into that part of the country, where the undaunted officer hoped to find a solution of several scientific problems. In spite of the representations made to him by the guide and the older men of the place, he started upon the formidable journey. Summoning up courage, already highly strung by the prospect of dreadful difficulties, he set out in the morning.

The loose sand shifted under his feet at every step ; and when, at the end of a long day's march, he lay down to sleep on the ground, he had never been so tired in his life. He knew, however, that he must be up and on his way before dawn next day, and his guide assured him that they should reach the end of their journey towards noon. That promise kept up his courage and gave him new strength. In spite of his sufferings, he continued his march, with some blasphemings against science ; he was ashamed to complain to his guide, and kept his pain to himself.

After marching for a third of the day, he felt his strength failing, his feet were bleeding, he asked if they should reach the place soon. " In an hour's time," said the guide. Armand braced himself for another hour's march, and they went on.

The hour slipped by ; he could not so much as see against the sky the palm-trees and crests of hill that should tell of the end of the journey near at hand ; the horizon line of sand was vast as the circle of the open sea.

He came to a stand, refused to go farther, and threatened the guide—he had deceived him, murdered him ; tears of rage and weariness flowed over his fevered cheeks ; he was bowed down with fatigue upon fatigue, his throat seemed to be glued by the desert thirst. The guide meanwhile stood motionless, listening to these complaints with an ironical expression, studying the while, with the apparent indifference of an Oriental, the scarcely perceptible indications in the lie of the sands, which looked almost black, like burnished gold.

" I have made a mistake," he remarked coolly. " I could not make out the track, it is so long since I came this way ; we are surely on it now, but we must push on for two hours."

" The man is right," thought M. de Montriveau.

So he went on again, struggling to follow the pitiless native. It seemed as if he were bound to his guide by some thread like the invisible tie between the condemned man and the headsman. But the two hours went by, Montriveau had spent his last drops of energy, and the skyline was a blank, there were no palm-trees, no hills. He could neither cry out nor groan, he lay down on the sand to die, but his eyes would have frightened the boldest ; something in his face seemed to say that he would not die alone. His guide, like a very fiend, gave him back a cool glance like a man that knows his power, left him to lie there, and kept at a safe distance out of reach of his desperate victim. At last M. Montriveau recovered strength enough for a last curse. The guide came nearer, silenced him with a steady look, and said, " Was it not your own will to go where I am taking you, in spite of us all ? You say that I have lied to you. If I had not, you would not be even here. Do you want the truth ? Here it is. *We have still another five hours' march before us, and we cannot go back.* Sound yourself ; if you have not courage enough, here is my dagger."

Startled by this dreadful knowledge of pain and human strength, M. de Montriveau would not be behind a savage ; he drew a fresh stock of courage from his pride as a European, rose to his feet, and followed his guide. The five hours were at an end, and still M. de Montriveau saw nothing, he turned his failing eyes upon his guide ; but the Nubian hoisted him on his shoulders, and showed him a wide pool of water with greenness all about it, and a noble forest lighted up by the sunset. It lay only a hundred paces away ; a vast ledge of granite hid the glorious landscape. It seemed to Armand that he had taken a new lease of life. His guide, that giant in courage and intelligence, finished his work of devotion by carrying him across the hot, slippery, scarcely discernible track on the granite. Behind him lay the hell of burning sand, before him the earthly paradise of the most beautiful oasis in the desert.

The Duchess, struck from the first by the appearance of this romantic figure, was even more impressed when she learned that this was that Marquis de Montriveau of whom she had dreamed during the night. She had been with him among the hot desert sands, he had been the companion of her nightmare wanderings ; for such a woman was not this a delightful presage of a new interest in her life ? And never was a man's exterior a better exponent of his character ; never were curious glances so well justified. The principal characteristic of his great, square-hewn head was the thick, luxuriant black hair which framed his face, and gave him a strikingly close resemblance to General Kléber ; and the likeness still held good in the vigorous forehead, in the outlines of his face, the quiet fearlessness of his eyes, and a kind of fiery vehemence expressed by strongly marked features. He was short, deep-chested, and muscular as a lion. There was something of the despot about him, and an indescribable suggestion of the security of strength in his gait, bearing, and slightest movements. He seemed to know that his will was irresistible, perhaps because he wished for nothing unjust. And yet, like all really strong men, he was mild of speech, simple in his manners, and kindly natured ; although it seemed as if, in the stress of a great crisis, all these finer qualities must disappear, and the man would show himself implacable, unshaken in his resolve, terrific in action. There was a certain drawing in of the inner line of the lips which, to a close observer, indicated an ironical bent.

The Duchesse de Langeais, realising that a fleeting glory was to be won by such a conquest, made up her mind to gain a lover in Armand de Montriveau during the brief interval before the Duchesse de Maufrigneuse brought him to be introduced. She would prefer him above the others ; she would attach him to herself, display all her powers of coquetry for him. It was a fancy, such a merest Duchess's whim as furnished a Lope or a Calderon with the plot of the *Dog in the Manger*. She would not suffer another woman to engross him ; but she had not the remotest intention of being his.

Nature had given the Duchess every qualification for the part of coquette, and education had perfected her. Women envied her, and men fell in love with her, not without reason. Nothing that can inspire love, justify it, and give it lasting empire was wanting in her. Her style of beauty, her manner, her voice, her bearing, all combined to give her that instinctive coquetry which seems to be the consciousness of power. Her shape was graceful ; perhaps there was a trace of self-consciousness in her changes of movement, the one affectation that could be laid to her charge ; but everything about her was a part of her personality, from her least little gesture to the peculiar turn of her phrases, the demure glance of her eyes. Her great lady's grace, her most striking characteristic, had not destroyed the very French quick mobility of her person. There was an extraordinary fascination in her swift, incessant changes of attitude. She seemed as if she surely would be a most delicious mistress when her corset and the encumbering costume of her part were laid aside. All the rapture of love surely was latent in the freedom of her expressive glances, in her caressing tones, in the charm of her words. She gave glimpses of the high-born courtesan within her, vainly protesting against the creeds of the duchess.

You might sit near her through an evening, she would be gay and melancholy in turn, and her gaiety, like her sadness, seemed spontaneous. She could be gracious, disdainful, insolent, or confiding at will. Her apparent good nature was real; she had no temptation to descend to malignity. But at each moment her mood changed; she was full of confidence or craft; her moving tenderness would give place to a heart-breaking hardness and insensibility. Yet how paint her as she was, without bringing together all the extremes of feminine nature? In a word, the Duchess was anything that she wished to be or to seem. Her face was slightly too long. There was a grace in it, and a certain thinness and fineness that recalled the portraits of the Middle Ages. Her skin was white, with a faint rose tint. Everything about her erred, as it were, by an excess of delicacy.

M. de Montriveau willingly consented to be introduced to the Duchesse de Langeais; and she, after the manner of persons whose sensitive taste leads them to avoid banalities, refrained from overwhelming him with questions and compliments. She received him with a gracious deference which could not fail to flatter a man of more than ordinary powers, for the fact that a man rises above the ordinary level implies that he possesses something of that tact which makes women quick to read feeling. If the Duchess showed any curiosity, it was by her glances; her compliments were conveyed in her manner; there was a winning grace displayed in her words, a subtle suggestion of a desire to please which she of all women knew the art of manifesting. Yet her whole conversation was but, in a manner, the body of the letter; the postscript with the principal thought in it was still to come. After half an hour spent in ordinary talk, in which the words gained all their value from her tone and smiles, M. de Montriveau was about to retire discreetly, when the Duchess stopped him with an expressive gesture.

"I do not know, monsieur, whether these few minutes during which I have had the pleasure of talking to you proved so sufficiently attractive, that I may venture to ask you to call upon me; I am afraid that it may be very selfish of me to wish to have you all to myself. If I should be so fortunate as to find that my house is agreeable to you, you will always find me at home in the evening until ten o'clock."

The invitation was given with such irresistible grace, that M. de Montriveau could not refuse to accept it. When he fell back again among the groups of men gathered at a distance from the women, his friends congratulated him, half laughingly, half in earnest, on the extraordinary reception vouchsafed him by the Duchesse de Langeais. The difficult and brilliant conquest had been made beyond a doubt, and the glory of it was reserved for the Artillery of the Guard. It is easy to imagine the jests, good and bad, when this topic had once been started; the world of Paris salons is so eager for amusement, and a joke lasts for such a short time, that everyone is eager to make the most of it while it is fresh.

All unconsciously, the General felt flattered by this nonsense. From his place where he had taken his stand, his eyes were drawn again and again to the Duchess by countless wavering reflections. He could not help admitting to himself that of all the women whose beauty had captivated his eyes, not one had seemed to be a more exquisite embodiment of faults and fair qualities blended in a completeness that might realise the dreams of earliest manhood. Is there a man in any rank of life that has not felt indefinable rapture in his secret soul over the woman singled out (if only in his dreams) to be his own; when she, in body, soul, and social aspects, satisfies his every requirement, a thrice perfect woman? And if this threefold perfection that flatters his pride is no argument for loving her, it is beyond cavil one of the great inducements to the sentiment. Love would soon be convalescent, as the eighteenth century moralist remarked, were it not for vanity. And it is certainly true that for everyone, man or woman, there is a wealth of pleasure in the superiority of the beloved. Is she set so high by birth that a contemptuous glance can never wound her? is she wealthy enough to surround herself with state which falls nothing short of royalty, of kings, of finance during their short reign of splendour? is she so ready-witted that a keen-edged jest never brings her into confusion? beautiful enough to rival any woman?—Is it such a small thing to know that your self-love will never suffer through her? A man makes these reflections in the twinkling of an eye. And how if, in the future opened out by early ripened passion, he catches glimpses of the changeful delight of her charm, the frank innocence of a maiden soul, the perils of love's voyage, the thousand folds of the veil of coquetry? Is not this enough to move the coldest man's heart?

This, therefore, was M. de Montriveau's position with regard to woman; his past life in some measure explaining the extraordinary fact. He had been thrown, when little more than a boy, into the hurricane of Napoleon's wars; his life had been spent on fields of battle. Of women he knew just so much as a traveller knows of a country when he travels across it in haste from one inn to another. The verdict which Voltaire passed upon his eighty years of life might, perhaps, have been applied by Montriveau to his own thirty-seven years of existence; had he not thirty-seven follies with which to reproach himself? At his age he was as much a novice in love as the lad that has just been furtively reading *Faublas*. Of women he had nothing to learn;

of love he knew nothing; and thus, desires, quite unknown before, sprang from this virginity of feeling.

There are men here and there as much engrossed in the work demanded of them by poverty or ambition, art or science, as M. de Montriveau by war and a life of adventure—these know what it is to be in this unusual position if they very seldom confess to it. Every man in Paris is supposed to have been in love. No woman in Paris cares to take what other women have passed over. The dread of being taken for a fool is the source of the coxcomb's bragging so common in France; for in France to have the reputation of a fool is to be a foreigner in one's own country. Vehement desire seized on M. de Montriveau, desire that had gathered strength from the heat of the desert and the first stirrings of a heart unknown as yet in its suppressed turbulence. A strong man, and violent as he was strong, he could keep mastery over himself; but as he talked of indifferent things, he retired within himself, and swore to possess this woman, for through that thought lay the only way to love for him. Desire became a solemn compact made with himself, an oath after the manner of the Arabs among whom he had lived; for among them a vow is a kind of contract made with Destiny, a man's whole future is solemnly pledged to fulfil it, and everything, even his own death, is regarded simply as a means to the one end.

A younger man would have said to himself, "I should very much like to have the Duchess for my mistress!" or, "If the Duchesse de Langeais cared for a man, he would be a very lucky rascal!" But the General said, "I will have Mme de Langeais for my mistress." And if a man takes such an idea into his head when his heart has never been touched before, and love begins to be a kind of religion with him, he little knows in what a hell he has set his foot.

Armand de Montriveau suddenly took flight and went home in the first hot fever-fit of the first love that he had known. When a man has kept all his boyish beliefs, illusions, frankness, and impetuosity into middle age, his first impulse is, as it were, to stretch out a hand to take the thing that he desires; a little later he realises that there is a gulf set between them, and that it is all but impossible to cross it. A sort of childish impatience seizes him, he wants the thing the more, and trembles or cries. Wherefore, the next day, after the stormiest reflections that had yet perturbed his mind, Armand de Montriveau discovered that he was under the yoke of the senses, and his bondage made the heavier by his love.

The woman so cavalierly treated in his thoughts of yesterday had become a most sacred and dreadful power. She was to be his world, his life, from this time forth. The greatest joy, the keenest anguish, that he had yet known grew colourless before the bare recollection of the least sensation stirred in him by her. The swiftest revolutions in a man's outward life only touch his interests, while passion brings a complete revulsion of feeling. And so in those who live by feeling, rather than by self-interest, the doers rather than the reasoners, the sanguine rather than the lymphatic temperaments, love works a complete revolution. In a flash, with one single reflection, Armand de Montriveau wiped out his whole past life.

A score of times he asked himself, like a boy, " Shall I go, or shall I not ? " and then at last he dressed, came to the Hôtel de Langeais towards eight o'clock that evening, and was admitted. He was to see the woman—ah ! not the woman—the idol that he had seen yesterday, among lights, a fresh innocent girl in gauze and silken lace and veiling. He burst in upon her to declare his love, as if it were a question of firing the first shot on a field of battle.

Poor novice ! He found his ethereal sylphide shrouded in a brown cashmere dressing-gown ingeniously befrilled, lying languidly stretched out upon a sofa in a dimly lighted boudoir. Mme de Langeais did not so much as rise, nothing was visible of her but her face, her hair was loose but confined by a scarf. A hand indicated a seat, a hand that seemed white as marble to Montriveau by the flickering light of a single candle at the further side of the room, and a voice as soft as the light said—

" If it had been anyone else, M. le Marquis, a friend with whom I could dispense with ceremony, or a mere acquaintance in whom I felt but slight interest, I should have closed my door. I am exceedingly unwell."

" I will go," Armand said to himself.

" But I do not know how it is," she continued (and the simple warrior attributed the shining of her eyes to fever), " perhaps it was a presentiment of your kind visit (and no one can be more sensible of the prompt attention than I), but the vapours have left my head."

" Then may I stay ? "

" Oh, I should be very sorry to allow you to go. I told myself this morning that it was impossible that I should have made the slightest impression on your mind, and that in all probability you took my request for one of the commonplaces of which Parisians are lavish on every occasion. And I forgave your ingratitude in advance. An explorer from the deserts is not supposed to know how exclusive we are in our friendships in the Faubourg."

The gracious, half-murmured words dropped one by one, as if they had been weighted with the gladness that apparently brought them to her lips. The Duchess meant to have the full benefit of her headache, and her speculation was fully successful. The General, poor man, was really distressed by the lady's simulated distress. Like Crillon listening to the story of the Crucifixion, he was ready to draw his sword against the vapours. How could a man dare to speak just then to this suffering woman of the love that she inspired ? Armand had already felt that it would be absurd to fire off a declaration of love point-blank at one so far above other women. With a single thought came understanding of the delicacies of feeling, of the soul's requirements. To love : what was that but to know how to plead, to beg for alms, to wait ? And as for the love that he felt, must he not prove it? His tongue was mute, it was frozen by the conventions of the noble Faubourg, the majesty of a sick headache, the bashfulness of love. But no power on earth could veil his glances; the heat and the Infinite of the desert blazed in eyes, calm as a panther's, beneath the lids that fell so seldom. The Duchess enjoyed the steady gaze that enveloped her in light and warmth.

"Mme la Duchesse," he answered, "I am afraid I express my gratitude for your goodness very badly. At this moment I have but one desire—I wish it were in my power to cure the pain."

"Permit me to throw this off, I feel too warm now," she said, gracefully tossing aside a cushion that covered her feet.

"Madame, in Asia your feet would be worth some ten thousand sequins."

"A traveller's compliment!" smiled she.

It pleased the sprightly lady to involve a rough soldier in a labyrinth of nonsense, commonplaces, and meaningless talk, in which he manœuvred, in military language, as Prince Charles might have done at close quarters with Napoleon. She took a mischievous amusement in reconnoitring the extent of his infatuation by the number of foolish speeches extracted from a novice whom she led step by step into a hopeless maze, meaning to leave him there in confusion. She began by laughing at him, but nevertheless it pleased her to make him forget how time went.

The length of a first visit is frequently a compliment, but Armand was innocent of any such intent. The famous explorer spent an hour in chat on all sorts of subjects, said nothing that he meant to say, and was feeling that he was only an instrument on whom this woman played, when she rose, sat upright, drew the scarf from her hair, and wrapped it about her throat, leant her elbow on the cushions, did him the honour of a complete cure, and rang for lights. The most graceful movement succeeded to complete repose. She turned to M. de Montriveau, from whom she had just extracted a confidence which seemed to interest her deeply, and said—

"You wish to make game of me by trying to make me believe that you have never loved. It is a man's great pretension with us. And we always believe it! Out of pure politeness. Do we not know what to expect from it for ourselves? Where is the man that has found but a single opportunity of losing his heart? But you love to deceive us, and we submit to be deceived, poor foolish creatures that we are; for your hypocrisy is, after all, a homage paid to the superiority of our sentiments, which are all purity."

The last words were spoken with a disdainful pride that made the novice in love feel like a worthless bale flung into the deep, while the Duchess was an angel soaring back to her particular heaven.

"Confound it!" thought Armand de Montriveau, "how am I to tell this wild thing that I love her?"

He had told her already a score of times; or rather, the Duchess had a score of times read his secret in his eyes; and the passion in this unmistakably great man promised her amusement, and an interest in her empty life. So she prepared with no little dexterity to raise a certain number of redoubts for him to carry by storm before he should gain an entrance into her heart. Montriveau should overleap one difficulty after another; he should be a plaything for her caprice, just as an insect teased by children is made to jump from one finger to another, and in spite of all its pains is kept in the same place by its mischievous tormentor. And yet it gave the Duchess inexpressible happiness to see that this strong man had told her the truth. Armand had never loved, as he had said. He was about to go, in a bad humour with himself, and still more out of humour with her; but it delighted her to see a sullenness that she could conjure away with a word, a glance, or a gesture.

"Will you come tomorrow evening?" she asked. "I am going to a ball, but I shall stay at home for you until ten o'clock."

Montriveau spent most of the next day in smoking an indeterminate quantity of cigars in his study window, and so got through the hours till he could dress and go to the Hôtel de Langeais. To anyone who had known the magnificent worth of the man, it would have been grievous to see him grown so small, so distrustful of himself; the mind that might have shed light over undiscovered worlds shrunk to the proportions of a she-coxcomb's boudoir. Even he himself felt that he had fallen so low already in his happiness that to save his life he could not have told his love to one of his closest friends. Is there not always a trace of shame in the lover's bashfulness, and perhaps in woman a certain exultation over diminished masculine stature? Indeed, but for a host of motives of this kind, how explain why women are nearly always the first to betray the secret?—a secret of which, perhaps, they soon weary.

"Mme la Duchesse cannot see visitors, monsieur," said the man; "she is dressing, she begs you to wait for her here."

Armand walked up and down the drawing-room, studying her taste in the least details. He admired Mme de Langeais herself in the objects of her choosing; they revealed her life before he could grasp her personality and ideas. About an hour later the Duchess came noiselessly out of her chamber. Montriveau turned, saw her flit like a shadow across the room, and trembled. She came up to him, not with a bourgeoise's enquiry, "How do I look?" She was sure of herself; her steady eyes said plainly, "I am adorned to please you."

No one surely, save the old fairy godmother of some princess in disguise, could have wound a cloud of gauze about the dainty throat, so that the dazzling satin skin beneath should gleam through the gleaming folds. The Duchess was dazzling. The pale blue colour of her gown, repeated in the flowers in her hair, appeared by the richness of its hue to lend substance to a fragile form grown too wholly ethereal; for as she glided towards Armand, the loose ends of her scarf floated about her, putting that valiant warrior in mind of the bright damosel flies that hover now over water, now over the flowers with which they seem to mingle and blend.

" I have kept you waiting," she said, with the tone that a woman can always bring into her voice for the man whom she wishes to please.

" I would wait patiently through an eternity," said he, " if I were sure of finding a divinity so fair ; but it is no compliment to speak of your beauty to you ; nothing save worship could touch you. Suffer me only to kiss your scarf."

" Oh, fie ! " she said, with a commanding gesture, " I esteem you enough to give you my hand."

She held it out for his kiss. A woman's hand, still moist from the scented bath, has a soft freshness, a velvet smoothness that sends a tingling thrill from the lips to the soul. And if a man is attracted to a woman, and his senses are as quick to feel pleasure as his heart is full of love, such a kiss, though chaste in appearance, may conjure up a terrific storm.

" Will you always give it me like this ? " the General asked humbly, when he had pressed that dangerous hand respectfully to his lips.

" Yes, but there we must stop," she said, smiling. She sat down, and seemed very slow over putting on her gloves, trying to slip the unstretched kid over all her fingers at once, while she watched M. de Montriveau ; and he was lost in admiration of the Duchess and those repeated graceful movements of hers.

" Ah ! you were punctual," she said ; " that is right. I like punctuality. It is the courtesy of kings, His Majesty says ; but to my thinking, from you men it is the most respectful flattery of all. Now, is it not ? Just tell me."

Again she gave him a side glance to express her insidious friendship, for he was dumb with happiness—sheer happiness through such nothings as these ! Oh, the Duchess understood *son métier de femme*—the art and mystery of being a woman—most marvellously well ; she knew, to admiration, how to raise a man in his own esteem as he humbled himself to her ; how to reward every step of the descent to sentimental folly with hollow flatteries.

" You will never forget to come at nine o'clock."

" No ; but are you going to a ball every night ? "

" Do I know ? " she answered, with a little childlike shrug of the shoulders ; the gesture was meant to say that she was nothing if not capricious, and that a lover must take her as she was.—" Besides," she added, " what is that to you ? You shall be my escort."

" That would be difficult tonight," he objected ; " I am not properly dressed."

" It seems to me," she returned loftily, " that if anyone has a right to complain of your costume, it is I. Know, therefore, *monsieur le voyageur*, that if I accept a man's arm, he is forthwith above the laws of fashion, nobody would venture to criticise him. You do not know the world, I see; I like you the better for it."

And even as she spoke she swept him into the pettiness of that world by the attempt to initiate him into the vanities of a woman of fashion.

"If she chooses to do a foolish thing for me, I should be a simpleton to prevent her," said Armand to himself. "She has a liking for me beyond a doubt; and as for the world, she cannot despise it more than I do. So, now for the ball if she likes."

The Duchess probably thought that if the General came with her and appeared in a ballroom in boots and a black tie, nobody would hesitate to believe that he was violently in love with her. And the General was well pleased that the queen of fashion should think of compromising herself for him; hope gave him wit. He had gained confidence, he brought out his thoughts and views; he felt nothing of the restraint that weighed on his spirits yesterday. His talk was interesting and animated, and full of those first confidences so sweet to make and to receive.

Was Mme de Langeais really carried away by his talk, or had she devised this charming piece of coquetry? At any rate, she looked up mischievously as the clock struck twelve.

"Ah! you have made me too late for the ball!" she exclaimed, surprised and vexed that she had forgotten how time was going.

The next moment she approved the exchange of pleasures with a smile that made Armand's heart give a sudden leap.

"I certainly promised Mme de Beauséant," she added. "They are all expecting me."

"Very well—go."

"No—go on. I will stay. Your Eastern adventures fascinate me. Tell me the whole story of your life. I love to share in a brave man's hardships, and I feel them all, indeed I do!"

She was playing with her scarf, twisting it and pulling it to pieces, with jerky, impatient movements that seemed to tell of inward dissatisfaction and deep reflection.

"*We* are fit for nothing," she went on. "Ah! we are contemptible, selfish, frivolous creatures. We can bore ourselves with amusements, and that is all we can do. Not one of us that understands that she has a part to play in life. In old days in France, women were beneficent lights; they lived to comfort those that mourned, to encourage high virtues, to reward artists and stir new life with noble thoughts. If the world has grown so petty, ours is the fault. You make me loathe the ball and this world in which I live. No, I am not giving up much for you."

She had plucked her scarf to pieces, as a child plays with a flower, pulling away all the petals one by one; and now she crushed it into a ball, and flung it away. She could show her swan's neck.

She rang the bell. "I shall not go out tonight," she told the footman. Her long, blue eyes turned timidly to Armand; and by the look of misgiving in them, he knew that he was meant to take the order for a confession, for a first and great favour. There was a pause, filled with many thoughts, before she spoke with that tenderness which is often in women's voices, and not so often in their hearts. "You have had a hard life," she said.

"No," returned Armand. "Until today I did not know what happiness was."

"Then you know it now ?" she asked, looking at him with a demure, keen glance.

"What is happiness for me henceforth but this—to see you, to hear you ? . . . Until now I have only known privation ; now I know that I can be unhappy——"

"That will do, that will do," she said. "You must go ; it is past midnight. Let us regard appearances. People must not talk about us. I do not know quite what I shall say ; but the headache is a good-natured friend, and tells no tales."

"Is there to be a ball tomorrow night ?"

"You would grow accustomed to the life, I think. Very well. Yes, we will go again tomorrow night."

There was not a happier man in the world than Armand when he went out from her. Every evening he came to Mme de Langeais's at the hour kept for him by a tacit understanding.

It would be tedious, and, for the many young men who carry a redundance of such sweet memories in their hearts, it were superfluous to follow the story step by step—the progress of a romance growing in those hours spent together, a romance controlled entirely by a woman's will. If sentiment went too fast, she would raise a quarrel over a word, or when words flagged behind her thoughts, she appealed to the feelings. Perhaps the only way of following such Penelope's progress is by marking its outward and visible signs.

As, for instance, within a few days of their first meeting, the assiduous General had won and kept the right to kiss his lady's insatiable hands. Wherever Mme de Langeais went, M. de Montriveau was certain to be seen, till people jokingly called him "Her Grace's orderly." And already he had made enemies ; others were jealous, and envied him his position. Mme de Langeais had attained her end. The Marquis de Montriveau was among her numerous train of adorers, and a means of humiliating those who boasted of their progress in her good graces, for she publicly gave him preference over them all.

"Decidedly, M. de Montriveau is the man for whom the Duchess shows a preference," pronounced Mme de Sérizy.

And who in Paris does not know what it means when a woman "shows a preference ?" All went on therefore according to prescribed rule. The anecdotes which people were pleased to circulate concerning the General put that warrior in so formidable a light, that the more adroit quietly dropped their pretensions to the Duchess, and remained in her train merely to turn the position to account, and to use her name and personality to make better terms for themselves with certain stars of the second magnitude. And those lesser powers were delighted to take a lover away from Mme de Langeais. The Duchess was keen-sighted enough to see these desertions and treaties with the enemy; and her pride would not suffer her to be the dupe of them. As M. de Talleyrand, one of her great admirers, said, she knew how to take a second edition of revenge, laying the two-edged blade of a sarcasm between the pairs in these "morganatic" unions. Her mocking disdain contributed not a little to increase her reputation as an extremely clever woman and a person to be feared. Her character for virtue was consolidated while she amused herself with other people's secrets, and kept her own to herself. Yet, after two months of assiduities, she saw with a vague dread in the depths of her soul that M. de Montriveau understood nothing of the subtleties of flirtation after the manner of the Faubourg Saint-Germain; he was taking a Parisienne's coquetry in earnest.

"You will not tame *him*, dear Duchess," the old Vidame de Pamiers had said. "'Tis a first cousin to the eagle; he will carry you off to his eyrie if you do not take care."

Then Mme de Langeais felt afraid. The shrewd old noble's words sounded like a prophecy. The next day she tried to turn love to hate. She was harsh, exacting, irritable, unbearable; Montriveau disarmed her with angelic sweetness. She so little knew the great generosity of a large nature, that the kindly jests with which her first complaints were met went to her heart. She sought a quarrel, and found proofs of affection. She persisted.

"When a man idolises you, how can he have vexed you?" asked Armand.

"You do not vex me," she answered, suddenly grown gentle and submissive. "But why do you wish to compromise me? For me you ought to be nothing but a *friend*. Do you not know it? I wish I could see that you had the instincts, the delicacy of real friendship, so that I might lose neither your respect nor the pleasure that your presence gives me."

"Nothing but your *friend!*" he cried out. The terrible word sent an electric shock through his brain. "On the faith of these happy hours that you grant me, I sleep and wake in your heart. And now today, for no reason, you are pleased to destroy all the secret hopes by which I live. You have required promises of such constancy in me, you have said so much of your horror of women made up of nothing but caprice; and now do you wish me to understand that, like other women here in Paris, you have passions, and know nothing of love? If so, why did you ask my life of me? why did you accept it?"

"I was wrong, my friend. Oh, it is wrong of a woman to yield to such intoxication when she must not and cannot make any return."

"I understand. You have merely been coquetting with me, and——"

"Coquetting ?" she repeated. "I detest coquetry. A coquette, Armand, makes promises to many, and gives herself to none ; and a woman who keeps such promises is a libertine. This much I believed I had grasped of our code. But to be melancholy with humorists, gay with the frivolous, and politic with ambitious souls ; to listen to a babbler with every appearance of admiration, to talk of war with a soldier, wax enthusiastic with philanthropists over the good of the nation, and to give to each one his little dole of flattery—it seems to me that this is as much a matter of necessity as dress, diamonds, and gloves, or flowers in one's hair. Such talk is the moral counterpart of the toilette. You take it up and lay it aside with the plumed head-dress. Do you call this coquetry ? Why, I have never treated you as I treat everyone else. With you, my friend, I am sincere. Have I not always shared your views, and when you convinced me after a discussion, was I not always perfectly glad ? In short, I love you, but only as a devout and pure woman may love. I have thought it over. I am a married woman, Armand. My way of life with M. de Langeais gives me liberty to bestow my heart ; but law and custom leave me no right to dispose of my person. If a woman loses her honour, she is an outcast in any rank of life ; and I have yet to meet with a single example of a man that realises all that our sacrifices demand of him in such a case. Quite otherwise. Anyone can foresee the rupture between Mme de Beauséant and M. d'Ajuda (for he is going to marry Mlle de Rochefide, it seems), that affair made it clear to my mind that these very sacrifices on the woman's part are almost always the cause of the man's desertion. If you had loved me sincerely, you would have kept away for a time.—Now, I will lay aside all vanity for you ; is not that something ? What will not people say of a woman to whom no man attaches himself ? Oh, she is heartless, brainless, soulless ; and what is more, devoid of charm ! Coquettes will not spare me. They will rob me of the very qualities that mortify them. So long as my reputation is safe, what do I care if my rivals deny my merits ? They certainly will not inherit them. Come, my friend ; give up something for her who sacrifices so much for you. Do not come quite so often ; I shall love you none the less."

"Ah !" said Armand, with the profound irony of a wounded heart in his words and tone. "Love, so the scribblers say, only feeds on illusions. Nothing could be truer, I see ; I am expected to imagine that I am loved. But, there !—there are some thoughts like wounds, from which there is no recovery. My belief in you was one of the last left to me, and now I see that there is nothing left to believe in this earth."

She began to smile.

"Yes," Montriveau went on in an unsteady voice, "this Catholic faith to which you wish to convert me is a lie that men make for themselves ; hope is a lie at the expense of the future ; pride, a lie between us and our fellows ; and pity, and prudence, and terror are cunning lies. And now my happiness is to be one more lying delusion ; I am expected to delude myself, to be willing to give gold coin for silver to the end. If you can so easily dispense with my visits ; if you can confess me neither as your friend nor your lover, you do not care for me! And I, poor fool that I am, tell myself this, and know it, and love you ! "

" But, dear me, poor Armand, you are flying into a passion ! "

" I flying into a passion ? "

" Yes. You think that the whole question is opened because I ask you to be careful."

In her heart of hearts she was delighted with the anger that leapt out in her lover's eyes. Even as she tortured him, she was criticising him, watching every slightest change that passed over his face. If the General had been so unluckily inspired as to show himself generous without discussion (as happens occasionally with some artless souls), he would have been a banished man forever, accused and convicted of not knowing how to love. Most women are not displeased to have their code of right and wrong broken through. Do they not flatter themselves that they never yield except to force ? But Armand was not learned enough in this kind of lore to see the snare ingeniously spread for him by the Duchess. So much of the child was there in the strong man in love.

" If all you want is to preserve appearances," he began in his simplicity, " I am willing to——"

" Simply to preserve appearances ! " the lady broke in ; " why, what idea can you have of me ? Have I given you the slightest reason to suppose that I can be yours ? "

" Why, what else are we talking about ? " demanded Montriveau.

" Monsieur, you frighten me ! . . . No, pardon me. Thank you," she added, coldly ; " thank you, Armand. You have given me timely warning of imprudence ; committed quite unconsciously, believe it, my friend. You know how to endure, you say. I also know how to endure. We will not see each other for a time ; and then, when both of us have contrived to recover calmness to some extent, we will think about arrangements for a happiness sanctioned by the world. I am young, Armand ; a man with no delicacy might tempt a woman of four-and-twenty to do many foolish, wild things for his sake. But *you!* You will be my friend, promise me that you will ? "

" The woman of four-and-twenty," returned he, " knows what she is about."

He sat down on the sofa in the boudoir, and leant his head on his hands.

" Do you love me, madame ? " he asked at length, raising his head, and turning a face full of resolution upon her. " Say it straight out ; Yes or No ! "

His direct question dismayed the Duchess more than a threat of suicide could have done ; indeed, the woman of the nineteenth century is not to be frightened by that stale stratagem, the sword has ceased to be part of the masculine costume. But in the effect of eyelids and lashes, in the contraction of the gaze, in the twitching of the lips, is there not some influence that communicates the terror which they express with such vivid magnetic power ?

"Ah, if I were free, if——"

"Oh ! is it only your husband that stands in the way ?" the General exclaimed joyfully, as he strode to and fro in the boudoir. "Dear Antoinette, I wield a more absolute power than the Autocrat of all the Russias. I have a compact with Fate ; I can advance or retard destiny, so far as men are concerned, at my fancy, as you alter the hands of a watch. If you can direct the course of fate in our political machinery, it simply means (does it not ?) that you understand the ins and outs of it. You shall be free before very long, and then you must remember your promise."

"Armand !" she cried. "What do you mean ? Great heavens ! Can you imagine that I am to be the prize of a crime ? Do you want to kill me ? Why ! you cannot have any religion in you ! For my own part, I fear God. M. de Langeais may have given me reason to hate him, but I wish him no manner of harm."

M. de Montriveau beat a tattoo on the marble chimneypiece, and only looked composedly at the lady.

"Dear," continued she, "respect him. He does not love me, he is not kind to me, but I have duties to fulfil with regard to him. What would I not do to avert the calamities with which you threaten him ?—Listen," she continued after a pause, "I will not say another word about separation ; you shall come here as in the past, and I will still give you my forehead to kiss. If I refused once or twice, it was pure coquetry, indeed it was. But let us understand each other," she added as he came closer. "You will permit me to add to the number of my satellites ; to receive even more visitors in the morning than heretofore ; I mean to be twice as frivolous ; I mean to use you to all appearance very badly ; to feign a rupture ; you must come not quite so often, and then, afterwards——"

While she spoke, she had allowed him to put an arm about her waist, Montriveau was holding her tightly to him, and she seemed to feel the exceeding pleasure that women usually feel in that close contact, an earnest of the bliss of a closer union. And then, doubtless she meant to elicit some confidence, for she raised herself on tiptoe, and laid her forehead against Armand's burning lips.

"And then," Montriveau finished her sentence for her, "you shall not speak to me of your husband. You ought not to think of him again."

Mme de Langeais was silent awhile.

"At least," she said, after a significant pause, "at least you will do all that I wish without grumbling, you will not be naughty ; tell me so, my friend ? You wanted to frighten me, did you not ? Come, now, confess it ? . . . You are too good ever to think of crimes. But is it possible that you can have secrets that I do not know ? How can you control Fate ?"

"Now, when you confirm the gift of the heart that you have already given me, I am far too happy to know exactly how to answer you. I can trust you, Antoinette; I shall have no suspicion, no unfounded jealousy of you. But if accident should set you free, we shall be one——"

"Accident, Armand?" (With that little dainty turn of the head that seems to say so many things, a gesture that such women as the Duchess can use on light occasions, as a great singer can act with her voice.) "Pure accident," she repeated. "Mind that. If anything should happen to M. de Langeais by your fault, I should never be yours."

And so they parted, mutually content. The Duchess had made a pact that left her free to prove to the world by words and deeds that M. de Montriveau was no lover of hers. And as for him, the wily Duchess vowed to tire him out. He should have nothing of her beyond the little concessions snatched in the course of contests that she could stop at her pleasure. She had so pretty an art of revoking the grant of yesterday, she was so much in earnest in her purpose to remain technically virtuous, that she felt that there was not the slightest danger for her in preliminaries fraught with peril for a woman less sure of her self-command. After all, the Duchess was practically separated from her husband; a marriage long since annulled was no great sacrifice to make to her love.

Montriveau on his side was quite happy to win the vaguest promise, glad once for all to sweep aside, with all scruples of conjugal fidelity, her stock of excuses for refusing herself to his love. He had gained ground a little, and congratulated himself. And so for a time he took unfair advantage of the rights so hardly won. More a boy than he had ever been in his life, he gave himself up to all the childishness that makes first love the flower of life. He was a child again as he poured out all his soul, all the thwarted forces that passion had given him, upon her hands, upon the dazzling forehead that looked so pure to his eyes; upon her fair hair; on the tufted curls where his lips were pressed. And the Duchess, on whom his love was poured like a flood, was vanquished by the magnetic influence of her lover's warmth; she hesitated to begin the quarrel that must part them forever. She was more a woman than she thought, this slight creature, in her effort to reconcile the demands of religion with the ever-new sensations of vanity, the semblance of pleasure which turns a Parisienne's head. Every Sunday she went to Mass; she never missed a service; then, when evening came, she was steeped in the intoxicating bliss of repressed desire. Armand and Mme de Langeais, like Hindoo fakirs, found the reward of their continence in the temptations to which it gave rise. Possibly, the Duchess had ended by resolving love into fraternal caresses, harmless enough, as it might have seemed to the rest of the world, while they borrowed extremes of degradation from the licence of her thoughts. How else explain the incomprehensible mystery of her continual fluctuations? Every morning she proposed to herself to shut her door on the Marquis de Montriveau ; every evening, at the appointed hour, she fell under the charm of his presence. There was a languid defence ; then she grew less unkind. Her words were sweet and soothing. They were lovers—lovers only could have been thus. For him the Duchess would display her most sparkling wit, her most captivating wiles ; and when at last she had wrought upon his senses and his soul, she might submit herself passively to his fierce caresses, but she had her *nec plus ultra* of passion ; and when once it was reached, she grew angry if he lost the mastery of himself and made as though he would pass beyond. No woman on earth can brave the consequences of refusal without some motive ; nothing is more natural than to yield to love ; wherefore Mme de Langeais promptly raised a second line of fortification, a stronghold less easy to carry than the first. She evoked the terrors of religion. Never did Father of the Church, however eloquent, plead the cause of God better than the Duchess. Never was the wrath of the Most High better justified than by her voice. She used no preacher's commonplaces, no rhetorical amplifications. No. She had a " pulpit-tremor " of her own. To Armand's most passionate entreaty, she replied with a tearful gaze, and a gesture in which a terrible plenitude of emotion found expression. She stopped his mouth with an appeal for mercy. She would not hear another word ; if she did, she must succumb ; and better death than criminal happiness.

" Is it nothing to disobey God ? " she asked him, recovering a voice grown faint in the crises of inward struggles, through which the fair actress appeared to find it hard to preserve her self-control. " I would sacrifice society, I would give up the whole world for you, gladly ; but it is very selfish of you to ask my whole after-life of me for a moment of pleasure. Come, now ! are you not happy ? " she added, holding out her hand ; and certainly in her careless toilette the sight of her afforded consolations to her lover, who made the most of them.

Sometimes from policy, to keep her hold on a man whose ardent passion gave her emotions unknown before, sometimes in weakness, she suffered him to snatch a swift kiss ; and immediately, in feigned terror, she flushed red and exiled Armand from the sofa so soon as the sofa became dangerous ground.

" Your joys are sins for me to expiate, Armand ; they are paid for by penitence and remorse," she cried.

And Montriveau, now at two chairs' distance from that aristocratic petticoat, betook himself to blasphemy and railed against Providence. The Duchess grew angry at such times.

" My friend," she said drily, " I do not understand why you decline to believe in God, for it is impossible to believe in man. Hush, do not talk like that. You have too great a nature to take up their Liberal nonsense with its pretension to abolish God."

Theological and political disputes acted like a cold douche on Montriveau ; he calmed down ; he could not return to love when the Duchess stirred up his wrath by suddenly setting him down a thousand miles away from the boudoir, discussing theories of absolute monarchy, whichshe defended to admiration. Few women venture to be democrats; the attitude of democratic champion is scarcely compatible with tyrannous feminine sway. But often, on the other hand, the General shook out his mane, dropped politics with a leonine growling and lashing of the flanks, and sprang upon his prey; he was no longer capable of carrying a heart and brain at such variance for very far; he came back, terrible with love, to his mistress. And she, if she felt the prick of fancy stimulated to a dangerous point, knew that it was time to leave her boudoir; she came out of the atmosphere surcharged with desires that she drew in with her breath, sat down to the piano, and sang the most exquisite songs of modern music, and so baffled the physical attraction which at times showed her no mercy, though she was strong enough to fight it down.

At such times she was something sublime in Armand's eyes; she was not acting, she was genuine; the unhappy lover was convinced that she loved him. Her egoistic resistance deluded him into a belief that she was a pure and sainted woman; he resigned himself; he talked of Platonic love, did this artillery officer!

When Mme de Langeais had played with religion sufficiently to suit her own purposes, she played with it again for Armand's benefit. She wanted to bring him back to a Christian frame of mind; she brought out her edition of *Le Génie du Christianisme*, adapted for the use of military men. Montriveau chafed; his yoke was heavy. Oh! at that, possessed by the spirit of contradiction, she dinned religion into his ears, to see whether God might not rid her of this suitor, for the man's persistence was beginning to frighten her. And in any case she was glad to prolong any quarrel, if it bade fair to keep the dispute on moral grounds for an indefinite period; the material struggle which followed it was more dangerous.

But if the time of her opposition on the ground of the marriage law might be said to be the *époque civile* of this sentimental warfare, the ensuing phase which might be taken to constitute the *époque religieuse* had also its crisis and consequent decline of severity.

Armand happening to come in very early one evening, found M. l'Abbé Gondrand, the Duchess's spiritual director, established in an armchair by the fireside, looking as a spiritual director might be expected to look while digesting his dinner and the charming sins of his penitent. In the ecclesiastic's bearing there was a stateliness befitting a dignitary of the Church; and the episcopal violet hue already appeared in his dress. At sight of his fresh, well-preserved complexion, smooth forehead, and ascetic's mouth, Montriveau's countenance grew uncommonly dark; he said not a word under the malicious scrutiny of the other's gaze, and greeted neither the lady nor the priest. The lover apart, Montriveau was not wanting in tact; so a few glances exchanged with the bishop-designate told him that here was the real forger of the Duchess's armoury of scruples.

That an ambitious abbé should control the happiness of a man of Montriveau's temper, and by underhand ways! The thought burst in a furious tide over his face, clenched his fists, and set him chafing and pacing to and fro; but when he came back to his place intending to make a scene, a single look from the Duchess was enough. He was quiet.

Any other woman would have been put out by her lover's gloomy silence; it was quite otherwise with Mme de Langeais. She continued her conversation with M. de Gondrand on the necessity of re-establishing the Church in its ancient splendour. And she talked brilliantly. The Church, she maintained, ought to be a temporal as well as a spiritual power, stating her case better than the Abbé had done, and regretting that the Chamber of Peers, unlike the English House of Lords, had no bench of bishops. Nevertheless, the Abbé rose, yielded his place to the General, and took his leave, knowing that in Lent he could play a return game. As for the Duchess, Montriveau's behaviour had excited her curiosity to such a pitch that she scarcely rose to return her director's low bow.

"What is the matter with you, my friend?"

"Why, I cannot stomach that Abbé of yours."

"Why did you not take a book?" she asked, careless whether the Abbé, then closing the door, heard her or no.

The General paused, for the gesture which accompanied the Duchess's speech further increased the exceeding insolence of her words.

"My dear Antoinette, thank you for giving love precedence of the Church; but, for pity's sake, allow me to ask one question."

"Oh! you are questioning me! I am quite willing. You are my friend, are you not? I certainly can open the bottom of my heart to you; you will see only one image there."

"Do you talk about our love to that man?"

"He is my confessor."

"Does he know that I love you?"

"M. de Montriveau, you cannot claim, I think, to penetrate the secrets of the confessional?"

"Does that man know all about our quarrels and my love for you?——"

"That man, monsieur; say God!"

"God again! *I* ought to be alone in your heart. But leave God alone where He is, for the love of God and me. Madame, you *shall not* go to confession again, or——"

"Or?" she repeated sweetly.

"Or I will never come back here."

"Then go, Armand. Good-bye, good-bye forever."

She rose and went to her boudoir without so much as a glance at Armand, as he stood with his hand on the back of a chair. How long he stood there motionless he himself never knew. The soul within has the mysterious power of expanding as of contracting space.

He opened the door of the boudoir. It was dark within. A faint voice was raised to say sharply—

"I did not ring. What made you come in without orders? Go away, Suzette."

"Then you are ill," exclaimed Montriveau.

"Stand up, monsieur, and go out of the room for a minute at any rate," she said, ringing the bell.

"Mme la Duchesse rang for lights?" said the footman, coming in with the candles. When the lovers were alone together, Mme de Langeais still lay on her couch; she was just as silent and motionless as if Montriveau had not been there.

"Dear, I was wrong," he began, a note of pain and a sublime kindness in his voice. "Indeed, I would not have you without religion——"

"It is fortunate that you can recognise the necessity of a conscience," she said in a hard voice, without looking at him. "I thank you in God's name."

The General was broken down by her harshness; this woman seemed as if she could be at will a sister or a stranger to him. He made one despairing stride towards the door. He would leave her forever without another word. He was wretched; and the Duchess was laughing within herself over mental anguish far more cruel than the old judicial torture. But as for going away, it was not in his power to do it. In any sort of crisis, a woman is, as it were, bursting with a certain quantity of things to say; so long as she has not delivered herself of them, she experiences the sensation which we are apt to feel at the sight of something incomplete. Mme de Langeais had not said all that was in her mind. She took up her parable and said—

"We have not the same convictions, General, I am pained to think. It would be dreadful if a woman could not believe in a religion which permits us to love beyond the grave. I set Christian sentiments aside; you cannot understand them. Let me simply speak to you of expediency. Would you forbid a woman at court the table of the Lord when it is customary to take the sacrament at Easter? People must certainly do something for their party. The Liberals, whatever they may wish to do, will never destroy the religious instinct. Religion will always be a political necessity. Would you undertake to govern a nation of logic-choppers? Napoleon was afraid to try; he persecuted ideologists. If you want to keep people from reasoning, you must give them something to feel. So let us accept the Roman Catholic Church with all its consequences. And if we would have France go to mass, ought we not to begin by going ourselves? Religion, you see, Armand, is a bond uniting all the conservative principles which enable the rich to live in tranquillity. Religion and the rights of property are intimately connected. It is certainly a finer thing to lead a nation by ideas of morality than by fear of the scaffold, as in the time of the Terror—the one method by which your odious Revolution could enforce obedience. The priest and the king—that means you, and me, and the Princess my neighbour; and, in a word, the interests of all honest people personified. There, my friend, just be so good as to belong to your party, you that might be its Sylla if you had the slightest ambition that way. I know nothing about politics myself; I argue from my own feelings; but still I know enough to guess that society would be overturned if people were always calling its foundations in question——"

"If that is how your Court and your Government think, I am sorry for you," broke in Montriveau. "The Restoration, madam, ought to say, like Catherine de Medici, when she heard that the battle of Dreux was lost, 'Very well; now we will go to the meeting-house.' Now 1815 was your battle of Dreux. Like the royal power of those days, you won in fact, while you lost in right. Political Protestantism has gained an ascendancy over people's minds. If you have no mind to issue your Edict of Nantes; or if, when it is issued, you publish a Revocation; if you should one day be accused and convicted of repudiating the Charter, which is simply a pledge given to maintain the interests established under the Republic, then the Revolution will rise again, terrible in her strength, and strike but a single blow. It will not be the Revolution that will go into exile; she is the very soil of France. Men die, but people's interests do not die. . . . Eh, great Heavens! what are France and the crown and rightful sovereigns, and the whole world besides, to us? Idle words compared with my happiness. Let them reign or be hurled from the throne, little do I care. Where am I now?"

"In the Duchesse de Langeais's boudoir, my friend."

"No, no. No more of the Duchess, no more of Langeais; I am with my dear Antoinette."

"Will you do me the pleasure to stay where you are," she said, laughing and pushing him back, gently however.

"So you have never loved me," he retorted, and anger flashed in lightning from his eyes.

"No, dear"; but the "No" was equivalent to "Yes."

"I am a great ass," he said, kissing her hands. The terrible queen was a woman once more.—"Antoinette," he went on, laying his head on her feet, "you are too chastely tender to speak of our happiness to anyone in this world."

"Oh!" she cried, rising to her feet with a swift, graceful spring, "you are a great simpleton." And without another word she fled into the drawing-room.

"What is it now?" wondered the General, little knowing that the touch of his burning forehead had sent a swift electric thrill through her from foot to head.

In hot wrath he followed her to the drawing-room, only to hear divinely sweet chords. The Duchess was at the piano. If the man of science or the poet can at once enjoy and comprehend, bringing his intelligence to bear upon his enjoyment without loss of delight, he is conscious that the alphabet and phraseology of music are but cunning instruments for the composer, like the wood and copper wire under the hands of the executant. For the poet and the man of science there is a music existing apart, underlying the double expression of this language of the spirit and senses. *Andiamo mio ben* can draw tears of joy or pitying laughter at the will of the singer ; and not unfrequently one here and there in the world, some girl unable to live and bear the heavy burden of an unguessed pain, some man whose soul vibrates with the throb of passion, may take up a musical theme, and lo ! heaven is opened for them, or they find a language for themselves in some sublime melody, some song lost to the world.

The General was listening now to such a song ; a mysterious music unknown to all other ears, as the solitary plaint of some mateless bird dying alone in a virgin forest.

" Great Heavens ! what are you playing there ? " he asked in an unsteady voice.

" The prelude of a ballad, called, I believe, *Fleuve du Tage*."

" I did not know that there was such music in a piano," he returned.

" Ah ! " she said, and for the first time she looked at him as a woman looks at the man she loves, " nor do you know, my friend, that I love you, and that you cause me horrible suffering ; and that I feel that I must utter my cry of pain without putting it too plainly into words. If I did not, I should yield—— But you see nothing."

" And you will not make me happy ! "

" Armand, I should die of sorrow the next day."

The General turned abruptly from her and went. But out in the street he brushed away the tears that he would not let fall.

The religious phase lasted for three months. At the end of that time the Duchess grew weary of vain repetitions ; the Deity, bound hand and foot, was delivered up to her lover. Possibly she may have feared that by sheer dint of talking of eternity she might perpetuate his love in this world and the next. For her own sake, it must be believed that no man had touched her heart, or her conduct would be inexcusable. She was young ; the time when men and women feel that they cannot afford to lose time or to quibble over their joys was still far off. She, no doubt, was on the verge not of first love, but of her first experience of the bliss of love. And from inexperience, for want of the painful lessons which would have taught her to value the treasure poured out at her feet, she was playing with it. Knowing nothing of the glory and rapture of the light, she was fain to stay in the shadow.

Armand was just beginning to understand this strange situation ; he put his hope in the first word spoken by nature. Every evening, as he came away from Mme de Langeais's, he told himself that no woman would accept the tenderest, most delicate proofs of a man's love during seven months, nor yield passively to the slighter demands of passion, only to cheat love at the last. He was waiting patiently for the sun to gain power, not doubting but that he should receive the earliest fruits. The married woman's hesitations and the religious scruples he could quite well understand. He even rejoiced over those battles. He mistook the Duchess's heartless coquetry for modesty ; and he would not have had her otherwise. So he had loved to see her devising obstacles ; was he not gradually triumphing over them ? Did not every victory won swell the meagre sum of lovers' intimacies long denied, and at last conceded with every sign of love ? Still, he had had such leisure to taste the full sweetness of every small successive conquest on which a lover feeds his love, that these had come to be matters of use and wont. So far as obstacles went, there were none now save his own awe of her ; nothing else left between him and his desire save the whims of her who allowed him to call her Antoinette. So he made up his mind to demand more, to demand all. Embarrassed like a young lover who cannot dare to believe that his idol can stoop so low, he hesitated for a long time. He passed through the experience of terrible reactions within himself. A set purpose was annihilated by a word, and definite resolves died within him on the threshold. He despised himself for his weakness, and still his desire remained unuttered.

Nevertheless, one evening, after sitting in gloomy melancholy, he brought out a fierce demand for his illegally legitimate rights. The Duchess had not to wait for her bond-slave's request to guess his desire. When was a man's desire a secret ? And have not women an intuitive knowledge of the meaning of certain changes of countenance ?

" What ! you wish to be my friend no longer ? " she broke in at the first words, and a divine red surging like new blood under the transparent skin, lent brightness to her eyes. " As a reward for my generosity, you would dishonour me ? Just reflect a little. I myself have thought much over this ; and I think always for us *both*. There is such a thing as a woman's loyalty, and we can no more fail in it than you can fail in honour. *I* cannot blind myself. If I am yours, how, in any sense, can I be M. de Langeais's wife ? Can you require the sacrifice of my position, my rank, my whole life in return for a doubtful love that could not wait patiently for seven months ? What ! already you would rob me of my right to dispose of myself ? No, no ; you must not talk like this again. No, not another word. I will not, I cannot listen to you."

Mme de Langeais raised both hands to her head to push back the tufted curls from her hot forehead ; she seemed very much excited.

" You come to a weak woman with your purpose definitely planned out. You say—' For a certain length of time she will talk to me of her husband, then of God, and then of the inevitable consequences. But I will use and abuse the ascendancy I shall gain over her ; I will make myself indispensable ; all the bonds of habit, all the misconstructions of outsiders, will make for me ; and at length, when our *liaison* is taken for granted by all the world, I shall be this woman's master.'—Now, be frank ; these are your thoughts ! Oh ! you calculate, and you say that you love. Shame on you ! You are enamoured ? Ah ! that I well believe ! You wish to possess me, to have me for your mistress, that is all! Very well then, No! The *Duchesse de Langeais* will not descend so far. Simple *bourgeoises* may be the victims of your treachery—I, never! Nothing gives me assurance of your love. You speak of my beauty; I may lose every trace of it in six months, like the dear Princess, my neighbour. You are captivated by my wit, my grace. Great Heavens! you would soon grow used to them and to the pleasures of possession. Have not the little concessions that I was weak enough to make come to be a matter of course in the last few months? Some day, when ruin comes, you will give me no reason for the change in you beyond a curt, 'I have ceased to care for you.'—Then, rank and fortune and honour and all that was the Duchesse de Langeais will be swallowed up in one disappointed hope. I shall have children to bear witness to my shame, and——" With an involuntary gesture she interrupted herself, and continued: "But I am too good-natured to explain all this to you when you know it better than I. Come! let us stay as we are. I am only too fortunate in that I can still break these bonds which you think so strong. Is there anything so very heroic in coming to the Hôtel de Langeais to spend an evening with a woman whose prattle amuses you?—a woman whom you take for a plaything? Why, half a dozen young coxcombs come here just as regularly every afternoon between three and five. They, too, are very generous, I am to suppose? I make fun of them; they stand my petulance and insolence pretty quietly, and make me laugh; but as for you, I give all the treasures of my soul to you, and you wish to ruin me, you try my patience in endless ways. Hush, that will do, that will do," she continued, seeing that he was about to speak, "you have no heart, no soul, no delicacy. I know what you want to tell me. Very well, then—yes. I would rather you should take me for a cold, insensible woman, with no devotion in her composition, no heart even, than be taken by everybody else for a vulgar person, and be condemned to your so-called pleasures, of which you would most certainly tire, and to everlasting punishment for it afterwards. Your selfish love is not worth so many sacrifices. . . ."

The words give but a very inadequate idea of the discourse which the Duchess trilled out with the quick volubility of a bird-organ. Nor, truly, was there anything to prevent her from talking on for some time to come, for poor Armand's only reply to the torrent of flute notes was a silence filled with cruelly painful thoughts. He was just beginning to see that this woman was playing with him; he divined instinctively that a devoted love, a responsive love, does not reason and count the consequences in this way. Then, as he heard her reproach him with detestable motives, he felt something like shame as he remembered that unconsciously he had made those very calculations. With angelic honesty of purpose, he looked within, and self-examination found nothing but selfishness in all his thoughts and motives, in the answers which he framed and could not utter. He was self-convicted. In his despair he longed to fling himself from the window. The egoism of it was intolerable.

What indeed can a man say when a woman will not believe in love ?—Let me prove how much I love you.—The *I* is always there.

The heroes of the boudoir, in such circumstances, can follow the example of the primitive logician who preceded the Pyrrhonists and denied movement. Montriveau was not equal to this feat. With all his audacity, he lacked this precise kind which never deserts an adept in the formulas of feminine algebra. If so many women, and even the best of women, fall a prey to a kind of expert to whom the vulgar give a grosser name, it is perhaps because the said experts are great *provers*, and love, in spite of its delicious poetry of sentiment, requires a little more geometry than people are wont to think.

Now the Duchess and Montriveau were alike in this—they were both equally unversed in love lore. The lady's knowledge of theory was but scanty; in practice she knew nothing whatever; she felt nothing, and reflected over everything. Montriveau had had but little experience, was absolutely ignorant of theory, and felt too much to reflect at all. Both therefore were enduring the consequences of the singular situation. At that supreme moment the myriad thoughts in his mind might have been reduced to the formula—" Submit to be mine ——' words which seem horribly selfish to a woman for whom they awaken no memories, recall no ideas. Something nevertheless he must say. And what was more, though her barbed shafts had set his blood tingling, though the short phrases that she discharged at him one by one were very keen and sharp and cold, he must control himself lest he should lose all by an outbreak of anger.

" Mme la Duchesse, I am in despair that God should have invented no way for a woman to confirm the gift of her heart save by adding the gift of her person. The high value which you yourself put upon the gift teaches me that I cannot attach less importance to it. If you have given me your inmost self and your whole heart, as you tell me, what can the rest matter ? And besides, if my happiness means so painful a sacrifice, let us say no more about it. But you must pardon a man of spirit if he feels humiliated at being taken for a spaniel."

The tone in which the last remark was uttered might perhaps have frightened another woman; but when the wearer of a petticoat has allowed herself to be addressed as a Divinity, and thereby set herself above all other mortals, no power on earth can be so haughty.

" M. le Marquis, I am in despair that God should not have invented some nobler way for a man to confirm the gift of his heart than by the manifestation of prodigiously vulgar desires. We become bond-slaves when we give ourselves body and soul, but a man is bound to nothing by accepting the gift. Who will assure me that love will last ? The very love that I might show for you at every moment, the better to keep your love, might serve you as a reason for deserting me. I have no wish to be a second edition of Mme de Beauséant. Who can ever know what it is that keeps you beside us ? Our persistent coldness of heart is the cause of an unfailing passion in some of you; other men ask for an untiring devotion, to be idolised at every moment; some for gentleness, others for tyranny. No woman in this world as yet has really read the riddle of man's heart."

There was a pause. When she spoke again it was in a different tone. "After all, my friend, you cannot prevent a woman from trembling at the question, 'Will this love last always?' Hard though my words may be, the dread of losing you puts them into my mouth. Oh, me! it is not I who speaks, dear, it is reason; and how should anyone so mad as I be reasonable? In truth, I am nothing of the sort."

The poignant irony of her answer had changed before the end into the most musical accents in which a woman could find utterance for ingenuous love. To listen to her words was to pass in a moment from martyrdom to heaven. Montriveau grew pale; and for the first time in his life, he fell on his knees before a woman. He kissed the Duchess's skirt hem, her knees, her feet; but for the credit of the Faubourg Saint-Germain it is necessary to respect the mysteries of its boudoirs, where many are fain to take the utmost that Love can give without giving proof of love in return.

The Duchess thought herself generous when she suffered herself to be adored. But Montriveau was in a wild frenzy of joy over her complete surrender of the position.

"Dear Antoinette," he cried. "Yes, you are right; I will not have you doubt any longer. I too am trembling at this moment—lest the angel of my life should leave me; I wish I could invent some tie that might bind us to each other irrevocably."

"Ah!" she said, under her breath, "so I was right, you see."

"Let me say all that I have to say; I will scatter all your fears with a word. Listen! if I deserted you, I should deserve to die a thousand deaths. Be wholly mine, and I will give you the right to kill me if I am false. I myself will write a letter explaining certain reasons for taking my own life; I will make my final arrangements, in short. You shall have the letter in your keeping; in the eye of the law it will be a sufficient explanation of my death. You can avenge yourself, and fear nothing from God or men."

"What good would the letter be to me? What would life be if I had lost your love? If I wished to kill you, should I not be ready to follow? No; thank you for the thought, but I do not want the letter. Should I not begin to dread that you were faithful to me through fear? And if a man knows that he must risk his life for a stolen pleasure, might it not seem more tempting? Armand, the thing I ask of you is the one hard thing to do."

"Then what is it that you wish?"

"Your obedience and my liberty."

"Ah, God!" cried he, "I am a child."

"A wayward, much spoilt child," she said, stroking the thick hair, for his head still lay on her knee. "Ah! and loved far more than he believes, and yet he is very disobedient. Why not stay as we are?

Why not sacrifice to me the desires that hurt me ? Why not take what I can give, when it is all that I can honestly grant ? Are you not happy ? "

" Oh yes, I am happy when I have not a doubt left. Antoinette, doubt in love is a kind of death, is it not ? "

In a moment he showed himself as he was, as all men are under the influence of that hot fever ; he grew eloquent, insinuating. And the Duchess tasted the pleasures which she reconciled with her conscience by some private, Jesuitical ukase of her own ; Armand's love gave her a thrill of cerebral excitement which custom made as necessary to her as society, or the Opera. To feel that she was adored by this man, who rose above other men, whose character frightened her ; to treat him like a child ; to play with him as Poppæa played with Nero—many women, like the wives of King Henry VIII, have paid for such a perilous delight with all the blood in their veins. Grim presentiment ! Even as she surrendered the delicate, pale, gold curls to his touch, and felt the close pressure of his hand, the little hand of a man whose greatness she could not mistake ; even as she herself played with his dark, thick locks, in that boudoir where she reigned a queen, the Duchess would say to herself—

" This man is capable of killing me if he once finds out that I am playing with him."

Armand de Montriveau stayed with her till two o'clock in the morning. From that moment this woman, whom he loved, was neither a duchess nor a Navarreins ; Antoinette, in her disguises, had gone so far as to appear to be a woman. On that most blissful evening, the sweetest prelude ever played by a Parisienne to what the world calls " a slip " ; in spite of all her affectations of a coyness which she did not feel, the General saw all maidenly beauty in her. He had some excuse for believing that so many storms of caprice had been but clouds covering a heavenly soul ; that these must be lifted one by one like the veils that hid her divine loveliness. The Duchess became, for him, the most simple and girlish mistress ; she was the one woman in the world for him ; and he went away quite happy in that at last he had brought her to give him such pledges of love, that it seemed to him impossible but that he should be but her husband henceforth in secret, her choice sanctioned by Heaven.

Armand went slowly home, turning this thought in his mind with the impartiality of a man who is conscious of all the responsibilities that love lays on him while he tastes the sweetness of its joys. He went along the Quais to see the widest possible space of sky ; his heart had grown in him ; he would fain have had the bounds of the firmament and of earth enlarged. It seemed to him that his lungs drew an ampler breath. In the course of his self-examination, as he walked, he vowed to love this woman so devoutly, that every day of her life she should find absolution for her sins against society in unfailing happiness. Sweet stirrings of life when life is at the full ! The man that is strong enough to steep his soul in the colour of one emotion, feels infinite joy as glimpses open out for him of an ardent lifetime that knows no diminution of passion to the end; even so it is permitted to certain mystics, in ecstasy, to behold the Light of God. Love would be naught without the belief that it would last forever; love grows great through constancy. It was thus that, wholly absorbed by his happiness, Montriveau understood passion.

"We belong to each other forever!"

The thought was like a talisman fulfilling the wishes of his life. He did not ask whether the Duchess might not change, whether her love might not last. No, for he had faith. Without that virtue there is no future for Christianity, and perhaps it is even more necessary to society. A conception of life as feeling occurred to him for the first time; hitherto he had lived by action, the most strenuous exertion of human energies, the physical devotion, as it may be called, of the soldier.

Next day M. de Montriveau went early in the direction of the Faubourg Saint-Germain. He had made an appointment at a house not far from the Hôtel de Langeais; and the business over, he went thither as if to his own home. The General's companion chanced to be a man for whom he felt a kind of repulsion whenever he met him in other houses. This was the Marquis de Ronquerolles, whose reputation had grown so great in Paris boudoirs. He was witty, clever, and what was more—courageous; he set the fashion to all the young men in Paris. As a man of gallantry, his success and experience were equally matters of envy; and neither fortune nor birth was wanting in his case, qualifications which add such lustre in Paris to a reputation as a leader of fashion.

"Where are you going?" asked M. de Ronquerolles.

"To Mme de Langeais's."

"Ah, true. I forgot that you had allowed her to lime you. You are wasting your affections on her when they might be much better employed elsewhere. I could have told you of half a score of women in the financial world, any one of them a thousand times better worth your while than that titled courtesan, who does with her brains what less artificial women do with——"

"What is this, my dear fellow?" Armand broke in. "The Duchess is an angel of innocence."

Ronquerolles began to laugh.

"Things being thus, dear boy," said he, "it is my duty to enlighten you. Just a word; there is no harm in it between ourselves. Has the Duchess surrendered? If so, I have nothing more to say. Come, give me your confidence. There is no occasion to waste your time in grafting your great nature on that unthankful stock, when all your hopes and cultivation will come to nothing."

Armand ingenuously made a kind of general report of his position, enumerating with much minuteness the slender rights so hardly won. Ronquerolles burst into a peal of laughter so heartless, that it would have cost any other man his life. But from their manner of speaking and looking at each other during that colloquy beneath the wall, in a corner almost as remote from intrusion as the desert itself, it was easy to imagine the friendship between the two men knew no bounds, and that no power on earth could estrange them.

"My dear Armand, why did you not tell me that the Duchess was a puzzle to you? I would have given you a little advice which might have brought your flirtation properly through. You must know, to begin with, that the women of our Faubourg, like any other women, love to steep themselves in love; but they have a mind to possess and not to be possessed. They have made a sort of compromise with human nature. The code of their parish gives them a pretty wide latitude short of the last transgression. The sweets enjoyed by this fair Duchess of yours are so many venial sins to be washed away in the waters of penitence. But if you had the impertinence to ask in earnest for the moral sin to which naturally you are sure to attach the highest importance, you would see the deep disdain with which the door of the boudoir and the house would be incontinently shut upon you. The tender Antoinette would dismiss everything from her memory; you would be less than a cipher for her. She would wipe away your kisses, my dear friend, as indifferently as she would perform her ablutions. She would sponge love from her cheeks as she washes off rouge. We know women of that sort—the thorough-bred Parisienne. Have you ever noticed a grisette tripping along the street? Her face is as good as a picture. A pretty cap, fresh cheeks, trim hair, a guileful smile, and the rest of her almost neglected. Is not this true to the life? Well, that is the Parisienne. She knows that her face is all that will be seen, so she devotes all her care, finery, and vanity to her head. The Duchess is the same; the head is everything with her. She can only feel through her intellect, her heart lies in her brain, she is a sort of intellectual epicure, she has a head-voice. We call that kind of poor creature a Laïs of the intellect. You have been taken in like a boy. If you doubt it, you can have proof of it tonight, this morning, this instant. Go up to her, try the demand as an experiment, insist peremptorily if it is refused. You might set about it like the late Maréchal de Richelieu, and get nothing for your pains."

Armand was dumb with amazement.

"Has your desire reached the point of infatuation?"

"I want her at any cost!" Montriveau cried out despairingly.

"Very well. Now, look here. Be as inexorable as she is herself. Try to humiliate her, to sting her vanity. Do *not* try to move her heart, nor her soul, but the woman's nerves and temperament, for she is both nervous and lymphatic. If you can once awaken desire in her, you are safe. But you must drop these romantic boyish notions of yours. If when once you have her in your eagle's talons you yield a point or draw back, if you so much as stir an eyelid, if she thinks that she can regain her ascendancy over you, she will slip out of your clutches like a fish, and you will never catch her again. Be as inflexible as law. Show no more charity than the headsman. Hit hard, and then hit again. Strike and keep on striking as if you were giving her the knout. Duchesses are made of hard stuff, my dear Armand ; there is a sort of feminine nature that is only softened by repeated blows ; and as suffering develops a heart in women of that sort, so it is a work of charity not to spare the rod. Do you persevere. Ah ! when pain has thoroughly relaxed those nerves and softened the fibres that you take to be so pliant and yielding ; when a shrivelled heart has learned to expand and contract and to beat under this discipline ; when the brain has capitulated—then, perhaps, passion may enter among the steel springs of this machinery that turns out tears and affectations and languors and melting phrases ; then you shall see a most magnificent conflagration (always supposing that the chimney takes fire). The steel feminine system will glow red-hot like iron in the forge ; that kind of heat lasts longer than any other, and the glow of it may possibly turn to love.

"Still," he continued, "I have my doubts. And, after all, is it worth while to take so much trouble with the Duchess ? Between ourselves a man of my stamp ought first to take her in hand and break her in ; I would make a charming woman of her ; she is a thoroughbred ; whereas, you two left to yourselves will never get beyond the A B C. But you are in love with her, and just now you might not perhaps share my views on this subject——. A pleasant time to you, my children," added Ronquerolles, after a pause. Then with a laugh : "I have decided myself for facile beauties ; they are tender, at any rate, the natural woman appears in their love without any of your social seasonings. A woman that haggles over herself, my poor boy, and only means to inspire love ! Well, have her like an extra horse—for show. The match between the sofa and confessional, black and white, queen and knight, conscientious scruples and pleasure, is an uncommonly amusing game of chess. And if a man knows the game, let him be never so little of a rake, he wins in three moves. Now, if I undertook a woman of that sort, I should start with the deliberate purpose of——" His voice sank to a whisper over the last words in Armand's ear, and he went before there was time to reply.

As for Montriveau, he sprang at a bound across the courtyard of the Hôtel de Langeais, went unannounced up the stairs straight to the Duchess's bedroom.

"This is an unheard-of thing," she said, hastily wrapping her dressing-gown about her. "Armand ! this is abominable of you ! Come, leave the room, I beg. Just go out of the room, and go at once. Wait for me in the drawing-room.—Come now !"

"Dear angel, has a plighted lover no privilege whatsoever ?"

"But, monsieur, it is in the worst possible taste of a plighted lover or a wedded husband to break in like this upon his wife."

He came up to the Duchess, took her in his arms, and held her tightly to him.

"Forgive, dear Antoinette ; but a host of horrid doubts are fermenting in my heart."

" *Doubts?* Fie !—Oh, fie on you ! "

" Doubts all but justified. If you loved me, would you make this quarrel ? Would you not be glad to see me ? Would you not have felt a something stir in your heart ? For I, that am not a woman, feel a thrill in my inmost self at the mere sound of your voice. Often in a ballroom a longing has come upon me to spring to your side and put my arms about your neck."

" Oh ! if you have doubts of me so long as I am not ready to spring to your arms before all the world, I shall be doubted all my life long, I suppose. Why, Othello was a mere child compared with you ! "

" Ah ! " he cried despairingly, " you have no love for me——"

" Admit, at any rate, that at this moment you are not lovable."

" Then I have still to find favour in your sight ? "

" Oh, I should think so. Come," added she, with a little imperious air, " go out of the room, leave me. I am not like you ; I wish always to find favour in your eyes."

Never woman better understood the art of putting charm into insolence, and does not the charm double the effect ? is it not enough to infuriate the coolest of men ? There was a sort of untrammelled freedom about Mme de Langeais ; a something in her eyes, her voice, her attitude, which is never seen in a woman who loves when she stands face to face with him at the mere sight of whom her heart must needs begin to beat. The Marquis de Ronquerolles's counsels had cured Armand of sheepishness ; and further, there came to his aid that rapid power of intuition which passion will develop at moments in the least wise among mortals, while a great man at such a time possesses it to the full. He guessed the terrible truth revealed by the Duchess's nonchalance, and his heart swelled with the storm like a lake rising in flood.

" If you told me the truth yesterday, be mine, dear Antoinette," he cried ; " you shall——"

" In the first place," said she composedly, thrusting him back as he came nearer—" in the first place, you are not to compromise me. My woman might overhear you. Respect me, I beg of you. Your familiarity is all very well in my boudoir in an evening ; here it is quite different Besides, what may your ' you shall ' mean ? ' You shall.' No one as yet has ever used that word to me. It is quite ridiculous, it seems to me, absolutely ridiculous."

" Will you surrender nothing to me on this point ? "

" Oh ! do you call a woman's right to dispose of herself a ' point ? ' A capital point indeed ; you will permit me to be entirely my own mistress on that ' point.' "

" And how if, believing in your promises to me, I should absolutely require it ? "

" Oh ! then you would prove that I made the greatest possible mistake when I made you a promise of any kind ; and I should beg you to leave me in peace."

The General's face grew white ; he was about to spring to her side, when Mme de Langeais rang the bell, the maid appeared, and, smiling with a mocking grace, the Duchess added, " Be so good as to return when I am visible."

Then Montriveau felt the hardness of a woman as cold and keen as a steel blade ; she was crushing in her scorn. In one moment she had snapped the bonds which held firm only for her lover. She had read Armand's intention in his face, and held that the moment had come for teaching the Imperial soldier his lesson. He was to be made to feel that though duchesses may lend themselves to love, they do not give themselves, and that the conquest of one of them would prove a harder matter than the conquest of Europe.

" Madame," returned Armand, " I have not time to wait. I am a spoilt child, as you told me yourself. When I seriously resolve to have that of which we have been speaking, I shall have it."

" You will have it ? " queried she, and there was a trace of surprise in her loftiness.

" I shall have it."

" Oh ! you would do me a great pleasure by 'resolving' to have it. For curiosity's sake, I should be delighted to know how you would set about it——"

" I am delighted to put a new interest into your life," interrupted Montriveau, breaking into a laugh which dismayed the Duchess. " Will you permit me to take you to the ball tonight ? "

" A thousand thanks. M. de Marsay has been beforehand with you. I gave him my promise."

Montriveau bowed gravely and went.

" So Ronquerolles was right," thought he, " and now for a game of chess."

Thenceforward he hid his agitation by complete composure. No man is strong enough to bear such sudden alternations from the height of happiness to the depths of wretchedness. So he had caught a glimpse of happy life the better to feel the emptiness of his previous existence ? There was a terrible storm within him ; but he had learned to endure, and bore the shock of tumultuous thoughts as a granite cliff stands out against the surge of an angry sea.

" I could say nothing. When I am with her my wits desert me. She does not know how vile and contemptible she is. Nobody has ventured to bring her face to face with herself. She has played with many a man, no doubt ; I will avenge them all."

For the first time, it may be, in a man's heart, revenge and love were blended so equally that Montriveau himself could not know whether love or revenge would carry all before it. That very evening he went to the ball at which he was sure of seeing the Duchesse de Langeais, and almost despaired of reaching her heart. He inclined to think that there was something diabolical about this woman, who was gracious to him and radiant with charming smiles ; probably because she had no wish to allow the world to think that she had compromised herself with M. de Montriveau. Coolness on both sides is a sign of love ; but so long as the Duchess was the same as ever, while the Marquis looked sullen and morose, was it not plain that she had conceded nothing ? Onlookers know the rejected lover by various signs and tokens ; they never mistake the genuine symptoms for a coolness such as some women command their adorers to feign, in the hope of concealing their love. Everyone laughed at Montriveau ; and he, having omitted to consult his cornac, was abstracted and ill at ease. M. de Ronquerolles would very likely have bidden him compromise the Duchess by responding to her show of friendliness by passionate demonstrations ; but as it was, Armand de Montriveau came away from the ball, loathing human nature, and even then scarcely ready to believe in such complete depravity.

" If there is no executioner for such crimes," he said, as he looked up at the lighted windows of the ballroom where the most enchanting women in Paris were dancing, laughing, and chatting," I will take you by the nape of the neck, Mme la Duchesse, and make you feel something that bites more deeply than the knife in the Place de la Grève. Steel against steel ; we shall see which heart will leave the deeper mark."

For a week or so Mme de Langeais hoped to see the Marquis de Montriveau again ; but he contented himself with sending his card every morning to the Hôtel de Langeais. The Duchess could not help shuddering each time that the card was brought in, and a dim foreboding crossed her mind, but the thought was vague as a presentiment of disaster. When her eyes fell on the name, it seemed to her that she felt the touch of the implacable man's strong hand in her hair ; sometimes the words seemed like a prognostication of a vengeance which her lively intellect invented in the most shocking forms. She had studied him too well not to dread him. Would he murder her, she wondered ? Would that bull-necked man dash out her vitals by flinging her over his head ? Would he trample her body under his feet ? When, where, and how would he get her into his power ? Would he make her suffer very much, and what kind of pain would he inflict ? She repented of her conduct. There were hours when, if he had come, she would have gone to his arms in complete self-surrender.

Every night before she slept she saw Montriveau's face ; every night it wore a different aspect. Sometimes she saw his bitter smile, sometimes the Jovelike knitting of the brows ; or his leonine look, or some disdainful movement of the shoulders made him terrible for her. Next day the card seemed stained with blood. The name of Montriveau stirred her now as the presence of the fiery, stubborn, exacting lover had never done. Her apprehensions gathered strength in the silence. She was forced, without aid from without, to face the thought of a hideous duel of which she could not speak. Her proud hard nature was more responsive to thrills of hate than it had ever been to the caresses of love. Ah ! if the General could but have seen her, as she sat with her forehead drawn into folds between her brows ; immersed in bitter thoughts in that boudoir where he had enjoyed such happy moments, he might perhaps have conceived high hopes. Of all human passions, is not pride alone incapable of engendering anything base ? Mme de Langeais kept her thoughts to herself, but is it not permissible to suppose that M. de Montriveau was no longer indifferent to her? And has not a man gained ground immensely when a woman thinks about him ? He is bound to make progress with her either one way or the other afterwards.

Put any feminine creature under the feet of a furious horse or other fearsome beast ; she will certainly drop on her knees and look for death ; but if the brute shows a milder mood and does not utterly slay her, she will love the horse, lion, bull, or what not, and will speak of him quite at her ease. The Duchess felt that she was under the lion's paws ; she quaked, but she did not hate him.

The man and woman thus singularly placed with regard to each other met three times in society during the course of that week. Each time, in reply to coquettish questioning glances, the Duchess received a respectful bow, and smiles tinged with such savage irony, that all her apprehensions over the card in the morning were revived at night. Ou lives are simply such as our feelings shape them for us ; and the feelings of these two had hollowed out a great gulf between them.

The Comtesse de Sérizy, the Marquis de Ronquerolles's sister, gave a great ball at the beginning of the following week, and Mme de Langeais was sure to go to it. Armand was the first person whom the Duchess saw when she came into the room, and this time Armand was looking out for her, or so she thought at least. The two exchanged a look, and suddenly the woman felt a cold perspiration break from every pore. She had thought all along that Montriveau was capable of taking reprisals in some unheard-of way proportioned to their condition, and now the revenge had been discovered, it was ready, heated, and boiling. Lightnings flashed from the foiled lover's eyes, his face was radiant with exultant vengeance. And the Duchess ? Her eyes were haggard in spite of her resolution to be cool and insolent. She went to take her place beside the Comtesse de Sérizy, who could not help exclaiming, " Dear Antoinette ! what is the matter with you ? You are enough to frighten one."

" I shall be all right after a quadrille," she answered, giving a hand to a young man who came up at that moment.

Mme de Langeais waltzed that evening with a sort of excitement and transport which redoubled Montriveau's lowering looks. He stood in front of the line of spectators, who were amusing themselves by looking on. Every time that *she* came past him, his eyes darted down upon her eddying face ; he might have been a tiger with the prey in his grasp. The waltz came to an end, Mme de Langeais went back to her place beside the Countess, and Montriveau never took his eyes off her, talking all the while with a stranger.

"One of the things that struck me most on the journey," he was saying (and the Duchess listened with all her ears), "was the remark which the man makes at Westminster when you are shown the axe with which a man in a mask cut off Charles the First's head, so they tell you. The King made it first of all to some inquisitive person, and they repeat it still in memory of him."

"What does the man say?" asked Mme de Sérizy.

"'Do not touch the axe!'" replied Montriveau, and there was menace in the sound of his voice.

"Really, my Lord Marquis," said Mme de Langeais, "you tell this old story that everybody knows if they have been to London, and look at my neck in such a melodramatic way that you seem to me to have an axe in your hand."

The Duchess was in a cold sweat, but nevertheless she laughed as she spoke the last words.

"But circumstances give the story a quite new application," returned he.

"How so; pray tell me, for pity's sake?"

"In this way, madame—you have touched the axe," said Montriveau, lowering his voice.

"What an enchanting prophecy!" returned she, smiling with assumed grace. "And when is my head to fall?"

"I have no wish to see that pretty head of yours cut off. I only fear some great misfortune for you. If your head were clipped close, would you feel no regrets for the dainty golden hair that you turn to such good account?"

"There are those for whom a woman would love to make such a sacrifice; even if, as often happens, it is for the sake of a man who cannot make allowances for an outbreak of temper."

"Quite so. Well, and if some wag were to spoil your beauty on a sudden by some chemical process, and you, who are but eighteen for us, were to be a hundred years old?"

"Why, the smallpox is our Battle of Waterloo, monsieur," she interrupted. "After it is over we find out those who love us sincerely."

"Would you not regret the lovely face that——?"

"Oh! indeed I should, but less for my own sake than for the sake of someone else whose delight it might have been. And, after all, if I were loved, always loved, and truly loved, what would my beauty matter to me?—What do you say, Clara?"

"It is a dangerous speculation," replied Mme de Sérizy.

"Is it permissible to ask His Majesty the King of Sorcerers when I made the mistake of touching the axe, since I have not been to London as yet?——"

"*Not so*," he answered in English, with a burst of ironical laughter.

"And when will the punishment begin?"

At this Montriveau coolly took out his watch, and ascertained the hour with a truly appalling air of conviction.

"A dreadful misfortune will befall you before this day is out."

" I am not a child to be easily frightened, or rather, I am a child ignorant of danger," said the Duchess. " I shall dance now without fear on the edge of the precipice."

" I am delighted to know that you have so much strength of character," he answered, as he watched her go to take her place in a square dance.

But the Duchess, in spite of her apparent contempt for Armand's dark prophecies, was really frightened. Her late lover's presence weighed upon her morally and physically with a sense of oppression that scarcely ceased when he left the ballroom. And yet when she had drawn freer breath, and enjoyed the relief for a moment, she found herself regretting the sensation of dread, so greedy of extreme sensations is the feminine nature. The regret was not love, but it was certainly akin to other feelings which prepare the way for love. And then—as if the impression which Montriveau had made upon her were suddenly revived—she recollected his air of conviction as he took out his watch, and in a sudden spasm of dread she went out.

By this time it was about midnight. One of her servants, waiting with her pelisse, went down to order her carriage. On her way home she fell naturally enough to musing over M. de Montriveau's prediction. Arrived in her own courtyard, as she supposed, she entered a vestibule almost like that of her own hotel, and suddenly saw that the staircase was different. She was in a strange house. Turning to call her servants, she was attacked by several men, who rapidly flung a handkerchief over her mouth, bound her hand and foot, and carried her off. She shrieked aloud.

" Madame, our orders are to kill you if you scream," a voice said in her ear.

So great was the Duchess's terror, that she could never recollect how nor by whom she was transported. When she came to herself, she was lying on a couch in a bachelor's lodging, her hands and feet tied with silken cords. In spite of herself, she shrieked aloud as she looked round and met Armand de Montriveau's eyes. He was sitting in his dressing-gown, quietly smoking a cigar in his armchair.

" Do not cry out, Mme la Duchesse," he said, coolly taking the cigar out of his mouth ; " I have a headache. Besides, I will untie you. But listen attentively to what I have the honour to say to you."

Very carefully he untied the knots that bound her feet.

" What would be the use of calling out ? Nobody can hear your cries. You are too well bred to make any unnecessary fuss. If you do not stay quietly, if you insist upon a struggle with me, I shall tie your hands and feet again. All things considered, I think that you have self-respect enough to stay on this sofa as if you were lying on your own at home ; cold as ever, if you will. You have made me shed many tears on this couch, tears that I hid from all other eyes."

While Montriveau was speaking, the Duchess glanced about her ; it was a woman's glance, a stolen look that saw all things and seemed to see nothing. She was much pleased with the room. It was rather like a monk's cell. The man's character and thoughts seemed to pervade it. No decoration of any kind broke the grey painted surface of the walls. A green carpet covered the floor. A black sofa, a table littered with papers, two big easy-chairs, a chest of drawers with an alarum clock by way of ornament, a very low bedstead with a coverlet flung over it—a red cloth with a black key border—all these things made part of a whole that told of a life reduced to its simplest terms. A triple candle-sconce of Egyptian design on the chimney-piece recalled the vast spaces of the desert and Montriveau's long wanderings; a huge sphinx-claw stood out beneath the folds of stuff at the bed-foot; and just beyond, a green curtain with a black and scarlet border was suspended by large rings from a spear handle above a door near one corner of the room. The other door by which the band had entered was likewise curtained, but the drapery hung from an ordinary curtain-rod. As the Duchess finally noted that the pattern was the same on both, she saw that the door at the bed-foot stood open; gleams of ruddy light from the room beyond flickered below the fringed border. Naturally, the ominous light roused her curiosity; she fancied she could distinguish strange shapes in the shadows; but as it did not occur to her at the time that danger could come from that quarter, she tried to gratify a more ardent curiosity.

"Monsieur, if it is not indiscreet, may I ask what you mean to do with me?" The insolence and irony of the tone stung through the words. The Duchess quite believed that she read extravagant love in Montriveau's speech. He had carried her off; was not that in itself an acknowledgment of her power?

"Nothing whatever, madame," he returned, gracefully puffing the last whiff of cigar smoke. "You will remain here for a short time. First of all, I should like to explain to you what you are, and what I am. I cannot put my thoughts into words whilst you are twisting on the sofa in your boudoir; and besides, in your own house you take offence at the slightest hint, you ring the bell, make an outcry, and turn your lover out at the door as if he were the basest of wretches. Here my mind is unfettered. Here nobody can turn me out. Here you shall be my victim for a few seconds, and you are going to be so exceedingly kind as to listen to me. You need fear nothing. I did not carry you off to insult you, nor yet to take by force what you refused to grant of your own will to my unworthiness. I could not stoop so low. You possibly think of outrage; for myself, I have no such thoughts."

He flung his cigar coolly into the fire.

"The smoke is unpleasant to you, no doubt, madame?" he said, and rising at once, he took a chafing-dish from the hearth, burnt perfumes, and purified the air. The Duchess's astonishment was only equalled by her humiliation. She was in this man's power; and he would not abuse his power. The eyes in which love had once blazed like flame were now quiet and steady as stars. She trembled. Her dread of Armand was increased by a nightmare sensation of restlessness and utter inability to move ; she felt as if she were turned to stone. She lay passive in the grip of fear. She thought she saw the light behind the curtains grow to a blaze, as if blown up by a pair of bellows ; in another moment the gleams of flame grew brighter, and she fancied that three masked figures suddenly flashed out ; but the terrible vision disappeared so swiftly that she took it for an optical delusion.

" Madame," Armand continued with cold contempt, " one minute, just one minute is enough for me, and you shall feel it afterwards at every moment throughout your lifetime, the one eternity over which I have power. I am not God. Listen carefully to me," he continued, pausing to add solemnity to his words. " Love will always come at your call. You have boundless power over men : but remember that once you called love, and love came to you ; love as pure and true-hearted as may be on earth, and as reverent as it was passionate ; fond as a devoted woman's, as a mother's love ; a love so great indeed, that it was past the bounds of reason. You played with it, and you committed a crime. Every woman has a right to refuse herself to love which she feels she cannot share ; and if a man loves and cannot win love in return, he is not to be pitied, he has no right to complain. But with a semblance of love to attract an unfortunate creature cut off from all affection ; to teach him to understand happiness to the full, only to snatch it from him ; to rob him of his future of felicity ; to slay his happiness not merely today, but as long as his life lasts, by poisoning every hour of it and every thought—this I call a fearful crime ! "

" Monsieur——"

" I cannot allow you to answer me yet. So listen to me still. In any case I have rights over you ; but I only choose to exercise one—the right of the judge over the criminal, so that I may arouse your conscience. If you had no conscience left, I should not reproach you at all ; but you are so young ! You must feel some life still in your heart ; or so I like to believe. While I think of you as depraved enough to do a wrong which the law does not punish, I do not think you so degraded that you cannot comprehend the full meaning of my words. I resume."

As he spoke the Duchess heard the smothered sound of a pair of bellows. Those mysterious figures which she had just seen were blowing up the fire, no doubt ; the glow shone through the curtain. But Montriveau's lurid face was turned upon her ; she could not choose but wait with a fast-beating heart and eyes fixed in a stare. However curious she felt, the heat in Armand's words interested her even more than the crackling of the mysterious flames.

" Madame," he went on after a pause, " if some poor wretch commits a murder in Paris, it is the executioner's duty, you know, to lay hands on him and stretch him on the plank, where murderers pay for their crimes with their heads. Then the newspapers inform everyone, rich and poor, so that the former are assured that they may sleep in peace, and the latter are warned that they must be on the watch if they would live. Well, you that are religious, and even a little of a bigot, may have masses said for such a man's soul. You both belong to the same family, but yours is the elder branch; and the elder branch may occupy high places in peace and live happily and without cares. Want or anger may drive your brother the convict to take a man's life; you have taken more, you have taken the joy out of a man's life, you have killed all that was best in his life—his dearest beliefs. The murderer simply lay in wait for his victim, and killed him reluctantly, and in fear of the scaffold; but *you . . . !* You heaped up every sin that weakness can commit against strength that suspected no evil; you tamed a passive victim, the better to gnaw his heart out; you lured him with caresses; you left nothing undone that could set him dreaming, imagining, longing for the bliss of love. You asked innumerable sacrifices of him, only to refuse to make any in return. He should see the light indeed before you put out his eyes! It is wonderful how you found the heart to do it! Such villainies demand a display of resource quite above the comprehension of those bourgeoises whom you laugh at and despise. They can give and forgive; they know how to love and suffer. The grandeur of their devotion dwarfs us. Rising higher in the social scale, one finds just as much mud as at the lower end; but with this difference, at the upper end it is hard and gilded over.

"Yes, to find baseness in perfection, you must look for a noble bringing up, a great name, a fair woman, a duchess. You cannot fall lower than the lowest unless you are set high above the rest of the world. —I express my thoughts badly; the wounds you dealt me are too painful as yet, but do not think that I complain. My words are not the expression of any hope for myself; there is no trace of bitterness in them. Know this, madame, for a certainty—I forgive you. My forgiveness is so complete that you need not feel in the least sorry that you came hither to find it against your will. . . . But you might take advantage of other hearts as child-like as my own, and it is my duty to spare them anguish. So you have inspired the thought of justice. Expiate your sin here on earth; God may perhaps forgive you; I wish that He may, but He is inexorable, and will strike."

The broken-spirited, broken-hearted woman looked up, her eyes filled with tears.

"Why do you cry? Be true to your nature. You could look on indifferently at the torture of a heart as you broke it. That will do, madame, do not cry. I cannot bear it any longer. Other men will tell you that you have given them life; as for myself, I tell you, with rapture, that you have given me blank extinction. Perhaps you guess that I am not my own, that I am bound to live for my friends, that from this time forth I must endure the cold chill of death, as well as the burden of life? Is it possible that there can be so much kindness in you? Are you like the desert tigress that licks the wounds she has inflicted?"

The Duchess burst out sobbing.

" Pray spare your tears, madame. If I believed in them at all, it would merely set me on my guard. Is this another of your artifices ? or is it not ? You have used so many with me ; how can one think that there is any truth in you ? Nothing that you do or say has any power now to move me. That is all I have to say."

Mme de Langeais rose to her feet, with a great dignity and humility in her bearing.

" You are right to treat me very hardly," she said, holding out a hand to the man who did not take it ; " you have not spoken hardly enough ; and I deserve this punishment."

" *I* punish you, madame ! A man must love still, to punish, must he not ? From me you must expect no feeling, nothing resembling it. If I chose, I might be accuser and judge in my cause, and pronounce and carry out the sentence. But I am about to fulfil a duty, not a desire of vengeance of any kind. The cruellest revenge of all, I think, is scorn of revenge when it is in our power to take it. Perhaps I shall be the minister of your pleasures ; who knows ? Perhaps from this time forth, as you gracefully wear the tokens of disgrace by which society marks out the criminal, you may perforce learn something of the convict's sense of honour. And then, you will love ! "

The Duchess sat listening ; her meekness was unfeigned ; it was no coquettish device. When she spoke at last, it was after a silence.

" Armand," she began, " it seems to me that when I resisted love, I was obeying all the instincts of woman's modesty ; I should not have looked for such reproaches from *you*. I was weak ; you have turned all my weaknesses against me, and made so many crimes of them. How could you fail to understand that the curiosity of love might have carried me further than I ought to go ; and that next morning I might be angry with myself, and wretched because I had gone too far ? Alas ! I sinned in ignorance. I was as sincere in my wrongdoing, I swear to you, as in my remorse. There was far more love for you in my severity than in my concessions. And besides, of what do you complain ? I gave you my heart ; that was not enough ; you demanded, brutally, that I should give my person——"

" Brutally ? " repeated Montriveau. But to himself he said, " If I once allow her to dispute over words, I am lost."

" Yes. You came to me as if I were one of those women. You showed none of the respect, none of the attentions of love. Had I not reason to reflect ? Very well, I reflected. The unseemliness of your conduct is not inexcusable ; love lay at the source of it ; let me think so, and justify you to myself.—Well, Armand, this evening, even while you were prophesying evil, I felt convinced that there was happiness in store for us both. Yes, I put my faith in the noble, proud nature so often tested and proved." She bent lower. " And I was yours wholly," she murmured in his ear. " I felt a longing that I cannot express to give happiness to a man so violently tried by adversity. If I must have a master, my master should be a great man. As I felt conscious of my height, the less

I cared to descend. I felt I could trust you, I saw a whole lifetime of love, while you were pointing to death. . . . Strength and kindness always go together. My friend, you are so strong, you will not be unkind to a helpless woman who loves you. If I was wrong, is there no way of obtaining forgiveness? No way of making reparation? Repentance is the charm of love; I should like to be very charming for you. How could I, alone among women, fail to know a woman's doubts and fears, the timidity that it is so natural to feel when you bind yourself for life, and know how easily a man snaps such ties? The bourgeoises, with whom you compared me just now, give themselves, but they struggle first. Very well—I struggled; but here I am!—Ah! God, he does not hear me!" she broke off, and wringing her hands, she cried out "But I love you! I am yours!" and fell at Armand's feet.

"Yours! yours! my one and only master!"

Armand tried to raise her.

"Madame, it is too late! Antoinette cannot save the Duchesse de Langeais. I cannot believe in either. Today you may give yourself; tomorrow, you may refuse. No power in earth or heaven can insure me the sweet constancy of love. All love's pledges lay in the past; and now nothing of that past exists."

The light behind the curtain blazed up so brightly, that the Duchess could not help turning her head; this time she distinctly saw the three masked figures.

"Armand," she said, "I would not wish to think ill of you. Why are those men there? What are you going to do to me?"

"Those men will be as silent as I myself with regard to the thing which is about to be done. Think of them simply as my hands and my heart. One of them is a surgeon——"

"A surgeon! Armand, my friend, of all things, suspense is the hardest to bear. Just speak; tell me if you wish for my life; I will give it to you, you shall not take it——"

"Then you did not understand me? Did I not speak just now of justice? To put an end to your misapprehensions," continued he, taking up a small steel object from the table, "I will now explain what I have decided with regard to you."

He held out a Lorraine cross, fastened to the tip of a steel rod.

"Two of my friends at this very moment are heating another cross, made on this pattern, red-hot. We are going to stamp it upon your forehead, here between the eyes, so that there will be no possibility of hiding the mark with diamonds, and so avoiding people's questions. In short, you shall bear on your forehead the brand of infamy which your brothers the convicts wear on their shoulders. The pain is a mere trifle, but I feared a nervous crisis of some kind, of resistance——"

"Resistance?" she cried, clapping her hands for joy. "Oh no, no! I would have the whole world here to see. Ah, my Armand, brand her quickly, this creature of yours; brand her with your mark as a poor little trifle belonging to you. You asked for pledges of my love; here they are all in one. Ah ! for me there is nothing but mercy and forgiveness and eternal happiness in this revenge of yours. When you have marked this woman with your mark, when you set your crimson brand on her, your slave in soul, you can never afterwards abandon her, you will be mine for evermore ? When you cut me off from my kind, you make yourself responsible for my happiness, or you prove yourself base ; and I know that you are noble and great ! Why, when a woman loves, the brand of love is burnt into her soul by her own will.—Come in, gentlemen ! come in and brand her, this Duchesse de Langeais. She is M. de Montriveau's forever ! Ah ! come quickly, all of you, my forehead burns hotter than your fire ! "

Armand turned his head sharply away lest he should see the Duchess kneeling, quivering with the throbbings of her heart. He said some word, and his three friends vanished.

The women of Paris salons know how one mirror reflects another. The Duchess, with every motive for reading the depths of Armand's heart, was all eyes ; and Armand, all unsuspicious of the mirror, brushed away two tears as they fell. Her whole future lay in those two tears. When he turned round again to help her to rise, she was standing before him, sure of love. Her pulses must have throbbed fast when he spoke with the firmness she had known so well how to use of old while she played with him.

" I spare you, madame. All that has taken place shall be as if it had never been, you may believe me. But now, let us bid each other good-bye. I like to think that you were sincere in your coquetries on your sofa, sincere again in this outpouring of your heart. Good-bye. I feel that there is no faith in you left in me. You would torment me again ; you would always be the Duchess, and—— But there, good-bye, we shall never understand each other.

" Now, what do you wish ? " he continued, taking the tone of a master of the ceremonies—" to return home, or to go back to Mme de Sérizy's ball ? I have done all in my power to prevent any scandal. Neither your servants nor anyone else can possibly know what has passed between us in the last quarter of an hour. Your servants have no idea that you have left the ballroom ; your carriage never left Mme de Sérizy's courtyard ; your brougham may likewise be found in the court of your own hôtel. Where do you wish to be ? "

" What do you counsel, Armand ? "

" There is no Armand now, Mme la Duchesse. We are strangers to each other."

" Then take me to the ball," she said, still curious to put Armand's power to the test. " Thrust a soul that suffered in the world, and must always suffer there, if there is no happiness for her now, down into hell again. And yet, oh my friend, I love you as your bourgeoises love ; I love you so that I could come to you and fling my arms about your neck before all the world if you asked it off me. The hateful world has not corrupted me. I am young at least, and I have grown younger still.

I am a child, yes, your child, your new creature. Ah ! do not drive me forth out of my Eden ! "

Armand shook his head.

" Ah ! let me take something with me, if I go, some little thing to wear tonight on my heart," she said, taking possession of Armand's glove, which she twisted into her handkerchief.

" No, I am *not* like all those depraved women. You do not know the world, and so you cannot know my worth. You shall know it now ! There are women who sell themselves for money ; there are others to be gained by gifts, it is a vile world ! Oh, I wish I were a simple bourgeoise, a working girl, if you would rather have a woman beneath you than a woman whose devotion is accompanied by high rank, as men count it. Oh, my Armand, there are noble, high, and chaste and pure natures among us ; and then they are lovely indeed. I would have all nobleness that I might offer it all up to you. Misfortune willed that I should be a duchess ; I would I were a royal princess, that my offering might be complete. I would be a grisette for you, and a queen for everyone besides."

He listened, damping his cigars with his lips.

" You will let me know when you wish to go," he said.

" But I should like to stay——"

" That is another matter ! "

" Stay, that was badly rolled," she cried, seizing on a cigar and devouring all that Armand's lips had touched.

" Do you smoke ? "

" Oh, what would I not do to please you ? "

" Very well. Go, madame."

" I will obey you," she answered, with tears in her eyes.

" You must be blindfolded ; you must not see a glimpse of the way."

" I am ready, Armand," she said, bandaging her eyes.

" Can you see ? "

" No."

Noiselessly he knelt before her.

" Ah ! I can hear you ! " she cried, with a little fond gesture, thinking that the pretence of harshness was over.

He made as if he would kiss her lips ; she held up her face.

" You can see, madame."

" I am just a little bit curious."

" So you always deceive me ? "

" Ah ! take off this handkerchief, sir," she cried out, with the passion of a great generosity repelled with scorn, " lead me ; I will not open my eyes."

Armand felt sure of her after that cry. He led the way ; the Duchess, nobly true to her word, was blind. But while Montriveau held her hand as a father might, and led her up and down flights of stairs, he was studying the throbbing pulses of this woman's heart so suddenly invaded by Love. Mme de Langeais, rejoicing in this power of speech, was glad to let him know all; but he was inflexible; his hand was passive in reply to the questionings of her hand.

At length, after some journey made together, Armand bade her go forward; the opening was doubtless narrow, for as she went she felt that his hand protected her dress. His care touched her; it was a revelation surely that there was a little love still left; yet it was in some sort a farewell, for Montriveau left her without a word. The air was warm; the Duchess, feeling the heat, opened her eyes, and found herself standing by the fire in the Comtesse de Sérizy's boudoir. She was alone. Her first thought was for her disordered toilette; in a moment she had adjusted her dress and restored her picturesque coiffure.

"Well, dear Antoinette, we have been looking for you everywhere." It was the Comtesse de Sérizy who spoke as she opened the door.

"I came here to breathe," said the Duchess; "it is unbearably hot in the rooms."

"People thought that you had gone; but my brother Ronquerolles told me that your servants were waiting for you."

"I am tired out, dear, let me stay and rest here for a minute," and the Duchess sat down on the sofa.

"Why, what is the matter with you? You are shaking from head to foot!"

The Marquis de Ronquerolles came in.

"Mme la Duchesse, I was afraid that something might have happened. I have just come across your coachman, the man is as tipsy as all the Swiss in Switzerland."

The Duchess made no answer; she was looking round the room, at the chimney-piece and the tall mirrors, seeking the trace of an opening. Then with an extraordinary sensation she recollected that she was again in the midst of the gaiety of the ballroom after that terrific scene which had changed the whole course of her life. She began to shiver violently.

"M. de Montriveau's prophecy has shaken my nerves," she said. "It was a joke, but still I will see whether his axe from London will haunt me even in my sleep. So good-bye, dear.—Good-bye, M. le Marquis."

As she went through the rooms she was beset with enquiries and regrets. Her world seemed to have dwindled now that she, its queen, had fallen so low, was so diminished. And what, moreover, were these men compared with him whom she loved with all her heart; with the man grown great by all that she had lost in stature? The giant had regained the height that he had lost for a while, and she exaggerated it perhaps beyond measure. She looked, in spite of herself, at the servant who had attended her to the ball. He was fast asleep.

"Have you been here all the time?" she asked.

"Yes, madame."

As she took her seat in her carriage she saw, in fact, that her coachman was drunk—so drunk, that at any other time she would have been afraid; but after a great crisis in life, fear loses its appetite for common food. She reached home, at any rate, without accident; but even there she felt a change in herself, a new feeling that she could not shake off. For her, there was now but one man in the world; which is to say, that henceforth she cared to shine for his sake alone.

While the physiologist can define love promptly by following out natural laws, the moralist finds a far more perplexing problem before him if he attempts to consider love in all its developments due to social conditions. Still, in spite of the heresies of the endless sects that divide the church of Love, there is one broad and trenchant line of difference in doctrine, a line that all the discussion in the world can never deflect. A rigid application of this line explains the nature of the crisis through which the Duchess, like most women, was to pass. Passion she knew, but she did not love as yet.

Love and passion are two different conditions which poets and men of the world, philosophers and fools, alike continually confound. Love implies a give and take, a certainty of bliss that nothing can change; it means so close a clinging of the heart, and an exchange of happiness so constant, that there is no room left for jealousy. Then possession is a means and not an end; unfaithfulness may give pain, but the bond is not less close; the soul is neither more nor less ardent or troubled, but happy at every moment; in short, the divine breath of desire spreading from end to end of the immensity of Time steeps it all for us in the selfsame hue; life takes the tint of the unclouded heaven. But Passion is the foreshadowing of Love, and of that Infinite to which all suffering souls aspire. Passion is a hope that may be cheated. Passion means both suffering and transition. Passion dies out when hope is dead. Men and women may pass through this experience many times without dishonour, for it is so natural to spring towards happiness; but there is only one love in a lifetime. All discussions of sentiment ever conducted on paper or by word of mouth may therefore be resumed by two questions—"Is it passion? Is it love?" So, since love comes into existence only through the intimate experience of the bliss which gives it lasting life, the Duchess was beneath the yoke of passion as yet; and as she knew the fierce tumult, the unconscious calculations, the fevered cravings, and all that is meant by that word *passion*—she suffered. Through all the trouble of her soul there rose eddying gusts of tempest, raised by vanity or self-love, or pride or a high spirit; for all these forms of egoism make common cause together.

She had said to this man, "I love you; I am yours!" Was it possible that the Duchesse de Langeais should have uttered those words—in vain? She must either be loved now or play her part of queen no longer. And then she felt the loneliness of the luxurious couch where pleasure had never yet set his glowing feet; and over and over again, while she tossed and writhed there, she said, "I want to be loved."

But the belief that she still had in herself gave her hope of success. The Duchess might be piqued, the vain Parisienne might be humiliated;

but the woman saw glimpses of wedded happiness, and imagination, avenging the time lost for nature, took a delight in kindling the inextinguishable fire in her veins. She all but attained to the sensations of love; for amid her poignant doubt whether she was loved in return, she felt glad at heart to say to herself, "I love him!" As for her scruples, religion, and the world she could trample them under foot! Montriveau was her religion now. She spent the next day in a state of moral torpor, troubled by a physical unrest, which no words could express. She wrote letters and tore them all up, and invented a thousand impossible fancies.

When M. de Montriveau's usual hour arrived, she tried to think that he would come, and enjoyed the feeling of expectation. Her whole life was concentrated in the single sense of hearing. Sometimes she shut her eyes, straining her ears to listen through space, wishing that she could annihilate everything that lay between her and her lover, and so establish that perfect silence which sounds may traverse from afar. In her tense self-concentration, the ticking of the clock grew hateful to her; she stopped its ill-omened garrulity. The twelve strokes of midnight sounded from the drawing-room.

"Ah, God!" she cried, "to see him here would be happiness. And yet, it is not so very long since he came here, brought by desire, and the tones of his voice filled this boudoir. And now there is nothing."

She remembered the times that she had played the coquette with him, and how that her coquetry had cost her her lover, and the despairing tears flowed for long.

Her woman came at length with, "Mme la Duchesse does not know, perhaps, that it is two o'clock in the morning; I thought that madame was not feeling well."

"Yes, I am going to bed," said the Duchess, drying her eyes. "But remember, Suzanne, never to come in again without orders; I tell you this for the last time."

For a week, Mme de Langeais went to every house where there was a hope of meeting M. de Montriveau. Contrary to her usual habits, she came early and went late; gave up dancing, and went to the card-tables. Her experiments were fruitless. She did not succeed in getting a glimpse of Armand. She did not dare to utter his name now. One evening, however, in a fit of despair, she spoke to Mme de Sérizy, and asked as carelessly as she could, "You must have quarrelled with M. de Montriveau? He is not to be seen at your house now."

The Countess laughed. "So he does not come here either?" she returned. "He is not to be seen anywhere, for that matter. He is interested in some woman, no doubt."

"I used to think that the Marquis de Ronquerolles was one of his friends——" the Duchess began sweetly.

"I have never heard my brother say that he was acquainted with him."

Mme de Langeais did not reply. Mme de Sérizy concluded from the Duchess's silence that she might apply the scourge with impunity to a discreet friendship which she had seen, with bitterness of soul, for a long time past.

"So you miss that melancholy personage, do you? I have heard most extraordinary things of him. Wound his feelings, he never comes back, he forgives nothing; and, if you love him, he keeps you in chains. To everything that I said of him, one of those that praise him sky-high would always answer, 'He knows how to love!' People are always telling me that Montriveau would give up all for his friend; that his is a great nature. Pooh! society does not want such tremendous natures. Men of that stamp are all very well at home; let them stay there and leave us to our pleasant littlenesses. What do you say, Antoinette?"

Woman of the world though she was, the Duchess seemed agitated, yet she replied in a natural voice that deceived her fair friend—

"I am sorry to miss him. I took a great interest in him, and promised to myself to be his sincere friend. I like great natures, dear friend, ridiculous though you may think it. To give oneself to a fool is a clear confession, is it not, that one is governed wholly by one's senses?"

Mme de Sérizy's "preferences" had always been for commonplace men; her lover at the moment, the Marquis d'Aiglemont, was a fine, tall man.

After this, the Countess soon took her departure, you may be sure. Mme de Langeais saw hope in Armand's withdrawal from the world; she wrote to him at once; it was a humble, gentle letter, surely it would bring him if he loved her still. She sent her footman with it next day. On the servant's return, she asked whether he had given the letter to M. de Montriveau himself, and could not restrain the movement of joy at the affirmative answer. Armand was in Paris! He stayed alone in his house; he did not go out into society! So she was loved! All day long she waited for an answer that never came. Again and again, when impatience grew unbearable, Antoinette found reasons for his delay. Armand felt embarrassed; the reply would come by post; but night came, and she could not deceive herself any longer. It was a dreadful day, a day of pain grown sweet, of intolerable heart-throbs, a day when the heart squanders the very forces of life in riot.

Next day she sent for an answer.

"M. le Marquis sent word that he would call on Mme la Duchesse," reported Julien.

She fled lest her happiness should be seen in her face, and flung herself on her couch to devour her first sensations.

"He is coming!"

The thought rent her soul. And, in truth, woe unto those for whom suspense is not the most horrible time of tempest, while it increases and multiplies the sweetest joys; for they have nothing in them of that flame which quickens the images of things, giving to them a second existence, so that we cling as closely to the pure essence as to its outward and visible manifestation. What is suspense in love but a constant drawing upon an unfailing hope ?—a submission to the terrible scourging of passion, while passion is yet happy, and the disenchantment of reality has not set in. The constant putting forth of strength and longing, called suspense, is surely, to the human soul, as fragrance to the flower that breathes it forth. We soon leave the brilliant, unsatisfying colours of tulips and coreopsis, but we turn again and again to drink in the sweetness of orange-blossoms or volkameria—flowers compared separately, each in its own land, to a betrothed bride, full of love, made fair by the past and future.

The Duchess learned the joys of this new life of hers through the rapture with which she received the scourgings of love. As this change wrought in her, she saw other destinies before her, and a better meaning in the things of life. As she hurried to her dressing-room, she understood what studied adornment and the most minute attention to her toilet mean when these are undertaken for love's sake and not for vanity. Even now this making ready helped her to bear the long time of waiting. A relapse of intense agitation set in when she was dressed ; she passed through nervous paroxysms brought on by the dreadful power which sets the whole mind in ferment. Perhaps that power is only a disease, though the pain of it is sweet. The Duchess was dressed and waiting at two o'clock in the afternoon. At half-past eleven that night M. de Montriveau had not arrived. To try to give an idea of the anguish endured by a woman who might be said to be the spoilt child of civilisation, would be to attempt to say how many imaginings the heart can condense into one thought. As well endeavour to measure the forces expended by the soul in a sigh whenever the bell rang ; to estimate the drain of life when a carriage rolled past without stopping, and left her prostrate.

"Can he be playing with me ?" she said, as the clocks struck midnight.

She grew white ; her teeth chattered ; she struck her hands together and leapt up and crossed the boudoir, recollecting as she did so how often he had come thither without a summons. But she resigned herself. Had she not seen him grow pale, and start up under the stinging barbs of irony ? Then Mme de Langeais felt the horror of the woman's appointed lot ; a man's is the active part, a woman must wait passively when she loves. If a woman goes beyond her beloved, she makes a mistake which few men can forgive ; almost every man would feel that a woman lowers herself by this piece of angelic flattery. But Armand's was a great nature ; he surely must be one of the very few who can repay such exceeding love by love that lasts forever.

"Well, I will make the advance," she told herself, as she tossed on her bed and found no sleep there ; "I will go to him. I will not weary myself with holding out a hand to him, but I will hold it out. A man of a thousand will see a promise of love and constancy in every step that a woman takes towards him. Yes, the angels must come down from heaven to reach men ; and I wish to be an angel for him."

Next day she wrote. It was a billet of the kind in which the intellects of the ten thousand Sévignés that Paris now can number particularly excel. And yet only a Duchesse de Langeais, brought up by Mme la Princesse de Blamont-Chauvry, could have written that delicious note ; no other woman could complain without lowering herself ; could spread wings in such a flight without draggling her pinions in humiliation ; rise gracefully in revolt ; scold without giving offence ; and pardon without compromising her personal dignity.

Julien went with the note. Julien, like his kind, was the victim of love's marches and countermarches.

" What did M. de Montriveau reply ? " she asked, as indifferently as she could, when the man came back to report himself.

" M. le Marquis requested me to tell Mme la Duchesse that it was all right."

Oh the dreadful reaction of the soul upon herself ! To have her heart stretched on the rack before curious witnesses ; yet not to utter a sound, to be forced to keep silence ! One of the countless miseries of the rich !

More than three weeks went by. Mme de Langeais wrote again and again, and no answer came from Montriveau. At last she gave out that she was ill, to gain a dispensation from attendance on the Princess and from social duties. She was only at home to her father the Duc de Navarreins, her aunt the Princesse de Blamont-Chauvry, the old Vidame de Pamiers (her maternal great-uncle), and to her husband's uncle, the Duc de Grandlieu. These persons found no difficulty in believing that the Duchess was ill, seeing that she grew thinner and paler and more dejected every day. The vague ardour of love, the smart of wounded pride, the continual prick of the only scorn that could touch her, the yearnings towards joys that she craved with a vain continual longing—all these things told upon her, mind and body ; all the forces of her nature were stimulated to no purpose. She was paying the arrears of her life of make-believe.

She went out at last to a review. M. de Montriveau was to be there. For the Duchess, on the balcony of the Tuileries with the Royal Family, it was one of those festival days that are long remembered. She looked supremely beautiful in her languor ; she was greeted with admiration in all eyes. It was Montriveau's presence that made her so fair. Once or twice they exchanged glances. The General came almost to her feet in all the glory of that soldier's uniform, which produces an effect upon the feminine imagination to which the most prudish will confess. When a woman is very much in love, and has not seen her lover for two months, such a swift moment must be something like the phase of a dream when the eyes embrace a world that stretches away forever. Only women or young men can imagine the dull, frenzied hunger in the Duchess's eyes. As for older men, if during the paroxysms of early passion in youth they had experience of such phenomena of nervous power ; at a later day it is so completely forgotten that they deny the very existence of the luxuriant ecstasy—the only name that can be given to these wonderful intuitions. Religious ecstasy is the aberration of a soul that has shaken off its bonds of flesh ; whereas in amorous ecstasy all the forces of soul and body are embraced and blended in one. If a woman falls a victim to the tyrannous frenzy before which Mme de Langeais was forced to bend, she will take one decisive resolution after another so swiftly that it is impossible to give account of them. Thought after thought rises and flits across her brain, as clouds are whirled by the wind across the grey veil of mist that shuts out the sun. Thenceforth the facts reveal all. And the facts are these.

The day after the review, Mme de Langeais sent her carriage and liveried servants to wait at the Marquis de Montriveau's door from eight o'clock in the morning till three in the afternoon. Armand lived in the Rue de Tournon, a few steps away from the Chamber of Peers, and that very day the House was sitting ; but long before the peers returned to their palaces, several people had recognised the Duchess's carriage and liveries. The first of these was the Baron de Maulincour. That young officer had met with disdain from Mme de Langeais and a better reception from Mme de Sérizy ; he betook himself at once therefore to his mistress, and under seal of secrecy told her of this strange freak.

In a moment the news was spread with telegraphic speed through all the coteries in the Faubourg Saint-Germain ; it reached the Tuileries and the Élysée-Bourbon ; it was the sensation of the day, the matter of all the talk from noon till night. Almost everywhere the women denied the facts, but in such a manner that the report was confirmed ; the men one and all believed it, and manifested a most indulgent interest in Mme de Langeais. Some among them threw the blame on Armand.

" That savage of a Montriveau is a man of bronze," said they ; " he insisted on making this scandal, no doubt."

" Very well, then," others replied, " Mme de Langeais has been guilty of a most generous piece of imprudence. To renounce the world and rank, and fortune, and consideration for her lover's sake, and that in the face of all Paris, is as fine a *coup d'état* for a woman as that barber's knife-thrust, which so affected Canning in a court of assize. Not one of the women who blame the Duchess would make a declaration worthy of ancient times. It is heroic of Mme de Langeais to proclaim herself so frankly. Now there is nothing left to her but to love Montriveau. There must be something great about a woman if she says, ' I will have but one passion.' "

" But what is to become of society, monsieur, if you honour vice in this way without respect for virtue ? " asked the Comtesse de Granville, the attorney-general's wife.

While the Château, the Faubourg, and the Chaussée d'Antin were discussing the shipwreck of aristocratic virtue ; while excited young men rushed about on horseback to make sure that the carriage was standing in the Rue de Tournon, and the Duchess in consequence was beyond a doubt in M. de Montriveau's rooms, Mme de Langeais, with heavy throbbing pulses, was lying hidden away in her boudoir. And Armand ?—he had been out all night, and at that moment was walking with M. de Marsay in the Gardens of the Tuileries. The elder members, of Mme de Langeais's family were engaged in calling upon one another, arranging to read her a homily and to hold a consultation as to the best way of putting a stop to the scandal.

At three o'clock, therefore, M. le Duc de Navarreins, the Vidame de Pamiers, the old Princesse de Blamont-Chauvry, and the Duc de Grandlieu were assembled in Mme la Duchesse de Langeais's drawing-room. To them, as to all curious enquirers, the servants said that their mistress was not at home ; the Duchess had made no exceptions to her orders. But these four personages shone conspicuous in that lofty sphere, of which the revolutions and hereditary pretensions are solemnly recorded year by year in the *Almanach de Gotha*, wherefore without some slight sketch of each of them this picture of society were incomplete.

The Princesse de Blamont-Chauvry, in the feminine world, was a most poetic wreck of the reign of Louis Quinze. In her beautiful prime, so it was said, she had done her part to win for that monarch his appellation of *le Bien-aimé*. Of her past charms of feature, little remained save a remarkably prominent slender nose, curved like a Turkish scimitar, now the principal ornament of a countenance that put you in mind of an old white glove. Add a few powdered curls, high-heeled pantoufles, a cap with upstanding loops of lace, black mittens, and a decided taste for *ombre*. But to do full justice to the lady, it must be said that she appeared in low-necked gowns of an evening (so high an opinion of her ruins had she), wore long gloves, and raddled her cheeks with Martin's classic rouge. An appalling amiability in her wrinkles, a prodigious brightness in the old lady's eyes, a profound dignity in her whole person, together with the triple barbed wit of her tongue, and an infallible memory in her head, made of her a real power in the land. The whole Cabinet des Chartes was entered in duplicate on the parchment of her brain. She knew all the genealogies of every noble house in Europe—princes, dukes, and counts—and could put her hand on the last descendants of Charlemagne in the direct line. No usurpation of title could escape the Princesse de Blamont-Chauvry.

Young men who wished to stand well at Court, ambitious men, and young married women paid her assiduous homage. Her salon set the tone of the Faubourg Saint-Germain. The words of this Talleyrand in petticoats were taken as final decrees. People came to consult her on questions of etiquette or usages, or to take lessons in good taste. And, in truth, no other old woman could put back her snuff-box in her pocket as the Princess could ; while there was a precision and a grace about the movements of her skirts, when she sat down or crossed her feet, which drove the finest ladies of the young generation to despair.

Her voice had remained in her head during one-third of her lifetime; but she could not prevent a descent into the membranes of the nose, which lent to it a peculiar expressiveness. She still retained a hundred and fifty thousand livres of her great fortune, for Napoleon had generously returned her woods to her; so that personally and in the matter of possessions she was a woman of no little consequence.

This curious antique, seated in a low chair by the fireside, was chatting with the Vidame de Pamiers, a contemporary ruin. The Vidame was a big, tall, and spare man, a *seigneur* of the old school, and had been a Commander of the Order of Malta. His neck had always been so tightly compressed by a strangulation stock, that his cheeks pouched over it a little, and he held his head high; to many people this would have given an air of self-sufficiency, but in the Vidame it was justified by a Voltairean wit. His wide prominent eyes seemed to see everything, and as a matter of fact there was not much that they had not seen. Altogether, his person was a perfect model of aristocratic outline, slim and slender, supple and agreeable. He seemed as if he could be pliant or rigid at will, and twist and bend, or rear his head like a snake.

The Duc de Navarreins was pacing up and down the room with the Duc de Grandlieu. Both were men of fifty-six or thereabouts, and still hale; both were short, corpulent, flourishing, somewhat florid-complexioned men with jaded eyes, and lower lips that had begun to hang already. But for an exquisite refinement of accent, an urbane courtesy, and an ease of manner that could change in a moment to insolence, a superficial observer might have taken them for a couple of bankers. Any such mistake would have been impossible, however, if the listener could have heard them converse, and seen them on their guard with men whom they feared, vapid and commonplace with their equals, slippery with the inferiors whom courtiers and statesmen know how to tame by a tactful word, or to humiliate with an unexpected phrase.

Such were the representatives of the great noblesse that determined to perish rather than submit to any change. It was a noblesse that deserved praise and blame in equal measure; a noblesse that will never be judged impartially until some poet shall arise to tell how joyfully the nobles obeyed the King though their heads fell under a Richelieu's axe, and how deeply they scorned the guillotine of '89 as a foul revenge.

Another noticeable trait in all the four was a thin voice that agreed peculiarly well with their ideas and bearing. Among themselves, at any rate, they were on terms of perfect equality. None of them betrayed any sign of annoyance over the Duchess's escapade, but all of them had learned at Court to hide their feelings.

And here, lest critics should condemn the puerility of the opening of the forthcoming scene, it is perhaps as well to remind the reader that Locke, once happening to be in the company of several great lords, renowned no less for their wit than for their breeding and political consistency, wickedly amused himself by taking down their conversation by some shorthand process of his own ; and afterwards, when he read it over to them to see what they could make of it, they all burst out laughing. And, in truth, the tinsel jargon which circulates among the upper ranks in every country yields mighty little gold to the crucible when washed in the ashes of literature or philosophy. In every rank of society (some few Parisian salons excepted) the curious observer finds folly a constant quantity beneath a more or less transparent varnish. Conversation with any substance in it is a rare exception, and bœotianism is current coin in every zone. In the higher regions they must perforce talk more, but to make up for it they think the less. Thinking is a tiring exercise, and the rich like their lives to flow by easily and without effort. It is by comparing the fundamental matter of jests, as you rise in the social scale from the street-boy to the peer of France, that the observer arrives at a true comprehension of M. de Talleyrand's maxim, "The manner is everything"; an elegant rendering of the legal axiom, "The form is of more consequence than the matter." In the eyes of the poet the advantage rests with the lower classes, for they seldom fail to give a certain character of rude poetry to their thoughts. Perhaps also this same observation may explain the sterility of the salons, their emptiness, their shallowness, and the repugnance felt by men of ability for bartering their ideas for such pitiful small change.

The Duke suddenly stopped as if some bright idea occurred to him, and remarked to his neighbour—

"So you have sold Tornthon ?"

"No, he is ill. I am very much afraid I shall lose him, and I should be uncommonly sorry. He is a very good hunter. Do you know how the Duchesse de Marigny is ?"

"No. I did not go this morning. I was just going out to call when you came in to speak about Antoinette. But yesterday she was very ill indeed ; they had given her up, she took the sacrament."

"Her death will make a change in your cousin's position."

"Not at all. She gave away her property in her lifetime, only keeping an annuity. She made over the Guébriant estate to her niece, Mme de Soulanges, subject to a yearly charge."

"It will be a great loss for society. She was a kind woman. Her family will miss her ; her experience and advice carried weight. Her son Marigny is an amiable man ; he has a sharp wit, he can talk. He is pleasant, very pleasant. Pleasant ? oh, that no one can deny, but—ill regulated to the last degree. Well, and yet it is an extraordinary thing, he is very acute. He was dining at the club the other day with that moneyed Chaussée-d'Antin set. Your uncle (he always goes there for his game of cards) found him there to his astonishment, and asked if he was a member. 'Yes,' said he, 'I don't go into society now ; I am living among the bankers.'—You know why ?" added the Marquis, with a meaning smile.

"No," said the Duke.

"He is smitten with that little Mme Keller, Gondreville's daughter; she is only lately married, and has a great vogue, they say, in that set."

"Well, Antoinette does not find time heavy on her hands, it seems," remarked the Vidame.

"My affection for that little woman has driven me to find a singular pastime," replied the Princess, as she returned her snuff-box to her pocket.

"Dear aunt, I am extremely vexed," said the Duke, stopping short in his walk. "Nobody but one of Buonaparte's men could ask such an indecorous thing of a woman of fashion. Between ourselves, Antoinette might have made a better choice."

"The Montriveaus are a very old family and very well connected, my dear," replied the Princess; "they are related to all the noblest houses of Burgundy. If the Dulmen branch of the Arschoot Rivaudoults should come to an end in Galicia, the Montriveaus would succeed to the Arschoot title and estates. They inherit through their great-grandfather."

"Are you sure?"

"I know it better than this Montriveau's father did. I told him about it, I used to see a good deal of him; and, Chevalier of several orders though he was, he only laughed; he was an encyclopædist. But his brother turned the relationship to good account during the emigration. I have heard it said that his northern kinsfolk were most kind in every way——"

"Yes, to be sure. The Comte de Montriveau died at St. Petersburg," said the Vidame. "I met him there. He was a big man with an incredible passion for oysters."

"However many did he eat?" asked the Duc de Grandlieu.

"Ten dozen every day."

"And did they not disagree with him?"

"Not the least bit in the world."

"Why, that is extraordinary! Had he neither the stone nor gout, nor any other complaint, in consequence?"

"No; his health was perfectly good, and he died through an accident."

"By accident! Nature prompted him to eat oysters, so probably he required them; for up to a certain point our predominant tastes are conditions of our existence."

"I am of your opinion," said the Princess, with a smile.

"Madame, you always put a malicious construction on things," returned the Marquis.

"I only want you to understand that these remarks might leave a wrong impression on a young woman's mind," said she, and interrupted herself to exclaim, "But this niece, this niece of mine!"

"Dear aunt, I still refuse to believe that she can have gone to M. de Montriveau," said the Duc de Navarreins.

"Bah!" returned the Princess.

"What do you think, Vidame?" asked the Marquis.

"If the Duchess were an artless simpleton, I should think that——"

"But when a woman is in love she becomes an artless simpleton," retorted the Princess. "Really, my poor Vidame, you must be getting older."

"After all, what is to be done?" asked the Duke.

"If my dear niece is wise," said the Princess, "she will go to Court this evening—fortunately, today is Monday, and reception day—and you must see that we all rally round her and give the lie to this absurd rumour. There are hundreds of ways of explaining things; and if the Marquis de Montriveau is a gentleman, he will come to our assistance. We will bring these children to listen to reason——

"But, dear aunt, it is not easy to tell M. de Montriveau the truth to his face. He is one of Buonaparte's pupils, and he has a position. Why, he is one of the great men of the day; he is high up in the Guards, and very useful there. He has not a spark of ambition. He is just the man to say, 'Here is my commission, leave me in peace,' if the King should say a word that he did not like."

"Then, pray, what are his opinions?"

"Very unsound."

"Really," sighed the Princess, "the King is, as he always has been, a Jacobin under the Lilies of France."

"Oh! not quite so bad," said the Vidame.

"Yes; I have known him for a long while. The man that pointed out the Court to his wife on the occasion of her first state dinner in public with, 'These are our people,' could only be a black-hearted scoundrel. I can see Monsieur exactly the same as ever in the King. The bad brother who voted so wrongly in his department of the Constituent Assembly was sure to compound with the Liberals and allow them to argue and talk. This philosophical cant will be just as dangerous now for the younger brother as it used to be for the elder; this fat man with the little mind is amusing himself by creating difficulties, and how his successor is to get out of them I do not know; he holds his younger brother in abhorrence; he would be glad to think as he lay dying, 'He will not reign very long——'"

"Aunt, he is the King, and I have the honour to be in his service——"

"But does your post take away your right of free speech, my dear? You come of quite as good a house as the Bourbons. If the Guises had shown a little more resolution, His Majesty would be a nobody at this day. It is time I went out of this world, the noblesse is dead. Yes, it is all over with you, my children," she continued, looking as she spoke at the Vidame. "What has my niece done that the whole town should be talking about her? She is in the wrong; I disapprove of her conduct, a useless scandal is a blunder; that is why I still have my doubts about this want of regard for appearances; I brought her up, and I know that——"

Just at that moment the Duchess came out of her boudoir. She had recognised her aunt's voice and heard the name of Montriveau. She was still in her loose morning-gown; and even as she came in, M. de Grandlieu, looking carelessly out of the window, saw his niece's carriage driving back along the street. The Duke took his daughter's face in both hands and kissed her on the forehead. "So, dear girl," he said, "you do not know what is going on?"

"Has anything extraordinary happened, father dear?"

"Why, all Paris believes that you are with M. de Montriveau."

"My dear Antoinette, you were at home all the time, were you not?" said the Princess, holding out a hand, which the Duchess kissed with affectionate respect.

"Yes, dear mother; I was at home all the time. And," she added, as she turned to greet the Vidame and the Marquis, "I wished that all Paris should think that I was with M. de Montriveau."

The Duke flung up his hands, struck them together in despair, and folded his arms.

"Then, cannot you see what will come of this mad freak?" he asked at last.

But the aged Princess had suddenly risen, and stood looking steadily at the Duchess, the younger woman flushed, and her eyes fell. Mme de Chauvry gently drew her closer, and said, "My little angel, let me kiss you!"

She kissed her niece very affectionately on the forehead, and continued smiling, while she held her hand in a tight clasp.

"We are not under the Valois now, dear child. You have compromised your husband and your position. Still, we will arrange to make everything right."

"But, dear aunt, I do not wish to make it right at all. It is my wish that all Paris should say that I was with M. de Montriveau this morning. If you destroy that belief, however ill grounded it may be, you will do me a singular disservice."

"Do you really wish to ruin yourself, child, and to grieve your family?"

"My family, father, unintentionally condemned me to irreparable misfortune when they sacrificed me to family considerations. You may, perhaps, blame me for seeking alleviations, but you will certainly feel for me."

"After all the endless pains you take to settle your daughters suitably!" muttered M. de Navarreins, addressing the Vidame.

The Princess shook a stray grain of snuff from her skirts. "My dear little girl," she said, "be happy, if you can. We are not talking of troubling your felicity, but of reconciling it with social usages. We all of us here assembled know that marriage is a defective institution tempered by love. But when you take a lover, is there any need to make your bed in the Place du Carrousel? See now, just be a bit reasonable, and hear what we have to say."

"I am listening."

"Mme la Duchesse," began the Duc de Grandlieu, "if it were any part of an uncle's duty to look after his nieces, he ought to have a position; society would owe him honours and rewards and a salary, exactly as if he were in the King's service. So I am not here to talk about my nephew, but of your own interests. Let us look ahead a little. If you persist in making a scandal—I have seen the animal before, and I own that I have no great liking for him—Langeais is stingy enough, and he does not care a rap for anyone but himself; he will have a separation; he will stick to your money, and leave you poor, and consequently you will be a nobody. The income of a hundred thousand livres that you have just inherited from your maternal great-aunt will go to pay for his mistresses' amusements. You will be bound and gagged by the law; you will have to say Amen to all these arrangements. Suppose M. de Montriveau leaves you——dear me! do not let us put ourselves in a passion, my dear niece; a man does not leave a woman while she is young and pretty; still, we have seen so many pretty women left disconsolate, even among princesses, that you will permit the supposition, an all but impossible supposition I quite wish to believe. ——Well, suppose that he goes, what will become of you without a husband? Keep well with your husband as you take care of your beauty; for beauty, after all, is a woman's parachute, and a husband also stands between you and worse. I am supposing that you are happy and loved to the end, and I am leaving unpleasant or unfortunate events altogether out of the reckoning. This being so, fortunately or unfortunately, you may have children. What are they to be? Montriveaus? Very well; they certainly will not succeed to their father's whole fortune. You will want to give them all that you have; he will wish to do the same. Nothing more natural, dear me! And you will find the law against you. How many times have we seen heirs-at-law bringing a law-suit to recover the property from illegitimate children? Every court of law rings with such actions all over the world. You will create a *fidei commissum* perhaps; and if the trustee betrays your confidence, your children have no remedy against him; and they are ruined. So choose carefully. You see the perplexities of the position. In every possible way your children will be sacrificed of necessity to the fancies of your heart; they will have no recognised status. While they are little they will be charming; but, Lord! some day they will reproach you for thinking of no one but your two selves. We old gentlemen know all about it. Little boys grow up into men, and men are ungrateful beings. When I was in Germany, did I not hear young de Horn say, after supper, 'If my mother had been an honest woman, I should be prince-regnant!' 'If?' We have spent our lives in hearing plebeians say *if*. *If* brought about the Revolution. When a man cannot lay the blame on his father or mother, he holds God responsible for his hard lot. In short, dear child, we are here to open your eyes. I will say all I have to say in a few words, on which you had better meditate: A woman ought never to put her husband in the right."

" Uncle, so long as I cared for nobody, I could calculate ; I looked at interests then, as you do ; now, I can only feel."

" But, my dear little girl," remonstrated the Vidame, " life is simply a complication of interests and feelings ; to be happy, more particularly in your position, one must try to reconcile one's feelings with one's interests. A grisette may love according to her fancy, that is intelligible enough, but you have a pretty fortune, a family, a name and a place at Court, and you ought not to fling them out of the window. And what have we been asking you to do to keep them all ?—To manœuvre carefully instead of falling foul of social conventions. Lord ! I shall very soon be eighty years old, and I cannot recollect, under any régime, a love worth the price that you are willing to pay for the love of this lucky young man."

The Duchess silenced the Vidame with a look ; if Montriveau could have seen that glance, he would have forgiven all.

" It would be very effective on the stage," remarked the Duc de Grandlieu, " but it all amounts to nothing when your jointure and position and independence is concerned. You are not grateful, my dear niece. You will not find many families where the relatives have courage enough to teach the wisdom gained by experience, and to make rash young heads listen to reason. Renounce your salvation in two minutes, if it pleases you to damn yourself ; well and good ; but reflect well beforehand when it comes to renouncing your income. I know of no confessor who remits the pains of poverty. I have a right, I think, to speak in this way to you ; for if you are ruined, I am the one person who can offer you a refuge. I am almost an uncle to Langeais, and I alone have a right to put him in the wrong."

The Duc de Navarreins roused himself from painful reflections.

" Since you speak of feeling, my child," he said, " let me remind you that a woman who bears your name ought to be moved by sentiments which do not touch ordinary people. Can you wish to give an advantage to the Liberals, to those Jesuits of Robespierre's that are doing all they can to vilify the noblesse ? Some things a Navarreins cannot do without failing in duty to his house. You would not be alone in your dishonour——"

" Come, come ! " said the Princess. " Dishonour ? Do not make such a fuss about the journey of an empty carriage, children, and leave me alone with Antoinette. All three of you come and dine with me. I will undertake to arrange matters suitably. You men understand nothing ; you are beginning to talk sourly already, and I have no wish to see a quarrel between you and my dear child. Do me the pleasure to go."

The three gentlemen probably guessed the Princess's intentions ; they took their leave. M. de Navarreins kissed his daughter on the forehead with, " Come, be good, dear child. It is not too late yet if you choose."

" Couldn't we find some good fellow in the family to pick a quarrel with this Montriveau ? " said the Vidame, as they went downstairs.

When the two women were alone, the Princess beckoned her niece to a little low chair by her side.

"My pearl," said she, "in this world below, I know nothing worse calumniated than God and the eighteenth century; for as I look back over my own young days, I do not recollect that a single duchess trampled the proprieties underfoot as you have just done. Novelists and scribblers brought the reign of Louis XV into disrepute. Do not believe them. The du Barry, my dear, was quite as good as the Widow Scarron, and the more agreeable woman of the two. In my time a woman could keep her dignity among her gallantries. Indiscretion was the ruin of us, and the beginning of all the mischief. The philosophists—the nobodies whom we admitted into our salons—had no more gratitude or sense of decency than to make an inventory of our hearts, to traduce us one and all, and to rail against the age by way of a return for our kindness. The people are not in a position to judge of anything whatsoever; they looked at the facts, not at the form. But the men and women of those times, my heart, were quite as remarkable as at any other period of the Monarchy. Not one of your Werthers, none of your notabilities, as they are called, never a one of your men in yellow kid gloves and trousers that disguise the poverty of their legs, would cross Europe in the dress of a travelling hawker to brave the daggers of a Duke of Modena, and to shut himself up in the dressing-room of the Regent's daughter at the risk of his life. Not one of your little consumptive patients with their tortoiseshell eyeglasses would hide himself in a closet for six weeks, like Lauzun, to keep up his mistress's courage while she was lying in of her child. There was more passion in M. de Jaucourt's little finger than in your whole race of higglers that leave a woman to better themselves elsewhere! Just tell me where to find the page that would be cut in pieces and buried under the floorboards for one kiss on the Königsmark's gloved finger!

"Really, it would seem today that the rôles are exchanged, and women are expected to show their devotion for men. These modern gentlemen are worth less, and think more of themselves. Believe me, my dear, all these adventures that have been made public, and now are turned against our good Louis XV, were kept quite secret at first. If it had not been for a pack of poetasters, scribblers, and moralists, who hung about our waiting-women, and took down their slanders, our epoch would have appeared in literature as a well-conducted age. I am justifying the century and not its fringe. Perhaps a hundred women of quality were lost; but for every one, the rogues set down ten, like the gazettes after a battle when they count up the losses of the beaten side. And in any case I do not know that the Revolution and the Empire can reproach us; they were coarse, dull, licentious times. Faugh! it is revolting. Those are the brothels of French history.

"This preamble, my dear child," she continued after a pause, "brings me to the thing that I have to say. If you care for Montriveau, you are quite at liberty to love him at your ease, and as much as you can. I know by experience that, unless you are locked up (but locking people up is out of fashion now), you will do as you please ; I should have done the same at your age. Only, sweetheart, I should not have given up my right to be the mother of future Ducs de Langeais. So mind appearances. The Vidame is right. No man is worth a single one of the sacrifices which we are foolish enough to make for their love. Put yourself in such a position that you may still be M. de Langeais's wife, in case you should have the misfortune to repent. When you are an old woman, you will be very glad to hear mass said at Court, and not in some provincial convent. Therein lies the whole question. A single imprudence means an allowance and a wandering life ; it means that you are at the mercy of your lover ; it means that you must put up with insolence from women that are not so honest, precisely because they have been very vulgarly sharp-witted. It would be a hundred times better to go to Montriveau's at night in a cab, and disguised, instead of sending your carriage in broad daylight. You are a little fool, my dear child ! Your carriage flattered his vanity ; your person would have ensnared his heart. All this that I have said is just and true ; but, for my own part, I do not blame you. You are two centuries behind the times with your false ideas of greatness. There, leave us to arrange your affairs, and say that Montriveau made your servants drunk to gratify his vanity and to compromise you——"

The Duchess rose to her feet with a spring. " In Heaven's name, aunt, do not slander him ! "

The old Princess's eyes flashed.

" Dear child," she said, " I should have liked to spare such of your illusions as were not fatal. But there must be an end of all illusions now. You would soften me if I were not so old. Come, now, do not vex him, or us, or anyone else. I will undertake to satisfy everybody ; but promise me not to permit yourself a single step henceforth until you have consulted me. Tell me all, and perhaps I may bring it all right again."

" Aunt, I promise——"

" To tell me everything ? "

" Yes, everything. Everything that can be told."

" But, my sweetheart, it is precisely what cannot be told that I want to know. Let us understand each other thoroughly. Come, let me put my withered old lips on your beautiful forehead. No ; let me do as I wish. I forbid you to kiss my bones. Old people have a courtesy of their own. . . . There, take me down to my carriage," she added, when she had kissed her niece.

" Then may I go to him in disguise, dear aunt ? "

" Why—yes. The story can always be denied," said the old Princess.

This was the one idea which the Duchess had clearly grasped in the sermon. When Mme de Chauvry was seated in the corner of her carriage, Mme de Langeais bade her a graceful adieu and went up to her room. She was quite happy again.

"My person would have snared his heart; my aunt is right; a man cannot surely refuse a pretty woman when she understands how to offer herself."

That evening, at the Élysée-Bourbon, the Duc de Navarreins, M. de Pamiers, M. de Marsay, M. de Grandlieu, and the Duc de Maufrigneuse triumphantly refuted the scandals that were circulating with regard to the Duchesse de Langeais. So many officers and other persons had seen Montriveau walking in the Tuileries that morning, that the silly story was set down to chance, which takes all that is offered. And so, in spite of the fact that the Duchess's carriage had waited before Montriveau's door, her character became as clear and as spotless as Mambrino's sword after Sancho had polished it up.

But, at two o'clock, M. de Ronquerolles passed Montriveau in a deserted alley, and said with a smile, "She is coming on, is your Duchess. Go on, keep it up!" he added, and gave a significant cut of the riding whip to his mare, who sped off like a bullet down the avenue.

Two days after the fruitless scandal, Mme de Langeais wrote to M. de Montriveau. That letter, like the preceding ones, remained unanswered. This time she took her own measures, and bribed M. de Montriveau's man, Auguste. And so at eight o'clock that evening she was introduced into Armand's apartment. It was not the room in which that secret scene had passed; it was entirely different. The Duchess was told that the General would not be at home that night. Had he two houses? The man would give no answer. Mme de Langeais had bought the key of the room, but not the man's whole loyalty.

When she was left alone she saw her fourteen letters lying on an old-fashioned stand, all of them uncreased and unopened. He had not read them. She sank into an easy-chair, and for a while she lost consciousness. When she came to herself, Auguste was holding vinegar for her to inhale.

"A carriage; quick!" she ordered.

The carriage came. She hastened downstairs with convulsive speed, and left orders that no one was to be admitted. For twenty-four hours she lay in bed, and would have no one near her but her woman, who brought her a cup of orange-flower water from time to time. Suzette heard her mistress moan once or twice, and caught a glimpse of tears in the brilliant eyes, now circled with dark shadows.

The next day, amid despairing tears, Mme de Langeais took her resolution. Her man of business came for an interview, and no doubt received instructions of some kind. Afterwards she sent for the Vidame de Pamiers; and while she waited, she wrote a letter to M. de Montriveau. The Vidame punctually came towards two o'clock that afternoon, to find his young cousin looking white and worn, but resigned; never had her divine loveliness been more poetic than now in the languor of her agony.

"You owe this assignation to your eighty-four years, dear cousin," she said. "Ah! do not smile, I beg of you, when an unhappy woman has reached the lowest depths of wretchedness. You are a gentleman, and after the adventures of your youth you must feel some indulgence for women."

"None whatever," said he.

"Indeed!"

"Everything is in their favour."

"Ah! Well, you are one of the inner family circle; possibly you will be the last relative, the last friend whose hand I shall press, so I can ask your good offices. Will you, dear Vidame, do me a service which I could not ask of my own father, nor of my uncle Grandlieu, nor of any woman? You cannot fail to understand. I beg of you to do my bidding, and then to forget what you have done, whatever may come of it. It is this: Will you take this letter and go to M. de Montriveau? will you see him yourself, give it into his hands, and ask him, as you men can ask things between yourselves—for you have a code of honour between man and man which you do not use with us, and a different way of regarding things between yourselves—ask him if he will read this letter? Not in your presence. Certain feelings men hide from each other. I give you authority to say, if you think it necessary to bring him, that it is a question of life or death for me. If he deigns——"

"*Deigns!*" repeated the Vidame.

"If he deigns to read it," the Duchess continued with dignity, "say one thing more. You will go to see him about five o'clock, for I know that he will dine at home today at that time. Very good. By way of answer he must come to see me. If, three hours afterwards, by eight o'clock, he does not leave his house, all will be over. The Duchesse de Langeais will have vanished from the world. I shall not be dead, dear friend, no, but no human power will ever find me again on this earth. Come and dine with me; I shall at least have one friend with me in the last agony. Yes, dear cousin, tonight will decide my fate; and whatever happens to me, I pass through an ordeal by fire. There! not a word. I will hear nothing of the nature of comment or advice—— Let us chat and laugh together," she added, holding out a hand, which he kissed. "We will be like two grey-headed philosophers who have learned how to enjoy life to the last moment. I will look my best; I will be very enchanting for you. You perhaps will be the last man to set eyes on the Duchesse de Langeais."

The Vicomte bowed, took the letter, and went without a word. At five o'clock he returned. His cousin had studied to please him, and she looked lovely indeed. The room was gay with flowers as if for a festivity; the dinner was exquisite. For the grey-headed Vidame the Duchess displayed all the brilliancy of her wit; she was more charming than she had ever been before. At first the Vidame tried to look on all these preparations as a young woman's jest; but now and again the attempted illusion faded, the spell of his fair cousin's charm was broken. He detected a shudder caused by some kind of sudden dread, and once she seemed to listen during a pause.

"What is the matter?" he asked.

"Hush!" she said.

At seven o'clock the Duchess left him for a few minutes. When she came back again she was dressed as her maid might have dressed for a journey. She asked her guest to be her escort, took his arm, sprang into a hackney coach, and by a quarter to eight they stood outside M. de Montriveau's door.

Armand meantime had been reading the following letter:—

"My Friend,—I went to your rooms for a few minutes without your knowledge; I found my letters there, and took them away. This cannot be indifference, Armand, between us; and hatred would show itself quite differently. If you love me, make an end of this cruel play, or you will kill me, and afterwards, learning how much you were loved, you might be in despair. If I have not rightly understood you, if you have no feeling towards me but aversion, which implies both contempt and disgust, then I give up all hope. A man never recovers from those feelings. You will have no regrets. Dreadful though that thought may be, it will comfort me in my long sorrow. Regrets? Oh, my Armand, may I never know of them; if I thought that I had caused you a single regret—— But, no, I will not tell you what desolation I should feel. I should be living still, and I could not be your wife; it would be too late!

"Now that I have given myself wholly to you in thought, to whom else should I give myself?—to God. The eyes that you loved for a little while shall never look on another man's face; and may the glory of God blind them to all besides. I shall never hear human voices more since I heard yours—so gentle at the first, so terrible yesterday; for it seems to me that I am still only on the morrow of your vengeance. And now may the will of God consume me. Between His wrath and yours, my friend, there will be nothing left for me but a little space for tears and prayers.

"Perhaps you wonder why I write to you? Ah! do not think ill of me if I keep a gleam of hope, and give one last sigh to happy life before I take leave of it forever. I am in a hideous position. I feel all the inward serenity that comes when a great resolution has been taken, even while I hear the last growlings of the storm. When you went out on that terrible adventure which so drew me to you, Armand, you went from the desert to the oasis with a good guide to show you the way. Well, I am going out of the oasis into the desert, and you are a pitiless guide to me. And yet you only, my friend, can understand how melancholy it is to look back for the last time on happiness—to you, and you only, I can make moan without a blush. If you grant my entreaty, I shall be happy; if you are inexorable, I shall expiate the wrong that I have done. After all, it is natural, is it not, that a woman should wish to live, invested with all noble feelings, in her friend's memory? Oh! my one and only love, let her to whom you gave life go down into the tomb in the belief that she is great in your eyes. Your harshness led me to reflect; and now that I love you so, it seems to me that I am less guilty than you think. Listen to my justification, I owe it to you; and you that are all the world to me, owe me at least a moment's justice.

"I have learned by my own anguish all that I made you suffer by my coquetry; but in those days I was utterly ignorant of love. *You* know what the torture is, and you mete it out to me! During those first eight months that you gave me you never roused any feeling of love in me. Do you ask why this was so, my friend? I can no more explain it than I can tell you why I love you now. Oh! certainly it flattered my vanity that I should be the subject of your passionate talk, and receive those burning glances of yours; but you left me cold. No, I was not a woman; I had no conception of womanly devotion and happiness. Who was to blame? You would have despised me, would you not, if I had given myself without the impulse of passion? Perhaps it is the highest height to which we can rise—to give all and receive no joy; perhaps there is no merit in yielding oneself to bliss that is foreseen and ardently desired. Alas, my friend, I can say this now; these thoughts came to me when I played with you; and you seemed to me so great even then that I would not have you owe the gift to pity—— What is this that I have written?

"I have taken back all my letters; I am flinging them one by one on the fire; they are burning. You will never know what they confessed—all the love and the passion and the madness——

"I will say no more, Armand; I will stop. I will not say another word of my feelings. If my prayers have not echoed from my soul through yours, I also, woman that I am, decline to owe your love to your pity. It is my wish to be loved, because you cannot choose but love me, or else to be left without mercy. If you refuse to read this letter, it shall be burnt. If, after you have read it, you do not come to me within three hours, to be henceforth forever my husband, the one man in the world for me; then I shall never blush to know that this letter is in your hands, the pride of my despair will protect my memory from all insult, and my end shall be worthy of my love. When you see me no more on earth, albeit I shall still be alive, you yourself will not think without a shudder of the woman who, in three hours' time, will live only to overwhelm you with her tenderness; a woman consumed by a hopeless love, and faithful—not to memories of past joys—but to a love that was slighted.

"The Duchesse de la Vallière wept for lost happiness and vanished power; but the Duchesse de Langeais will be happy that she may weep and be a power for you still. Yes, you will regret me. I see clearly that I was not of this world, and I thank you for making it clear to me.

"Farewell; you will never touch *my* axe. Yours was the executioner's axe, mine is God's; yours kills, mine saves. Your love was but mortal, it could not endure disdain or ridicule; mine can endure all things without growing weaker, it will last eternally. Ah! I feel a sombre joy in crushing you that believe yourself so great; in humbling you with the calm, indulgent smile of one of the least among the angels that lie at the feet of God, for to them is given the right and the power to protect and watch over men in His name. You have but felt fleeting desires, while the poor nun will shed the light of her ceaseless and ardent prayer about you, she will shelter you all your life long beneath the wings of a love that has nothing of earth in it.

"I have a presentiment of your answer; our trysting place shall be—in heaven. Strength and weakness can both enter there, dear Armand; the strong and the weak are bound to suffer. This thought soothes the anguish of my final ordeal. So calm am I that I should fear that I had ceased to love you if I were not about to leave the world for your sake.

"ANTOINETTE."

"Dear Vidame," said the Duchess as they reached Montriveau's house, "do me the kindness to ask at the door whether he is at home."

The Vidame, obedient after the manner of the eighteenth century to a woman's wish, got out, and came back to bring his cousin an affirmative answer that sent a shudder through her. She grasped his hand tightly in hers, suffered him to kiss her on either cheek, and begged him to go at once. He must not watch her movements nor try to protect her.

"But the people passing in the street," he objected.

"No one can fail in respect to me," she said. It was the last word spoken by the Duchess and the woman of fashion.

The Vidame went. Mme de Langeais wrapped herself about in her cloak, and stood on the doorstep until the clocks struck eight. The last stroke died away. The unhappy woman waited ten, fifteen minutes; to the last she tried to see a fresh humiliation in the delay, then her faith ebbed. She turned to leave the fatal threshold.

"Oh, God!" the cry broke from her in spite of herself; it was the first word spoken by the Carmelite.

Montriveau and some of his friends were talking together. He tried to hasten them to a conclusion, but his clock was slow, and by the time he started out for the Hôtel de Langeais the Duchess was hurrying on foot through the streets of Paris, goaded by the dull rage in her heart. She reached the Boulevard d'Enfer, and looked out for the last time through falling tears on the noisy, smoky city that lay below in a red mist, lighted up by its own lamps. Then she hailed a cab, and drove away, never to return.

When the Marquis de Montriveau reached the Hôtel de Langeais, and found no trace of his mistress, he thought that he had been duped. He hurried away at once to the Vidame, and found that worthy gentleman in the act of slipping on his flowered dressing-gown, thinking the while of his fair cousin's happiness. Montriveau gave him one of the terrific glances that produced the effect of an electric shock on men and women alike.

"Is it possible that you have lent yourself to some cruel hoax, monsieur ?" Montriveau exclaimed. "I have just come from Mme de Langeais's house ; the servants say that she is out."

"Then a great misfortune has happened, no doubt," returned the Vidame, "and through your fault. I left the Duchess at your door——"

"When ?"

"At a quarter to eight."

"Good evening," returned Montriveau, and he hurried home to ask the porter whether he had seen a lady standing on the doorstep that evening.

"Yes, my Lord Marquis, a handsome woman, who seemed very much put out. She was crying like a Magdalen, but she never made a sound, and stood as upright as a post. Then at last she went, and my wife and I that were watching her while she could not see us, heard her say, 'Oh, God !' so that it went to our hearts, asking your pardon, to hear her say it."

Montriveau, in spite of all his firmness, turned pale at those few words. He wrote a few lines to Ronquerolles, sent off the message at once, and went up to his rooms. Ronquerolles came just about midnight.

Armand gave him the Duchess's letter to read.

"Well ?" asked Ronquerolles.

"She was here at my door at eight o'clock ; at a quarter-past eight she had gone. I have lost her, and I love her. Oh ! if my life were my own, I could blow my brains out."

"Pooh, pooh ! Keep cool," said Ronquerolles. "Duchesses do not fly off like wagtails. She cannot travel faster than three leagues an hour, and tomorrow we will ride six.—Confound it ! Mme de Langeais is no ordinary woman," he continued. "Tomorrow we will all of us mount and ride. The police will put us on her track during the day. She must have a carriage ; angels of that sort have no wings. We shall find her whether she is on the road or hidden in Paris. There is the semaphore. We can stop her. You shall be happy. But, my dear fellow, you have made a blunder, of which men of your energy are very often guilty. They judge others by themselves, and do not know the point when human nature gives way if you strain the cords too tightly. Why did you not say a word to me sooner ? I would have told you to be punctual. Good-bye till tomorrow," he added, as Montriveau said nothing. "Sleep if you can," he added, with a grasp of the hand.

But the greatest resources which society has ever placed at the disposal of statesmen, kings, ministers, bankers, or any human power, in fact, were all exhausted in vain. Neither Montriveau nor his friends could find any trace of the Duchess. It was clear that she had entered a convent. Montriveau determined to search, or to institute a search, for her through every convent in the world. He must have her, even at the cost of all the lives in a town. And in justice to this extraordinary man, it must be said that his frenzied passion awoke to the same ardour daily and lasted through five years. Only in 1829 did the Duc de Navarreins hear by chance that his daughter had travelled to Spain as Lady Julia Hopwood's maid, that she had left her service at Cadiz, and that Lady Julia never discovered that Mlle Caroline was the illustrious duchess whose sudden disappearance filled the minds of the highest society of Paris.

The feelings of the two lovers when they met again on either side of the grating in the Carmelite convent should now be comprehended to the full, and the violence of the passion awakened in either soul will doubtless explain the catastrophe of the story.

In 1823 the Duc de Langeais was dead, and his wife was free. Antoinette de Navarreins was living, consumed by love, on a ledge of rock in the Mediterranean; but it was in the Pope's power to dissolve Sister Theresa's vows. The happiness bought by so much love might yet bloom for the two lovers. These thoughts sent Montriveau flying from Cadiz to Marseilles, and from Marseilles to Paris.

A few months after his return to France, a merchant brig, fitted out and munitioned for active service, set sail from the port of Marseilles for Spain. The vessel had been chartered by several distinguished men, most of them Frenchmen, who, smitten with a romantic passion for the East, wished to make a journey to those lands. Montriveau's familiar knowledge of Eastern customs made him an invaluable travelling companion, and at the entreaty of the rest he had joined the expedition; the Minister of War appointed him lieutenant-general, and put him on the Artillery Commission to facilitate his departure.

Twenty-fours hours later the brig lay to off the north-west shore of an island within sight of the Spanish coast. She had been specially chosen for her shallow keel and light mastage, so that she might lie at anchor in safety half a league away from the reefs that secure the island from approach in this direction. If fishing vessels or the people on the island caught sight of the brig, they were scarcely likely to feel suspicious of her at once; and besides, it was easy to give a reason for her presence without delay. Montriveau hoisted the flag of the United States before they came in sight of the island, and the crew of the vessel were all American sailors, who spoke nothing but English. One of M. de Montriveau's companions took the men ashore in the ship's longboat, and made them so drunk at an inn in the little town that they could not talk. Then he gave out that the brig was manned by treasure-seekers, a gang of men whose hobby was well known in the United States; indeed, some Spanish writer had written a history of them. The presence of the brig among the reefs was now sufficiently explained. The owners of the vessel, according to the self-styled boatswain's mate, were looking for the wreck of a galleon which foundered thereabouts in 1778 with a cargo of treasure from Mexico. The people at the inn and the authorities asked no more questions.

Armand, and the devoted friends who were helping him in his difficult enterprise, were all from the first of the opinion that there was no hope of rescuing or carrying off Sister Theresa by force or stratagem from the side of the little town. Wherefore these bold spirits, with one accord, determined to take the bull by the horns. They would make a way to the convent at the most seemingly inaccessible point; like General Lamarque, at the storming of Capri, they would conquer Nature. The cliff at the end of the island, a sheer block of granite, afforded even less hold than the rock of Capri. So it seemed at least to Montriveau, who had taken part in that incredible exploit, while the nuns in his eyes were much more redoubtable than Sir Hudson Lowe. To raise a hubbub over carrying off the Duchess would cover them with confusion. They might as well set siege to the town and convent, like pirates, and leave not a single soul to tell of their victory. So for them their expedition wore but two aspects. There should be a conflagration and a feat of arms that should dismay all Europe, while the motives of the crime remained unknown; or, on the other hand, a mysterious, aerial descent which should persuade the nuns that the Devil himself had paid them a visit. They had decided upon the latter course in the secret council held before they left Paris, and subsequently everything had been done to insure the success of an expedition which promised some real excitement to jaded spirits weary of Paris and its pleasures.

An extremely light pirogue, made at Marseilles on a Malayan model, enabled them to cross the reef, until the rocks rose from out of the water. Then two cables of iron wire were fastened several feet apart between one rock and another. These wire ropes slanted upwards and downwards in opposite directions, so that baskets of iron wire could travel to and fro along them; and in this manner the rocks were covered with a system of baskets and wire-cables, not unlike the filaments which a certain species of spider weaves about a tree. The Chinese, an essentially imitative people, were the first to take a lesson from the work of instinct. Fragile as these bridges were, they were always ready for use; high waves and the caprices of the sea could not throw them out of working order; the ropes hung just sufficiently slack, so as to present to the breakers that particular curve discovered by Cachin, the immortal creator of the harbour at Cherbourg. Against this cunningly devised line the angry surge is powerless; the law of that curve was a secret wrested from Nature by that faculty of observation in which nearly all human genius consists.

M. de Montriveau's companions were alone on board the vessel, and out of sight of every human eye. No one from the deck of a passing vessel could have discovered either the brig hidden among the reefs, or the men at work among the rocks; they lay below the ordinary range of the most powerful telescope. Eleven days were spent in preparation, before the Thirteen, with all their infernal power, could reach the foot of the cliffs. The body of the rock rose up straight from the sea to a height of thirty fathoms. Any attempt to climb the sheer wall of granite seemed impossible; a mouse might as well try to creep up the slippery sides of a plain china vase. Still there was a cleft, a straight line of fissure so fortunately placed that large blocks of wood could be wedged firmly into it at a distance of about a foot apart. Into these blocks the daring workers drove iron cramps, specially made for the purpose, with a broad iron bracket at the outer end, through which a hole had been drilled. Each bracket carried a light deal board which corresponded with a notch made in a pole that reached to the top of the cliffs, and was firmly planted in the beach at their feet. With ingenuity worthy of these men who found nothing impossible, one of their number, a skilled mathematician, had calculated the angle from which the steps must start; so that from the middle they rose gradually, like the sticks of a fan, to the top of the cliff, and descended in the same fashion to its base. That miraculously light, yet perfectly firm, staircase cost them twenty-two days of toil. A little tinder and the surf of the sea would destroy all trace of it forever in a single night. A betrayal of the secret was impossible; and all search for the violators of the convent was doomed to failure.

At the top of the rock there was a platform with sheer precipice on all sides. The Thirteen, reconnoitring the ground with their glasses from the masthead, made certain that though the ascent was steep and rough, there would be no difficulty in gaining the convent garden, where the trees were thick enough for a hiding-place. After such great efforts they would not risk the success of their enterprise, and were compelled to wait till the moon passed out of her last quarter.

For two nights Montriveau, wrapped in his cloak, lay out on the rock platform. The singing at vespers and matins filled him with unutterable joy. He stood under the wall to hear the music of the organ, listening intently for one voice among the rest. But in spite of the silence, the confused effect of music was all that reached his ears. In those sweet harmonies defects of execution are lost; the pure spirit of art comes into direct communication with the spirit of the hearer, making no demand on the attention, no strain on the power of listening. Intolerable memories awoke. All the love within him seemed to break into blossom again at the breath of that music; he tried to find auguries of happiness in the air. During the last night he sat with his eyes fixed upon an ungrated window, for bars were not needed on the side of the precipice. A light shone there all through the hours; and that instinct of the heart, which is sometimes true, and as often false, cried within him, "She is there!"

"She is certainly there! Tomorrow she will be mine," he said to himself, and joy blended with the slow tinkling of a bell that began to ring.

Strange unaccountable workings of the heart! The nun, wasted by yearning love, worn out with tears and fasting, prayer and vigils; the woman of nine-and-twenty, who had passed through heavy trials, was loved more passionately than the lighthearted girl, the woman of four-and-twenty, the sylphide, had ever been. But is there not, for men of vigorous character, something attractive in the sublime expression engraven on women's faces by the impetuous stirrings of thought and misfortunes of no ignoble kind ? Is there not a beauty of suffering which is the most interesting of all beauty to those men who feel that within them there is an inexhaustible wealth of tenderness and consoling pity for a creature so gracious in weakness, so strong with love ? It is the ordinary nature that is attracted by young, smooth, pink-and-white beauty, or, in one word, by prettiness. In some faces love awakens amid the wrinkles carved by sorrow and the ruin made by melancholy; Montriveau could not but feel drawn to these. For cannot a lover, with the voice of a great longing, call forth a wholly new creature ? a creature athrob with the life but just begun breaks forth for him alone, from the outward form that is fair for him, and faded for all the world besides. Does he not love two women ?—One of them, as others see her, is pale and wan and sad ; but the other, the unseen love that his heart knows, is an angel who understands life through feeling, and is adorned in all her glory only for love's high festivals.

The General left his post before sunrise, but not before he had heard voices singing together, sweet voices full of tenderness sounding faintly from the cell. When he came down to the foot of the cliffs where his friends were waiting, he told them that never in his life had he felt such enthralling bliss, and in the few words there was that unmistakable thrill of repressed strong feeling, that magnificent utterance which all men respect.

That night eleven of his devoted comrades made the ascent in the darkness. Each man carried a poniard, a provision of chocolate, and a set of house-breaking tools. They climbed the outer walls with scaling-ladders, and crossed the cemetery of the convent. Montriveau recognised the long, vaulted gallery through which he went to the parlour, and remembered the windows of the room. His plans were made and adopted in a moment. They would effect an entrance through one of the windows in the Carmelite's half of the parlour, find their way along the corridors, ascertain whether the sister's names were written on the doors, find Sister Theresa's cell, surprise her as she slept, and carry her off, bound and gagged. The programme presented no difficulties to men who combined boldness and a convict's dexterity with the knowledge peculiar to men of the world, especially as they would not scruple to give a stab to ensure silence.

In two hours the bars were sawn through. Three men stood on guard outside, and two inside the parlour. The rest, barefooted, took up their posts along the corridor. Young Henri de Marsay, the most dexterous man among them, disguised by way of precaution in a Carmelite's robe, exactly like the costume of the convent, led the way, and Montriveau came immediately behind him. The clock struck three just as the two men reached the dormitory cells. They soon saw the position. Everything was perfectly quiet. With the help of a dark lantern they read the names luckily written on every door, together with the picture of a saint or saints and the mystical words which every nun takes as a kind of motto for the beginning of her new life and the revelation of her last thought. Montriveau reached Sister Theresa's door and read the inscription, *Sub invocatione sanctæ matris Theresæ*, and her motto, *Adoremus in æternum.* Suddenly his companion laid a hand on his shoulder. A bright light was streaming through the chinks of the door. M. de Ronquerolles came up at that moment.

"All the nuns are in the church," he said; "they are beginning the Office for the Dead."

"I will stay here," said Montriveau. "Go back into the parlour, and shut the door at the end of the passage."

He threw open the door and rushed in, preceded by his disguised companion, who let down the veil over his face.

There before them lay the dead Duchess; her plank bed had been laid on the floor of the outer room of her cell, between two lighted candles. Neither Montriveau nor de Marsay spoke a word or uttered a cry; but they looked into each other's faces. The General's dumb gesture tried to say, "Let us carry her away!"

"Quick!" shouted Ronquerolles, "the procession of nuns is leaving the church. You will be caught!"

With magical swiftness of movement, prompted by an intense desire, the dead woman was carried into the convent parlour, passed through the window, and lowered from the walls before the Abbess, followed by the nuns, returned to take up Sister Theresa's body. The sister left in charge had imprudently left her post; there were secrets that she longed to know; and so busy was she ransacking the inner room, that she heard nothing, and was horrified when she came back to find that the body was gone. Before the women, in their blank amazement, could think of making a search, the Duchess had been lowered by a cord to the foot of the crags, and Montriveau's companions had destroyed all traces of their work. By nine o'clock that morning there was not a sign to show that either staircase or wire-cables had ever existed, and Sister Theresa's body had been taken on board. The brig came into the port to ship her crew, and sailed that day.

Montriveau, down in the cabin, was left alone with Antoinette de Navarreins. For some hours it seemed as if her dead face was transfigured for him by that unearthly beauty which the calm of death gives to the body before it perishes.

"Look here," said Ronquerolles when Montriveau reappeared on deck, "*that* was a woman once, now it is nothing. Let us tie a cannon ball to both feet and throw the body overboard; and if ever you think of her again, think of her as of some book that you read as a boy."

"Yes," assented Montriveau, "it is nothing now but a dream."

"That is sensible of you. Now, after this, have passions; but as for love, a man ought to know how to place it wisely; it is only a woman's last love that can satisfy a man's first love."